BBC

DOCTOR WHO

THE ESSENTIAL TERRANCE DICKS VOLUME ONE

TERRANCE DICKS

BOOKS

BBC Books, an imprint of Ebury Publishing
20 Vauxhall Bridge Road, London SW1V 2SA

BBC Books is part of the Penguin Random House group of companies
whose addresses can be found at global.penguinrandomhouse.com

First published by BBC Books in 2021
Paperback edition published by BBC Books in 2022

www.penguin.co.uk

A CIP catalogue record for this book is available from the British Library

ISBN: 9781785946653

Printed and bound in Great Britain by Clays Ltd, Elcograf S.p.A.

The authorised representative in the EEA is Penguin Random House Ireland,
Morrison Chambers, 32 Nassau Street, Dublin D02 YH68

Penguin Random House is committed to a sustainable future for our
business, our readers and our planet. This book is made
from Forest Stewardship Council® certified paper.

DOCTOR WHO

THE ESSENTIAL TERRANCE DICKS VOLUME ONE

CONTENTS

DOCTOR WHO AND THE ABOMINABLE SNOWMEN

DOCTOR WHO THE WHEEL IN SPACE

DOCTOR WHO AND THE AUTON INVASION

DOCTOR WHO AND THE DAY OF THE DALEKS

FOREWORD

The early adventures of *Doctor Who* lit my life with fear and wonder. On my first day at school, I experimentally – and I thought heroically – kicked a nun. Her combination of veil and floor-length skirt made her look to me like a small blue Irish Dalek. Almost everyone I know has stories like this. And almost everyone I know owes a debt to these books. Because the Target novels *were Doctor Who*. If you'd missed a series because some fool in your house preferred *Opportunity Knocks* then these books were your only recourse. There were no videos or streams and not that much chance of a repeat. I actually kept a separate *Doctor Who* diary in which I wrote down as much as I could remember of each episode. I was that scared that I might forget.

But all that is nostalgia.

Why should you read these stories *now*? Now that you could watch the adventures.

When the great day came that my generation – the watching-from-behind-the-couch, nun-kicking generation – finally got to see those old episodes again we discovered something. These books were a better record of those adventures than the episodes themselves. We had watched these adventures through the eyes of childhood. We'd seen wild and windy Himalayas, overwhelming hordes of Daleks, freezing wastes of space. When we looked again the Daleks were a bit tinny and thin on the ground, and the Himalayas were unmistakably Welsh. On the TV. But not in the books. The pace, the grandeur, the intensity that our childhood imagination had brought to the series, were there in these books, waiting to be unleashed. These books showed Russell T Davies what *Doctor Who* could be.

They also showed us what a book could be.

Terrance Dicks was writing during a glorious moment when TV and books had a rich, antagonistic relation. The same Terrance Dicks, who turned Doctor Who's adventures into books also turned classic novels and stories – The Invisible Man, The Prisoner of Zenda, The Diary of Anne Frank – into TV. He used to joke that he wouldn't have to novelize Dickens or Conan Doyle because they'd already written the novels. Though I'd happily stump up to read Terrance's version of Jane Eyre.

This is the real reason you should read these books: Terrance Dicks was a terrific writer and these books are some of his best work. Look at Day of the Daleks. The TV series is famously flawed. Its ending is comically abrupt. The Ogrons clutter up the narrative space that would have been better left to the Daleks. The book on the other hand crackles with pace and intelligence. It's famously the story in which the Blinovitch Limitation Effect is first formulated. It brilliantly plays with the conventions of the big house ghost story. But it's the way Dicks messes with your moral compass that really stays with you. Is Reginald Styles good or bad? Are the guerrillas freedom fighters or terrorists (and by the way, imagine posing that question in 1972 on prime time TV when the IRA were just beginning their campaigns)? In the TV series the Controller is described as a Quisling – a straightforward traitor – but in the book he's a superior slave, a much more complicated and conflicted position. Somehow Dicks brought this new complexity and scale to the story without betraying the book's original purpose – which was simply to help us remember the TV series.

I think often of the humility that Dicks showed when he sat down to write these books. There was no kudos in it for him. There is no more despised genre than the 'novelization'. Yet he put all of himself into them. For the same reason that he did those classic serials. Because he believed culture belonged to all of us. It was the very fact that these books were so low status – because they were sold for a few pence in Woolworths and Smiths – that they got into our hands and inspired us. Terrance Dicks believed that children deserved the very best, and that if you gave them the best, they would grow up to give of their best. He was prepared to go without praise and prestige himself just to make sure we got the best.

And that in the end is why you should read these books. Because they are the best gift of a very good human.

Frank Cottrell-Boyce

DOCTOR WHO AND THE DALEK INVASION OF EARTH

1

RETURN TO TERROR

Through the ruin of a city stalked the ruin of a man. His clothes were tattered and grimy, his skin blotched and diseased over wasted flesh. On his head was a gleaming metal helmet. He walked with the stiff, jerky movements of a robot—which was exactly what he had become.

The robot man moved through the shattered rubble of a once-great city, a fitting inhabitant of a nightmare landscape.

In time he came to a river, a sluggish, debris-choked, polluted stream which had once carried great ships. He quickened his pace, sensing that the water would provide the thing he sought—a way to end an existence of misery and pain.

When he came to a gap in the embankment wall, he marched stiffly through it and plunged into the water below. He fell, like a log or a stone, making no attempt to save himself. Dragged down by the weight of the helmet, his head sank beneath the grimy waters. There was something inhuman about the manner of his death—but then, he had not been truly human for a very long time.

Not far away, on the rubble-littered remains of what had been a building site, something very strange happened. There was a wheezing, groaning sound and suddenly a square blue police box materialised out of thin air, light flashing busily on top.

Inside the police box, things were stranger still. There was a large, brightly lit, ultra-modern control room. In the centre was a many-sided control panel, its surfaces covered with a complex array of knobs, switches, levers and dials. From the size of the control room it was clear that the police box must be bigger on the inside than on the outside.

Around the centre console stood an oddly-assorted group of people.

The oldest was a man who appeared to be somewhere in his sixties, though in reality he was very much older. He wore check trousers, a frock-coat and a long black tie. He had flowing white hair and a proud, imperious face, with more than a touch of ruthless cunning.

The three others were more ordinary in appearance. There was a young man and a young woman, both somewhere in their twenties, and a dark pretty girl in her teens. All three were casually dressed in the clothes worn on Earth in the last part of the twentieth century.

The young man was called Ian Chesterton, the woman Barbara Wright. Once, though it seemed a very long time ago, they had both been schoolteachers. Led by their curiosity about Susan, the youngest member of the party, then one of their pupils, they had followed her home. To their amazement, they had discovered that she appeared to live in this police box with a mysterious old man known only as the Doctor, who she said was her grandfather. They had been even more astonished to find themselves inside the police box, and to discover that it was a kind of Space/Time ship, called the TARDIS—a name formed from the initial letters of Time and Relative Dimensions In Space.

Then had begun a series of terrifying journeys through Time and Space. The TARDIS had many extraordinary qualities, but accuracy of steering did not appear to be one of them. The Doctor's attempts to return them to their own time and place resulted only in an incredible number of unplanned arrivals, sometimes on alien planets, sometimes on Earth, though always at completely the wrong period. They had seen many wonders, and undergone many strange adventures. Such is the adaptability of the human spirit that they had now adjusted to a life of Space/Time travel. Though they still hoped to see twentieth century Earth again, their old life had begun to seem more and more like a kind of dream.

Now the TARDIS had made yet another landing. They were all waiting with mingled anticipation and apprehension to discover what lay ahead this time. Moreover, to the Doctor's extreme annoyance, they were all being rather sceptical about his assurances that they were back on Earth, and in the twentieth century.

'Let's take a look on the scanner,' suggested Ian practically.

The Doctor switched on, and they all peered into the viewing screen. The picture was dark and fuzzy, like an old TV set in a poor reception area. 'Oh dear, oh dear, it's not clear,' said the Doctor peevishly. 'It's not clear at all.' He glared at them accusingly, as if it were all their fault.

'I wonder where we really are,' said Ian thoughtfully.

Barbara sighed. 'Somewhere quiet and peaceful, I hope.' She knew from bitter experience that the TARDIS never seemed to take them anywhere *safe*.

Susan gave her a quick smile. 'Yes, we could all do with a holiday, couldn't we?'

Barbara peered at the murk on the scanner. 'I can't see *anything*.'

Ian looked over her shoulder. 'Don't worry, neither can I!'

The Doctor indicated sluggish movement on the screen. 'That could be water. A river, perhaps.' Ian gave him a sceptical look, and the Doctor turned away in a huff. 'Susan, perhaps you'll be kind enough to give me the instrument readings?'

Susan was already studying dials on one of the control panels. 'Radiation nil, oxygen and air pressure normal.'

'Normal for *where*?' snapped the Doctor. He hated any kind of imprecision, especially in matters of science.

'Normal for Earth, grandfather,' said Susan excitedly. 'This is a typical Earth reading.'

The Doctor gave a self-satisfied sniff, as if he'd known the answer all along. 'I don't want to boast, my friends,' he said loftily, 'but that might well be London out there!'

Ian and Barbara exchanged rueful looks. In theory the Doctor's words were true enough. It might indeed be twentieth-century London out there. But on his previous record, it might equally well be some savage alien planet—or the Earth of some completely different age.

Ian braced himself. 'Well, what are we waiting for? Let's go and take a look.'

Barbara agreed. 'Doctor, open the door, please. We'll chance it!'

For a moment the Doctor continued to look sulky. Then he gave one of his sudden charming smiles. 'Yes, of course, my dear.'

He touched the controls, the door swung open, and they all went outside.

They found themselves in an open area, surrounded by high buildings. In front the ground sloped down towards a wide river.

There were scattered piles of building material all around, bricks, timber, steel girders in enormous stacks. Many of the stacks were partially collapsed—the one nearest the TARDIS was in a particularly perilous state.

There was an ironic gleam in the Doctor's eye as he looked at Chesterton. 'Well, here you are, my boy— home at last. There's the Thames.'

'We've come a pretty roundabout way, Doctor.'

The Doctor nodded. 'And arrived more by luck than judgement,' he said, with one of his disarming flashes of honesty. He looked distastefully at the rubble all around. 'This is a pretty horrible mess, isn't it?'

Barbara nodded in agreement. It wasn't a particularly pretty spot to choose for a homecoming. But at least it was Earth.

'Where do you think we are, Ian?'

'Looks like a building-site, down by the Docks. It all seems pretty deserted. We can follow the river into central London, there'll be people about there.'

Ian and Barbara began making plans to find their homes and friends again. The Doctor watched them, frowning. He ran his hand along the nearest girder, then inspected it. His fingers were covered in thick rust. The Doctor's frown deepened. Building material was valuable. You didn't leave it out in the open to decay unused.

'I wonder which year we're in,' he muttered.

Ian caught the worried tone. 'What's the matter, Doctor?'

'Eh? Oh, I was just worrying about the time factor, my boy.'

'After all our travels, we're not going to quibble about a year here or there!'

The Doctor sniffed. For all their recent experiences, these young people didn't realise the dangers and paradoxes in time travel. Suppose they met their own grandparents while they were still children? Or worse still, arrived at a time when all their family and friends were already dead? He kept these gloomy thoughts to himself and said, 'For both your sakes, I hope we're very near to your own time. But bear in mind, we may have arrived in the early nineteen hundreds—or in the twenty-fifth century!'

Barbara refused to be downhearted. 'Well, it's still London. No mistaking that, I can feel it in the air,' she said cheerfully.

Suddenly they realised Susan was no longer with them. She'd grown bored with the conversation of her elders, and slipped away. Ian hunted round for her unsuccessfully. Then it occurred to him to look up. Sure enough Susan was far above their heads, scrambling up the pile of girders. 'What do you think you're doing?' he yelled.

'Just having a look around. Can't see a thing from down there.'

Ian was about to order her down when he was distracted by the Doctor, who said mysteriously, *'Decay!'*

Ian and Barbara stared at him. The Doctor went on talking as if to himself. 'That's the word I was looking for—decay!'

Barbara put a hand on his arm. 'Doctor, what's worrying you?'

'Look at all this! Preparations for some great constructional work. A new bridge across the river, perhaps. Not a small undertaking. Yet all around us is this air of neglect. This place has been *abandoned*—and for quite some time too.'

Ian could see the force of the Doctor's arguments, but he didn't want to admit, even to himself, that the Doctor might be right. The thought that perhaps they weren't home safely after all was too awful to be faced. 'There's always a lot of mess in construction work, Doctor,' he said unconvincingly.

The Doctor was staring into space, his mind trying to solve the problem on the little evidence available. 'Perhaps, my boy, perhaps,' he murmured. 'And yet …'

Barbara shivered. Like Ian, she didn't want her hopes of a safe return snatched away. 'Doctor, you're spoiling it all.'

The Doctor's keen glance went from one to the other of them. 'I'm sorry, my dear. The last thing I want to do is spoil your homecoming. But I think we ought to be wary …'

Susan's voice floated down from above. 'I'm nearly at the top now. Still can't see much, though. I'll just go a bit higher …'

Enjoying her own daring, Susan continued upwards. Suddenly the girder beneath her feet rocked a little. Nervously she said, 'Oops!'

But the girder steadied again. She worked her way along it and on to the very top of the pile. Balanced precariously, she stared at the view below in shocked disbelief.

Although she wasn't a native of Earth, Susan had lived there with the Doctor for quite some time. She was very familiar with the way that London ought to look. The sight of the deserted, half-ruined city came as as big a shock to her as it would have done to Ian or Barbara.

Susan wondered when they must have arrived. Somewhere in the nineteen-forties, perhaps? She knew London had been damaged in World War Two—but she couldn't remember hearing that the damage was as bad as this ... And how was she going to break the news to Ian and Barbara?

She heard Ian calling. 'Susan, be careful! What's it like up there?'

'Doesn't seem to be anyone about,' she called back. 'And the whole city's ...' The girder beneath her feet twisted sideways, and Susan lost her footing. She made a desperate grab at the nearest girder but her hand slipped, and she began a bumpy slide down the side of the pile.

The others looked on horrified and helpless, as she tumbled from the pile, landing almost at their feet. Barbara ran to her, kneeling by her side. Susan stirred and muttered, 'Ruined ... all ruined,' then fell back unconscious. Barbara felt her head with skilful hands. There was a slight trickle of blood on Susan's forehead.

'She grazed her head on the way down but there doesn't seem to be any real injury. She'll be all right.'

The Doctor looked down at Susan, disguising his very real concern with an air of irritation. 'She will go dashing about,' he said disapprovingly—forgetting that he spent his whole life in dashing about on a far greater scale.

Ian helped Barbara to sit Susan up. 'Daft kid,' he grumbled, sounding very much like the schoolteacher he'd once been. 'She's lucky it wasn't worse—'

The Doctor rested a hand on the nearest girder. It was *vibrating*. 'I'm afraid it is worse,' he said urgently. 'That pile was finely balanced, and Susan disturbed the equilibrium.'

They stared upwards and saw a huge steel girder, balanced see-saw like across another, tilt slowly to one side. There was a rumbling, grinding sound as the whole pile began to shift. Susan's fall, though minor in itself, had been like the shout that starts an avalanche ...

'The whole lot's going,' yelled Ian. 'Let's get out of here!'

The Doctor had already spotted the only safe shelter—the arched doorway of a half-completed building nearby. 'Come on,' he called.

AND THE DALEK INVASION OF EARTH

'Over here!' Dragging Susan between them, Ian and Barbara followed him.

From beneath the shelter of the archway they watched the collapse of the pile of girders. It was an impressive spectacle, accompanied by an ear-splitting clang of metal and clouds of dust.

The last girder clattered to the ground and there was a deafening silence. Coughing and choking, the Doctor peered out. 'Everybody all right? Splendid!' He seemed rather exhilarated by the adventure.

'We're all right,' said Ian. 'What about the TARDIS?'

The Doctor smiled complacently. 'How many times must I tell you, Chesterton, my boy, the TARDIS is indestructible.'

The dust was settling now, and the Doctor left the shelter of the arch and began making his way towards the TARDIS. Suddenly he called in an alarmed voice. 'The Ship, Chesterton, the Ship!'

Ian ran to join him, then stopped in horror. The police box was still visible—but only just. An impenetrable tangle of twisted steel girders blocked the way to its entrance. The TARDIS was safe right enough— but they couldn't get back inside it.

9

2

THE ROBOMAN

The Doctor began tugging crossly at one of the obstructing girders. Ian came to help him, but they were wasting their strength. Ian shrugged and gave up, stepping back and wiping his hands. 'We'll need help to shift this lot, Doctor. We'd better try and find someone.'

The Doctor didn't move. He stood gazing at the twisted pile of wreckage, rubbing his chin thoughtfully. 'Remember where we are, Chesterton.'

'We're in London—oh, yes, I see what you mean. Why do we want to get into a police box, people will ask.'

'Ironic, isn't it?' The Doctor was still studying the wreckage. 'Now as I see it, this girder here is the main problem. Shift that and we could open the door of the Ship far enough to squeeze inside.'

Ian looked at the girder. Luckily it was thinner than the rest. 'I could cut through it with an oxy-acetylene torch.'

'Easier said than done, my boy. One can't just whistle up machinery and tools at a moment's notice.' The Doctor looked at Ian with an infuriating air of expectancy. His manner suggested that he already had the answer to the problem, and was waiting to see if Ian could work it out for himself. Since Ian had a shrewd suspicion that the Doctor had no idea what to do next, he found this attitude particularly annoying. Ian glanced about him. 'That building over there looks like a warehouse of some kind. We might find something in it. Even a few crowbars would be a help.'

The Doctor shook his head disappointedly, like a teacher whose favourite pupil had let him down. 'I'm impressed by your optimism, my boy. But brute strength will never move that girder. No, a cutting flame is the right answer.'

Ian's temper boiled over. 'I'm sure of one thing, Doctor,' he snapped. 'We won't achieve anything just standing here. And we must be able to get into the TARDIS before we start looking round—just in case we run into trouble.'

The Doctor was quite unruffled. 'Good, good, Chesterton,' he said approvingly. 'A very intelligent observation.' Clearly the favourite pupil was doing better. Ian opened his mouth for a sharp retort, when the Doctor lowered his voice and led him a little further from the two girls. 'I have a feeling, Chesterton, an intuition if you like, that we're not in your time.'

A wave of disappointment swept over Ian, all the stronger because he himself shared the Doctor's suspicions. 'Just a feeling, Doctor?' he asked, hoping against hope.

The Doctor shook his head. 'Consider this, my boy. Here we are by the Thames. We've been here some little while. And what have we heard? Nothing. No sound of birdsong, no voices, no shipping, not even the chimes of Big Ben. Just an uncanny silence.'

Suddenly Ian realised the truth of the Doctor's words. Apart from the noises they'd made themselves, there'd been nothing but dead silence. Now deeply worried, he followed the Doctor back to the two girls.

Susan was trying to stand up, with Barbara supporting her. 'Ow, my foot!' She sank to the ground, looking apprehensively up at the Doctor. 'Sorry about what happened.'

The Doctor sniffed, showing no signs of his relief that Susan wasn't badly hurt. 'Oh, you're sitting up and taking notice, are you?'

'There don't seem to be any bones broken,' said Barbara encouragingly. 'Just a bit of a sprain.'

Susan was still looking at the Doctor. 'Don't be angry. After all, there's no real harm done.'

'Oh isn't there? Just look at all this mess in front of the Ship. We can't get in.'

Susan looked as if she was about to burst into tears. Hurriedly Ian said, 'We're going to take a look at that warehouse over there, see if we can find some tools.'

Barbara looked worried. 'Can't we all go?'

Susan tried standing up again, then collapsed with a wince of pain. 'My ankle seems to have got worse. It's all swelling up.'

Ian said, 'I'm afraid that settles it. We'll be back as soon as we can.'

Unhappily Barbara watched Ian and the Doctor move away. She turned back to Susan, who was rolling down her sock. 'That ankle does look swollen, doesn't it? Can you move your toes?'

Susan gave an experimental wiggle. 'Yes, it's fine until I put my whole weight on it. I've just twisted it a bit, that's all.'

Barbara looked towards the river. 'Suppose I go and soak my handkerchief with water for a sort of compress? That might relieve it a bit.'

Susan was already struggling to her feet. 'You're not leaving me here alone,' she said determinedly. 'Give me a hand and I can manage to walk.' She put her arm round Barbara's shoulders for support, and they started hobbling towards the water.

By the time they reached the embankment Susan was exhausted. They stopped at the head of some steps leading down to the water and sat on the ground to rest. Barbara looked around. 'It's all too quiet. No traffic … this isn't my time, Susan. It can't be.'

Susan managed a smile. 'Well, back to the TARDIS and off we go again—as soon as we can get the door open.' She saw the sadness in Barbara's face. 'I'm sorry you're not home again after all.' Then she added honestly. 'Sorry for you, but not for me. I suppose I'm selfish, wanting us all to stay together.'

Barbara gave her a consoling hug. 'No, of course not.'

Susan looked at the silently flowing river. 'I think this must be long after your time. We can't expect things to stay as they are. They have to change, don't they?'

'I suppose so,' said Barbara sadly. 'Maybe London's been abandoned. Or maybe they've just done away with noise altogether! You stay there, I'll go down and get some water.'

Barbara made her way down the steps to the river's edge, and took out her handkerchief. By laying face down and stretching her arm, she was just able to dip her handkerchief in the murky water. As she straightened up, something caught her eye, and she jumped back, shuddering.

The body of a man was floating face-down in the water. His clothes were tattered and grimy, and his body seemed thin and emaciated inside them. Some unhappy tramp who'd decided to end everything, thought Barbara—then she noticed the gleaming metal helmet clamped to his head. The body drifted slowly away downstream.

Barbara stood up, half-inclined to drop the water-soaked handkerchief back in the river. But she told herself not to be silly and started climbing the steps.

She was still wondering whether to tell Susan what she'd seen when she reached the top. But there was no one to tell. Susan had vanished. Barbara gazed round wildly. Susan couldn't have walked off, not with that ankle. She must have been *taken*. Suddenly she sensed a flicker of movement behind. Before she could react, a large, grimy hand clamped over her mouth, and she felt herself being dragged away ...

The Doctor and Ian had to go round the back of the warehouse before they found an unlocked door. It creaked open to reveal a flight of steps leading upwards into darkness. 'I'll go first, Doctor,' said Ian firmly. He led the way up the stairs. 'Keep close behind me—and be careful.'

He heard the Doctor's cross voice behind him. 'I'm not a half-wit, you know, Chesterton.' Ian smiled to himself. It would do the Doctor good to be treated like a child—a taste of his own medicine.

Halfway up the stairs Ian paused and called, 'Hallo! Hallo ... anybody there?' His voice echoed in the silence and he went on climbing. The staircase led to a long gloomy landing broken up with several doors. The nearest one, on their right, stood invitingly open, and Ian and the Doctor moved inside. (Intent on what was ahead of them, neither noticed when a door further down the corridor was pushed slightly ajar by a cautious hand. Through the crack, someone was watching them.)

They found themselves in a long high storeroom, empty except for a few scattered crates and boxes, and an old-fashioned roll-top desk in the far corner. Ian looked round. 'Well, there's nothing here.'

The Doctor agreed. 'I'm afraid the place has been abandoned for some time.'

There were shuttered windows on the far side of the room, and Ian threw them open. As the shutters creaked back, sunlight streamed into the dusty room. Ian looked out of the high window, his eyes widening at the panorama of ruined London before him. Below, the river flowed sluggishly through a desert of half-ruined buildings. 'Doctor,' he called. 'Come over here and look!'

The Doctor shook his head sadly at the view. 'Just as I feared. Some unimaginable catastrophe has over-taken London.'

Ian pointed to a square building just across the river. 'Look, there's Battersea Power Station,' he said dazedly. 'It's only got three chimneys. What's happened to the other one?'

The Doctor waved at the surrounding desolation. 'What's happened to all London, my boy? That's the real question.'

The Doctor moved away from the window and began hunting through the desk in search of clues. Suddenly he said, 'Ah,' and triumphantly held up a grimy sheet of paper. 'Well, at least we know the century. This is the remains of a calendar.'

Ian ran across the room and almost snatched the paper from the Doctor's hand. It was a calendar right enough, the familiar pattern of numbered squares. Ian looked unbelievingly at the bold black figures at its head. They read '2164'.

He stared at the numbers, unable to take in what they meant. Slowly realisation dawned. He'd travelled two hundred years into 'his' future.

The Doctor put a consoling hand on his shoulder.

'I'm sorry, my boy, believe me. We must get back in the TARDIS and try again. I'll get you home.'

Ian nodded, unable to speak. The sounds from across the river came as a sudden distraction. 'What's that?'

The Doctor went over to the window. 'Gunfire! This city isn't quite dead after all.'

'Well, we'd better carry on searching. We may find *something* we can use.'

The Doctor slapped him on the back. 'That's the spirit, my boy.' They started searching the room, rooting through crates and boxes, most of which were empty or filled with useless junk.

The Doctor pulled aside an empty crate to get at the one behind— and a figure slumped to the floor at his feet. 'Chesterton! Over here,' he called.

Ian knelt to examine the body, which had fallen face-upwards. It was a middle-aged man, his body as grimy and neglected as his uniform. Clamped to his head was a strange helmet-like device, a gleaming metal affair fitting round the neck and over the head. Ian looked up. 'He's quite dead, Doctor. What's this metal thing for?'

The Doctor bent to take a closer look. 'Just what I was asking myself. Not for ornament, we can be sure of that.'

'Could it be some kind of surgical device—support for a fractured skull, or broken neck?'

'It's too complex for that,' said the Doctor thoughtfully. 'You know what I think, Chesterton—it's an extra ear, a device for picking up ultra high frequency radio waves.'

'A kind of communications system?'

'That—or some method of radio-control ...'

Ian noticed a couple of objects thrust into the dead man's belt. A truncheon—and a whip. He pulled out the whip, a vicious-looking device with a stubby black handle and long leather thongs, tipped with lead. He passed it over to the Doctor, who examined it with distaste. 'Worse and worse. Whoever this chap was, I'm glad we didn't run into him while he was still alive.'

'Any idea *what* killed him, Doctor?'

'He doesn't seem to be lying quite flat. If we turn the body over ...' They turned the body on its face. The black hilt of a knife was jutting out from under the left shoulder blade. 'Just as I thought,' said the Doctor grimly. 'He was murdered.'

From outside the room came the sound of a creaking floorboard.

Ian grabbed the truncheon from the dead man's belt and crept stealthily towards the door. He peered out into the corridor. It was empty. The Doctor close behind him, Ian crossed the corridor and pushed open the door of the room on the opposite side. 'Just another storeroom—and it's empty.' They went back into the corridor and Ian looked up and down it. 'The sounds were coming from somewhere out here.' He moved along the corridor and tried another door. It was locked. Ian rammed it with his shoulder, the door burst open, and he found himself shooting into empty space ... The Doctor quickly grabbed him by his coat and heaved backwards, and they both landed up in a heap in the corridor. Ian scrambled up and looked cautiously out of the door. Once it had led to a wooden staircase running down the outside of the building. But now the staircase was shattered and the door gave on to a sheer drop. Ian helped the Doctor to his feet. 'Well no one could have gone that way,' he said grimly.

The Doctor dusted himself down. 'Only someone like you would even try,' he replied acidly. 'I suggest we abandon this fruitless search and return to the others.'

It was clear that the Doctor had had enough. Ian was inclined to agree with him. It wasn't very likely they'd find a full set of oxy-acetylene tools lying about waiting for them. And maybe hunting for the unseen killer wasn't such a brilliant idea either. 'All right, Doctor, come along.' Ian turned and led the way back downstairs.

They'd reached the warehouse door, and were about to step out into the open when the Doctor grabbed Ian's arm. 'Chesterton, *look*!' The Doctor's other hand was pointing upwards. Ian looked, and gave a gasp of sheer incredulity. Drifting low over the ruined buildings, for all the world like a plane coming in to land, was a flying saucer.

Instinctively Ian ducked back. The Doctor muttering, 'Fascinating, fascinating,' stepped out into the open to get a better look. Ian grabbed him and pulled him back into cover.

From the shelter of the doorway they watched the saucer drift slowly downwards. It looked exactly like the classic flying saucer of science-fiction films and drawings, silvery-coloured, oval in shape, and with rows of windows round the exterior. It made a low droning sound as it moved, disappearing behind some buildings.

Ian shook his head wonderingly. 'There were rumours of flying saucers in my time, Doctor. But I never thought I'd see one as close as this.'

The Doctor rubbed his hands together. 'Well, it settles one question. Whatever happened to London was not caused by the people of Earth. That was an interplanetary spaceship, my boy. Earth has been invaded by some other world.'

'Which explains the dead man we found,' said Ian thoughtfully. 'That thing on his head must have been some kind of alien control-device. And that gunfire we heard means somebody's still resisting the invaders.' Ian looked at the Doctor in sudden alarm. 'Barbara and Susan! We've got to find them and warn them what's going on.'

They ran back to the TARDIS at top speed. Barbara and Susan were nowhere to be found.

Ian looked angrily round the building site. 'Why will they do it?' he demanded. 'Why must they always go wandering off?'

'Perhaps they heard the gunfire from across the river,' suggested the Doctor. 'Or they might have seen the saucer, and run to hide.'

Ian sighed. 'Well, I suppose we'll just have to look for them.'

They searched the building site without success, then started working their way towards the river. At the top of the embankment steps they found their first clue…a grubby, water-soaked handkerchief.

The Doctor nodded keenly, looking, thought Ian, like a rather elderly Sherlock Holmes. 'So far so good, Chesterton, my boy. They came here for water, something frightened them, and they ran off again.'

'Why didn't they run back to find us?'

The Doctor frowned at the interruption to his fine flow of deduction. 'I can't imagine,' he snapped. 'We shall just have to look further afield.'

They turned to leave—and found four uniformed men barring their way. They were ragged, gaunt, emaciated—and each one wore a shining metal device clamped to his head. They held truncheons in their hands.

Ian and the Doctor stood quite still. 'We won't get past them, Doctor,' Ian whispered.

'Then we must go down the steps.'

'Swim for it?'

'What else?'

Ian looked at the Doctor. For all his tetchiness, he was certainly a game old boy. 'All right. They don't seem to have guns. I'll try talking first.' Ian called out a hearty 'Hello!' At the same time he and the Doctor began edging their way down the steps.

The four men moved steadily after them. One was a little ahead of the rest. Suddenly he bellowed, 'Stop!' His voice was slurred and dragging, like a record played at the wrong speed. As he spoke he picked up a jagged chunk of masonry, and the other men did the same.

Ian and the Doctor continued their steady retreat. As they neared the water Ian whispered. 'When I give the word, turn and dive!'

'Ready when you are, my boy.'

'Right—now!'

They both turned, and froze in horror. A Dalek was rising from the water and advancing menacingly towards them.

3

THE FREEDOM FIGHTERS

When the flying saucer passed overhead, Barbara and Susan were already fleeing through the ruins of London with a man who called himself
Tyler. He was a tough looking character, burly and middle aged, and
although his manner was curt and brusque he didn't seem to be hostile.

When he'd grabbed Barbara at the steps, he'd released her almost
at once, saying he'd just wanted to make sure she didn't scream. 'They'
had their patrols everywhere, and he'd already carried Susan to shelter
so she wouldn't be spotted.

He'd taken Barbara to Susan, who was laying under one of the
arches of the bridge, confused and frightened. Lifting Susan in his
arms, he'd bustled them both on their way, promising to take them to
a safe hiding place, and come back later for their friends.

When the drone of the saucer filled the air, Tyler immediately flung
Susan and himself to the ground. 'Get down,' he whispered fiercely.
Barbara obeyed, though she couldn't resist raising her head to watch
the gleaming shape of the saucer glide out of sight. Then Tyler was
on his feet again, picking Susan up. Ignoring their questions, he said
brusquely, 'We must keep moving, we can talk later. We shan't be safe
till we get underground.'

Still carrying Susan, Tyler led the way to the broken entrance
of what had once been an underground railway station. He started
carrying Susan down the stairs, but she struggled till he had to put her
down. 'Wait! What about my grandfather and our friend?'

Tyler shrugged. 'We'll do the best we can for them.'

Susan wasn't satisfied. 'That's not what you said before!'

Barbara joined in. 'You promised you'd get the others. We don't
want to be separated.'

'There isn't time to argue,' said Tyler savagely. 'If we stay on the surface we'll all be killed, and then who'll help your friends? Now *come on*.' They moved on down the steps, Barbara and Tyler supporting Susan between them.

Tyler led the way along dusty silent corridors and on to the platform. Strange posters covered the walls, not the usual announcements of films and plays and exhibitions, but severe looking official notices in heavy black type. Barbara paused to read one.

PUBLIC WARNING. DO NOT DRINK RAINWATER.
ALL WATER MUST BE BOILED BEFORE CONSUMPTION.

In smaller letters beneath were the words, 'Issued by the European Emergency Commission.'

Tyler reached out and pressed the letter 'o' in 'NOT'. Part of the wall slid back to reveal a tiny gap. A grim-looking young man appeared, rifle in hand. Tyler said, 'O.K. David, it's me.' David stood aside and Tyler helped Barbara and Susan through the gap. The door closed silently behind them.

They were in a small tiled ante-room, furnished with a few battered tables and chairs. Barbara guessed it had originally been accommodation for London Transport staff. Susan collapsed thankfully into a chair, rubbing her ankle.

The young man called David looked curiously at the two girls. 'Hullo, then, what have you got here?' There was a faint Scots burr in his voice.

'Found 'em wandering about down by the river. Sitting targets.'

Barbara was annoyed by his scornful tone. 'We've only just got back to London. We didn't know there was any danger.'

Tyler looked incredulous. 'Didn't know? No, I suppose you couldn't have known or you wouldn't have acted so stupidly.'

'Now, *listen* ...' began Barbara angrily. 'You drag us here ...'

David held up his hand. 'All right, you two, let's not fight among ourselves. Time for introductions. You already know Jim Tyler. My name's David Campbell.'

His friendly smile transformed the grim young face, and Barbara couldn't help smiling back. 'I'm Barbara, and this is Susan.'

'I hope you can cook.'

Barbara gave him a surprised look. 'After a fashion.'

'Good. We're short of cooks down here ... and my cooking's terrible.'

He turned back to Tyler, his manner serious again. 'One of the Robomen jumped me in the warehouse. I had to deal with him. We'd better stop using the place for storage though.'

Tyler nodded. 'All right. Tell Dortmun.'

Susan had only been half-listening to this conversation, but the mention of a warehouse made her look up. 'Are you talking about the warehouse near that building site—beside the river?'

David nodded. 'That's right. Just opposite the old power station.'

Susan tried to get up, then sank down again, wincing from the pain in her ankle. 'Then you must have seen the Doctor and Ian—they went in there.'

'There *were* two men—but I hid from them. I thought they must be enemies—'

An inner door opened and a wheelchair shot through it, halting abruptly. In the chair sat a middle-aged man with a strong deeply-lined face. The upper part of his body was muscular and powerful, and he propelled the wheelchair along with big hands gripping the wheels. But his legs were wasted and shrunken, covered by an old army blanket. His voice was deep and commanding, with nothing of the invalid about it. 'Where the devil have you been, Tyler?'

Tyler was obviously used to the newcomer's abrupt manner, and his reply was equally spirited. 'I got delayed. Ran into these two. What are you doing up here? You're supposed to stay below in the operations room.'

'I'm just as active as anyone, and don't you forget it.'

Tyler grinned. 'All right, Dortmun, all right.' Somehow Susan sensed that despite the angry way they talked to each other, these two men were old and close friends.

Dortmun spun the wheelchair to face Barbara and Susan. 'Well, I suppose we can use two more pairs of hands,' he said gruffly.

David winked at Susan, as if telling her not to be too put off by Dortmun's abrupt manner. 'This is Susan. And this is Barbara—she says she can cook!'

'Good!' Dortmun glared at Susan. 'And what can you do?'

Susan grinned cheekily at him. 'Me? I can eat.'

For a moment Dortmun glared at her, then he gave a grim smile. 'Well mind you leave some for me. David, where do you think you're going?'

The young man was already at the door. 'These two have friends, two men, still on the surface. I know roughly where they'll be—I thought I'd go and bring them in.'

Dortmun considered for a moment—and Barbara and Susan held their breath. Then he nodded. 'All right. But take care—and don't be too long.'

As David passed by her chair, Susan whispered, 'Thank you. Be careful.'

'Don't worry, I'll see you later.'

As David left, Dortmun headed his wheelchair towards the inner door. 'Come along. We'd better get below.' He stopped as he saw Tyler and Barbara helping Susan to get up. 'What's the matter with her?'

Susan hobbled to her feet. 'I happen to have sprained my ankle,' she said sharply. 'Don't worry, I'll manage. I'm just as active as anyone.'

Dortmun gave an approving nod. Clearly he liked people to stand up to him. 'All right, let's get moving.'

He sped the wheelchair through the inner doors, and Tyler, Barbara and Susan followed him.

Ian and the Doctor watched horror struck as the Dalek rose slowly from the water and glided along the bank towards them. Instinctively they turned to run. But the nightmarish figures of the metal-helmeted men had moved down the steps to cut off their escape.

The Dalek spoke in the harsh, grating tones Ian remembered from Skaro.* 'Robomen! Why are these humans wandering freely in a forbidden zone?'

In his slurred, dragging voice the leader of the Robomen replied, 'No explanation.'

'Where is the Robopatrol for this section?'

'Not known.'

---

*See 'Doctor Who and the Daleks'

'You will take his place until he is found. The human beings will be taken to the landing area.'

'Daleks,' whispered Ian. 'What are they doing here on Earth?'

'Leave this to me, my boy.' The Doctor marched boldly up to the Dalek. 'I demand that you release us at once.'

'We do not release prisoners.'

'Indeed? And by what right do you take prisoners in the first place?'

'We are the masters of Earth.'

The Doctor snorted disdainfully. 'Not for long, I promise you.'

The Dalek was both astonished and enraged by this defiance. 'You will obey us or die!'

The threat only made the Doctor more indignant. 'Die? And who are you to condemn us to death? That settles it. Whatever you're up to, I shall pit myself against you and defeat you.' The Doctor folded his arms and glared defiantly at the Dalek. Ian closed his eyes and held his breath, mentally willing the Doctor to shut up. He was all in favour of opposing the Daleks, but he saw no use in getting themselves blasted on the spot.

The Doctor's words seemed to touch off one of those typical speeches, a mixture of threats and boasts, which seemed to be the Daleks' only form of communication with other species. 'We have heard many such speeches from the human leaders. All have been destroyed. Resistance is useless. It must cease immediately.'

'Oh must it? You surely don't expect the people of Earth to welcome you with open arms. Even Daleks can't be that stupid.'

'We have already conquered Earth.'

'Don't you pathetic creatures realise? You'll never conquer Earth, not unless you destroy every living being—'

The Dalek's patience was clearly exhausted. 'Take them! Take them!' it screeched.

Robomen grabbed Ian and the Doctor by their arms and dragged them away. In their ears echoed the angry voice of the Dalek. 'We are the masters of Earth. We are the masters of Earth. We are the masters of Earth ...'

From his hiding place nearby, David Campbell watched helplessly as the Doctor and Ian were led away. He had arrived just in time to see their capture. There was little he could do to help them, not with

Robomen present in such force. But at least he could find out where they were being taken. Slipping cautiously through the ruins, David began trailing the Robomen and their prisoners.

'Survivors of London. The Daleks are the masters of Earth. Surrender now and you will live. Those wishing to surrender must stand in the middle of any street and obey the orders they will receive. Obey the Daleks!'

The radio went silent. Dortmun crashed his fist on the table, making the set jump and rattle. 'Obey motorised dustbins! We'll see about that! Tyler, come to the office, I want to talk to you.'

Barbara and Susan looked at each other. They were in a long underground room, filled with rows of trestle tables, at which people sat quietly working. Some were cleaning or assembling weapons, others were working on radio sets and a variety of technical equipment. One corner was sectioned off into a kind of canteen, where women and girls were preparing food, and in another was the partitioned-off room into which Dortmun had just disappeared. Susan noticed that everyone in the room was tired and grim-faced. The place was obviously the main headquarters of the anti-Dalek resistance movement.

Tyler hesitated a moment before following Dortmun. He called, 'Jenny, come over here a moment, will you?'

A small dark girl got up from the nearest table and walked across to them. She stood before Tyler unsmiling, as if resenting the interruption to her work. 'Well?'

'Two newcomers. See if you can find them something to eat. One of them has a bad ankle.'

The girl looked unsmilingly at Susan and Barbara, no hint of welcome in her face. 'All right.'

Tyler turned to go. 'David will be back soon. I'm sure he'll have news of your friends. He might even have them with him.' He disappeared after Dortmun.

Jenny said briskly, 'Right, who's got the bad ankle?'

Susan held out her foot. 'I have.'

Jenny knelt beside her chair and examined the ankle with skilful but ungentle fingers, ignoring Susan's groan of protest. She straightened up. 'Just a strain, no bones broken. Why haven't you put a cold compress on it?'

'Because I've only just got here,' said Susan spiritedly. She'd no intention of being bullied by someone no older than herself, and she'd taken an immediate dislike to this cold-faced and bossy girl.

Jenny turned to Barbara. 'I'll see to this ankle. You go over there and get some food. While you're at it, put your names down for a work detail.'

Protectively Barbara said, 'Susan won't be able to do much, not till her foot's better.'

'She can work sitting down, can't she? We've no room for useless mouths here.' Jenny moved away.

Barbara glared after her angrily. Like Susan, she didn't take kindly to being bossed about. But she reminded herself that they were dependent upon these people, not only for food and shelter, but for help in finding Ian and the Doctor. It wouldn't do to upset them—at least until Susan's ankle was better. Barbara gave Susan a rueful grin, and went meekly to fetch the food. From inside the little office came the noise of voices raised in anger. No one took any notice. It was only Dortmun and Tyler having another shouting-match. Everyone was used to that ...

Dortmun slammed his fist on the desk. 'We must attack them, Tyler. We must attack now!'

'That's all very fine. But how? We've got about twenty able-bodied men and women, the rest are old folk, and kids.'

'Ample!' snapped Dortmun defiantly.

Tyler groaned. 'Ample? To attack the Daleks? Remember the wars in the twentieth century, Dortmun, when men with bayonets attacked machine-gun posts? They got mown down, defeated by superior technology. So would we be ...'

'Don't lecture me, Tyler!'

'Then don't ask the impossible. You haven't been in the streets for quite some time. The Daleks have increased the Robopatrols, tightened up their security. It's almost suicide to go out there these days.'

Dortmun hammered the arm of his wheelchair. 'All right, I know. I'm *in this*! I send others, but I don't have to go myself!'

Tyler's tone softened. 'I didn't mean that and you know it. Now then, how's this new bomb of yours getting on?'

The distraction worked, just as Tyler had hoped. Eagerly Dortmun wheeled his chair to a table in the corner of the office, where shining glass spheres were set out on a blanket. 'All finished,' he said proudly.

'Have you tested it yet?'

'Tested it? It doesn't need testing, it's perfect. This is the bomb that will destroy the Daleks! Look, here's the casing, the new formula explosive, the detonating device ...' Eagerly Dortmun began to explain the workings of the bomb on which he had laboured so long.

He was still doing it when David Campbell slipped into the room some minutes later. David had seen Barbara and Susan as he came in, but they'd had their backs turned and he'd been able to slip into the office without their noticing him. Dortmun looked up. 'We're just discussing the next attack, David. How did you get on?'

'I brought back some more tinned food. There's quite a bit left in that department store.'

Tyler nodded. 'All right, I'll send out a foraging party. What about the two strangers?'

'Just as I got to the embankment I saw them being taken away. I followed them part of the way. Judging by the direction, they were taking them to Heliport Chelsea, where the Dalek saucer landed.'

Dortmun shrugged dismissively. 'Then that's the end of them. Once the Daleks get them inside that saucer, they're done for!'

David thought for a moment. Then he said, 'Not necessarily Dortmun. You listen to me ...'

4

INSIDE THE SAUCER

Guarded by Robomen, the Doctor and Ian were standing in what had once been the Chelsea Helicopter Port—Heliport for short. It was a wide stretch of open tarmac, surrounded by ruined buildings. Towering above them rose the immense gleaming shape of the Dalek spaceship. Together with a group of other prisoners, the Doctor and Ian were being held at the foot of a ramp which led up into the ship. Dalek patrols glided to and fro, guarding the perimeter of the Heliport.

Ian moved closer to the Doctor. 'Why are they keeping us waiting about here?' he whispered.

'I imagine this is an assembly point, my boy. They're going to take all their prisoners on board at once.' The Doctor nodded towards the other side of the Heliport. A group of Robomen were marching two more prisoners to join the main group.

Ian looked round at his fellow captives. They were grimy, ragged and defeated-looking. He turned back to the Doctor. 'I still don't understand all this. The Daleks were destroyed. We were there on Skaro, we saw it happen.'

Sadly the Doctor shook his head. 'The devastation may not have been as complete as we imagined. The Daleks have incredible tenacity, tremendous powers of survival. There may have been other colonies, on other parts of Skaro …' He looked at the scene around them, the ruined city, the enormous spaceship, the blank-faced, helmeted Robomen standing guard over their prisoners. 'Anyway, however it happened, the Daleks have survived. And they've evolved too.'

Ian studied one of the Daleks as it glided past. 'I see what you mean. These do look a bit different. I wonder if that's got anything to do with their increased power of movement. On Skaro they could only travel in their own metal city.'

'Quite true. But this is an invasion force, remember. They've found ways to adapt themselves to new planets. Something on the hover-craft principle I should imagine.'

By now the two newcomers had been herded across to the main group. They were tough looking characters, one tall and wiry, the other short and thickset. Ian thought they looked less cowed than the other prisoners. A Dalek glided up to the Robomen guards accompanying them. 'Where are the other members of your patrol?'

In a slurred emotionless voice one of the Robomen answered, 'These men killed them both.'

Angrily the Dalek spun round, its gun-stick pointing at the prisoners. 'What are your names?'

'Bill Craddock,' said the taller man defiantly.

With equal truculence the thick-set man said, 'And I'm Mick Thomson. Want to put us in your hall of fame, do you?'

The Dalek's eye stalk swivelled towards them. 'Craddock and Thomson,' it repeated. 'You will be punished for your crimes. Robomen, continue your patrol.'

The Robomen moved away, and the Dalek addressed the group of prisoners. 'You will remain here without moving until it is time to enter the ship.'

Ian heard the man called Thomson mutter, 'We'll never escape once they get us inside there. I'm going to try something now, are you with me?'

Craddock glanced around. Daleks were on patrol everywhere, constantly moving round the edges of their group. 'Don't be a fool, man. You haven't got a chance.'

There was a note of hysteria in Thomson's voice. 'They're not getting me back in their filthy mine.'

A Dalek moved closer. 'The prisoners will be silent.'

Suddenly Thomson shoved Craddock to one side, dodged around the Dalek, and began tearing across the Heliport at full speed. Almost immediately a Dalek appeared to block his path. Thomson changed direction, wheeling to his left, but here too a Dalek was waiting. He dodged desperately to and fro, like a chess-pawn threatened by more

28

powerful pieces, but the Daleks were ahead of him at every turn. At last a group of them encircled him—there was nowhere to run. Thomson called desperately to his friend. 'Craddock—help me!'

Instinctively Craddock took a step forward, but the Doctor held him back. 'Don't be a fool! There's nothing you can do. Our time will come.' Such was the confidence and authority in the Doctor's voice that Craddock found himself obeying without question.

They heard a grating Dalek voice. 'Kill him!' Several Daleks fired at once, and Thomson twisted and spun under the agonising impact of the Dalek death-ray. His body crumpled to the ground.

A Dalek moved menacingly back towards the horror-struck prisoners. 'Any further defiance will be punished in the same way. Prisoners will wait until it is time to enter, the ship.'

In a corner of the main operations room, David was breaking the news of the Doctor's capture to Susan. He glanced across to the other side of the room, where Barbara was helping to prepare a meal. 'I thought perhaps we wouldn't tell Barbara—not just yet anyway.'

'Oh, but I must,' protested Susan.

'Listen,' said David urgently. 'Dortmun's keen to make an immediate attack on the Daleks. He's got a new type of bomb he wants to test. Now, I managed to persuade him that the saucer would be a natural target. We can put off telling Barbara until the attack is over.'

Susan was beginning to understand what he meant. 'If the attack's a success, there's a chance that Ian and the Doctor will be rescued?'

David took her hand. 'Exactly. And if it isn't—well, they'll have just disappeared. At least there'll still be hope.'

They were interrupted by Jenny, who held out a batch of Roboman helmets to David. 'You wanted these?'

'Yes I did, thank you.'

'Well, here they are, take them. I've got more important things to do than wait on you.'

'You're a model of patience and charm, aren't you, Jenny?'

'I don't believe in wasting time.' Jenny glanced at David's hand, which was still holding Susan's. 'And I don't believe in sentiment, either.'

Her work finished, Barbara came over to them. She looked curiously at the pile of helmets. 'What's all this?'

'An invention of the Daleks,' said David grimly. 'We took them off dead human beings—human beings who'd been turned into Robomen.'

'There aren't that many Daleks on Earth,' explained Jenny, 'so they need helpers. They operate on some of their prisoners and turn them into sort of human robots, radio-controlled by these helmets. David's trying to find some way to block the Dalek transmissions that's why we're collecting these things.'

David picked up a helmet. 'The Daleks call the operation the Transfer. These helmets here transmit the Dalek orders direct to the human brain—at least for a time. Eventually the effectiveness of the operation wears off.'

Susan looked at the gleaming metal helmets and shuddered. 'What happens then? Do the people become human again?'

Jenny shook her head. 'The process burns out the circuits of the brain. In the end the Robomen go mad and die. They seem to get a sort of suicidal urge. They throw themselves off buildings, into the river … That's why the Daleks need so many prisoners—to keep up their supply of Robomen.' David frowned warningly at Jenny, but she went on with her story. 'They take them to their flying saucer and operate on them. Once they've got you on board, there isn't a hope.'

Unaware of the shattering effect of her news on Susan, Jenny moved away. Susan looked at David. Perhaps it was just as well they hadn't told Barbara what had happened to the Doctor and Ian.

'Move!'

Obedient to the Dalek voice, the line of prisoners began shuffling up the ramp. The Doctor looked up at the Dalek ship as they moved inside. 'A work of genius, Chesterton.'

Ian was less enthusiastic. 'It's impressive enough. And it looks escape proof.' The interior of the Saucer was built in the Dalek style that Ian remembered from Skaro. Walls, doors, floors and ceilings were all of gleaming metal, everything utterly bleak and functional.

The Doctor rubbed his hands. 'Only on the surface, my friend. There's always a weak point—if you can find it.'

The Daleks were marching them along a curving metal corridor. The leading Dalek stopped, and touched a control. 'The first three prisoners will move into this cell.' The Doctor, Ian and the man named

Craddock were the first three in line. The Dalek herded them into a cell and closed the door after them. 'Remaining prisoners—move!' Obediently the line of prisoners shuffled on.

In the control room, a Dalek stood watching the scanner screen. This Dalek was larger than the others, and its casing was a dull jet black. This was the Dalek Supreme, the Black Dalek, Commander of the expedition to Earth. On the scanner was a view of a prison cell, with the Doctor, Ian and Craddock sitting on the floor, their backs against the wall. The Dalek Supreme touched a control and the hidden camera zoomed in until the Doctor's face filled the screen. 'This is the one?'

Another Dalek replied. 'That is so, Commander. He defied us, spoke of resistance. His words betrayed superior intelligence and determination.'

The Dalek Supreme turned away. 'We shall await the results of the experiment.'

Unaware that he was the subject of a Dalek experiment, the Doctor was chatting to his fellow-prisoners, discussing the only subject of real interest—escape. 'I had a good look in that corridor outside. Plenty of scanners about.'

Craddock glanced round the cell. 'Can't see any in here. They may be hidden. What do you make of this thing, Doctor?' He pointed to a semi-transparent crystal box, packed with complex machinery, which was mounted on the wall near the cell door.

'I've a theory about that. I'll investigate it in a moment. Let's continue to survey the general situation.'

'I noticed what looked like a loading bay, Doctor,' Ian contributed. 'It should lead to the ground. There might be a guard outside, though.'

'There will be,' said Craddock gloomily.

Our task is to escape,' said the Doctor sharply. 'You'll do no good sitting here moping.'

'And you'll do no good fooling yourself,' growled Craddock. 'Once the Daleks have got you, that's it!'

The Doctor shook his head reprovingly, and moved across to the crystal box. He began studying it closely. Ian said, 'How did all this start—the invasion of Earth, I mean?'

Craddock stared at him. 'Where've you been, on one of the moon stations?'

'Something like that,' replied Ian vaguely. 'I never got the full story.'

Craddock was silent for a moment, then he began to speak in a low, bitter voice. 'The meteorites came first. They bombarded Earth about ten years ago. A freak cosmic Storm, the scientists said ... Then people started dying—some new kind of plague.'

'Germ warfare?' suggested Ian.

Craddock nodded. 'The Daleks were waiting, up there in space, waiting for Earth to get weaker. Whole continents were wiped out. Asia, Africa, America. Everywhere you went, the air smelled of death. The doctors tried all kinds of new drugs, but none of them worked. By now the world was split up into tiny struggling communities, too far apart to help each other. About six months after the plague had begun, the first of the flying saucers landed ...'

Ian listened in fascinated horror as Craddock went on with his story. The Daleks had flattened whole cities, striking ruthlessly at any sign of resistance. They had captured untold numbers of human beings, turning them into Robomen, discarding them when they died and creating new ones. Other human beings had simply been enslaved, made to toil in the Dalek mines under the whips of the Robomen.

The catalogue of horrors went on, until Ian could bear it no longer. 'Why?' he interrupted. 'That's the one thing you haven't told us. Why are they doing all this? What has Earth got that they want so much?'

Craddock looked dully at him. 'I don't know, no one knows. But it's something under the ground. They've turned most of Bedfordshire into one gigantic mining area ...'

The Doctor, who had been only half-listening, turned round impatiently. 'Never mind all this blab about Bedfordshire. I think I've discovered how this thing works.'

Ian went over to him. 'All right, Doctor. What is it?'

The Doctor pointed to a small metal rod clamped into a holder beside the box. Fixed next to it was a lens with a handle, looking like a pocket magnifying glass. 'Just hand me that, will you, my boy?'

'I wouldn't touch it,' warned Craddock.

Ian looked at the Doctor, who beamed infuriatingly at him. Carefully Ian took out the rod and handed it to the Doctor. 'There you are. Now what?'

'First, an experiment.' The Doctor moved the rod close to the transparent box. As if in sympathy, a similar but much larger metal rod *inside* the box began to move. 'You see, it's magnetic.'

'Marvellous,' said Craddock sarcastically. 'How does it help us?'

'And why's the box here at all?' asked Ian. 'What do the Daleks use it for?'

The Doctor nodded approvingly. 'An excellent question, my dear chap. Now, suppose you were a Dalek shut in here, how would you get out?'

Craddock frowned. 'Push up the door?'

The Doctor shook his head reproachfully. 'A Dalek has no hands, only a sucker. They rely on brain, not brawn.'

Ian looked at the crystal box, the lens and the metal rod. 'Are you telling me this set-up is some kind of key?'

'Precisely. All we have to do is open the box and use the key. Now then, pass me that lens, will you?'

Ian handed it over, examining the handle. 'You know I think you're right, Doctor. This thing is obviously made for a Dalek to hold.'

The Doctor gave him an encouraging smile. 'You're a good lad, Chesterton, you really do try hard. Now we must find the correct refractive index, or the box will probably explode.'

The Doctor began moving the lens about near the top of the box. Craddock watched him sceptically. 'Refractive rubbish,' he muttered. 'You don't think the Daleks would leave the key in here for us to find.'

'They have only contempt for human intellect,' said the Doctor sharply. 'And if all their prisoners are like you, I'm not so sure they're wrong ...' The Doctor started muttering abstruse calculations to himself. 'Did you ever do applied three dimensional graph geometry at your school, Chesterton?'

Ian shook his head. 'Only Boyle's Law.'

'Let's boil down this problem then, shall we?' Chuckling at his own excruciating pun, the Doctor added, 'Cover your eyes, gentlemen, this may be nasty.'

Craddock shook his head scornfully. 'I suppose it'll turn into a great big pumpkin or—' He broke off in astonishment. The lid of the crystal box had sprung silently open. 'Hey, it's a flaming miracle.'

Ian slapped the Doctor on the back. 'Doctor, sometimes you amaze me!'

'Only sometimes?' The Doctor chuckled. 'Now, all we've got to do is find the way to use this bar … it'll be something to do with static electricity, I imagine. Now, if I push the bar in the box back with this one …'

Craddock looked at the two bars. The one in the Doctor's hand was tiny, the one in the box large and heavy. 'You're going to push *that*—with *that*?'

'Exactly. And since similar poles repel, and both bars are magnetic …'

The Doctor moved the small bar close to the large one. Immediately the large bar slid back—and the cell door moved smoothly upwards.

Craddock looked admiringly at the Doctor. 'You're a genius!'

The Doctor waved a deprecating hand. 'Oh it was nothing, nothing at all … Now let's get out of this infernal flying machine and find Susan and Barbara.'

They ran out into the corridor and straight into a waiting group of Daleks and Robomen. The Black Dalek dominated the group. 'He has passed the escape test. Take him.' Robomen grabbed the Doctor and dragged him away. Others held back Ian as he tried to follow. He turned angrily to the Black Dalek. 'What are you going to do with him?'

The toneless Dalek voice replied, 'He will be robotised.'

5

ATTACK THE DALEKS!

The voice of the Dalek Supreme seemed to shake the little radio set. 'Rebels of London. This is your final warning. Leave your hiding places. Show yourself in the open streets. You will be fed and watered. Work is needed, but in return the Daleks offer you life. Continue to resist and we will destroy London. You will all die, the males, the females, the young of the species. Rebels of London, come out from your hiding places.'

The radio went silent. Dortmun gestured exultantly at the pile of shining glass grenades. 'We'll come out all right—with these. We don't need to hide any more, we can make *them* run.'

Barbara looked round the operations room, which was packed with grim-faced freedom fighters. Dortmun had called a meeting to listen first to the Dalek speech, and then to make one of his own. 'We'll answer their ultimatum for them—tonight. We're going to make a frontal attack on their flying saucer. Now *we* have the superior weaponry. One success and people will hope again. One victory will set this country alight. Then Europe, then the world. That's all we need—one victory!'

There was a roar of enthusiasm. Jenny's sceptical voice cut through it. 'How do we get within throwing range at the Heliport? The Daleks guard the perimeter—and they can fire long before we're near enough to use the bombs.'

Tyler didn't care for opposition. 'This will be a surprise attack, at night.'

Jenny wasn't convinced. 'The surprise will be over when the first bomb is thrown.'

Barbara jumped up. 'I've got it! You can use *these*.' She pointed to the pile of Robomen helmets at the back of the room. 'Some of the men can disguise themselves as Robomen. The rest can be prisoners they're bringing in. You'll be able to get right into the middle of the Heliport before they suspect!'

Tyler picked up one of the helmets and put it over his head. 'It'll work,' he said slowly.

Dortmun smiled grimly. 'Yes. It'll work. Let's prepare for the attack.'

Barbara, David and Susan crouched in a ruined house, overlooking the edge of the Heliport. The open area before them was brightly lit, the gleaming shape of the flying saucer towered above them. Patrolling Daleks moved silently around the perimeter.

All three were carrying satchels full of grenades. David tapped his meaningfully. 'Sure you've got it straight? As soon as Tyler and his attack group move in, we start chucking these.'

The two girls nodded. There was nothing to do now but wait. Susan rubbed her ankle, hoping it wouldn't let her down. Though still a little sore, it was almost better. She'd been determined not to be left out of the attack ...

Inside the saucer the Doctor had been taken to a small room packed with intricate electronic machinery. Its central feature was a long table. Above one end was suspended an elaborate helmet-like device from which projected two metal prongs. For what seemed a very long time the Doctor was subjected to a variety of measuring devices which had recorded his blood-pressure, his temperature, the electrical activity of the brain, and indeed his total physical condition. The Robotising process was elaborate and time-consuming, and the Daleks did not care to waste it on subjects who might ruin everything by dying on them. At last the battery of tests was complete, and a Dalek scientist droned, 'Prisoner suitable subject for operation. Take him to the table.'

Two Robomen bustled the Doctor over to the table and stretched him out on it. Before he could move metal clamps were applied to hold him in place. His sleeve was pushed back and he felt a prick in his right arm. Immediately a numbing paralysis spread over his entire body.

The Doctor discovered he was unable to move a muscle. But although his body was immobilised, his brain was fully alert. Surely there was something he could do … Surely something would turn up to save him. Or was this really the end, after all?

The Doctor lay quite still on the metal table. Dalek scientists glided around him, making final adjustments to the. machinery that was designed to turn the Doctor into their helpless slave.

In the ruined house, David suddenly tensed. A dispirited-looking group of prisoners was being marched to the bottom of the saucer ramp, under the charge of a squad of Robomen. David drew a deep breath. 'Here they come. Get ready.' He took a grenade from his satchel, and prepared to throw.

Roboman helmet weighing heavy on his head, Tyler marched his squad of fake Robomen, with their equally fake prisoners, straight towards the ramp. The nearest Dalek guard moved up to him. 'Stop. What are you doing?'

Tyler made his reply in the slow dragging tones of the Robomen. 'I am taking the prisoners into the ship.'

'Wait. In which area were these prisoners captured?'

Tyler answered at random. 'Sector Four.'

'No patrol was ordered in Sector Four.'

Tyler did his best to bluff. 'New orders were given by the Dalek Supreme.'

Before the Dalek could reply there came the dull crump, crump, crump of exploding grenades from all around the Heliport. Barbara, Susan and David, and several other groups of freedom fighters, hurling grenades at random from widely different points, tried to create the impression of an attack from all sides. Forgetting Tyler, the Dalek guard began to scream, 'Attack warning. Attack warning!'

A siren started blaring from inside the ship. Daleks were rushing around in all directions. In his Roboman voice Tyler shouted, 'I will take the prisoners into the ship.' He marched his party quickly up the ramp.

Daleks were all round the perimeter of the Heliport now, firing in the direction of the explosions. But since the attackers were so few in number, and well spaced out, they were very hard to find.

A Dalek sped close to the building in which David and the girls were hiding, firing almost at random. David yelled, 'Get down!' and swept the two girls to the floor. The blast of a Dalek ray-gun sizzled through the open window and set fire to the wall above their heads. A man ran past the window then dropped screaming as the Dalek fired again. David struggled to his feet. 'Right, that's it. They must be inside by now. Time for us to pull back.' They ran from the blazing building and disappeared into the darkness.

Tyler and his men dashed along the metal corridors of the Dalek ship. 'Right,' called Tyler, 'spread out. Free as many prisoners as you can before you use the bombs.' One of the freedom fighters began blasting open the door of the cell which held Ian and Craddock.

The noise of battle came only faintly to the Robotising room, and the Dalek scientist continued his work undistracted. Suddenly a harsh voice blared from a hidden speaker. 'We are under attack. Report to main ramp. General alert. Report to main ramp.'

Obediently the Robomen and the Dalek scientists began filing from the room. The last Roboman was about to leave when a Dalek scientist stopped him. 'The prisoner is already prepared. You will remain and supervise the operation.' The Roboman touched a control. The Robotising machinery started to hum and throb with power. The pronged, helmet-like device began to descend, coming closer and closer to the Doctor's head. Just as the prongs seemed about to sink into his forehead Tyler dashed into the room, and wrenched the helmet device to one side. It blew up in a shower of sparks. The Roboman ran forward, there was a brief struggle, and he dropped with Tyler's knife between his ribs.

Another freedom fighter ran in. Tyler called, 'Baker! Help me get this man off the table.' They unfastened the clamps and lifted the Doctor clear. He slumped limply in their arms. Tyler made a quick attempt to bring him round and then gave up: 'No good, you'll have to carry him. See if you can get him clear.' Baker began dragging the Doctor from the table. A Dalek voice blared from the speaker. 'All reserve Robomen into action. Destroy the invaders!'

From a new hiding place behind a ruined wall, David, Susan and Barbara surveyed the scene. Fires were blazing all round the perimeter of the heliport. The Daleks had now abandoned the search for their elusive attackers and were retreating back to their ship. Barbara gripped David's arm. 'Tyler's going to be trapped inside the ship! Are those bombs of Dortmun's really any use against Daleks?'

Susan said, 'I didn't see the bombs stop any Daleks. But there's too much smoke to see what's going on.'

David said nothing. He too had his doubts about Dortmun's bombs.

Jenny came tearing towards them, pausing only to hurl a grenade at the Dalek ship. David seized on her arrival with relief. 'Jenny, take these two back to H.Q. I'm going to see if I can get Tyler out of that ship.'

As David ran off, Jenny said, 'I'm not playing nurse to you two. I'm going with David.' She looked scornfully at Barbara and Susan. 'I should have thought you'd have wanted to come too. After all, your two friends are in there.'

Barbara looked at her in astonishment, then turned to Susan. The look on Susan's face told her the whole story. 'You knew. You knew all along.'

Susan was shamefaced. 'We didn't want to worry you before—'

Barbara was already running towards the Dalek ship. Susan followed, and caught her by the arm. 'Barbara, where are you going?'

'To help David find Ian and the Doctor. We've got to get them out of there.' Pulling free of Susan's grasp, Barbara ran off.

Susan turned to find Jenny looking at her. 'Well, are you coming?'

'I suppose so, though what good we can do ...'

Jenny wasn't listening. 'We'll do no good if we don't try. Come on, this way.'

Jenny ran off and Susan, still hobbling a little, did her best to keep up with her.

By now Tyler and his men were already rushing down the ramp, bringing with them all the released prisoners they could find. Ian was somewhere near the back of the confused bunch of men.

At the foot of the ramp, the Daleks were waiting to meet them. They fired into the crowd at point blank range, and men screamed and dropped all around. Tyler shouted, 'The bombs. Use the bombs!' He pulled a grenade from his satchel and hurled it at the nearest Dalek. There was an explosion, a blaze of flame, and a cloud of smoke. Then, through the drifting smoke, Tyler saw the Dalek moving inexorably towards him, quite unharmed. Dortmun's bombs were a failure. Tyler yelled, 'Scatter all of you. Run! The bombs are no good!'

Freedom fighters and escaping prisoners began to run in all directions. Remorselessly the Daleks pursued, shooting them down. Since he'd been at the back of the escaping crowd, Ian was still on the ramp when the battle started. He got a grandstand view of the unequal struggle. He saw the useless bombs exploding all around, producing flame and smoke, but doing very little damage. Two freedom fighters tipped a Dalek on to its side by main force—only to be themselves blasted down by more Daleks. Suddenly, he saw a familiar face appear out of the darkness. 'Barbara,' he yelled desperately. 'Barbara, get back!' Barbara saw him and waved then she disappeared, swept up by the milling crowd.

Ian jumped down from the ramp, just as the ramp itself began retracting with a hum of power. Two Daleks appeared round the curve of the Dalek ship, their gun sticks trained on Ian. The lifting of the ramp had left a small gap between the base of the ramp and the ship itself. Instinctively Ian flung himself into the gap—just as the ramp started to come down again, closing the opening and trapping Ian inside the Dalek ship. Gun-sticks blazing, Daleks poured down the ramp ...

Barbara shielded her eyes from the smoke, dodged the blast of a Dalek gun-stick, and stumbled straight into Jenny. One glance at the disaster and chaos around them had convinced even Jenny that the attack was hopeless. She grabbed Barbara's arm and started dragging her away. 'Come on. We're getting out of here.'

Barbara pulled away from her. 'But Ian's there—I saw him on the ramp. And where's Susan?'

'We got separated. I think she's with David. They'll both have to take their chances. There's a way through the sewers. If you don't come now, you'll get killed.'

Without waiting for a reply, Jenny ran off. After a last agonised glance at the spaceship, Barbara ran after her.

In the control room of the Dalek ship, the Black Dalek watched the scene outside the saucer on a scanner. The screen showed a confused picture of blasting Daleks, exploding grenades, and falling freedom fighters. The area around the saucer was littered with the crumpled bodies of those who had failed to escape.

The Black Dalek transmitted orders to those outside. 'The enemy are retreating. Recapture as many prisoners as possible. Block all exits from the area. Find the enemy attackers and exterminate them.'

Tyler was ushering the last of the survivors down an open manhole cover, in an alley behind a burning building. 'Hurry,' he shouted. 'They'll be here soon.'

He was just about to duck down the manhole himself, when he heard pounding footsteps. He hesitated, then yelled, 'Come on, over here ... Quickly!'

A man tore round the corner of the building, hesitated for a moment then started running towards Tyler. Seconds later a Dalek appeared in pursuit. It fired immediately, and the man screamed once then dropped to the ground. Tyler disappeared down the manhole like a rat into its hole, pulling the cover over his head.

The Black Dalek turned away from the scanner screen.

'The attack has been defeated.'

His number two came forward eagerly. 'Many prisoners have been recaptured. Most of the attacking rebels have been killed or wounded. Only a very few are still at large.'

There was cold fury in the voice of the Black Dalek. 'Find them. Find all survivors and destroy them. They must be exterminated!'

In a ghastly chorus, the surrounding Daleks took up their leader's chant. 'Exterminate them! Exterminate them! Exterminate them!'

6

THE FUGITIVES

The freedom fighters' operations room was almost empty. Jenny was bathing a cut on Barbara's head with a wet cloth, while Dortmun looked on in gloomy silence. There was no one else. The rest must have been captured or killed, thought Barbara wearily. She looked up at Jenny. 'You're sure you didn't see what happened to Susan? She was with you the last time I saw her.'

Jenny's voice was gruff. 'I told you. She caught up with David—we were going to look for you. Then there were all those explosions, and I just lost sight of her.' Barbara sighed, and Jenny's voice softened at the sight of her unhappy face. 'Don't worry, she may still turn up. There, your head's fine now. Just a scratch.'

There came the sound of movement from the corridor outside. Barbara looked up hopefully—but it was Tyler who came into the room.

'Your bombs are useless, Dortmun.'

The man in the wheelchair looked up. 'How many were killed?'

'It was a massacre. We didn't stand a chance.'

'How many?'

Tyler sighed. 'I don't know. Almost all of them, I think. A few got away before the Daleks sealed the area, one or two got out through the sewers ...' He picked up a rucksack and started to fill it with supplies.

Barbara said dully, 'The Doctor and Ian were in that saucer. I saw Ian ... just for a moment ...' her voice faltered, then she regained control. 'What about the Doctor? Did you see any sign of him?'

'There was an oldish man,' said Tyler slowly. 'We found him in the Robotiser Chamber. Baker got him clear of the ship, but after that

…' He shrugged, then turned to Dortmun. 'We'll have to get out of London.'

'Why? The Daleks have never looked for us down here.'

'That was before we attacked their precious flying saucer. We've stirred them up now. They'll search every inch—*destroy* every inch.'

'But I *must* stay here. I need to work on my bomb.' He looked up at Tyler appealingly. 'It only needs a little more work, the principle is sound …'

'Forget your bomb. It's a waste of time.'

'It's the answer. It's the *only* answer …' There was a mad obsessive determination in Dortmun's voice.

'And who's going to use it for you?' asked Tyler. 'Me? These two girls here? Use your intelligence, man.'

Jenny joined in. 'Tyler's right. London will be too hot for us now.'

'If we could just stay a few days longer,' persisted Dortmun.

Tyler shook his head decisively. 'No. I'm going to see if I can find any more survivors, then I'm heading North.'

Barbara got to her feet. 'Can I come with you? If Ian and the Doctor did escape, we might find them …'

Tyler shouldered the rucksack. 'I'm sorry, but you'd slow me down. I've got to go alone. Good luck.'

Barbara called, 'If you do see any of my friends …' But Tyler had already gone.

Jenny said, 'We must get out of here too.'

Dortmun looked at them with sudden eagerness. 'There's the other H.Q. People will be gathering there—your friends too, maybe. I can go on working on my bomb—there's a laboratory there …'

'Dortmun, *please*—' began Jenny.

Dortmun was beyond reason. 'That's it, we'll go to the Transport Museum.' He looked hopefully at them. 'It means crossing London, going over one of the bridges …'

Barbara sighed. 'All right, we'll come with you.'

Dortmun spun his wheelchair, and headed for his office. 'I'll just get my things together. You'd better pack some supplies.'

Jenny moved closer to Barbara, and said in a low voice. 'We'd stand a lot more chance on our own.'

'Maybe. But he won't stand *any* chance without us. You needn't come—if you don't want to.'

Jenny hesitated, then shrugged. 'Might as well. Maybe Dortmun's right ... people might start collecting at the other H.Q.'

By the time they had loaded two more rucksacks, Dortmun came out of the office, a satchel slung over his shoulder. 'We'd better be moving. It's nearly light now.'

He headed his chair for the door. As she followed him, Barbara said, 'Do you really think my friends might end up at this Museum?'

Dortmun nodded vigorously. 'It's possible. Yes, it's distinctly possible.'

Possible, but not very probable, thought Barbara wearily. In her heart she feared she would never see her missing friends again.

The Black Dalek was addressing his aides. 'Orders from Dalek Supreme Command. Rebels must be totally crushed. An intensive search of London is to be made. If necessary, the city will be totally destroyed.'

'Do you intend to remain in the city?' asked the second-in-command.

'No. The ship will now take me to the mine workings in the Central Zone.'

'We have recaptured many escaped prisoners.'

'They will be put to work in the mine. Feed and water them. They must be strong in order to work.'

'I obey.'

The second-in-command began issuing orders into a communications network. Dalek and Robomen patrols would cover all central London, seeking out and destroying rebel hiding places.

The Black Dalek swivelled to face the spaceship's flight operators. 'Prepare ship for lift-off!'

Although the Daleks didn't know it, there was at least one escaped prisoner who was still free, and still on the ship. After his dive into the hatch below the ramp, Ian had found himself in a service tunnel somewhere in the bowels of the ship. Wriggling between humming and throbbing Dalek machinery, he had gradually worked his way back to the upper levels. Immediately he headed for the Robotiser room, in the hope of finding the Doctor.

He slipped inside, glancing with a shudder at the central table and sinister electronic apparatus suspended above it. The place was completely empty, no Doctor, no Daleks.

He heard movement in the corridor outside and ducked behind a bank of instruments. Two men came into the room. One was slight and wiry, with curly black hair. Behind the first man, holding him in a painful armlock, was a tall figure that Ian recognised immediately.

He stepped from his hiding place. 'Craddock!'

Releasing his prisoner, Craddock swung round. His face was expressionless, and there was a gleaming metal device on his head. His voice was slurred and dragging. 'You are to be Robotised.'

Ian backed away. 'Craddock—it's me …'

Craddock lurched forward and grabbed Ian's arm, trying to bend it behind his back. Ian struggled desperately. Although his movements were slow and clumsy, the Robotised Craddock seemed abnormally strong, and quite impervious to pain. A savage blow to his ribs produced only a grunt, and there was no slackening in the steady pressure on Ian's arm.

Ian decided to use skill rather than strength. Grabbing Craddock by sleeve and coat, Ian twisted round, bent and sent his opponent hurling over his shoulder in a judo throw. Craddock crashed to the floor, with enough force to stun any normal man. But Craddock was no longer normal. He scrambled immediately to his feet and advanced on Ian, hands outstretched. Despairingly Ian realised he was fighting not a man but a machine—a machine that couldn't be hurt, would never get tired and never give up …

As Craddock's hands closed on Ian's throat, the wiry man joined in the struggle. He threw himself on Craddock, gripped the helmet-device with both hands, and ripped it from Craddock's head. The results were immediate and dramatic. Craddock let out a series of terrifying screams, his hands clutching his head. His body flopped to the floor and thrashed frantically like a stranded fish. His back arched in a final convulsion and he went limp and still.

Ian got up slowly, rubbing his throat. He examined Craddock's body. As he'd expected, the man was quite dead. He looked at the wiry man and held out his hand. 'Thank's for the help—my name's Ian.'

The other returned the handshake. 'Larry. And thank *you*. I was on my way to ending up like *him*.' He nodded towards the body on the floor. 'He caught me hiding in one of the storerooms. I smuggled myself on board quite a while ago.'

'You did *what*?'

'This saucer makes periodic trips to the mine workings in Bedfordshire. My brother's one of the slaves there. I'm going to find him and get him out.'

'So you're hitching a lift with the Daleks? You don't choose the safest way to travel, do you?'

Larry grinned. 'Maybe not. But it's the quickest. What about you? What are you doing here?'

Quickly Ian explained how he'd been captured by the Daleks, freed during the raid, and trapped in the ramp housing straight afterwards. 'I'm looking for the friend who was captured with me,' he finished. 'Though I'm not even sure if he's still on board. There's a chance he got away during the raid.'

Larry started dragging Craddock's body towards the wall. 'We'd better put this down the disposal chute. They'll start hunting for us if it's found in here.'

Ian helped Larry to drag the body to a hatch set in the far corner. Larry slid back the hatch-cover, and immediately they felt a powerful suction dragging them towards the opening.

Between them they wrestled the body into the hatch-way. Immediately the force of the suction snatched it down into the chute. Larry slid the cover back into place. 'Right, we'd better get out of here and find somewhere safer to hide.'

Suddenly there was a hum of power, and a steady vibration all around them. Ian put a hand on the wall to steady himself. 'Looks as if you might get your trip to Bedfordshire after all. I think we're taking off!'

In the Control Room, the Black Dalek ordered, 'Maximum repulsion. Set course for mine workings in Central Zone.'

The Dalek spacecraft lifted slowly from the Heliport, which was still littered with the bodies of those who had died in the attack. It rose smoothly into the air and began skimming northwards over London, just as dawn was breaking.

*

46

From their hiding place, Susan and David watched the saucer disappear from sight. Susan wondered if the Doctor and Ian were still on board, or if they'd managed to get away during the raid. She had only a confused and nightmarish memory of her own escape. Daleks firing into the crowd of freedom fighters and escaping prisoners, the screams of the dying, the roar of explosions, sheets of flame and clouds of smoke. Somewhere in all the confusion David had grabbed her hand and pulled her clear. They'd escaped from the area just before the Daleks sealed it off, and they'd been stumbling through the ruins ever since. At last they'd arrived in the cellar of a ruined house, and here they'd stopped to rest. David explained it. was one of the freedom fighters' regular hiding places. Although the house above it was in ruins, the cellar itself was warm and dry. It was furnished with battered old beds and chairs, and there were even stores of food, water, weapons and ammunition. A flight of steps led up from the cellar into an alleyway between rows of ruined houses.

From the cellar doorway, Susan saw the flying saucer disappear over the rooftops. 'Does that mean the Daleks have gone?'

David shook his head wearily. 'The saucer comes and goes regularly, ferrying prisoners to the mines. There are still plenty of Daleks and Robomen on the ground.' Suddenly he broke off. 'Get down—there's a patrol coming.'

They ducked back inside the cellar. Despite David's warning Susan couldn't resist peeping round the door. Two Daleks were gliding along the alleyway above them. Alert and suspicious, their eye-stalks swivelled to and fro, scanning all around them. Susan shrunk back inside the cellar, closing her eyes. After a moment, David touched her gently on the shoulder. 'It's all right—they've gone. We'll give them time to get well clear and then move on.'

'Move on where?'

'We'll have to try to get out of London, join up with one of the other groups.'

From the alleyway came the sound of pounding footsteps. A Dalek voice grated, 'Stop! Surrender or you will be exterminated!'

The footsteps faltered then ran on. There was a scream of 'No ... no ...' and the crackle of a Dalek gun-stick. Then silence.

Susan shuddered and threw herself into David's arms. 'Why did we ever come here,' she said hysterically. 'Why, why? If only we could get back in the TARDIS and just go away ... I'm sure the Doctor would let you come with us ...'

David said sadly, 'You get away if you can. But I can't.'

'Why not?'

'This is my world. My Earth. I can't just leave it, clear off somewhere else.'

Susan looked at him wonderingly. 'I've never felt like that about anywhere. I left my own planet when I was very young, and we've been travelling ever since. I've never really *belonged* anywhere.'

David looked seriously at her. 'Someday you ought to stop travelling and really *arrive* somewhere—get down, someone's coming.'

'Daleks?'

'Don't think so. Human footsteps. Could be Robomen ...'

Pushing Susan down into cover, David crouched in readiness at the bottom of the stairs. He slipped something from his belt, and Susan saw light glinting on the blade of a knife.

They waited as the dragging footsteps came closer ...

REUNION WITH THE DOCTOR

Susan cowered back as a monstrous, deformed shape appeared at the top of the steps. The huge misshapen figure began to descend the stairs … As it came nearer, Susan realised she was looking not at one man but *two*, one carrying the other on his shoulders. And the man being carried was the Doctor!

Joyfully she ran forward calling, 'Doctor, it's me, Susan!'

David meanwhile had recognised the other man. He put his knife away, and helped the newcomer to lower the Doctor's body to the ground. 'Baker! Are you all right?'

Baker grunted with relief as he lowered the Doctor's body. 'I'm O.K. Worried about him, though.'

The Doctor was very still. His eyes were wide open but he seemed unable to move or talk. Susan looked anxiously at Baker. 'What is it? What's the matter with him?'

'Daleks drugged him. Should be beginning to wear off by now.'

The Doctor stared up at them. Slowly, very slowly, his lips moved and he said, 'Susan …' Susan hugged him in happy relief.

Shrugging aside Susan's thanks, Baker told them of the disastrous aftermath of the attack, of how he'd managed to get the Doctor away early on. 'We were lucky. I think most of the others were killed or captured.'

'What will you do now?' asked David. 'Do you want to join up with us?'

Baker, a burly, taciturn character, was clearly something of a loner. 'No, the bigger the group, the bigger the risk. I'll make for the Cornish coast. Not so many Daleks down there.'

David handed over a flask and a packet of food. 'Here, take these. You'll need them.'

'What about you?'

'We'll manage. Plenty of food stored here—and not many left alive to eat it.'

Baker took the supplies and made for the cellar door. 'Thanks. I'm off then. Good luck.' He disappeared up the stairs, and they heard his footsteps moving along the cobbles of the alleyway.

Suddenly a metallic voice shouted, 'Halt!'

David ran to the top of the steps and peered out. He could see Baker halfway down the alley. A Dalek had appeared at the other end. Baker spun round. A second Dalek was blocking the alleyway behind him.

As both Daleks advanced towards him, Baker dropped his rifle and raised his hands. The second Dalek screeched, 'Exterminate!' Both Daleks fired at once. Caught in the double blast, Baker twisted in mid-air and died immediately. His body dropped to the ground. For a long moment the two Daleks scanned the alley with their eye-stalks. Then they glided silently on their way.

Shaken, David crept back to Susan. 'The Daleks just shot him down, wouldn't even let him surrender. They must have decided to kill everyone on sight.'

Susan was cradling the Doctor in her arms, getting him to drink a little water. 'Where can we go, David? What can we do?'

'Dortmun set up a second Command H.Q.—in the old Transport Museum. If your friends have survived, that's probably where they'll make for. There are more supplies there too, bombs and weapons. Dortmun had quite a laboratory ...'

The Doctor groaned and started to sit up, and Susan helped him into a chair. 'How are you feeling now?'

The Doctor spoke with surprising clarity. 'The Daleks paralysed my body and my willpower, but not my mind. Really a most interesting experience.' He flexed his legs and found he could move them a little. 'It's wearing off, though. Wearing off fast.'

Susan hugged him again. 'You just have a good rest. As soon as you feel better, we're going to go and find Barbara.'

*

For Barbara and Jenny, the long journey across London was fraught with danger. Although it was now broad daylight, the fact that Dortmun was in a wheelchair meant they had to keep to roads and paths in fairly good repair, and prevented them from using the safe routes across the rubble and through the sewers. Time and time again they had to shove the chair into some doorway for cover, and crouch motionless while a patrol of Daleks glided by.

Most dangerous of all was crossing the river. They had decided to use Westminster Bridge, since that part of Central London seemed fairly free of Daleks. They had almost reached the bridge itself when Jenny called, 'Look out!' and they rushed into a shop doorway for cover. Barbara never forgot the sight that met her eyes when she peeped out. A patrol of Daleks gliding over Westminster Bridge, their sinister shapes profiled against the ornately decorated façade of the Houses of Parliament. It made an unforgettably symbolic picture. The squat metallic shapes of the alien invaders stood out against the building that represented so many centuries of human progress and tradition—a tradition the Daleks had ended with brutal abruptness. They watched in silence as the Daleks filed over the bridge and disappeared.

Dortmun nodded satisfied. 'There shouldn't be another patrol for a while. Come on, let's try to get across while we can.'

They pushed the wheelchair across the bridge and through the deserted streets of Belgravia without running into any more Daleks. The Civic Transport Museum was housed in an elegant exhibition hall, in a quiet side street.

Dortmun led them to a back entrance in a mews, and produced a key that opened a locked side-door.

They found themselves in a shadowy darkened hall, rather like a huge bus garage. All around stood vehicles of various kinds, roped off with explanatory placards nearby. There were milk-floats, taxis, old-fashioned open-topped buses, dust-carts—all the many kinds of vehicles that are part of the life of a big city. Some of the vehicles had still been in use in Barbara's day, and she wondered what had replaced them in this future age. Had Londoners *ever* solved their traffic problem? If they hadn't, thought Barbara, remembering the empty streets, the Daleks had certainly dealt with it for them.

At the back of the hall were various rooms intended for museum staff, including a workshop where Dortmun had established his laboratory. He made for it immediately, forgetting the two girls in his anxiety to get back to work on his one obsession—the creation of a bomb that would destroy the Daleks. Jenny disappeared too, scouting the area for signs of the enemy.

Several hours later, Barbara was prosaically employed in boiling a kettle in one corner of the hall. Behind a small screen she'd found a tiny kitchen alcove. There was a table and a gas-ring, a packet of tea in one of the cupboards, and an unopened tin of milk. The logical thing to do seemed to make a cup of tea. The typically English response to any crisis, thought Barbara with a smile as she poured water into a chipped china teapot.

A side-door flew open and Dortmun propelled himself towards her. The satchel over his shoulder was once more filled with gleaming grenades. 'It's finished,' he announced triumphantly. 'I've boosted the explosive charge. The problem is to crack the Daleks' outer casing. It's made from a metal called Dalekenium.'

Barbara looked doubtfully at the grenades. Would they really work this time? Dortmun had been just as confident before the disastrous raid on the Dalek flying saucer. She passed him a cup of tea. 'This Dalekenium … could that be what they're mining for in Bedfordshire?'

'I doubt it. I imagine they mine Dalekenium on their own planet.'

'Then what are they looking for? Oil maybe? Some other metal?'

Dortmun shook his head. 'They could have picked on a hundred planets to find those things. But they're after something … Something buried deep in the heart of Earth.'

Footsteps echoed through the great hall as Jenny came towards them. 'I've checked over the whole building,' she announced. 'Not a sign of anyone. But I think the Dalek patrols *have* been here—and I *know* some of our people have.'

Barbara poured her some tea. 'How can you be so sure?'

Jenny pointed to a mysterious symbol scrawled on a wall nearby. 'That's one of our message-signs. It means some of our people have been here and moved off towards the South Coast. Don't blame, them either. London seems to be swarming with Daleks.'

Dortmun frowned. 'You think they've landed another force in London?'

'You saw for yourself. We were lucky to make it here through the streets. If things go on building up, we haven't a chance. We'll have to move on.'

Barbara's heart sank at the thought of another pointless, dangerous journey. 'Where can we go? What's the good of just running all the time?'

Jenny looked coldly at her. 'We're surviving, aren't we? That's what counts.'

Dortmun patted his satchel of grenades. 'We'll all survive. Now I've got this new-formula explosive ...'

Barbara looked despairingly at her two companions. Dortmun obsessed with perfecting the bomb that had become his reason for living, Jenny thinking only of running and hiding like some hunted animal. They needed someone who could look at the problem with a wider perspective. Barbara spoke her thoughts aloud. 'I wish the Doctor were here.'

Jenny looked surprised. 'He's just an old man, isn't he? What could he do?'

'He happens to be a brilliant scientist. He could *think*—which is more than the rest of you seem to be doing!'

'A scientist, you say?' Dortmun was immediately interested. 'I'd like to discuss my work with another scientist. If only we knew where he was ...'

'I've been thinking about that, trying to put myself in his place. I'm sure he'd be intrigued by those mines in Bedfordshire. He'd want to take a look at them.'

Jenny said brutally, 'If he's still alive.'

'Of course he's still alive,' said Barbara angrily.

'Why? What's so special about your Doctor? He doesn't wear some invisible shield, does he?'

Dortmun spoke with sudden authority. 'Jenny! Go and take another look around.' As Jenny moved sulkily away, Dortmun said apologetically, 'She's not really callous, you know. She's been fighting the Daleks for most of her life.' Barbara nodded understandingly and he went on. 'I'd like you to try to find your friend the Doctor and give him this—it's the notes for my bomb.' He handed her a tightly folded bunch of papers, scrawled over with notes and incomprehensible diagrams ...

Barbara looked at the papers in astonishment. 'Why can't you give them to him yourself?'

'I can, I can … if we ever meet. But meanwhile I'd like you to take care of them. I'm not exactly mobile like this, am I? If something happened, I'd like my work to go on.'

For all his bitterness, thought Barbara, no one could deny Dortmun's courage. Crippled, defeated, hunted, his one thought was to go on fighting. She took the papers and laid them on the table. 'All right, I'll look after them if you like. But I'm not leaving you …'

Dortmun gave one of his rare smiles. 'Thanks. Now then, if you'll round up Jenny, we can set out for those mines …'

Barbara didn't have to go far to look for Jenny. There were stairs on the other side of the hall, and Jenny came running down them, her footsteps echoing. 'Daleks! I saw them from an upper window. They're all over the place.'

Jenny's voice rang out across the hall. Nearby, Dortmun heard it, and came to a sudden decision. Clutching the bombs on his lap, he wheeled his chair towards the main doors.

Barbara and Jenny missed him as they ran down the other side of the hall. Barbara stopped in astonishment when she saw Dortmun wasn't where they'd left him. Jenny looked round. 'Where is he? He can't have gone outside, he wouldn't be so stupid.'

Barbara saw the papers on the table. 'Look, he's left the plans—but he's taken the bombs. I think he's gone to try them out!'

There was an echoing crash from the front of the hall. Daylight streamed in as the main doors were flung open. They turned and saw Dortmun in the doorway, heard his voice raised in defiant challenge.

'Daleks! Where are you, Daleks?'

The group of Daleks outside the museum's main door seemed frozen in astonishment as Dortmun appeared in the doorway. To be defied and attacked was a new experience for them, and they hesitated, fearing some trap.

Dortmun wheeled himself forwards straight at the nearest Dalek. When he was close enough he hurled the entire satchel of grenades. There was a shattering explosion, and a sheet of flame. A corner of the building collapsed, and Dortmun and his Dalek enemy disappeared beneath the rubble. Daleks milled about in confusion, shouting 'Emergency! We are being attacked!'

Picking up Dortmun's papers, Barbara pulled Jenny back into the shadows. 'They'll be here any minute. We've got to hide!'

Daleks moved cautiously into the hall, eye-stalks scanning the exhibits on either side. One of them trained its gun-stick on the waxwork of a milkman, posed stiffly beside his float. 'Halt! Who are you?' The waxwork, naturally enough, didn't move. Another Dalek examined it more closely. 'It is a sub-cultural effigy. Proceed with the search.'

Methodically the Daleks continued to search the hall. Barbara and Jenny retreated before them, dodging from one antiquated vehicle to another. Despairingly, Barbara realised they were being driven into a corner. The Daleks moved closer and closer, tightening the circle around the two girls ...

The Doctor was staggering determinedly to and fro across the little cellar, working off the remaining effects of the Dalek drugs. His face was grim and set as he fought to ignore the shooting cramp-like pains in arms and legs. Susan watched him in concern, realising the Doctor was quite likely to go on till he dropped. She caught him by one arm, and gently led him to a chair. 'Easy does it. That's enough for a first try.'

Thankfully the Doctor stretched his aching limbs. 'I never realised walking could be so exhausting. The numbness is most certainly wearing off though. I shall be able to travel in a short while.'

'Good. David says we should move North, join up with the resistance groups there.'

Susan saw at once that she'd made a mistake. The Doctor frowned and said sharply, 'My dear child, I don't care what that young man says. I make the decisions, and I think it best that we return at once to the TARDIS.'

'But we can't even get inside. David says London's swarming with Daleks. We'd never even get there alive.'

The autocratic side of the Doctor's nature came to the fore. 'Are you questioning my authority, child?'

'No, but David says ...'

'David says, David says,' mimicked the Doctor savagely. 'You seem to trust this young man's judgement more than you do mine!'

With a shock Susan realised the Doctor was quite right. Somehow she *had* grown to rely on David, to trust his judgement in every crisis. She felt safe when they were together. That was why she didn't want to leave him. Perhaps there were other reasons too ...

Returning from his scouting expedition, David heard raised voices, and listened to the last stages of the argument. He paused at the head of the cellar steps, realising he would have to move carefully. He was getting very fond of Susan, and he didn't want them to be separated. He ran down the steps into the cellar. The Doctor and Susan were glaring at each other, and scarcely seemed to notice him. David ignored the tension in the atmosphere. 'I didn't even get as far as the river. There are patrols everywhere. We'll never make it to the Museum.'

The Doctor snorted. 'I take it you're saying it would be impossibly dangerous to go back to the river too?'

David nodded. 'I'm afraid so. There are Daleks in this area of course, but not nearly so many.' He grinned reassuringly at Susan and turned back to the Doctor. 'I wanted to ask you—what would you suggest as our next move?'

The Doctor sat bolt upright. 'Me? Why do you ask me?'

'You're the senior member of the party, sir. Naturally, I'd like the benefit of your superior experience.'

The Doctor beamed. Clearly this young fellow David was a sensible chap after all. He considered carefully. 'Well, if you really want my advice ... I think we should head North, join up with some of the resistance groups there. I'm very keen to see what the Daleks are up to in this mine of theirs!'

Susan flung her arms round the Doctor and hugged him. 'Grandfather! Oh, Grandfather!' The Doctor returned her hug, winking at David over her shoulder. 'My dear child, what is all the fuss about?'

The Commander of the Dalek ground forces glided into the control room of the London base. 'Message from Dalek Supreme, now *en route* for mining area. Report on the destruction of rebel hiding places.'

The Dalek engineer gestured with his sucker towards an illuminated wall-chart. 'Destruction is proceeding. Rebel hiding places in areas one to three destroyed. Areas four to eight now in flames. Proceeding to lay charges in vicinity of suspected rebel hideout in area nine.' The sucker indicated a spot on the map ...

Two Daleks glided along the alleyway outside the basement in which the Doctor and his friends were hiding. Between them they pushed a small trolley on which stood a large metal canister. Dials and switches were set into the canister lid. One of the Daleks touched a control, and the canister began emitting a steady electronic bleep.

Leaving the trolley just at the head of the stairs, the Daleks turned and glided away. From somewhere in the distance there came the noise of an explosion.

Susan looked up at the sound of the distant rumble. 'What was that?'

'The latest Dalek tactic,' said David grimly. 'Blockbuster bombs. They destroy whole sections of the city at a time. Anywhere the Daleks think we've a hideout, they just blow up the entire area.'

The Doctor was on his feet. 'Shouldn't we be on our way, my boy? If they suspect you've a hideout in *this* area ... ?'

Susan shivered. 'Must we? I don't like the sound of those explosions—and there may still be Daleks about.'

David put an arm round her shoulders. 'All right, we'll hang on a little longer. But the Doctor's right, we must go soon.'

A needle flickered on the detonation dial of the canister outside. The electronic bleep quickened as countdown entered the final phase ...

8

THE MINE OF THE DALEKS

Suddenly the Doctor held up his hand. Susan stared at him. 'What's the matter?'

'Listen!'

In the silence the electronic bleep sounded clearly. It was speeding up, and getting louder. The Doctor and his companions ran out of the basement. They stopped in horror at the sight of the gleaming metal canister at the top of the steps. 'What is it?' whispered Susan.

David's face was grim. 'One of the Dalek blockbuster bombs.'

Susan tugged at his arm. 'Quick, let's get clear ... run!'

David didn't move. 'No use. That thing's due to go off any moment. There's no way we could get out clear of the range of the blast.' He stood staring at the bomb as if paralysed by horror.

'In that case we'd better dismantle the thing,' said the Doctor briskly. He ran nimbly up the steps and leaned over the canister, studying the controls set into its top. 'Now then, this dial with the needle is the time mechanism. The red area at twelve o'clock signifies the detonation point, I imagine.'

David looked over his shoulder. 'So when the needle reaches the red, that will be it?'

The Doctor nodded. 'Help me prise the front off this thing, will you, my boy? I must destroy the timing control.'

David produced his knife and thrust it into the join between the main body of the canister and its lid. He heaved with all his strength— and the knife blade broke in two.

'I need some kind of a lever,' snapped the Doctor. 'Look around, both of you. A nail, a piece of metal, anything will do.'

Obediently David and Susan began searching the rubble. The Doctor went on working with the broken blade but without much success. The stub of the blade was too thick to go in the crack. He tossed it aside. Susan found a twisted piece of iron. 'How about this, Doctor?'

'Too big. There must be *some* way we can get in ... some tool.'

Suddenly David said, 'Acid! Those bombs of Dortmun's—the detonation mechanism is acid-based. Maybe we could burn through the casing.'

The Doctor nodded eagerly. 'It's a chance. Let's have one of them here. Quickly now!' David ran down into the cellar, reappearing almost immediately with his bomb-satchel. He ran back up the steps and handed the Doctor one of the fragile glass spheres.

The Doctor took it from him, and held it carefully on the top of the canister, just over the point where he estimated the timing mechanism to be. 'Pass me your piece of iron, Susan. Now, *if* I can manage to release the acid without detonating this bomb ...' Using the iron as a hammer, the Doctor gave the sphere a carefully measured tap, like a man cracking a boiled egg with a spoon. A crack appeared in the sphere and a colourless liquid started to trickle out. As it ran over the lid of the canister it *smoked*.

'Look,' whispered Susan. 'It's starting to burn through ...'

A patch of the metal was beginning to crack and crumble. The Doctor jabbed cautiously with the piece of iron, and the metal flaked and crumbled away. 'Splendid! Now your knife again, young man.' Feeling like the assistant surgeon at an operation, David passed the Doctor the broken knife.

The Doctor glanced at the detonation dial. The needle was now only a fractional distance from the red zone, and the bleep was rising even higher. But the Doctor's face was calm and his hand steady as he jabbed at the delicate mechanism with the improvised tool.

'Now, if I remove the fuse ...' Carefully he lifted out a small section of the bomb's 'works' ...

Suddenly the bleeping stopped. The needle on the detonation dial became still, and the Doctor leaned on the canister for support as he drew a deep gasping breath ...

The Daleks finished their search of the Transport Museum and assembled outside. 'There are no more rebels in the building,' announced the patrol leader in confident tones. 'We shall continue the search elsewhere.'

The Dalek patrol moved away, leaving behind them a pile of rubble which entombed one of their number and the rebel leader Dortmun.

Inside the museum, Barbara and Jenny crept from the vintage corporation dustcart in which they'd been hiding. Although it was an unglamorous hiding place it had proved quite effective. The Daleks had searched all round the parked vehicles, but hadn't bothered to look inside any of them, perhaps not understanding the purpose of these alien machines.

Barbara peered out of the still-open front door. 'They've gone. But there's no saying they won't be coming back. We've got to get away from here.'

'How? With Dalek patrols everywhere, we'd be shot down as soon as we set foot in the streets.'

'Then we won't set foot.' Barbara waved her hand. 'With transport all around us, why should we have to walk?'

Ignoring Jenny's protests that the whole scheme was crazy and would never work, Barbara started checking over the vehicles in the hall. Some were too clumsy and antiquated, others too slow, and she settled at last on the sturdy corporation dustcart in which they'd hidden.

A search of the garage attached to the Museum produced tools, a foot-pump, and best of all, half a dozen cans of petrol under a tarpaulin. Soon Jenny was pumping up the dustcart's tyres while Barbara checked over the engine. She'd run her own little car in her teaching days, and had learned the basics of car-maintenance just to save on garage bills. Jenny collapsed, out of breath, and Barbara lowered the bonnet of the dustcart. 'All right, let me take a turn.'

'What's the engine like?'

'Fine as far as I can see. They're usually pretty well maintained in this sort of place. I imagine they used to drive them out occasionally, for parades and exhibitions.'

'Surely the Daleks are bound to hear when we start the engine?'

Barbara stopped pumping, and gave the tyre an experimental kick. 'There, that'll do.' She disconnected the pump. 'We'll just have to chance the noise. It'll still be better than walking.'

Jenny was pessimistic. 'You realise we won't get very far in this old thing?'

'Probably not,' said Barbara patiently. 'But at least it will give us a start out of London.'

'Anyway, do you even know the way to Bedfordshire.'

'Yes, of course ...' Barbara hesitated. 'At least, I used to.'

'What does that mean?'

'Things may have changed. I'm not sure how much damage the Daleks have done.'

'Just wait till you see it,' said Jenny, with a kind of gloomy relish.

Barbara sighed. There were times when she could have wished for a more *cheerful* companion. Once again her thoughts turned to Susan and the Doctor. What were they doing now? And Ian ... What had happened to him?

Crouched in an empty storeroom, Ian and Larry were talking in low voices. Both were tense and watchful. There had recently been a change in the note of the spaceship's engines, and Ian was convinced they would soon be landing. Would they be in Bedfordshire as he hoped? More important, would they be able to get off the ship without being recaptured?

Larry was talking about his missing brother Phil, and his determination to find out what the Daleks were doing. 'Phil got himself sent to the mines on purpose. He reckoned if we knew what the Daleks were doing we'd stand a better chance of defeating them.'

Ian nodded abstractedly, his ears alert for more signs of a landing. 'I suppose that makes good sense.'

'Phil sent back just one message from the mines. He'd worked out some kind of theory ... he reckoned the Daleks were drilling to reach the magnetic core of the Earth ...'

A sudden jolt sent them reeling across the storeroom, and Ian lost interest in Larry's brother and his theories. 'We're down,' he said excitedly. 'Now—how do we get out of here?'

Larry nodded towards the corner of the room, where there was the usual disposal chute. 'Only one way out. Through there. As soon as we get out, make for cover. I'll go first.'

Larry moved over to the chute, but Ian moved in front of him. 'You realise we've no idea what's out there?'

Larry pushed him aside. 'Only one way to find out.'

He flung open the hatch cover, swung his legs over the edge, and was immediately sucked away by the powerful down-draft. Ian hesitated for a moment. But Larry was right, there was no alternative. They'd never make it down the ramp. He swung his legs over the hatchway and followed Larry. Immediately the suction swept him away. He was whizzing through darkness, sliding down what felt like a giant drain pipe. Suddenly the pipe came to an end and Ian found himself flying through open air. He landed with a thump on solid ground, rolled over on his shoulder and came up running, heading for the shelter of a clump of bushes ahead. He flung himself into the midst of them—and landed on top of Larry, who'd obviously followed exactly the same route.

As soon as he had his breath back, Ian gasped, 'Where do you reckon we are? Is it Bedfordshire?'

Larry parted the bushes. 'Take a look.'

Ian peered through the leaves, and gasped in astonishment. The saucer had landed on what looked like the biggest mining area in the world, an immense muddy valley torn out of what had once been wooded English countryside. It was dotted with mine shaft entrances at regular intervals. There were earth moving machines all around, some of Dalek origin, others obviously commandeered from the humans. Rows and rows of little shacks dotted the site, giving it the air of a mining camp in gold-rush days. A gleaming metal pylon dominated the area, with beside it, a crater like an extinct volcano.

The enormous site was swarming with activity. Slave workers trudged to and fro in long lines, guarded by metal-helmeted Robomen with whips and guns. Here and there Daleks glided up and down on tours of inspection. Ian felt a new respect for Larry's missing brother and his theories. The Daleks were engaged in some colossal undertaking. Surely it held the answer to the mystery of their presence on this planet—and, perhaps, the key to their defeat. He turned to Larry. 'You'll have quite a job, finding your brother in this lot.'

'I'm going to have a darned good try. Come on, let's get on to the site. With any luck we can mingle with the slave workers.'

Making no attempt at concealment, Larry started marching across the site. Ian trudged beside him, hoping they looked like a couple of industrious workers on some errand for the Daleks. They certainly looked as ragged and hungry as the rest of the slaves.

They reached the shelter of a huge excavating machine and paused to survey the activity around them. 'If we can get a chance to grab one of these blokes going by,' whispered Larry, 'we can ask him for news of my brother.'

The familiar hated tones of a Dalek voice rang out. 'Section Beta Zero. Parade for Robotisation selection at hut thirty.'

'I think we ought to find better cover,' muttered Ian. 'There's a bit too much going on round here.'

A voice spoke from behind them. 'And who are you two?' They whirled round. A thin-faced middle-aged man had just come round the other corner of the excavator. He was as ragged-looking as the rest of the slave workers, but at the same time he had an air of natural authority about him. He looked at them impatiently, waiting for their answer.

Larry looked defiantly at him. 'Never mind about us. Who are you?'

'My name's Wells. I'm a section leader. Why aren't you with your work detail? It makes trouble for all of us if you dodge your share of work.' They didn't reply, and he looked more closely at them. 'Escaping, are you? I suppose you know there are Robomen just the other side of this machine?' He reached under the machine and grabbed a pile of picks, tossing some to Ian and Larry. 'Grab these—and leave the talking to me.'

A Roboman appeared round the side of the machine. He stopped, looked searchingly at them and spoke in the familiar slurred voice. 'Who are these two men?'

'I took them from a work detail,' said Wells quickly. 'I needed them to collect more tools.'

'Which work detail?'

Wells waved an arm vaguely. 'I don't know, somewhere over there.'

Ian and Larry stood quite still as the Roboman came closer and looked at them with his dead eyes. 'They must attend for Robotisation.'

Wells shook his head. 'They're needed on their work details. I'll take them back with me.'

'No. They must attend.' The Roboman moved closer to Ian. 'Why do you wait? Move!'

Slowly, very slowly, Ian and Larry began walking away. The Roboman turned to Wells. 'You. Come here.'

Slowly Wells walked across to him. As soon as Wells was close enough, the Roboman swung his arm in a brutal arc, clubbing Wells to the ground with the butt of his gun. Wells collapsed face down in the mud, moaning and clutching his head.

Emotionlessly the Roboman said, 'In future, refer all decisions to your masters.'

Ian ran across to Wells and helped him to his feet. After a second's hesitation, Larry ran to join him. Between them they got Wells to his feet, blood streaming from a gash in his forehead.

The Roboman suddenly realised what was going on. 'What are you doing?'

Ian said furiously, 'You can't just leave him like this.'

'Do not disobey orders.'

'Get some other orders!' said Ian contemptuously. Between them Ian and Larry took Wells across to the shelter of the nearest hut.

The Roboman stood quite still, and made no attempt to pursue them.

They laid Wells on the table, and Ian wiped away the blood with his handkerchief. After a moment Wells struggled to sit up. 'I'm O.K. Sorry I got you into that —it was all I could think of.'

'We should be thanking you,' said Ian. He ran over to the window and looked out. The Roboman was still standing quite still. Then he nodded his head abruptly, as if in response to some unheard voice. Gun at the ready, he began marching towards the hut.

The Roboman stepped through the doorway. Wells was sitting on the table, and Larry stood beside him. That was the last thing the

Roboman saw. Ian stepped from behind the door and clubbed him down with a savage swing of his pickhandle.

Wells got shakily to his feet. 'We'll have to get out. The Daleks always know when a Roboman is attacked. It cuts off the radio-link. Pick up some tools and try to mingle with one of the working parties. This place is so big there's a chance they'll lose you in the crowd.'

Ian nodded and picked up a couple of picks, passing one to Larry. 'What about you?'

'I know a good hiding place not far away. I've got to stay in the area, I'm meeting Ashton here later.'

'Someone important?' Ian guessed that Wells was one of the leaders of whatever resistance movement existed in the mines.

'Ashton's a rat,' said Wells dispassionately. 'He smuggles in extra food, and sells it to us for whatever we can raise—rings, jewels, anything people have got hidden away. He's useful, though. That extra food has saved quite a few lives.' He looked curiously at Ian. 'I still don't know about you two. Are you trying to break out?'

Ian grinned. 'Believe it or not, we're breaking in. Larry here's looking for his brother, and I'm looking for a friend of mine. I want to take a look around as well, see what the Daleks are up to.'

'You must be mad,' said Wells simply.

'Maybe. Look, whatever happens we'll want to get out of here sooner or later. Will this Ashton smuggle us back to London?'

'Maybe—for a price. Meet me back here when it gets dark—should be safe again by then. I'll tell you what he says.'

Ian shouldered his pick. 'Right, we'll see you later. Come on, Larry, it's time to go down the mine.'

All three slipped quietly out of the hut. They trudged through the mud and attached themselves to a file of slave workers heading towards one of the mine entrances. No one seemed to notice them. Ian guessed that the sheer scale of the enterprise made it impossible for the Daleks to keep tabs on *all* their slaves.

As they headed into the darkness of the mine, Ian suddenly wondered what on earth he was doing. Larry had a definite mission—to find and rescue his brother. But Ian had only the vaguest of plans. First he wanted to look for the Doctor. Knowing the old chap's insatiable curiosity, Ian thought it was a fair bet that the Doctor would come to see what the Daleks were up to. And if he didn't find the Doctor, he'd gather as much useful information as he could, then return to London and take up the search for his companions there. As a scheme it was somewhat on the vague side. But Ian felt a curious sense of excitement as he trudged into the darkness. Somewhere in the depths below lay the secret of the Dalek invasion of Earth. If he could find out what it was, he might yet have a hand in their defeat …

9

DANGEROUS JOURNEY

Barbara swung the starting handle of the dustcart. The engine coughed, spluttered, then began to turn over. She withdrew the handle and climbed behind the wheel. Jenny finished flinging back the main doors and jumped in the cab beside her. Slowly the dustcart rumbled out of the museum where it had stood for so many years.

As they came into the street, Jenny glanced briefly at the pile of debris covering Dortmun. A single hand projected from the rubble ... she looked hurriedly away. 'I wonder why he did it?'

Barbara drove cautiously through the empty streets. 'Mostly because he just wouldn't give up.'

'It was senseless,' said Jenny harshly. 'He threw his life away.'

'Depends how you look at it, doesn't it?'

'You've got some romantic idea about this resistance business, haven't you? There's nothing heroic about dying uselessly.'

'Does it occur to you that Dortmun sacrificed himself to save *us*, to draw off the Dalek attack? If he hadn't we probably wouldn't be alive now!'

They drove on in silence for a while. Suddenly Jenny shouted, 'Look out—Dalek!' A Dalek had appeared at the end of one of the side turnings. Barbara put her foot down, and the Dalek disappeared from view as they sped past.

Jenny looked back nervously. 'Do you think it saw us?'

'Even if it didn't it must have heard the noise.'

'Then we're really in for trouble. It'll send a message ahead ...'

Barbara increased speed. 'We'll worry about that problem when we come to it.'

They came to it very quickly. A turn in the road revealed a line of Daleks stretched across their path. 'What shall we do?' shouted Jenny. 'Jump for it?'

Barbara stamped on the accelerator. 'No! Hold tight, I'm going through!'

Roaring and rattling, the old dustcart sped straight for the line of Daleks, scattering them like skittles. Barbara was vaguely conscious of hitting one head-on, sending it flying through the air. The dustcart lurched as she ran over another one, crushing it beneath the heavy wheels. A Dalek blast sizzled past the open window and then they were through, the line of Daleks scattered in confusion behind them. One or two blasts were fired after them, but Barbara swung the dustcart round a corner and they were safely out of sight. Jenny was bouncing exultantly in her seat. 'We went straight through them, we went straight through them!'

Barbara smiled in satisfaction. 'I enjoyed it too. We can't go on much longer in this thing though. They'll really be after us now.'

On the flight deck of the Dalek spaceship, a message was received from central ground control. 'Rebels travelling north in motorised vehicle. Have broken through Dalek cordon. You will intercept this vehicle and destroy!'

'I obey. Give position of rebel vehicle.' The saucer prepared for take-off.

They were driving along a quiet country lane when suddenly a low droning filled the air. Jenny stuck her head out of the open window and craned her neck to gaze up above. 'It's the Dalek saucer, coming in low!'

Barbara nodded, grim-faced. 'All right. Jump for it Jenny—now! I'll follow you.'

Jenny flung open the door and jumped, rolling over and over on the dusty road. Barbara saw thankfully that the road stretched dead straight ahead of them. She decreased speed slightly, adjusted the steering wheel carefully, then opened her door and jumped clear … She rolled over as she hit the ground, flinging herself desperately to the side of the road.

High above in the control room of the Dalek ship, a scanner showed the old vehicle trundling along the lane like some bright orange bug.

The Dalek commander said, 'Target located. Destroy!' Another Dalek reached out and touched a control ...

A ray shot from the hovering ship and bathed the dustcart in a glow of light. Seconds later it exploded in a cloud of flame and smoke.

The Commander sent a message back to central control. 'The rebel vehicle has been located and destroyed.'

The Dalek ship glided higher and sped on its way back to the mines.

From the roadside ditch, Jenny and Barbara looked regretfully at the blazing remains of the dustcart. Both had jumped clear at the last possible moment. It was Barbara's hope that the Daleks would believe they had died in the flames and call off the hunt. She got to her feet. 'Come on, Jenny, time to move. It's still a long way to Bedfordshire.'

Susan tramped wearily along behind David, wrinkling her nose at the ripe mixture of smells that floated up from the murky waters below. They were following the course of the main sewer, walking along a sort of tow-path beside an underground canal.

'David,' she called. 'Can't we rest for a moment?'

David's heart softened at the weariness in her face. 'Yes, of course we can.'

Susan sank thankfully to the ground. 'How long do we stay down these sewers?'

'Just as long as we can. It's smelly, but it's safe!'

Something tinkled by Susan's foot and she held it up. 'Look—a cartridge case.'

David took it and examined it. 'Could be Robomen—though they don't usually come down here.'

'Some of your friends then?'

'Not necessarily. We're not all allies, you know. There are people about who just think of their own survival. They'd kill you for a few scraps of food.' David tapped his rifle. 'This isn't too much use against Daleks, but it will keep anyone else away.'

Suddenly they heard footsteps. A shadow moved down the tunnel towards them. David raised his rifle. 'All right, who are you?'

The shadow stopped. 'David? Is that you? It's me, Tyler.'

David jumped up and ran forward, overjoyed to see his old friend again. Tyler explained that he'd abandoned his search for other guerrilla bands, and decided to go North on his own. 'Did they manage to find that Doctor chap?' he asked.

David nodded. 'He's back there. We left him to rest while we made sure it was all clear ahead!'

'You'd better get back to him. There are renegades about down here, I scared a couple off with this.' Tyler brandished his rifle.

Susan held up the cartridge. 'Did you shoot at one?'

Tyler looked. 'That's mine all right. I wasn't shooting at renegades though.'

'What then?'

'Alligators.' He saw Susan's look of horror and smiled grimly. 'Quite a lot of animals escaped from zoos after the invasion. Most of them died off. But the big reptiles flourished—down here.'

Susan jumped to her feet. 'Come on, David. Let's get back to the Doctor!' She had immediate visions of alligators creeping up to the Doctor's dozing form.

Tyler said, 'Better let me scout ahead, just in case. You two follow.'

David nodded, and Tyler moved away.

Susan called, 'Mr Tyler, you haven't any news of our other friends?'

Tyler said curtly, 'Barbara got back to H.Q. with Dortmun. I left her there—that's all I can tell you.' He disappeared into the darkness. David and Susan waited a few minutes then followed him down the tunnel.

Somehow during their journey he drew further ahead of them, gradually disappearing from sight. They came to a main junction in the tunnels and David stopped. 'This is where we left the Doctor.' He called out, 'Doctor? Tyler?' There was no reply.

'There are these ladders to upper and lower tunnels. Susan pointed. 'Maybe they took one of those.' She moved across to a ladder and began to climb down. 'Mr Tyler? Grandfather, are you down there?'

There was a rusty creaking sound from Susan's ladder. David yelled, 'Be careful,' but he was too late. The top end of the ladder pulled away from the wall and pivoted round on its lower fastening. Susan clung on desperately, and found she was suspended just a few inches over the water. She heard David's voice. 'Hang on! I'll come and get you.' He leaned over, trying to pull her back.

Susan's eyes were fixed on the rushing flood beneath her. Surely there was something moving? To her horror she saw a squat shape gliding nearer. A long jaw lined with savage teeth appeared from the murky water. Susan screamed as the alligator's teeth clashed within inches of her dangling foot.

The alligator dropped back into the water and turned for a second try. Its jaws opened ...

A bulky shape appeared above her, there was the crack of a rifle. Tyler fired straight into the open mouth of the alligator and it dropped back into the water with a coughing roar. Seconds later Tyler and David had grabbed the ladder and dragged it and Susan back to safety. She collapsed into David's arms. 'Where's Grandfather?'

Tyler pointed upwards. 'Don't worry. I got him to one of the upper levels. It's not really safe down here.'

Susan looked at the murky water and shuddered. 'I believe you.'

David put an arm round her shoulders. 'Don't worry, you'd probably have given the poor old chap indigestion!'

They started to climb the ladder after Tyler.

It lay curled and asleep on one of the throbbing machines. The machine was warm, and it didn't care for the cold on this planet. Suddenly it quivered and woke. Its keen hearing had picked up voices ... human voices. And humans meant food. It slithered from the machine and began sliding quietly through the darkness.

Ian stopped moving and listened intently. 'I tell you I heard something. A sort of slithering noise.'

Larry peered into the darkness. 'Which direction?'

'I'm not sure. It seemed to come from all round ...'

They stood waiting tensely. Their exploration of the mine had not proved a great success. Security was tighter than Ian had imagined, and all the deeper levels were closely guarded. He'd been unable to pick up any real clue as to what was going on here. Nor had they found any trace of the Doctor, or of Larry's brother. Most of their time had been taken up with dodging the constantly patrolling Robomen and their Dalek masters. Now they were back where they'd started, close to the hut where they'd parted from Wells. But this time it was dark— and something very nasty was hunting them through that darkness.

A huge shapeless bulk slithered towards them, making a kind of screaming roar. They jumped back. A Dalek searchlight cut through the darkness, and Ian and Larry flung themselves down. Ian caught a glimpse of a hideous bloated shape, slithering off into the darkness, The searchlight passed by and they picked themselves up. Larry was trembling violently. 'Ian, did you *see*? What was that thing?'

'Search me. Luckily for us it doesn't seem to like the light. Come on, let's get under cover.'

They ran to the little hut and threw themselves inside. Ian closed the door and turned round. Larry was standing absolutely still. From the shadows a man was covering them with a rifle.

'Now you can turn round and go out again,' said a cold sneering voice. The man stepped forwards into the moonlight which shone through the window. He wore a soft hat and heavy raincoat, not old and ragged but new and of good quality. His face was round, even a little plump, not gaunt and thin like the slave workers. Suddenly Ian realised who the man was. 'I take it you're Ashton?'

'How do you know that?'

'Wells told us. We came to meet you.'

'You're lying. You came to steal my food. Now get out.' He jerked the rifle barrel towards the door.

Ian didn't move. 'With that thing out there?'

'It didn't see you come in—it needn't see you go out.'

From outside came the roar of the creature that was roaming the darkness. Ian decided he wasn't going outside again whatever happened. The thing was to keep talking. If he could get close enough to jump the man ... Edging a few inches nearer Ashton, Ian said, 'Maybe we can do business together. I want to get back to London.'

'Indeed?' Ashton seemed intrigued. 'And why can't you just die here?'

'I'm not planning to die anywhere yet. I've got friends in London and I want to find them. Can you get me there?'

'Of course I can. For the right price.'

'And what's the right price?'

'As much as you can afford. I'll take anything. Stones, precious metal, jewellery, rings ... I'm not particular ...'

'I'm afraid I don't have very much in that line.'

Ashton smiled coldly. 'Then goodbye. I *do* hope you avoid the Slyther on the way back.'

'We're not leaving.'

'No?' Ashton raised the rifle and worked the bolt. Ian tensed himself to spring ...

Suddenly the door opened. 'Ashton? It's all right, these two are friends of mine.' Wells slipped into the hut, closing the door behind him.

Ashton lowered his gun. 'You came up with the character references just in time. You've got the goods?'

Wells produced a bundle of objects tied in a handkerchief. He opened it and Ian saw a pathetic collection of wedding rings, cuff-links, ear-rings, bracelets ... whatever valuables the inmates of the mines had managed to hide. Ashton examined it. 'Not much—but it'll have to do.'

From a corner Ashton produced a small sack, and tossed it across to Wells. 'There you are, then. Now why don't we all have something to eat, boys?'

Wells hefted the sack. 'This has to go round a lot of people. I'll share with my *friends* here—but you're not included, Ashton.'

For a moment Ashton flushed, but he forced a sneering smile back on his face. 'Don't worry. I've brought my own.' He produced a silver hip flask, pushed the top off with his finger and thumb and took a swig. The whole operation was performed one-handed. The other hand still held the rifle, and it was still pointed in their direction.

Ian looked across at Wells. 'Know all the best people, don't you?'

Wells was checking the contents of the sack. 'I told you—he's our only source of real food. You can hardly survive on the slop the Daleks dish out.'

The weird howl echoed through the hut. Ian looked up. 'What is that thing out there?'

'We call it the Slyther. The Black Devil keeps it as a sort of pet.'

'The Black Devil?'

Impatiently Ashton joined in. 'Where've you been—Fairyland? The Black Dalek. Otherwise known as the Dalek Supreme. He's the big boss Dalek.'

'And what's this Slyther thing doing roaming about loose? Is it on guard?'

Wells nodded. 'In a way. There's a curfew, see? The Black Dalek turns the thing loose to deter people from wandering about at night. It wanders round in search of food.'

The howl rang out again. 'What kind of food.?' asked Larry nervously.

It was Ashton who answered the question. 'People,' he said simply. 'The Daleks can always spare it a slave or two. They've got plenty more.'

Wells fished out two tins of spam and two tins of peaches, tossing one of each to Ian and Larry. 'Here, we can spare you these. No, don't argue. Take it, you'll need it.' He fished out two tins for himself, and produced a can-opener.

They made a strange, uneasy, meal in the darkened hut, digging the food from the cans with their fingers. Ashton watched them sardonically, taking the occasional swig from his flask. He passed the time checking through the little hoard of jewellery. 'You're a fool, Wells,' he said conversationally. 'There's enough here to buy you a passage out of this place. I could take you to nice empty countryside, plenty of food … Why don't you forget your ridiculous resistance movement, look after yourself?'

Wells swallowed his last half peach and drained the juice from the can. 'I'll get out … when everyone gets out.'

'Suit yourself. Some people never learn.'

Larry slipped a signet ring from his finger and tossed it to Wells. 'Here, this is for our supper.'

Wells stowed the ring away. 'I'll take it too, if you don't mind. It'll help to buy the next lot from our greedy friend here.'

Whether it was the sound of their voices or the scent of the food they were eating, they never knew, but something led the Slyther to their hut. Suddenly there was a shattering roar and the door burst open. *It* was there filling the doorway. They cowered back as the terrible bulging shape *slithered* towards them …

10

TRAPPED IN THE DEPTHS

Ian saw a vast lumpy blob of a body, powerful flailing tentacles, two tiny deep-set eyes shining with malice … Moving incredibly fast, the creature lurched towards them.

It was Ashton who saved their lives, though he was only trying to preserve his own. It was his last good deed, perhaps the only one in his mis-spent life. The rifle was still in his hand, and instinctively he raised it to his shoulder and began blazing away at the Slyther. He succeeded only in attracting its attention. The horrible creature paused for a moment then began rolling swiftly towards him. He fired again and again with no result. Ashton was still screaming when the creature flowed over him and engulfed him entirely.

Ian didn't like to leave even Ashton to the mercy of the Slyther, but it was dreadfully clear that there was nothing they could do for him. 'Quick,' he yelled. 'Now's our chance.' Leaving the Slyther to its feast, Ian, Larry and Wells ran from the hut into the darkness outside. Immediately they were caught in the beam of a Dalek searchlight. 'Scatter!' yelled Wells, and they all split up, Wells running one way, Larry and Ian the other. From behind them came the screaming roar of the Slyther as it abandoned Ashton to pursue the rest of its prey.

Ian and Larry struggled to the surface of a low mound of earth. In its centre was a crude mine shaft, a deep round hole. A wooden derrick straddled the hole, and from the derrick hung an enormous iron bucket, obviously designed for carrying earth.

They paused, wondering whether to run round the excavation or go back—when the Slyther appeared over the top of the mound, rushing towards them at amazing speed.

Ian acted without thinking. He took a flying leap through the air, clutched the side of the earth-bucket and scrambled inside. Larry hesitated, took a look at the approaching Slyther, and followed his example. Ian grabbed him and hauled him inside the bucket.

Howling with rage the Slyther ranged to and fro on top of the mound, its prey just out of reach. 'It's still after us,' shouted Ian. 'I hope it can't jump!'

Larry grabbed Ian's arm. 'It's going to try!'

Larry was right. The Slyther somehow *gathered* itself, then flew through the air in a tremendous leap. It landed on the edge of the bucket and began scrambling over the side.

Terrified by the thought of being trapped inside the bucket with the voracious monster, Ian and Larry fought like demons. They heaved and kicked and punched at the Slyther's flabby bulk, shoving it out of the bucket with maniacal fury, dodging the flailing blows from its enormous tentacles. A last desperate heave sent it over the edge. With a long final scream, the monster disappeared. There was a squelching thud as it struck the edge of the crater, then screaming in rage and pain it slithered off into the darkness …

For a moment Ian and Larry crouched in the bucket, panting for breath. Then Larry gasped, 'Come on, let's get out of here.' He started to climb the side of the bucket, but Ian held him back. 'No— someone's bound to have heard all that racket. Let's just stay here till things quieten down.'

In the mine control room deep below the surface, a Dalek engineer was studying his work-chart. He turned to his assistant, 'There is no work party in shaft nine. Why?'

The assistant consulted another chart. 'The section is completed. A labour force is now being assembled for clearing operations.'

'Work must proceed to schedule. There must be no delay.'

'All will be ready. I shall now lower the waste bucket into shaft nine.' The assistant touched a control.

Ian listened cautiously. Everything seemed silent 'It's all clear now.'

'Might as well take a chance,' agreed Larry. 'Can't stay here all night.'

There was a shuddering, a clanking sound—and Ian and Larry felt the bucket jerk into sudden movement. 'What's happening?' yelled Larry.

'Hold tight,' shouted Ian. 'We're going down!' And so they were. Slowly the bucket clanked down into the darkness below.

'I must say this is a nice state of affairs,' announced the Doctor peevishly. 'All this time and we're still hiding in sewers.'

David grinned, well used to the Doctor by now. 'Better to hide down here, Doctor, than be caught by the Robomen. As soon as Tyler says the coast is clear we can travel on the surface again.'

They had climbed up from the deeper parts of the sewer system and were now in a stone walled antechamber directly below street level. A ladder led up through a manhole, and Tyler had just gone ahead to see if it was safe for the rest of them to emerge.

There was a scrambling sound and Tyler shot down the ladder, rifle in hand. Susan looked up hopefully. 'Is it clear?'

'It is *not*,' announced Tyler grimly. 'Ran straight into a patrol. I couldn't get under cover, they came after me.'

David grabbed his rifle. 'How many?'

'Just two of them.'

Tyler started back up the ladder. 'David and I will deal with them, you stay under cover.'

'Just a moment,' said the Doctor mildly. 'Wouldn't it be better to— er, lure them down here? If they succeeded in communicating with their fellows and summoning reinforcements ...'

Tyler shook his head ruefully. 'I suppose if we stick together long enough I'll learn to do what you say the first time. All right, David, you draw them in. Don't shoot unless you have to, ricochets might get one of us.

David climbed up the ladder, emerged through the manhole, and ran a little way into the street. The Robomen saw him immediately and wheeled round in pursuit. They raised their guns, but David had already disappeared down the manhole.

Crouched in the corner of the little chamber, the Doctor and Susan waited. David and Tyler were also waiting, one each side of the ladder. The first Roboman came to the top of the ladder, paused, then slowly began to descend. As soon as he was down, Tyler grabbed him round the throat and pulled him to the floor.

The second Roboman more cautious, paused half way down the ladder. David grabbed his feet and pulled him down. The two men collapsed in a wildly struggling heap. The Roboman's gun went off, but luckily the shot went up through the open hatchway. Quickly David raised his rifle and used the butt to club the Roboman into unconsciousness.

The Doctor went over to Tyler, who was methodically choking the life out of his victim. 'That will do, Tyler,' he said sharply. 'I never countenance the taking of life unless my own is directly threatened.' The astonished Tyler let go of the Roboman who slumped unconscious, to the floor. The Doctor made his way to the ladder. 'Now then, let's be on our way to this mine, and then we shall discover how to deal with the Daleks. We'll leave these poor creatures to their own devices. David, you lead the way, my boy. Come along, everybody.' Very much in command, the Doctor bustled his party up the ladder.

Barbara and Jenny were tired and footsore by the time they came to the little cottage in the forest. It was nearly dark now, and there was an ominous rumbling in the sky, with occasional lightning flashes. They'd cut across country, keeping off the roads for greater safety, but now night was coming and they were lost somewhere in thick woods.

Jenny looked at the cottage. 'It seems deserted. What do you think, shall we try it?'

Barbara hesitated. There was something sinister about the tumbledown old cottage. It looked curiously like the witch's house in some fairy tale. She told herself she was being over-imaginative. 'Well, there's a storm coming on. We'd be much better off under shelter.'

They moved cautiously up to the front door. Suddenly it swung open and a hag-like old woman dressed in rags stood glaring at them, a lantern held over her head. Jenny jumped back with a scream, and Barbara thought wildly that perhaps it was a witch's house after all …

The old woman snarled, 'What do you want?'

Barbara made her voice calm and reassuring. 'We're lost. We were looking for shelter.'

'Just the two of you?' The old woman gave a sudden cackle of a laugh. 'Tired are you?'

'Yes … yes, we are.'

Jenny looked at the old woman uneasily, 'Barbara, I think we should be moving on.'

The smaller, equally ragged figure of a younger woman appeared beside the first in the doorway.

'Dogs'll get you,' it piped suddenly.

'Dogs?' Barbara echoed nervously.

The old woman took up the chorus. 'Terrible beasts. After the plague they formed a pack. They hunt travellers. You'd better come in.'

Reluctantly Barbara and Jenny stepped inside. The cottage was dirty and primitive, like something out of the Middle Ages. A bed, a stove, a ricketty table and some battered wooden chairs were all the furniture of its single room. Barbara looked at the two women who stood nodding and smiling. It was clear from their close resemblance that they were mother and daughter. Barbara told herself that she was wrong to feel repelled by them. They were poor and ignorant that was all, and small wonder in this horrible world the Daleks had made. 'Where are you making for?' asked the old woman suddenly.

Barbara sank into a chair, suddenly realising how tired she was. 'The Dalek mines. We have friends there. We're trying to find them.'

The younger woman shook her head dolefully. 'Nobody ever gets away from the mines. You'll be caught yourselves.'

The old woman nodded. 'You're lucky you got this far—and found us. Patrols pass here all the time.'

Jenny was still suspicious. 'Then how is it you're still free. They must know you're here.'

The old woman cackled. 'Oh, they know all right. But we can't harm them.'

'We helps 'em,' piped up the younger one.

The old woman scowled at her, swiftly changing to a smile as she turned back to Barbara. 'We make clothes for the slave workers,' she explained. 'We're more use to them doing that than we would be in the mines.'

'How do you manage for food?'

'They give us a bit from time to time, payment you might say. We go hungry most days though.'

Even Jenny was won over by their sad faces. 'We've got a little food with us,' she said gruffly. 'You can share it if you like.'

The old woman gave a toothless grin. 'Why thank you, my child. We've little to offer in return, but if you like you can sleep here for the night. We can make up a bed in that corner, you'll be comfy enough.'

There was another rumble of thunder, and rain began lashing down. Barbara realised she couldn't face going out again. 'Thank you,' she said wearily. 'We'll stay the night if we may.'

Jenny unpacked the meagre supplies—apples, a tin of meat, some rather stale biscuits. The old woman put out some plates, four battered tin mugs and a jug of water.

Barbara noticed that the younger woman was wrapping herself in a heavy hooded cloak. 'Where are you going?' she demanded.

'I have to go out to deliver these clothes.'

'In this weather?'

The old woman sighed. 'Daleks don't care about the weather, my dear. We have to keep up our quota—and these are late already.'

'What about those dogs you told us about?' asked Jenny.

'She follows the patrols,' explained the old woman.

The younger nodded eagerly. 'That's right, I follow the patrols.'

'She'll come to no harm,' said the old woman soothingly. 'She's done it often enough before. Now why don't we sit down and enjoy our meal? The girl will have hers when she gets back.'

Jenny shared out their food with scrupulous fairness, putting aside a portion for the younger woman, and they sat down to eat.

Barbara and Jenny ate the scanty meal in tired silence, but the old woman was excited and talkative. She plied Barbara with questions about London. 'What's it like now, dearie, still as wonderful?'

'I'm afraid not. The Daleks have destroyed quite a lot of it.'

'Destroyed? Well I never I When I went it was all *so* pretty. The shops and the moving pavements … and I went to the Astronauts' Fair …'

The old woman rambled on about her once-in-a lifetime day trip to London, and all the wonderful things she'd seen. Barbara's head began nodding. It was pathetic really, she thought, she should feel sorry for the poor old thing. But somehow she still felt uneasy. The old woman was nervous too, glancing constantly at an old alarm clock on a shelf, and looking out of the window. Probably worrying about her daughter.

Suddenly bright light flooded into the room as the clearing outside was lit up with a blazing searchlight. Jenny screamed as the cottage door smashed open. In the doorway stood a Dalek, flanked by Robomen guards. 'Both of you will follow me. Do not try to escape or you will be exterminated!'

Stunned, Barbara and Jenny stood up, and gathered their few possessions. How had the Daleks found them so easily? The thin figure of the daughter dodged round the Dalek and scuttled to her mother's side. She held out a little sack. 'Look, ma. There's bread, and oranges and sugar …'

The old woman chuckled. 'Good, good. I knew they'd give us food if we told them.'

Impatiently the Dalek shouted, 'Move!' As Barbara and Jenny were marched out of the cottage, the other two women were excitedly rummaging through the sack. The older one looked out of the window as the Robomen led their captives away. 'Such a pity,' she muttered. 'Still, they'd have been captured anyway, in the end.' Eagerly she sucked the juice from her orange. She hadn't tasted an orange for years and years …

The giant wastebucket clanked down through the darkness on a seemingly endless journey, taking its human cargo deeper and deeper into the Dalek mine. Ian supposed he shouldn't complain, since he'd wanted to get into the mine anyway. But he hadn't bargained for travelling this way. He heard Larry's nervous voice from the darkness beside him. 'How long do you think we've been going down now?'

'Must be nearly twenty minutes.'

'It's getting warmer, isn't it?'

'Yes … pressure's increasing too, my ears are popping.'

Larry shuddered. 'I'd rather be dead than work down here.'

'I hope we don't have to make the choice!'

'We're stopping,' said Larry excitedly. 'We must be nearly at the bottom.' He craned his head over the side of the bucket. 'Look—lights, just below!'

Ian saw a huge open space, the junction of several earth-walled tunnels supported by wooden pit props, lit by dim working-lights. Piles of earth and rock were everywhere. 'Let's get out of here, before this bucket tips over and chucks us out.'

They clambered on to the rim of the giant bucket. This was by no means an easy job, since the bucket tended to tip with the movement of their weight. Ian wriggled over the edge, hung by his hands and dropped. The fall was a long one, but he landed unhurt in a pile of soft earth.

Larry wasn't so lucky. He landed with a thud right beside Ian, but when he tried to get up he groaned and clutched his leg. 'It's my knee. I hit it on the bucket coming down.'

Ian looked round. 'We must hide for a bit till you can walk. It's too open here. Come on, put your weight on me.'

He helped Larry away from the open area and into one of the side tunnels. They crouched in the semidarkness, resting thankfully.

After a few minutes Ian said, 'How's the leg?'

Larry straightened it, and gave another groan. 'Seems to be stiffening up. I don't think I'll be able to walk.'

'Don't worry. We'll stay here for a while.' Ian looked out of the tunnel and into the main area. There were lots of tunnels leading off, enormous piles of earth and stones, and that was all. 'This mine doesn't make sense to me. All they seem to be digging is rocks. I suppose they could be processing ore somewhere.'

'You remember what my brother Phil said—the Daleks want to tunnel through to the magnetic core of the Earth.'

'But why? What are they up to?'

Larry shrugged. 'You can't tell much from here. This is only a sort of clearance area. Perhaps the important work's going on somewhere else.'

'You may be right at that.' Ian felt a surge of impatience. It was maddening to be so close to the Daleks' secrets without learning more. 'Larry, would you be all right if I went to have a look around?'

'Yes, sure.'

Ian got to his feet and moved out of the tunnel into the main area. He chose the largest of the tunnels leading off, and made his way along it. Soon he heard voices and movement coming towards him, and ducked behind a pit prop for cover. Cautiously he peered out. A procession of gaunt ragged men and women was stumbling along the tunnel, driven by the whips of Robomen guards. They clutched a variety of containers, and some carried picks and shovels. Ian turned and ran back to Larry.

'Lay low and keep quiet. There's a crowd of workers and Robomen coming this way.'

Larry and Ian watched from hiding as the workers flooded into the central area. The huge bucket in which they'd travelled down suddenly dropped the rest of the distance to the ground, tipping over on its side. Immediately workers began carrying earth and rocks from the piles and tipping them into the bucket. They worked at a feverish pace and the whips of the Robomen lashed out at anyone who slowed down or stumbled.

A Roboman spoke briefly to one of the, slaves who collected a small group of workers. The Roboman started leading them across the area and into the tunnel in which Ian and Larry were hiding ... Gun in hand, he marched straight towards them ...

11

ACTION UNDERGROUND

A few yards from Larry and Ian, the Roboman halted his party, and set them to work on the nearest rock-pile.

Ian put his lips to Larry's ear and whispered, 'We'll have to move back! They're clearing this whole section ...'

Desperation gave Larry the power to overcome the pain in his twisted knee. Ian helped him to his feet and they started edging their way deeper into the tunnel.

Larry's foot slipped, and he fell back against the tunnel wall with a moan of pain. The Roboman left his workers and ran towards them, covering them with his gun. 'Halt!'

Ian and Larry stood quite still. The Roboman stared intently at them. Ian guessed that the Robotising process reduced the human mind to the lowest level, capable of giving and receiving only the simplest of commands. Finally the Roboman worked things out. 'You are not in the working party. Who are you?'

Larry gripped Ian's arm in a painful grip. 'It's Phil,' he whispered. 'Ian, it's my brother Phil.' He moved closer to the Roboman, staring into his face. 'Think, Phil. You must remember me. I'm your brother, Larry. *Remember me!*'

There was no change in the Roboman's voice or expression. With the same painful slowness, he came to another conclusion. 'You are runaways.'

'Angela,' said Larry desperately. 'Remember your wife, Angela. I can take you to her.'

'You must both be punished. I shall take you to the Daleks. Follow me.'

The Roboman turned, taking obedience for granted—and immediately Ian jumped him. The Roboman fired at once but Ian shoved the gun barrel upwards and the blast hit the ceiling. They wrestled fiercely for possession of the weapon. Once again Ian realised the inhuman strength of the Robomen, their total imperviousness to pain.

Helplessly Larry watched Ian and the Roboman roll over and over, finishing up almost at his feet. His back to Larry, the Roboman wrenched free of Ian and stood up. He levelled the gun at Ian's still prone body—and with a scream of 'No, Phil, no!' Larry launched himself at his brother's back, ripping the Roboman helmet from his head ...

The gun exploded again, missing Ian and bringing rock down from the wall. The Roboman screamed and convulsed, collapsing in his death agony. Sobbing Larry held the body in his arms. He knew he hadn't really killed his brother. The Daleks had done that a long time ago, when they'd taken away his humanity.

Stunned and shocked, Ian scrambled to his feet. Larry was still clutching Phil's body, tears streaming down his face. Behind them in the main area an alarm signal was ringing out, and there was a confused shouting.

'Come on, Larry, run!' shouted Ian. 'Here, I'll help you ...'

Larry shook his head. 'You run, Ian, while you've got the chance. They'd only get both of us ...'

From the tunnel behind them came a voice shouting 'Halt!' A Dalek was at the end of the tunnel, a Roboman behind him. Ian flung himself to one side and the Roboman fired a long raking blast. Larry's body jerked convulsively, and he collapsed on top of his dead brother. Ian turned and ran into the darkness of the tunnel. Behind him he could hear the Dalek's blaring voice. 'Emergency, emergency in shaft nine. Seal all exits! Emergency!' Ian ran blindly on into the darkness.

The Doctor stood on a wooded hill overlooking the Dalek mine-workings, his face solemn. He studied the shafts, the machinery, the immense ordered pattern of activity for a moment longer, then turned to his companion. 'Thank you, Mr Tyler, I've seen all I need to see.' They turned and made their way back through the wood.

As they walked back to their little camp, the Doctor mused how often there seemed to come a period of tranquillity in the time of greatest danger. After their fight with the Robomen in the sewer, they'd had a surprisingly peaceful journey to Bedfordshire. They'd even travelled by road for a part of the way in an abandoned car that Tyler had managed to get working.

It was certainly an idyllic scene that met them as they returned to the camp. They'd established themselves by a little stream, and David had produced fishing gear from his pack and started to fish. Clearly he'd been successful, for Susan was frying trout over a small fire, while David himself could be seen coming downstream with another fine fish in his hand.

The Doctor watched smiling as David crept up behind Susan and suddenly thrust the fish over her shoulder. Susan screamed and jumped up. David caught her in his arms, and kissed her. Astonished, Susan stood quite still. The Doctor cleared his throat very loudly, and made a deliberate crashing noise as he came through the bushes.

The two young people jumped apart and David babbled, 'Ah, yes, there you are, Doctor. We were, that is, I was just …'

The Doctor looked at the sizzling frying pan. 'Yes, I could see something was cooking,' he said dryly. He looked closely at Susan. How deeply was she involved with this young man? For some time now the Doctor had been aware that Susan was fast growing up, and that their wandering way of life posed problems that would one day have to be faced … Still, time enough for that later on. First they had to solve the problem of the Daleks. Unless *that* was dealt with, they'd none of them have a future to worry about.

The meal was the most enjoyable one they'd had in quite some time, and the Doctor's instincts told him it might be even longer before they got another. The food was simple enough, fish, biscuits, the remains of their tinned fruit. Tyler even produced some long-hoarded coffee from his pack. It was jet black, milkless and sugarless, but still delicious.

As they sat round sipping it, David asked, 'Now you've actually seen the Dalek base, Doctor, what do you think?'

'Well, young man, it's quite obvious to me that these mine workings are the centre of their entire operations.' He gave Tyler a reproving glare. 'I really can't think why you didn't focus all your resistance efforts down here.'

Tyler grunted. 'That's all very well, Doctor. We've been fighting the Daleks wherever we could. Fighting to stay alive mostly!'

David came to his support. 'We assumed they were just mining for Earth's minerals, looting the planet.'

'No,' said the Doctor decisively. 'These workings hold the answer to the one question that is of any importance to you. *Why* are the Daleks here?'

David looked puzzled. 'Why? Surely they're here because they've invaded us? It's as simple as that.'

'Indeed it isn't, young man. It goes much deeper. The Daleks have no interest in Man as such. He's just a work machine, an insignificant specimen of life scarcely worth conquering. It doesn't *matter* to the Daleks whether you live or die.'

'All right,' said David. 'Suppose you're right, Doctor. What *are* the Daleks up to?'

'I'm not quite sure yet, my boy. There must be something about this planet, something no other planet can offer. It's nothing near the surface, or they'd have collected it and gone. Instead there they are, burrowing like metal moles, deep into the Earth's crust!'

Tyler scratched his head. 'I'm no scientist, Doctor, but surely … if they penetrate the Earth's crust they'll cause an enormous earthquake—something nobody will survive?'

'That is so—unless they've found some way of controlling the flow of living energy.' The Doctor looked round the little group. 'The Daleks are daring to tamper with the forces of creation—and we must dare to stop them!'

There was a moment of silence. The Doctor's words had made them all aware of the tremendous issues they were facing.

Suddenly the Doctor stood up. 'Time to pack up camp and be on our way,' he ordered. 'We have a great deal to do.' No one questioned the order. Once again, the Doctor had taken charge.

Ian ran on through the darkness until he saw a glimmer of light ahead. He slowed down and went more carefully. The tunnel widened ahead, and joined up with several others. Rows of slave workers were filling their buckets and emptying them into wheeled trucks, which others pushed away. Robomen stood on guard and occasionally a Dalek moved past. It all looked very familiar, and suddenly Ian realised why. He'd stumbled upon another clearing area, a point where the endless debris from the Dalek's drilling was collected and hauled to the surface. Ian looked along the line of workers. A tall, dark-haired woman was emptying a bucket of rocks. Ian gave a silent gasp of astonishment. It was Barbara. He started creeping nearer …

Barbara and Jenny had been toiling for hours now, and Jenny was beginning to crack up. She was carrying yet another basket of rocks to the wastebucket when she stumbled and fell, spilling most of the painfully gathered rocks. She crouched by the overturned basket, almost sobbing with despair. 'It's no good, Barbara, we're beaten. We'll never get out of here, never.'

Barbara knelt to help her. 'Steady, Jenny, that's no way to talk. We wanted to get to the mine and here we are.'

'But there's nothing we can *do*.'

'We can get this bucket filled for a start,' said Barbara practically.

Already a whip-carrying Roboman was moving towards their part of the mine. 'Move,' he shouted. 'Continue with your task.'

Barbara went on tossing rocks into the basket. 'We can try to find their main control room. That's what the Doctor would do.'

Jenny sniffed. 'And what do we do then?'

'I don't know, Jenny, but at least we could try to do *something*. If we don't succeed, we'll just end up back here.'

From his hiding place nearby, Ian saw one of the Robomen address a crouched over slave worker. 'You! Collect more containers from the nearest storage section.'

The man straightened up, and started moving towards Ian. To his joy he saw it was Wells, the man who'd helped him and Larry earlier. As Wells passed his hiding place Ian hissed softly. 'Wells, it's me, Ian.'

Wells pretended to have trouble with his shoe, bent to fix it. 'Ian? Should have thought you'd have been out of here by now.'

'That tall girl over there—I know her. See if you can get a chance to speak to her. Tell her I'm here.'

Wells picked up the last bucket. 'I'll try. But I've got to get the buckets first.' He trudged off along the tunnel and Ian settled down to wait for his return.

On the work line, Jenny was still objecting. 'They'll never let us get *near* their control room.'

Something crackled inside Barbara's coat as she bent down for another rock. 'Jenny, I've just realised. I've still got Dortmun's notes.'

'A lot of use they are!'

Barbara suddenly lost patience with Jenny's pessimism. It was time to act. A Dalek was coming towards them. Deliberately Barbara straightened up and stepped out in front of it. The Dalek stopped, eye-stalk swivelling round in astonishment. 'Continue work.'

Barbara stood her ground. 'I have important information for you. Rebels are planning a revolution against the Daleks.'

The Dalek's reaction was immediate. 'There will be no revolution. The Daleks are masters of Earth.'

'You don't understand. This is no ordinary uprising. They have scientists working with them.'

'You are lying. It is a trick.'

'No. I have proof.' Barbara held out Dortmun's notes.

The Dalek scanned the first page. 'These contain details of the acid bomb used in the unsuccessful attack on the Dalek spaceship.'

'There's more,' said Barbara quickly. 'We know the names of the rebels, the places where they plan to attack.'

'You will tell me immediately.'

Barbara shook her head. 'No, I must speak to someone in authority. You'll have to act at once on what I tell you, and it's all very complicated.'

The Dalek paused, considering. Barbara held her breath. Then the Dalek spoke. 'Very well. I will take you both to the Dalek Supreme. If you are lying you will be killed. Follow me.'

The Dalek set off down the tunnel, Jenny and Barbara following behind.

Ian watched all this from hiding, not really understanding what was going on. Wells came back down the tunnel, loaded with buckets.

'All right. Take some buckets, and follow me. I'll try to get you to your friend.'

'Too late. The Daleks have just taken her off.'

'They've probably taken her to the control room for questioning.'

'Then that's where I'm going. Just you point me in the right direction. Come on! Give me some of those buckets.'

Ian stepped out boldly behind Wells, and walked along the line of workers handing out buckets. The Robomen didn't seem to notice him. Wells took him to the far end of the line and pointed. 'That tunnel at the end there, runs towards the control area. Good luck.'

Wells turned back towards the line of workers, and Ian ran off down the tunnel.

Very soon the nature of the tunnel started to alter. Earth and rock walls gave way to metal. There was better lighting and the hum of powerful machinery nearby.

At the end of the tunnel was an open door, and through it Ian could see a long room lined with banks of strange machinery and complex control panels. Daleks glided to and fro, tending the instruments. Ian crept quietly to the door and slipped inside.

The place was so enormous, the Dalek scientists so absorbed in their many tasks, that Ian found it easy to slip from machine to machine and work his way to the centre of the area. He saw no sign of Barbara. What he did see was a circular hole in the centre of the area, about the size of a large well. From the concentration of Daleks and instruments around this spot, something very important was going on. Ian crept closer, looking for a good hiding place, near enough to allow him to eavesdrop.

Facing him, and just on the edge of the area was a curious container, rather like half of a giant metal egg. Cables ran into its top. It was partly filled with machinery, but there was just room for Ian to duck inside and crouch down out of sight. He was near enough now to hear the voices of the Daleks as they moved busily around their instruments.

He saw the Daleks in the group wheel round as a large Black Dalek approached. 'Give me your report.'

'The main drills have penetrated the final strata. We are within four miles of the Earth's outer core.'

'When will final breakthrough occur?'

'As soon as the slave workers have finished clearing the top of the fissure, we shall put into position the penetration explosive. The charge is already prepared in the capsule.'

The Black Dalek addressed those around it, rather like a professor delivering a lecture to students. 'The charge will be timed to detonate in the fissure in the Earth's crust. The fissure will expand and the molten core will be released. We will then control the flow until all the gravitational and magnetic forces in the Earth's core are eliminated. I shall now announce to Dalek Earthforce the near completion of Project Degravitate.'

The Black Dalek moved across to a communications console.

Ian listened eagerly. He had arrived at a crucial moment, just as the secret of the Daleks' plans was to be revealed. He heard the voice of the Black Dalek once more, this time echoing through a whole series of loudspeakers. Clearly the announcement was being relayed over the entire control area.

'This is the Supreme Controller. Our mission to Earth is nearly completed. We were sent here to remove the core of this planet. Once the core is removed we shall replace it with a power system. This will enable us to pilot the planet anywhere in the Universe. All that remains is to put into position the penetration explosive capsule. Daleks controlling this device will now report.'

There came another voice. 'The device is ready.'

'Capsule to closed position.'

Inside his hiding place, Ian's mind was reeling at the sheer audacity of the Dalek plan. To steal an entire planet, to steer it around the Universe as a moving base for conquest ... No doubt something about the structure of the Earth had made it exactly the kind of planet the Daleks needed. They weren't taking anything *from* Earth—they were stealing Earth itself!

Lost in thought, it took Ian a moment too long to notice that something was happening. The container in which he had hidden was gliding across the floor. Another identical metal shape, its opposite half, was moving towards it. The two halves clicked together to form a giant metal egg, shutting Ian inside.

The capsule glided across the control room floor until it was suspended above the central well. The overhead cable was paid out and the container slowly descended into the bomb-shaft.

The Black Dalek's voice rang out in triumph. 'Once the capsule has been guided into position, it will be released. It will travel to the fissure in Earth's crust and then explode.'

The penetration explosive capsule was on its way—and Ian was trapped inside.

12

REBELLION!

Inside the capsule Ian was struggling frantically. The metal container was completely sealed, the only possible exit a small hatch in one side. Ian set his back against one side of the capsule and kicked frantically at the hatch with his heels. The capsule swung violently to and fro on the end of its cable.

Suddenly it jerked to a halt.

In the control room above there was pandemonium. A panic-stricken Dalek scientist reported, 'Capsule oscillating violently, due to operation of unknown forces. Descension mechanism has ceased to function.'

The Black Dalek was in a fury. 'Recover capsule and re-check immediately.'

'Descension mechanism now jammed. Capsule must be drawn up manually. Alert Robomen working party. Emergency!'

Soon the capsule began moving upwards again, more slowly now, as a party of sweating Robomen heaved on the cable. It was still spinning to and fro as Ian inside kicked frantically at the hatch.

In the control room a Dalek scientist announced. 'Capsule now arrived at sub-station immediately below this level. Still vibrating violently.'

The Black Dalek decided to take no chances. 'Arrest capsule at sub-station. Ascertain cause of breakdown.'

The capsule jerked to a halt, just as Ian finally kicked the hatchway open. He peered out of the hatch. He was at a point where an intersecting tunnel cut at right angles across the vertical shaft. Down that tunnel a Dalek was speeding straight towards him.

Ian jumped from the capsule and looked round for an escape. There was only one way to go—down.

A coil of rope lay amidst a jumble of timbers at the edge of the shaft. Ian tied the rope round a pit prop, threw the other end into the shaft and started climbing down.

The Dalek arrived at the shaft and spun round angrily, puzzled by the disappearance of its prey. Then its eye-stalk swivelled on to the knotted rope. It fired at the beam and the rope blazed and snapped in two …

Ian began whizzing down the smooth metal shaft, scrabbling desperately at the sides. The edge of another tunnel intersection flashed by and he flung himself forward frantically. He hit the edge with an impact that drove the breath from his body. Painfully, Ian pulled himself up into the lower tunnel. With the last of his strength, he crawled slowly away into the darkness. Halfway down the tunnel he slumped forward, unconscious.

Barbara and Jenny heard the Dalek Supreme's announcement while they were waiting in the outer control area. Like Ian they were astonished at the scope of the Dalek scheme. Soon they were taken to the centre of the control area and ordered to wait until the Black Dalek was free. It was clear by the number of Daleks bustling about, and their evident agitation, that there was some kind of crisis.

Barbara looked curiously at the opening to the bomb shaft. No doubt this was where the penetration capsule had been lowered. She whispered to Jenny, 'See if you can get to one of the control panels and do some damage. I'll try to hold their attention.'

She could hear agitated Dalek voices. 'Dalek unit reports human being discovered in capsule. Human fell down bomb shaft in attempt to escape.'

The Black Dalek was still issuing orders. 'Every error must be corrected. The penetration explosive *must* strike the fissure correctly if we are to extract the molten core. Are all slave worker tasks completed?'

'Only final clearance remains.'

'Once clearance is completed, you will confine all slave workers below ground level. When the molten core breaks through they will be completely exterminated.'

Completely unmoved by this order to commit mass murder, the aide moved to the communications console. 'To all Robomen. Herd all human slaves to lower galleries as soon as clearance is complete!'

Jenny looked at Barbara in horror. 'Did you hear what they're planning to do?'

Barbara was thinking furiously. 'That's where they control the Robomen ...'

'Maybe we can put it out of action,' said Jenny eagerly.

'Better than that—we can use it.'

A Dalek guard ordered them forward, driving them to stand before the Black Dalek. 'Here are the humans who reported an imminent revolt.'

The Black Dalek scanned them. 'Speak!'

Barbara held out Dortmun's notes. 'This is the bomb—'

'We are not interested in the bomb. Give information on planned revolt.'

Barbara racked her brains for a sufficiently colourful story. 'Well, it's planned to start quite suddenly, like the Indian Mutiny.'

'We have already conquered India.'

Barbara rattled on, ignoring the interruption. 'I'm talking about Red Indians of course, in disguise, like the Boston Tea Party. General Lee and the Fifth Cavalry will attack from the North while Hannibal's forces move in from the Southern Alps ...'

While the bemused Daleks were listening to this historical mish-mash, Jenny made a sudden dash for the communications console. Immediately a nearby Roboman grabbed her—but the diversion gave Barbara *her* chance. She ran to the console. 'Attention all Robomen. You will attack the Daleks. Attack the Daleks—'

Like a huge metal dodgem car, the Black Dalek shoved Barbara aside. 'Cancel last order. Resume normal operations.'

The order given, the Black Dalek swung menacingly towards Barbara and Jenny. An aide came forward, 'They were lying to trick us. Shall I exterminate them?'

The Black Dalek considered for a moment. 'No. Hold them here for interrogation. I will deal with them later. There is still much to be done!' Moving to the communications console, the Black Dalek began issuing a further stream of orders.

'Spaceship will hover above main crater, ready to evacuate all Dalek personnel. Repair capsule and descension mechanism. Return capsule to main control ...'

As they were marched away, Barbara whispered, 'Sorry, Jenny.'

'What for? It was a marvellous try—and it nearly worked.'

Their Roboman guard shouted, 'Silence!' Robomen smartly grabbed Barbara and Jenny and manacled them to clamps on a nearby pillar. All around the bustle of Dalek activity continued.

At the edge of an enormous crater, David and Susan were waiting while Tyler and the Doctor crawled round the rim of the excavation.

'Any idea what they're up to?' asked David.

Susan shook her head. 'The Doctor never explains anything. He'll tell us when he's ready.'

David sighed. 'Well whatever it is, I just hope it works. The Doctor seems to be our only hope.' He paused. 'Susan—if we are successful—what will you do?'

'Go on travelling with grandfather, I suppose, moving from place to place ...'

'Wouldn't you *like* to belong somewhere? Like here—with me?'

Susan looked at him in distress. 'Please, David, don't ask me that. I just don't know.' She looked at his unhappy face. 'I'm sorry, David, really ...'

They moved apart as the Doctor and Tyler came back to them. The Doctor rubbed his hands together briskly. 'David, my boy, have you any of those bombs left?'

'Just three, I think.'

'That will be sufficient. Now, you see that radio-mast over there with the cables leading away? I want you and Susan to destroy it. Use the bombs, you can detonate them from a distance with your gun. Off you go—and don't stop to pick flowers on the way.'

As David and Susan scrambled away, the Doctor turned to Tyler. 'I don't think they'll run into any trouble—but I can't say the same for us! We're going down this crater. Come along!'

The Doctor started scrambling rapidly down the steeply sloping sides. Tyler shook his head in reluctant admiration, and started climbing after him.

Ian was never sure how long he'd been unconscious but it couldn't have been very long. He came to, suddenly, in the darkness of the lower tunnel, his mind still full of the Daleks' terrible plan. If there was only something he could do to frustrate them ... He had just one advantage. He was still very close to the shaft down which the bomb capsule must pass. If he could only stop or divert it ...

Ian walked slowly back along the tunnel to the bomb shaft. He peered upwards, to where the light shone down from the Dalek control room. They'd hauled the bomb-capsule back up by now. Soon they'd have it repaired, and ready to drop. Released from its cable it would plummet down the bomb shaft, into the fissure and then explode. Unless ...

Just as there had been on the level above, there was a pile of timber close to the end of the tunnel. Ian looked thoughtfully at the heavy planks. Heaving and struggling, he dragged a plank off its pile and laid it like a bridge right across the bomb shaft. He pulled out another plank, and another ... Some time later, his work completed, Ian ran back up the tunnel. He was looking for a way through to the upper levels. If his plan worked, the tunnel he was in now would soon be a very unhealthy place.

Tyler and the Doctor stood by a massive metal door let into the side of a tunnel. The Doctor was rubbing his chin. 'Since it isn't *guarded*, there's probably a photo-electric alarm ...'

He examined the lower edge of the door. 'Ah yes, here ... and here. One to trigger the alarms, one to open the door. Now, I need something shiny.'

Tyler produced his knife. 'Will this do?'

'Excellent.' Using the shiny blade of the knife as a mirror, the Doctor reflected the light beam of one cell into the other. 'By glancing one beam on to the other, we open the door and neutralise the warning system ... so!' There was a crackle of electricity, a shower of sparks and the door sprang open.

Tyler scratched his head. 'I'll say one thing, Doctor, life with you is never dull!' They passed into the Dalek Base.

Manacled and helpless in the control room, Barbara and Jenny watched as the re-checked capsule was swung out over the bomb shaft. The Dalek Supreme ordered, 'Commence lowering capsule!'

The huge metal egg, this time without a human passenger, was lowered slowly down to the bomb shaft.

The Dalek scientist moved to a control. 'Am releasing capsule—now!'

(The penetration explosive capsule dropped only a short distance further down the bomb shaft, before it hit the wooden barrier constructed by Ian. Deflected from its intended path, the capsule rolled down the side-tunnel, hit the earth wall, then stopped, hidden in the darkness.)

Proudly the Black Dalek announced 'The Capsule is on its way to the core of this planet. When it reaches its destination it will detonate automatically. We shall go to the edge of the mine workings for greater safety. We shall remain in the Dalek spaceship until we are certain it is safe to return. All Daleks will now evacuate this base.'

Barbara gave Jenny an agonised glance. The Dalek plan looked like succeeding after all. And they were being left behind—to die.

13

EXPLOSION!

Tyler and the Doctor jumped back into an intersection, as a long line of Daleks moved down the corridor ahead of them. Tyler popped his head out. 'That was a near one.'

The Doctor nodded. 'They seem to be on the move. Let's go to where they've come from.'

Jenny and Barbara were still struggling with their manacles when Tyler and the Doctor made their way into the now deserted control area. The reunion was excited and ecstatic. 'My poor Barbara,' said the Doctor indignantly. 'Mr Tyler, help me get these things off.' Tyler set to work on the manacle locks with his knife, and soon Barbara and Jenny were free again.

Briefly Barbara explained what she'd gathered about the Daleks' plan. The Doctor seemed unsurprised. 'I thought it would be something like that. I'm working on a scheme to circumvent them. Now, let me see if I can work this scanner.'

The Doctor swiftly adjusted controls and a little screen in front of him sprung to life. It showed various shots of the mines, then suddenly a picture of Susan and David laying bombs around the base of an enormous radio mast. 'They're trying to blow up the mast and so fracture the outer cable ring,' explained the Doctor.

Jenny was none the wiser. 'What good will that do?'

'You know the Daleks communicate by a sort of radio network? Well, if the radio-link is suddenly broken it will give them a most tremendous shock. A kind of brainstorm. It should immobilise them completely, at least for a while ...'

A Dalek voice crackled from a nearby speaker. 'Interference to scanner settings in main control area. One Dalek unit will return to investigate!'

Tyler ran to the doorway. 'There's a Dalek coming along the corridor now!'

On the screen David and Susan continued their task with maddening slowness.

From the doorway Tyler called, 'Doctor—the Dalek's nearly here!'

He ran back to join them at the scanner. Seconds later a Dalek glided into the control area.

The Doctor stood quietly at the scanner, ignoring the approaching Dalek completely.

On the screen they saw David and Susan finish laying their charges, and retreat to a safe distance. David raised the rifle to his shoulder, then a flash filled the screen. When it cleared they saw the radio mast toppling slowly to the ground.

The Doctor beamed triumphantly, turned round—and saw the Dalek heading straight towards him.

Tyler tried to pull him aside. 'Run, Doctor, it hasn't worked.'

The Doctor shook him off, and stepped directly in front of the Dalek, hands clutching his lapels.

The Dalek said, 'Halt! Who *aaare* ...'

Its voice seemed to wind down, and trail away into silence. The Dalek stopped moving.

Tyler gave a huge sigh of relief. 'You certainly took a chance.'

'Science, my dear chap, not chance. It took a little time for the effect to be felt, that's all.'

'What will you do now, Doctor, stop the bomb?'

After this latest display, Tyler was quite prepared to believe the Doctor could do anything.

'All in good time,' replied the Doctor calmly. 'I'm not sure how long this little shock will hold the Daleks. We must find some more permanent way of dealing with them.'

Barbara said excitedly, 'The Robomen, Doctor. That console controls them. I tried ordering them to attack the Daleks, but they caught us. Let me try again.'

The Doctor gave an assenting wave of his hand and Barbara rushed to the console. 'Robomen, this order cannot be countermanded. Attack the Daleks! Destroy them!'

The Doctor stepped up to the console. 'Slave workers—here is your freedom. Use it. Destroy the Daleks.' He turned away from the console, rubbing his hands with glee. 'Now come along all of you. Let's see what happens!'

They walked along the corridor towards the mining area. Soon they heard a clamour and a shouting, the ringing of metal on metal. They turned a corner to find a seething mob of slave workers and Robomen battering and smashing at a Dalek with pails and picks, until it was no more than a hunk of twisted metal. The crowd rushed past them, obviously searching for more Daleks to destroy.

A grimy ragged figure dashed out of the crowd and caught Barbara in his arms, hugging her till she was breathless. 'Ian,' she cried delightedly. 'Ian!'

'Bless my soul, it's young Chesterton!' said the Doctor. 'Where did you spring from, my boy?'

Ian shook the Doctor's hand like a pump handle. 'Doctor! I might have guessed you were behind all this. Just listen to them!'

From all over the mine came the sound of exultant shouting, the roar and clamour of battle. The Doctor smiled. 'The people of Earth are fighting back at last.'

They made their way back to the control room, exchanging a babble of congratulations, explanations and recitals of all their different adventures.

The Doctor listened gravely as Ian told of his attempt to deflect the bomb. Ian crossed to a chart on the wall which showed the bomb shaft plunging down to join the fissure in the Earth's crust. He put his finger on the chart. 'If the contraption works, the bomb's jammed here—just a couple of levels below us.'

'A brave scheme, my boy,' said the Doctor, 'But not without its perils to the rest of us. The bomb won't release the Earth's core as the Daleks had hoped. But there will be the most tremendous explosion in a very short time!'

'How long have we got, Doctor?'

The Doctor crossed to the bomb control area. 'If I read these dials correctly—something in the order of ten more minutes!'

Barbara ran to his side. 'Can you switch it off to delay the explosion?'

The Doctor shook his head. 'The bomb was intended to explode deep within the Earth's core, remember. The detonation device is automatic—and self-contained.'

'Then we've got to get out of here!' said Tyler urgently. 'And we've got to get everyone else out too!'

The Doctor went over to the communications console. 'The public address system will still be working. It's on a separate circuit.' He cleared his throat and spoke into it. 'Robomen and slave workers. This mine is about to explode. You must make for the surface and leave the area immediately. Never mind the Daleks. Leave them to their fate. I repeat, this mine is about to explode. Leave the area immediately.' He turned to the others. 'We've done all we can. It's time to look to our own safety. Follow me. We'll go out the way I came in!'

Swiftly the Doctor led them out of the control area along the corridors, out into the tunnel, and finally in a last frantic scramble up the sloping sides of the crater. They found Susan and David waiting for them at the top. 'Don't talk—run!' ordered the Doctor breathlessly, as they joined the crowds fleeing desperately from the mine.

They witnessed the end of the Dalek invasion of Earth from the hill overlooking the mine area. The place looked like a disturbed ant-hill, long lines of people streaming away from it in all directions. The Dalek spaceship hovered over the main crater, but made no attempt to attack, waiting no doubt for the results of the experiment.

As the last few escapers fled from the mine there was a low subterranean rumble … It grew steadily until, suddenly, the whole of the mine workings erupted in a great belching cloud of smoke and flame. The noise was shattering, and they all dropped to the ground, hands over their ears. All except the Doctor, who stood watching the holocaust with keen scientific interest.

The incredible noise ended at last, dying down to a low, constant rumble. They looked up to see a huge mountain of earth, the crater on its top belching smoke and flame. 'Quite a sight, eh, Mr Tyler,' said the Doctor. 'An active volcano in England!'

Jenny looked upwards. 'What happened to the Dalek spaceship?'

'Totally destroyed,' said the Doctor with satisfaction. 'I saw it. They were caught in the first up-blast of the explosion.'

Jenny stood looking at the sky. Barbara put an arm round her shoulders. 'It's all right, Jenny, it's over ...'

'Over,' said Jenny quietly. Barbara saw tears streaming down her cheeks. Suddenly she realised—in all their adventures together, it was the first time she'd ever seen Jenny cry.

14

THE FAREWELL

It took them a very long time to make their way back to London, the riverside, and the building-site where the TARDIS had been trapped so long ago. So many people wanted to congratulate them, to hear the story of their adventures and final triumph. But they arrived at last, and now the Doctor stood looking on in quiet satisfaction while a willing gang of Tyler's men cleared the last of the girders away from the TARDIS door.

London was already a very different place from the ruined city in which they'd arrived. There were people in the streets again and even a few cars, and boats on the river. Everywhere was a spirit of hope, the sense of life starting again. London was being reborn before their eyes.

Tyler stood beside the Doctor and looked round at the bustling scene. 'It's a pity Dortmun isn't here to see this. Dortmun and lots of others like him.'

'It's up to you to build their memorial,' said the Doctor quietly. 'A new London, a better Earth. I'm certain you'll succeed.'

The TARDIS was clear at last. Tyler nodded towards it. 'There's your police box, Doctor. And I won't ask questions. As far as I'm concerned you're welcome to every police box in London.'

The Doctor smiled. 'This one will do, thank you.' A sound rang out, a sound once familiar to every Londoner, one that had been missing for a very long time—the chimes of Big Ben. Tyler smiled contentedly.

The Doctor left him listening happily to the chimes, and scrambled down to Susan. She was sitting on a beam of timber, absently toying with her TARDIS key, which hung as usual on a chain around her neck. 'All alone, child?' he asked gently.

Susan smiled. 'I've already let Barbara and Ian into the ship. I was just—thinking.'

The Doctor sat down beside her. 'Hasn't been much time for that recently. I'm afraid you must blame me—I seem to have a nose for trouble.'

Susan gave him an affectionate hug. 'You know I wouldn't blame you for anything, Grandfather.'

They sat in silence for a while. Several times the Doctor seemed about to speak, and then changed his mind. Susan seemed plunged in a fit of abstraction. Suddenly she stood up and said, 'Ah well——' then broke off, wincing.

The Doctor jumped up too. 'Susan, you're hurt ...'

Susan stood on one foot. 'No, I'm all right. I just trod on a sharp stone.' She held up one shoe to reveal a gaping hole in the bottom. 'The journey to the mines wore them out completely.'

The Doctor took the shoe from her, pursing his lips. 'Dear me. Still it's nothing to worry about. I'll soon mend it for you.'

Susan smiled at him affectionately. The funny thing was that he was quite serious. It was typical of the Doctor that he was quite as willing, and as able, to repair a worn-out shoe as he was a damaged spaceship computer. 'It's all right, Doctor, I've got plenty more pairs in the TARDIS.'

The Doctor frowned. 'That reminds me, I'd better go and check up on the ship.' He gave Susan a pat on the head and wandered off, the shoe clutched in his hand.

Susan was still sitting on the beam when David came quietly up to her. He sat beside her, his arm round her shoulders.

'Susan, stay with me,' he pleaded.

'David, I can't! I don't belong on your world or in your time.'

'I love you, Susan. I'm asking you to marry me.'

'I have to stay with grandfather. He's old now, he needs me. Please—don't ask me to choose between you.'

David took a deep breath. 'You told me once you'd never really belonged anywhere. That's what I'm offering you now, Susan. A place and a time of your own.'

Susan stood up and started limping towards the TARDIS. There were tears in her eyes. 'Goodbye, David. I'm all right. I just trod on a nail.' She limped off towards the waiting police box. As she moved away she said quietly to herself 'But I do love you, David. I do ...'

The Doctor stood at the TARDIS console, still holding Susan's shoe. Behind him Ian and Barbara stood hand in hand. They knew the dilemma the Doctor was facing, but there was nothing they could do to help.

Suddenly the Doctor stood very erect. He put Susan's shoe down carefully, reached for a particular control-switch and slammed it over, hard.

Susan had almost reached the TARDIS when its door closed in her face. She took the key from round her neck and tried to open it. Nothing happened. 'Grandfather,' she screamed. 'Grandfather!'

Suddenly she heard the Doctor's voice. 'Susan, please listen. I've safety-locked the door—you can't get in.'

Inside the TARDIS the Doctor could see Susan's puzzled face looking at him on the scanner. Gently he said, 'All these years I've been taking care of you—and all the time, you really felt you were taking care of me ...'

He heard Susan's voice. 'But I belong with you ...'

'Not any more, Susan. Your future is with young David, not with an old buffer like me.' He saw that David had come to join Susan, his arm around her. 'Look after her, David, my boy. Be kind. Work hard both of you. You'll find that life on Earth can be an adventure too.'

For a moment the Doctor's voice faltered, then he recovered himself. 'Now then, both of you, no regrets. And look to the future. Remember, both of you, love's the thing. That's what really counts. Goodbye. One day I'll come back. One day ... Goodbye ...'

Susan and David stepped back, as the dematerialisation noise began, and the TARDIS disappeared.

Quietly David said, 'He knew, Susan. He knew you could never leave him. That's why he left you.'

As David took Susan in his arms the TARDIS key slipped from her fingers, and lay unregarded on the ground. Susan made no attempt to pick it up because she knew she wouldn't be needing it again.

Inside the TARDIS the Doctor turned away from the scanner with a sniff. He glared at Ian and Barbara, as if daring them to comment. When they said nothing, his face broke into a smile. 'I'll get over it,' he said briskly. 'Bound to happen one day. Now then, I really must get you two home again. Right place *and* the right time, eh? Let's see what we can do!'

As the Doctor leaned over the console, his fingers moving over the controls, Ian gave Barbara a nudge. 'I wonder where the old boy will land us up this time!'

'I'd be willing to bet you it's not Earth,' she whispered.

Through the Space Time Vortex, the TARDIS sped on its way. The Doctor still had two faithful companions, and many more adventures lay before them.

Doctor Who And The Abominable Snowmen

1

THE SECRET OF
THE SNOWS

High on the Himalayan mountainside the little camp fire was burning low. Edward Travers shivered, and huddled deeper inside his sleeping-bag. He was drifting in and out of an uneasy slumber, fantasy and reality merging and blurring in his mind. In his dream, he was at the Royal Geographical Society, addressing a scornful and hostile audience.

'Gentlemen, I assure you – the body of evidence that has accumulated over the years is undeniable. The Abominable Snowman does exist.'

He heard again the hated voice of his old rival, Professor Walters. 'If you're as sure as that, my dear Travers, I suggest you go and look for the beast!'

Once more Travers heard the scornful laughter that followed. He heard his own voice. 'Thank you for the suggestion, sir. Perhaps I will.'

Travers twisted and muttered in his sleep. Scene followed scene in his mind, like a jerky, speeded-up old film: the desperate struggle to raise money for his expedition; the final, half-scornful agreement of a Fleet Street editor to back him; the long journey to India; the endless days of overland travel to reach the slopes of the Himalayas; still more days spent climbing, always climbing, to reach this remote point. And all for nothing.

Soon they would have to turn back, the expedition a failure. Back in London there would be polite sympathy, concealing quiet amusement. Only Mackay would stand by him. Mackay, his oldest and best friend, the only man who had agreed to join his expedition. Yet now it seemed that even Mackay had turned against him. Mackay was laughing at him, screaming insults.

111

Suddenly Travers jerked fully awake. He really could hear Mackay's voice. It was calling to him. Screaming for help ... Travers rubbed his eyes and looked across the circle of light round the camp fire. Mackay's sleeping-bag was empty. There were tracks leading out into the darkness. Travers fumbled for his rifle and struggled from his sleeping-bag. Then he set off towards the sound of Mackay's voice. He scrambled over the edge of the little plateau, and down the rocky slope.

In the darkness ahead of him he could see two struggling figures. One was Mackay. But the other ... It was enormous – a giant, shaggy form. Travers tried to call out, but could only produce a sort of croak. Instantly the creature flung Mackay to the ground. It whirled round to attack Travers. He raised his rifle, but before he could fire it was wrenched from his hands. Travers caught a brief glimpse of glowing eyes and savage fangs. Then a blow from a giant, hairy paw smashed him to the ground.

Back at the little camp-site the fire was almost out. The guttering of the flames threw a feeble light on the two empty sleeping-bags. The shadow of a huge shuffling figure fell over the site. Something was tossed contemptuously into the dying fire. It was Mackay's rifle. The barrel was bent almost double, the stock shattered into matchwood. The giant shape moved away and vanished into the night.

Next morning, a little higher on that same Himalayan peak, a wheezing, groaning sound shattered the peace and stillness of the mountain air. An old blue police box appeared from nowhere, transparent at first, but gradually becoming solid. It perched on a snowy ledge, looking completely out of place.

Inside the police box was an ultra-modern control room, with a centre console of complex instruments. There was something very odd about this police box. Somehow it was bigger on the inside than on the outside.

There were three people in the control room. One was a middle-aged, middle-sized man with a gentle, rather comical face, and a shock of untidy black hair. He was wearing an old black coat, and a pair of rather baggy check trousers. Watching him were a brawny youth in highland dress, complete with kilt, and a small, dark girl dressed in the style of Earth's Victorian age. Appropriately enough, since her name was Victoria.

She was the daughter of a Victorian antique dealer, who had lost his life during a terrifying adventure with the Daleks. Alone and friendless, Victoria had been taken under the protection of a mysterious traveller in Space and Time known only as the Doctor.

Much the same thing had happened to Jamie, the Scots lad, whose fate had become caught up with the Doctor's during the Jacobite rebellion. Now both young people, wrenched from their own times, spent their lives travelling through Time and Space with the Doctor in the strangely disguised craft known as the TARDIS. (The Doctor had told Victoria that the initials stood for Time and Relative Dimensions in Space – which left her none the wiser.)

Victoria sometimes wondered if her decision to join the Doctor had been a wise one. He was very kind, in his vague, erratic way, and she was very fond of him. But he did seem to have a knack of wandering into the most appalling danger. Victoria, like most girls of her time, had had a rather sheltered upbringing. Her travels with the Doctor had brought her a number of rather nerve-shattering experiences. But despite her initial timidity, she was discovering unexpected resources of courage inside herself.

Jamie, on the other hand, was completely different. He welcomed each new adventure with tremendous gusto. Jamie was a fighter by nature. English Redcoat soldier or alien monster, it was all the same to Jamie. He grabbed his trusty claymore and charged.

Victoria looked on indulgently as the Doctor peered into the little scanner screen, almost hopping up and down with excitement. As usual, she and Jamie had no idea *where* or *when* they were – or for that matter, *why*. No doubt the Doctor would get round to telling them in his own good time.

'Marvellous,' the Doctor was chortling. 'Absolutely marvellous! And after all this time!' He adjusted the scanner controls and the picture of snowy wastes changed to that of a distinctively-shaped peak.

Jamie looked over the Doctor's shoulder. 'I dinna see what's so marvellous about a lot of snowy mountains.'

The Doctor looked up in amazement. 'But it's the Himalayas, Jamie! The Himalayas!'

'The Hima—what?' Geography wasn't Jamie's strong point. Anywhere outside Scotland was unknown territory to him.

Victoria leaned forward. 'The Himalayas. They're a range of mountains. On the border between India and Tibet, I think.'

The Doctor turned away from the scanner. 'That's right! Tibet, that's where we are. Tibet!' The Doctor beamed at Victoria, then said briskly, 'Well, come on then, no time to waste. Help me find the ghanta.' He rushed across the TARDIS, opened a wall-locker and dragged out an enormous old chest, covered in antique carving. 'Now I'm sure I put it in here somewhere!' The Doctor started ferreting inside the chest, rather like a dog at a rabbit hole, throwing things over his shoulder with gay abandon. Jamie and Victoria looked on in amazement. After a moment, the Doctor's head popped up indignantly. 'Come on, you two. Aren't you going to help me?'

They came over to join him. 'That's all verra well,' said Jamie. 'Can you no' tell us what we're looking for?'

'I've already told you. The ghanta!' The Doctor went on burrowing.

'Yes, but what's a ghanta?' Victoria asked gently.

The Doctor was amazed. 'You mean you don't know? It's a Tibetan holy relic. A bell actually. Quite small. You see it was given to me to look after when …'

The Doctor broke off as he pulled an enormous fur coat from the bottom of the chest. 'Ah,' he exclaimed delightedly, 'now I'll have that. Just the thing for this climate.' The Doctor began to struggle into the coat. It completely swamped him, coming right down to his ankles. 'Tell you what, I'll just go and have a scout around.' Suddenly he couldn't wait to be off.

Jamie looked up from the chest. 'What about this precious ghanta?'

The Doctor looked uneasy. 'Ah. Well, I thought you and Victoria might find it for me.' He looked pleadingly at them, like a small boy begging to be allowed to go out and play.

Victoria smiled. 'All right, Doctor, off you go. We'll find your bell for you. But what do you want it for? Why's it so important?'

The Doctor paused at the door. 'Because when we get down there, it'll guarantee us the welcome of a lifetime.'

'Down *where?*' called Victoria. But the Doctor was already gone, the door of the TARDIS closing behind him.

Jamie sighed. 'When you've been with the Doctor as long as I have, you'll realise ye canna hope to know what he's talking about most of the time. Let's find his bell, there'll be no peace till we do!'

Jamie went on rummaging in the chest. Victoria wandered over to the scanner and switched it on, hoping to see where the Doctor was off to. Suddenly she jumped back from the screen in terror. 'Jamie, look!'

Jamie came over to the scanner, and peered in amazement at the huge, hairy form on the little screen. 'It's a beastie,' he muttered, 'a huge hairy beastie!'

Victoria felt a sudden stab of fear. 'We must warn the Doctor …'

Jamie held up a restraining hand. 'Just a wee moment. Let's have another look.' He adjusted the scanner controls to give a closer view of the shambling figure. Then he looked up, grinning. 'Ye needna worry about warning the Doctor. Yon great hairy beastie *is* the Doctor!'

And indeed the Doctor did look rather like a huge animal as he plodded up the mountain path in his enormous fur coat. He gazed around him with child-like pleasure.

The surrounding peaks seemed to sparkle in the clear frosty atmosphere. The Doctor took deep, satisfying breaths of the fresh, sharp mountain air, puffing it out again like steam. The path climbed sharply upwards, and soon the Doctor was breathing hard. He reached the point he was making for and leaned thankfully against a boulder. A hidden valley lay far below him. And there nestling in the valley was the Monastery. The Doctor sighed with quiet satisfaction. For once the TARDIS, and his navigation, hadn't let him down. He'd come to exactly the right spot. Clumps of snow had built up on the Doctor's boots, making walking difficult. He began kicking his boots against a boulder to clean them. Suddenly he stopped, his eye caught by something at his feet. It was an enormous footprint, many times the size of his own.

The Doctor began to cast about the area, like a hunting dog. There were other footprints, a line of them, leading to the other side of the boulder. Cautiously, the Doctor followed the tracks. On the other side of the boulder there were more footprints, deeper ones. The snow was churned as though the creature had stood for some time. There were other tracks leading away down the mountainside.

The Doctor stood, pondering. The story in the snow was clear. Some enormous creature had climbed to this spot, and stood there, looking down at the Monastery below. Then it had moved away. Not long ago, either. The tracks leading away from the boulder were still fairly fresh.

The Doctor's scientific curiosity was roused. Could it be – he'd heard the stories, of course, on previous visits to Earth – The Abominable Snowman? Known to the Tibetans as the Yeti. A giant man-like creature that lived somewhere on the remotest peaks, seen only in glimpses by terrified natives. But surely the creature had never been heard of in this part of Tibet? The Doctor was puzzled. For a moment he was strongly tempted to follow the tracks still further.

The Doctor had seen so many amazing creatures on so many planets that he was prepared to believe in anything. Then he checked himself. What would he do with the creature if he found it? Come to that, what would it do with him? There was the Monastery to be visited. And Jamie and Victoria still waiting in the TARDIS. Congratulating himself on his self-control, the Doctor turned and retraced his steps.

Suddenly he stopped. Had there been a flash of movement, higher up the mountain? There, behind the clump of boulders? The Doctor peered, but could see nothing. He continued on his way, back to the TARDIS.

Behind those same boulders there was a stir of movement. An enormous hairy hand appeared on the top of a sheltering boulder. A giant, shaggy form pulled itself upright. It stood looking down at the tiny figure of the Doctor, plodding on his way far below.

Jamie rose from the empty trunk in disgust. 'He must have put this ghanta thing somewhere else. It's no' in here!'

Victoria looked round at the amazing collection of objects spread over the TARDIS floor: clothes, weapons, curios and carvings from a hundred different planets. There was something of the magpie in the Doctor, she thought despairingly. 'Are you sure the trunk's empty? Really empty?'

'Och, see for yourself!'

Victoria groped in the inner recesses of the enormous trunk, practically disappearing inside. 'I'm afraid you're – wait a minute!' Her fingers touched a scrap of cloth wedged in a corner. Stretching, she pulled a tiny bundle from the trunk. 'Look, there's a label on it. "Ghanta of Det-sen Monastery."' Victoria unwrapped the bundle. Triumphantly, she held up an ornately carved bronze bell.

'Wouldn't you know it'd be the verra last thing?' groaned Jamie disgustedly. The TARDIS door opened and the Doctor came in. He saw the little bell in Victoria's hand.

'Found it, have you? Splendid. Knew it wasn't far away.' Gently he took it from Victoria and slipped it in his pocket.

'It took a wee bit of searching, ye ken,' said Jamie dryly.

The Doctor frowned abstractedly. 'Yes, I'm sure it did …'

Jamie looked at him. 'You've seen something, haven't you? Out there?'

The Doctor glanced quickly at Victoria. 'Oh, nothing really, Jamie. Probably nothing.' He came to a decision. 'I've just got to pay a quick visit to the Monastery, and then we'll be on our way. Stay here in the TARDIS, will you, Jamie?'

'Would it no' be better if I came too?'

The Doctor shook his head. Victoria looked from one to the other. 'Look, what's happening? Is there something dangerous out there?'

The Doctor smiled. 'Just a lot of snow! I'll be as quick as I can.' The Doctor left the TARDIS, closing the door behind him.

Victoria turned to Jamie. 'There is something the matter, isn't there?'

Jamie nodded reluctantly. 'Something's worrying him, right enough. But don't go asking me what, for I dinna ken!'

Victoria looked at the litter of objects on the floor. 'Come on, Jamie. Let's put this lot away.'

The Doctor was slowly picking his way along the uneven track that led down towards the Monastery. Every now and again he would stop, looking around him uneasily. He kept getting the feeling that something malevolent and hostile was watching his every movement. Sometimes he thought he saw a flicker of movement on the slopes above him. But always it vanished before he could pin it down. Warily the Doctor plodded on his way.

He followed the path round the curve of the mountain, and on to a little plateau. It formed a kind of natural camp-site, and the Doctor saw that someone had indeed made camp there. A few charred sticks marked the remains of a fire. Close by were two empty sleeping-bags. Something glinted in the cold ashes of the fire. The Doctor fished it out. It was the barrel of a rifle, bent almost double. The charred, splintered stock was burnt almost completely away. The Doctor wondered what kind of strength could bend the steel of a rifle barrel like plasticine.

Footprints, human footprints, led over the edge of the plateau. Peering over the edge, the Doctor saw a huddled shape a little further down. He scrambled towards it.

The body lay face down in the snow. Gently the Doctor turned it over. To his surprise he saw that the man was a European. As he shifted the body, the head lolled over at a strange angle. The man was dead, his neck broken by a single savage blow.

2

THE CREATURE IN THE CAVE

The Doctor straightened up, and stood looking down at the body. For a moment he considered going straight back to the TARDIS. All around him he sensed the presence of some alien evil. Then he remembered the ghanta.

Slipping his hand in his pocket, the Doctor took out the little Tibetan bell. He gazed at it for a moment, and sighed. A promise was a promise. But as soon as he had returned the ghanta to the Monastery, he would go back to the TARDIS and whisk Jamie and Victoria off to a safer place and time. Not far from the dead man, a rucksack lay in the snow. It held maps, warm clothes, brandy, concentrated foods – the provisions of an experienced explorer. Perhaps he would find the owner at the Monastery – if he had survived the attack on the camp.

After a long and weary journey, the Doctor finally reached the lower slopes of the mountain. The path sloped sharply, leading him at last to the Det-sen Monastery. With a sigh of relief, he looked up at the huge old building he remembered so well. Protected by its high stone walls, the Monastery huddled as if for shelter in the valley between two mountains. It had been many years since his last visit, yet nothing had changed. Or had it? In former days, the massive bronze doors had always stood open, welcoming the entry of pilgrims and travellers. The monks of Det-sen were peaceful, hospitable men, always willing to provide shelter. But now the gates were closed. An oppressive silence seemed to hang over the Monastery.

The Doctor took a deep breath. 'Hello! Hello! Anyone about?' His voice echoed round the high forbidding walls. He hammered on the doors, but his fists made almost no sound. The Doctor put his shoulder to the heavy, bronze doors and shoved – more as a kind of gesture than with any hope of success. To his surprise, he felt them shift a little. Using all his strength, he managed to push one of the doors ajar, creating just enough of a gap to slip through. Once through the doors, the Doctor gazed round him. The long rectangular courtyard was unchanged. The stone flagstones were worn smooth by the sandalled feet of generations of monks. Doorways and cloisters led off into different parts of the rambling old Monastery. But still this mysterious silence and emptiness. The Det-sen Monastery had always buzzed like a beehive – the chatter of pilgrims, the cries of pedlars in the courtyard, the low humming of the temple bells, the endless drone of the monks at their prayers. It had been a lively, bustling place. Now it was as quiet as a tomb. The Doctor shivered. He walked to the middle of the courtyard, his footsteps echoing hollowly. 'Hello! Where is everyone?'

Suddenly there came a shattering clang. The Doctor whirled round. The bronze doors had been pushed to, and barred. A little group of men stood watching him. They wore the simple robes of the Det-sen monks, but they carried bows and swords. They ran forward and surrounded the Doctor, weapons raised.

Their leader, a tall man with a dark, hawk-like face, towered over him.

'Who are you? Why do you come here?'

Quite unintimidated, the Doctor smiled up at him. 'First may I ask *who* you are? By what right do you question me?'

'I am Khrisong, leader of the warrior monks.' The tall man indicated a younger monk who stood at his side. 'This is Thomni – my guard captain. Now – you will answer. Who are you?'

Gently the Doctor said, 'You can call me the Doctor.' He looked at the group. 'Warrior monks – that's a contradiction in terms, isn't it? I thought the monks of Det-sen were men of peace.'

There was grim irony in Khrisong's reply. 'Most of them still are. But these are dangerous times. If the men of peace are to survive, they need men of war to protect them.' His tone hardened. 'Now – you would do well to answer quickly. Who are you? What is your business at the Monastery of Det-sen?'

Before the Doctor could answer a man ran out of the cloisters and up to the little group. He flung himself on the Doctor, wrenching the rucksack from his shoulders.

'You murderous devil. We've got you now!'

The Doctor looked curiously at his attacker. He was a European, dressed in a ragged, travel-stained anorak. His eyes were red-rimmed with exhaustion, and a stubble of beard covered his chin. His manner was hysterical, like a man in the grip of some over-mastering obsession. He glared angrily at the Doctor.

Khrisong turned to the newcomer. 'Travers! Do you know this man?'

'No – but this rucksack's mine all right. He must have stolen it when he attacked my camp.' Travers hugged the rucksack protectively.

'You told us that a beast attacked you,' said Khrisong sharply.

'Well, that's what I thought. I just saw a shape in the darkness – felt the fur. But look at his coat! That's what I felt. It *must* have been him. How else did he get my rucksack?'

The little group of armed men gathered menacingly round the Doctor. 'Why did you attack this man?' snapped Khrisong.

The Doctor kept his voice low and calm. 'I attacked no one. I found this rucksack by a wrecked camp. There was a dead man—'

'Yes – and you killed him!' shrieked Travers. Dropping the rucksack, he hurled himself at the Doctor. Thomni and another of the warrior monks held him back.

Khrisong said, 'We have heard enough. Seize him!' Before the Doctor could move, two brawny young monks had grabbed his arms.

'Look,' said the Doctor mildly, 'this is ridiculous. I've killed no one. I brought the rucksack here to return it to its owner. I came on a most important …'

'Silence,' interrupted Khrisong. 'You have been accused of a crime. There have been many other such crimes of late. All strangers are suspect. If you are guilty, be sure you will be punished. Take him away!'

Lifting him almost off his feet, the two warrior monks carried the protesting Doctor away. At a nod from Khrisong, Thomni released

Travers. He seized Khrisong's arm, looking up at the tall monk with a kind of crazy intentness. 'He's a dangerous man, Khrisong. Watch him carefully!'

Thomni, the young guard captain, said thoughtfully, 'We do not *know* that this man is the killer ...'

'Of course we do,' Travers interrupted. 'I've just told you so.'

Thomni ignored him. 'After all,' he went on, 'we still do not know *why* he came here.'

'That, too, we shall discover – in good time,' said Khrisong impassively.

The two warrior monks half-carried, half-dragged the Doctor along the endless stone corridors of the Monastery, ignoring his spirited protests. 'Do put me down, you chaps. I can walk, you know. Anyway, I've got something important to tell you ...'

The monks came to a halt before a massive wooden door, studded with iron. They opened it, thrust the Doctor inside, slammed the door and bolted it. Then they turned and marched away.

The Doctor looked around him. He was in a bare stone cell, with a little window high up in the wall. There was a wooden stool, and a wooden bed with a straw mattress along one wall. The Doctor sank down on the bed and sighed. He remembered his own words, back in the TARDIS. 'The welcome of a lifetime!' said the Doctor ruefully.

Jamie and Victoria sat looking at each other blankly. The contents of the massive chest had been tidied away long ago. Now they were just sitting waiting – and waiting. Jamie gave a massive yawn.

'I'm getting very bored,' Victoria said. 'Couldn't we take a look outside?'

Jamie shook his head. 'The Doctor said to wait here.'

'I'll go by myself.' Victoria stood up decisively.

Jamie sighed. It was in the nature of females to be contrary. 'Och, all right. Just a wee look round. We'd better wrap up warm.'

Victoria gave him a happy smile, and rushed to the TARDIS' clothing locker, which held garments in every imaginable size to suit every possible climate. Soon the two of them were kitted out like polar explorers in warm, fur-lined anoraks, with fur gloves and fur-lined boots.

Victoria rushed to the door. 'Come on, Jamie!'

'Just a wee moment.' Jamie went back to the big chest, and rummaged inside. He fished out a huge curved sword – a kind of Turkish scimitar.

'What on earth do you want that for?'

'Aye, well, ye never know what ye'll run in to.' Grasping the sword firmly, Jamie ushered Victoria outside. If there was something dangerous out there, he was ready for it.

Standing on the little ledge, Victoria looked entranced at the panorama of mountain scenery spread out before them. 'Look how clear everything is, Jamie. Even the furthest peaks seem close enough to touch. Aren't the Himalayas beautiful?'

'Aye, well, they're no' so bad.' As far as Jamie was concerned there were bigger and better mountains at home in Scotland.

'Let's climb a little higher, Jamie. Maybe we'll see the Doctor coming back.'

They scrambled up the mountain track, which became steeper and narrower. Suddenly Victoria stopped. 'Jamie, look!' She pointed downwards. Just to one side of the path was an area of churned-up snow. Leading away from it was a set of enormous footprints. They stooped to examine them.

Jamie whistled. 'Will you look at the size of that? Something's been prowling round here, right enough. A bear, mebbe.'

Suddenly Victoria gave a little gasp of excitement. 'Jamie! Perhaps it's the Yeti – the Abominable Snowman!'

'The abominable what?'

'There have been stories and legends about them in the Himalayas for ages. Huge furry creatures. Something between a bear, an ape and a man. Let's track it, Jamie!'

'We will not! Look at those footprints. Ye can see how big the beastie must be.'

Victoria jumped up and down in excitement. 'You don't understand, Jamie. People have been trying to find the Abominable Snowman for ages. Scientific expeditions and everything. No one's succeeded. It'd be marvellous if we found it.'

'That's all verra well. Suppose it finds us first?'

'There's nothing to worry about, Jamie. All the reports say it's a timid creature. It'll run as soon as it sees us.' Jamie still looked dubious. Cunningly, Victoria continued, 'Of course, if you're *afraid* . . .'

Jamie was outraged. 'Me? Afraid? I'll have you know, my girl, we Highlanders fear nothing. Come on!' Brandishing his sword, Jamie set off. Victoria smiled to herself, and followed him.

The trail of huge footprints led them higher and higher up the mountain slope. They scrambled over boulders and across icy patches. The creature they were following was obviously strong and agile, able to move over the roughest ground. Eventually, the tracks led them straight into the side of the mountain. They found themselves at the entrance to a small cave. 'Well, there you are then,' said Jamie. 'That's where the beastie lives.'

Victoria peered curiously into the darkness of the cave mouth. Just to the right of it stood a huge boulder, just a little larger than the cave mouth itself. 'It looks almost like a door,' said Victoria. 'Couldn't we just have a quick look inside the cave?'

'And mebbe wake the beastie up? We'll do no such thing. Come on, my girl, it's back to the TARDIS for us.' Obediently Victoria started back down the mountainside. On second thoughts, she was rather pleased not to be going inside that dark cave. There was something rather spooky about it. Suddenly she realised that Jamie wasn't following her. He had moved closer to the cave entrance, and was looking inside.

'Hey, Victoria, look at this. Just inside the cave. Wooden beams!'

Victoria came to join him. Intrigued, Jamie went up to the cave entrance. 'Aye, it's beams, right enough. Kind of supports. Mebbe this thing we're following is no' a beastie after all.' And before Victoria could stop him, Jamie plunged into the darkness of the cave.

'Come back, Jamie,' she called. 'You said we should go back to the TARDIS.'

Jamie's voice came from within the cave, booming hollowly. 'That was when I thought we were tracking a wild animal. I'm no' afraid of a *man*.'

Victoria decided that she was more frightened of being left outside than of going in. She followed Jamie into the cave. Actually it turned out to be more of a tunnel leading into the heart of the mountain, just inside the entrance the walls were supported by what looked like pit-props. They could see other props further down the tunnel. Jamie examined the nearest beam curiously. 'Now what kind of a beastie builds a thing like this?'

There came a grinding noise from the cave entrance. A huge shadow fell across the light, blocking it out completely. Suddenly they were in darkness. Victoria clutched Jamie's arm in fear. 'What is it? What's happened?'

It took Jamie a moment to work things out. Then he realised. 'You remember yon big rock by the entrance ... the one you said looked like a door?' Victoria nodded. 'Well,' said Jamie grimly, 'someone's just shut that door!'

Outside the cave, two huge hairy paws finished jamming the boulder into place. Then a massive shaggy form turned and lumbered away down the mountainside.

By dragging the wooden bed under the window, putting the wooden stool on the bed, and climbing on top of the stool, the Doctor was just able to peer out of the high barred window of his cell. He looked down on the courtyard far below. He grasped the bars and shook them but they were set firmly in the stone-framed window.

There was a rattle from behind the Doctor, and a barred grille in his cell door slid open. He turned and saw the face of Travers peering through at him.

'It's a forty-foot drop down there, you know,' said Travers. 'There's no way out.'

The Doctor clambered down from his perch. 'I didn't really think there would be.' He smiled placidly at Travers, who glared back at him, and asked fiercely, 'How did you track me down?'

'My dear chap, I don't even know who you are.'

There was a sharp note of hysteria in Travers' reply. 'Don't you play the innocent with me. You all laughed at me, didn't you? "Travers, the mad anthropologist!" And now that I'm close to success, you want to steal my glory. Just as I've found them at last.'

'Found what?'

'You know what I'm talking about. They're here, on this mountain. The Yeti – the Abominable Snowmen.'

The Doctor nodded. 'Yes, I rather thought they might be. But don't you see, my dear fellow, that makes nonsense of your accusing me. Obviously, a Yeti attacked your camp.'

'Nonsense! The Yeti are timid, harmless creatures. Everyone knows that.'

The Doctor tried another tack. 'Whoever – whatever – attacked your camp and killed your poor friend must have had enormous strength. Isn't that so?'

Reluctantly, Travers nodded. The Doctor rose to his modest height and spread out his hands. 'Well, could I have done it? Could I? Just look at me!' The Doctor could almost see the self-evident truth of this statement fighting to get through to Travers' brain. All at once, a look of childish cunning came over Travers' face. 'Not going to discuss it any longer. I've got work to do. And as for you, while you're safely locked up here, you won't be able to steal my credit.' Abruptly Travers' face disappeared and the grille slammed shut. The Doctor sighed, stretched out on the hard, lumpy mattress, and prepared for a little doze.

At that very moment, the Doctor was the subject of fierce discussion. In the nearby Great Hall, Khrisong and Thomni were confronting a group of older men in saffron-coloured robes. These were lamas, the priests of Det-sen Monastery, whose lives were spent in peaceful meditation and prayer. Despite their gentle and unworldly manner they had a sort of spiritual strength, a kind of gentle obstinacy, that never failed to infuriate Khrisong. He leaned forward urgently in an attempt to carry his point.

'We have the word of the Englishman, Travers. Why should he lie?'

Sapan, oldest and wisest of the lamas said gently, 'The man Travers has had a most terrible experience. His mind has been affected. The man is consumed with fear and ambition. He has strayed far from the way of truth!'

Khrisong's voice was fierce. 'The death of Travers' companion is the latest of many deaths. You know how many of our brethren have been killed. We live in terror. The Abbot has sent away most of the brethren to other monasteries for their own safety. The pilgrims, the travellers, the merchants come no more to Det-sen. Only a handful of us remain. My warriors, who fear nothing – and you ...' Khrisong broke off in confusion.

Rinchen, another old monk, smiled gently. 'We who are so old and feeble and useless that death holds no terrors.'

Khrisong said gruffly, 'I mean no disrespect, holy one. You know that all I have said is true.'

'Indeed it is, my son. But we agreed, did we not, that the Yeti were the cause of all our troubles?'

'True, Rinchen. And we wondered why. They were so rarely seen, so timid. Suddenly they became savage. Now here is this stranger, and Travers accuses him. I ask you again, let me put this man to the proof.'

Sapan shook his head. 'You ask us to condemn a man to almost certain death.'

'I am chief warrior. It is my duty to protect you.'

'Not by taking a man's life,' said Sapan firmly. 'You cannot use a human as live bait.'

Khrisong leaped to his feet. 'If it is necessary – yes, I demand that you ...'

Sapan spoke quietly as always, but there was an authority in his voice that made Khrisong fall silent. 'No, Khrisong. The price is too high.' There was a murmur of assent from the other lamas, which was interrupted by the boom of a temple gong.

'Come, my brothers,' said Sapan placidly. 'It is time for prayer.' He turned to Khrisong. 'After our meditations, I shall consult with the Abbot.' The little group of lamas filed from the room. Once they were gone, Khrisong exploded with rage.

'This is madness. Must more of our brothers die before we act?'

Thomni looked at him in astonishment. 'But the holy ones have decided. There is no other way.'

'There is for me,' said Khrisong. 'Let them meditate. Let them consult. I, Khrisong will act. Bring me the prisoner!'

Panting with exhaustion, Jamie abandoned his attempt to shift the boulder that blocked their exit. 'Och, it's no use. I canna shift it at all.' Victoria shivered beside him in the darkness, wishing desperately that they'd never left the TARDIS.

'Jamie, what are we going to do now?'

Jamie considered. What was it that the Doctor was always on about? The exercise of logical thought. 'Well, since we canna go back, and we dinna want to stay here – we'll just have to go forward, or rather I will. There's mebbe another exit!'

'But there might be more of those things in there.'

'Aye, there might. That's why I want you to wait here. Just yell if you need me.'

'Don't worry,' said Victoria. 'I'll yell all right.'

Jamie gave her an encouraging pat on the shoulder. Gripping his sword tightly, he set off down the dark tunnel.

For quite a while he had to feel his way along the walls. Then, to his astonishment, he saw a gleam of light ahead of him. Not daylight, though. More a kind of eerie glow. Summoning up all his courage, he moved towards it. As the glow grew brighter he saw that it came from the entrance to some kind of chamber leading off the tunnel. Jamie moved to the entrance, and then stepped inside, looking round in wonder.

He was in a completely circular cave with smooth stone walls. In the centre of the cave stood the source of the light – a little pile of silver spheres, arranged as a pyramid. Each of the spheres was glowing gently, and their combined radiance lit up the cave. Wonderingly, Jamie approached the spheres. He was just reaching out to touch one when a sudden scream echoed down the tunnel.

'Jamie! Jamie, come back!' He turned and ran down the tunnel towards the sound of Victoria's voice.

As he dashed up to her he saw that a rim of light was appearing around the edge of the boulder. He could hear the noise of rock grinding on rock. 'It's coming back,' whispered Victoria fearfully. 'It's taking away the boulder.'

'Aye, that it is,' said Jamie. 'You flatten yourself against the wall. It'll likely go past without seeing you.'

'But what about you?'

Jamie hefted his sword. 'I'll give yon beastie a welcome it doesna expect.'

Jamie backed away as the boulder was swung completely clear. Light flooded into the tunnel, silhouetting the enormous shaggy figure in the cave mouth. With a blood-curdling roar, claws outstretched, it bore down on Jamie. Gripping his sword in both hands, the Highlander brought it round in a savage slashing cut that should have struck the beast's head from its shoulders. But to Jamie's amazement the sword simply bounced off, as though the creature was made of steel. The Yeti lunged forward, wrenched the sword from Jamie's grasp, and snapped it in two like a matchstick. Remorselessly the Yeti lumbered forward, clawed hands outstretched to grasp him ...

3

LIVE BAIT TO CATCH
A MONSTER

Jamie backed away before the advancing Yeti. 'Stay back, Victoria!' he yelled. 'I canna stop it!' Terrified of being separated from Jamie, Victoria edged along the wall of the tunnel. She was actually following behind the Yeti, which didn't seem to have noticed her. Jamie retreated along the tunnel as far as the inner cave. Trying to run backwards, he crashed full into one of the pit-props supporting the tunnel. A trickle of rubble fell from the tunnel roof. The Yeti suddenly stopped, as if alarmed by the falling rock.

Jamie flung his arms round the base of the loose beam and pulled with all his might. It shifted! There was a steady rumble as more rubble trickled down. Victoria shrieked, 'No, Jamie, don't! We'll be buried alive.' But Jamie ignored her. With a final mighty heave he wrenched the supporting beam free. A cascade of rock began pouring down from the roof. 'Back, Victoria, back!' yelled Jamie.

With Victoria on one side, and Jamie on the other, the great pile of falling rock landed neatly on the Yeti between them, burying the creature completely, except for one paw, which stuck out from under the pile.

Dust filled the tunnel as the rock stopped falling at last. Coughing and spluttering, Jamie called, 'Victoria! Where are you? Are you all right?' To his vast relief he heard the sound of more coughing. Dimly he saw Victoria's dust-covered form clambering over the rocks towards him. He grabbed her arm and led her into the little inner chamber. Victoria dusted herself down in an attempt to recover her composure.

'That horrible creature,' she gasped. 'What was it?'

'I dinna ken, lassie. But it was verra strong. Did you see what it did to my sword?' said Jamie indignantly.

Looking round the cave Victoria saw the pyramid of spheres. 'What *are* those things?'

Jamie picked one up, and hefted it in his hand. 'Feels like some kind of metal ...'

Victoria suddenly shivered. 'Jamie, let's get out of here.'

Jamie nodded. 'We're lucky that rock-fall didna block the whole tunnel!'

Slipping the sphere into his pocket, Jamie grabbed Victoria's hand and pulled her out of the cave, back towards the pile of rock. For a moment she hung back, afraid to go too near the buried Yeti.

'Dinna be afraid,' said Jamie reassuringly. 'The thing's dead right enough! Nothing could survive a ton of rock on its head.'

Victoria clambered over the pile of rocks, keeping as far away as she could from the projecting hand. Suddenly she screamed and clutched at Jamie. 'Look!'

The Yeti's hand was clenching and unclenching slowly, as if making an attempt to grab her. Before their horrified gaze, the hand, and part of the arm, began to wriggle out of the pile of rocks. The creature was alive, and struggling to free itself.

'Come on!' said Jamie grimly. He almost dragged Victoria over the rocks, down the tunnel and out into the open air.

Victoria looked round in amazement. 'It's starting to get dark. We were in there for ages.'

For a moment the two of them stood gasping, drawing the sharp, fresh air into their lungs. From inside the cave came a rumble of rock, and then the savage roar of the Yeti. 'Come on,' said Jamie. 'It'll be after us any minute.'

They began running down the mountain slope, towards the TARDIS.

Thomni the guard captain was a worried young man as he went along the corridor towards the Doctor's cell. He could sympathise with Khrisong's impatience. The lamas didn't realise that not every problem could be solved by prayer and meditation. But even so, to disobey the will of the holy ones in the way that Khrisong was planning ...

Thomni unbolted the door of the cell, and threw it open. The stranger was sleeping peacefully on the bed. Thomni looked down at him. The face was gentle and relaxed with something of the serenity of the holy ones themselves about it. Thomni jumped, as the man on the bed spoke without opening his eyes. 'Have you come to release me?'

Thomni felt strangely at a disadvantage. 'Er, no ... sir.'

The Doctor sat up on the bed and beamed at him. 'It's Thomni, isn't it? Captain of the Guard? By the way, I'm usually called "The Doctor".'

Somehow the name was familiar to Thomni. 'You must come with me, Doctor,' he said.

'Let's have a little chat first, shall we?'

'Khrisong is waiting ...'

'What's come over this place?' asked the Doctor plaintively. 'No one wants to listen to me. You seem a reasonable sort of lad. What's going on, eh? Why is everything so military? You'd think there was a war on.'

'So there is – and we are besieged. The Yeti have turned on us. At least, that is what we thought until ...' Thomni stopped, confused.

'Until I turned up. And friend Khrisong decided, on very slender evidence, that it's all my fault. You know, the last time I visited Det-sen, there was trouble. Something about a threatened attack by Chinese bandits.'

Thomni stared at him in amazement. 'You must be mistaken. That attack was many hundreds of years ago ... It was then that the holy ghanta was lost.'

The Doctor smiled. 'Indeed? What happened to it?'

'It is hard to be sure. Some say that it was stolen by the bandits when they attacked. But there is a legend that it was given to a mysterious stranger for safe-keeping. One known only as—'

'As the Doctor?' interrupted the man on the bed.

Thomni nodded, surprised. 'I see you have studied our history. The legend tells us that the stranger swore to return it. Yet he warned that this might not happen for many hundreds of years ...' Thomni stopped, puzzled. 'You said *you* were called the Doctor!'

The cell burst open and Khrisong entered, armed monks at his back. 'Why this delay? Seize him and take him to the gate!'

The monks grabbed the Doctor and pulled him to his feet. As he was bustled out of the cell, he stumbled against Thomni. To his astonishment, Thomni heard the Doctor whisper, 'Under straw, in the mattress – tell Abbot …' Before he could say more, the Doctor was dragged away, down the corridor.

Thomni stood puzzled. He went to the bed and examined the straw mattress. Just where the Doctor had been sitting, a little hole had been picked. Thomni felt inside. His fingers touched a little cloth-wrapped bundle. He pulled it out, and unwrapped it. There in his hand was the holy ghanta of Det-sen. The ghanta which had been lost for over three hundred years.

Hand in hand, Jamie and Victoria pelted down the mountainside. Every now and again, Victoria managed a quick glance over her shoulder, but the creature from the cave didn't seem to be following them. All the same, she sighed with relief when at last they came in sight of the TARDIS. Soon they would be safe.

But as they ran towards the TARDIS, a huge shaggy shape could be seen in the gloom. Jamie and Victoria skidded to a halt. 'It's here before us,' gasped Victoria. 'But how *can* it be – we'd have seen it.'

'Then it canna be the same beastie,' said Jamie. 'There's more than one of them!'

Jamie studied the creature cautiously, fascinated by his first clear look at a Yeti. It was massive, about seven or eight feet tall, Jamie guessed, and covered in shaggy, brown fur. The powerful body was immensely broad, so that the thing seemed somehow squat and lumpy, in spite of its great height.

The huge hairy hands, and the black snout, were gorilla-like. The little red eyes, and the yellow fangs were like those of a bear. He remembered Victoria's description – something between a bear, an ape and a man. All in all, thought Jamie, it was the biggest, nastiest, hairiest beastie he had ever seen.

Victoria tugged urgently at his arm. 'Jamie, what are we going to do?' Jamie looked again at the Yeti. It was making no attempt to attack them, though they were now quite close. It stood like a kind of weird sentry, quite motionless, waiting.

Jamie rubbed his chin. 'Well, we canna get back into the TARDIS, yon beastie's blocking the way. We'll just have to go on – down to this Monastery place. Maybe we can find the Doctor and warn him what's going on.'

Now too exhausted to run, Jamie and Victoria stumbled down the mountainside towards the Monastery.

In the Monastery courtyard, dusk was falling. The Doctor, guarded by armed warrior monks, stood shivering inside his fur coat. He was the subject of a heated argument between the old lama, Sapan, and a very angry Khrisong.

'Do not interfere, holy one,' said the warrior monk furiously.

Sapan's voice was gentle as always. 'Did we not agree, Khrisong, that we would consult the Abbot Songtsen, before taking further action in this matter?'

'No, holy one, we did not agree!' Khrisong said bitterly. 'You decided, as always. But I tell you, I cannot always wait to consult the Abbot before I act.'

'Be reasonable, Khrisong …'

The Doctor stopped listening as the argument raged on. He thought wryly that no one wanted to know what *he* thought, even though his fate was under discussion. Not that he was worried. Once that boy got the sacred ghanta to the Abbot, Songtsen would put a stop to whatever nonsense Khrisong was planning. Something about a test, as far as the Doctor could make out.

A curiously furtive movement caught the corner of the Doctor's eye. He turned and saw Travers about to slip out of the main door. He was fully kitted-out for travel, a loaded rucksack on his back.

'Travers!' the Doctor called. 'Don't you think all this has gone far enough?' He indicated the arguing monks, the armed guards at his elbow. 'For Heaven's sake, tell them you were mistaken.'

Travers shook his head. 'Sorry, nothing I can do.'

'What do you expect to gain by all this?'

'Time,' said Travers fiercely. 'Time to find the Yeti, even though I'm on my own. You won't get another chance to get in my way. *Your* little expedition stops right here.'

The Doctor was indignant. 'I am not an expedition, and I'm not interested in your precious Yeti. But you've put me in a very nasty position. These chaps are liable to do something silly.'

Travers laughed. 'Don't worry, the monks won't harm you. They're men of peace.' Settling his rucksack on his shoulders, Travers turned away, and slipped through the main door, disappearing into the evening shadows.

The Doctor turned back to the arguing monks, just in time to hear Khrisong say, 'I tell you the stranger is a killer. We have Travers' word for that. I believe this man may have found some way to control the Yeti, and make them savage. I shall tie him to the main doors. If the Yeti come to rescue him, my warriors will be waiting …'

'You cannot use a human being as live bait,' Sapan protested.

Overriding the old lama, Khrisong turned to the Doctor's guards. 'Take him outside, and tie him to the door.'

Cupping the ghanta in reverent hands, Thomni crept timidly into the ante-chamber of the Abbot Songtsen. He looked around him in fear and wonder. He had never dared enter this part of the Monastery before. The room was dimly lit by the prayer lamps. There were no windows. All around were ornate carvings, statues and hangings. Many of the treasures of Det-sen Monastery were here, sacred objects of immense value, treasured and worshipped through the ages. But none were so valuable, or so holy, as the little bronze bell, the ghanta, that Thomni held.

Thomni froze like a statue as the door of the Inner Sanctum creaked open, apparently by itself. This was the most sacred place of all, the very heart of the Monastery. The Abbot Songtsen emerged. Terrified, Thomni prostrated himself. The Abbot backed away from the Sanctum doors, which closed behind him. He turned and crossed the Anteroom, his wise, wrinkled old face still and trance-like. He seemed not even to notice Thomni, and would have walked right past him. Thomni managed to produce a terrified whisper, 'Master Abbot!' Songtsen stopped, consciousness slowly returning to his face. 'Master Abbot!' Thomni whispered again.

A look of horror came over the old man's face as he saw the boy crouching at his feet. 'Thomni – you know well that only I may enter this sacred place.'

Silently, Thomni held out his hands, the ghanta cupped in their palms. The Abbot leaned forward and peered at the little bell. 'What is this? Where did you get it?'

Thomni's voice was low and reverent. 'Master Abbot, is this not the sacred ghanta which was lost?'

Suddenly another voice spoke. It came from nowhere, and yet from everywhere in the room. It was old and wise, yet strong and vigorous too. The voice said, 'It is indeed the holy ghanta, my son. Lost to us for three hundred years. How came you by it?'

Terrified, Thomni looked round for the source of the voice. But, apart from himself and the Abbot, the Anteroom was empty. Yet the power of the speaker's personality filled the entire room. Too frightened to speak, Thomni looked to the Abbot, who said gently, 'It is the Master, Padmasambvha. Do not be afraid.'

The voice spoke again. 'Bring the ghanta to me – both of you.' The Abbot bowed his head in assent, and indicated that Thomni should follow him. Thomni scrambled to his feet, and followed the Abbot through the door to the Inner Sanctum. The doors opened silently as they approached.

The handles of the great doors of Det-sen Monastery were in the form of huge, bronze rings. To one of these rings, the Doctor was being firmly lashed with leather thongs. Khrisong gave a final check to the knots, and nodded in satisfaction. He turned to the little group of warriors around him. 'Place yourself at the windows, on the walls, and in cover behind the doors. Be ready with your bows.' As the warrior monks went off to take their places Khrisong looked grimly at the Doctor. 'If your servants attempt to rescue you, we shall slay them!'

The Doctor sighed wearily. 'This is all very pointless, you know. I assure you, no one's going to rescue me – least of all an Abominable Snowman.' Khrisong turned to go back inside the Monastery. 'And there's something else,' yelled the Doctor. 'Does it occur to you that whatever has been killing your monks might also kill me?'

Khrisong said ironically, 'If the Yeti attack *you*, that will be proof of your innocence. Then, of course, we shall rescue you – if we can.' He turned and went back inside the Monastery.

The Doctor sighed wearily. 'This is all very point—' and then gave up. It was almost dark now, and gloomy shadows covered the mountain path and the area before the Monastery doors. Everything looked odd and sinister in the half-light. The Doctor wondered what was happening to Thomni. Perhaps he hadn't even found the ghanta. And what about Jamie and Victoria? They must be getting pretty bored by now ...

Jamie and Victoria were far too frightened to be bored. It was no easy task, picking their way down to the Monastery in the fast-gathering gloom. Several times they had wandered off the snow-covered path, finding their way back only with difficulty. As the gloom thickened and the shadows grew darker and longer, every rock and boulder seemed a Yeti waiting to pounce.

Victoria clasped Jamie's hand tighter and wailed, 'Oh, Jamie, I'm sure we're lost again.'

Jamie did his best to sound confident. 'I tell you we canna be lost. The path leads down the mountain, and the Monastery's at the bottom. All we've got to do is keep going.'

But Victoria wasn't listening. She stopped and whispered, 'There's something moving. Ahead of us, down there.'

Jamie sighed. 'Ever since we set off, you've been seeing things ...'

'I'm not imagining it this time. Listen!'

Jamie peered through the gloom, straining his ears. Sure enough, there was something ... a sound of shuffling feet, and heavy breathing. Jamie looked round for a weapon. He grabbed a football-sized rock from the side of the path, and stood poised and ready. A shadowy figure loomed up out of the darkness, huge and threatening. Victoria gave a little scream and Jamie was just about to let fly, when the figure spoke. 'Hey, you two! What are you doing here?'

Jamie dropped the rock with a sigh of relief. The figure came nearer and was revealed as a man wearing a rucksack. But Jamie was still cautious. 'I might ask you the same,' he said stoutly.

'My name's Travers. I'm a sort of explorer.'

'We're on our way to the Monastery,' said Victoria.

'Are you now? You wouldn't be anything to do with a feller calls himself the Doctor, would you?'

'Aye, that we would,' said Jamie. 'Have you seen him? Is he all right?'

The man laughed. 'Oh yes, I met him at the Monastery. He's perfectly all right.'

'Come on, Jamie, we'd better go and find him,' said Victoria.

'Yes, why don't you do that,' said the man. 'I expect the monks will give you quite a welcome.' He nodded and set off up the path.

Jamie hesitated. He hadn't taken to the man at all. His eyes were bright and feverish, and there was something odd about his manner. All the same, it was only fair to warn him.

Jamie called after the retreating figure. 'I'd watch your step, Mister, if I were you. There's some kind of great hairy beasties prowling about. They live in a cave higher up the mountains.'

The man turned and ran back towards them. 'You've seen the Yeti? You've actually found their lair?' He grabbed Jamie's arm and tried to pull him off by force. 'You've got to take me there. Now, right away.'

Jamie pulled his arm away firmly. 'I will not. I've seen enough of those things to last a lifetime.'

'But I've got to find them. I've got to.' Travers was almost babbling with excitement.

Jamie was unmoved. 'Ye canna go up there now, man. It's nearly dark. I couldna find the place myself.'

'Will you take me there tomorrow?'

'Aye, mebbe. But on one condition.'

Travers glared at him suspiciously. 'What's that, then?'

'You say you've come from the Monastery?'

Travers nodded.

'Then you can just guide us back there – now. That's if you want my help tomorrow.'

Travers hesitated, obviously still wanting to get after the Yeti right away. But it *was* nearly dark. And if this boy had found their lair …

'All right, then. Come on.' Travers turned and set off back down the path.

Jamie took Victoria's arm and gave her a reassuring grin. They both hurried off after their guide. Travers waited for Jamie to catch up and said, 'Tell me exactly where you found this cave …'

The Inner Sanctum was even darker and more mysterious than the Anteroom. In its centre was a raised dais, upon which was set a kind of ornate golden chair, like a throne. There were thin veils arranged in a canopy, a transparent tent obscuring the throne and the figure upon it. A giant golden statue of the Lord Buddha stood against the far wall.

Thomni and his Abbot stood before the throne. Both had the blank expressionless faces of men under deep hypnosis. Padmasambvha spoke. Even though he was now seated before them, his voice still seemed to come from everywhere and nowhere, filling the room. 'We are grateful for the return of our holy ghanta. The Doctor is our friend. Thomni, you will go to Khrisong. Tell him that the Abbot orders the Doctor's release.'

Thomni bowed. Still in the same trance-like state, he turned to leave. The voice spoke again. 'Remember, these words were spoken by the Abbot. You have never seen me or heard my voice. You have never entered this room.'

Thomni bowed again and left. He did not even notice when the doors of the Sanctum opened and closed behind him of their own accord.

In the Anteroom, Thomni seemed to wake up with a jerk. He gazed around him wildly. Then he remembered. He had been given a most important errand, by the Abbot Songtsen himself … Thomni ran from the room.

In the Sanctum, the voice of Padmasambvha was saying, 'We must make certain, Songtsen, that the Doctor learns nothing of what is happening here. He may not be in sympathy with the power that now guides us. He might even seek to hinder the Great Plan. It would be well if he were to depart as soon as possible.'

The Doctor was starting to feel cold and cramped as he hung in his bonds from the ring on the Monastery door. Khrisong and his warriors were cold and cramped too, waiting high on the walls. But they stood guard bravely, spears and bows ready to hand. Suddenly one of them turned excitedly to Khrisong. 'There – coming down the path. Three of them.'

Khrisong looked. 'Yes, I see them. Your eyes are keen, Rapalchan! Make ready, all of you!' Khrisong's archers fitted arrows to their bows. Others balanced spears, ready to hurl.

Nearby, on the mountain path, Jamie and Victoria had just seen the lights of the Monastery.

'There it is, Jamie. Look – there's the Doctor waiting for us by the door.' In her excitement, Victoria began to run ahead. Jamie ran to catch up with her. Travers, behind them, broke into a trot.

On the Monastery walls, Khrisong and his warriors waited, bows drawn and ready, watching the three figures running towards them in the darkness. 'The Yeti are coming, brothers,' whispered Khrisong exultantly. 'As soon as they are in bowshot – slay them! Kill them all!'

4

JAMIE TRAPS A YETI

The Doctor strained his eyes, trying to pick out the three shapes running down the mountain path towards him. For a moment the distance and the gloom misled him. Perhaps the Yeti really were coming to rescue him. He looked again, then chuckled to himself. Of course – Victoria and Jamie! And that looked very like Travers behind them.

Suddenly a terrifying thought struck the Doctor. If *he* could mistake the three for attacking Yeti, might not Khrisong and his warrior monks do the same? Tired, nervous men, bows and spears in their hands, waiting in the darkness to be attacked. They'd let fly at anything that moved!

Frantically the Doctor yelled, 'Victoria, Jamie, keep back. They'll kill you!'

On the mountainside Victoria could just hear the Doctor's voice, but the wind carried away his actual words. 'All right, Doctor, we're coming!' she cried, and ran even faster.

Up on the wall, a young monk panicked. Without waiting for Khrisong's order, he drew his bow and fired.

An arrow thudded into the snowy ground at Victoria's feet. Jamie came up beside her. 'Look,' cried Victoria. 'They're shooting at us.'

Travers joined them and gazed in amazement at the arrow. 'Damn fools – what do they think they're doing?'

Khrisong meanwhile was leading a picked band of warriors down from the wall, and out of the main gate, ready to do battle with the Yeti. As Khrisong emerged, the Doctor called, 'Please! Don't shoot! Those are friends of mine.'

'We know that, Doctor,' shouted Khrisong, 'but your Yeti shall not rescue you!'

The Doctor strained at his bonds. 'They're not Yeti, man. They're hardly more than children.'

Khrisong ignored him. 'Ready, brothers?' The little band of monks prepared to shoot at the three figures on the path. Bows were drawn, spears raised in readiness. It was Travers who saved them all. Shouldering Jamie and Victoria aside, he ran straight at the little group of warriors, ignoring the danger. 'Stop all this nonsense at once – it's me, Travers. You know me!'

'Perhaps it is witchcraft,' one of them muttered. 'The Yeti try to trick us with their magic, speaking with the voice of Travers. Better to kill, and be sure.' He raised his spear.

Khrisong stopped him, knocking the spear aside. 'No. It is Travers!'

Travers puffed up to him angrily. 'Look here, what do you think you're doing?' he shouted.

Khrisong said, 'I am sorry. It was a mistake. Who are these others?'

'Couple of kids I met on the mountain. Say they're friends of the Doctor's.' Travers called over to his two companions. 'It's all right, come down. It's safe now.'

Jamie and Victoria ran to the Doctor. Furiously, Jamie asked Khrisong, 'What's going on? Why's the Doctor tied up like that?'

'He is a suspected criminal,' said Khrisong sternly. 'So too are you, if you are his friends. Seize them!'

One of the monks tried to grab Victoria. Jamie promptly knocked him down, snatching away his spear. He turned threateningly on the approaching monks. Trouble seemed inevitable. Another monk ran out from inside the Monastery. It was Thomni. 'Wait, Khrisong,' he called. 'I have a message for you from the Abbot.'

Khrisong held up his hand to restrain the warriors. 'Well?'

'This man has brought back the sacred ghanta. We must treat him with all kindness and respect. Those are the commands of the Abbot.'

Khrisong swung round on the Doctor, 'Why did you not tell me of this?'

The Doctor smiled. 'Would you have listened?'

Khrisong glared at him for a moment, then nodded to one of the monks. The monk stepped forward and began cutting the Doctor's bonds. 'I'm sure the Abbot meant his words to apply to my friends as well,' said the Doctor mildly. The warriors menacing Jamie and

Victoria stood back. Victoria ran to the Doctor. 'Are you all right?' she said.

The Doctor rubbed his wrists. 'Oh, I think so. A little stiff, perhaps. They were using me as Yeti bait, you see! But there's no real harm done.' Looking sternly at Travers, the Doctor continued sternly, 'But there might have been, Mr Travers. We might all have been killed. All through that ridiculous story of yours. Isn't it time you told the truth?'

'What truth?' asked Khrisong sternly.

Travers looked thoroughly abashed. 'I'm sorry, Khrisong. I'm afraid I misled you. It couldn't have been the Doctor who attacked me. The thing was huge – not human at all. I just wanted him safely locked up. I didn't mean you to hurt him.' Khrisong turned in disgust and strode back inside the Monastery.

Thomni said apologetically, 'Doctor, the Abbot has given orders for comfortable quarters and refreshments to be prepared for you. Later, when you are rested, he would like to see you and thank you. Shall we go inside?'

The Doctor said, 'An excellent idea. Come along, you two. You come as well, Mr Travers. You may have got us into trouble but at least you helped to get us out.'

They all went back inside the Monastery and the great bronze doors clanged to behind them.

High on the mountainside, three enormous, shaggy shapes were standing motionless near the mouth of the cave where Jamie and Victoria had been trapped. Suddenly they jerked into life. As if in obedience to a common command, they began lumbering down the path, towards the Monastery.

In the simple guest room provided by the monks, the Doctor finished a mug of scalding Tibetan tea and sighed with pleasure. 'My thanks to your Abbot, Thomni. A truly splendid meal.' Jamie and Victoria exchanged glances.

'Och, yes,' muttered Jamie. 'It was verra nice.'

'Yes, it was lovely,' added Victoria.

Actually neither of them were very impressed with Tibetan food. The pile of yellow rice, covered with strange meats and vegetables, had been palatable enough, especially since they were both ravenous with hunger. But the milkless, unsweetened tea with Yak butter floating in it had been too much for them. Travers had eaten and drunk with gusto. Victoria supposed he must be used to strange foods. As for the Doctor, he seemed ready, as usual, to eat and drink anything, anywhere, with anyone.

Thomni flushed with pleasure at their praise. 'When you have rested further the Abbot will wish to see you and thank you, Doctor.' He bowed and withdrew. Travers poured the Doctor another mug of tea. 'You certainly seem to be well in with the monks, Doctor.'

The Doctor smiled. 'Well, it is my second visit, you know.'

'I thought I was one of the first white men to reach here,' said Travers. 'When *was* your first visit?'

'Oh, about three hundred years ago,' replied the Doctor airily. Ignoring Travers' astonished reaction, he went on. 'Jamie, let's have another look at this sphere you found in the cave.' Jamie fished it out, and handed it over. The Doctor stared at it, lost in thought.

'I still don't believe those things that attacked us were my Yeti,' said Travers argumentatively. 'All the reports agree – the creature is shy and timid. The monks confirm it too. In the old days the Yeti were hardly ever seen.'

'Yet all at once they've become bold and savage,' said the Doctor thoughtfully. Travers nodded.

'According to the monks they've been killing all sorts of people, attacking the camps of the pilgrims and merchants, just as they did mine.'

'Maybe they don't want people to come here any more,' suggested Victoria.

'They, or whoever's controlling them,' chimed in Jamie. They all looked at him in surprise. Jamie felt suddenly embarrassed.

'Go on, Jamie,' said the Doctor encouragingly. He knew that although the Scots lad was more of a fighting man than a thinker, he had a shrewd, quick mind, especially where practical problems were concerned.

'I've been thinking, Doctor,' said Jamie. 'Yon beastie – there was something awful strange about it. What kind of an animal can get smashed over the head with a pile of rocks and scramble out as good as new? And the other one, by the TARDIS, it didna attack at all. I'm no' sure they're just animals at all. They're not *natural* somehow.'

The Doctor sighed. 'I'd like to see one of these things, I really would.'

As if in answer to the Doctor's wish, Thomni rushed into the room. 'Mr Travers, Doctor, you must come at once. The Yeti are approaching the Monastery!'

Travers, Jamie and Victoria leaped to their feet and followed Thomni from the room. Before he left, the Doctor placed the silver sphere which Jamie had given him carefully on the bed, under the pillow. Then he followed the others.

In the torch-lit courtyard, there was a scene of bustle and activity. Khrisong had every available warrior monk armed, and on duty. Some were being sent to the observation platform, others waited by the doors in case the Yeti should try to break through.

The Doctor and his little party stood on an observation platform, looking out over the walls. It was dark now, and they could just make out the bulk of the mountain as it loomed over the Monastery. The area just before the gates was lit up by blazing torches on the walls, but beyond their circle of light, it was hard to see anything at all. 'Well, where are they?' grumbled Travers.

'Wait,' said Khrisong. 'When the moon comes from behind those clouds, you will see them. They are very close.' As he spoke the moon began to appear. Its rays lit up the snow-covered mountain, the track leading upwards. Then they saw them. A group of shaggy forms, milling about just beyond the circle of torch-light.

'That's them, right enough,' said Jamie. 'There's a whole gang of them now!'

Travers had a pair of battered binoculars to his eyes. His face was radiant. 'At last,' he was muttering. 'At last. Look at them! Aren't they magnificent?'

Victoria wasn't so enthusiastic. 'Doctor, look,' she whispered. 'They're coming nearer.' And, indeed, the lumbering figures seemed to be edging closer and closer to the Monastery gates.

The Doctor tapped Khrisong's shoulder. 'Do you think they'll attack?' Khrisong's face was grim.

'I cannot tell, Doctor. We can only be ready. But they have never come so close before.'

The Doctor had taken the binoculars from a reluctant Travers and was staring eagerly at the creatures. 'You know, Jamie, I see what you mean. There's something about the way they move ...' He handed the binoculars back. 'Oh, I do wish I could examine one properly. Do you think you could capture one for me?'

Jamie chuckled. 'Oh, aye, nothing to it. Shall we wrap it up for you, Doctor?'

Khrisong looked at the Doctor in amazement. 'We will kill them, Doctor – if we can. But why should we wish to capture one?'

'Because *if* you can get me one to examine, I may be able to find out why the Yeti have suddenly become killers. I might even be able to find a way for you to defeat them.'

Jamie cleared his throat. 'You're really serious, Doctor? About needing one of those beasties?'

'Very much so, Jamie.'

'Och, well, I think I can get hold of one for you. I'll need some equipment, Khrisong, and the help of those warriors of yours.'

Khrisong looked dubiously at Jamie. 'You are little more than a boy ...'

'Believe me, Khrisong,' said the Doctor firmly, 'if Jamie says he can do it – he can do it. I've seen him in some very tight corners indeed.'

Khrisong turned to Jamie. 'Well, boy, what do you need?'

'Come on, Victoria,' said the Doctor. 'I think we'd better get out of the way. It's time we paid our respects to the Abbot Songtsen.'

The Great Hall was the biggest room in the Monastery. It was filled with long tables and benches, enough to hold hundreds of monks when they gathered for food and prayer. Now only a handful of lamas were assembled.

'Do not fear, brethren,' Songtsen was saying, 'I am sure that the return of the sacred ghanta means better times for us at Det-sen.'

'Master Abbot,' Sapan objected mildly, 'even now the Yeti gather at our gates to attack us.'

The Abbot smiled reassuringly. 'Have faith. Khrisong and his warriors will protect us.'

Sapan frowned. 'Khrisong is a rash and angry man. He disobeyed me, Lord Abbot. So sure was he that the Doctor was a danger to us.'

There was a deprecating cough from the doorway. The lamas looked up to see the Doctor and Victoria standing in the doorway. 'Me, a danger?' said the Doctor. 'I can assure you I'm not. In fact, I very much hope I can help you.'

The Abbot came forward, smiling. 'You have helped us greatly already, Doctor, by returning the sacred ghanta. We owe you much.'

In the Monastery courtyard, Jamie had taken charge of things with a will. Except for a few sentries, he had all the warrior monks, and Travers too, assembling a kind of improvised net. All the available ropes in the Monastery had been woven together into a sort of tangled cat's cradle. Khrisong looked on, half resentful and half amused, as Jamie harried the monks into doing exactly what he wanted. 'Och, no, ye great loon. The rope goes over *there*, and under *here*. Then tie it *there*. And make those knots good ones. If the beastie gets loose, we shall all be for it.'

At last the work was complete. The improvised net lay spread out in the courtyard, long ropes tied to each corner. Under Jamie's instructions, a party of monks carried the net out through the doors, and spread it on the ground just under the wall. 'Right,' said Jamie. 'Off you go, the lot of you.' The monks, all except for Thomni and Khrisong, went back inside. Jamie waited a moment then yelled, 'Ready inside?' He grabbed one of the long ropes attached to a corner, coiled it, and threw it over the wall. He did the same thing with the ropes at the other three corners of the improvised net. Quickly, Jamie dashed back inside the courtyard to check.

The ends of the four ropes were now dangling over the wall inside the courtyard. A couple of brawny young monks had hold of each rope. Travers was in charge of them. 'Remember,' said Jamie grimly, 'when you hear me yell "Now!", tug with all your might, and dinna let go.' Travers nodded determinedly, Jamie grabbed a flaming torch from the wall, and went outside where Khrisong and Thomni were waiting, both armed with heavy spears.

Jamie looked at the outspread net, the ropes at each corner stretching away over the wall. 'All we need now is a Yeti,' he said cheerfully. 'I'll just awa' and whistle one up!'

'You are brave, stranger,' said Thomni. 'Our prayers go with you.'

Holding his blazing torch in front of him, Jamie set off up the mountain path towards the waiting Yeti.

All this time the little group of Yeti had stayed on the mountain, sometimes advancing, sometimes retreating, but never far away. Jamie whistled to keep his spirits up as he came closer to them. He picked the nearest Yeti, and marched boldly towards it.

The Yeti stood motionless as he approached. Just like the one outside the TARDIS, thought Jamie. Even when he was almost within touching distance, the creature didn't move. Jamie held up his torch. The light glinted on the Yeti's yellow fangs, and was reflected fierily in its little red eyes. Jamie summoned up all his courage, and yelled at the top of his voice, 'Garn, ye great hairy loon. I'll have you for a doormat, so I will!' He thrust the flaming torchlight right under the Yeti's nose, close enough to singe its whiskers.

With a nerve-shattering roar the Yeti came to life. A giant, hairy hand aimed a savage slash at Jamie's head. Jamie ducked, turned, and ran back down the path at full speed. He could hear the angry howls of the Yeti as it lumbered after him.

He timed his speed carefully, letting the Yeti get as close as he could without actually being caught. He didn't want the beast to get discouraged and give up. Soon Jamie was nearly at the Monastery gates, where Khrisong and Thomni waited, spears in hand. Now if he could only lure the creature on to the net ...

Jamie was almost there, when he slipped and fell on the icy ground. The Yeti loomed over him, the great clawed hands reaching out. Jamie, the breath knocked out of him, lay helpless on the ground.

Khrisong and Thomni ran forward, thrusting at the Yeti with their spears. The creature whirled round on them, shattering Thomni's spear at a single blow. Khrisong held it off alone, jabbing and thrusting with his spear while Thomni helped Jamie to his feet.

Khrisong fought hard, but his blows had no effect. He was forced to fall back before the attacking monster. The Yeti lumbered further and further forward. It advanced until it was standing right on the net. 'Khrisong, get back!' shouted Jamie. With a final spear-thrust Khrisong leaped backwards, and Jamie gave a mighty yell of 'Now!' at the top of his voice.

In the courtyard, Travers shouted 'Heave!' The warrior monks pulled hard on the ropes. The corner ropes jerked taut, and, caught in the net, the Yeti was lifted off its feet. It was slammed against the wall, then tugged higher and higher off the ground. The Yeti thrashed about frenziedly in the tangle of ropes, roaring with rage. More armed monks ran from the courtyard and began belabouring the Yeti with swords, spears and clubs. None of their blows had the slightest effect. The maddened creature still continued its thrashing and roaring. It ripped savagely at the net and, to his horror, Jamie saw some of the ropes beginning to fray and snap. To make matters worse, no one told the monks inside the courtyard to *stop* pulling. The entangled monster was jerked higher and higher up the wall, until it was out of reach of those attacking it from below.

'They'll pull it over the top and inside with them in a minute,' thought Jamie, 'and the beast's alive and kicking!'

He turned to go and warn the monks in the courtyard, when suddenly he saw that it was already too late. The net was coming apart like a wet paper bag. With the Yeti hanging almost at the top of the high wall, it flew to pieces. There was a tremendous thud as the Yeti slammed down on to the icy ground below, and lay completely still. Cautiously the ring of warrior monks approached it. Khrisong jabbed it with his spear. The Yeti didn't stir. 'The thing is dead,' said Thomni.

Jamie nodded. 'It wasna just as I'd planned it, but it's worked out well enough. Come on. Let's get the puir beastie inside.'

As the monks began to drag the Yeti into the courtyard, Jamie turned and looked up the mountain path. The little group of Yeti stood motionless, watching. Then, moving with one accord, they turned and shambled into the darkness.

Jamie turned and followed the monks inside. One of the warrior monks began clearing up the remains of the broken net from the place where the Yeti had fallen. As he did so, his sandalled foot came down on a little silver sphere, pressing it down further into the icy mud.

In the Great Hall, the Yeti lay stretched out on the huge central dining table. The Hall was brightly lit, for the Doctor had called for extra torches. Outside waited a hushed group of monks and lamas. At first they had all crowded round the table, eager to see the captured Yeti.

But the Doctor had chased them away, saying he couldn't work in the middle of a Rugby scrum. Only Travers, Jamie, Victoria, Khrisong and Thomni were allowed to stay.

The Doctor leaned over the prostrate Yeti. Victoria thought he looked rather like a surgeon at the operating table. She stood well at the back of the little group. She wasn't going to get too close to the Yeti, even if it was dead. Victoria and the Doctor had come running at the news of the Yeti's capture, and she had scolded Jamie for taking such terrible risks.

The Doctor looked up. 'Well, I can tell you one thing. This creature isn't flesh and blood. Look!' He beckoned them forward and indicated a place on the massive arm. He had removed a patch of fur. Beneath it they could see the unmistakable glint of metal. 'You were right – it's not your Abominable Snowman after all, Travers,' the Doctor added.

'Then what is it, Doctor?' Travers asked.

'It is witchcraft,' snarled Khrisong. 'The thing is a servant of the devil.'

The Doctor shook his head. 'Not quite. It's some kind of robot, I think.'

'No wonder we couldna kill it with spears,' said Jamie.

'The thing is,' said the Doctor, 'why did it stop working?' He returned to his examination.

'Maybe something inside it got broken in the fall?' suggested Victoria.

The Doctor was examining the fur on the creature's massive chest. 'Wait a moment,' he muttered. 'Jamie, lend me your knife.' Jamie slipped the dagger from his stocking, and passed it to the Doctor. Slipping the point into a crevice in the fur, the Doctor prised open a little trapdoor, revealing a hollow, empty space.

'There's nothing in there,' said Victoria.

'No, but there should be. When you trapped it, Jamie, you must have dislodged its control unit. That's why it went dead.'

'So if it gets its control unit *back*,' said Jamie slowly, 'it could come to life?'

The Doctor nodded gravely. 'Yes, Jamie, I think it could.'

*

Outside the Monastery, the silver sphere embedded in the ground stirred feebly, trying to free itself. But the icy mud held it gripped fast. It began to pulse rhythmically, sending out some kind of signal.

In the Doctor's quarters, the little silver sphere came to life. It, too, pulsed with a signal. Then it rolled slowly from the bed, on to the floor and out of the room.

A kitchen monk came along the corridor, on his way to clear away the remains of the Doctor's meal. As he approached, the little sphere rolled into a dark corner. Once the monk had gone, the sphere resumed its journey, moving inch by inch towards its ultimate destination – the 'dead' Yeti on the table in the Great Hall. It had a long way to go. The Great Hall was in a distant part of the Monastery. But it would get there in the end.

5

THE SECRET OF THE
INNER SANCTUM

Hands deep in his pockets, the Doctor paced up and down the Great Hall. 'We've got to find that control unit. It's far too dangerous to be left around.'

Jamie nodded in vigorous agreement. 'You're telling me. We dinna want yon beastie coming to life again. Especially now we've brought it in here with us.'

'Exactly,' said the Doctor. 'Come on.' He set off briskly for the door, but the tall figure of Khrisong barred his way.

'Where are you going?' demanded Khrisong sternly.

The Doctor looked up at him impatiently. 'To have a look outside the gates.'

'No, I will not allow it.'

The Doctor sighed. 'My dear chap, why ever not?'

'You say someone made this creature and sent it against us? Why? Who wishes harm to the monks of Det-sen? I will trust no stranger until these questions are answered.'

Jamie glared at Khrisong furiously. 'Have we no' convinced you yet? We're on your side!'

'Khrisong,' said the Doctor patiently, 'why won't you let us help you?'

'I do not need your help. Thomni, guard these strangers well.' Khrisong turned and strode from the room.

The Doctor shook his head. 'My word, he's an obstinate fellow.'

Travers cleared his throat. 'Afraid you're right, Doctor. Still, that's it. Nothing more we can do. Think I'll get some sleep. Night everybody.' Travers bustled from the room, suddenly in a great hurry.

He ran along the corridor and out into the courtyard. Over by the closed and barred door, he could hear Khrisong talking to the sentry. 'No one is to leave the Monastery. And be watchful. The Yeti are even more dangerous than we feared. Send men to fasten with chains the one that we captured.' As Khrisong strode back across the courtyard, Travers intercepted him.

'Khrisong! I must talk to you.'

Khrisong paused reluctantly. 'Well?'

Travers' voice was low and urgent. 'We know now that the creatures who've been attacking you are robots. They're not the real Yeti at all. I've always said the Yeti were timid and harmless. You've got to let me go out and find their cave. Perhaps there may still be some real Yeti there. I *must* know. Otherwise the whole point of my expedition will be lost.'

'No. I will not allow anyone to leave.'

'You can't give *me* orders, you know,' said Travers truculently. '*I'm* not one of your monks.'

'I command here. And I say no one is to leave. Anyone may be controlling these monsters. Even you.'

Travers was about to argue further, then a sudden thought struck him. He glanced over at the sentry, not far away. 'Thank you, Khrisong, old chap. Thank you very much!' said Travers in a suddenly loud voice. He saw the sentry glance towards them.

'Why do you thank me?' snapped Khrisong.

Travers smiled. 'For making me see sense,' he said quietly. Then, raising his voice again, 'Well, thanks again. Good night.'

Khrisong stared at him as if he were mad, and strode away. Travers waited until he was out of sight, then walked quickly across to the sentry at the gate. 'I've just been having a word with Khrisong,' he said. 'He's given me permission to leave the Monastery.'

In the Great Hall, the Doctor was getting nowhere.

'I'm sorry, Doctor,' said Thomni firmly. 'I myself would trust you. But I must obey the orders of Khrisong.'

'I suppose you must,' said the Doctor sadly. He wandered back to the table where the Yeti lay stretched out.

'Doctor,' said Victoria timidly, 'that space you found in the Yeti's chest – it's round, isn't it?'

The Doctor nodded. 'That's right, my dear. Why do you ask?'

'Well,' said Victoria, 'that silver sphere thing we took from the cave … that was round, too. It would just about fit in that space.'

'Aye, so it would,' said Jamie excitedly. 'It could be one of those control units too!'

The Doctor struck his forehead and groaned. 'I'm an idiot. An absolute imbecile. You're quite right, of course. Let's go and find it.'

Guided by a puzzled but helpful Thomni, they hurried down the endless corridors of the rambling old Monastery, on the way back to the Doctor's room. 'It's a good job you're with us,' gasped Victoria. 'This place is a real rabbit-warren.'

At the sound of their approaching feet in the corridor, the little silver sphere rolled swiftly under the base of a statue of Buddha which stood nearby. The Doctor and his party hurried past. Once they were gone, the sphere rolled from under the statue, and, hugging the darkest corners, moved slowly on its way.

In his room, the Doctor was rummaging frantically on his bed. 'I left it here, just under the pillow. I *know* I did!'

Victoria and Jamie joined in the search. 'Well, it's no' here now,' said Jamie when they had finished. 'Someone must have taken it.'

'Travers!' said Victoria suddenly. 'I thought it was odd, the way he rushed off.'

'It does seem a possibility,' agreed the Doctor. 'I hate to accuse anyone without proof – but perhaps we'd better ask him.'

'I will take you to his room,' said Thomni. 'It is next to yours.' He led them a little way along the corridor to a small bare room, much like the Doctor's. 'You see,' said Victoria triumphantly. 'He's not here – and he said he was going to sleep.'

'We could search the place,' suggested Jamie.

The Doctor frowned. 'I don't think that would be any use. If he has taken it, he'll have it on him. We'll have to find him.'

'All verra well,' said Jamie, 'but where do we start in a place this size?'

The Doctor was already on his way to the door. 'At the main gate, I think. Since he isn't in his room, he's probably trying to leave the Monastery.'

After another dash along the corridors, they reached the courtyard. The Doctor rushed up to the sentry at the doors. 'Have you seen Mr Travers, by any chance?'

The sentry nodded. 'It was some time ago. He has gone now.'

'Gone?' snapped Thomni. 'Out of the Monastery?'

'Yes, Captain. He told me Khrisong had given his permission.'

'That is impossible. He has tricked you.'

Thomni turned to the Doctor. 'We must inform Khrisong of what has happened. He is with the Abbot Songtsen. Will you come with me, please?'

As they walked across the courtyard, the Doctor said thoughtfully, 'I still can't believe Travers has anything to do with controlling these robots. Or with taking the sphere come to that.'

Victoria looked at him affectionately. As usual, the Doctor was being far too trusting. He always found it hard to think ill of anybody. 'Well, one thing's certain, Doctor,' she told him. 'That sphere couldn't have moved off on its own.' She had no idea that, in a corridor not far away, the little silver sphere was doing exactly that.

With the Abbot Songtsen at his side, Khrisong strode into the Great Hall. 'The monster is here, Lord Abbot. I have had it fastened down with chains ...' Khrisong stopped short at the sight of Sapan and Rinchen. The two old lamas were building an elaborate framework of wood and coloured threads, which completely surrounded the prostrate body of the Yeti. 'What are you doing?' Khrisong asked impatiently.

The Abbot smiled. 'They are constructing a ghost trap, Khrisong. Is it not so, my brethren?'

Sapan nodded proudly. 'We have built a spirit trap about the monster, to restrain its evil, my Abbot.'

'It was well thought of,' said the Abbot gently. 'You are wise, Sapan.'

Khrisong laughed. 'I think my chains will be of more use,' he said. 'See, Lord Abbot.' Khrisong pointed to the heavy chains which now fastened the Yeti to the great stone table.

Offended, the two old lamas prepared to go. Sapan paused by the door. 'You should never have allowed this monster to be brought into

154

the Monastery, Khrisong,' he reproved. And with this parting shot, he followed his friend down the corridor.

Khrisong shouted after him. 'What I allow is my business, Sapan.'

Songtsen held up a restraining hand. 'Gently, my son.'

Khrisong looked rather ashamed of himself. 'I am sorry, my Abbot. Sapan and his fellow lamas find much fault in me of late.'

'Harsh words are like blunted arrows, my son. Only the truth can make them sharp.'

'I have only tried to do my duty, my Abbot. The protection of the Monastery is in my hands.'

'I know, Khrisong. Your task is not an easy one.'

Khrisong gazed down at the tethered Yeti. 'And such is our adversary. It is against these creatures that I must protect you. My life is nothing if I fail.' He gestured angrily towards the monster, still terrifying as it lay motionless. 'Can I combat *this* with mildness?'

'Our ways are the ways of peace, my son. You must not seek to change them.'

'I fight to preserve them, my Abbot. There is no other way.'

A strange, faraway expression came over the old Abbot's face. 'There is. It is merely obscured to our simple minds. I will seek guidance of our Master, Padmasambvha.' The Abbot sank cross-legged to the floor, in the classic position for meditation.

The Doctor rushed into the room, followed by Thomni, Jamie and Victoria. With a quick glance at Songtsen, who didn't appear even to see him, the Doctor said, 'Khrisong! Did you give Travers permission to leave the Monastery?'

'Of course not.'

'Well, he's awa',' said Jamie.

Briefly the Doctor explained what had happened.

Khrisong marched to the door. 'You will come with me, Doctor.' The Doctor looked pleased. 'Going to let me help at last, are you?'

'No, Doctor. I merely wish to make sure that you do not vanish also.' With that, Khrisong strode from the room, the Doctor and Jamie following him.

Victoria hung back for a word with Thomni. She rather liked the shy young warrior monk. She indicated the Abbot, still sitting motionless. 'Is he all right?'

'Oh yes,' whispered Thomni reverently. 'He is in a trance. We must leave him.'

Victoria jumped, as suddenly the old Abbot spoke, in a distant faraway voice. 'Yes, Master, I will obey. I come.' Moving like a sleep-walker, the Abbot rose and walked slowly from the room.

'Who was he talking to?' whispered Victoria.

Thomni's voice was hushed in awe. 'To our Master, Padmasambvha, in the Holy Sanctum.'

'Your Master? I thought the Abbot was in charge?'

'And so he is. But above him is the Most Holy Padmasambvha, who rules us all.'

'What's he like?' asked Victoria curiously.

'I do not know. I have never seen him.' Thomni believed he was speaking the truth – his visit to the Inner Sanctum had been wiped from his mind.

'How long has he been here?'

Thomni shrugged. 'Forever, perhaps. He is ageless.'

A look of mischief came over Victoria's face. 'Can't we go to this Sanctum place, and take a peep at him?'

Thomni was appalled. 'Most certainly not. Only the Abbot may enter the Sanctum.'

'Don't you want to know what your Master looks like? Surely you do?'

Thomni was firm. 'No, I do not. It is forbidden, and I have been brought up in the path of obedience. Now, Victoria, I think I must take you to your room. You will be safe there, till your friends return to look after you.'

Victoria sighed to herself, as Thomni marched her off. He was very nice, but he really was rather a stick-in-the-mud. Path of obedience, indeed. Victoria had her own ideas about that. But for the moment she said nothing. Smiling meekly at Thomni she followed him down the corridor.

At the main gate the unfortunate sentry was wishing he had never been born. 'But I saw you speak to him, Khrisong. I heard him thank you. Naturally, I thought ...'

'You are a fool,' snapped Khrisong.

'Well, what's done is done,' interrupted the Doctor 'The important thing is that we examine a control unit. The one Jamie brought down from the mountains has vanished.'

'Aye, that's right,' Jamie joined in. 'So you've got to let us go outside and look for the other one – the one that fell from the Yeti when we trapped it. It canna be far.'

For a long moment, Khrisong stood silent, considering. Then he nodded. 'Very well.' Jamie sighed with relief, and made for the doors. Khrisong held up a forbidding hand. 'No. I will go.'

Jamie watched resentfully, as the sentry opened the doors just enough for Khrisong to slip out into the night.

'Never mind, Jamie,' said the Doctor consolingly. 'At least *someone's* looking for the thing.'

Not far away, in the hush of the Inner Sanctum, Padmasambvha sat brooding. There was a small table just before him, the kind that might have been used to hold a chessboard. On it there stood instead a kind of model landscape – a relief-map of the Monastery, the mountain, and all the surrounding terrain. Little figures stood on the map, models of the Yeti, each about three inches high. Padmasambvha stretched out a withered, claw-like hand. For a moment, the hand hovered over the board, as the old Master focused the power of his will on the symbolic map. Then the hand picked up first one and then another of the Yeti models, and moved them from a position on the lower slopes of the mountain to one very close to the Monastery doors.

Out on the cold, dark mountainside two Yeti were standing. At the precise moment that Padmasambvha's withered hand moved their model counterparts, the two Yeti began lumbering towards the Monastery.

Crouched behind a nearby boulder, a dark shape stirred. Travers watched as the two Yeti moved away. He was shivering with a mixture of excitement and terror. He got up, and continued his journey up the mountain.

Padmasambvha looked up from the board. The Abbot Songtsen was beside him, eyes glazed and face blank, held in a trance by the force of his Master's will. 'The Doctor is wise,' said Padmasambvha softly. 'His eyes are not closed in ignorance. But his mind is too complex. I cannot control it, as I control yours, Songtsen.' There was a hint of something cold and gloating in the thin, old voice. It was as though something else, some other being, spoke through the old monk's mouth.

'I must make sure that the Great Plan is imperilled no further.'

Again the withered hand stretched out and moved the two Yeti. This time they were almost at the Monastery doors.

In the circle of torchlight outside the Monastery doors Khrisong continued his search, unaware of the two giant, shaggy forms moving closer and closer.

6

A Yeti Comes to Life!

The Doctor and Jamie peered anxiously out of the Monastery door. In the torchlight they could see Khrisong, methodically searching the trampled ground in the area where the Yeti had fallen.

'Khrisong,' called the Doctor. 'Why don't you let us come out and give you a hand?'

'No!' Khrisong shouted back. 'You will stay where you are.' The sentry raised his spear, barring their exit.

Suddenly, Khrisong stooped down. At his feet was something that looked like a large pebble. But surely it was *too* round, *too* smooth? He prised it from the icy mud, and scraped it clean. Suddenly the sphere glowed in his hand, and emitted a high-pitched note. Khrisong jumped back, dropping the sphere in amazement.

The sphere gave out a second high-pitched note. As if in response to a signal, two Yeti loomed out of the darkness.

From the gateway, the Doctor shouted a warning. 'Khrisong! Look out! Yeti!' Khrisong looked up to see the two giant shapes bearing down on him. He backed away in horror. Then suddenly he stopped, holding his ground. The Yeti came menacingly on.

'Leave it, Khrisong!' the Doctor shouted. 'Come back in, you don't stand a chance.'

But in an act of lunatic courage, Khrisong dashed forward, snatching up the sphere from under the Yeti's feet. He turned to run for the doors, only to find the second Yeti barring his way. With terrifying speed a massive paw shot out and grabbed his wrist. Khrisong was a big, heavy man, but the Yeti held him dangling in the air, like a doll in the hand of a careless child. Khrisong screamed with pain, twisting and thrashing about, but he was utterly helpless.

Jamie snatched the spear from the sentry's grasp, and ran out of the gates. A shout from the Doctor summoned more warrior monks, and they too ran out to the rescue. Led by Jamie, the warriors began to rain blows upon the two Yeti, who responded with savage roars and slashing blows. The one holding Khrisong wrenched the sphere from his hand, and threw him to the ground like a discarded toy. Ignoring the attacking warriors, the two Yeti turned and disappeared into the darkness.

The Doctor and Jamie half-dragged, half-carried Khrisong back through the Monastery gates.

'Inside, all of you,' the Doctor yelled to the warrior monks. 'Don't follow them. You can't hurt them, you'll just get killed for nothing.'

Soon everyone was back inside and the doors were barred once more.

The Doctor and Jamie lowered the burly Khrisong to the ground. 'Is he all right?' asked Jamie. Before the Doctor could reply, Khrisong struggled angrily to his feet.

'Of course I'm all right, boy,' he growled, rubbing his brawny arm. The Doctor examined it – the marks of the Yeti's paws could be seen, clearly embedded in the flesh.

'Just a little bruising,' the Doctor said. 'You're lucky you weren't killed.'

'Aye,' Jamie agreed. 'That was the daftest thing I ever saw – and the bravest.'

Khrisong ignored this. He looked at the Doctor in puzzlement. 'Why did they just leave? They had us at their mercy.'

'Because they got what they came for, I imagine. They didn't *want* to fight, they were after that control unit.'

Khrisong frowned. 'You speak as though these monsters were intelligent, Doctor.'

'They're being controlled,' explained the Doctor. 'Somehow that sphere was important to them. They *had* to get it back.'

'Did ye hear the screech it gave?' demanded Jamie.

'Some kind of signal – and that's a help. With the right kind of equipment, signals can be traced.'

'You have such equipment?' asked Khrisong.

'Yes, but not here, I'm afraid.' The Doctor looked significantly at Jamie. 'I'm afraid we've got to get back to the TARDIS.' Turning to Khrisong he explained. 'All my equipment is in my, er, camp, some way up the mountainside.'

'Then you must fetch it at once,' declared Khrisong.

Jamie looked at him in amazement. 'You're letting us go? Just like that?'

Khrisong looked a very shaken man, as he answered. 'I have no choice. My warriors are powerless. I *must* trust you, Doctor.'

'We'll try not to let you down,' said the Doctor. 'Let's just get our coats, Jamie, and we'll be on our way.'

They ran back to their rooms and struggled into warm clothing. There was no sign of Victoria. 'Probably wandering around somewhere,' said Jamie. 'Maybe it's better if she doesna know where we're going. She'd only worry.' With the Doctor in his huge fur coat, and Jamie in his anorak, they returned to the courtyard. Khrisong was waiting by the gate.

'Good fortune go with you,' he murmured gruffly. At Khrisong's signal the door was unbarred and opened, and Jamie and the Doctor slipped out into the night. Khrisong said to the sentry, 'Let no one pass. Call me if there is news. I shall be in my quarters.'

Padmasambvha looked up from his board. 'The Yeti have accomplished their task. Now I have a task for you, Songtsen.' The old Master held out his hand. In it was a small transparent pyramid. It seemed to glow with a sort of inner fire, as though there was a kind of life within it. Padmasambvha gestured towards the board, where three of the little Yeti models were grouped together. 'These three Yeti are waiting to escort you. Take this pyramid, which I have prepared, to the cave. Then, the Great Intelligence will have its focus on this planet. Its wanderings in space will be over, and my task will be done. Go now, Songtsen!'

The Abbot bowed, took the strangely glowing pyramid, and left the Sanctum. Once again the doors opened and closed behind him of their own accord.

The Abbot glided along the corridors of the Monastery, and crossed the courtyard to the main gate. Surprised to see his Abbot, the sentry bowed. As the man straightened up, Songtsen passed a hand lightly across his face. Immediately the sentry stood motionless, waiting. In a quiet, faraway voice, Songtsen said, 'You will open the doors and let me pass. You will close them behind me. You will remember nothing.'

The sentry moved at once to the doors and opened them. The Abbot passed through. The sentry closed and barred the doors again. For a brief moment he stood motionless again. Then he seemed to wake with a start. He looked round, reassured to see that all was quiet and normal.

'Must have dozed off,' he thought. 'Lucky Khrisong wasn't around.' Confident that all was well, he resumed his watch.

The Doctor and Jamie trudged wearily up the mountain path, neither of them feeling very happy.

They were doing their best to keep a look-out in all directions at once. A cold wind howled round them. The moon kept drifting in and out of black clouds, so that they were alternately plunged in pitch darkness, or bathed in sinister, ghostly moonlight. Their footsteps sounded very loud as they crunched through the frozen snow. Every now and again, Jamie thought he could hear someone behind them, but when he stopped to listen the sound had gone. 'Och, I'm just getting jumpy,' he thought. 'And no wonder. Surely we're getting near the TARDIS by now?'

The Doctor came to a sudden halt. 'Jamie, look!' A little way ahead, just off the main path, stood the still forms of three Yeti. 'They're not moving,' whispered the Doctor. 'Maybe they're switched off. If I could just examine ...'

Jamie tugged at his arm. 'Aye, and what if someone switches them on while you're doing it? Come on, let's get to the TARDIS while we still can.'

The Doctor sighed. 'I suppose you're right.'

The two moved off, looking back at the three Yeti until a turn in the path hid them from sight.

The three Yeti stood in the same spot, completely motionless.

After a few minutes the Abbot Songtsen came softly up the path. His sandalled feet made almost no sound, and in spite of his thin robes he didn't appear to feel the biting cold. With the same gliding, sleep-walking motion he went up to the three Yeti.

He held out the glowing pyramid in his palms. The Yeti jerked into life. They formed themselves round him in a kind of hollow triangle. With his three strange escorts surrounding him, the Abbot Songtsen struck off away from the main path, heading for the cave of the Yeti.

Bored, and a little frightened, Victoria wandered round the echoing corridors. The Monastery seemed to be almost empty. She had looked in dormitory after dormitory, all deserted. She remembered Thomni telling her that most of the monks had been sent to other Monasteries for safety. She had wandered along corridors, down dusty staircases and through echoing halls, all now confused and identical in her mind.

Bored with waiting in her room, she had decided to go and hunt for the mysterious Inner Sanctum. Almost immediately she had become lost. She had long ago abandoned her plan to look for Padmasambvha, and would have been happy to settle for finding her own room again. Suddenly she saw a gleam of light ahead. She ran forward and found herself at the entrance to the Great Hall. Happy to be back on familiar ground, she crept inside.

The huge room was empty, except for the giant bulk of the Yeti stretched out on the table at the far end. Victoria walked towards it, half-fearful, half-fascinated. She looked in puzzlement at the complicated arrangement of wood and coloured threads surrounding it, and with relief at the chains that fastened it to the table.

As she was about to leave, she saw something silvery moving at her feet. It was the little silver sphere that Jamie had brought from the mountain. She bent down and picked it up. 'Now how did you get all the way over here?' she said. As she glanced at the stretched-out Yeti, she saw the empty cavity that the Doctor had found in its chest. The little sphere would just fit inside, she thought. Victoria's hand began to stretch out towards the Yeti, and the sphere pulsed with light, and gave out a high-pitched signal. Victoria felt as though the sphere was moving her hand, rather than she the sphere.

Before she knew what was happening, she had slipped the silver ball into the little space on the Yeti's chest. The cavity snapped shut, and Victoria pulled back her hand.

For a moment nothing happened. Then the little red eyes of the Yeti snapped open. It began thrashing about in its bonds, shattering Sapan's spirit trap to pieces. To her horror, Victoria saw that the heavy chains were snapping almost as easily as the coloured threads of the ghost trap. In a matter of minutes the Yeti would be free!

7

A Plan to Conquer Earth

Not for the first time, Victoria's well-developed lungs came to her rescue. Too frightened to move, she let out a series of ear-splitting screams that echoed through every corridor of the Monastery. Warriors and lamas came running from every direction.

Thomni was first into the Great Hall, dashing in just as the Yeti broke through the last of its chains, and started making for Victoria. He grabbed the frightened girl, and bundled her into the corridor. 'Run, Victoria, run. Fetch Khrisong!'

As Victoria ran down the corridor, Thomni grabbed a heavy bronze incense-holder, almost as tall as himself, and prepared to use it as a club. He smashed it down on the Yeti's head. The blow landed with a tremendous impact that jarred Thomni's arms. He swung back the incense-holder for a second blow, but the Yeti roared angrily, and wrenched it from his grasp. Grasping the heavy metal pillar in both paws, the Yeti twisted it in two like a wax candle. Then it slashed out at Thomni. The glancing blow sent him spinning across the room and he crashed into a stone pillar. Ignoring him, the Yeti made for the doorway.

Thomni's attack had delayed it long enough to allow a little group of warrior monks to arrive. The Yeti burst through them, its sweeping blows smashing men to one side and the other. Several of the warriors struck at the monster with swords or spears, but the Yeti didn't even pause. Leaving a pile of wounded and bleeding warriors behind it, it shambled purposefully down the corridor.

As Victoria reached the courtyard she met Khrisong, and the main body of the warriors. Khrisong gripped her wrists fiercely.

'What has happened? Why are you screaming?'

'The Yeti, Khrisong! It's alive. It's broken free.'

Khrisong stared at her in disbelief. 'It's true,' she screamed. 'It's all my fault – I put back the sphere …'

Suddenly the Yeti appeared from the cloisters, and began moving towards the barred main doors. Khrisong smiled in grim satisfaction. 'This time we shall destroy it. Attack!'

Victoria crouched sobbing in a corner as Khrisong and his warriors fought their gallant and useless battle. The Yeti seemed almost uninterested in its human opponents. It simply continued its progress towards the main doors. Bowman after bowman loosed his arrows at point-blank range. Arrows thudded into the Yeti's hide until it looked like a porcupine. They didn't have the slightest effect. Savage blows from spears, swords, even axes simply rebounded from the monster's body. Whenever a rash warrior got too close, a single smashing blow from the Yeti put him out of the fight.

Victoria saw Thomni stagger into the courtyard, his face covered with blood. 'You've got to stop them,' she sobbed. 'They'll all be killed. They can't hurt it. It isn't alive. It's a robot.'

Thomni watched the useless battle for a moment, and saw that she was right. Running to the main doors, he unbarred them, and flung them wide. Immediately the Yeti began heading towards them. 'Close the doors,' yelled Khrisong furiously. 'We *must* destroy it.'

'No, brothers,' called Thomni. 'Let it go, or it will kill us all.'

Hurling aside the warriors in its way, the Yeti lumbered through the open doors and out into the night. Thomni, helped by some of the other monks, slammed the doors shut after it, and collapsed against them, panting for breath! All around, the courtyard was a shambles of dead and wounded men.

Dawn was breaking, as the Doctor and Jamie toiled up the mountain path on the last stages of their journey to the TARDIS. It was a beautiful and spectacular sight to see the sun rising over the snow-covered peaks, but they were both too tired and apprehensive to appreciate it properly.

The Doctor stopped for a moment, resting his back against a boulder. He huddled inside his big fur coat, gazing round the bleak terrain.

Jamie toiled up the path and leaned beside him, panting a little. Although the Doctor was small in stature, he seemed to have limitless resources of energy and strength. It was Jamie who was feeling the effects of the journey most. 'What's the matter, Doctor?' he asked, stamping his feet to bring back some feeling. His breath came out in little steamy puffs in the cold, clear morning air.

The Doctor gazed around abstractedly. 'Nothing, Jamie. Just taking a breather.'

Jamie looked at him, puzzled. The Doctor's head was cocked, like a hunting dog.

'You've heard something?'

'No. Nothing.'

'Let's be getting on then.'

The Doctor held up his hand. 'Just a moment. Something's worrying me.'

'I canna hear or see anything,' said Jamie, exasperatedly.

'Exactly. That's what's so worrying. It's all too quiet. Not a sign of the Yeti since we saw those three back there.'

'Aye, well, let's just be grateful, and get on to the TARDIS.'

As they set off again, the Doctor muttered, 'I still don't like it. There's something happening on this mountain. Something evil. I can feel it.'

Jamie looked round and shivered. 'Och, come on, will you? You're giving me the willies.'

Still further up the mountain, Travers was keeping watch on the cave of the Yeti. At least, he hoped it was their cave. On the journey to the Monastery, after he had first met Jamie and Victoria, he had made Jamie give him a detailed description of the cave and how to find it. Now he had been forced to wait until daylight to locate the place, and for hours he had been crouched in hiding, hoping desperately that it was the right cave.

He looked again at the huge boulder, standing in the cave mouth as a kind of door. It *must* be the place. Despite the cold and his lack of sleep, his fanatical enthusiasm kept him bright and alert.

He ducked further into cover. Two Yeti were moving towards the cave. One of them held something in its paw. As the Yeti came closer, Travers could just make out that it was holding a glowing silver sphere. The Yeti came up to the cave entrance, and then stopped. They made no attempt to move the boulder but simply stood like sentries, one each side of the door. Obviously they were waiting for something. But what? Travers studied them eagerly. Could they *all* be robots, as the Doctor said? Were there perhaps *real* Yeti, somewhere inside the cave? Travers settled down to wait.

Rounding a turn in the steep mountain path, the Doctor and Jamie came in sight of the rocky ledge where stood the TARDIS. A Yeti was standing beside it. Immediately, they moved back into cover.

'I said we'd been too lucky,' whispered the Doctor.

'What now?' asked Jamie.

The Doctor frowned ferociously. 'We've jolly well got to get in to the TARDIS.'

Jamie was aghast at the unfairness of it all. 'What's the thing *doing* there? It can't have known we'd turn up.'

'It's just a robot, Jamie. It merely follows instructions. Now – I wonder ...'

Suddenly, the Doctor stepped out of cover and into plain sight of the Yeti.

'Come back,' hissed Jamie. The Doctor ignored him, and walked closer to the monster. Nothing happened. Nothing at all. The Yeti just stood there, motionless. Cautiously, Jamie joined the Doctor, who turned and beamed at him.

'Do you know, Jamie, I think I know how to deal with it? I shall arrange a test!'

Jamie looked at him with respect. Trust the Doctor to come up with one of his brilliant scientific plans. 'What are you going to do?' he asked.

The Doctor chuckled. 'Bung a rock at it.' To Jamie's horror, the Doctor grabbed a rock from the ground and did just that. The rock whizzed through the air and bounced off the Yeti's nose. It still didn't react.

'Just as I thought. Can't see, can't hear, can't feel. Completely de-activated. Come on.' The Doctor marched right up to the Yeti and examined it at close range. He prodded it gently. 'Still, we'd better make sure. Lend me your knife, Jamie.'

Jamie was appalled. 'Dinna be so daft, Doctor. You might switch it on by mistake.'

'Oh, I don't think so. Just the opposite, I hope.'

Taking the little dagger, the Doctor probed the Yeti's chest, just as he'd done with the captured one at the Monastery. After a little fumbling, he prised open the chest cavity, revealing the little silver sphere. The Doctor reached in, and slowly and carefully removed it. With a sigh of relief he tossed the sphere to Jamie, and they moved towards the TARDIS.

'It's a wonder there wasn't some kind of protective mechanism,' said the Doctor thoughtfully. 'You'd think whoever built it would have thought of that!'

Jamie laughed. 'How many people do you think would go up to yon beastie, and start poking it with a wee dagger? The thing is, Doctor, they just didna reckon on anyone as daft as you!'

The Doctor gave him a mock-offended look, and opened the door of the TARDIS.

'How about some breakfast?' he suggested cheerily.

Outside the cave of the Yeti, Travers' long vigil was at last rewarded. He saw a group of shaggy figures moving across the mountainside towards him. Three more Yeti. Travers' eyes widened in amazement. In the centre of the little group of Yeti walked the Abbot Songtsen.

Songtsen marched up to the boulder outside the cave. He took the sphere from the Yeti holding it. The other Yeti lifted the enormous boulder aside and Songtsen entered the cave. The Yeti grouped themselves around the entrance, motionless once more.

In the Inner Sánctum the prayer lamps flickered, casting shadows in the gloom. The Master Padmasambvha was communing with the alien power that had dominated his being for so many weary years.

'Oh, Great Intelligence, the time for your Experiment has come at last. Abbot Songtsen makes the final preparations now. I ask only that you release me, as you have promised.' He sank back on the golden throne in infinite weariness.

The Abbot Songtsen was indeed busy about his preparations. Obeying the orders placed in his mind by Padmasambvha, who was himself performing the wishes of the Great Intelligence they both served, Songtsen was arranging the glowing spheres that Jamie had found into an intricate pattern. When the design was complete, Songtsen placed the pyramid given him by Padmasambvha reverently in the centre. Then he turned and walked from the cave. The pyramid began to pulse and flicker with life. Then, slowly, but surely, it began to grow ...

Outside, Travers watched as Songtsen emerged. The Abbot set off down the mountain path. All the Yeti followed him.

Travers could scarcely believe his good fortune. The Yeti were gone, and the boulder at the mouth of the cave had not been replaced. He crept forward slowly, and entered the cave.

It was just as Jamie had described it – the pit-props, the tunnel, and, in the distance, a glowing pulsating light. Jamie had not said how fierce and bright it was. And there was a kind of high-pitched noise ... Eagerly, Travers crept up to the entrance of the inner cave. He looked through, and then fell back, shielding his eyes. In the centre of the pattern of spheres, the pyramid was pulsing and glowing, blazing with light. A high-pitched screaming sound filled the cave. It seemed full of a kind of exultant madness. Travers could feel it affecting his mind ...

As Travers watched, the swollen pyramid cracked open. A bubbling, glutinous substance, shot with fiery colours, began to ooze forth. More and more of it poured forth, and then more and more still. It spread across the cave floor in a heavy mass, trickling slowly towards him. And it was still coming, far more than the pyramid could possibly hold! The thought flashed through Travers' confused mind that the pyramid was really a sort of gateway, a channel between some other, alien universe and this one. And that the other universe was pouring this evil substance through to this one. Pouring and pouring and pouring endlessly. Soon it would envelop the whole world ...

With a mighty effort, Travers wrenched himself away. Half-demented, he ran from the cave, out through the tunnel and on to the mountainside. He began to run madly downwards, stumbling, falling, rising, and stumbling on, ignoring his hurts and bruises. He had to get away, away from the horror in the cave. What Travers found really unbearable about the heaving, bubbling mass, was the fact that he felt it was *alive*.

Jamie was happily spooning down the last of an enormous bowl of well-salted porridge. The Doctor was polishing off a plate of bacon and eggs. Somewhere in the TARDIS there was a machine that could produce any kind of food you could think of, piping hot and in a matter of seconds. Jamie had never been more glad of it. 'Och, that's better,' he said, pushing aside his bowl. 'But hadn't we better be getting back, Doctor?' The Doctor nodded, his mouth too full to speak. Wrapping themselves up for the outside, they prepared to leave.

'Mustn't forget this,' said the Doctor, picking up a little black box, covered with dials. 'My tracking device.'

Jamie picked up the sphere they had taken from the Yeti. 'What about this?'

'Oh, bring it along. I'll study it back at the Monastery.' They left the TARDIS, and the Doctor locked it behind them. The de-activated Yeti still stood motionless in the snow. The Doctor gave it an affectionate pat. 'Come on, Jamie,' he said, and set off down the mountain. Suddenly, he realised that Jamie wasn't following him. 'Come on, Jamie,' he repeated.

Jamie's voice was desperate. 'I canna, Doctor. I just canna. It's pulling me towards it.'

Turning, the Doctor saw Jamie. The sphere in his outstretched hand was being dragged by some invisible force closer and closer to the Yeti. The sphere was pulsing and glowing, emitting a high-pitched signal. 'Don't put it back,' yelled the Doctor. 'Whatever you do, don't put it back!' He rushed up to Jamie, grabbed him by the waist and tried to pull him away from the Yeti. But the invisible force exerted by the glowing sphere was more than a match for both of them. Step by step, Jamie and the Doctor were pulled closer and closer to the waiting Yeti.

'It's no good,' gasped Jamie. 'I'll have to let it go.'

'No, Jamie, you mustn't. You've *got* to hold on.' Letting go of Jamie's waist, the Doctor moved round in front of him. Just as the sphere slipped from Jamie's hands, he interposed his own body between the sphere and the Yeti. It thudded into the Doctor's ribs with painful force, ramming him back against the monster's body. The Doctor found he couldn't move. The pressure on his ribs increased. It seemed obvious that the sphere was determined to get back to the Yeti, even if it had to drill a hole through the Doctor to do it!

Jamie tried to move the sphere away from the Doctor, but he couldn't budge it. Painfully, the Doctor gasped, 'Jamie ... get rock ...'

'What's that, Doctor – I dinna understand.'

The pressure on the Doctor's ribs was now agonising. 'Find rock,' he sobbed. 'Same size ... put in chest ...'

All at once, Jamie saw what the Doctor meant. He abandoned his attempt to move the sphere, and groped round frantically for a suitably sized rock. All the stones around seemed too big or too small. He scrabbled frantically in the icy mud and snow, the sound of the Doctor gasping for breath in his ears. At last, he saw a rock the same size and shape as the silver sphere. It was half buried in ice, and he couldn't shift it. Jamie kicked frantically at the rock with his boot heel. As soon as it came free, he dashed across to the Yeti and rammed it into the hole in the Yeti's chest.

Immediately, the pressure from the sphere cut off. It dropped harmlessly into Jamie's cupped hands.

The Doctor drew a deep, sobbing breath, and rubbed his aching chest. 'Are you all right?' asked Jamie anxiously.

'Just a bit breathless,' said the Doctor. 'No, don't do that – we may need it.' Jamie had drawn back his arm like a shot-putter, and was about to send the sphere whizzing over the horizon.

'But the thing nearly killed you, Doctor.'

'Not on purpose, though – it's simply programmed to return to ... oh, my word!' The Doctor broke off as a sudden thought struck him.

It struck Jamie at the same time. 'The one back in the Monastery – maybe Travers didna take it!'

'Exactly,' agreed the Doctor. 'Victoria said it couldn't move by itself – but it can!'

'Aye,' said Jamie, 'and if it finds its way back to that Yeti we captured … we've got to warn them!'

Unaware that the catastrophe they feared had already happened, Jamie and the Doctor set off down the mountainside.

REVOLT IN THE
MONASTERY

The Monastery courtyard still showed the after-effects of battle. Injured monks were having their wounds dressed and bandaged. The dead were being carried away on stretchers, their faces covered.

Victoria finished bathing Thomni's forehead. 'There,' she said. 'That's better.' The young monk's face had been covered with blood, but most of it came from a long, shallow cut on his forehead. To Victoria's relief the injury wasn't nearly so bad as it looked. She was wringing out the cloth in a stone basin when Khrisong appeared. He glared furiously down at Thomni. 'Why did you disobey my orders?' he demanded.

Thomni tried to stand. He reeled dizzily, and had to hold on to Victoria. Gathering his strength, he replied, 'Because it was the only thing to do.'

'Had you not opened the gate,' growled Khrisong, 'the creature would not have escaped.'

Victoria came to Thomni's defence. 'If he hadn't opened the gate, you'd have *all* been dead by now,' she said spiritedly.

Khrisong rounded on her. 'And you – did you not say it was all *your* fault. What did you mean by that?'

Victoria was silent, staring at the ground.

'You'd better answer, Victoria,' said Thomni gently.

Without looking up, Victoria said, 'I put the control unit back in the Yeti. That's what brought it to life again.'

Khrisong called over two of his warriors. 'Seize her. Put her in the cell.'

'You don't understand,' sobbed Victoria. 'I didn't mean to do it. The sphere *made* me.'

'Spare her, Khrisong,' urged Thomni. 'She would not deliberately harm us. She must surely have been bewitched.'

Baffled and angry, Khrisong glared from one to the other. 'You are much of one mind, are you not? You disobey my orders, and she defends you. She confesses her crime, and you speak for her. Do you plot against me?'

'This is madness,' protested Thomni. But Khrisong was not listening.

'Take them both,' he ordered. 'Lock them up together. Let them do their plotting behind bars.'

Angrily he strode away across the courtyard, while the warrior monks closed in on Thomni and Victoria.

The Doctor and Jamie were trudging on down the mountainside, the Doctor carrying his detection device, Jamie gingerly carrying the silver sphere. Much to his relief, the sphere had stopped its signalling once they were away from the immobilised Yeti. 'The number of times we've traipsed up and down this mountain …' Jamie was grumbling. Then he broke off short. The sphere had started its high-pitched signalling note again. 'Hey, Doctor,' he called. 'It's away again.'

The Doctor listened intently. 'That's a different sort of signal,' he said thoughtfully. 'Slightly different pitch.' He held his detection device close to the sphere, and studied the flickering dials intently.

Not far away the Abbot Songtsen and his escort of three Yeti were descending the mountain by a different route. Suddenly, the Yeti stopped. They paused as if listening, then, moving as one, they changed direction, setting off on a course which took them towards the Doctor and Jamie. The Abbot Songtsen, apparently unaware of what was happening, continued his journey down the mountain alone.

The Doctor peered excitedly at the flickering dials. 'You know, Jamie,' he said happily, 'I think I picked up some kind of answering signal! Isn't that splendid?'

Jamie was less enthusiastic. 'Can we no' just get back to the Monastery?' he asked plaintively. 'You can do all your detecting behind those nice high walls. So come on, will you?' And he set off down the mountain.

Obediently, the Doctor followed him. 'The trouble with you is, Jamie,' he said reproachfully, 'you lack the proper scientific spirit. This is a perfect opportunity to try and trace the main transmitter.'

'Aye,' said Jamie. 'And it's a perfect opportunity to get ourselves killed. While you're fiddling away with that machine, this thing's probably calling up all the Yeti in creation.'

For a while they plodded on in silence. The signal from the sphere stopped. Jamie began to hope they might reach the Monastery safely after all. Then, suddenly, the signal started up again. 'I wish you'd keep quiet,' muttered Jamie. He tried to muffle the sphere inside his anorak. 'Can we no' just throw it away, Doctor?'

'Too late for that, I'm afraid,' said the Doctor ruefully. 'Look!' Barring the path ahead, there stood three of the Yeti.

'We could maybe double back,' said Jamie. But when he looked over his shoulder, he saw that two more Yeti were blocking the path behind them. They were trapped.

For a long moment nobody moved. Then the Doctor said quietly, 'Jamie, give me the sphere. You take the detection device.' Quickly they made the exchange.

'Now what?' asked Jamie.

'We move forward. Very slowly.'

As they moved, the Yeti moved too, closing in on them.

The Doctor whispered urgently, 'When I say run, you run like the wind. Don't stop, and don't worry about me.'

'Och, no, Doctor—' protested Jamie.

The Doctor held up his hand. 'Please, Jamie, just run. Don't try to do anything heroic. Promise?'

'Aye, verra well.' By now they were almost up to the three Yeti in front of them.

'Run, Jamie, run!' yelled the Doctor. Jamie sprinted down the path, dodging between the three Yeti like a centre-forward making for goal. They ignored him, and continued their advance on the Doctor. When they were almost within touching distance, the Doctor twisted round and bowled the silver sphere back up the path, towards the other two Yeti. He stood perfectly still.

The three Yetis lumbered closer and closer. Almost brushing against him, they lumbered up the path, after the sphere. The Doctor heaved a sigh of relief. 'It worked!' he said to himself in mild astonishment. Then he ran off down the path after Jamie.

Khrisong hurried across the courtyard to the main doors where Rapalchan, one of his young warriors, was keeping guard.

'Rapalchan! Has the Doctor returned?' he asked impatiently.

The sentry shook his head. 'No, Khrisong. No one has entered or left!'

Khrisong paused, indecisively. A man of action above all, he felt baffled and frustrated. Terrible perils menaced his beloved Monastery, and he could do nothing to fight them. Instead he was forced to rely on the promises of this strange Doctor, a madman springing from nowhere. Even the trusty Thomni had turned against him, led astray by that devil-girl Victoria.

Glaring round the courtyard he found a new target for his anger. The two old lamas, Sapan and Rinchen, were strolling placidly across the courtyard on their way to morning prayer. Nothing must disturb their invariable routine, thought Khrisong, even though the whole Monastery was in peril. He crossed over to them and asked, 'Where is the Abbot Songtsen?'

'We have not seen him for many long hours,' said Sapan.

'Indeed, that is so,' agreed Rinchen. 'No doubt he seeks guidance from the Master Padmasambvha.'

Khrisong laughed scornfully. 'Seeks guidance – or seeks to evade his responsibilities?'

Sapan was shocked. 'You ought not to speak so,' he reproved.

'Why not? Has anyone ever seen this legendary immortal?' Khrisong walked quickly away, leaving the two old lamas staring after him aghast. What blasphemy! To query the very existence of the most holy one ... Whatever was the world coming to? Shaking their heads, the two old men went on inside the Monastery.

For a moment all was peaceful in the courtyard. It was the hour of morning prayer, and all those not on duty would be in the Great Hall. The silence was broken by a gentle tapping at the main door. A quiet voice said, 'Open. It is I, your Abbot Songtsen.' The astonished Rapalchan opened the door – it was indeed the Abbot. Songtsen entered. Songtsen brushed his hand lightly over the young sentry's face. 'You have not seen me, Rapalchan. None has entered, none has left.'

Rapalchan stood in a trance, eyes staring ahead, while Songtsen crossed the courtyard and entered the Monastery. Once he was out of sight, Rapalchan came to, with a little start and resumed his vigil. None had entered, none had left.

Minutes later, Songtsen stood at the side of the shrouded figure of Padmasambvha. 'You have done well, Songtsen,' the incredibly old voice whispered. 'The Great Intelligence takes on material form. Now it will grow and grow. For their own safety, our brothers must leave the Monastery.'

'I understand, Master,' said the Abbot tonelessly. 'And the strangers?'

'I will tell you how to deal with them *if* they return.'

Victoria paced impatiently up and down the cell. Angrily she turned to Thomni who sat placidly on the floor in the posture of meditation.

'How can you take everything so quietly?' she demanded. 'After the way Khrisong spoke to you …'

'Khrisong carries many burdens,' said Thomni gently. 'Their weight makes him angry. He knows in his heart we are innocent. When his anger cools, he will release us.'

'Oh, will he? Well, if you think I'm sitting here quietly until he has a change of heart …'

Thomni looked at her in mild surprise. 'There is nothing else we can do, Miss Victoria. What is written is written …' He returned to his meditation.

There was a rattle at the door. Victoria looked up alertly. If they gave her the slightest chance … Rinchen entered, with a tray of food and drink. Eagerly Victoria seized one of the stone beakers. 'Oh, good, I'm so thirsty.' She drained the beaker at a gulp.

For a moment she stood gasping, her hand at her throat. 'The taste,' she gasped. 'So strange …' Suddenly she crumpled to the floor.

Horrified, Thomni knelt beside her. 'Miss Victoria, Miss Victoria …' She was quite still. Rinchen hovered indecisively. 'I will fetch help. Stay with her, Thomni.' The old lama scuttled off, leaving the door open behind him in his panic. Thomni went to the bed to fetch a blanket. He heard movement behind him and turned. Victoria was on her feet and by the door, her eyes sparkling with mischief. 'Sorry, Thomni,' she said, and nipped through the door, slamming and barring it behind her.

In the Great Hall, all the warrior monks and lamas were assembled, summoned by the Abbot Songtsen.

'I have sought guidance from the Master Padmasambvha,' he was saying solemnly. 'In his wisdom he has told me that there is no defence against the Yeti. We must flee at once, or we will all be slain.'

'No!' There was a shout from the doorway and they turned to see Khrisong. 'The Doctor has returned. He brings with him a way to fight this evil.'

The Abbot said sternly, 'Khrisong, the Master has decided …'

'The Master, always the Master,' interrupted Khrisong. 'I have felt the strength of these Yeti. See, I bear their scars on my arm. Yet I will not meekly turn away. I mean to fight! Who is with me? Come!'

A confused babble broke out in the Hall. But only a few of the warrior monks followed Khrisong as he strode out. The rest, afraid to defy their Abbot, stayed with the lamas and Songtsen.

The Abbot's voice cut through the noise. 'Brothers, Khrisong has been led astray by the strangers. He has forgotten his vows of obedience. Follow him, and bring him back to the path of wisdom! I will pray for guidance.' In a confused mass, monks and lamas poured excitedly from the Great Hall. Songtsen was left standing alone.

At once he closed his eyes, and went into a state of trance.

'Advise me, Padmasambvha,' he implored. 'Khrisong turns his warriors from the path of obedience. Not all of them will obey your command to go …'

From all around him, he heard the ghostly voice of Padmasambvha. 'If they will not be led from the Monastery – then they must be driven. This is what you must do …'

The Doctor and Jamie were waiting in the courtyard amidst a scene of utter confusion. A little crowd of monks and lamas milled about arguing and disputing. Some supported the Abbot, some were for following Khrisong.

The Doctor looked round in amazement. 'What's going on?' he said wonderingly.

'Search me,' said Jamie. 'Seems they've all gone daft.'

Khrisong shouldered his way through the throng, a little knot of warriors around him. 'We must act quickly, Doctor. The Abbot has ordered us to evacuate the Monastery ...'

He was interrupted by a frantic knocking and scrabbling at the doors. A faint voice called, 'Let me in. Please, let me in!'

Cautiously Khrisong opened the doors. A tattered, scarecrow figure staggered inside, and collapsed at their feet. It was Travers.

The Doctor and Jamie bent over him. He was in a terrible state, ragged, dirty and bleeding. He had tumbled down the mountain like a falling boulder, with no concern for his own safety. His lips were cracked, his eyes wide and staring, filled with the recollection of that horrible living mass that was bubbling and growing in the cave ...

'Pyramid,' he muttered feverishly. 'It was growing ... growing ... the noise ...' Travers' head lolled back, and he fainted dead away.

Jamie was thoroughly confused. 'What was all that about, Doctor?'

Before the Doctor could reply, there came a further shock. The Abbot Songtsen appeared. 'Seize the strangers,' he ordered. 'They must all be locked up at once. The girl Victoria has escaped. She too must be taken and imprisoned.'

At once utter pandemonium broke out. Everyone started talking and shouting at once.

'Victoria escaped?' yelled Jamie furiously. 'Escaped from where? Where is she? What's been going on?'

'Abbot Songtsen, please,' called the Doctor. 'You really must listen to me.' The Doctor's voice was drowned in the general babble. Khrisong shouldered him aside, and forced his way through the little crowd to the Abbot.

'I cannot allow this!' he protested fiercely.

The Abbot's voice was stern. 'You cannot allow? These are the orders of the Master. You *must* obey.'

'These people can help us, Lord Abbot.'

'The Master says there is *no* help against the Yeti. He orders us to leave or we will all die.'

A frightened murmuring from the monks and lamas showed the effect of his words. Songtsen saw that he had the upper hand. 'Take the strangers and lock them up,' he ordered.

A horde of panic-stricken monks descended upon the Doctor and Jamie, and bustled them away, ignoring their protests and those of Khrisong. The Doctor was almost carried off towards the cell, and Jamie, struggling furiously, was bundled along after him. Other monks picked up the unconscious Travers and carried him along, too.

The Abbot turned to Khrisong and the little group of rebellious warriors around him. 'Khrisong! Defy me no further. Take your warriors and find the girl.' For a moment it seemed that Khrisong would still refuse. Then, defeated, he bowed his head, and led his warriors away.

Except for the sentry at the doors, the Abbot was now alone in the great courtyard. He walked across to the doors and said to the sentry, 'Go and join in the search, my son.' He passed his hand lightly over the sentry's face, and the young monk froze for a moment, then ran off after his fellows. Once he was out of sight, Songtsen unbarred the great doors and then opened them wide. The Monastery of Det-sen was defenceless. 'It is done, Master,' said the Abbot Songtsen. Then he walked slowly away.

Since her escape from the cell, Victoria had been hiding in the empty guest quarters, uncertain what to do with herself once she was free. She wondered where everyone was, not realising that Travers, the Doctor and Jamie had just returned to the Monastery.

Eventually, she crept cautiously out into the corridor and moved towards the courtyard. Soon she began to hear the noise and shouting of the excited monks. Afraid to venture further, she waited. Suddenly the noise started coming nearer. She could hear yells and shouts. 'Find her. Find the devil girl!' With a shock, Victoria realised that they were hunting *her*. Terrified, she turned and fled, the sounds of pursuit echoing behind her.

For what seemed an endless time she was hunted up and down the gloomy corridors. More than once she eluded her pursuers by hiding in some dark corner, while they all raced by. But they always seemed to pick up her trail again.

By the time she managed to shake them off, Victoria was in a part of the Monastery that she had never visited before. She found herself in a little windowless room, lit only by flickering prayer lamps. On the walls were rich hangings and tapestries. All around were carved statues, devil masks, rare ornaments. Victoria knew enough about antiques to realise that the contents of the little room were virtually priceless.

At the far end of the room, she saw a pair of ornately carved double doors, Victoria looked at them curiously, wondering what was beyond them. She decided not to try and find out. This place was quiet enough, but it was far too spooky to be comfortable. She turned to leave, and found that she couldn't move. Something, some force, held her unmoving.

'Enter, my child,' said a voice. It came from nowhere and yet from everywhere. It was quiet and gentle, yet it filled the room. The doors opened before her of their own accord. 'Come in,' said the voice again. 'You *must* come in, you have no alternative.'

Victoria tried to hang back, but the invisible force made her walk slowly into the Inner Sanctum. Ahead of her she could see the raised dais, the golden throne with its seated figure. She was drawn closer and closer. The canopy round the throne had been pulled back. The seated figure raised its head and looked at her. Victoria was the first in many hundred years to look upon the face of Padmasambvha. She opened her mouth in a gasp of pure terror, too frightened even to scream...

9

ATTACK OF THE YETI

Victoria's first thought was that the man before her was incredibly old. Older than Sapan or Rinchen, or any of the other venerable old men at the Monastery. Older than anyone she had ever seen or imagined. So old that the shrunken body seemed like that of a child, swaddled inside the long, flowing robes.

The face was quite incredible. Completely hairless, with huge forehead, sunken cheeks and bony jaw. In contrast to the wizened face and shrunken body, the eyes were huge and dark and alive, shining with the blaze of an almost superhuman intelligence. The Master Padmasambvha had indeed gone beyond the flesh. His body was merely the worn-out husk which barely contained his soul and spirit.

He looked up at Victoria, and smiled with a curious gentleness. 'Do not be afraid, my child. Why do you come here?'

Victoria tried to babble some explanation. 'I'm sorry, I was lost, and I was afraid. They were chasing me, you see, and …'

Gently, Padmasambvha interrupted her. 'You need help, do you not?'

'Yes, I'm afraid I do,' said Victoria thankfully. 'You see, I can't find the Doctor and …'

Padmasambvha held up his hand, cutting her off. 'One moment, child.'

He leaned forward, brooding over the board in front of him. 'The courtyard is empty, and the gates are open,' he said mysteriously. Victoria leaned forward, peering at the model landscape with its tiny figures.

'I must do what I am compelled to do,' said Padmasambvha sadly. He picked up one of the little figures from the board.

'What is it?' asked Victoria curiously. She was getting over her fear now.

There was something pathetic about the old man. Yet, at the same time, something frightening, and unpredictable too.

'Come and see,' invited the Master, holding up the little figure.

Victoria came closer and looked at it. 'It's one of those horrible creatures – a Yeti.'

Again Padmasambvha gave that curiously sad smile. 'That is so, my child. But you have not seen it.' He passed his hand gently in front of her eyes. Immediately Victoria went into a trance, her eyes wide open and staring. Padmasambvha placed the Yeti model down in the courtyard of the miniature Monastery.

He reached out for another model. 'I must do what I am compelled to do,' whispered Padmasambvha again.

The courtyard of the Monastery still stood empty. The doors were open wide. One after another, four of the Yeti lumbered into the courtyard. Once inside, they split up, each making for a different part of the Monastery, as if by some prearranged plan.

Things were uncomfortably crowded in the little cell. Travers lay on the bed. He had fallen into a deep, exhausted sleep, broken by occasional muttering and twitching.

The Doctor perched on the wooden stool by the bed, watching Travers thoughtfully. Thomni sat cross-legged by the wall in his meditation position. Jamie was pacing up and down the cell, pausing now and again to bang on the door, or yell through the grille.

'So that's why they locked up poor Victoria,' he was saying to Thomni. 'She was telling the truth, you know. Those wee balls *can* make you put them back in the Yeti. One of them nearly did it to me, didn't it, Doctor?'

The Doctor nodded absently, his eyes still fixed on the face of the sleeper.

Suddenly Travers opened his eyes, and stared in amazement at the Doctor. 'Where am I? What happened to me?'

'We were rather hoping you could tell us that,' said the Doctor gently.

Travers shook his head vaguely. 'I left the Monastery then … it's no use … it's all a blank … there's just a feeling of evil … I felt a shadow on my mind. I felt as if I might drown …'

'Aye, man, but what did you see?' asked Jamie impatiently. 'Where did all this happen?'

Travers closed his eyes again. 'I don't know … I can't … I'm so tired …' His eyes closed and sank back into sleep.

'What do you think?' asked Jamie.

The Doctor sighed, and scratched his head. 'He must have seen something very nasty indeed, I fear. Perhaps whatever's behind all this trouble we're having. If only he could tell us.'

There came a tremendous crash from somewhere inside the Monastery. It was followed by shouts of alarm, cries of fear, and the sound of running feet. 'The Yeti are coming,' yelled a panic-stricken voice. 'Flee, my brothers, flee!'

Jamie rattled at the door. 'What's going on? Let us out of here.'

But the Doctor, with a pleased expression, had pulled his detection device from under the bed and was carefully noting the readings.

Khrisong's face appeared briefly at the grille. 'The Yeti have broken into the Monastery. Stay where you are, you are safe there.'

'What about Victoria,' yelled Jamie frantically. 'Where is she? Have you found her?' But Khrisong had gone. Jamie turned back to the Doctor. 'Isn't there something we can …'

The Doctor hushed him with an upheld hand. Jamie saw that he was bent intently over the detection device, studying every little flicker of the dials.

The Abbot Songtsen, Khrisong and most of the monks and lamas, were gathered together in the Great Hall. From throughout the Monastery came the sound of destruction, as the Yeti carried on their rampage. Occasionally there was a scream, as some unfortunate monk was caught in their path. Khrisong tried to organise his warriors into a defensive force, but they were all too panic-stricken.

He said bitterly to Songtsen, 'Forgive me, my Abbot. I have failed you.'

The Abbot looked at him pityingly. 'You have not failed, my son. This disaster was written. Man cannot alter his destiny.'

Meanwhile, the Yeti raged unhindered through the Monastery. Dormitories were wrecked, statues cast down, priceless treasures mutilated and destroyed. Yet they did not seem intent on taking life. They attacked only those who attacked them, or sought to hinder their work of methodical destruction. It was in the storage cellars that most terrible havoc was wreaked. The Yeti smashed open food barrels, burst water tanks so that the food cellars were flooded, and mixed fuel, food, clothing and medicines into one unusable pile.

Then, as if their work were done, they began to withdraw from the Monastery.

A terrified monk rushed into the Great Hall to give the news to the Abbot. 'The Yeti are falling back,' he cried.

'Come, brethren, do not be afraid,' said the Abbot. He led his little band from the Great Hall into the courtyard.

All but two of the Yeti were gone. These two stood waiting by a great golden statue of Buddha that dominated the courtyard, the Buddha that was the very spirit and symbol of Det-sen Monastery. The appearance of the Abbot and his followers seemed to serve as a signal. The remaining two Yeti lumbered forward, seized the statue in their mighty paws, and began to tilt it forward. The old lama, Rinchen, ran forward from the crowd in horror. 'No! No!' he cried. 'You shall not.' Stretching out his feeble hands, he made a vain attempt to prevent the great golden figure from falling. Slowly the Buddha crashed to the stones of the courtyard, crushing the life from old Rinchen in the process. The head of the Buddha was smashed from the body. It rolled slowly across the courtyard. The two Yeti turned and left.

Khrisong looked from the broken statue to the broken body of Rinchen. 'The Monastery of Det-sen is accursed,' he said bitterly. 'It is time for us to leave.'

Padmasambvha was communing with the Great Intelligence. Beside him stood Victoria, unseeing and unhearing in her trance.

'Now it is complete,' whispered Padmasambvha. 'Now the monks will leave. By nightfall the Monastery will be deserted, the entire mountain yours.' He turned his attention to Victoria. 'And what of you and your friends, my poor child? The Doctor is not so easily frightened as my poor monks. Therefore you must help me. Together we will make sure that he leaves. Come closer.'

Unable to resist, Victoria stepped forward.

Jamie watched impatiently as Thomni finished scratching a plan of the Monastery on the cell wall with a piece of chalk fished from the Doctor's capacious pocket.

'This is the courtyard,' said Thomni, pointing. 'We are here – to the south. The north lies – here.' And he chalked an 'N' on the map.

The Doctor took the chalk from him and drew a line across the map.

'Does your science provide an answer, Doctor?' asked Thomni.

'Only half an answer, I'm afraid. We know that the transmissions come from *somewhere* on this line. But we need a second reading, a cross reference to give us the actual place. That could give us the *where*.' Absent-mindedly, the Doctor scratched his head with the piece of chalk. 'Of course we still won't have the most important thing.'

'Oh aye, and what's that?' said Jamie impatiently.

The Doctor looked at him in surprise. 'The *why* of course. That's what we really need to know.'

Travers came to life with a sudden start. He sat up, looked round, and said cheerily, 'Hullo, Doctor, Jamie. How are you all?'

'Oh, fine, just fine,' said Jamie dryly.

'What's going on?' said Travers. 'What are we doing here?'

'There's been a spot of trouble,' said the Doctor gently.

'With the Yeti,' added Jamie,

'Oh, really,' said Travers. 'Must have missed it all while I was sleeping.'

'You had a spot of trouble yourself,' prompted the Doctor. 'On the mountainside. You saw something pretty nasty. Do you remember?'

'Not a thing,' said Travers. 'Got a bit of a headache, actually. Think I'll get a breath of fresh air.' He got up, went to the door and tried to open it. 'I say,' he said indignantly, 'do you chaps realise we're locked in?'

*

In the courtyard, the monks had managed to move the heavy statue. Some of them were lifting Rinchen's body on to a stretcher. Khrisong's head was bowed in grief.

'Do not blame yourself,' said the Abbot Songtsen. 'Death is inevitable.' He turned to the monks with the stretcher. 'Rinchen will accompany us on our journey. There will be time to mourn our brother. The rest of you gather what is needed. Save what provisions you can. Soon it will be the hour for meditation. Then we must depart.'

'What of the strangers?' asked Sapan.

'They will be taken with us to a place of safety.'

'And the Master Padmasambvha?'

'His powers are great,' said the Abbot. 'He will remain.'

There was a sudden stir amongst the crowd. Many of the monks fell to their knees. Turning, Songtsen saw that Victoria had come into the courtyard. In her hands was the holy ghanta. A murmur of awe swept through the crowd.

For a moment Victoria stood immobile, eyes wide and staring hands outstretched. Then she spoke. But the voice that came from her lips was that of Padmasambvha. 'I have chosen to speak to you through the lips of this maiden,' said the low, compelling voice that seemed to come from all around them. 'She holds the holy ghanta. Bear it away with you for safe keeping. Treat her with kindness – she and the other strangers are innocent of malice. They wish to help you against the Yeti but I tell you there is no help. Det-sen must be abandoned. When the wind destroys its nest, the bird will build another.'

Victoria fell silent. She tottered, and the monks rushed to support her.

'Release the strangers,' said Songtsen. 'Bid them make ready to depart.'

Victoria was in the guest room, sitting on the bed and gazing straight in front of her, when the Doctor, Jamie and Travers were brought in by Khrisong and Thomni.

'Victoria, are you all right?' asked Jamie anxiously. She did not move,

'Victoria,' said the Doctor. The sound of *his* voice provoked an instant reaction.

'Doctor,' she said, 'there is great danger. You must take me away! Take me away!' She spoke in a sort of formal chant. She stopped, and fell into her silent trance. 'Victoria, what is it? What's the matter?' said Jamie. She ignored him.

'Khrisong, how long has she been like this?' asked the Doctor.

But before Khrisong could reply, Victoria reacted once more to the Doctor's voice.

'Doctor, there is great danger. Take me away from here. Take me away.' Like a switched-off record she fell silent.

'She's reacting to my voice,' said the Doctor. He moved away. 'I'd better start whispering.'

'She is still in a trance,' said Khrisong gravely. Briefly he told the Doctor what had happened.

'She must have reached the Sanctum,' said Thomni. 'She has seen the Holy Padmasambhva.'

The Doctor looked up sharply. 'Padmasambvha, the Master? Surely he must have died long ago – I met him on my last visit, and he was incredibly old then. He can't have lived for another three hundred years.'

'Padmasambvha is ageless, Doctor,' said Khrisong gravely. 'But how could you have known him three hundred years ago? Are you ageless, too?'

The Doctor didn't reply. 'Padmasambvha – still here,' he muttered to himself. 'Why does nobody *tell* me anything?' He moved to the door. 'Take care of Victoria for me, Jamie,' he whispered. 'I shan't be long.'

'Can you no' help her?' demanded Jamie.

'I think so, Jamie. But I have to find out something first. Khrisong, will you walk with me for a moment?'

As they walked along the corridor together, the Doctor said, 'Khrisong, a while ago you wanted my help. Now, you're preparing to leave. Don't you want to save the Monastery any more?'

'I must obey the Abbot,' said Khrisong. 'He wishes us to leave.'

'Somebody wishes it,' replied the Doctor. 'That's why all this was arranged. To get you to leave. That's why someone opened the gates to the Yeti, so they could spoil all your supplies and terrify your monks. Are you going to do what this someone wants?'

Khrisong was silent.

'I am very close to success,' said the Doctor. 'But I still need help.'

They stopped at a junction of corridors. 'If you need my help, you shall have it,' said Khrisong.

The Doctor smiled. 'Thank you. Now if you'll excuse me – I must visit an old friend; one I haven't seen for many years.'

'You go to the Sanctum, Doctor? Do you wish me to accompany you?'

'That won't be necessary, Khrisong. I already know the way.' With a farewell nod, the Doctor set off.

As he walked through the wrecked and deserted Monastery his mind was a ferment of ideas. Padmasambvha, still alive! He must be nearly four hundred years old – an incredible feat, even for a Tibetan master. Padmasambvha was a good man, thought the Doctor. One of the best men I've ever known. Who or what could change him? Lost in thought, the Doctor walked on towards the Inner Sanctum.

In the Sanctum itself, the frail body of Padmasambvha was twisting and writhing on his chair, locked in some terrible inner struggle. 'Oh, Great Intelligence,' he gasped, 'you promised me release, yet still you hold your grip on my old body. Is not your plan complete? Will not the mountain content you ...'

A vision of the cave on the mountain filled the Master's mind. The glutinous living mass still seeped from the pyramid. More and more and more ... it filled the cave ... it was filling the tunnel. When would it stop? How much territory would it cover? 'You said *only* the Mountain for your Experiment,' shrieked Padmasambvha. 'If you do not stop, you will cover the planet. You have lied to me ... tricked me.' The sound of hellish cosmic laughter seemed to fill his ears. The old Master slumped in his chair. In an appalled whisper, he said, 'I have brought the world to its end!'

For some time he sat on the golden throne, his breath only a shallow flutter. Then his mind sensed someone in the Anteroom. He looked at the doors. 'Enter,' he whispered, and the doors opened.

The Doctor walked slowly towards the throne. He looked at the shrunken figure upon it, saddened by the toll the years had taken of his old friend. Padmasambvha had been old when the Doctor first met him – well over a hundred. But he had still been vigorous, clear-skinned and bright-eyed. Now he was a shattered husk of a man, his life prolonged beyond any natural length. But why, the Doctor wondered, and how?

Padmasambvha's voice was a little more than a breath. 'Greetings, Doctor. It is good to see your face after so long.'

The Doctor said quietly, 'What has happened to you, old friend?'

Padmasambvha could speak only with a tremendous effort. 'I have been kept alive,' he whispered feebly. 'I did not know ... did not realise ... Intelligence ... formless ... on the Astral plane ... it wished for form ... substance ... said it was experiment ... long life and knowledge, in return for my help.'

The Doctor leaned forward. The thin reedy voice was scarcely audible. It was as though something was trying to stop the Master from speaking. The thin whisper went on ... 'Refused to let me go ... on and on ... not experiment but conquest!' The last word came out in a sudden gasp.

Then the body of Padmasambvha writhed and twisted. It actually rose in the air and hung suspended. Then it dropped to the chair, limp, like a rag doll.

The Doctor leaned forward urgently. He felt the heart, the pulse, held his magnifying glass before the withered lips to test for breath. Nothing. Grim-faced, the Doctor turned and left the room.

For a moment there was silence. Then suddenly the body of Padmasambvha jerked and twisted. It sat bolt upright on the throne filled with new vigour. The eyes that glared after the Doctor were ablaze with malevolence. The Great Intelligence was back in control.

10

PERIL ON THE MOUNTAIN

Jamie sat uneasily watching the still-motionless Victoria. They were alone. Travers had wandered off somewhere. Jamie had tried speaking to her loudly and commandingly, gently and persuasively, all to no avail. In sudden exasperation, he picked up a stool and slammed it down on the ground just behind her. The stool shattered to pieces. Victoria didn't stir.

'What on earth are you doing, Jamie?' He looked up to see the Doctor in the doorway. Before Jamie could answer, Victoria reacted to the Doctor's voice. 'Doctor, there is great danger! You must take me away! You must take me away! Take me away!' This time there was an added note of sheer hysteria in her voice.

'You've got to do something, Doctor,' said Jamie desperately. 'I've tried everything and she takes no notice at all. She sounds as if she's getting worse!'

The Doctor went over to the bed, and stood over Victoria. He said gently, 'Victoria, my dear—'

This time her voice was a scream of terror. 'Doctor – take me away! Take me away!'

'No, Victoria!' There was a whiplash crack of authority in the Doctor's voice. Victoria stopped her screaming, and gazed up at him in panic … 'Listen to me, Victoria,' said the Doctor firmly. 'You are no longer in the Monastery, you are back in the TARDIS. You are safe, do you understand. Safe in the TARDIS.'

She looked up at him wonderingly. 'Safe?' she whispered.

'Look at me,' murmured the Doctor soothingly. 'You are tired, your eyes are closing, let yourself relax ...'

Victoria's eyes closed and her head nodded. So did Jamie's. The Doctor jabbed him in the ribs. 'Not you, Jamie!'

Jamie came awake with a jerk, grinned sheepishly, and said, 'What now?'

'I've got to try to erase this implanted fear, if I can,' said the Doctor. 'It's increasing all the time.'

'Suppose you can't?' Jamie asked anxiously.

'We'll have to do as she says and take her away. Otherwise she'll go out of her mind.'

Jamie looked at him in horror. 'That's the object of all this,' said the Doctor gently. 'To make sure we leave with the others.'

He snapped his fingers in front of Victoria's face. Her eyes opened. 'Listen, Victoria, you are not in the TARDIS. You are in the cell with Thomni. Do you understand?' Victoria nodded slowly. The Doctor went on in the same compelling tone. 'Jamie and I have come to release you. We have taken you back to the guest room. You have been dozing. You will wake up in a moment, happy but still a little tired. Do you understand?' Again Victoria nodded. She slipped back slowly on to the bed, her eyes closing. She was asleep.

'I've erased the memory of whatever happened after she left the cell,' said the Doctor. 'She should be all right now.'

Jamie looked at him with respect. 'I didna realise you could do that sort of thing, Doctor.'

'I don't *like* to do it, Jamie. It's a serious thing to tamper with the mind. But in an emergency like this ...'

Suddenly Victoria sat up, yawning. She smiled at them. 'I must have dropped off. I am glad you came and got me out of that cell. I was so bored ...'

She turned to Jamie who was staring at her open-mouthed. 'What are you gawping at, Jamie? Anyone would think there was something wrong with me!'

The Doctor chuckled. 'Stay with her, Jamie. I've got work to do.' Gathering up his detection device, he slipped away before Jamie could ask him what he'd discovered.

*

The Doctor found Travers on one of the observation platforms, gazing up the mountainside with his old binoculars. 'They're still up there, Doctor,' he said. 'Look.' He handed over the field glasses.

Peering through them, the Doctor could see several Yeti dotted about the mountainside, motionless and waiting ... 'I must go back up there,' he said softly. 'One more reading and I can track their control source. I could do with some help.'

Travers looked at him uneasily. 'What about the boy?'

'He's staying here to look after Victoria. They'll leave with the monks.'

Travers nodded. 'All right, Doctor, I'm your man. I reckon I owe you something.'

Some time later, the Doctor and Travers were well on the way up the mountainside. They rounded a bend and saw three Yeti guarding the path a little way ahead. The Doctor turned to Travers. 'Now we need to provoke it enough to send out a signal. If you'll take the reading ...' He started to hand over the black box.

Travers shook his head. 'I don't know how that thing works, Doctor. You take the readings and I'll stir 'em up.'

The Doctor looked dubious. 'I don't like to ask you to take the risk ...'

'Rot,' said Travers stoutly, 'I can take care of myself.'

He came out from behind the boulders and marched boldly up to one of the Yeti. It didn't move. 'Boo!' Travers yelled. Still nothing. Then, suddenly, all the Yeti came to life. They started moving forwards. 'Are you getting your readings, Doctor?' yelled Travers, backing away in alarm. He jumped aside, out of their way.

The Doctor, head bent over the flickering dials, did not reply. He seemed oblivious of the little group of Yeti marching straight towards him. 'Look out, Doctor,' Travers yelled. The Yeti marched on, past the Doctor, ignoring him completely. They veered off at a tangent across the mountainside, and disappeared from sight behind some boulders. Travers shook his head. 'Wonder what caused *that*?' he muttered. He went back to the Doctor, who was still studying his dials. 'I said did you get your reading?' he asked. The Doctor nodded, his face worried.

'Yes,' he said, 'I'm afraid I did. We'd better be getting back.'

Followed by a puzzled Travers, the Doctor started scrambling down the path. He was frowning furiously, lost in some very unpleasant thoughts.

Supervised by the Abbot Songtsen, a sad little procession of monks and warriors was assembling in the courtyard. They were bundled up in their warmest robes. The young warriors were making up heavy packs, containing such provisions as they had been able to salvage from the wreckage. Jamie and Victoria stood looking on.

Khrisong entered the courtyard from the Monastery and hurried over to them. 'My warriors have searched every room. There is no sign of the Doctor, or of Travers,' he whispered. Going over to Songtsen he said, 'It is as you wished, my Abbot. Every room in the Monastery is empty.'

'It is well,' said Songtsen gravely. 'I will ask a final blessing of the Master, Padmasambvha, then we shall leave.' He went inside the Monastery.

Victoria frowned. 'Master? Padmasambvha? That sounds ...'

'Dinna think about it,' said Jamie fiercely. 'Think about something else. Anything!'

Victoria looked at him in puzzlement. Luckily there was an immediate distraction. The Doctor and Travers came into the courtyard. Victoria rushed up to the Doctor and hugged him in delight. 'You're back! Where have you been?'

The Doctor disengaged himself with an absent-minded 'There, there,' and went over to Khrisong and Thomni. 'I've found it,' he said urgently. 'Khrisong, I've found the source of the transmissions controlling the Yeti!'

Khrisong indicated the little procession forming up for departure. 'I fear you are too late.'

'You don't understand,' interrupted the Doctor. 'As I suspected all along, it's here, in the Monastery.' He looked at his box. 'It's transmitting now, at this very moment.'

Khrisong looked round. 'But we are all here, in this courtyard ... all but ... the Abbot Songtsen!'

The Doctor nodded. 'I fear so. Now that the Master is dead, he's the only one left.'

'The Master dead?' said Thomni.

The Doctor nodded sadly. 'I should have told you earlier. We'd better find Songtsen.'

'No!' said Khrisong fiercely. 'I will deal with him. It is my right.'

The Doctor looked at him dubiously. 'He too has great powers,' he said.

'He is still my Abbot,' said Khrisong confidently. 'He will not harm me.' He turned and left. The Doctor was worried. Could Khrisong deal with the Abbot? The Doctor knew that if Padmasambvha had been alive, Khrisong wouldn't have stood a chance. But since it was only Songtsen ...

Travers said suddenly, 'Songtsen! He was *with* them. He was with the Yeti on the mountainside. And there was a cave ...'

A look of horror came over Travers' face as memory flooded back to him. Briefly, he described seeing Songtsen escorted by Yeti, and the growing, swelling horror in the cave.

'If Songtsen can control the Yeti, he's more dangerous than I'd thought,' said the Doctor. 'I think I'd better go and help Khrisong.'

Khrisong marched into the Anteroom, a burly, warlike figure, sword in hand. He towered over the frail figure of the Abbot who stood, in an attitude of prayer, before the doors to the Sanctum. 'You must come with me, Lord Abbot,' said Khrisong, gruffly. 'You must come away from this place.'

Songtsen looked up at him with mild surprise. 'What madness is this?'

'The Doctor has discovered your guilt,' said Khrisong. 'You must answer to the brethren for your crimes.'

He seized the Abbot as if to drag him away by force. Then a voice spoke out of the air. 'Khrisong!'

Khrisong glared round. 'Padmasambvha. The Doctor told us you were dead.'

'I am deathless, Khrisong.' There was a cold gloating note in the voice.

'Do not try to frighten me. I demand to know what is happening here!'

Songtsen was appalled. 'Demand, Khrisong? You are in the presence of the Master.'

'A Master of the Yeti?' demanded Khrisong. 'A Master who has destroyed his own monastery?'

Songtsen turned towards the closed door. 'Forgive him, oh Master.'

'Of course,' said the cold voice. 'But our brother must not depart thinking that I am other than I am. Bring him to me, Songtsen!'

Songtsen said tonelessly, 'I obey, master.' Looking down at him, Khrisong saw that the Abbot seemed almost in a state of trance, his eyes staring sightlessly ahead.

'What is this?' he growled suspiciously.

The doors to the Sanctum swung open. 'You may enter,' said Songtsen. 'But give me your sword. You may not go armed into the presence of Padmasambvha.'

Khrisong hesitated. 'Do you fear us, Khrisong?' asked the voice. 'We are two old men!'

Khrisong handed over his sword. He went towards the doors. Songtsen, the sword in his hands, was behind him.

Khrisong stopped cautiously on the threshold to the Sanctum. He peered through the gloom at the figure on the throne. His eyes widened in awe. 'Padmasambvha,' he whispered. 'So you are not dead!'

'No, my son, but you are,' said the cold voice.

Behind Khrisong, Songtsen raised the sword, and thrust with savage force. Khrisong gasped and wheeled round. His eyes, filled with pain and unbelief, fixed on those of his Abbot. Khrisong took a couple of tottering steps forward and collapsed. The doors to the Sanctum swung to.

In the Sanctum, the body of Padmasambvha writhed on the throne. For a moment a different voice emerged from the withered lips, as the personality of the real Padmasambvha broke through. 'Why do you make me do this? Release me, I beg of you …'

Then, as the Intelligence reasserted its control, the cold voice filled the room. 'You have done well, Songtsen. Take the monks from the Monastery, and never return.'

In the Anteroom, Songtsen said, 'I obey, master.' He was about to leave when the Doctor, Thomni and Jamie rushed into the room. They found him standing over Khrisong's body, the bloodstained sword in his hands.

The little group stopped at the threshold, appalled. 'Lord Abbot!' called Thomni in horror. He rushed to kneel by Khrisong's body.

Songtsen looked down in horror. 'What has happened? Who has slain Khrisong?' he asked.

Thomni looked up. 'You killed him, you!' he sobbed.

Songtsen looked in utter amazement at the bloody sword in his hands ... 'I?' he said wonderingly.

A cold voice filled the room. 'Slay them, Songtsen. Slay them all!'

The blankness of trance came over Songtsen's face and he raised the sword. 'Kill! Kill! Kill!' he hissed.

'Look out!' yelled the Doctor. He dodged the blow and grabbed the Abbot's sword arm.

Despite his modest size, the Doctor could exert amazing strength when he needed to. But he was helpless in Songtsen's grip. The frail old body was vibrating with supernatural force. Thomni and Jamie, both young and strong, joined in the struggle. It took every ounce of their combined strengths to subdue the Abbot and wrench the sword from his hands. Suddenly Songtsen slumped in their grip. The Doctor stood back panting. 'Get him out of here,' he gasped. 'Quickly!'

Jamie and Thomni dragged the Abbot away. The Doctor looked grimly at the closed doors to the Sanctum. 'I was wrong, then,' he thought grimly. 'Whatever is controlling Padmasambvha will not let him die!'

The Doctor turned and left, and the Anteroom was filled with the mad, icy laughter of the Intelligence.

As the Doctor walked along the corridor he met an excited Travers. 'You'd better come at once, Doctor. There's going to be a riot!'

198

11

THE FINAL BATTLE

A confused and angry crowd filled the courtyard. They surrounded Jamie and Thomni, and the frightened and confused Songtsen. 'Indeed, it is true, brothers,' Thomni was shouting. 'Khrisong *was* slain by the Abbot. But Songtsen was under an evil spell, placed on him by the Master.'

One of the young warrior monks thrust himself to the front of the crowd. 'Tell us it is not so, my Abbot,' he implored.

For a moment Songtsen gazed at him uncomprehendingly. Then, grabbing the still bloody sword from Thomni's hand he hissed, 'Kill! Kill! Kill!' and swung the sword at the astonished monk. Once again it took the combined efforts of several strong young warriors to hold down the frail body. Then the fit was over and the Abbot went limp.

A roar of fear and terror rose from the crowd. 'He is bewitched,' they shouted. 'He is possessed by demons. Slay him now before he kills us all.' Another warrior stepped forward, sword raised high above Songtsen's head. Ignoring the weapon, Jamie gave the man a hearty shove that sent him staggering back into the crowd.

'I'm thinking we've had enough killing,' he said grimly. 'Stand back!'

'Do not interfere, stranger,' said the monk angrily, and the warriors began to close in. Jamie slipped the highland dagger from his stocking, and shoved the Abbot behind him.

'Wait, my brothers,' called Thomni, but the warriors would not listen.

As the Doctor entered the courtyard with Travers, he took in the ugly situation at a glance. In times of crisis, his normally modest and unassuming personality took on a new force.

'Stop this nonsense at once,' he ordered, pushing through the crowd.

'Your Abbot is not responsible for his crime. Neither for that matter is the Master, Padmasambvha. Both are being controlled by a greater force.'

The monks fell silent. 'What must we do, Doctor?' asked old Sapan.

'Leave the Monastery. There is great evil here. One day soon, if I am successful, you will be able to return.'

'The Doctor is right, my brethren,' shouted Thomni. 'Let us obey him and leave now!'

There was a murmur of agreement. Their anger subsiding, the confused and frightened monks began to gather up their belongings. Thomni said, 'And what of you, Doctor?'

'I shall stay here,' said the Doctor simply. 'If this evil isn't stopped it will spread ... And the root of it is here, in this Monastery.'

'Well, if you're staying, I'm staying too,' said Victoria firmly.

'Aye, and me!' added Jamie.

'I too will stay and help you, if I may, Doctor,' said Thomni.

The Doctor smiled. 'Thank you, all of you. It may be dangerous, but I won't pretend I'm not glad of your help.'

'What's the first step?' asked Jamie.

'There are things I need to know,' said the Doctor thoughtfully. 'And Songtsen is the only one who can tell me.'

'How will you make him do that, Doctor?' asked Thomni. 'His mind is controlled.'

The Doctor sighed. 'There's more than one kind of control, Thomni. Let's take him inside, shall we?'

Travers walked slowly back to his room. He was convinced that, for all his cleverness, the Doctor was wrong. The source of the evil wasn't some old monk in the Monastery, it was the evil throbbing mass in that cave up the mountain.

There was nothing Travers wanted less than to see that cave again. But he reckoned it was up to him. He picked up his rifle and loaded it. He'd blast that pyramid thing with a clip full of bullets, and see if that stopped it.

Unnoticed by the busy monks, Travers slipped out of the gate and began climbing up the mountain path. It was getting dark now. For a moment he stopped, and looked back longingly at the lights of the Monastery. Then, he began to climb the path, dreading what he might find at the end of his journey.

In the Great Hall, the Abbot Songtsen sat on a high-backed stone chair. His eyes were wide open and he stared unseeingly ahead of him. But this time, the voice he heard and obeyed came not from Padmasambvha, but from the Doctor.

'What about the robots, the false Yeti?' the Doctor was prompting.

'They were designed to serve the Intelligence. Their purpose was to frighten all travellers and pilgrims from Det-sen, lest they hinder the Great Plan.'

'And just what is this plan?' the Doctor asked.

'At first the Intelligence said that it wished only to create substance for itself – as an experiment. It wanted only the cave. Then it demanded the whole mountain. The Monastery, too. Its appetite is insatiable. It seeks to overwhelm the whole world.'

The Doctor remembered Travers' description of the glowing, ever-growing mass in the cave. He had a sudden horrific vision of the whole Earth, hanging in space, one heaving, pulsating mass. And what then? Suppose it travelled through space. All the planets in the Universe could be under threat. The Doctor shivered. Somehow he had to stop it.

'Tell me, Songtsen,' he said. 'How are the Yeti controlled?

'By Padmasambvha.'

'What about the control units? Where did they come from?'

'Under the guidance of the Intelligence, the Master laboured for nearly three hundred years. He made the control units, the Yeti, all the other wonderful machines …'

'But there still has to be some kind of master transmitter,' insisted the Doctor. 'The power source that amplifies the commands of Padmasambvha's mind. Where is it?'

Songtsen said, 'It is in the Sanctum.'

The Doctor was puzzled. 'I've been in the Sanctum, very briefly, it's true, but I saw nothing.'

'There is a secret room …'

'Where is it, Songtsen? How do we get in there?'

There was no reply. The Abbot sat staring into space.

The Doctor leaned forward, his voice commanding. 'How do we reach the secret room, Songtsen? You must tell us. You *must* tell us ...'

In the Inner Sanctum the body of Padmasambvha jerked into life as the Intelligence took over. The withered hand hovered over the board, picked up a Yeti and moved it down towards the Monastery.

Out on the mountain, in the fast-gathering dark, Travers plodded on, rifle in hand. Not that he really expected the weapon would do him any good against a Yeti. It was just that its presence gave him a certain comfort.

He heard the sound of huge shuffling feet ahead of him and dropped into cover. Two Yeti lumbered past, then another and another. Making for the Monastery, thought Travers. He hoped those poor devils of monks had got safely away. And what about that fellow, the Doctor? What were his plans?

Travers got to his feet and started to move on. As he climbed he became aware of something very strange. On the lower slopes of the mountain, it had been getting darker and darker as the night drew on. But now that he was actually getting closer to the cave it seemed to be getting lighter. It was as though the entire mountain was somehow glowing.

The strange light continued to increase. Then as he came within sight of the cave, Travers understood why. The cave itself was the source of the light.

The pulsating, glowing mass of the Intelligence's physical form was flooding out of the cave at an absolutely incredible rate. Spreading out from the cave, it seemed to be seeping into and absorbing the very substance of the mountain.

It was moving in both directions, upwards as if to consume the topmost peak of the mountain, and downwards too. If it went on spreading it would eventually ooze down the mountain slopes and engulf the entire Monastery.

Travers realised the foolishness of his plan to attack the pyramid in the cave. There was nothing he could do against the kind of power that was exultantly displayed here. Perhaps the Doctor had been right all along. Perhaps the Monastery did hold the key to it all. Travers remembered the Yeti he had seen trooping down the mountainside. With a sudden sense of urgency, he began to run back down the path.

In the Great Hall, the Doctor handed Songtsen over to the care of the old lama Sapan, who was now the leader of the monks. 'I have done my best to erase the memory of evil from his mind,' said the Doctor. 'But he will be troubled for a long time. He has suffered much.'

'We will care for him, Doctor,' promised Sapan. Two other lamas gently led the old Abbot out of the hall.

The Doctor turned to those left behind – Thomni, Jamie and Victoria. 'Now remember,' he said. 'As soon as *all* the monks and lamas are safely away, we'll have to make our attack on the control room of the Intelligence. You two lads have got to smash up the equipment. Whatever you find in there, wreck it utterly and completely, do you understand?' The two young men nodded.

'I thought these would be useful,' said Thomni. He produced a pair of long, heavy, iron-tipped staffs. Jamie took one and swung it appreciatively.

'Aye,' he said happily, 'that ought to do it.'

'It won't be any picnic,' warned the Doctor. 'The Intelligence has supernormal powers and it will use them all.'

'What kind of powers?' asked Victoria nervously.

'Well, it'll probably try to hypnotise you,' said the Doctor. 'Thomni, you teach her the "jewel in the lotus" prayer. That'll give her something to concentrate on …'

Their conference was interrupted by a chorus of shouts and screams from outside. Led by the Doctor, they rushed outside to see what was wrong.

In the courtyard the procession was ready to move off. But all the monks were gazing upwards, at the mountain. 'Look, Doctor,' called Sapan. 'The mountain is burning.'

The Doctor looked. The night was now so dark, and the flowing substance from the cave had now spread so far, that it could be clearly seen from the Monastery. It seemed as though the whole peak of the mountain was glowing and burning. And the glow was moving downwards.

The Doctor turned quickly to Sapan. 'There is even less time than I feared. You must lead your brethren away at once.'

Obediently the old lama began to give orders. The warrior monks marshalled the procession into line. They began to hand out torches for the steep climb down to the lower valley.

'Our brethren in the plains will give us shelter,' said Sapan. 'But I fear for you, Doctor. Will you not let our brave warriors stay and help you?'

'They are needed to guard you and your fellow lamas, Sapan,' replied the Doctor. 'Thomni is staying with me – he will be all the help I need.' The Doctor thought to himself that if the few of them couldn't succeed, a larger party would do no better. 'Go now, Sapan,' he said.

The little procession began to wind its way out of the courtyard and down the path. Standing by the doors, the Doctor and his companions watched the line of torches disappear into the darkness. Floating up to them came the sound of monks chanting the 'jewel in the lotus' prayer that Thomni had just taught Victoria.

'Om, mane, padme, hum.' The sound was curiously moving and beautiful.

At last the lights died away, the sounds faded and they were left alone. Victoria shivered. How strange and eerie to be the sole inhabitants of the Monastery! Except, that is, for whatever was lurking in the Sanctum.

'Will we shut the doors, Doctor?' asked Jamie.

The Doctor shrugged. 'No point, Jamie. We're fighting something inside as well as outside.' He glanced grimly up at the glowing, burning mountain for the last time, and led them back inside the Monastery.

As the little party disappeared inside the building, there was movement outside the doors. Yeti appeared from the darkness. Grouped in a semicircle, they stood waiting outside the gates.

Back in the Great Hall, the Doctor gave his companions a final briefing. 'As soon as we're in the control room, I'll tackle the Intelligence. Thomni and Jamie, move away the statue of Buddha at the end of the room. Get inside there and—'

'Aye, you've told us,' said Jamie. 'Smash the lot to bits!' He and Thomni picked up their massive, iron-tipped staffs. Jamie spun his, whistling it through the air.

'What about me?' asked Victoria. 'What do I do?'

'Nothing, I hope,' said the Doctor briskly. 'But you never know. Something may turn up.'

He hadn't the heart to tell Victoria she was only being included in the expedition because she would find it even more frightening to be left on her own. Moreover, win or lose, she'd be as safe with them as she would anywhere.

'Everybody ready?' asked the Doctor. 'Right, off we go.'

As they moved cautiously along the gloomy corridors, Jamie had a sudden thought.

'Hey, what happened to yon fellow Travers? I havena seen him.'

'Maybe he's deserted us,' suggested Victoria.

'I somehow doubt it,' said the Doctor. 'More likely he's gone off on some scheme of his own.'

'Well, he's no' here now, at any rate,' said Jamie. 'We'll just have to manage without him!' By the light of their flickering torches they crept forward along the echoing stone corridors towards the Inner Sanctum.

Travers, in fact, was very near. He was running full tilt down the last stretch of the path towards the Monastery. Far below him in the darkness he could see the torch-lit procession of the departing monks, and even hear their chanting.

As he came to the gates of the Monastery, Travers came to a sudden halt.

Standing grouped in a semicircle around the door was a group of Yeti – four of them. He wondered if they were activated or not. He picked up a big rock and rolled it towards them. Instantly all the Yeti swung round, alert to the movement. They were alive all right, thought Travers. Alive and waiting. There was nothing for it – he would have to wait, too.

Glancing back over his shoulder, he saw that the glowing mass was covering more and more of the mountain. It was moving nearer and nearer to the Monastery. Soon he would *have* to leave. Yet somehow, Travers felt that things were coming to a climax. He decided to wait as long as he could. Those Yeti were waiting for something, too.

*

The Doctor and his friends stopped in the corridor outside the Anteroom. 'Everyone remember what to do?' asked the Doctor. They all nodded. Jamie and Thomni took a firmer grip of their staves. 'All right,' said the Doctor. 'In we go!'

Their actual entrance into the Anteroom was something of an anti-climax. All was still and quiet. The prayer lamps were burning low and the place was shrouded in gloom and silence. Led by the Doctor, the little group moved forward.

The Doctor went up to the doors of the Inner Sanctum. He tried them, but they were fast closed. Suddenly, the voice of the Intelligence spoke to them, out of the air. There was a subtle change in its quality. It was harsher, colder, more inhuman, the traces of Padmasambvha's personality almost completely erased.

'Why are you here?' the voice said. 'Why do you not heed my warnings? You are stubborn, Doctor.'

'Who are you?' said the Doctor steadily. 'Or should I rather ask – what are you?'

A terrible mock-sweetness came into the alien voice. 'You know me well, Doctor. Am I not your old and treasured friend, Padmasambvha?'

'No!' said the Doctor. 'No, you are not. You have captured his spirit and abused his body. You have taken the mind and being of a good and great man, and corrupted and abused it. I ask again, who are you? Where do you come from?'

'I come from what you would call another dimension. I was exiled into yours, without physical substance; condemned to hover eternally between the stars. Then I made contact with the mind of Padmasambvha. He had journeyed further on the mental plane than any other of your kind. I tempted him, promised him knowledge and long life. Gradually I took him over, and made him my own. But I have rewarded him well.'

'You have enslaved him,' said the Doctor angrily. 'Now you withhold from him the one thing he craves – the boon of a natural death. You are evil. You are what men once called a demon!'

Jamie, Thomni and Victoria waited motionless behind the Doctor while this exchange was going on. 'It's all verra well standing here name-calling,' thought Jamie. 'How's he going to get the thing to open the door?'

Similar thoughts were passing through the Doctor's mind. His one hope was that the Intelligence had not realised that the power of Hypnotism was shared by the Doctor. So long as it was unaware of the extent and the value of the information he had drawn from the mind of Songtsen, they still had a fighting chance.

'You are unwise to anger me, Doctor,' said the voice. 'My purposes are beyond the understanding of such a puny brain as yours. And I have power. Much power ...'

The Doctor made his voice deliberately contemptuous. 'You? Much power?'

Suddenly, one of the heavy bronze lamps flared up in a sheet of flame. It whizzed through the air like a cannon ball, missing the Doctor's head by inches, and crashed into the wall. The three others gasped in terror, but the Doctor didn't turn a hair.

'A little simple teleportation?' he said scornfully. 'Are you going to keep us here watching conjuring tricks? What next? Rabbits out of hats?'

'Aye, you're a cunning wee fellow, Doctor,' thought Jamie. 'Playing on its vanity. I hope it works. If we canna get into that Sanctum, we're done for.'

'Why don't you open those doors?' the Doctor said mockingly. 'Afraid to face us, are you?'

There was a moment of silence. Then slowly the doors swung open. The Doctor turned round to his companions.

'Anything may happen now. Anything at all. Trust me. And, above all – don't panic.' Slowly he led them through the doors and into the Inner Sanctum.

Once inside, Jamie and Thomni looked in astonishment at the golden throne. The drapes were pulled now, obscuring it, but they could still see the little figure crouched over his table. A memory of some old fear passed through Victoria's mind, but she pushed it aside. She began to repeat the prayer that Thomni had taught her.

'Om, mane, padme, hum, om, mane, padme, hum.' She repeated the soothing words over and over.

Jamie looked at the little figure almost with pity. 'Och, is that all?' he thought. 'You could blow the wee fellow away with a sneeze.' Then, before he could move another step toward the dais, his whole body was caught by some terrifying invisible force.

He literally could not move a muscle. Thomni and Victoria were held in the same way. So too, it seemed, was the Doctor. Or was he? Slowly, with infinite effort, the Doctor managed to take first one step and then another. He directed the entire force of his will towards the little shrouded figure on the golden chair. The build-up of energy in the little room was overpowering. Suddenly, the blast of a mighty wind ripped through the room, sweeping away the draperies around the throne. Padmasambvha was revealed sitting bolt upright, eyes blazing with malignancy.

'Now!' yelled the Doctor. 'Now!'

Jamie felt the grip on him slacken. He saw that the Doctor was standing in a half-crouch, one foot on the steps of the dais. His eyes were locked with those of the wizened figure on the throne. The effort required to do battle with the will of the Intelligence was distorting his face.

'Come on, Thomni,' yelled Jamie. 'Let's get to work.'

They ran to the golden statue of Buddha and swung it aside, following the instructions from Songtsen. The entrance to the hidden control room was revealed. But before they could enter, a high-pitched sound filled the room. Blinding lights flickered before their eyes. Jamie saw that the Doctor was sinking slowly to his knees. Then, with agonising slowness, the Doctor began to straighten up. His eyes fixed on those of the possessed Master, he took another step forward. A low ghastly moan filled the room as the Intelligence realised the strength of the mind that was opposing it.

'Come on, Thomni,' yelled Jamie. The two young men dashed into the secret control room. It was bare, and very small. All the walls were covered with an incredible tangle of equipment, of all ages and in all conditions – a mad, lunatic lash-up of electronics. At one end of the room a plain metal pyramid reposed on an altar. At the other end a glowing sphere, larger even than the ones which Jamie and Victoria had seen in the cave, caught their attention.

For a moment the two young men stood amazed. Then Jamie heard a strangled shout from the Doctor.

'Hurry, Jamie, hurry. Can't hold out much ...'

Jamie raised his staff and smashed it down on a control panel. Thomni did the same. They worked frantically with great sweeping blows. Soon the entire control room was well on the way to being wrecked.

Outside in the Sanctum, Victoria watched as the Doctor waged his battle of wills with the Intelligence. She sensed a deadlock. Neither could afford the slightest distraction. Then to her horror she saw the withered hand of Padmasambvha creeping out towards the board.

'Look out, Doctor,' she called. 'He's going to bring the Yeti in.'

The Doctor redoubled his concentration, but he was unable to stop the movement of the hand. One by one, four of the Yeti models were placed on the map of the Monastery.

Outside the Monastery doors, Travers saw four of the Yeti move swiftly inside. Once they were under way, he started to follow them.

The Yeti seemed to move at a far greater speed than normal. As if impelled by some signal of great urgency, they rushed along the corridors, Travers trailing cautiously behind them.

Inside the Sanctum, the Doctor was still locked in struggle with the Intelligence. Like two wrestlers of exactly even strength, neither of them could move.

But the Doctor knew that the alien strength of the Intelligence would soon wear him down. And once he weakened, all would be over ... They would all die.

Victoria watched helplessly. From inside the hidden control room came the sound of smashing equipment. Jamie and Thomni were going about their task with savage gusto. Then, from the corridor she heard the sound of roaring. The Yeti were coming!

'Victoria – get the models ...' gasped the Doctor. 'Move them back ...'

Victoria forced herself to go forward to the table. But the strength of the Intelligence's will was too much for her. Even locked in struggle with the Doctor, it stopped her from reaching the models.

'Resist it,' urged the Doctor. 'Say the prayer!'

Victoria tried. 'Om, mane, padme, hum. Om, mane, padme, hum …' But it was no use. She could *not* move her hand. And then it was too late. The Yeti burst into the room. As they lumbered towards him, the Doctor managed to yell, 'Jamie, Yeti … here …'

In the control room, Jamie and Thomni looked at each other.

'We have smashed all that controls them,' said Thomni. Jamie looked round.

'Aye, except this,' he said, and moved towards the sphere on the altar. Raising his staff above his head, he brought it smashing down on the sphere.

A Yeti, its arm drawn back to attack the Doctor, staggered back with a roar. There was an explosion from somewhere inside it, and it reeled away smoking, a hole blown in its chest. The control unit had exploded. The same happened to all its companions. They collapsed, shattered wrecks, on the floor.

The voice of the Intelligence said, 'You have destroyed my servants, but you have not destroyed me!'

Travers rushed into the room. Raising his rifle, he emptied the whole magazine into the figure on the throne.

It brushed its hand across its face as though swatting a fly, and then held out the hand. In it lay the spent bullets. The Intelligence gave its terrible laugh. 'Oh foolish man,' it said. 'Did you not realise my power in the cave?'

The cave, thought the Doctor with the part of his mind that was still free. What did Travers tell me about the cave? Raising his voice, he yelled, 'Jamie, is there a pyramid in there?'

'Aye, there is that!' Jamie called back.

'Then smash it. Smash it now!'

In the control room Jamie and Thomni lashed with all their force at the pyramid. Suddenly it shattered into fragments as though made of glass.

Padmasambvha's body gave out a last terrible scream.

From somewhere outside came a series of rumbling explosions that shook the building. The cave in the mountain had exploded.

The body on the throne gave a sudden leap, falling from the throne. It landed across the little table, knocking it to the ground. With a final convulsive twitch, the Intelligence left it.

The Doctor lifted the shrivelled body in his arms. Worn out by years of slavery, it was almost weightless. Suddenly Padmasambvha's eyes opened. He saw the Doctor looking down at him, and smiled.

Victoria realised that, for the first time, they were seeing the real Padmasambvha, free of the Intelligence. When he spoke, his voice was warm and gentle, the voice of a wise old man.

'At last, I shall have peace … I waited so long, Doctor. I knew you would come, and save me from myself …'

The old man's head fell back.

'Goodbye, old friend,' said the Doctor, and lowered the frail body to the ground. Jamie and Thomni emerged from the control room.

'It worked,' said the Doctor. 'The Intelligence is destroyed. My old friend Padmasambvha can rest at last.'

They all walked slowly from the Sanctum, and made their way back to the courtyard.

'Look,' said Travers, and pointed. They all looked up. The glow had gone from the mountain. The explosion in the cave had destroyed the physical being of the Intelligence.

'Yes,' said the Doctor. 'It's really over at last.' He yawned and stretched.

'You know, I think I could do with some sleep.'

12

THE ABOMINABLE
SNOWMAN

Next morning, as the Doctor, Jamie, Victoria and Travers came out into the courtyard, they were greeted by a deafening clang. Thomni was solemnly banging an enormous gong. 'What on earth are you doing?' asked Victoria, her hands over her ears.

'It is the hour for morning prayer, Miss Victoria,' explained Thomni.

Victoria frowned. 'But there's no one here but you.'

'All the more reason that I should strictly observe the rituals, until my brothers return,' said Thomni. 'They will hear the gong and know that all is well.'

'Time we all said goodbye, I'm afraid,' said the Doctor.

Thomni looked disappointed. 'Can you not stay until my brethren return? They will wish to thank you.'

'I'm afraid not,' said the Doctor hastily. 'You see, I'm worried about my equipment. It might have been damaged when the top of the mountain exploded.'

Thomni looked at the mountain. It was now quite a different shape at the top, part of the upper peak having been blown away. 'Very well then, Doctor. Goodbye and thank you again.' After more farewells, Travers said, 'I'll see you safely up the mountain, Doctor!'

Nothing they could say would dissuade him, and they all set off up the mountain path together. Looking back, they could see that once again the doors of Det-sen Monastery stood wide and welcoming. Victoria just caught a fleeting glimpse of Thomni setting off for prayers in a one-man procession. She smiled. He really had been very nice. But very solemn.

Jamie came up close to the Doctor and whispered, 'You're not really worried about the TARDIS, are you, Doctor?'

The Doctor shook his head. 'The TARDIS is indestructible, Jamie, you know that. No, I just thought it was time we were leaving.'

Jamie indicated Travers, who was happily marching on ahead.

'What about him, Doctor? The TARDIS will be a bit of a shock to him.'

'I know,' said the Doctor. 'That's been worrying me rather. But he won't take any hints!'

There came a shout from Travers. He had stopped, and was waving to them. 'Look at this!' The shattered body of a Yeti lay across the path. 'Its chest unit must have exploded at the same time as those in the Sanctum,' said Jamie.

'Wonderful machines, those,' said the Doctor. 'Almost a shame to have destroyed them. Something for you to take back from your expedition at any rate, Mr Travers.'

Travers sighed. 'They'd only say it was a fake. If they won't believe in the real Yeti, they certainly wouldn't credit what's happened here.'

Walking round the shattered robot, they went on. 'You really needn't trouble to come with us any further, Mr Travers,' said the Doctor.

'Ay, that's right,' agreed Jamie eagerly. 'No doubt you'll want to be off hunting your beasties!'

'I'm thinking of giving all that up,' said Travers gloomily. 'I'm only getting myself laughed at. Wretched thing's probably only a legend anyway.'

'Don't give up, whatever you do,' urged the Doctor. 'It's a splendid thing to have a dream … even if it does turn out to be a legend.'

'Maybe,' said Travers, but he didn't sound convinced. 'Let's get on,' he suggested. 'I'm looking forward to seeing this camp of yours.'

The Doctor and his companions exchanged glances, and they all walked on. The journey became more difficult now as they climbed higher. The explosion at the cave had thrown down rocks and boulders which covered the path, and they had to clamber over and round them. 'Much further, is it?' puffed Travers.

The Doctor shook his head resignedly. 'Not far. Once we get through that clump of boulders we'll be there.'

A few minutes later, Travers was staring in utter amazement at the old blue police box perched incongruously on a mountain ledge. 'My word,' he said. 'What the blazes is that doing here?'

The Doctor cleared his throat. 'Well, as a matter of fact, Mr Travers,' he began. There came a sudden scream from Victoria. 'Look – another Yeti. It's moving.'

'That's impossible!' said the Doctor. They all looked where she was pointing. Not far away, behind some boulders, a creature was peering shyly at them.

'It's different!' said Victoria. 'Not like the others at all!' And so it was. It was taller and less bulky. The fur was longer and silkier, and had a more reddish tint. Above all, the face was different, rather like that of a lemur, with dark, soft eyes. Travers was looking at it entranced. 'Don't you see?' he said. 'It's a Yeti. It's a real Yeti, not some wretched robot. I've found it. I've found it at last!'

Travers began stumbling towards the Yeti, across the mountain slope. For a moment the creature watched him approach. Then it gave a curiously high-pitched squeal of fright and disappeared behind a boulder. Travers broke into a run, and soon he too had disappeared from view.

'I rather think this is our opportunity,' said the Doctor. 'No need to worry about Mr Travers' reaction to the TARDIS. By now he's forgotten its existence.'

'Do you think he'll catch his Yeti, Doctor?' asked Victoria.

'That doesn't really matter,' said the Doctor gently. 'The important thing is, he's found his dream again.'

Jamie shivered. 'Let's be away then, Doctor,' he said. 'It's no' a bad place, this Tibet of yours, but it's awful chilly. Next time you want to visit some old friends, can you no' make it somewhere warmer?'

'Honestly, Jamie, you're always grumbling,' said Victoria. 'Anyway, you know the Doctor's got no idea where the TARDIS will finish up next.'

'That's most unfair, Victoria,' protested the Doctor. 'There may be the occasional navigational error, but basically I am fully in control – well, more or less.'

Wrangling amiably the three companions walked across the snow and disappeared inside the TARDIS. After a moment, a strange groaning noise echoed through the mountain air, and the old blue police box shimmered and vanished. The Doctor and his friends were off on their next adventure.

DOCTOR WHO THE WHEEL IN SPACE

1

GOODBYE TO VICTORIA

Victoria was waving goodbye.

She looked very small on the TARDIS's monitor screen, lost and alone on the wide stretch of empty beach.

Two very different figures stood gazing sadly at the monitor screen. One was that wandering Time Lord known as the Doctor, a rather shabby little figure in frock coat and baggy check trousers. His deeply lined face, which could look young or old, wise or foolish, was crowned with a mop of untidy black hair. Beside him stood a brawny young man in the kilt of a Scottish Highlander. This was James Robert McCrimmon – Jamie for short. Like Victoria, Jamie had been the Doctor's companion through a number of dangerous and terrifying adventures.

Now Victoria was leaving them and Jamie was taking it hard. Somehow it didn't make things any better that Victoria was leaving them of her own accord. She had had all the adventure and excitement she could take and she had decided to stay behind on Earth with a family who would be glad to adopt her as their daughter.

Somehow Jamie just couldn't accept it. 'We can't just – leave her, Doctor.'

'We're not leaving her, Jamie. It was her decision to stay,' the Doctor said reassuringly. 'She'll be happy with the Harrises, don't worry.'

Jamie hated showing his feelings. 'I'm no' worrying, I'm just – och, get us away from here, will ye?'

'All right,' said the Doctor obligingly. He moved over to the many-sided central control column. 'Where would you like to go?'

Theoretically, all space and time were available to them.

Theoretically.

In practice, as Jamie well knew, the combination of the TARDIS's erratic navigational circuitry and the Doctor's even more erratic steering, meant they were liable to fetch up almost anywhere – and anywhen, come to that.

But for once this suited Jamie fine. 'I couldna care less!' The Doctor gave him a sympathetic look. 'I was fond of her too, you know, Jamie.'

His hands moved over the controls and moments later the central column of the control panel began its rise and fall. The TARDIS was about to take off.

On the beach, the incongruous square blue shape of the police box gave out a strange wheezing, groaning sound and faded slowly away.

Victoria looked on sadly, her eyes filling with tears …

On the monitor screen her figure grew even smaller, receding into the distance.

The Doctor switched off the monitor and turned away.

It was some time later before the rising and falling of the centre column began slowing down.

The Doctor looked up from the controls. 'We're landing, Jamie!'

There was no reply.

The Doctor turned and saw Jamie fast asleep in his chair. Like the good fighting man he was, Jamie took every opportunity for a nap.

'Jamie! We're landing!'

Jamie blinked. 'Mmm? What?'

'Let's see what's on the scanner shall we?'

The Doctor switched on the screen, but it remained blank. He frowned and jiggled the switch.

Still nothing.

'I thought you said we'd landed,' said Jamie grumpily.

'We have – but we seem to have lost the picture.' The Doctor flicked another switch. 'Let's try a bit of extra power, shall we?'

Nothing happened.

'You're sure you're using the right one?' asked Jamie sceptically.

The Doctor was indignant. 'Of course I am! Just take a look at the fault indicator, will you? Just there to your right.'

Jamie opened the lid of a small black box built into the console. Inside he saw an oscillation meter, its glowing lines pulsing in a regular pattern. It meant absolutely nothing to him. 'Seems right enough,' he said hopefully.

The Doctor glanced at the meter. 'Yes, no abnormal movement at all. I don't understand it.' He checked the other dials. 'Air normal, temperature normal ... seems to be quite an amount of metal all around us ...'

'What's that, Doctor? I canna hear ye when you mumble to yourself.'

Suddenly the Doctor caught sight of the monitor screen. 'Look, the picture's coming through again.'

There on the monitor was a beautiful lake and as they watched a flock of cranes rose lazily from its surface and flew gracefully away.

Jamie cheered up. 'Och, that looks all right.'

The picture changed and now they were looking at a waterfall, its cascading waters gleaming in the moonlight.

The Doctor frowned. 'That's funny, it's changed to night now.'

'That's a wee bit quick, surely?' muttered Jamie.

The picture changed again. Now they saw a tropical island, white sands, waving palms, all set in a bright blue sea.

'Och, now the whole place is different. What's going on?'

'Oh dear, I know what it is,' said the Doctor suddenly. 'Those pictures aren't of the outside world at all, I'm certain of it!'

'Then why are they appearing?'

'Temptations, Jamie. The TARDIS is telling us to leave wherever we are and go to somewhere more pleasant. I must have connected the automatic defence network by mistake.'

'And what's that?'

'One of the optional extras built into this particular model. I don't often use it; it's a perfect nuisance to be honest.'

'What does it do?'

'Well, if there's danger outside it tries to warn us – or as in this case, to tempt us – into going somewhere else.'

'That's guid enough,' said Jamie. 'Let's go!'

The Doctor sighed. 'Jamie, if I took any notice of that silly gadget, we'd never even leave the TARDIS. It's so *fussy*. That's why I usually disconnect it.'

'No wonder we always end up in trouble!'

The Doctor was struggling with the switch that would turn the automatic defence network off, but it refused to budge. 'Oh dear, now I can't seem to move it. Where's my spanner ... ?'

Jamie glanced casually at the fault indicator – its lid was still open – and his eyes widened. 'Hey! There's a light flashing ...' The Doctor looked. Sure enough an alarm-light was flashing wildly, and the lines on the oscillation meter were pulsing furiously. 'Something's gone wrong,' said Jamie worriedly.

The Doctor wrinkled his nose and sniffed. Tracing the acrid reek to its source, he saw wisps of smoke coming from the control console. 'There's too much power ...' He rushed to the main power switch and tried to thrust it back. It refused to budge, and Jamie came to help him. Suddenly there was a bang and a flash and a cloud of smoke and the Doctor and Jamie were hurled across the control room. They struggled to their feet. By now it was obvious that something was badly wrong.

The central column was rising and falling rapidly, and lights were blinking on and off all over the console. The TARDIS's usually inaudible electronic hum had turned into a steadily rising shriek.

'The fluid links must have gone,' muttered the Doctor.

Jamie pointed to the base of the central column. 'Look, Doctor!'

The Doctor saw a silvery fluid leaking from the base of the column. 'The mercury's vaporising!' As if to confirm his theory, Jamie coughed and clutched at his throat. 'Doctor!' he gasped.

Now they really were in trouble, thought the Doctor. Mercury vapour was a deadly poison. 'We've got to get out of here.'

'How?' croaked Jamie.

The Doctor took his arm and led him to the TARDIS doors. He touched a concealed button and a little panel slid back in the wall. Behind it, clamped to the wall, was a golden rod, black at either end.

'Hold on to me, Jamie,' ordered the Doctor.

'What are you going to do?'

'Just hold on!'

Jamie enfolded the Doctor in a kind of awkward bear-hug, and the Doctor reached out and pulled the gold rod away from its fitting.

Jamie heard a sound like a rushing wind and the control room seemed to swirl around him. It began pulsing in and out of existence, more and more rapidly, and suddenly everything was extinguished in a blaze of light. The last thing Jamie heard was the anguished electronic howling of the console …

Jamie opened his eyes.

He was still clutching the Doctor and they were jammed together in some kind of enclosed space, somewhere small and square. The Doctor struggled free and Jamie followed him.

To his astonishment, he found himself standing outside the TARDIS. The outside was the familiar square blue shape, but glancing behind him, Jamie saw that the inside was totally different. There was no sign of the impossibly large control room – instead there was just the amount of space you'd expect to see inside. 'Doctor, what have you done? You've shrunk the TARDIS!'

The Doctor held up the golden rod. 'I disconnected the Time Vector Generator.'

'What does that do?'

'It controls the size of the interior of the TARDIS amongst other things. Once it's removed, the interior becomes an ordinary police box once again.'

Jamie looked stunned.

The Doctor closed the TARDIS doors. 'Come and sit over here, Jamie.'

For the first time, Jamie became aware of his surroundings. He was in a kind of metal cave, surrounded by massive metallic shapes. 'Where are we?'

'Oddly enough, we seem to be in the motor section of some sort of rocket.'

The Doctor led Jamie to a kind of ledge surrounding one of the vast pieces of machinery and sat him down. He himself wandered over to an instrument panel set into the wall. A row of dials was labelled 'Gravity Field Strength'.

The Doctor studied the readings. 'Yes, there's an artificial gravity system on the ship …'

'And what's that?'

'Gravity, Jamie. We shouldn't be able to stand up otherwise, we'd be floating about.'

'Oh aye?' Jamie licked his lips. 'There's no water around anywhere, is there?'

The Doctor looked round. 'Not in here, no.' He paused. 'There doesn't appear to be any movement either.'

'We're on the ground then?'

'I don't know, Jamie. Perhaps. Aha!'

The Doctor was fishing in his pockets.

'Well come on, don't keep me in suspense,' grumbled Jamie.

The Doctor fished out a crumpled paper bag. 'Have a sherbet, it'll help to quench your thirst!' The Doctor gave Jamie a sweet, took one himself and began a renewed study of their surroundings.

There was a metal door at the far end of the motor area, and the Doctor bent down and studied the floor just in front of it. Twin track marks led directly to the door.

Jamie rose and came to join him. 'That warning system of yours must have thought there was something wrong out here. But what can the danger be? Everything's so – dead in here.'

The Doctor indicated the tracks. 'Something's been here, Jamie.' He bent down and rubbed a finger across one of the track marks, and then sniffed it. 'Oil. It must have been a machine of some kind. In here fairly recently too …'

Jamie wandered up to the door and saw a button set into the wall just beside it. Impulsively he pressed it and the door slid smoothly open.

Jamie jumped back in alarm. 'Sorry, Doctor!'

But the door revealed nothing more alarming than a short section of metal corridor with yet another door at the other end. The Doctor and Jamie moved cautiously into the corridor. The Doctor noticed that the tracks led along the corridor and up to the door ahead of them. Set into the wall at the left of the door was a bank of monitor screens with a control panel beneath them. On the right they could see the outline of two closed hatches set into the corridor wall.

The Doctor crept cautiously up to the next door and put his ear to it.

'Doctor –' began Jamie.

The Doctor waved him to silence. 'Ssh, Jamie! We don't know what may be on the other side …'

2

THE UNSEEN ENEMY

The Doctor paused for a moment, thinking hard. They couldn't just stay where they were – they'd starve apart from anything else – but he was reluctant to move ahead without knowing what might be waiting ...

He turned and studied the bank of monitors, and began fiddling with the controls. 'This one? No, should be this one by rights.' One of the screens lit up.

The Doctor and Jamie studied it. There on the screen was what was obviously some kind of control room – computer banks, control consoles, a central cockpit area with chairs for the crew.

The whole place was silent – and completely empty. Low-level maintenance lights glowed dimly here and there, but the recesses of the control room were lost in shadowy gloom. In the centre of the floor was a strangely sinister oblong shape. It looked like a metal coffin. Just to one side of it stood a big crate, also made of some metallic substance.

Jamie peered uneasily at the screen. 'Well, it *looks* safe enough ...'

'But what caused the defense mechanism of the TARDIS to signal danger? And why isn't there anyone on board?' The Doctor studied a dial set beside the control console. 'Well, there seems to be plenty of air in there. Let's take a look.' The Doctor pressed what should have been the door opening control. Nothing happened. He tried a number of other controls. They didn't work either. The Doctor glared indignantly at the door, trying to work out what to do next.

'I'll have a nose about back here,' said Jamie tactfully. He turned and wandered back to the two hatchway doors set in the wall. There was something set into each door that looked very like a handle. Curious as ever, Jamie turned it – and the first hatchway door slid open.

It was the door to a little cabin, three-quarters filled with variously shaped metallic containers stacked against the walls. Jamie closed the door, went along to the next one and opened that. This door too gave on to a cabin, but the cabin was furnished with two bunks, a central table and two padded chairs, all built in.

Jamie became aware that the Doctor had come over to join him. The Doctor looked round the little cabin. 'Living quarters?'

Jamie nodded. 'Aye. Stores in the other one.'

There was some kind of machine standing upright against the far wall – a dispensing-machine, thought the Doctor. They went over to examine it.

'Hey, it says "water" on here!' said Jamie.

They began experimenting with the controls . . .

There was movement in the empty control room. A squat bulbous shape glided silently out of the shadows. It was a servo-robot, a simply designed affair that was little more than a metal cylinder on running tracks with bulblike sensors on its upper surface. It was making a routine inspection. Trundling up to the control room door the robot paused for a moment. One of its sensor-globes glowed and the door slid open. The robot moved off down the corridor.

After a lot of jiggling and fiddling, the Doctor managed to persuade the dispensing-machine to produce two plastic cups filled with ice-cold distilled water. They stood sipping the water gratefully.

Jamie looked round. 'I'd have thought a rocket this size would have carried more than two people.'

The Doctor nodded. 'It does. Four, I imagine; two resting, two on duty.'

He went to the cabin's viewing hatch, which was covered by a metal shutter. The Doctor began unscrewing the clamps that held it closed.

'The TARDIS must have gone crazy,' said Jamie. 'There's nothing on board here with us, so there's no danger!'

'Isn't there?' The Doctor beckoned Jamie over to the window. 'Come and look!'

Jamie looked. Through the viewing hatch he saw – nothing. The infinite blackness of space.

'We appear to be drifting aimlessly in space, Jamie. Maybe that's what the TARDIS was trying to warn us about.'

Jamie shrugged. 'What does it matter?'

'Matter!' said the Doctor indignantly. 'We're just a piece of drifting space flotsam, don't you realise that?'

'Aye, all right then. All you have to do is replace yon rod what d'you call it, the dimension thingy ...'

'The Time Vector Generator,' said the Doctor patiently. 'It controls the temporal drive.'

'Aye, that thing. You just put it back and we go on somewhere else.'

'I'm afraid it isn't as simple as that, Jamie, remember? First we need mercury to replace the fluid links.'

'Aye, well, there must be some on board here.' Jamie was ever optimistic.

The Doctor however was still feeling vaguely uneasy. 'Besides, what happened to the crew, Jamie? They didn't just pop out for a little constitutional, you know!'

'We might find that out if we get inside that control room.'

The Doctor nodded thoughtfully. 'Perhaps, Jamie. Perhaps.' His mind was busy with a dozen theories – and none of them were particularly reassuring.

When the TARDIS warned of danger, it was never wrong and the Doctor felt things were happening on this ship, somewhere out of view.

'Well, let's start looking,' he said, and they began their search.

They searched every inch of the motor section and the whole of the store room as well. They found stores, supplies, fuel, tools, protective clothing, space suits, any number of useful and interesting things – but not what they were looking for.

'Not a drop of mercury anywhere,' said the Doctor despairingly. They were back where they'd started, in the little cabin.

'Maybe we'd better try the control room,' suggested Jamie.

'I think you're right, Jamie. We'll have a bit of a rest and try there next.'

Jamie eyed the dispensing-machine. 'D'you think we might get food as well as water out of that thing?'

'I can give you another sherbert.'

'I was hoping for something a wee bit more substantial, Doctor.'

'Right! Let's see what we can do then.' The Doctor went over to the machine and studied the controls. He was beginning to get the hang of it now. 'What do you fancy, Jamie?'

'Oh ... roast beef and all the trimmings.'

'What vegetables?'

'Potatoes and cabbage.'

'And you'd like a fruit salad?'

'Aye, I would.'

The Doctor's hands moved over the controls. 'And I'll have ... pork chop, potatoes, carrots and ... and some ice cream.'

A moment later two small paper plates emerged from the machine's dispensing compartment. They held a selection of cubes of jelly, in different colours and sizes. The Doctor handed one to Jamie. 'There you are, complete with gravy.'

Jamie stared down at his plate in horror. 'Ye dinna expect me to eat this stuff, do you?'

'Why not? I'm sure it'll be delicious.'

Jamie looked at his plate and then at the Doctor who was already munching one of his cubes with every sign of enjoyment.

Jamie sighed. 'I didn't expect a five-course dinner, but this is ridiculous!'

'It's perfectly good, Jamie. Come on, sit down and eat up!'

Jamie sat down obediently and began munching gloomily on one of the cubes. It had a vague, faint ghost of a fruity taste, and Jamie realised he must have started on his dessert by accident. Still, what did it matter?

'What do you think Victoria's doing now, Doctor?'

The Doctor smiled. 'All depends when "now" is Jamie. If I knew that I might be able to hazard a guess.'

'Och, you know what I mean.'

'Victoria will be all right,' said the Doctor reassuringly. 'She chose a good time in Earth's history to stay in, no wars, great prosperity, a time of plenty. She'll be happy, never fear.' He noticed that Jamie had pushed his plate of food concentrate aside. 'Filling, isn't it?'

'Aye,' said Jamie sourly. 'Well, what do we do now?'

'We'll give ourselves time to digest our food, then we'll have a go at getting into that control room.'

'Aye, good idea. I think I'll just have a wee lie down.' Yawning, Jamie stretched out on one of the bunks. 'What do you think's happened to the crew?'

'I don't know, Jamie, I wish I did. I'm inclined to suspect that there was some sort of disaster. Perhaps we shall find some clue to the answer in the control room.'

In its methodical patrol through the corridors of the space rocket, the servo-robot came to the door that the Doctor had opened some time earlier. It stood studying the open door for a moment, its sensor-globes flashing agitatedly. The door was open. It was supposed to be closed, according to the information on the robot's built-in data bank.

Something was badly wrong.

The Doctor was staring out of the viewing port. 'At least this ship doesn't seem to be in any immediate danger. However, I'd very much like to know what really happened.' The only answer was a long rattling snore. The Doctor turned and saw that Jamie was fast asleep.

The servo-robot was standing in front of the TARDIS, its sensor-globes flashing wildly in robot astonishment. Faced with an event totally outside its programming, it was completely and utterly at a loss.

Attached to the control console in the rocket control room was a strangely alien looking device. Somehow it was clear that it was the product of a very different technological culture from the one that had originally built the ship. It was some kind of clock device with three separate hands. One revolved swiftly and silently, like the second hand on a watch.

The second made a series of sudden jumps at regular five-second intervals. The third moved less frequently, covering a whole quarter section of the dial at a time. Above the clock was a small digital register. It was currently reading one thousand and twenty-five.

*

The robot abandoned the problem of the TARDIS's presence on board. Since it was impossible it could not have happened so it was not a problem.

Trundling back along the corridor, it applied itself to the problem of the open door. Passing through, it turned to face the door from the other side. It flashed its sensor-globes at the control panel and the door slid shut. The robot extruded a metal rod from the upper part of its body. Light glowed at the end of the rod, and the robot moved the laser-beam carefully around the edges of the door, sealing them shut.

Satisfied it moved back towards the control room.

Tucking a space-blanket around Jamie's sleeping form, the Doctor straightened up and headed for the cabin door. He had decided to let Jamie sleep, and to make the attempt to reach the control room on his own.

Just as he reached the door, he paused listening. Had there been some kind of sound from the corridor outside? A sound of movement? Cautiously he opened the cabin door and stepped out into the corridor.

Looking down he saw track marks on the floor. *Fresh* track marks, overlaying the ones he'd already seen. Yet the corridor was empty …

The Doctor moved along to the bank of monitor screens. He operated controls, but this time he got nothing but a swirl of static.

By now the servo-robot was back in the control room. It was standing next to the main computer bank, extruding a power cable from its body. The cable locked home, plugging in to a socket on the computer bank. Needles flickered, lights flashed, and the ship's computer, with its pre-programmed automatic pilot, hummed into life. Orders were transmitted across the ships operation circuits – and suddenly the rocket motors surged into life.

Changing direction abruptly, the ship set off on its new course …

The sudden lurching of the ship took the Doctor unawares as he was leaning forward to study the monitor controls. Hurled across the corridor, he struck his head on the steel wall and slumped unconscious to the ground.

3

HUNTED

The lurch that threw the Doctor into the wall sent Jamie hurtling from his bunk. He thumped onto the floor, rolled over, and scrambled to his feet – to find the Doctor gone. He hurried out of the cabin to look for him.

At the far end of the corridor he saw the Doctor stretched out on the ground. As Jamie watched, the Doctor stirred and began making feeble attempts to get to his feet.

Jamie ran to help him. 'Doctor! What's happening?'

The Doctor groaned. 'Hit my head ...'

Jamie helped him to sit up. All around them was the deep hum of machinery, the subdued roar of the rocket's motors. 'We're moving, Doctor ... The rocket's moving!'

'I know ...' The Doctor clasped his aching head. 'There must be someone inside the control room.'

'Let's have a look, then!'

The Doctor shook his head dazedly. 'No, Jamie, help me back to the TARDIS, that's the safest place for us.'

'But we still havena found the mercury ...'

'Never mind that now ... back to the TARDIS, Jamie.'

Jamie helped the Doctor to rise, half supporting him as they staggered along the corridor, heading for the spot where they'd left the TARDIS. The door that led out from the motor section was closed. Jamie stabbed at the controls, but nothing happened. He examined the edges of the door. 'It's sealed, Doctor!'

The Doctor stared blankly at him – and collapsed.

Catching him just in time, Jamie half-dragged, half-carried him back to the little cabin and laid him down on the bunk. The Doctor revived for a moment. 'Lock the door, Jamie.'

'But Doctor ...'

'Lock it ...' The Doctor's head fell back.

Jamie went over to the door, closed it, and operated what seemed to be a locking device. He turned back to the bunk. 'Doctor ...'

But the Doctor was unconscious.

In the rocket control room, a complicated series of events was unfolding, according to a pre-determined plan.

The servo-robot had disconnected itself from the computer bank and was concerning itself with the coffin-like metal pod that occupied the centre of the control room. The robot's sensor lights flashed and the top of the pod slid open revealing rows of opaque globular objects resembling some kind of alien eggs. A hatchway opened in the rocket wall, and the metal pod slid inside it. The hatchway door closed.

In the control room the alien clock clicked down to zero – and a strident signal sound filled the control room ...

A hatchway opened on the exterior of the rocket and the alien eggs began drifting away into space, one by one ... When the pod was empty the hatchway closed.

Its tasks completed, the servo-robot turned towards a monitor screen. Sensors flashed and the screen sprang into life. On it there appeared the Wheel, a giant man-made space station, one of humanity's distant outposts in this remote part of the cosmos.

From the cabin porthole Jamie was staring in fascination at the Wheel.

It was vast, colossal, dominating what had seemed, only minutes ago, to be an empty sector of space. To Jamie's eyes it looked like a giant metal spinning top, with a saucer-like superstructure and some kind of supporting framework underneath.

So absorbed was Jamie by this astonishing sight that he failed to notice that the Doctor was sitting up on the bunk and gazing dazedly around him. He rose unsteadily and moving like someone sleepwalking, opened the door and staggered off down the corridor. By this time the Doctor was suffering from mild concussion, and he had only one idea in his head. 'Must get door open ... get Jamie to safety ...'

*

Kept moving only by sheer determination, the Doctor staggered up to the sealed door. He fished in his pocket and pulled out the black-tipped gold rod that he had taken from the TARDIS.

The Time Vector Generator was in itself a tremendously powerful energy-source – one which could be adapted in emergency to many strange uses ...

The Doctor slipped the black cap from one end of the rod to reveal a fiercely-glowing tip. He pointed it like a torch, running it along the sealed edges of the door. There was a crackle of power, and smoke drifted from the sealed edges. The Doctor re-capped the gold rod, slipped it back in his pocket. Shaking his aching head to clear it, he turned his attention to the door controls. They seemed to surge and ripple before his eyes. Shaking his head determinedly he forced his bleary eyes to focus and reached out for the controls. Then he sensed rather than heard that there was something behind him.

Slowly the Doctor turned – and found himself facing the servo-robot.

As the Doctor turned the robot shot back several feet – almost as if it was frightened of the Doctor. Then it extruded the nozzle of the laser-gun from its body. The Doctor was not part of the Plan. He was an error. Errors must be erased.

Recovering from his astonished reaction to the Wheel at last, Jamie turned to the Doctor. 'Hey Doctor, come and look –' But the Doctor was gone. The crumpled space blanket trailed from the end of the bunk and the door stood open.

Snatching up the blanket – he had a confused idea that the Doctor ought to be kept warm – Jamie shot out of the cabin and into the corridor ...

He dashed along it, arriving just in time to see the confused, half-conscious Doctor being menaced by the robot's laser gun. Jamie acted instantly.

Draping the blanket over the servo-robot's squat form, he gave the robot a powerful shove that sent it shooting down the corridor. Grabbing the Doctor by the shoulders, Jamie ran him back down the corridor into the comparative safety of the cabin, closing and locking the door behind them.

To do this he had to let go of the Doctor, who slid quietly to the floor, completely unconscious ...

A blast of the servo-robot's laser sent the blanket shooting into the air in charred and tattered fragments. The robot glided swiftly down the corridor after the Doctor and Jamie, coming to a halt outside the locked cabin door ...

The nozzle of the laser-gun glowed fiercely, and smoke began rising from the metal door ...

As Jamie heaved the Doctor back on to the bunk a fierce crackle of energy came from the direction of the door. Jamie looked and saw smoke rising and a pin-point hole that was growing steadily larger.

The Doctor opened his eyes and saw what was happening. Fumbling in his pocket he took out the gold rod and thrust it into Jamie's hand. 'Use it like a torch, Jamie ... burn ... be careful ... careful ...' The Doctor gestured feebly towards the door – the hole was much bigger now.

In the corridor, the servo-robot had already melted away a sizeable patch of the metal door – there was a puddle of molten metal at its feet. Soon the door would be melted and the two mistakes could be erased.

Obeying the Doctor's feebly muttered instructions, Jamie took the end off the gold rod and directed the energy-beam through the hole in the door. The beam struck the servo-robot in the centre of its mid-section.

Results were immediate and spectacular. The robot shot backwards at enormous speed, smashed into the still closed door and blew up, disintegrating into smoking metallic fragments.

Jamie settled the Doctor on the bunk and found another blanket to cover him. 'We seem to be safe for a little while. But no more gallivanting about, Doctor.'

Exhausted by his efforts, the Doctor was dead to the world. Jamie settled him as comfortably as he could and then went over to the porthole, looking out at the gleaming shape of the Wheel. There had to be people on a thing like that, he thought. Maybe they would come and help ...

*

The control room of the Wheel was very different from that of the rocket. It was huge and brightly lit, with a big semi-circular control station with places for all the crew members.

Leo Ryan sat in the command chair, a big, handsome fair-haired giant of a man, cheerful and confident, sometimes to the point of arrogance. Next to him was Tanya Lernov, a slim attractive young woman with a bell of fair hair framing her sensitive face. Standing behind them was Gemma Corwyn, medical officer of the Wheel, a pleasant-looking sensible woman in her mid-thirties.

'Hold it steady,' snapped Ryan. 'Get a proper fix on that thing!'

Gemma said mildly, 'It seems to have stopped moving.'

Ryan glanced at Tanya. 'How is it now, Tanya?'

'Stable. Exactly the same.'

Gemma said, 'Isn't there a slight drift still?'

Ryan shook his head. 'No. The movement's not real. It's an illusion caused by slight polar precession.'

A stocky, balding bearded man came into the control room and there was an immediate respectful silence.

This was Jarvis Bennett, Commander of the Wheel. Dressed like his subordinates, in quilted black and white space coveralls, he was in his own quiet way a figure of considerable authority. 'Well, how's our mystery rocket?'

Gemma shrugged. 'Suddenly lifeless, apparently.'

Ryan frowned. He hated mysteries. 'It doesn't make sense, Commander. It must have been driven by *something*.'

'There's been no radio contact at all,' added Gemma.

Jarvis Bennett said, 'I'm not surprised. I've just checked out its description on the Register. It's a Phoenix Mark Four, named Silver Carrier.'

'Register even,' said Tanya. 'No crossover reading.'

Ryan said, 'It's definitely stopped moving. No momentum at all now.'

Gemma looked at Jarvis Bennett. 'Silver Carrier, you said?'

'That's right. Supply ship for Station Five. It was reported overdue about nine weeks ago. It's only about ninety million miles off course.'

Ryan glanced towards the dark, silent man at a nearby sub-console. 'Try radio contact again, Rico.'

Enrico Casali was the Wheel's communications officer. Olive-skinned, brown-eyed and curly-haired, his appearance, like his name reflected his Indian origins, though there was no trace of accent in his voice. 'Space Station Three to Silver Carrier. Station Three to Silver Carrier. Come, in please. Come in please.'

'Ninety million miles?' said Gemma. 'It couldn't have drifted all that way, Commander.'

'No, it couldn't.'

'Try the emergency channel, Leo,' suggested Tanya.

Ryan leaned forward to his console mike. 'Station Three to Silver Carrier. Operate red band switch for emergency transmission.' They all waited tensely, but there was no reply.

Gemma Corwyn said, 'Maybe their radio's dead.'

'We have to try,' said Tanya.

Jarvis Bennett nodded approvingly. 'Standard procedure. I'm afraid we're wasting time, but waste it we must.'

'Any reaction, Tanya?' asked Ryan.

'No, nothing. No response at all.'

'So how does the Silver Carrier turn up in this part of the cosmos?' mused Gemma.

Jarvis Bennett said thoughtfully, 'Say something happens to the crew, illness or accident. One of them manages to put on the automatic pilot. The rocket's travelled so far by now the power feed-back is probably failing. So the rocket could start up and stop again more or less any time.'

'And what about the crew?' asked Gemma. 'Do you think they're still alive?'

Jarvis Bennett looked at Ryan, who shook his head.

'We've tried everything, sir. Can't raise a thing.'

Jarvis Bennett said, 'If I'm right about that faulty automatic system, that rocket could accelerate at any moment – and whip straight towards us. And there can't be any life on board after all this time – can there?'

Like soap bubbles from the bubble pipe of a child, the alien eggs drifted through the space between the rocket and the Wheel …

236

As the eggs struck the surface of the Wheel, they seemed to sink right through it, as if somehow the Wheel was absorbing them.

Tanya looked up from her instruments with a frown. 'I'm getting some kind of reading. Like very small meteorites hitting our outer rim. No damage, but there's a very slight drop in air pressure.'

'Can't be meteorites, surely,' said Gemma. 'We'd have had some warning.'

'Well, there's something,' said Tanya. 'These readings are jumping all over the place.'

Jarvis Bennett had the explanation. 'I imagine minor objects, with small mass and high density, have escaped from the Silver Carrier.'

'In that case,' said Gemma, 'such objects would be clinging close to the rocket, not descending on us.'

Jarvis Bennett didn't care for having the flaws in his theories pointed out. 'It really doesn't matter, Gemma, let's not start looking for mysteries. The point is, I daren't risk that rocket homing in on the Station and smashing into us.'

'So what are you going to do?'

Jarvis Bennett smiled. 'You're about to experience something rarely seen by human beings. Is the laser projector on standby, Leo?'

'Yes, sir. Moving into position now.'

As the rumble of heavy machinery filled the control room Jarvis Bennett said, 'I'm going to turn our laser-cannon on the Silver Carrier. In a few moments you will see the complete destruction of a rocket in space.'

From the cabin of the rocket, Jamie stared out at the Wheel. He glanced briefly at the still unconscious Doctor. Surely the people on that thing would see them and send help ...

Unaware that it was preparing to blast him from existence, Jamie stared hopefully out at the Wheel ...

4

COMMAND DECISION

As Jamie watched, a hatch slid back on the upper part of the Wheel and a massive metal tube slid slowly into view. Jamie looked thoughtfully at it. His knowledge of space technology was patchy to say the least, but his fighting-man's instinct knew a weapon when he saw one. This thing looked unpleasantly like the muzzle of a gun. And it seemed to be pointing straight towards him ...

In a sectioned-off area of the control room, Bill Duggan, a thick-set, amiable-looking defence officer was supervising Laleham and Vallance, two technicians who were preparing the laser-cannon for operation.

Jarvis Bennett stood watching them. 'Got the range, Bill?'

'Locked on now, sir.'

'That's the idea. Don't get much fun, do we Bill? Better make the most of it!'

Bill Duggan grinned. 'Makes a change from blasting the occasional meteorite, sir.'

Jarvis Bennett nodded. 'Tanya? How about taking a visual recording?'

'Can do, sir.'

'Right. I'd better make a crew announcement.'

Gemma Corwyn hurried over to him. 'Could I have a word first, Jarvis? It's important.'

Glancing across the control room, Jarvis Bennett caught Leo Ryan's eye and smiled. 'More bogies,' he said in a stage whisper. But he allowed Gemma to take his arm and lead him aside.

Tanya Lernov looked at Ryan and snapped, 'I don't know what you're grinning about!'

Hurriedly Ryan straightened his face. 'Neither do I.'

'This isn't funny, Leo. The Commander's so keen to use the laser, he's like a kid with a new toy.'

'Don't say you agree with old stick-in-the-mud Gemma Corwyn?'

'Doctor Corwyn isn't old and she's no stick-in-the-mud either. She's quite right to be cautious.'

'Oh come on, Tanya,' said Ryan wearily. 'That rocket is nine weeks overdue and ninety million miles off course. There can't possibly be anyone alive on board ...'

Jamie's instincts had led him to an almost uncannily accurate estimate of the situation. For some reason, the Wheel had decided that the rocket was a danger to it, and it was going to destroy the intruder.

His only hope was to make some kind of signal. He tried to wrench a light panel from the wall, but with no success. The light wouldn't be bright enough anyway. Jamie looked desperately at the Doctor, hoping he would be recovered enough to give some advice.

The Doctor was still unconscious – but the gold rod was lying beside him on the bunk.

Well, it had worked a treat on the robot, thought Jamie. It was worth a try.

Since she believed that rows between senior personnel were best held in private, Gemma Corwyn had taken the Commander back to her living quarters.

Much larger and more luxurious than the cramped living quarters on the rocket, Gemma's rooms were soothingly decorated in pastel shades. She was the Wheel's psychiatrist as well as medical officer, and her quarters doubled as her consulting room.

Jarvis Bennett had a nasty suspicion that he was being viewed as a potential patient.

'Don't subject me to your psychoanalysis,' he roared. 'You think I'm acting like a kid again don't you? Bang, bang, blow up the balloon! Well, you're wrong!'

'Am I?'

'The Silver Carrier is a menace to the Wheel.'

'Only if you equate menace with automatic power drive, which I don't. You want me to believe some emergency occurred on the Silver Carrier, the pilot switched over to automatic, then – tragedy. Is that it, Jarvis?'

'Right!'

'And the crew are all dead?'

'Right again!'

'Where was the Silver Carrier bound for?'

'I told you, it was servicing Station Five.'

'Then wouldn't the automatic have taken it to Station Five?' asked Gemma triumphantly.

Jarvis Bennett stared at her. 'That's good reasoning. But the emergency might well have damaged the control sensors – which would explain why the rocket went off course.'

'Assumptions, Jarvis. Guesswork. It would be so easy to *check*.'

'We can't risk that rocket crashing into the station,' said Jarvis obstinately. 'She'd blast a hole right through us.'

Jamie stood hesitating by the porthole, the gold rod in his hand. If the Wheel interpreted his signal as an attack ... Still, something had to be done.

Aiming the gold rod at the Wheel, Jamie whipped the black tip off one end – seconds later he replaced it.

Tearing the earphone from his head, Enrico Casali staggered back from the console. Rudkin, a neighbouring technician did the same.

Ryan ran over to them. 'What is it, Enrico?'

'Some kind of power surge ... static, noise. Tremendous noise! Right through me like a knife. Swamped everything ...'

All over the control room, astonished technicians were cursing and rubbing their ears. Lights were flashing wildly on all the consoles.

Bill Duggan shouted, 'What's going on? The whole system's gone crazy!'

'Tanya, get Doctor Corwyn,' ordered Ryan.

'The internal communications are out.' Tanya jumped up. 'I'll go and get her.'

Ryan went over to help Enrico, who was easing Rudkin, much more badly affected than he was himself, away from the controls.

'All right, Rudkin,' Enrico said soothingly.

'Lie him down over here,' said Ryan.

They settled the unfortunate Rudkin, who was still moaning and clasping his ears, on a bench at the side of the control room.

Enrico massaged his ears. 'I don't want to go through that again …'

'Listen!' said Ryan.

The energy pulse could still be distinctly heard, coming through the sets of ripped-off headphones. It was coming in a steady, but, uneven beat – like some kind of signal.

'Don't argue with me, Gemma,' shouted Jarvis Bennett. 'The decision is mine. I command this Station and all the people in it.'

The door was flung open and Tanya dashed in. 'Doctor Corwyn, Rudkin's hurt.'

'What happened?'

'Colossal static pulses, swamping all the detectors.'

Jarvis Bennett glared angrily at Gemma. 'I knew that rocket was a menace!'

They hurried from the room.

Unaware of the havoc he was causing, Jamie stood by the rocket porthole, capping and uncapping the gold rod at irregular intervals.

Tanya, Gemma and Jarvis Bennett came back into the control room at a run.

'Tanya, you get back to your console,' ordered Jarvis Bennett. 'See if you can pin this static down. Gemma, see what you can do for Rudkin and the others.'

As Gemma began organising the transfer of Rudkin and the worst-hit of the other technicians to the medical bay, Jarvis took his seat at the console. 'All right, Leo, that rocket's given us more than enough trouble. Knock it out!'

'Commander!' called Tanya urgently.

'Yes, what is it?'

'That static – it's a signal.'

'It can't be!'

Leo Ryan held up his hand. 'She's right, sir. Listen!'

They listened.

It was quite clear that the irregular beat of the static was forming some kind of pattern.

'Get me a fix on it, Tanya,' snapped Ryan.

'If I can. It's no code I've ever heard of, but there's definitely a repetitive order to it.'

'You think it's coming from the rocket?' asked Jarvis Bennett.

'I just want to make sure, Commander.'

Tanya looked up. 'The rocket it is, sir. There's no doubt.'

Jarvis Bennett was a good enough commander to admit it when he was wrong. 'Then there's someone on board that thing. Leo, I want two men to cross over.'

'Right, sir.'

Jarvis Bennett shook his head unbelievingly. 'Ninety million miles off course. If anyone is still alive on that ship, they must be in a pretty bad way ...'

Jamie had given up on his signalling by now, and was staring down at the still unconscious Doctor in despair. Suddenly he heard a tapping from the porthole. Swinging round he was shocked to see a helmeted head peering at him from outside the rocket.

Then realising that the longed-for help had arrived, Jamie grinned broadly and waved. The helmeted figure pointed towards the front of the rocket. Jamie nodded and hurried from the cabin.

As he hurried along the corridor, he stepped gingerly over the shattered remains of the servo-robot, then made his way towards the control room.

As he reached the door it opened before him and he went inside. One space-suited figure was already there, and seconds later, a second emerged from the air-lock.

'Quick!' shouted Jamie urgently. 'I've got someone hurt back there.'

The two space-suited figures hurried after him.

It was some time later and for the moment the Wheel seemed almost back to normal.

Ryan and the other technicians were acting as deep space traffic controllers and weather men, confirming the routes of space freighters, issuing warnings of meteor showers and generally smoothing the complex process of interplanetary travel.

Leo Ryan looked up as Tanya came into the control room. 'How are our guests?'

'Doctor Corwyn's looking after them now. They both seem to be in shock.'

'What happened to them?'

'Nobody knows. It's still a mystery.'

Ryan grinned. 'Jarvis won't like that.' Something on one of the read-out screens caught his attention. 'What's that interference on Green System, Chang?'

The technician looked up. 'It's very odd, sir. Been getting funny signs here and there for some time. As soon as you check them out – they vanish!'

'You've been logging them?'

'Yes, sir.' Chang frowned. 'It's as if we had magnets touching the outer skin of the Wheel then letting go again. Localised field effects, that's all.'

His co-technician, a massive Irishman called Flanagan said, 'But all field detectors check out normal, sir. Can't be anything serious.'

Ryan nodded. 'Keep logging it – and keep me up-to-date.' He smiled at Tanya. 'More mysteries.'

Tanya didn't return the smile. 'I know. And what about those sudden drops in air pressure? Small enough and they soon adjusted themselves – but I still don't like it.'

'How small?'

'One degree – sometimes one-and-a-half.'

Ryan shrugged. 'Could be a minor fault in the air supply pumps.'

'In so many different parts of the Wheel?'

'Did you tell the Commander?'

'Of course. And he bit my head off.'

Ryan nodded sympathetically. 'That figures. Did you tell Doctor Corwyn?'

'Not yet. She's busy with the new arrivals. I didn't like to disturb her.'

Ryan said seriously, 'I'd start a check on the whole air supply system if I were you, Tanya.'

'I already have. Leo?'

'What?'

'All these mysteries. The temporary faults in your systems, the air pressure drops. They all started with the rocket, didn't they?'

Ryan chuckled. 'Reckon there are little green men on board, do you?'

But Tanya didn't smile. 'What about those two people they brought back from the rocket?' she asked. 'They weren't exactly normal.'

'I tell you what, Tanya – if you get scared I'll let you hold my hand, okay?'

He gave her one of his cheeky grins, and Tanya couldn't help smiling in return. 'Leo, I'm serious.'

Ryan raised his eyebrows. 'So am I!'

Meanwhile, outside the Wheel, a string of silvery bubbles drifted onto the outer skin then disappeared, somehow seeming to pass through the metal.

The long-prepared invasion had begun.

5

UNDER SUSPICION

Jamie was sitting uneasily in the medical bay, stripped to the waist. Gemma Corwyn was passing a stethoscope-like instrument over his chest.

'Breathe in ... out. Now a deep breath and let it out slowly.'

Meekly Jamie obeyed.

'Good,' said Gemma Corwyn crisply. 'You can get dressed now.'

Jamie rose and began struggling into his shirt. 'How's the Doctor?'

'Well, he's certainly suffering from concussion. I'm waiting for X-rays to see if there's a fracture.' She paused. 'Look, your clothes ... fancy dress or something?'

Jamie was stung. 'Have you thought what you'd look like if you walked down the street in those clothes – people might think *you* were a wee bit strange!'

'But we're in space – you're the ones who aren't conforming.'

Jamie changed the subject. 'How about the medical. Do I pass?'

'If it's any comfort, you're in excellent physical shape. What's your full name?'

'James Robert McCrimmon – Jamie for short.'

'And your friend?'

'The Doctor?'

'I can't just put that down.'

Jamie glanced round for inspiration. 'Er, Smith. John Smith.'

As she fitted the stethoscope back into the diagnostic machine and lifted the whole thing back into its container, she noticed the name on the open lid. 'John Smith and Co. London'.

Jamie followed her gaze. 'Er – there's a lot of them about.'

'Yes indeed,' said Doctor Corwyn drily. 'You and your friend were passengers – on the Silver Carrier?'

'What? Oh, aye, we were. Could I have a drink of water, please?'

Gemma went to a dispensing-machine and returned with the usual plastic cup of distilled chilled water. She handed it to Jamie who took a couple of sips and put down the cup. 'What happened to the crew?' she asked.

'I dinna ken.' Jamie swallowed hard, desperately wishing the Doctor was here. He could talk his way out of anything. Jamie floundered on. 'I was ill in my cabin, terrible raging fever. I was raving for days. When I got up there was no one about, the doors were closed against us and the Doctor was hurt ... Then your people came and rescued us.'

'Your friend couldn't tell you what had happened?'

'No. He was too ill.'

'All right, Jamie, that will do for now. The Commander will want to have a chat with you – and of course we must see about getting you home.'

'Home. That'll be the day,' said Jamie wryly, thinking of the Scotland of 1746. He'd no chance of reaching that without the Doctor – precious little with him, he sometimes thought. Jamie became aware that Doctor Corwyn was staring at him and said hurriedly, 'Aye home. Yes, of course.'

'There's another ship passing through in a week or two.'

Jamie pulled on his jacket and began knotting his scarf. 'Can I go now?'

Gemma was still looking curiously at him. 'You haven't finished your water.'

'No, well, that's all right ...' Jamie began edging away.

'Would you like to see round the Wheel?' asked Gemma suddenly. 'I could arrange it for you.'

'Aye, why not – nothing else to do,' said Jamie rather ungraciously.

Gemma Corwyn pointed. 'If you go through that door and along the corridor you'll find a door marked Parapsychology Library.'

'Parawhat?'

'It's on the far side of the Wheel, about eight sections on. I'll ask Zoe to show you around.'

'Zoe?'

'She's our – well, you might call her our librarian.'

'Right, fine,' said Jamie. 'You'll let me know how the Doctor gets on?'

'Of course.'

Jamie nodded and hurried away.

Gemma Corwyn picked up a mike from a nearby console. 'Doctor Corwyn calling Parapsychology.'

After a moment a young girl's face appeared on a monitor screen. 'Library. What reference do you require, Doctor Corwyn?'

'No reference, thank you Zoe. I need your help in another way. One of the people retrieved from the rocket is coming to see you. I want you to show him over the Wheel – and observe him. Discreetly, of course.'

'Do you wish these observations recorded?'

'Yes please, Zoe.'

'Right,' said the girl briskly. 'Should be interesting. Any other facts known?'

Gemma Corwyn smiled. 'Well, he's a nice lad. His name is –'

'Just a minute,' interrupted Zoe. 'I was half-way through a RNA analysis, just let me clear my head …' She clicked her tongue, shook her head then smiled. 'Right, fire away!'

It took Jamie quite some time to find the Parapsychology Library, but he managed it at last and tapped hesitantly on the door. It opened immediately. Jamie stepped through and it closed behind him.

He found himself in a small completely bare room, in the centre of which was a semi-circular desk, also completely bare. Behind the desk sat a very small girl, or rather young woman. She wore the same black and white coverall outfit as everyone else on the Wheel and her appealing rather pixie-like face was framed with shortish black hair.

She was rattling something off into the microphone of the video-link built into the otherwise empty desk. '… with the exception of the Hercules cluster. Computation shows that one of the stars in the Messier Thirteen group is entering a nova phase – information on gamma radiation level is available …'

The girl broke off as Jamie came in. 'You must be James Robert McCrimm –' She stopped again, with a little gurgle of laughter.

'Aye, McCrimmon,' completed Jamie. 'What are you laughing at?'

The girl was looking at the kilt that swung round Jamie's brawny knees. 'You're wearing female clothes!'

'Female!' Jamie was outraged. 'This is a kilt. Have you no' seen one before?'

'Kilt?' She frowned and closed her eyes, as if calling up the information. '"Kilt: a primitive form of garment, worn by a kiltie." Are you of Scandinavian origin?'

'No I am not. I'm a true bred Scot!'

'Ah, Scot – Scotland. Pre-century history isn't really my field.'

Jamie had had quite enough of being patronised by some bossy wee girl. 'Mebbe not – but you'd better not give me any more of your Sassenach lip, or I'll bend you over my knee and larrup you!'

The girl looked at him with delighted amusement. 'Oh this is going to be fun – I can learn a great deal from you, James Robert McCrimmon. Come on, I'll show you round. My name's Zoe, by the way ...'

Some time later, Jamie was feeling tired and more than a little dazed. He had seen the generator area, the computer section, the astro-navigational guidance complex, the space meteorology area, and a whole lot more, and his guide, the wee girl Zoe seemed to know absolutely everything about everywhere they'd seen.

Impressed and amused by her enthusiasm, Jamie had done his best to look interested, but he couldn't help thinking how much more the Doctor would have got out of the tour.

Now at last they were somewhere Jamie could take an interest in – a sort of mini greenhouse which their host, a stocky, cheerful fair-haired man called Bill Duggan had set up in the Wheel's main power room.

The rows of exotic alien plants in their carefully laid-out growing trays made a strange contrast to the gleaming technological environment all around them.

'This is my little kingdom,' said Bill Duggan proudly. 'How do you like my greenhouse?'

Jamie nodded appreciatively. 'Just fine. Where do you collect all these things?'

'Floating seeds, most of them. The only place they seem to flourish is down here in the power room. The Commander kicked up a dust storm at first, but Doc Corwyn said it was good therapy or something

– me, I just like flowers.' Lovingly he stroked the petals of an exotic black and scarlet blossom. 'This one comes from Venus. Imagine that, all those millions of miles away!'

'Twenty-four million, five hundred and sixty-four thousand miles at perihelion, one hundred and sixty-three million three hundred and fifty thousand at aphelion ...' Zoe rattled off the information as if someone had touched the read-out button on a computer.

'Aye, thanks,' said Jamie. 'I was just dying to know!'

Bill Duggan grinned and led them into the main body of the room. 'This is the capacitator bank for the laser-cannon, Jamie. Without it the gun's useless.' He indicated a massive central installation, shaped rather like a giant mushroom, its transparent dome crammed with complex electronic circuitry.

Jamie studied it respectfully. 'What do you need a cannon for, out here in space?'

Duggan shrugged. 'Self-defence – we can blot out any attackers for ten thousand miles in any direction!'

'Reassuring,' said Jamie drily.

Bill pointed to another similar installation. 'Anti-magnetic field generators over there. They fend off even medium-sized meteorites for up to five miles.'

Jamie turned to Zoe. 'The Doctor will be verra keen to see all this!'

'This Doctor friend of yours,' asked Zoe curiously. 'Is he a scientist?'

'Aye.'

'What's his speciality? Is he a physicist, bio-chemist, astronomer, bio-metrician ...'

'Aye,' said Jamie. 'That's right!'

'He sounds an interesting character,' said Bill Duggan. 'When's he going to be up and about?'

Jamie sighed. 'I wish I knew ...'

The Commander was asking Doctor Corwyn exactly the same question.

She looked thoughtful. 'Well, if the concussion's not too serious, before very long.'

Jarvis Bennett wasn't happy with her answer. 'That doesn't tell me much. I want some facts.'

'I don't blame you.'

'Landed with a couple of strays,' grumbled Jarvis. 'All these mystery panics from the crew. Routine's getting shoddy, I don't like it.'

'What panics?'

'Mysterious untraceable faults, air presure drops. Nothing serious. People are getting edgy.' He strode restlessly about the consulting room. 'Out in space people need routine, ordinariness. Confuse them and you get trouble.'

Gemma Corwyn watched him thoughtfully, thinking that it was his own feelings that he was really expressing.

As if sensing her thoughts Jarvis said hurriedly. 'Of course I'm used to emergencies, trained to cope. But all this nonsense …'

'What you call mysteries, panics …'

'Exactly! I don't want to know, Gemma!'

And that was the literal truth, thought Gemma Corwyn. Jarvis Bennett was a man for procedures, routines. The unknown would always be his greatest fear.

'Do you want to hear my preliminary report on the boy Jamie?'

'All right, go on.'

'He's lying. Not completely, and apparently reluctantly. He's very fit, mentally and physically, with a nice constructive personality. His blood pressure suggests he hasn't been long in space.'

'What has he lied about?'

'He said he'd had fever on the Silver Carrier, but he hadn't – his blood shows no trace of it.'

'But why lie about that?'

'I asked him to explain what had happened to the crew – fever was his excuse for not knowing. I think he lied about his companion's name – John Smith.'

'Well, they do exist, you know!'

Gemma showed him the label on the diagnostic machine. 'He was looking at this at the time. Coincidence possibly, but I doubt it. What's the most precious thing in deep space, Jarvis?'

'Air, water … take your pick …'

'And the training that teaches you not to waste them. Even one-journey travellers know that.' She leaned forward. 'He asked me for a drink of water – *and then left it!* He might have been on Earth. The boy hasn't had space training, Jarvis. He must be a stowaway …'

Immediately Jarvis Bennett's fear surfaced again. 'Sabotage!' he said explosively. 'He must be some kind of agent! But whose …'

'Well, plenty of people on Earth think we should suspend the space programme, use the resources to tackle Earth's problems. Some of them have tried to enforce their ideas …'

Jarvis Bennett seized on the theory enthusiastically. 'So these two stowed away on the Silver Carrier, disposed of the crew, pretended to drift here helplessly. We take them in and they start to sabotage the Wheel. Of course, everything fits!'

'It's a possibility, Jarvis – there are others …'

'We'll discuss them later.' Jarvis Bennett was already heading for the door. 'This could be serious. I'll deal with these people myself!'

6

BIRTH OF TERROR

Unaware that her guest had been branded a secret agent and potential saboteur, Zoe was still showing Jamie round, and explaining all about the operation of the Wheel. 'Now, this is the main Operations and Communications area – the control room in other words.'

Jamie looked round the control room. 'Aye – but what's the Wheel doing up here in space?'

'It's a radio-visual station for Earth, a half-way house for deep-space travel, a space research station, a stellar early warning system for potentially dangerous space phenomena ...'

Jamie grunted. 'Aye well, ask a silly question!' He dropped into one of the swivel chairs behind the main console.

'Not there,' said Zoe hurriedly. 'That's the Commander's chair!'

Jamie got up and he and Zoe moved over to Leo Ryan, who swung round and beamed cheerfully at them. 'You two are in for a treat.'

Bill Duggan, who'd tagged along on the tour said, 'The old man's going ahead, then?'

'Too right he is!'

Tanya Lernov looked up. 'I thought Doctor Corwyn had talked him out of it?'

'Only because she thought someone might be on board.' He grinned at Jamie. 'Lucky for you, young feller.'

Jamie gave him a baffled look. 'Sorry, you've lost me.'

Zoe explained. 'The Commander, Jarvis Bennett ... apparently he wanted to destroy the rocket.'

'We got your message just in time,' said Tanya.

Leo Ryan nodded. 'I'll say. Only minutes in it, the lasers were all primed and ready to go.'

Tanya said, 'And now Jarvis has given the go–ahead to try again?'

'That's right. I've run a new co-ordinate fix to be sure. The whole thing's primed and ready, all we need is the final signal.'

Jamie was horrified. 'You're no' going to blow up the rocket? What for?'

'Commander reckons it's unsafe,' said Ryan. 'Might go out of control and ram us. So, to be on the safe side, we blast it out of existence first.'

Tanya said, 'Jarvis asked for a visual record, I'd better re-position the camera. Zoe, come and help me recalculate will you, you're quicker than the computer.'

As Zoe and Tanya moved across to the nearby camera console, Jamie began edging towards the door ...

'Should be very interesting this,' Ryan was saying. 'It'll be quite an explosion.'

Jamie slipped out of the door. Nobody noticed him go.

Jamie strode boldly along the corridors of the Wheel. One or two of the technicians looked curiously at him, but no one challenged him.

He had a good sense of direction, and he managed to find his way back to the power room without two much trouble. There were Bill Duggan's flowers, and there close by was the capacitator bank – vital to the operation of the laser-cannon. Jamie began looking around. He opened a locker, and studied a row of aerosol cans on a shelf ...

Jarvis Bennett meanwhile had just strode into the control room in search of Jamie. He was far from pleased to be told that the boy seemed to have disappeared. 'He was definitely here?'

Zoe said, 'Yes, Commander, Doctor Corwyn asked me to look after him.'

'We were showing him round,' added Bill Duggan helpfully. Jarvis Bennett winced. 'Round where?'

'Everywhere. We'd just come from the power room ...'

'The power room,' said Jarvis thoughtfully. He beckoned Duggan aside and whispered urgently. 'Bill, don't say anything to the others. Just follow me out quietly when I go. Zoe, not a word about this to anyone.'

'Right, sir,' said Zoe obediently.

With a warning frown, the Commander marched out of the control room.

Zoe gave Bill Duggan a puzzled look. He shrugged. 'Don't look at me, I've no idea what's going on!'

Tanya Lernov came over to join them. 'Problems, Bill?'

'I don't know,' said Bill Duggan awkwardly. 'All in your mind, dear.' He hurried off.

By now Tanya was sure something was going on. 'What was the Commander talking to Bill Duggan about, Zoe?'

'Nothing important,' said Zoe. 'At least, I don't think so – I don't know. Does it matter?' She too hurried away.

Thoughtfully, Tanya went back to the console.

'What's all the whispering about?' asked Leo.

'I wish I knew. Leo, did I ever tell you about my nose?'

'What about it?'

'It's like a barometer, it never lets me down ... and I smell trouble.'

'Can you pin point where?'

'I think it's got something to do with that rocket out there. There's something sinister about it ...'

They turned to look at a monitor screen. On it there was a picture of the abandoned rocket, drifting in space.

On board the rocket, something was happening.

The alien clock which had counted down to zero had re-set, and now the number on the digital read-out was mounting: 997, 998, 999 ...

As the count reached a thousand, a harsh electronic screeching filled the control room. Lights came on in a darkened section to reveal two giant silver spheres. Power leads connected them to a machine of the same alien design as the countdown clock. The machine began to hum with power and the silvery spheres started to glow.

As they lit up they became semi-transparent, revealing inside the crouched shapes of giant humanoid figures, bent over, knees to chin, like some ghastly parody of a human embryo.

The transparent membranes of the spheres began to expand as the figures inside stirred, slowly flexing arms and legs. It was like some weird and uncanny process of birth. The difference was that these creatures would not be born small and helpless but huge and powerful, ready to conquer and destroy.

A massive silver fist smashed open one of the spheres, and the towering monster within began rising to its full height ...

7

MENACE

'I tell you, Leo,' said Tanya Lernov obstinately, 'There's trouble on the way. My nose never lets me down!'

Gently Leo touched the nose in question with his finger. 'Well, don't over-work it, it's much too pretty to risk damaging its shape.'

'Just don't say I didn't warn you. That rocket's dangerous.'

'Not for much longer it isn't. Once Jarvis gives the go-ahead, we'll blast it out of existence.'

Thoughtfully Jamie studied the label on the aerosol can in his hand. 'Liquid Plastic'. Underneath was written, 'Unmeltable, Unbreakable, Everlasting'.

'That ought to do it,' thought Jamie grimly and, lifting off the protective dome, he began spraying the plastic right into the heart of the capacitator bank. He shot the plastic in at random, aiming for the most complex looking sections of the equipment in the hope of doing as much damage as he could.

Suddenly a hand gripped his wrist, wrenching the can away from the machinery, twisting the wrist savagely so that Jamie was forced to drop the can.

'Red-handed!' said an angry voice in Jamie's ear.

Twisting round, Jamie saw he was in the grip of a stocky, balding, bearded man. Beside him was a horrified Bill Duggan. Grabbing a pair of gloves from the bench, Duggan grabbed a can of solvent from the locker and began squirting it into the machine. He shot Jamie a reproachful look. 'What do you think you're doing you fool?'

The bearded man tightened his grip on Jamie's wrist. 'Oh no, he's not just a fool, Bill. He's a saboteur!'

Bill Duggan stopped his spraying, and shook his head. 'It's no good, Commander. He's wrecked it.'

'Completely?'

Bill nodded. 'The stuff's had time to harden.'

'Watch him,' ordered the Commander. He shoved Jamie towards Bill, who stepped back and snatched up a spanner from the work bench.

Jamie held up his hands. 'All right, I'll not give you any trouble.'

'Too right you won't,' said Bill grimly.

Jarvis Bennett was talking into a wall communications unit.

'This is the Commander. Now hear this: all men on security duty are to draw side-arms immediately. Yellow Alert to be put into operation immediately. Two men from Security to report to the power room on the doubled.'

In the control room, Ryan turned to Tanya. 'Yellow Alert? What's the sudden panic?' He rose. 'I'll have to go and log out the blasters. Keep an eye on the Hercules cluster, will you, Tanya? Zoe thinks one of the stars in Messier Thirteen is going nova.'

'That's all we need, a star blowing itself to a million pieces. I told you my nose was never wrong!'

Two massive silver figures now sat at the rocket controls. Approximately man-shaped, they were much bigger than any man, a good seven feet tall, perhaps more. They seemed to be formed of some uniform silvery material, something with the qualities of both metal and plastic. Faces, bodies, arms and legs and the complex apparatus that formed the chest-unit, all seemed to be of a piece, made from the same gleaming silvery material. Their faces were blank, terrifying parodies of the human visage, with small circles for eyes and a thin letter-box slit for a mouth. The heads rose to a sort of crest into which was set what looked like a kind of lamp. Two strange handle-like projections grew out from the head in place of ears.

The Doctor, had he been there would have recognised them instantly. They were Cybermen.

At the moment they were busy with the communications equipment that had been installed in the rocket by their fellow

Cybermen. A monitor screen had been fitted on to the rocket control console, with a control panel beneath.

As one of the Cybermen adjusted controls with a giant silver hand, first a sleek and sinister-looking space ship appeared. After a moment the ship faded, and the screen was filled by the head of the Cyber Planner.

The head, shaped similarly to that of the Cybermen themselves, was even more featureless, semi-transparent so that the convolutions of the great brain within could be dimly seen.

The Cyber Planner was a creature of pure thought. He had no physical functions as such, and was, in fact, no more than a vast living brain.

'Report,' said the Planner from the screen. His voice had a blurred electronic quality.

The first Cyberman replied in the same eerie voice. 'Phase One complete.'

'The Cybermats are launched?'

'Phase Two complete.'

'You are undetected on the rocket?'

'Phase Three now prepared.'

'Report again after completion of Phase Three.'

The screen went dark.

'Yellow Alert,' blared the communications system. 'Yellow Alert all sections.'

Security men hurried along the corridor, buckling on their hand blasters.

Zoe and Doctor Corwyn came along the corridor.

'You'd better check your theory with the computer,' Gemma Corwyn was saying.

'Oh, I know I'm right,' said Zoe confidently. 'Hercules 208 in Messier Thirteen is definitely on the blink. I can tell what the radiation effect will be on Earth if you like.'

'Not now, Zoe,' said Gemma Corwyn gently.

They came to the corridor junction where their ways separated.

'I suppose you're going to see the fun, whatever it is,' said Zoe.

Gemma Corwyn said, 'Somehow, Zoe, I don't think this is going to be fun.'

Flanked by two armed security guards, Jamie was watching Bill Duggan complete his examination of the damaged machinery.

Jarvis Bennett stood looking on impatiently. 'Well?'

Duggan straightened up, glaring at Jamie. 'You did a good job, boy!'

'What's the exact damage?' demanded the Commander.

'It's very serious, sir. All the primary relay contacts are fused shut. The whole unit will have to be stripped down.'

'How long?'

'Depends how much plastic he used, and how far it penetrated.'

'Haw long?'

'I don't honestly know, Commander.'

'Surely you can give me some idea. You know as well as I do, without the laser-cannon we're virtually helpless.'

'Well, if we assume the worst – that the central storage charge unit is absolutely finished – it could take best part of a week.'

Gemma Corwyn hurried in and took in the tense scene. 'What's the trouble, Jarvis?'

He gestured savagely at Jamie. 'This young idiot has ruined the laser – poured quick-seal plastic right into the relay lines for the Branston mirrors.'

'But why?'

'Sabotage – just as we said.'

'No!' protested Jamie.

Jarvis Bennett swung round on him. 'What – are you one of these "Pull Back To Earth" maniacs? I suppose your friends are out there in deep-space, waiting to attack us now you've put our laser out of action …'

'You're talking rubbish,' said Jamie.

Bill Duggan looked up from the machinery. 'You can't deny it. We saw you.'

'I'm not denying anything,' said Jamie sulkily.

Gemma Corwyn was looking shocked. 'Is the laser really out of action, Jarvis?'

'It is.'

'But Zoe calculated there's a new star going nova. We haven't checked fully yet, but she's usually right.'

Jarvis Bennett looked grim. 'How bad is it?'

'Zoe calculates that the radiation flux will swing the meteor shower straight in on us. With the cannon we could knock the worst of them out.'

'I'd better get on with this as quick as I can,' said Bill Duggan. He hurried to the communicator. 'Maintenance! Get me maintenance ... All hands to the power room, immediate and urgent!'

Jarvis Bennett said, 'We'll go and check Zoe's calculations on the radar computers. Bring the boy along!'

The Commander, Doctor Corwyn, Jamie and his two guards all left the power room, leaving Bill Duggan to contemplate the ruined capacitator bank, and await the maintenance team.

He shook his head sadly. 'What a mess!' Suddenly a flash of movement caught his eyes. Something small and silvery had scuttled out of an open cupboard. Bill Duggan knelt to examine it.

At first glance it seemed like a sort of metal mouse, but when you examined it closer it was more like some kind of insect. Its scaled, segmented body was roughly triangular, with a sort of fringe around the base, and two huge red eyes glowed on the top of its head.

It shot backwards a foot or two as Bill approached, and then froze motionless. 'Hang on,' said Bill gently. 'I'm not going to hurt you.' He reached out slowly, and when the creature didn't move he carefully picked it up. 'Well, well, well, where do you come from, eh?' He tapped the hard metallic shell. 'You're a strange little creature aren't you? Some kind of space bug ...'

Perhaps it had come on board with one of his alien plants, he thought, grown maybe from some kind of egg – the cosmos was full of strange and wonderful things.

Whatever it was, Bill Duggan felt a sort of proprietary interest in it. When he heard the footsteps of the maintenance men approaching he said, 'I think I'd better hide you, Billy Bug – they'll think I've gone bonkers.'

He popped the creature back into the storage cupboard and closed the door.

*

Jarvis Bennett swung round from the computer read-out screen. 'Radar computers Two and Five both confirm Zoe's calculations.' He jabbed an angry finger at Jamie. 'Didn't know what you were letting yourself in for, did you boy? Ever been in a sky station when the meteorites hit?'

'Look, I'm sorry,' growled Jamie.

'Why did you do it?' asked Gemma.

Jamie turned to the Commander. 'They said you were going to give orders to blow up the rocket.'

Jarvis nodded. 'So?'

'I couldna let you, that's all.'

'Why not?'

Jamie looked round the circle of angry and concerned faces. 'Because the Doctor told me to protect the rocket.'

'Oh well, that's marvellous, isn't it?' said the Doctor bitterly. '"The Doctor told me to protect the rocket". Don't bother about a convincing reason, will you? Just leave me to get you out of trouble!'

They were in the Doctor's room in the medical section. Jamie had refused to say another word until he had a private meeting with the Doctor, and after a lot of what Jamie called havering, his request had been granted.

The Doctor, looking very much better, was stretched out on a couch, clearly in a sort of half-way stage between being ill in bed and properly up and about.

'Look, I had to stop them destroying the rocket, didn't I?' said Jamie desperately.

'I suppose so.'

'You know very well so! What about the TARDIS eh? Fine thing if they'd blown that to pieces!'

The Doctor sighed. 'And I was so enjoying this little rest.'

'What are you going to tell them, Doctor?'

'I've no idea – Jamie – what exactly did happen on that rocket? And there's no need to look at me like that!'

'Ye canna remember?'

'Well, it is a bit hazy.'

'I found you out in the corridor, by that locked door. Something must have shook up the rocket. It tumbled me out of bed. It must have made you stumble and hit your head as well.'

'I hit my head?'

'Don't you remember anything, Doctor?'

'Oh, I will. I will. Things keep lurking at the back of my mind.'

'How about that robot thing in the corridor? The one that was about to attack you. Do you remember *that*?'

'I'm afraid I don't.'

Jamie sighed despairingly. How was the Doctor going to solve their problems if he couldn't remember what they were?

The Doctor was staring into space. 'But there's something in the back of my mind, Jamie ... Some warning. Some menace ...'

The Cyber Planner's head was once more on the rocket's monitor screen. 'Report progress.'

The leading Cyberman said flatly. 'All phases proceeding as planned.'

'Excellent! Prepare Phase Four ...'

8

THE FIRST DEATH

Enrico Casali and his colleagues were busy at the radar computer console. Leo Ryan, Tanya and Zoe were clustered round, anxious to learn the news that might determine their fate.

'Band eighteen,' ordered Enrico.

The technician adjusted the controls.

Enrico nodded. 'Too far – now back a bit. Try a cross–fix ... just a touch more ... it's coming clearer now.'

'Getting it?' asked Leo urgently.

'I think so ... that's it ... there! Hold on that and turn up the gain.' Enrico turned to the others, indicating the star chart on the screen. 'You see? It's all happening in the Hercules cluster all right.'

'I told you,' said Zoe brightly. 'The same thing happened in the Perseus cluster a week ago, remember?'

Tanya said, 'Only then we had the laser-cannon to deflect the biggest meteorites.'

Casali tapped the screen. 'You see? It's beginning to emit hard gamma already.'

'Is it bigger than the Perseus one, Enrico?' asked Leo.

'At least four magnitudes up.'

Leo Ryan winced. 'Well, better give the Commander the bad news.'

Tanya touched his arm. 'What are we going to do – if they can't repair the laser in time?'

'There's still the forcefield ...'

Zoe shook her head. 'That won't help us. When a star of this magnitude goes nova it deflects meteorites with a mass of two hundred tons or more.'

Tanya shuddered. 'Two *hundred*?'

'At least,' said Zoe cheerfully.

'Aren't you *ever* wrong?' snarled Ryan.

'Rarely.'

'It's all a problem in solid geometry to you, isn't it? Don't you care what happens to us?'

'Of course. I'm only telling you what's going to happen.'

'Yes, just like a robot. Facts, calculations. Little brain child, all brain and no heart!' Ryan strode away, and with an apologetic look at Zoe, Tanya followed him.

Zoe stared after them, a puzzled frown on her face.

Bill Duggan was supervising a team of maintenance men as they lifted the central core out of the capacitator bank. 'That's it … steady. Get that down to the workshops and start stripping it right away … I'll be along in a moment.'

As the men staggered out of the door with the heavy piece of machinery, Bill Duggan glanced down and saw a flash of silver. It seemed to be coming from the bottom of a half-open cupboard door. He bent down and saw the silvery bug shooting out of the door. It froze as he bent down.

'Hello, Billy Bug. You should've stayed where I put you …' Duggan stared into the cupboard his eyes widening. There was a metal bar just inside the cupboard on the floor – or rather, half a metal bar. The other half was corroded, eaten away.

Bill Duggan stared at the bug. 'Hey, did you do that?'

He opened the cupboard door. There was a tumbled pile of metal bars scattered inside the cupboard. Every one of them was partially eaten away. Duggan picked up one of the bars and was astonished to feel it crumble between his fingers like rotten wood.

'What have you done?' he said appalled. He looked down, but the silvery space bug had disappeared.

A technician called Rudkin came into the power room, and Bill Duggan wheeled around, wild-eyed.

Rudkin looked curiously at him. 'What's the matter?' 'Nothing,' said Duggan hurriedly. 'How's it going?'

'The Commander asked me to come down and see if you needed any help. He asked how things were going.'

'You can tell him we're doing our best. Actually, there is something you could do for me. Look in on spares and ask them to give me a stock position on Bernalium, would you?'

'Sure.' Rudkin went out and Duggan turned back to the devastated store cupboard.

He unearthed an untouched stack of Bernalium bars at the very back and gave a sigh of relief. 'That lot's all right anyway. I'll murder that little beast ...'

He turned away, closing the cupboard door firmly behind him. A silver space bug flashed across the floor, and froze just by the cupboard door. Its eyes glowed, the door opened and the space bug shot inside ...

Gemma Corwyn was examining the Doctor, using a diagnostic machine much like the one she'd used on Jamie. The Doctor still in shirtsleeves submitted meekly to her tests, watching with interest as the bleeping electronic stethoscope passed over his body, flashing its results on the little screen.

Gemma Corwyn sat back, putting the instrument away. 'You and your friend are amazingly healthy specimens, Doctor. Though some of these readings are ...'

'Well, we all keep fit as best we can,' said the Doctor hurriedly. 'Does this mean I've got to get up?'

'Not quite yet, I'm afraid.'

'Oh good.'

'Does your head ache?'

'It did at first, but it's better now.'

'Any loss of memory?'

'Just a little.'

'Does that make you anxious?'

The Doctor smiled. 'Not unduly. I think you'll find my psyche quite in order.'

'Possibly. But you mustn't strain to remember. Concussion does interfere with memory – like having a word on the tip of your tongue. There's quite a bit we don't know about the memory bank.' She smiled, then added casually, 'I suppose the bit you can't remember is why you told Jamie to protect the rocket.'

'Oh no, I remember that all right,' said the Doctor cheerfully. 'We're not saboteurs, you know. The last thing we want is to interfere with your work, or put you in any danger. You saved our lives and we're very grateful.'

'But you have interfered,' Gemma pointed out coolly. 'We're in the path of a meteorite storm and we've no defence against it.'

'I didn't know about the meteorites,' said Jamie. 'I didna really ken what they were!'

The door opened and Zoe shot in. 'Is it all right? The guard on the door let me in.'

The Doctor frowned. 'Guard?'

'We can't let you roam wherever you want to,' Gemma pointed out. 'Not any more.'

'We're under arrest,' said Jamie glumly.

'How did you pilot the rocket so far, Doctor?' asked Zoe.

The Doctor frowned. 'I don't think we've met.'

Gemma Corwyn said, 'Zoe, this is Doctor … John Smith, isn't it?'

'What? Oh yes, that's me,' said the Doctor hurriedly. 'And what do you do on the Wheel, Zoe?'

'I'm an astrophysicist – a pure mathematics major.'

'Really? I'm impressed.'

'We use Zoe as our second opinion,' explained Gemma.

Zoe wasn't to be put off. 'You didn't answer my question, Doctor.'

'What question?'

'How did you pilot the rocket ship so far? There's a record of the last contact with the Silver Carrier. It had seven million miles to touchdown and fuel for twenty million. It couldn't have *drifted* ninety million miles off course in the time involved. It must have been driven and piloted. Somehow the rocket was refuelled in space, provided with at least another twelve fuel rods.'

'That's a very interesting theory, Zoe.'

'It isn't a theory, Doctor, it's fact. Pure logic.'

'Logic, my dear Zoe, merely allows you to be wrong with authority. Suppose a faulty automatic pilot was at work?'

'Driving a rocket ninety million miles on fuel for twenty million? That rocket was driven here somehow, Doctor. I know it was!'

The worrying thing, thought the Doctor, was that Zoe was almost certainly quite right.

The Cybermen were once again in conference with their Planner.

'We have ionised a star,' announced the Planner. 'Soon meteorites will strike the Wheel.'

The Cyberman said, 'Phase Three is in operation.'

'The Cybermats will consume Bernalium,' droned the Planner. 'Without Bernalium the Wheel cannot deflect the meteorites.'

The Cyberman said, 'They will discover Bernalium aboard this ship. Phase Four is ready.'

'Remove telemeter control from Cybermats,' ordered the Planner. His image faded from the screen.

One of Bill Duggan's space bugs – a Cybermat, to give it its proper name – was crouching in a corner of the power room. Suddenly its eyes glowed a fiercer red and it seemed to pulse with malignant energy.

The telemeter control, the device that rendered the Cybermats harmless when they had specific tasks to perform had been removed.

Now they were killers.

Rudkin came info the power room. 'Bill?' he called.

Bill Duggan was nowhere to be seen. Rudkin was just about to leave when the wall intercom flashed. Rudkin went over, touched a control and the face of a technician appeared on the screen. 'Vallance from spares here. Bill Duggan around?'

Rudkin said, 'No, I'm looking for him myself.'

'You know we're checking the Bernalium stock?'

'Yes, Bill asked me to check up on it. I had a word with Chang.'

'Well, we're a bit puzzled – most of the Bernalium stock was transferred over to him in the power room weeks ago. Bill must have got his wires crossed. Have a look round will you, see if you can locate it?'

'Sure.'

'Call me back, will you?'

'Will do.'

The screen went blank.

Rudkin started a methodical search of the many cupboards and storage lockers that lined the power room.

A Cybermat glided out of hiding and moved towards him, its eyes flaring red ...

Bill Duggan was in Doctor Corwyn's consulting room, pouring out his unlikely story. His conscience wouldn't allow him to keep silent any longer – even if the doctor did think he was potty. '... and now the Bernalium's useless, Doc.'

'What about the reserve?'

'I asked for a check, but later I remembered. I'm already holding most of it in the power room. You know how much we rely on the Bernalium rods. They're the only things that stand up in the laser-cannon.'

'And what about these creatures of yours ... I'm far more concerned about them.'

'There's only one – at least, that's all I found.'

'Did anyone else see it?'

'No.'

'Did you tell anyone about it at the time?'

'You must be joking. They already think I'm a nut for messing about with my flowers. How d'you think they'd react if I started telling them I'd found a space bug?'

Gemma looked thoughtfully at him. It could all be delusion – but it didn't sound like it. 'What did this bug look like?'

Duggan held his hands a little way apart. 'About so big ... cross between a fish and a rat. Big red eyes. Body feels like metal or some light tensile material ...'

'And you say it eats metal?'

'Not exactly. It sort of draws all the life out of it – corrodes it. You should see what it does to Bernalium!'

'But how did this thing get on the Wheel?'

'Search me – I'm just the one who found it. Could have got in through a loading bay, or one of the air locks.'

Gemma looked dubious. 'It's possible, I suppose.'

Duggan said worriedly, 'What's the matter? You think I'm a nut, don't you?'

Gemma rose. 'No, I don't. But I'd like to see this thing for myself.'

Bill Duggan jumped up. 'Okay, be my guest. I'll introduce you to Billy Bug with pleasure.'

They were in the corridor near the power room when they heard the scream. It was a terrible choking howl, like nothing either had heard before. They began to run. The scream echoed through the corridors of the Wheel. The Doctor, Jamie and Zoe heard it in the medical section and Jamie flung open the door of the Doctor's room. He found himself facing an armed security guard, a massive heavy-featured Irishman called Flanagan. 'You can't come out,' he announced.

'What was that scream?' asked Jamie.

'It sounded like all the devils of hell,' said Flanagan. 'But you still can't come out!' He shoved Jamie back into the room and closed the door.

Bill Duggan and Gemma Corwyn rushed into the power room – and found Rudkin sprawled on his back across the trays of flowers. He was dead, and his face was twisted in horror, as if death had frozen the scream in his throat …

9

THE TRAP

Gemma Corwyn knelt to examine the body. After a moment she rose, shaking her head.

Bill Duggan was looking inside the open cupboard. The last pile of Bernalium had been scattered and corroded like the rest.

There was an empty aerosol spray can lying near the body ... And there was something else.

Gemma Corwyn knelt down and touched it. 'What's this?' Sealed to the floor was an irregularly shaped lump of what seemed to be solid plastic ...

Some time later, the plastic lump was reposing on a tray by the Doctor's couch, with the Doctor, Zoe and Jamie all peering at it.

'The Commander's mounting a full enquiry,' said Zoe. She tapped the lump. 'But what I'm interested in is this!'

The Doctor said thoughtfully, 'Found by the body, was it?'

'They had to get one of the men to take up a floor plate. The polymer strength of this plastic is higher than chrome steel. You can't cut through it.'

'The Gordian Knot couldn't be untied either,' said the Doctor quietly.

'What does that mean?'

'I think he means there's always a solution,' whispered Jamie.

'And the Bernalium is useless, is it?' asked the Doctor.

Zoe nodded. 'Completely. We've got a few spares, but nowhere near enough.'

'And the laser, the main defence of the Wheel relies on Bernalium ...'

'Maybe there's a real saboteur on the Wheel,' suggested Jamie. 'Yon Bennett talked about some group or other ...'

'There are people who want to stop the space programme,' said Zoe.

'Aye well, mebbe they planted someone on board. The rocket comes along with us on board, and the saboteur uses the opportunity and strikes.'

'And murders?' asked the Doctor.

'If he was caught, he might have had to kill.'

'It's an interesting theory,' said the Doctor.

'Well, everything fits,' said Jamie.

The Doctor tapped the lump of plastic. 'Except this.'

'Och, it's just a spare part. The man tried to defend himself with the plastic and it misfired and went over some lump of machinery.'

'There's one way we can find out,' said the Doctor.

'How?' asked Zoe.

'Use the X-ray machine!' said the Doctor simply.

In the control room, the Commander's enquiry was in progress. Jarvis Bennett sat behind a table, Doctor Corwyn beside him. A miserable-looking Bill Duggan stood before the table. 'You'll be sent back to Earth when the next ship comes in,' the Commander was saying. 'I want a written report on the whole affair in my hands first thing tomorrow. That's all.' As Bill Duggan turned away Jarvis Bennett said, 'He's to be confined to quarters. Leo, you'll have to take over some of his operations. Tanya, you'll have to cover for Leo.'

'Very well, Commander.'

Jarvis turned back to Leo Ryan. 'Remember, I want the laser working as soon as possible.'

'Right, Commander.'

Jarvis swung round. 'Enrico, is the boarding party ready?'

'Laleham and Vallance are standing by, sir. Just waiting for the go-ahead.'

'Then give it!'

'Commander.'

As Enrico spoke into the intercom, Jarvis Bennett turned to Gemma. 'I want a word with you in your quarters, Doctor Corwyn. As for the rest of you, let's get back to normal working conditions.' Leaving a flurry of activity behind him, Jarvis Bennett strode away.

*

Bill Duggan was talking quietly to Tanya.

'Sorry, Bill,' she said quietly.

'It was my own fault, I was a fool.'

'You didn't do anything.'

'I should have told somebody straightaway when I saw that creature. The old man doesn't believe me, but it was there.'

Leo said, 'We searched the whole power room, Bill. There was a hell of a mess, but we didn't see anything like your bug.'

'Well, I didn't dream it … What's the use? Rudkin's dead, and talking won't bring him back.' He moved sadly away.

In Gemma Corwyn's quarters the Commander was letting off steam. 'What's the matter with you people? You can't turn round without dreaming up some little bit of emotionally based fantasy. Did you hear that nut Duggan? Space rodents! The man's a wreck!'

Gemma Corwyn drew a deep breath. 'Jarvis, will you listen?'

'If it's sensible, yes.'

Gemma began counting on her fingers. 'One: the rocket drifts near us. Two: drops in temperature and air pressure, adjusted back to normal. Three: two meteorite storms, both above average dimensions, both within seven days. Four: two strangers brought to the Wheel, one of them sabotages the laser. Five: Bill Duggan's apparitions, call them what you like, turn up and corrode our Bernalium … just when we're facing a big meteor storm. I tell you Jarvis, that rocket is the base of all our troubles.'

'Don't worry about it,' said Jarvis complacently. 'I've just sent two men across to look it over. But, let's have no more mysteries …'

After a certain amount of fiddling, the Doctor got the plastic lump into the scanning field of the X-ray machine beside his couch. Zoe was busy processing the prints. The results would appear on the machine's little monitor screen. At the moment the screen simply showed the plastic lump.

'Right, they're ready,' said Zoe. She slipped the negative into the machine and flicked a switch.

Suddenly the plastic lump seemed to melt away, revealing a picture of the creature entombed inside.

Zoe heard the Doctor and Jamie gasp. 'What is that thing?' she asked.

'A Cybermat,' whispered the Doctor.

Jamie said, 'But that means there are Cybermen here too then?'

'That's right, Jamie. And there's only one place they could be – on that rocket!'

Propelling themselves by little thrusts from their oxygen cylinders, Vallance and Laleham drifted across space towards the rocket. A few minutes later they were clambering through the air lock, and making their way into the control room.

There was a crate in the centre of the control room, its lid already pried off. Valance and Laleham went over to it, and saw that it was piled high with Bernalium ...

They heard heavy footsteps, and turned to find two giant silver forms towering over them. Laleham reached for the blaster at his hip, but as he did so a bright light beamed from the head of the Cyberman nearest him and he slumped, dropping the blaster. A similar beam from the second Cyberman was transfixing Valance. The beams brightened and the two spacemen straightened up, their bodies rigid.

The first Cyberman said, 'You will take us to the Wheel. Inside the Wheel you will help us. Obey!'

10

TROJAN HORSE

Jarvis Bennett stared at the image on the X-ray machine's monitor screen – it showed a Cybermat entombed inside the lump of plastic. 'And what's this supposed to mean?'

The Doctor said sombrely, 'It means that the Wheel is under threat from Cybermen.'

Jarvis laughed scornfully. 'Cybermen? Where did you dream up a name like that?'

Zoe was staring blankly ahead of her. 'The study and comparison of systems of control and communications in living organisms and machines,' she recited.

'What are you talking about?' snapped Jarvis Bennett.

'Cybernetics,' said Zoe.

'I know what Cybernetic means, young lady, and I don't need any lectures from you!'

'I tell you, Commander, these Cybermen do exist,' said the Doctor. 'You must believe me – you must!'

'On the evidence of one faked X-ray?'

'It's not faked,' said Zoe indignantly. 'I took and developed it myself, Commander.'

Jarvis Bennett looked angrily at the Doctor. 'So what exactly are these Cybermen?'

The Doctor's voice was grave. 'They were men once – human beings like you. They come from the planet Mondas. Now they are more machine than man.'

'You mean – half and half?' asked Jarvis Bennett uneasily.

'More than that,' said the Doctor. 'Their entire body is mechanised. Their brains have been treated neuro-surgically to remove all

273

human emotion, all awareness of pain. They are ruthless inhuman killers.'

Jarvis Bennett laughed nervously. 'You expect me to believe all this rubbish?'

'It isn't rubbish, Commander, believe me. They'll kill anyone who stands in their way. You've *got* to believe me!'

Laleham and Vallance looked on unmoving while the first Cyberman climbed into the enormous crate, now standing quite empty.

The second Cyberman said, 'You will take us to the Wheel. Inside the Wheel you will help us. Now obey your instructions.' The second Cyberman climbed into the crate.

Working together silently, the two men picked up the false top that lay propped against the crate and fitted it into place, so that it formed a sort of shallow tray, taking up the top quarter of the crate. Into this space they put the boxed bars of Bernalium. When they had finished the whole crate appeared to be full. They fitted on the lid, hammering it into place.

Then Vallance moved to the communication unit. 'Rocket to Wheel, Rocket to Wheel ...'

The Doctor was still trying to convince the Commander of the danger they were facing. 'Don't you understand? Somehow the Cybermen will get inside the Wheel.'

'Nothing gets on and off the Wheel just like that. What do you think this is, a heliport?'

'Listen to him will ye?' urged Jamie. 'He's telling you the truth.'

Jarvis turned on him. 'No, I'll tell you what he's doing – what too many others are trying to do – spreading fear ... alarm and terror. Do you think I can't see it? It must be some kind of space sickness ...'

Gemma Corwyn said, 'Jarvis, you might at least *listen* ...'

'How could anything get inside the Wheel?' demanded Jarvis. 'How will these creatures get through the airlocks? Or will they just float through the loading bay in full view of everybody?'

'It's still worth listening, and taking precautions,' said Gemma. 'Just in case there *is* some truth in all this.'

'Don't try to tell me my job, Gemma. I'm still Commander of the Wheel, and things will be done my way. Any orders to the contrary will have to come from Earth Control, and that's what ... that's ...' His voice trailed off. Suddenly he turned and marched from the room.

The Doctor shook his head. 'How do you convince a man like that?'

'I think Bill Duggan should see that X-ray,' said Gemma. 'Go and get him, will you please, Zoe?'

'Isn't he still confined to quarters?'

'Have him brought here under guard if necessary – you can use my authority – but get him, Zoe. I'll be responsible.' As Zoe hurried from the room, Gemma Corwyn continued, 'Jarvis was right about one thing, Doctor. These Cybermen of yours can't just walk on to the Wheel.'

'You don't know the Cybermen as I do,' said the Doctor. 'Believe me, they'll find a way.'

Vallance and Laleham were floating back towards the Wheel, propelling themselves by puffs of oxygen from their cylinders. Between them slung on a harness of ropes, there floated the enormous crate.

Vallance's voice crackled from a speaker in the control room. 'Survey party returning. We are coming in through the loading bay.'

Tanya frowned. 'Ask why. We've prepared airlock five.'

Casali said, 'Is anything wrong, survey party? Airlock five is ready for you.'

'Survey party to Control. We have discovered a large crate of Bernalium on the rocket, and are bringing it over with us.'

'This'll cheer the old man up!' whispered Casali.

Tanya nodded. 'I'd better check with him though.'

'Checking with Commander, survey party,' said Casali. 'Please await confirmation.'

Tanya was already talking to Jarvis Bennett on the internal visiphone. 'Survey party report a find of Bernalium on the rocket, Commander. They want to bring it on board. Shall I give the go-ahead?'

Jarvis Bennett's face beamed cheerfully from the screen. 'Yes indeed, we need it badly. Somebody's using their brains at last. Good work!'

Tanya nodded to Casali, and he spoke into his communications mike. 'All clear for cargo, survey party. Loading bay will be clear for your arrival.'

*

Bill Duggan was staring in astonishment at the picture of the Cybermat on the X-ray screen. 'That's old Billy Bug all right! What is it?'

'An alien machine,' said the Doctor. 'Destructive, capable of killing.'

'I thought it was some kind of space rodent – I know you all think I'm crazy ...'

'It's a pity you didn't tell someone about it straightaway,' said the Doctor severely.

Bill Duggan's voice was defensive. 'I told the old man eventually – and look what happened? I got confined to quarters!'

'I'd better take you back,' said Zoe. 'Then I've got to do some calculations on those meteorites – half the space fleet might be flying into them.'

'The meteorites, yes, of course,' said the Doctor suddenly. 'The Cybermats must have been sent to put your laser out of action – that's why they attacked your stocks of Bernalium.'

Jamie looked relieved. 'So even if I hadn't put the laser out of action, the Cybermats would have done it anyway.'

'Are there any other defences?' asked the Doctor.

There are magnetic field projectors,' said Gemma. 'The Meson Shields. But they can only ward off small meteorites.'

'Maybe their destruction of the Bernalium had some other purpose,' said the Doctor thoughtfully. 'Wait a minute – the rocket. There must be Bernalium on board the rocket ...'

The doors of the loading bay were open on to the blackness of space. With eerie slowness the two spacemen floated inside, bringing the crate between them. A space suited technician stood waiting by the loading bay controls. Once the two space-walkers and their cargo were safely inside, he touched a control and the massive double doors slid closed. Slowly he brought up the artificial gravity field and the two men and their burden settled gently to the floor. There was a sudden whoosh as he fed air into the chamber. He studied the dials for a moment, then gave the two men a thumbs up sign. Removing their helmets, all three men climbed the steep flight of steps leading up out of the loading bay.

The huge wooden crate was left on the floor of the loading bay. The Trojan Horse of the Cybermen was on board the Wheel.

11

TAKEOVER

Zoe was reeling off a string of calculations into her voice-recorder when Jamie wandered into her library. 'Hey, what are you doing, talking to yourself?'

'I was recording some very important readings, James Robert McCrimmon – and now you're recorded too!'

'I'm not!'

Zoe touched a control and Jamie heard himself saying, 'Hey, what are you doing, talking to yourself?'

He gave her an astonished look. 'Och, have I ruined it?'

'Not really. I thought you were confined to quarters?'

'Och, I was going crazy – Doctor Corwyn told the guard I needed to get out for a while – she's keeping the Doctor as a hostage!'

'Well, you got off to a bad start, sabotaging the laser-gun.'

'I had to do that,' said Jamie.

'Why?'

'I canna tell you.'

Zoe looked curiously at him. 'Tell me something else then. Is the Doctor telling the truth – about these Cybermen? Do they really exist?'

'They exist all right. I've seen them!'

'Of course, such creatures are theoretically possible,' said Zoe thoughtfully. 'Given advanced cybernetic technology ...'

'Well, dinna be frightened,' said Jamie reassuringly. 'I'll look after you.'

'Oh, I'm not frightened, just curious. I should very much like to see one.'

Jamie realised she was quite sincere. 'Och, you're a funny wee thing. You take it all so calmly.'

'All brains and no heart?'

'I didna say that,' protested Jamie.

'No, Leo Ryan did.'

'Well, he's plain daft then!'

Zoe smiled at him, 'Jamie, these calculations *are* urgent ...'

'Och, I can take a hint – I'm away!' Jamie wandered off.

Feeling strangely cheered up, Zoe went back to her work.

Jarvis Bennett strode purposefully into the power room, Bill Duggan trailing behind him and surveyed the busy scene. Leo Ryan and the burly Irish technician Flanagan were hard at work on the capacitator bank, which seemed to be lying in dis-assembled sections all over the power room.

'How's it going, Leo?' asked the Commander.

Leo Ryan straightened up. 'Not too badly, sir. We've been working non-stop.'

'I'm giving you Bill Duggan here, Leo. No reason he can't make himself useful. Keep up the good work!' Beaming cheerfully, the Commander strode away.

Ryan said, 'Boy, am I glad to see you Bill! This thing's your baby, not mine.'

Bill Duggan cast a skilled professional eye over the machinery. 'How's it looking?'

'Well, we've had a bit of luck. The central deployment complex didn't get as much plastic as we feared. Maintenance have sorted it out and sent it back.' He pointed to the central core which was scattered in pieces around the main console.

Bill Duggan nodded. 'That's great! How about the Bernalium problem?'

'I haven't got around to that one yet!' Leo turned to Flanagan.

'Go on, you, hoppit!'

'I'll grab a snack and be back in five minutes,' promised Flanagan.

'You'll take forty-five minutes and like it,' ordered Ryan.

As Flanagan grinned wearily and went off Bill Duggan said, 'What about you, Leo, you look done in.'

'Can't leave you here all alone Bill, it's a two-man job.'

The technician, Chang, came in just in time to over hear him. 'Some people have all the luck – the Commander just nabbed me, said you needed some help. Of course, I've only done two watches in a row!'

'Congratulations,' said Ryan drily. 'I've just done three!'

'Go on, Leo, clear off,' said Bill Duggan. 'Chang and I can handle things here.'

Leo Ryan said, 'I'll just have a quick bite and – all right, I know!'

'You'll take forty-five minutes and like it!' said Chang and Bill Duggan in chorus.

Ryan grinned and went away.

'Right,' said Chang. 'What do I do?'

The Doctor was studying another X-ray picture, not of a Cybermat this time but of his own skull.

'You may get the odd headache for a while,' said Gemma Corwyn. 'But at least there's no lasting damage. It's an extraordinary X-ray, though. In fact, your whole physical make-up ...'

'I'm so glad there's no damage,' said the Doctor hurriedly. 'Well done, Miss Corwyn.'

'It's Mrs,' said Gemma Corwyn quietly. 'At least, it was. My husband died three years ago in the asteroid belt.'

'I'm so sorry,' said the Doctor gently.

'My name's Gemma. Why don't you call me that?'

'Thank you, Gemma,' said the Doctor solemnly. 'Now, tell me about your Commander, Mr Bennett. Isn't he a strange man to be in a position like this?'

Gemma found herself torn between loyalty to Jarvis Bennett and a desire to confide in the Doctor. 'Well, not in ordinary circumstances ...'

'Are there any ordinary circumstances in space?'

'Jarvis simply can't accept phenomena outside the known laws of science ...'

The Doctor nodded. 'I think that's a very accurate – er ...'

'Diagnosis, you were going to say?'

'You're very perceptive, Gemma.'

She looked anxiously at him. 'You think Jarvis's attitude is a weakness – medically, I mean?'

'Don't you?'

'Normally Jarvis is more than capable of commanding the Wheel. It's a continuous, merciless responsibility ...'

'Exactly! But what does a man like that do when faced with a problem for which he doesn't have a solution?'

'I've been – concerned,' said Gemma slowly. 'I've a feeling that there are some things that Jarvis just can't face. He may have blocked off a part of his mind …'

Jarvis Bennett marched purposefully into the control room, and stood surveying the technicians, working busily at their consoles. 'Everything going all right here? Yes, I can see it is. Good, good. Well done!' Nodding and smiling at everyone who caught his eye, the Commander did a complete circuit of the control room and disappeared out of the door.

Tanya Lemov gave Casali a baffled look. 'Enrico?'

He looked up from his console. 'Mmm?'

'Did you notice anything – odd, about the Commander?'

'No – why?'

'He seemed a bit – detached.'

'Yeah?'

Tanya shrugged. 'Probably just my imagination.'

The Doctor was struggling into his coat when Jamie came back into the room. 'Well, here I am. Are you better now, Doctor?'

'He needs more rest,' said Gemma. 'You shouldn't be up and about yet, Doctor.' She turned to Jamie. 'Can't you persuade him to rest?'

'Och, it's no use trying to stop the Doctor doing what he wants!'

'Do be reasonable Gemma,' said the Doctor. 'I've got to get up – I know the danger we're in. The Cybermen want the treasures of Earth, you see, they want to colonise …'

'But you're not even supposed to leave this room, Doctor. Jarvis gave orders –'

'He isn't fully responsible!'

'I'm sorry, Doctor. I can't countermand the Commander's orders.'

'But you let Jamie out.'

'Only briefly. He's got to stay here now – and so must you.'

Jamie grinned. 'Hey, Doctor, she's as stubborn as you are.'

The Doctor was about to protest further, when Jarvis Bennett strode into the room. 'Everything in order here? Good, good. Up and about, eh, Doctor? I've done the tour, Gemma, and everything's running like clockwork!'

'That's fine, Jarvis. I think we ought to talk about the rocket ...'

'Yes, yes, everything's going well,' said Jarvis. 'You must want to stretch your legs a bit, have a wander around.'

The Doctor shot Gemma a quick look. 'Er, yes, thank you. you'll tell the guard?'

'Yes, I'll deal with it.' He opened the door and addressed the bewildered guard. 'Off you go, everything's in order!' The guard moved away.

'Jarvis!' said Gemma sharply.

He swung round. 'Make a note about morale, Doctor Corwyn. Never been better. Everything's in order ...' His voice tailed off. 'Tired now, better turn in. Sleep, that's the idea, I'll be needed at first watch ...' Reviving, he beamed at them. 'Well, keep up the good work!' With a cheery nod, Jarvis Bennett turned and marched away, a happy man in a world in which everything was in order.

A world of his own.

In the power room, Bill Duggan was gloomily examining the handful of un-corroded Bernalium rods that he'd been able to scrape together. 'These are no good to us anyway – they're all covered in plastic.'

'Didn't anyone tell you?' said Chang. 'They brought back a whole load of Bernalium from the rocket. It's still in the loading bay.'

'Well, don't just stand there, go and grab me half a dozen rods. With a bit of luck we can have this lot reassembled in a few more hours.'

'On my way,' said Chang, and hurried out.

A few minutes later, Chang came down the steps to the loading bay. The place was in semi-darkness. The crate from the rocket stood in a little pool of light in the centre of the bay. Chang went to the box, lifted the lid, and took one of the boxes of Bernalium rod from the inside.

Removing the box revealed the wooden surface of the false top, and with a shock of astonishment, Chang realised that the top layer of Bernalium was all there was. He took out the rest of the boxes and then lifted out the false top, revealing the empty blackness beneath.

As he peered inside a giant silver hand reached out of the shadows behind him, and gripped his shoulder, pulling him back. Chang swung round, wrenching himself free and staggered back against the crate. For a moment he stared up in unbelieving horror at the giant silver form towering over him. Then he snatched up one of the boxes of Bernalium rods he'd just unpacked and hurled it at his attacker's chest.

The Cyberman staggered back, and Chang ran for the stairs ... A second Cyberman appeared out of the darkness, blocking his escape. He turned, spun around – and saw Laleham and Vallance come out of the shadows.

'Help me!' he screamed.

But neither man moved or spoke. Chang turned again, dodged round the Cyberman blocking his path and made a desperate doomed run for the steps. The chest units of both Cybermen glowed fiercely for a moment, and caught in the fierce light Chang twisted, screamed briefly and died.

One of the Cybermen walked to the foot of the stairs, scooped up Chang's body and carried it away, thrust almost casually under one arm ...

12

INTO DANGER

Tanya Lernov glanced up as an indicator light came up on a side-console. 'Enrico, someone's using the incinerator in the loading bay. Have you got it down?'

Casali punched up information on a read-out screen. 'Nothing here.'

Leo Ryan wandered in, looking fresh and rested. 'What's the problem, Tanya?'

'Somebody just used the loading bay incinerator.'

'Looks like a spot of unauthorised waste-disposal,' said Casali. 'Better log it, Tanya. Someone'll catch it …'

Bill Duggan was hard at work reassembling the capacitator bank when Laleham and Vallance came into the power room. He looked up. 'Hullo, boys. Where's Chang?'

Laleham said flatly. 'He cut his hand. He has gone to the medical bay.'

Both men, Duggan saw, were carrying boxes of Bernalium rods. 'Trust him. Poor old Chang!'

Vallance said, 'What is to be done?'

'Open a box of those rods will you?' said Duggan. 'I've nearly beaten this job. I only hope the rods are the right size.'

'They are,' said Laleham.

Bill Duggan shot him a quick glance. 'Didn't know you were an expert.'

In the same toneless voice Laleham said, 'The laser must be made operative, or the meteorites will destroy the Wheel.'

'No!' said Bill Duggan sarcastically. 'What do you think I'm sweating over here for?'

Laleham handed him a Bernalium rod. 'It is the right size.'

Duggan slotted the rod in place. 'It is too! You must be psychic. Better not tell the old man, he doesn't believe in it.'

'When will the repair be finished?' asked Vallance.

Bill Duggan was finding his two visitors a bit of a pain. 'It won't get done at all if you don't stop nattering at me.'

'The meteorites must not harm the Wheel,' said Vallance again.

Bill Duggan returned to his work. 'Worried about the storm, are you? Well, don't be. It'll be a close thing, but I reckon on having the laser assembled and ready for operation in, oh, six or seven hours maximum.' He looked up at them and grinned. 'So you two can sleep like babes, daddy won't let anything happen to you!' Once again he bent over his work, whistling tunelessly.

Vallance walked over to the door and opened it. A Cyberman came into the room.

Still bent over his work Bill Duggan said, 'Look, if you two want to make yourself useful ...' He looked up, and saw the Cyberman. Slowly he straightened up. He opened his mouth to scream but a beam from the Cyberman's helmet transfixed him and he went rigid, staring straight ahead of him – just like Laleham and Vallance.

The Cyberman said, 'The Wheel must be protected from the meteorites. We will re-assemble your laser. You will go to the control room. Here are your orders ...'

Gemma Corwyn was in her quarters, studying a medical file on her computer read-out screen. The file was headed: Jarvis Bennett.

She looked up almost guiltily as someone came into the room. Hurriedly she switched off the screen. 'What is it, Zoe?'

Zoe said worriedly. 'It's rather difficult ... I've just made a report, some calculations ... I've been told to forget them.'

'Ordered by whom? What report?'

'My calculations on the path of the meteorite storm. I found evidence of a critical state, reported it to the Commander –'

'And he ignored it?'

Zoe nodded. 'You don't seem very surprised.'

'He's getting worse,' said Gemma almost to herself.

'Is he ill?' asked Zoe.

'I'm not sure, yet.'

'If he is ill,' said Zoe seriously, 'he's chosen a rather inconvenient time, hasn't he?'

'Not very emotional, are you, Zoe?'

'Emotional?' Zoe frowned. 'Leo Ryan said I was all brain and no heart.'

'It's just your training, Zoe. I shouldn't worry about it.'

'Oh, but I do,' said Zoe solemnly. 'Don't want to be a freak. Maybe Leo's right. My brain's been pumped so full of facts and figures … I want to feel things too.'

Gemma Corwyn said gently, 'Some people with your training do have trouble developing their human emotions.'

'You don't think I'll be like that, do you?'

Gemma Corwyn smiled, 'No, you appear to have survived your brainwashing very well.'

'Good,' said Zoe.

'Now then,' said Gemma Corwyn. 'Tell me about these calculations of yours …'

In the control room, the Doctor and Jamie, apparently restored to favour were being given the tour.

'… and this last one here is how we check all energy expenditure,' Tanya was saying. 'Any device on the Wheel that uses energy shows up somewhere on the board … from a coffee grinder upwards.'

'Have you got any coffee?' asked the Doctor hopefully.

Tanya shook her head. 'I've got a coffee tablet – would you like one?'

The Doctor shook his head and wandered away.

'You won't forget to keep an eye out for some mercury, Doctor,' whispered Jamie.

'I haven't forgotten, Jamie. I'm very worried about the TARDIS. If I'm right and there are Cybermen aboard that racket …'

Zoe and Gemma hurried into the control room, and were soon engaged in a low-voiced conference with Leo Ryan, Tanya and Casali.

The Doctor beckoned to Zoe, who came over to them. 'What's going on?'

'I did some calculations on the meteorites – they're heading towards us faster than I'd first thought.'

'Don't you ever have any cheerful news?' growled Jamie.

'Facts are facts,' said Zoe primly. 'And these are indisputable.'

'I wouldn't dream of arguing,' said the Doctor hurriedly. 'Can you get the laser repaired in time?'

'Apparently. The real worry's the Commander. He just brushed my warning about the meteorites aside. That's the worry, not the laser.'

'He's getting worse,' muttered the Doctor.

Zoe nodded. 'That's what Doctor Corwyn said. He is ill, isn't he?'

Blatantly the Doctor changed the subject. 'Why aren't you more worried about the laser? Even if you get it fixed in time, I thought all the Bernalium had been destroyed.'

'Oh no,' said Zoe confidently. 'Some more turned up.'

'Oh good!'

'Yes, two of the men brought a crate of it over from the rocket.'

'What did you say?'

'That's what Flanagan said – I met him coming off duty.'

The Doctor went and grabbed Gemma Corwyn's arm and marched her away from the group. 'Did you know about this Bernalium from the rocket?'

'Yes, Tanya told me just now.'

'Don't you see? The Cybermen came over in that crate!'

'But our men wouldn't have brought them across.'

'Maybe they were tricked.' The Doctor frowned. 'Or maybe they knew what they were doing. Cybermen have ways of making people carry out orders.'

'Hypnotism?' asked Gemma.

'Something like that.'

'But all Wheel personnel are protected against brain control. There's an implanted Silenski capsule. It gives off a signal if there's any interference with the brain of the wearer.'

'How can we check?' asked the Doctor.

Gemma led him over to Tanya. 'I want to check the Silenski circuit.'

'I'll have to activate the whole detection network.'

'Do it,' said Gemma. 'I'll authorise the extra power.'

Tanya adjusted the controls and a large monitor screen came to life, with a network of electronic trace-lines running endlessly across it. 'If the lines are even, everything's normal … I'll scan this room first.'

As Tanya began her check, Bill Duggan came into the control room. He hovered uncertainly in the doorway.

Jamie moved over to Zoe. 'What's he hanging round like that for?'

Zoe frowned. 'I thought he was confined to quarters.' She went over towards the door. 'Hullo, Bill, has the Commander ...'

Bill Duggan went on in to the control room, ignoring her.

The lines on Tanya's scanner began fluctuating wildly. 'Look!'

'Someone is affected,' said Gemma. 'You were right, Doctor!'

'It's someone in this room,' whispered Tanya.

'Can we pin it down?' asked the Doctor quietly.

'I'll scan the room,' said Tanya. 'She adjusted controls. 'Somewhere over ... *that* way ...'

She pointed – and they saw Bill Duggan raise a big spanner high above his head and smash it down on the communications console, again and again ...

'Stop him!' yelled the Doctor.

Jamie hurtled across the room and tried to pull Bill away, but was thrown off with apparently superhuman strength. The spanner smashed down again. Sparks crackled across the console, and Casali was suddenly hurled backwards out of his chair. As the spanner rose again, Leo Ryan drew his blaster and fired ... Bill Duggan crashed to the ground.

The Doctor ran to the body and knelt to examine it. 'He's dead. The Cybermen must be here, on the Wheel. They took over this poor fellow and sent him to stop you from getting a message to Earth.' He turned to Gemma. 'If you'll take my advice, you'll alert the whole Wheel. You'll need something to stop your people from being taken over. Small sheets of metal will do, taped to the back of the neck. It interferes with the Cyber control signal.'

'I'll see to it,' said Leo Ryan, who had come to join them.

'What do we do? asked Jamie.

'We're going hunting,' said the Doctor grimly.

'Oh aye? Are you sure you know who's to be hunted?'

The Doctor and Jamie moved off.

Zoe watched them go. She shivered. 'I feel cold, Doctor Corwyn.'

'It's shock,' said Gemma gently. 'Just sit quietly and keep out of the way.'

Zoe sat down shivering. She had never felt more frightened – or more useless.

The Doctor and Jamie came down the steps into the loading bay. The empty crate stood in its little pool of light.

'Well, there it is,' said Jamie.

'Sssh,' whispered the Doctor.

They crept cautiously over to the crate. The loading bay seemed to be empty. The Doctor and Jamie studied the crate, working out the purpose of the false top. They saw the boxes of Bernalium bars, stacked beside the crate. The only thing they didn't see was the giant silver form of the Cyberman as it descended the steps behind them …

13

CYBERMAT ATTACK

Suddenly Jamie heard the scrape of metal on metal, turned round and saw the descending Cyberman.

It was still at the top of the steps, staring arrogantly straight ahead, and for the moment it didn't seem to have seen them. Jamie grabbed the Doctor by the arm and heaved him out of sight behind the crate, and into the shadows beyond. The Cyberman descended to the floor of the loading bay, picked up one of the boxes of Bernalium rods, turned and went back up the steps.

As it disappeared, Jamie gave a silent whistle of relief. 'That was close.'

'I can't understand them,' said the Doctor. 'It's so easy now.'

'Eh? What are you talking about?'

'Destroying the Wheel, Jamie. That's what I'm talking about. From the outside it's strong enough, but now that the Cybermen are inside ...'

'Aye, I see ... What d'you think they're planning then?'

'I don't know, Jamie, not yet – but it's obvious that they don't want to destroy the Wheel.'

'What do they want then?'

'I wish I knew. But the first thing we must do is protect these people.'

'Aye, but how do we do that?'

'What's the one thing we need to survive that Cybermen don't?'

'Food?' suggested Jamie, thereby reminding himself he was feeling peckish.

'Always thinking of your stomach,' said the Doctor reprovingly. 'No, air ... that's what, air!' The Doctor rose and went over to the wall communication unit. 'Now, I wonder how this works?'

*

In the control room, Tanya called Gemma Corwyn and Leo Ryan over to her console. 'It's the Doctor, calling from the loading bay.'

They saw the Doctor's face on Tanya's monitor. 'It would be wise to seal off all the airlock doors,' he was saying. 'Can you do that?'

Tanya glanced at Leo, who nodded. She turned back to the Doctor. 'Yes, we can. Why?'

'The Cybermen are definitely on the Wheel. Jamie and I have just seen one. They may try to interfere with the air supply.'

'Doctor,' whispered Jamie.

'Yes, what is it?'

Jamie pointed. 'I think I saw something move, over there in the shadows. I just caught a glimpse of it in the corner of my eye.'

The Doctor turned, peering into the shadows.

'What's wrong?' asked Gemma.

Tanya said, 'I don't know.'

'Shall I seal off the airlock doors, Gemma?' asked Leo.

Gemma considered for a moment, then nodded. 'Yes, do it.'

Leo went over to another console and began issuing instructions. Tanya looked up at Gemma Corwyn and said quietly, 'I suppose we can trust the Doctor?'

'I'm not sure why I do, but I do,' said Gemma. 'Anyway, sealing off the airlocks is good common sense.'

Jamie pointed again. 'There, look!'

The Doctor saw a Cybermat, gliding from a patch of shadow into the light. It didn't appear to have seen them as yet ... The Doctor turned back to the intercom, speaking in an urgent whisper. 'Listen to me very carefully. Please, just do as I ask and don't delay. There's a Cybermat very close to us. Any moment it'll tune into our brainwaves ...'

Jamie had been keeping the Cybermat under observation. 'It's turning, Doctor,' he whispered. 'And look, there's another!'

The Doctor whispered into the wall mike. 'Hook up a vario audio-frequency to this channel – at once please!'

Tanya looked at Gemma for a decision.

'Do it please, Enrico,' she ordered.

Casali began making rapid adjustments of a console.

They heard the Doctor's voice. 'Hurry! Please hurry!'

'Come on, Enrico,' pleaded Gemma.

Casali flipped a switch. 'That's it – power on.' They heard a low, oscillating electronic howl.

In the loading bay the sound was coming from the communications mike which the Doctor had deliberately left swinging from its wall fitting.

The Cybermats began gliding forwards.

The Doctor and Jamie retreated slowly towards the steps ...

'Come on, let's run for it!' urged Jamie.

The Doctor shook his head. 'They've got a range of at least ten feet ...'

The Cybermats made a sudden dart forwards, as if to attack. But the move brought them within range of the sound from the dangling wall mike ... Suddenly they began swinging to and fro in erratic curves, like disorientated dodgem cars. Their paths intersected and they collided with a metallic crash. For a moment they were still, then one began zooming round in circles while the second sped straight for the wall. The circling Cybermat began giving out smoke, ground slowly to a halt and expired in a final puff of smoke. The second Cybermat smashed into the bulkhead and blew up, disappearing in smoke and flame.

In the control room the Doctor appeared on the monitor, waving his hands. 'That's quite enough, thank you!'

Casali switched off the electronic howl.

The Doctor ducked down then popped up again with the defunct Cybermat displayed on a box lid. 'This is what you saved us from!'

Tanya peered at it unbelievingly. 'What is it?'

Zoe, who had been looking on silently all this time said, 'It's a Cybermat.'

'Exactly,' said the Doctor. 'We're coming back as soon as we can.'

As the Doctor's face vanished from the screen, a light began flashing on a nearby console.

'Leo?' called Tanya.

He came across to her, and she indicated the light. 'It seems to be a signal from the power room.'

Leo studied the indicator light, puzzled. 'Yeah – and it doesn't seem to be coming from our power source. Let's check it out ...'

In the power room a Cyberman was operating a Cyber-Communications Unit, reporting to the Planner. 'The Cybermats have been destroyed.'

'By what method?'

'By the use of high-current phase contrast.'

'Some human has knowledge beyond our prediction. Continue report.'

'The laser-cannon is now repaired and operative.'

'And the communication beam to Earth?'

'Attacked and damaged.'

The Planner said, 'Excellent. Phase Six will now be completed. The Wheel is to be taken over.'

Enrico Casali looked down at the shattered communication beam console, shaking his head. 'Bill Duggan knew the spots to attack all right. What a mess!'

'How about radar?' asked Tanya.

'That's okay. But the Earth communication circuits are done for.'

'What time's the next check with Earth Central?'

'Two hours time.'

'Better set up a fix on the first wave of the meteorites.'

Casali shrugged. 'Doesn't seem much point, not without a laser to knock them away with.'

'Don't be a pessimist, Enrico. They may not hold on a crash course to us. Anything can happen.'

Casali grinned. 'Everything has!'

Leo Ryan looked up his face concerned. 'I've been checking the different sections on the intercom.'

Tanya looked puzzled. 'And?'

'I can't raise anyone ...' He looked worriedly at her. 'We might be alone on the Wheel.'

14

METEOR STORM

Tanya's eyes widened in alarm. 'Have you told Gemma Corwyn?'

'Not yet. I reckon she's got enough on her plate. I'll go on checking...'

On the other side of the control room Jarvis Bennett was sitting in his command chair, with Gemma, Zoe, Jamie and the Doctor grouped around him. Gemma had persuaded him to leave his quarters for the control room in the hope that familiar surroundings might help to restore him to normality, but it wasn't working. Jarvis Bennett's earlier euphoric mood had faded, and he was slumped down in the chair a picture of depression while Zoe held a lifeless Cybermat up in front of him.

'Jarvis, look at it,' pleaded the Doctor. 'Bring it forward, Zoe, into his line of sight.'

Zoe held the Cybermat directly in front of the Commander's face. Jarvis Bennett's eyes widened. He began shivering, and twisted his head away. 'No ... it's not true ... not true ...'

Gemma Corwyn said, 'All right, Zoe, put that thing away somewhere.' She looked at the Doctor. 'It looks like complete withdrawal.'

'Not necessarily complete,' said the Doctor. 'Catatonic features, certainly.'

'I could try E.C.T. ... maybe he could be shocked back to normal.'

'Give him a little more time,' said the Doctor. 'You've thrown a force-field around this section – strong enough to keep the Cybermen out?'

'Strong enough to keep anything out!' She looked worriedly at Jarvis, who was staring gloomily at the ground.

'It's no good, Gemma,' said the Doctor gently. 'You're the second in command – you'll have to take over.'

'Take over what?' asked Gemma bitterly. 'We've been invaded, we've no contact with Earth, and we're in the path of a storm of meteorites, and we can't fight them off because there's no laser!'

Zoe took the Cybermat over to Jamie, and put it down on top of a console. Jamie nodded towards Jarvis. 'How is he?'

'Hopeless, he's just closed himself away. Doctor Corwyn's second in command – I suppose she'll take over. Though what she can do ... or any of us, for that matter. I feel so useless, Jamie.'

Jamie patted her clumsily on the shoulder. 'You're just not trained for this sort of emergency.'

'That's the whole point! What good am I? I've been created for a false kind of existence where there are only known emergencies. What good is that to me now?'

'Hey, we're not done yet, you know,' said Jamie. 'We'll survive this mess yet!'

Zoe didn't look convinced.

Leo Ryan was still going on with his check. 'Section twelve? Make contact section twelve!'

There was no reply.

Section twelve was the oxygen supply room. There was no answer to Leo Ryan's call because the duty technician lay dead on the floor, a Cyberman towering over him.

Flanagan came into the power room, and looked around, surprised to find it empty. The wall communications unit was buzzing and he went to answer it.

Suddenly Vallance appeared from around the side of a storage locker and stepped forward, barring his way.

'So there you are,' said Flanagan. 'Why don't you answer that thing, someone sounds a bit violent.'

Vallance said flatly, 'It is not important.'

'It could be the old man himself, for all you know!'

Laleham stepped out from behind another storage locker.

Suddenly Flanagan noticed that the capacitor bank for the laser-cannon, which he had last seen in numerous pieces, seemed to have been reassembled as good as new. 'Is the laser working again?'

Laleham said, 'The repair is finished.' He spoke in the same flat tone as Vallance.

'So we're not to be riddled by meteorites after all then? Sure that's a relief, and me with a whole year's Earth leave due!'

The intercom was still buzzing, and instinctively Flanagan went to answer it again, and again Vallance barred his way. 'Do not touch that.'

'You can't just ignore it!' To Flanagan's utter astonishment, Vallance drew his blaster. 'Have you gone mad?' demanded Flanagan.

Vallance said, 'Do as you are told.'

Contemptuously Flanagan swept the blaster aside. 'What's the matter with you, boy?' He gave Vallance a shove that sent him staggering back.

Laleham too drew his blaster.

Flanagan promptly knocked it out of his hand, and knocked Laleham down for good measure. Flanagan backed away, raising his fists. 'All right, come on! If it's a fight you're after, I'm your man. Come on both of you!' Flanagan was a big powerful man, and an accomplished brawler.

Laleham and Vallance, their reflexes dulled by Cyberman control were just no match for him.

Vallance came forward, aiming a clumsy blow, and Flanagan side-stepped and knocked him down with scientific precision.

Laleham scrambled to his feet and rushed at him, a heavy spanner in his hand. The spanner swept towards Flanagan's head, Flanagan dodged aside, and the spanner smashed into a metal bench with a force that jarred it from Laleham's grasp.

Now thoroughly enraged, Flanagan grabbed Laleham and began shaking him to and fro. 'Now that wasn't sporting! You want a few lessons in the Noble and Manly Art, me friend.'

Shaking his head, Vallance scrambled over to his fallen blaster, snatched it up, and got to his feet, aiming the weapon at Flanagan's back. He fired … Just as Laleham, in a frantic effort to break free from Flanagan's grip, twisted himself around – and stumbled full into the path of the blaster bolt.

Laleham staggered and fell dead to the ground.

Flanagan and Vallance stood motionless for a moment, Flanagan shocked out of his fighting fury, Vallance shaken free of the Cyberman's control.

'You've killed him!' gasped Flanagan.

Vallance stared at him, too shocked to speak. Then his eyes widened as he stared over Flanagan's shoulder, and his body went rigid.

Flanagan swung round, and saw the giant silver form of a Cyberman looming over him.

Before Flanagan could move or speak, he was transfixed by the beam from the Cyberman's helmet. His body went rigid, and he stood passive, waiting.

The Cyberman spoke. 'The laser has been repaired?'

Vallance bowed his head. 'Yes.'

'A force field is in operation around the control room. How is it operated?'

'From within the control room itself.'

The Cyberman glanced down at Laleham's body. 'Dispose of this human.' It turned and stalked away.

Obediently, Flanagan and Vallance lifted Laleham's body ...

Zoe was feeding Jarvis Bennett water from a beaker. He took a sip or two, then turned his head away like a sulky child. 'No more ...'

'Just give him what he wants,' said Gemma.

She went to join the Doctor and Jamie, who were grouped around Casali who was operating the radar screen.

'They're coming through now.'

A whooshing, humming sound was coming from the radar complex. 'It's a big one,' said Casali. 'Even bigger than we thought.'

'All right, all right, don't make it worse,' said Leo Ryan nervously.

Gemma said, 'We've still got the anti-matter field projectors.'

'You don't think meteorites like this are going to bounce off that, do you?' said Casali. 'We're talking about things weighing two or three hundred tons here!' He adjusted his screen and suddenly they could see a swarm of blips, travelling across the screen. 'There they are – swarms of them – and they're headed straight for this Wheel!'

15

POISON IN THE AIR

There was a moment's awed silence.

'How far away are they?' Gemma Corwyn asked.

Casali studied his instruments. 'Under a million miles now. Closing in on an elliptical path, tilted ten degrees.'

As yet, the danger wasn't imminent. But it was unavoidable.

Suddenly there came a buzz from the communication-unit, and Flanagan's face appeared on screen. 'Power room here.'

'Flanagan! Where have you *been*?' said Leo Ryan explosively.

'We have been repairing the laser capacitator bank. Work has now been completed.'

Leo Ryan was too excited to register Flanagan's flat voice and stilted manner. 'Are you telling me the laser's working again?'

'Ready for testing.'

Leo swung round to the others. 'Hear that? The laser's repaired! Stand by to run a test.' He turned back to the screen. 'Why didn't you answer me, Flanagan? I've been calling for ages!'

'There must be a fault on the line,' said Flanagan in the same dull voice. 'Vallance is with me. We're ready when you are.'

Gemma, the Doctor, Jamie and Zoe stood watching as Leo and his team ran through a series of checks.

'What's the range of this thing?' asked the Doctor.

'Fifty-thousand miles for total destruction, ninety for partial,' said Gemma.

'Hmm … won't do to miss any, will it?'

'Some of the forerunners will be in range now. We can use them to test. We'll try a random shot,' said Leo. 'At least it'll tell us how the power bank reacts. Blue control.'

Casali said, 'Red on standby. Angle eighty-eight to zero four zero one. Distance closing, five four nine, four eight … zero!'

'Fire!' said Ryan. 'Tanya give me a power reading.'

'Power normal at maximum. Meteor has been destroyed.'

Leo Ryan sat back satisfied. It had been just one shot, one meteor destroyed out of untold numbers … But steering and power had responded perfectly. Leo Ryan said cheerfully, 'Well, everybody, I think we stand a chance.'

It was some time later. The control room was humming with activity. More and more of the meteorites were coming in range now and Leo and Tanya and the rest of their team were steadily deflecting or destroying them.

Against the steady background of information, orders and reports the Doctor and Gemma were talking quietly.

'I think it's safe to assume that the Cybermen caused this meteor storm,' said the Doctor. 'They must have made the star go nova.'

'Why?' asked Gemma. 'To destroy the Wheel?'

'No, they just wanted to make you use the laser. The Cybermats were sent in to attack the laser, by ruining the Bernalium.'

'Aye, that's right,' said Jamie. 'Then you'd be sure to search that drifting rocket, find the crate and bring it on board – with Cybermen hidden inside!'

The Doctor nodded. 'It was all a cunning plan to get on to the Wheel.'

Gemma said, 'And you really think it was the Cybermen who repaired the laser?'

'They had to,' said Jamie, 'or the Wheel would have been smashed up!'

'This isn't just an attack on the Wheel,' said the Doctor. 'The Cybermen have an overriding ambition to invade Earth and plunder its mineral wealth. Somehow they must be able to see a way of doing that through this Wheel …' The Doctor began patting his pockets. 'Jamie, the Time Vector Generator – where is it?'

'You've got it. I put it back in your pocket when we were on board the rocket.'

'But I haven't got it!'

'It must have fallen out of your pocket, just before they brought you across. Is it important?'

'Important?' spluttered the Doctor. 'It's vital! Someone will have to go over to the rocket and find it.'

'Well, good luck to them whoever they are! Who's going?'

'Well, Jamie, if Doctor Corwyn can spare someone to help you make the crossing – you are!'

'Me?'

'You're the only one besides me who knows what to look for, and I'm needed here. Besides, it's your fault it's lost!'

In the power room the Cyberman was making a further report to the Planner. 'The meteorite shower is now approaching the Wheel. The weapons of the humans have been tested and are operative.'

'Phase Six can now be completed.'

'The humans have set up a force field barrier around the section containing their control room.'

The Planner said, 'To complete Phase Six it will be necessary to initiate plan three.'

The Cyberman switched off the communicator and turned to Vallance, who had been waiting silently in the comer. 'Follow me.'

Jamie, Zoe and Gemma Corwyn stood waiting at a corridor junction. The air before them seemed mildly hazy. Looking through it, things on the far side looked blurred, and if you tried to walk through you would have been held motionless. Gemma looked at her watch, and suddenly the haze vanished. Gemma hurried across the junction, motioning Jamie and Zoe to follow her.

On the far side, she picked up a wall communicator. 'Replace the force field barrier – we're through.'

Zoe said, 'I'll check that it's clear ahead.' She moved on a little.

'Don't see what you've landed me with her for,' grumbled Jamie.

'She knows enough space drill to get you across to the rocket – and she's the only one I can spare.'

'I still think I'd do better by myself!'

Gemma smiled. 'Do you? Don't be too sure.'

Meanwhile in the control room, Leo Ryan and the Doctor were having a furious row about the same subject.

'Zoe agreed to go,' said the Doctor obstinately.

'She'd no right to agree – and you'd no right to ask her.'

'It had to be done. Jamie will look after her.'

'Have you any idea what it could be like between the Wheel and that rocket. The whole area's bound to be bombarded with debris ...'

'They know the risks,' said the Doctor quietly. 'Zoe calculated them.'

'And what about Gemma? She'll have to make her way back here on her own.' He glared at the Doctor. 'From now on you don't do anything without checking with me first, OK?' He glared angrily at the Doctor, and the Doctor scowled mutinously back at him.

'Meteorite coming in range – now!' called Casali.

Leo went back to his console.

The route to the airlock led through the oxygen supply room – and there Gemma and her party had stumbled on the body of the dead technician.

Shocked, Gemma knelt to examine the body.

'Is he dead?' whispered Jamie.

Gemma straightened up. 'I'm afraid so. Zoe, the emergency exit.' She led the way to a hatch in the wall and opened it. 'That'll take you to the air-lock. You'll find space equipment in the supply locker.'

'Right, come on, Jamie,' said Zoe. She clambered into the dark space, and Jamie scrambled after her.

'Good luck,' said Gemma as she closed the hatch behind them. Crossing over to the wall unit she called the control room. 'They'll be away any minute. Shouldn't be any problems.'

In the control room, Casali called, 'This is the main concentration ... coming into range now.'

'Crossover on vector link,' said Ryan. 'Countdown as from now ...'

They bent tensely over their instruments.

Out in deep-space the massive meteor swarm was still hurtling swiftly and silently towards them. Hundreds of meteors had been deflected or destroyed, but there were hundreds more to come. It would only take one to destroy the Wheel and everyone on it.

*

Gemma Corwyn was about to set off back to the control room when she heard movement in the corridor and ducked into hiding behind an instrument console.

A Cyberman stalked into the room, Vallance behind him. The Cyberman surveyed the oxygen room. 'Each section of the Wheel has its own oxygen supply?'

'Yes,' said Vallance.

The Cyberman handed him a metal container, which held rows of silver capsules. 'Insert one capsule into the supply for each section. The oxygen will turn into pure ozone and the humans will die ...'

'Fire!' commanded Ryan. Another meteorite exploded in space.

'We're hitting them,' called Casali. 'But there are so many ... It's hopeless.'

'Shut up,' snapped Ryan, hunched over his console. 'Fire!'

Suddenly the monitor screen came to life and Gemma's face appeared. 'Gemma Corwyn to control room.'

The Doctor, the only one not fully occupied, leaned forward. 'Yes, Gemma, what is it?'

'The Cybermen are going to poison the air supply. Do you understand? Tell Leo Ryan to switch over to the emergency sectional supply units. Do you understand?'

The Doctor peered into the monitor. Gemma was looking not at the screen but at something just behind her. 'How do you know, Gemma?' called the Doctor. 'What's happening there? You must get back here right away.'

The screen went blank.

Hanging up the mike, Gemma Corwyn turned to face the giant silver form that was looming over her. The communication unit had been in a corner some way from Vallance and the Cyberman. She knew that she would be heard – but she also knew that the call must be made.

Drawing her hand blaster, Gemma trained it on the Cyberman and fired. It stopped, staggered bade, then continued its remorseless advance. Before she could fire again, the Cyberman's chest unit glowed fiercely, and Gemma twisted and fell.

*

Jamie and Zoe, space-suited and steering with their oxygen packs, were over half way to the rocket when the fringe of the meteorite storm reached them. Jamie saw it first. 'Zoe, look!'

It was an astonishing, terrifying sight; the debris of a shattered star, chunks of rock the size of golf balls, footballs, others as big as a house, and icebergs, some very like small mountains.

Jamie heard Zoe's voice sounding inside his space helmet. 'It's the meteorites, Jamie – and they're heading straight for us!'

16

PERILOUS JOURNEY

'Fire!' shouted Leo Ryan,

Somewhere a meteorite, heading for the Wheel, exploded in smoke and flame.

'We're still hitting them!' said Casali grimly.

'What about Jamie and Zoe?' asked the Doctor. 'They're out there too you know.'

Tanya said, 'They'll be in danger from shock, from radiation and blast …'

'They'll have to take their chances,' said Leo savagely. 'I can't think about anything except stopping those meteorites.' He returned his attention to the firing console. 'Fire!'

Tanya looked up at the Doctor. 'They'll be blown out of space!'

'Zoe calculated the risks,' said the Doctor. 'Let's hope she was right!'

Explosions all around them, holding hands in an attempt to keep together, Jamie and Zoe cartwheeled through space, flung to and fro by the explosions all around them.

A final, violent explosion very close to them blasted them apart and they spun off in different directions …

'The radar screen's clear,' said Casali. 'We've done it!'

'Any sign of Jamie and Zoe?' asked the Doctor anxiously.

'Can't pick 'em up on screen till all the static's cleared.'

'We'll stay on Blue stand-by for the moment,' said Leo. 'There'll be a cloud of small stuff following behind. Check all circuits, maintain power levels till further notice.'

Leo Ryan rose and stretched, glanced curiously at Jarvis Bennett, who was still slumped motionless in his chair, and went over to the Doctor. 'You realise what you've done, Doctor? Those two kids have probably been either burnt up by radiation, or fried by thermal blast – always assuming they weren't actually hit by all that rubbish.'

'Do you think I'm not aware of that?' said the Doctor bitterly. 'It was a calculated risk – one which had to be taken.'

'Why?'

'Because there's something on board the rocket we need if we're to defeat the Cybermen.'

'Something that justified risking two lives?'

'In order to save many – yes. Incidentally, we'll all die very soon unless you switch over to sectional emergency air supply.'

'What?'

'The Cybermen are planning to poison your air.' Leo Ryan stared at him. 'How do you know?'

'Gemma Corwyn told me.'

'Where is she?'

'In the oxygen room but –'

'I want to talk to her.' Ryan headed for the communicator.

'I'm afraid you can't,' said the Doctor sadly. 'She's dead.'

Leo Ryan went and punched up a picture of the oxygen room on the monitor. It showed a section of floor, with the lower part of Gemma Corwyn's crumpled body.

'She sacrificed herself to warn us,' said the Doctor.

Casali looked up from his radar screen. 'Here comes the following wave!'

'Right,' said Leo. 'We'll try three second interval shots, but we'll reinforce the anti-matter shield around the Wheel as well. Maybe we can deflect some of this lighter stuff off course. Tanya, switch over to sectional emergency air supply.'

The rattle of readings, instructions and commands filled the control room once more as the second wave of meteorites were either deflected or destroyed.

Suddenly the Doctor said, 'Where's Jarvis?' The Commander's chair was empty.

*

Jarvis Bennett marched purposefully along the corridors, away from the control room. He had lost his former apathy and looked determined, even exalted.

Tanya was flicking the monitor screen through various channels in an attempt to locate him when the communicator screen lit up, showing Jarvis Bennett's face.

'Jarvis, what are you doing?' called Ryan. 'You must come back!'

'No, I'm going on,' said Jarvis calmly. 'They killed Gemma, you know. I lifted the force field to get out – you'd better replace it right away.'

Leo Ryan rose and headed for the door, but the Doctor caught his arm. 'Where are you going?'

'To fetch Jarvis back.'

'I'm afraid it's already too late for that. Look!' The Doctor pointed to the monitor.

They saw Jarvis turn away from the screen and move off down the corridor – straight towards an approaching Cyberman.

Jarvis Bennett smiled, as if pleased to come face to face with his enemy. He drew his blaster and fired, blast after blast at the approaching Cyberman – but to no effect. Hurling the weapon at the Cyberman Jarvis Bennett closed with it, in an attempt to wrestle it to the ground.

His action was as suicidal as it was brave.

The Cyberman caught and held him in an inflexible steel grip, simply ignoring his attempt to attack. It raised him high above its head then smashed him to the ground. Even then, Jarvis wouldn't give up.

As he struggled feebly to rise, the Cyberman's chest unit glowed fiercely and caught in the killing beam, Jarvis's body writhed and twisted grotesquely for a moment, then fell back, dead.

The Cyberman stepped over the body and moved on.

In the control room a horrified audience watched his death struggle on the monitor.

Tanya turned away. 'Please, turn it off …'

The Doctor flicked the control and the screen went blank.

*

Jamie had good reason to be grateful for Zoe's brief bit of space training. Somehow he'd managed to brake himself with his air jet then steer himself over to the rocket, where he found Zoe just about to enter the airlock. Now they were both on board the rocket, feeling somewhat astonished to be alive.

Jamie was fetching Zoe some water from the dispenser.

'Thanks, Jamie,' she said, sipping it gratefully.

Jamie looked at her in concern. 'How do you feel?'

'I really didn't think we were going to get through,' she said. 'I feel as if someone's been hitting me all over with hammers!'

'Take it easy while I look round.'

Zoe got up. 'No I'll help.' She looked round the control room. 'What is it that we're looking for?'

Jamie held his hands apart. 'It's a rod, about so big, with black and gold tips to it. Come on then, let's start looking.'

The Cyberman said, 'You have inserted the capsules into the air supply unit?'

'Yes,' said Vallance dully.

'Inject it into the system.'

Vallance operated a lever and there was a hiss of air.

The Cyberman said, 'Effective penetration should be immediate. Report!'

Vallance studied the oxygen room instrument dials. 'They have already switched over to the emergency supply.'

'Can that be reached?'

'No. The controls are inside the force field.'

The Cyberman hesitated – then called up the Planner on the Cyberman communication unit.

The eerie transparent head appeared on the little screen, 'Do you report success?'

'No. Our plans have been anticipated.'

'Wait. The Data will be re-computed.' There was a high-pitched electronic twittering and symbols flowed across the screen.

The Planner reappeared. 'One of the Earthmen must have experience of our method. Projection of all identities on the Wheel is essential …'

*

Jamie found the missing rod in the corridor, just outside the little cabin. He came hurrying back into the control room. 'Here it is, Zoe, I found it. We can go back now –'

Zoe waved him to silence. After a perfunctory search of the control room she had started fiddling with the communication equipment – with very unexpected results.

On a monitor screen, Jamie could see one of the Wheel technicians, a Cyberman beside him, using some kind of communication device.

'Come and look, Jamie,' said Zoe excitedly. 'This could be important. I seem to have broken in on the Cyberman frequency ...'

17

THE INVASION

'Stare into the device,' ordered the Cyberman. The light on its helmet glowed gently.

Vallance obeyed.

The Cyberman said, 'Now think of each individual human on the Wheel. Form the image in your mind.'

The Cyberman Planner sat staring straight ahead, concentrating on the images that appeared in conjunction with Vallance's voice.

'Tanya Lernov. Astrologer, second class.' A young, fair-haired human female.

'Negative,' said the Planner.

'Leo Ryan, Communications Officer.' A large human male.

'Negative.'

'Jarvis Bennett, Station Commander.' An older human.

'Negative.'

'Zoe Heriot, Astrophysicist, Astrometricist, first class.' A small human female.

'Negative.'

'That's me,' said Zoe. 'They seem to be running through all the crew of the Wheel, one after the other.'

'But why?' said Jamie wonderingly. 'What are they after?'

The figure of a small male dark humanoid appeared, and for the first time Vallance's voice faltered. 'Doctor … The Doctor … I don't know his name.'

'Repeat image,' ordered the Planner. 'Concentrate!'

In the control room a conference was in progress.

'But what possible use could these Cybermen have for the Wheel, Doctor?' Leo Ryan was asking.

'That remains to be seen,' said the Doctor infuriatingly.

'Why shouldn't they simply be attacking us?'

'Why would they go to all this trouble just to knock out one space station?'

Tanya interrupted them. 'Leo, there's something on radar.'

The Doctor and Leo went over to the radar screen.

'Not a meteorite,' said Casali. 'Look, it's changing course.'

'No ships are due in this sector of space,' said Tanya, checking her log.

Casali said, 'Too big for one of ours anyway.'

'It could be a Cyberman ship,' said the Doctor quietly.

'Moving in for the kill?' suggested Leo.

'Possibly.'

Leo turned to Casali. 'What about the Earth communication system, Enrico? We must try to contact Earth for assistance.'

'Not a chance,' said Casali. 'Oh, I could repair it all right, given time, but I'd need some valve transistors and some replacement circuitry, and they're all in the power room.'

'Then someone will have to go and get them,' said Leo.

'Positive,' said the Planner. 'Positive; the Doctor is known and recorded as an enemy of the Cybermen. He must be lured outside the force field and destroyed.'

In the rocket control room, Jamie leaned forward and switched off the scanner. 'They're going to try and trap the Doctor. We must get back and warn him.'

They began putting on their space helmets.

The Doctor, Tanya and Leo Ryan were poring over a map of the Wheel.

'This is the route to the power room,' said Tanya, tracing the corridors with her forefinger.

Leo Ryan frowned. 'Trouble is, we don't know where the Cybermen will be – the direct route's no good.'

'Well, how else will you get there. Through the cable tunnels?' He shook his head. 'They're blocked off – here and here. That leaves the emergency air tunnels …'

They were interrupted by the buzz of the communicator, and turned to find Flanagan's face on the screen.

'Flanagan, where are you?' said Ryan.

'In a corridor near the workshops. I've got a whole bunch of them locked up in a workshop.'

'Well done, Flanagan! Is the way to the power room clear?'

'It is for now. But they're trying to melt down the doors, I may not be able to hold them for much longer.'

'Well try to keep them bottled up as long as possible,' said Ryan. 'One of us has to come through for some radio spares.'

'Right, I'll seal off some more compartments, sir. But you'd better send someone for those spares pretty quickly. They may be trying the other doors.'

'Tell him I'll go for the spares,' whispered the Doctor.

'It's better if I go,' said Ryan. 'I know just where –'

'It's essential that I go,' insisted the Doctor.

Ryan shrugged. 'All right, Doctor, it's your neck.' He turned back to the intercom. 'Flanagan, the Doctor's coming for the spares. Hold the Cybermen back as long as you can.'

'Right, sir. I'll meet the Doctor in corridor six.'

The screen went blank.

The Doctor took Ryan aside. 'When Flanagan turns up here, let him in through the force field – then grab him!'

Tanya said, 'But he isn't coming here. He said he'd meet you in corridor six.'

The Doctor smiled. 'I don't think so.' He picked up the map. 'Now don't forget, don't trust him. Check the safety plate on his neck. Turn off the force field so I can get out will you? Oh, and tell me where the spares are, will you?'

Ryan told him, and the Doctor hurried away.

In corridor six, Flanagan stood stiffly before a Cyberman. 'The Doctor will come here, to corridor six.'

'Excellent. You will return to the control room. Once they have admitted you, you must destroy the machinery that sets up the force field.'

Flanagan turned and moved away.

It was dark and eerie in the deserted power room. A grille moved in the wall, and the cover was lifted off from inside. The Doctor clambered down into the room and looked around. Following Ryan's directions, he located a shelf of spares above a workbench, and filled his pockets with the vital equipment. On a nearby shelf he found a phial of mercury. Beaming delightedly he stowed it away in a separate pocket. On his way out, the Doctor paused by the main work bench, still cluttered with odds and ends after the repair of the laser capacitator. Some Bemalium rods, coils of wire, connectors and plugs – and a handy power point nearby . . .

'Yes, I think so,' said the Doctor. 'Worth a try!'

Picking up a coil of wire he set to work . . .

Zoe and Jamie had a much calmer journey from the rocket to the Wheel. They reached the airlock without incident, and returned to the oxygen room through the same hatchway by which they'd left it. They slipped out of the door and moved off down the corridor. Suddenly a massive figure stepped out of a side corridor.

Zoe looked up at him. 'Flanagan!'

'And what are you doing wandering about? Don't you know them creatures is everywhere? You two come with me now, this way's quicker.'

He led them off down the side corridor.

Not far away, in corridor six the Cyberman turned to Vallance. 'The Doctor has not come.'

'He must have gone another way. There's an air tunnel leading to the power room.'

'Show me,' ordered the Cyberman.

They moved away.

The Planner's orders had to be obeyed – the Doctor must be found and destroyed.

*

In the control room, Ryan and Casali were waiting, one each side of the door. Tanya stood waiting too, a blaster in her hand. They were waiting for Flanagan.

Just as the Doctor predicted, Flanagan had called in on a communicator and asked them to let down the force field so that he could come into the control room. He was bringing Jamie and Zoe with him.

The door opened, and Flanagan came in.

Ryan and Casali jumped him. They wrestled him to the ground, face down, and Tanya passed Leo one of the Doctor's improvised metal plates to clamp on his neck.

Jamie and Zoe, who had followed Flanagan in, looked on appalled.

'What are you doing?' demanded Zoe. 'He helped us, he guided us back here.'

'He's controlled by the Cybermen,' said Tanya.

Ryan finally managed to get the metal plate fixed to the back of Flanagan's head. He bucked and reared wildly for a few moments, and then lay still. After a moment he groaned, clutching his head.

Ryan got to his feet, still panting. 'He'll be all right now. Let's get him sat down, Enrico.' Between them they got Flanagan into a chair.

Jamie looked round. 'Where's the Doctor? We overheard the Cybermen planning to lure him into a trap.'

Tanya said, 'But he's already –' She was interrupted by the buzz of the communicator.

The Doctor's face appeared on screen. 'I've got the spares.'

Jamie hurried over. 'Doctor!'

'Jamie! Are you and Zoe all right?'

'Aye, we're fine. Listen, Doctor, the Cybermen know you're on the Wheel. They're planning to trap you.'

'Yes, I thought they might. Jamie, did you find the Time Vector Generator?'

'I have it right here, Doctor.'

'Just bring it to me, would you Jamie? Get someone to show you the way through the air tunnels. I'm afraid I'm expecting visitors.'

The screen went blank.

'Visitors?' Jamie frowned. 'What does he mean – visitors?'

*

The Doctor made a final connection to the power box and straightened up. He had built up a structure of Bernalium rods on either side of the door, and both were connected by cables to the power box. His work was finished, just in time.

A Cyberman was standing in the doorway.

'Oh, are you waiting for me?' asked the Doctor politely.

'You are the Doctor? You know our ways.'

'Yes, I thought you'd realise that someone did, sooner or later,' said the Doctor modestly. 'I imagine you have orders to destroy me?'

'Yes,' said the Cyberman.

The Second Cyberman appeared beside the first.

'Tell me,' said the Doctor conversationally. 'Why did you make Duggan destroy the radio communication beam to Earth. That is why you want the Wheel, isn't it? As a way to reach Earth?'

'He was instructed to destroy only the transmitting complex.'

'Of course,' said the Doctor. 'How interesting. I suppose your giant Cyber-ship holds your invasion fleet, and the smaller ships inside need the guidance of a radio beam from Earth?'

'You know our ways,' repeated the Cyberman. 'You are to be destroyed.'

'Yes, I thought we'd get back to that sooner or later. Do come in!'

The Cyberman stepped into the doorway.

The Doctor stooped down and threw the power switch. Electricity crackled between the two sets of Bernalium rods. Caught in the powerful force field the Cyberman writhed and twisted in a sort of grotesque dance – a dance of death. Smoke poured from its helmet and chest unit and suddenly the Cyberman went rigid and crashed to the ground like a felled tree. The second Cyberman's chest unit glowed – but the Doctor's electric force-field repelled the deadly ray.

'It's no good you know,' said the Doctor calmly. 'You can't break through the field.'

'Others are coming, Doctor,' said the Cyberman threateningly. 'You will be destroyed.' It backed slowly away, disappearing down the corridor.

The Doctor heard a sound and spun round. The grille was being lifted away from inside. A moment later, Jamie appeared, followed by Flanagan.

'Ah, Jamie,' said the Doctor happily. He looked suspiciously at Flanagan. 'Is he all right now?'

'Aye, he's fine,' said Jamie. 'Aren't you, Mr Flanagan?'

'Except for a head like a big bass drum I am,' growled Flanagan. 'And somebody's going to pay for it.'

Jamie looked down at the dead Cyberman. 'Looks as if you've made one pay already, Doctor.'

'Yes, but they're sending in re-inforcements, Jamie. Probably through the loading bay. Just give me the Time Vector Generator, will you?'

Jamie handed it over.

'I'm going to try to fix this into the laser gun circuitry,' explained the Doctor. 'With luck it'll boost the power energy to destroy the Cyber-ship. You'll have to hold them off at the loading bay for me – I need time!'

'Leave it to me,' said Flanagan.

'There's still one Cyberman left on the Wheel,' warned the Doctor. 'You'll have to deal with him first.' He fished in his pocket. 'Oh, and here's a protective plate for Vallance when you find him.'

'Right, sir,' said Flanagan taking it. He grabbed a can of spray plastic from a shelf. 'Let's see how them creatures like this! Well, come on Jamie, let's be at them!'

Flanagan and Jamie hurried off, and the Doctor headed for the laser gun capacitator bank.

The final stage of the Cyberman invasion was about to begin.

18

AN END AND A
BEGINNING

Casali looked up from the radar scanner. 'That ship's moving closer. It's colossal!'

Ryan was talking to the Doctor over the intercom.

'I'm trying to put more power into your laser,' said the Doctor. 'Line the cannon on the Cyberman space ship and I'll tell you when I'm ready.'

'You'd better be ready soon,' said Ryan. 'That ship's on the move.'

'I know,' said the Doctor. 'They're planning to invade the Wheel.'

Flanagan marched Jamie into the loading bay, both of them now wearing space suits. Vallance, also space suited stood waiting, and beside him was the waiting Cyberman.

'I couldn't get into the power room for the force field,' explained Flanagan. 'I caught this feller on the way back.'

'He is not important,' said the Cyberman. 'Guard him. He may be useful later.'

Luckily the Cyberman had a lot to worry about, thought Jamie. They all stood, waiting.

The Doctor was working rapidly on the laser bank, trying to find a way of building in the Time Vector Generator without blowing the whole installation.

Ryan was watching him on the intercom. 'Hurry, Doctor. That ship's still moving in!'

In the loading bay the Cyberman moved towards the door controls.

'Now,' yelled Flanagan.

Jamie leaped on Vallance, bearing him to the ground, trying to clamp the metal plate Flanagan had given him onto the man's neck. Vallance stuggled furiously …

As the Cyberman turned, Flanagan brought up the plastic gun and emptied it into the Cyberman's chest unit. The Cyberman staggered back choking. Smoke began pouring from its helmet. It reeled back, collapsing – but before it fell, it managed to press the button that opened the loading bay doors. The doors slid back onto the blackness of space.

Jamie managed to clamp the metal plate to the back of Vallance's neck – and the man went limp. Struggling to his feet, Jamie looked out through the opening doors and gasped.

The horizon was filled by the colossal bulk of the Cyber-ship, now incredibly close. And from the ship there was streaming an army of Cybermen, jetting towards them through space.

Flanagan ran to the control, and the doors began to close. But not quickly enough. The leading Cybermen were almost on them now, and the first managed to jam itself in the doors before they were quite closed. Incredibly, its strength was such that it could stop the doors from closing.

With limitless others to help, the Cybermen would be able to wrench the doors open again, Jamie realised. 'Use the plastic!' he yelled.

He heard Flanagan's frantic voice inside his helmet. 'Can't … emptied it onto the other one …'

Through the gap, Jamie could see more Cybermen arriving to aid the first.

In the control room, the laser-cannon was aligned on the colossal Cyber-ship – the ship that held the invasion fleet destined for Earth. They were waiting for the Doctor now.

His voice came over the intercom. 'Right, everything's ready here!'

'Fire,' yelled Leo Ryan.

A beam of extraordinarily intense light shot from the Wheel's boosted laser cannon, striking the Cyber-ship at point blank range.

The ship was bathed in a fierce glow of light – and exploded in smoke and flame.

The glare lit up the loading bay like lightning.

The Cyber-ship might be gone, thought Jamie – but they still had swarms, of angry Cybermen, clustering around like wasps – and any moment now they'd be inside.

Flanagan had opened up a panel in the wall, and was throwing switches. 'I'm going to operate the neutron field barrier. Hold on!' He threw the last switch and the loading bay, and indeed the whole of the exterior of the Wheel hummed with power.

The force field was designed to repel the smaller meteorites – but it repelled Cybermen as well.

Shot off from the Wheel, they spun away into the blackness of space, cartwheeling away into infinity.

The door closed and Flanagan touched the control that flooded air back into the loading bay.

'We've done it!' gasped Jamie, and sank exhausted to the ground.

'Wheel to Earth Control,' said Casali. 'Stand by for emergency report.' He looked round. 'Where's Zoe, by the way?'

'Taking the Doctor and Jamie back to the rocket,' said Tanya.

A voice from the speaker said, 'Earth Control standing by. Report.'

Leo Ryan drew a deep breath. 'This is Leo Ryan, Acting Commander of Station Three. Radio contact with Earth lost at 1252 hours, due to attack by alien force …'

Leo became aware of Tanya's cool hand removing the protective metal plate from his neck.

He caught one of her hands and held it as he poured out the incredible story of recent events on the Wheel in space …

Jamie and Zoe were standing in the control room of the rocket.

'So you've really got to go back?' said Zoe.

Jamie nodded awkwardly. 'I'm afraid so.'

'You won't tell me anything about this TARDIS of yours – Time and Relative Dimensions in Space – that's what the Doctor said it meant. But you won't explain it?'

'Look, it's like … well, like two different worlds. You have yours, and we have ours.' Jamie thought of the shock it had been for him to leave his own place and time, and of how sometimes his heart still ached for his native highlands. He heard the Doctor calling him.

'Look, Zoe,' he said, 'You've been – well, we won't forget you.' He turned and hurried away, leaving Zoe staring after him.

The Doctor meanwhile had been having a very busy time. He had replaced the Time Vector Generator, restoring the TARDIS to its normal size. Normal, for the TARDIS that is, since it was once again bigger on the inside than the outside. Now he was topping up the mercury level once again, pouring the mercury he'd found on the Wheel into the TARDIS console by means of an old tin kitchen funnel. He looked up as Jamie came in.

'All set, Doctor?' asked Jamie.

'Yes, I've even got a little mercury left over.'

'Then we can go?' Jamie seemed to be in a hurry – as if leaving was a wrench and he wanted to get it over with.

Over Jamie's shoulder, the Doctor watched amusedly as Zoe crawled into the TARDIS on her hands and knees, and climbed inside an ornate wooden chest he kept in the control room for its decorative value.

'There's just one little matter to settle first, Jamie,' said the Doctor gently. He went over to the chest and opened the lid. Zoe climbed shamefacedly out.

'Hey, I told you –' began Jamie.

Zoe said firmly. 'I want to go with you!'

'Well, ye canna'. It's impossible.'

'Not impossible, Jamie,' said the Doctor. 'What we have to decide is – is it wise? You might be sorry one day, Zoe, wish you'd changed your mind.'

'I won't.'

The Doctor smiled. 'I wonder.' He opened a panel in the TARDIS console, and took out a kind of headset. He fitted it on and settled himself in a chair. 'Look at that screen up there …'

Jamie was baffled. 'What are you going to do, Doctor?'

'I'm going to show Zoe the sort of thing she might be in for, if she stays.'

318

Zoe looked at the headset and at the screen. 'Thought patterns, Doctor?'

'Yes. I shall make them into a complete story ... Have you ever heard of the Daleks, Zoe?'

'No.'

'Then watch,' said the Doctor impressively.

Shapes began to appear on the screen, squat menacing metallic shapes.

The Daleks ...

Jamie realised that the Doctor was telling Zoe the story of one of their recent adventures, the one in which they'd first met poor Victoria.

Jamie wondered if she was happy in her new life. He hoped so. Curiously, he was finding it hard to remember her face – especially with Zoe's vivid little face gazing enthralled at the screen. Jamie noticed something else.

Consciously or unconsciously, the Doctor must have operated the controls before sitting down. The TARDIS doors were closed and the centre column was rising and falling. The TARDIS was already in flight.

Jamie hoped Zoe wouldn't be too scared by the Doctor's Dalek story. Because now, like it or not, she was on her way.

DOCTOR WHO AND THE AUTON INVASION

1

PROLOGUE: EXILED TO EARTH

In the High Court of the Time Lords a trial was coming to its end. The accused, a renegade Time Lord known as the Doctor, had already been found guilty. Now it was time for the sentence.

The Doctor looked very out of place standing amongst the dignified Time Lords in their long white robes. To begin with, he was quite a small man. He wore an ancient black coat and a pair of check trousers. He had a gentle, rather comical face and a shock of untidy black hair. But there was strength in that face, too, and keen intelligence in the blue eyes.

A hush fell as the President of the Court rose, and began to speak. 'Doctor, you have been found guilty of two serious offences against our laws. First, you stole a TARDIS and used it to roam through Time and Space as you pleased.'

'Nonsense,' said the Doctor indignantly. 'I didn't steal it. Just borrowed it for a while.'

The President ignored the interruption. 'More important, you have repeatedly broken our most important law: interference in the affairs of other planets is a serious crime.'

Again the Doctor interrupted: 'I not only admit my interference, I am proud of it! You just observe the evil in the galaxies. I fight against it.'

'We have accepted your plea, Doctor, that there is evil in the Universe which must be fought. You still have a part to play in that great struggle.'

At once the Doctor began to look hopeful. 'You mean you're going to let me go?'

'Not entirely. We have noted your interest in the planet Earth. You have visited it many times. You must have special knowledge of that world and its problems.'

'I suppose I have,' agreed the Doctor.

'You will be sent to Earth in the Twentieth Century Time Zone. You will remain there for as long as we think proper. And for that time the secret of the TARDIS will be taken from you.'

The Doctor was indignant. 'You can't condemn me to exile on one primitive planet, in one particular time.'

The President's voice was cold. 'We can, and we do. That is the verdict of this Court.'

A new thought struck the Doctor. 'Besides, I'm known on Earth already. It could be most embarrassing for me.'

'Your appearance has changed before. It will change again. That is part of your sentence.'

The Doctor continued to protest. 'You can't just change what I look like without asking me!'

'You will have an opportunity to choose your new appearance,' said the President patiently. 'Look!'

As if by magic, a huge screen appeared on one wall of the Court. Upon it the Doctor saw a wide variety of faces and forms. At once the Doctor started to make trouble. He rejected each one with the utmost scorn. 'Too thin. Too fat. Too young. Too old. No, I certainly don't want to look like that, I can tell you.'

The President of the Court sighed. They were letting the fellow off lightly. He ought to be humble and grateful, not kick up all this fuss. 'You are wasting time, Doctor,' said the President. 'Since you refuse to take the decision, we shall take it for you.'

The Doctor made no secret of his indignation.

'Well, I've got a right to decide what I'm going to look like,' he grumbled. 'They attach a great deal of importance to these things on Earth. I mean, it's not my fault if this is the best you can do, is it? I've never seen such a terrible looking bunch!'

Ignoring the Doctor's protests and complaints, the President sent a thought-impulse to a fellow Time Lord who sat at a nearby control panel. The Time Lord's fingers moved swiftly over the rows of buttons.

Immediately the Doctor was held in the grip of a force-field. Unable to move, he felt the entire courtroom dissolve round him into a sort of spinning blackness.

Sam Seeley moved through Oxley Woods like a rather tubby ghost. Sam was the most expert poacher for miles around, and proud of it. Many a time he'd slipped by within inches of a watching gamekeeper. Soundlessly he moved through the woods, stopping from time to time to check his rabbit traps.

He mopped the sweat from his brow as he moved along. No business to be as hot as this, not in October. Worse than a midsummer night it was. Seeley blamed it on those atom bombs. Suddenly a fierce whizzing and hissing filled the air around him. Terrified, Seeley dropped to the ground, muffling his head in his poacher's sack. The terrifying noise continued. He heard soft thumping sounds, as if heavy objects were burying themselves in the forest earth around him. At last there came silence.

Sam looked up cautiously. Within a few feet of his head the ground was smoking gently. Cautiously Sam reached for a stick and started to scrape away the earth. Within minutes he uncovered the top half of a buried sphere, roughly the size of a football. The sphere was smooth, almost transparent. It pulsed and glowed with an angry green light. It seemed somehow alive. Sam reached out to touch it, then pulled back his hand. The thing was red hot.

Hurriedly, Sam replaced the earth over his find and moved away. He'd come back again when it had cooled down, in daylight. He set off for home.

But Sam Seeley was in for an even more terrifying experience as he crossed the dark woods. Just as he came to a moonlit clearing, a strange wheezing and groaning filled the air. Sam slipped behind a tree and froze as still as any rabbit.

Before his unbelieving gaze an old blue police box was appearing out of thin air. It took shape, becoming solid as he watched. The weird groaning sound died away and the box just stood there, looking sad and lost in the moonlit clearing. Slowly, the door started to open.

Not daring to move, Sam watched as a man came out of the police box. A tall thin man, with a deeply lined face and untidy white hair.

325

Terrified as he was, Sam noticed that the man's old black coat and check trousers were both far too small for him.

The man looked around as if in a daze. He looked straight at Sam, yet didn't seem to see him. Frowning with concentration, the man produced a key and carefully looked the door of the police box behind him. Then he took a couple of wobbly steps and collapsed.

At this Sam Seeley's nerve finally broke. He crashed off through the woods, running for home like a man chased by demons.

2

THE MYSTERY OF THE METEORITES

Elizabeth Shaw was very angry indeed. It didn't help a bit that the tall army officer sitting on the other side of his desk seemed to find her anger mildly amusing.

'Now see here, General,' she began angrily.

'Just "Brigadier", Miss Shaw. Brigadier Alastair Lethbridge-Stewart, at your service.'

'Since you seem to be in charge of this silly James Bond outfit—'

Again the Brigadier interrupted, this time sounding rather hurt. 'I take it you're referring to UNIT – the United Nations Intelligence Taskforce?'

'I don't care what you call yourselves. I'm just trying to make it clear to you that I'm not interested in playing secret agents with you. I happen to have a very important research programme under way at Cambridge.'

The Brigadier looked through a file on the desk in front of him. 'I'm well aware of your scientific qualifications, Miss Shaw. An expert in meteorites, degrees in physics, medicine and a dozen other subjects. Just the sort of all-rounder I've been looking for!' The Brigadier sat back, stroking his clipped moustache with an infuriatingly self-satisfied air.

Liz Shaw took a deep breath, and made a tremendous effort to control herself. 'You scoop me up from my laboratories in Cambridge, whizz me down here in a fast car, and expect me to join some ridiculous spy outfit, just like that! Why me, for Heaven's sake?'

The Brigadier said, 'We need your help, Miss Shaw. You'll find the laboratory facilities here are really first class.'

'And what am I supposed to do with them? Invent a better kind of invisible ink?'

'I think you have rather a mistaken idea of our work here at UNIT. We're not exactly spies, you know. If I could explain?'

Liz realised that, in spite of her anger, she was really rather curious about what was going on. 'All right,' she said. 'Just what do you do – exactly?'

The Brigadier paused for a moment, obviously choosing his words with great care. 'We deal with the odd – the unexplained. We're prepared to tackle anything on Earth. Or even from beyond the Earth, if necessary.'

Liz looked at him in amazement. To her astonishment he seemed quite serious. 'You mean alien invaders?' she said incredulously. 'Little blue men from Mars with three heads?'

'Early this morning,' said the Brigadier, 'a shower of about fifty meteorites landed in Essex.'

Liz's scientific curiosity was aroused at once. 'Landed? Most meteorites don't even reach the Earth's surface. They burn up in the atmosphere.'

The Brigadier nodded. 'Exactly. But these didn't.'

'Were they exceptionally large?'

'Rather small if anything. And they came down through a funnel of thin, super-heated air twenty miles in diameter – for which no one has been able to provide an explanation.'

Liz frowned. 'Some kind of freak heat-wave?'

'Perhaps. But the temperature in that area was over twenty-eight Centigrade. A few miles away there was ground-frost.'

'There must be an explanation,' said Liz thoughtfully. 'A natural one, I mean.' She didn't sound very convincing, even to herself.

'I hope there is. I've cordoned off the area and I've got men searching now. But we didn't find anything last time.'

Liz looked up sharply. 'Last time?'

Grimly the Brigadier nodded. 'Six months ago, a smaller shower of meteorites, five or six of them, landed in the same area.'

'That's impossible!' said Liz. 'The odds against two lots of meteorites landing in the same place must be enormous.'

With some satisfaction the Brigadier looked at the girl in front of his desk. At last she was beginning to realise the true seriousness of the situation.

Liz went on: 'In fact the odds are so high as to be scientifically unacceptable.' She stood up and paced about the office, thinking aloud. 'So if we rule out coincidence, there can be only one other explanation. Those meteorites – both showers – must have been ...' Her voice tailed off as she couldn't bring herself to say the final words.

The Brigadier finished the sentence for her. 'That's right. The meteorite swarms must have been directed. Deliberately aimed at this planet.'

In the reception hall of Ashbridge Cottage Hospital Captain Munro, of UNIT, was arguing with an irate casualty officer. Fortunately, Munro, a dark-haired, smoothly handsome young man, was something of a diplomat. He was used to smoothing down awkward civilians, and he answered all Doctor Henderson's objections with infuriating politeness. In the background, two soldiers, Regular Army men on attachment to UNIT, waited patiently, carrying between them a stretcher on which lay a still, blanket-covered form.

'Dammit man,' said Doctor Henderson crossly, 'why didn't you take him to a military hospital?'

Munro sighed. 'For one thing, sir, there isn't one in the area. And for another ...' Munro turned to the stretcher and pulled back the blanket. 'As you can see, the chap's obviously a civilian.'

Henderson looked in amazement at the tall, thin figure on the stretcher. Coat and trousers were both far too small, leaving bony wrists and ankles stretching out in a scarecrow fashion. 'Not a very military figure, I agree,' admitted Doctor Henderson. 'All right, I suppose I'd better take a look at him.' He turned to the soldiers carrying the stretcher. 'Take him through into Casualty, will you? The porter will show you the way.' At a nod from Munro, the soldiers carried the stretcher through the swing-doors into the casualty ward.

'You've no idea who he is, I suppose?' asked Henderson. Munro shook his head. 'Haven't a clue, sir. There's no identification on him, I'm afraid.'

Henderson heaved a sigh. 'You don't realise the amount of paperwork these cases involve,' he said wearily. 'Reports to the police, memos to the Hospital Committee. All in triplicate.'

Like any good soldier, Captain Munro knew when it was time to beat a retreat. 'You really have been awfully good sir,' he said smoothly. 'I'm sure the Brigadier will be most grateful.' Munro looked at his watch. 'Which reminds me, I really ought to 'phone in a report. I wonder if I might ...'

'Over there,' said Henderson, nodding towards a 'phone booth in the corner. 'Mind you, this chap's still your responsibility.'

Munro didn't commit himself. 'Thanks again, sir,' he said with his most charming smile. 'Now, if you'll excuse me ...'

Hastily Munro disappeared inside the 'phone booth. Henderson, realising he'd been out-manoeuvred, turned and went through the swing-doors after his new patient.

Back at UNIT H.Q., Brigadier Lethbridge-Stewart was still trying to persuade Liz Shaw to accept the unbelievable.

'Don't you see, Miss Shaw, it's just *because* everyone takes your attitude, refuses to believe the evidence, that the Earth is in so much danger.'

'Why is Earth any more likely to be attacked now than at any time during the last fifty thousand years?' said Liz obstinately.

'Isn't that obvious? Space probes, rocket launches, men on the moon ...' The Brigadier leaned forward, his voice urgent. 'We have drawn attention to ourselves, Miss Shaw.'

Liz sank back into her chair. 'I'm sorry,' she said, 'but I just can't swallow it. I admit I've got no explanation for your meteor swarms – but invasion from outer space!'

For a moment the Brigadier was silent, then he seemed to come to a decision. 'And if I were to tell you that to my personal knowledge there have been two attempts to conquer the planet Earth, both by intelligent life forms from beyond this galaxy?'

All Liz could do was stare at him open-mouthed. He's cracking up, she thought wildly. Over-work probably. Been reading too much science-fiction. The Brigadier was still talking, quietly and calmly, apparently very much in control of his wits.

'UNIT was formed as a direct result of the first attempt. And I am proud to say that it played a very large part in preventing the second invasion.'

'Well done,' said Liz faintly. She wondered if she ought to start heading towards the door, before the Brigadier suddenly decided she was a Martian spy.

The Brigadier seemed lost in his memories. 'Though, of course, we weren't alone. We had help. Very valuable help.' He looked up and smiled. 'To be perfectly honest, Miss Shaw, you weren't my first choice for the post of UNIT's Scientific Adviser.'

Despite herself, Liz felt a bit resentful. 'Oh? And who was then?'

'A man called "the Doctor",' answered the Brigadier.

'Doctor?' said Liz. 'Doctor who?'

The Brigadier chuckled. 'Who indeed? I don't think he ever told us his name. But he was the most brilliant scientist I have ever met. No disrespect, Miss Shaw.'

'So why didn't you get this mysterious genius to be your Scientific Adviser, instead of practically kidnapping me?'

'Don't think I didn't try,' said the Brigadier ruefully. 'Unfortunately, he tends to appear and disappear as he pleases. I tried to get hold of him when they decided we needed a resident scientist. The Intelligence services of the entire world were unable to turn up any trace of him.'

'So you decided to make do with me?'

'And a great success you'll make of it, I'm sure,' said the Brigadier. Liz couldn't help smiling at the compliment. Despite his stiff military manner, there was something very likable about the Brigadier.

The 'phone on the Brigadier's desk buzzed, and with a gesture of apology to Liz the Brigadier picked it up.

'Munro here, sir,' said the voice at the other end. 'I'm at the Ashbridge Cottage Hospital.'

'Have you found any trace of those meteorites?'

'No sir. All we've found so far is one unconscious civvie. I've just turned him over to the local hospital.'

'Captain Munro,' said the Brigadier acidly, 'if you've nothing better to report than the finding of a drunken tramp sleeping it off in the woods, I suggest you get off the 'phone and get on with the search.'

'The chap wasn't drunk sir. Half-dead more like it. And I don't think it was a tramp. Weirdest thing you ever saw, sir. A police box slap in the middle of the woods, and this fellow lying spark-out beside it.'

'A police box?' said the Brigadier. 'You did say a *police box*?' His voice was suddenly eager and excited.

'That's right, sir,' said Munro cheerfully. 'Suppose I ought to tell the police, really. I mean they may want the thing back.'

The Brigadier's voice was brisk. 'On no account, Munro. I want an armed guard on that police box right away. Nobody's to be allowed near it. Nobody! Is that clear?'

'Yes sir,' said Munro automatically. 'But I don't quite understand, sir …'

The Brigadier's voice cut in. 'This man you found. You say he's at the hospital?'

'In Casualty now sir. The Doctor's taking a look at him. The man seems to be in a sort of a coma.'

'Right,' said the Brigadier crisply. 'Armed guard on him too, Munro. Nobody's to talk to him till I arrive.'

'Very good sir,' said Munro, by now thoroughly puzzled.

'I'll come down right away. Oh – and Munro, I'll be bringing our new Scientific Adviser with me. Meanwhile, keep the patrols searching.'

The Brigadier slammed down the 'phone and sat for a moment lost in thought. 'It can't be,' he said, almost to himself. 'But a police box! And it would be just like him, turning up like that out of the blue.'

'Just like who?' said Liz, now thoroughly curious.

The Brigadier grinned. 'Come and see for yourself. I'd like you to come down to Essex with me right away.'

'But why? What's going on?'

'That,' said the Brigadier, 'is exactly what I hope to find out. If my chaps do turn up any of these meteorites you'll be able to do an on-the-spot examination. And I want to see this man they've found for myself. Shall we go?'

Liz Shaw hesitated for a moment. She realised that this was her last chance to insist on her rights, to refuse the ridiculous hush-hush job she was being offered and return to the quiet, sane, sensible world of scientific research.

'Shall we go, Miss Shaw?' repeated the Brigadier.

Liz looked at him and saw the appeal behind the formal manner. Suddenly she realised that the Brigadier really was worried, that he really did need her help. Why me, she thought, why me? There must be heaps of people better qualified.

But she also realised that she was now much too caught up in this mysterious business of invading alien forces, intelligent meteorites and mysterious men with police boxes, to draw back now. If she did, she'd be torn with curiosity for the rest of her life. She got up and strode to the door which the Brigadier was holding open for her. 'Come along then, Brigadier,' she said briskly, 'what are we wasting time for?'

The Brigadier stood astonished as Liz strode past him and marched off down the corridor. Then, deciding not for the first time that he would never understand the ways of women, he hurried after her.

3

THE MAN FROM SPACE

In a small private room, Ashbridge Cottage Hospital's latest arrival lay motionless on the bed. Henderson stood over him, his face a picture of astonishment. He'd expected all along that the new arrival would mean trouble. But not this kind of trouble. Hovering as it seemed between life and death, the new patient was showing reflexes and reactions that Henderson had never encountered before.

Henderson looked up eagerly as a nurse entered with a batch of X-ray plates. Surely these would throw some light on things. The nurse looked at the still figure on the bed. 'How is he, Doctor?'

Henderson turned away to look at the X-rays. 'I only wish I knew,' he said honestly. The nurse leaned over the patient, automatically smoothing the pillows and straightening the sheets. The man on the bed was quiet and still, scarcely breathing. She studied the still features for a moment. It was a strange face. Sometimes it seemed handsome and dignified, sometimes quizzical, almost comic. The seams and wrinkles, the shock of almost white hair should have made it an old face, yet somehow there was a strong impression of energy and youth.

Suddenly the nurse drew back in amazement as two very blue eyes flicked open, and studied her with interest. Then solemnly one of them winked. Both eyes closed and the man seemed to subside into his coma.

'Nurse!' Henderson's voice made her jump. It was cold with anger. 'Would you mind coming over here, please?'

The nurse trembled. Like all the other nurses in the hospital, she was terrified of Henderson and his sharp tongue. What could be wrong now, she thought. Maybe those idiots in radiology had sent up the wrong plates. Whatever it was, she'd be the one to get the blame.

Inwardly quaking, she crossed to where Henderson was examining the X-rays on a lighted stand. 'Is there anything wrong, Doctor?' she said, trying to keep her voice calm.

Henderson pointed to the X-ray. 'You have, I take it, studied the human anatomy as part of your training?'

The nurse sighed. 'Of course, Doctor.'

Henderson jabbed a quivering finger at the X-ray plate. 'Then perhaps you would be kind enough to tell me what that is?'

She followed the direction of the finger. 'It's the patient's heart, Doctor.'

Henderson's finger moved across to the other side of the plate. 'Then what's this, then, eh? What's this?' By now he was so angry that his voice came out only as a sort of strangulated shriek.

The nurse, now completely terrorised, leaned forward and peered nervously at the X-ray. Then she drew a deep breath. 'It appears to be another heart, sir.'

'Exactly,' said Henderson grimly. 'Another heart. And that, as we know, is impossible, isn't it, nurse? Now then, which of your jolly medical student friends is responsible for this little prank, eh?'

The nurse struggled to control her quavering voice. 'I don't know, Doctor, honestly. All I did was wait till the plates were ready and bring them back to you.'

Henderson studied her narrowly and saw that she was much too terrified to be relating anything except the truth. As always, he regretted his quick temper. 'All right,' he said gruffly, 'probably wasn't your fault. But someone in that X-ray Department is playing games with me, and I'm going to find out who it is.' He was about to stride from the room when the internal 'phone bleeped. The nurse picked it up. An angry voice said in her ear: 'This is Lomax. Pathology Lab. Is Doctor Henderson there?'

The nurse almost dropped the 'phone from pure terror. If there was anyone more feared than Doctor Henderson, it was old Doctor Lomax in Pathology. Silently she handed the 'phone to Doctor Henderson. He took it and said, 'Doctor Henderson. Well?'

The fierce Scottish voice jabbed at his eardrums. 'No, Doctor Henderson, it's no' well at all. Not when ye've the time to play wee stupid tricks on a busy man like me.'

Henderson's bad temper returned full blast. He and Lomax were old enemies. 'What the blazes are you talking about?'

'I am talking, Doctor Henderson, about the sample of blood ye've just sent us for cross matching. Ye admit ye sent the sample?'

'Of course I did. It's routine. You know that. What's the matter with it?'

The voice on the 'phone was airily sarcastic. 'Oh nothing, Doctor Henderson, nothing. Except that it's not human blood, as you very well know.'

Henderson said angrily. 'What do you mean, not human? I took it from the patient myself.'

'It is not human blood,' said Lomax emphatically. 'The platelet stickiness is quite different and it corresponds to no known human blood-type.'

'Now you listen to me, Doctor Lomax. I took that blood sample from an adult male patient who is lying on the bed in front of me now. You tell me it's not human. His X-ray tells me he's got two hearts. Now I don't know whether that makes me a doctor, a vet or a raving lunatic, but as far as I'm concerned those are the facts.'

Henderson slammed down the 'phone, feeling considerably better for his outburst. He turned to the nurse, who braced herself for another blast, and was astonished when Henderson said gently, 'It seems I owe you an apology, nurse.' He crossed to the bed and looked down at the sleeping man. 'Well, whoever or whatever you are, old chap, you're still a patient, and it's my job to look after you.' Henderson turned to the nurse with a worried smile. 'The only thing is – I haven't the faintest idea where to start.'

They both looked down at the man on the bed. The nurse said, 'I thought he was coming round a moment ago, but he seems to have …'

She stopped as the man on the bed opened his eyes again. This time he was frowning. He said clearly, 'My lord, I wish to protest in the strongest terms … the sentence is … I insist on my rights …'

The voice tailed away and the patient slept again. In the corridor outside, Mullins, the hospital porter, abandoned a half-mopped floor and moved off towards the foyer. No one paid Mullins any attention as he slipped across the foyer and into the 'phone booth. He was a seedy little man, easy to ignore. Quickly he dialled the local paper, hands trembling with excitement. In a moment he was speaking to one of the junior reporters.

'Listen, I've got something for you.'

In a clump of bushes at the edge of Oxley Woods, Sam Seeley crouched as motionless as one of the rabbits he had so often poached. In the distance he could hear the crashing of heavily booted feet, the sound of shouted orders as the army patrols called to each other on their search.

With military precision the soldiers had divided the woods into sections, and were methodically combing them, one by one. The woods were thick and dark, the ground between the trees heavily overgrown with gorse and bracken. The search was taking a long time. So far they had found nothing. They certainly hadn't found Sam Seeley, who slipped through the patrols at will, sometimes passing within a few feet of them.

The sounds of search came nearer. Sam peered through a gap in the bushes and saw a three-man patrol approaching. Two of the soldiers were carrying some kind of mine-detector, while the third, a corporal, was directing their search. Sam grinned to himself. He knew what they were looking for. What's more, he knew where to find it.

After his terrifying experience in the woods, the previous night, Sam had been glad to slip back to his little cottage and creep into bed. His wife, Meg, pretended to be asleep as he crept into bed beside her. She knew well enough where he'd been, but preferred not to show it. Although she would never admit that Sam was a poacher, she'd no objection to the plump rabbits or partridges that appeared on the kitchen table from time to time, some to go into her stewpot, some to be sold by Sam down at the village pub.

Sam had been tossing and turning in bed, thinking over the things he'd seen. The glowing green sphere of the meteorite, the man who'd appeared by magic. Who should he tell? Above all, how could he turn a profit out of it all?

He had been wakened from an uneasy sleep just a few hours after dawn by the rumble of lorries past his window. Slipping out of bed and drawing back the curtain, he had seen the troops go by, lorry-load after lorry-load of grim silent men, clutching rifles.

As he crouched in the bushes, watching the patrol move away past him, Sam became more and more convinced that he was doing the right thing. Anything that was worth so much trouble must also be worth a lot of money. Let the soldier boys crash round the woods as much as they liked. Then, when they were desperate, they'd be ready to pay and pay well for the thing he'd found. Some piece of Government equipment, he reckoned. Something they'd shot up in the air that hadn't come down where it was meant to. Well, they could have their nice green ball back. But not for nothing. Meanwhile he'd better get his find to a safe place, just in case one of those soldiers happened to get lucky. The patrol was almost out of sight now. Sam slipped into the woods, making for the clearing where he'd found the glowing ball. This time there was a shovel and a sheet of the wife's new-fangled kitchen foil in the sack he carried.

Retracing his steps of last night, Sam skirted the edge of the clearing where the strange blue box had appeared. The man had gone but the box was still there. Now, in the daylight, he could see that it was nothing more than an old blue police box. A sentry stood guarding it. He was young and nervous looking. In his curiosity Sam forgot to watch his footing and stepped into a crackly patch of dry bracken. Immediately the sentry's rifle swung round.

'Halt. Who goes there? Answer, or I fire!' Sam dropped to the ground and froze. The sentry's voice was high-pitched with nerves. The sentry swung his rifle around, covering the thick forest. Except for some distant bird song, the silence was complete. Shaking his head at his own nervousness, the sentry shouldered his rifle, went back to guarding the police box. How much longer were they going to leave him here, anyway? What was the point of guarding a police box that some idiot had stolen and carried out here?

In the trees, Sam heaved a sigh of relief and slipped away. After a narrow shave with another patrol – the soldier was having a crafty doze and Sam almost stepped on him – he found himself back in the part of the woods where he'd made his find. To most people that bit of wood looked like any other, but to Sam it was as easily identifiable as if there'd been street names and signposts. That oddly shaped branch there, that little fold of land there, little thorn bush here … Sam lined up his landmarks, produced his spade and began to dig.

In a few moments the blade of the shovel touched something hard and smooth. Sam began to dig cautiously round the sphere. Whatever it was, he didn't want to damage it. Soon the green globe was fully uncovered. It still pulsated, but it seemed quieter, more subdued, in the daylight. Sam reached out and touched it cautiously. Still warm, but none of the searing heat of the night before. He produced his sheet of kitchen foil and began to wrap up his find.

In the hospital bed the mysterious new patient stirred. His eyes shot open. Suddenly he sat bolt upright in the bed, looking keenly around him. Apart from himself, the room was empty. He frowned and rubbed his chin as if he'd forgotten something very important. Suddenly he lurched forward, face down across the bed, and began to grope underneath it. It was in this position that the nurse found him when she re-entered the room.

Shocked, she rushed forward, grabbed him by the shoulders and pushed him back onto the bed.

'You really mustn't, you know,' she said firmly. 'You're not strong enough to get up yet.'

The patient struggled feebly, but it was no use. 'Shoes,' he said with sudden clarity, 'must find my shoes.'

The nurse ignored him. With professional skill she settled him back into the bed and tucked him in. 'You don't need your shoes,' she said brightly, 'because you're not going anywhere. Now try to rest.'

The man on the bed regarded her with evident disgust. 'Madam,' he said with old-fashioned politeness, 'I really must ask you … must ask you …' The voice became faint and he sank back into sleep.

The nurse was smoothing his pillows and straightening the coverlet as Doctor Henderson entered. 'Any change?'

'He recovered consciousness, Doctor, just for a few minutes. He tried to get up but I managed to calm him.'

'Did he say anything?'

'Not really. He seemed to be worried about his shoes.'

Henderson shook his head as he looked down at the patient. The man was sleeping calmly now, though a faint frown still wrinkled his forehead. 'Probably still irrational, poor chap. Well, some bigwig from UNIT's coming down to see him. Perhaps he'll know what to make of you,' said Henderson to the sleeping man, 'because I'm blowed if I do.'

At this particular moment the bigwig from UNIT, accompanied by a rather amused Liz Shaw, was trying to push his way politely but firmly through a crowd of eagerly inquisitive newspapermen and photographers in the hospital entrance hall. The Brigadier's moustache twitched with disgust as a particularly keen photographer shot off a flash-bulb right under his nose. As the leader of a supposedly secret organisation, the Brigadier felt it was all wrong to be photographed for the newspapers, and he had no idea how all these people had turned up. He only knew that they *were* there, and he very much wished that they weren't.

A tall man pushed his way to the front of the crowd. 'Wagstaffe, sir, Defence Correspondent of *The Daily Post*.'

A second reporter cut in – 'Can you give us a statement, sir?'

The Brigadier's tone was not encouraging. 'What about?'

Wagstaffe was courteous, but persistent. 'What's UNIT doing down here, sir? Is it true you've got some kind of man from space in there?'

'Nonsense,' said the Brigadier firmly. 'I don't know where you chaps get these stories from.'

'Can we have some pictures of him, sir?' said the photographer, getting another quick shot of the Brigadier meanwhile.

'Certainly not.'

'Why not, sir? Can we tell the readers they'd be too horrible to publish?' said one of the reporters hopefully. 'Have you got some kind of monster in there, sir?'

'Ridiculous,' said the Brigadier, 'I assure you there is no monster and no story for you, either, so you might as well go home.'

Wagstaffe returned to the attack. 'Then why are you here, sir? Why have your men cordoned off the whole of Oxley Woods? What are they searching for?' The questions came thick and fast now, from all the others. 'What about the freak heat-wave last night?' 'And the meteorite shower. Is there some connection?' 'What about this man from space? Is it true he's not really human?' 'Where did you find him? Have you found his space-ship yet?' 'Who's the young lady, sir? Has she come to identify the man?'

It was many years since the Brigadier had been on a barrack square, but his voice could still carry the arresting sharpness of command.

'One moment, gentlemen, *if* you please!' A rather startled silence fell. The Brigadier looked round. Beneath his assured exterior his mind was frantically searching for a plausible story. Oddly enough, he hit upon the same idea that Sam Seeley had worked out for himself in the woods. 'All I can tell you at the moment is this. Last night some top secret Government equipment, something to do with the space programme, descended off-course and landed in this area. My men are searching for the fragments, if any, now.' Pretty convincing, that, thought the Brigadier, might almost be true. He gave himself a mental pat on the back. Indicating Liz Shaw, he said, 'This is our Scientific Adviser. She's come to help identify anything we turn up.'

'Then what about this mystery man in there?' Wagstaffe again, not to be easily put off.

The Brigadier thought fast. 'In there, gentlemen, is some unfortunate civilian who was found unconscious in the woods early this morning. We hope he may have seen the device land. He may even be able to tell us where it is.'

'And that's really all there is to it, sir?'

'That's all I can tell at the moment,' said the Brigadier rather neatly avoiding a direct lie. 'Now if you'll excuse me?'

He strode through the swing-doors into Casualty, Liz Shaw following behind. The Brigadier would have been less pleased with himself if he could have known that his flight-of-fancy had endangered the life of the man he had come to see.

As the Brigadier was beginning his explanation, a man had entered unobserved. He was standing now at the back of the crowd. The man was middle-aged, immaculately dressed, with regular, handsome features. He might have been a distinguished surgeon, or a wealthy visitor for one of the hospital patients.

One of the reporters glanced casually at him, wondering who he was. Then the reporter looked again. There was something about this man, something odd. The clothes were too immaculate, the handsome features too calm and regular. He looks like a wax dummy, thought the reporter uneasily. Like a waxwork come to life.

Sensing that he was being stared at, the new arrival looked up. The reporter recoiled physically, as if struck by a sudden blow. The stranger's eyes were staring at him, fiercely alive, almost glowing with the light of an intelligence that seemed somehow – alien. Those eyes scorched the reporter for a moment, then the man turned away, strode across the foyer, making as if to follow the Brigadier.

Mullins, the hospital porter, rather aghast at the results of his 'phone call, had been placed on guard by the door. He was being extra efficient, as if trying to make up for his previous indiscretion. As the stranger tried to follow the Brigadier, Mullins barred his way. 'Can't go in there sir, sorry. No one allowed in there at all.' The stranger raised those burning eyes and Mullins too, recoiled. But he stood firm.

'No use you glaring at me like that, mate,' he said, his voice quavering a little. 'You can't go in there and that's that. You want me to call the soldiers?'

Much to Mullins' relief the man turned on his heel and strode swiftly away, making for the telephone in the corner.

Mullins mopped his brow and swore that he'd never call the papers again.

The stranger stepped beneath the acoustic hood and stood motionless. There was no expression on the blank face. The burning eyes stared into the distance, the head was cocked a little as if listening. The smooth white hands made no move to pick up the 'phone. The man simply stood there, completely motionless. Like a waxwork ...

4

THE FACELESS
KIDNAPPERS

Brigadier Lethbridge-Stewart strode along the hospital corridor, Liz Shaw struggling to keep up with him. Captain Munro came hurriedly to meet him.

'Where the blazes did that lot come from?' snapped the Brigadier, gesturing behind him.

'No idea sir,' said Munro. 'They just appeared like swallows in the spring.' He looked enquiringly at Liz, who gave him a friendly smile.

The Brigadier grunted. 'Miss Shaw, this is Jimmy Munro, my number two.' Munro nodded a greeting and fell into step beside them.

'Got that police box under guard?' said the Brigadier.

'Yes sir. The sentry's got orders to let no one near it.'

'This man we're going to see,' said Liz. 'I gather you think he may be your mysterious Doctor?'

'I'm certain of it, Miss Shaw.'

'Why? Because of the police box?'

'Just so,' said the Brigadier. 'Because of the police box.'

'Here we are, sir,' said Munro. 'They've put him in a private room.' A sentry was guarding the door. The Brigadier acknowledged his salute and strode into the room.

Doctor Henderson stood waiting by his bed. Nothing could be seen of the bed's occupant, who had wriggled down under the covers. Briefly Munro made the necessary introductions.

'I understand you may be able to cast some light on our mystery man, Brigadier?' said Henderson. The Brigadier nodded. 'In that case,'

Henderson went on, 'I'd be very grateful for some explanation of his physical make-up.'

Liz looked puzzled. 'How do you mean?'

'His whole cardio-vascular system is different from anything I've ever encountered. He appears to have *two* hearts. Moreover, his blood belongs to no known human type.'

Lethbridge-Stewart nodded, obviously delighted by this news. 'Splendid. That sounds exactly like the Doctor.' He peered at the little that could be seen of the patient. 'Hair was black, though, as I remember. Could be shock, I suppose.'

Cautiously the Brigadier drew back the sheet from the face of the man on the bed. He peered for a moment, then straightened up, his face a study in disappointment.

Liz said, 'Well? *Do* you know him?'

The Brigadier shook his head sadly. 'The man's a complete stranger.'

'You're sure?' asked Henderson.

'Of course I'm sure.' Disappointment made the Brigadier speak sharply. He looked down again at the sleeper. 'Never seen the feller before in my life.'

The eyes of the man on the bed opened wide, staring straight at the Brigadier. A sudden charming smile spread over his face.

'Lethbridge-Stewart, my dear fellow. How nice to see you again!'

'You may not know him, sir,' said Munro, 'but he seems to know you all right.'

Baffled, the Brigadier stared at the patient, who seemed to be drifting off to sleep again.

'But he can't do. It's impossible.' The Brigadier bent over the bed and prodded the sleeper awake.

'Steady on, Brigadier,' protested Doctor Henderson. 'He's still very weak, you know.'

But the Brigadier ignored him. 'Look here, my man, can you hear me? Who are you?'

The man opened his eyes indignantly. 'Don't be silly, my dear chap. You know who I am. I'm the Doctor.'

'You most certainly are not!'

'Come, come now, old chap. Remember the Yeti? And the Cyber-men? You can't have forgotten already.' And struggling to a sitting position, the Doctor looked at his old friend in astonishment. 'Don't you recognise me?' he asked plaintively.

'I am quite positive that we have never met before.'

The Doctor passed his hand over his face in puzzlement. It didn't feel right. 'Oh dear,' he said. 'You really are sure? I can't have changed that much.' He seemed to brace himself, then asked, 'I wonder if I might borrow a mirror?'

At a nod from the Brigadier, Henderson produced a mirror from the bedside locker and handed it over. The Doctor looked into it. The face of a stranger was looking back at him.

The Doctor's mind reeled under the sudden shock. Fragments of the recent past flashed disjointedly before his eyes. His capture by the Time Lords. The trial. The faces of Jamie and Zoe as they said goodbye. The Doctor looked round him wildly. He saw the young army officer, the girl, the doctor, Lethbridge-Stewart peering at him suspiciously. Suddenly their faces began to spin round him, like the faces they'd offered him to choose from at the trial. He made an unsuccessful attempt to stand up, then collapsed backwards upon the bed.

The Brigadier made an attempt to re-awaken him, but Henderson stepped firmly between them.

'Whoever or whatever this man is, Brigadier, he's still my patient. He's tired and weak and he needs rest.'

The Brigadier rubbed his chin. 'Extraordinary business. Quite extraordinary.' He came to a decision. 'When will this man be well enough to travel?'

Henderson shrugged. 'Hard to say at the moment.'

The Brigadier turned to Munro. 'As soon as he's well enough, I want him transferred to the sick-bay at UNIT H.Q. Meanwhile, carry on with the search!'

'Very good, sir,' said Munro. They moved away from the bed.

'And keep that police box under guard. I'll send a lorry with some lifting tackle down to bring it back to H.Q.' The Brigadier looked again at the man on the bed and shook his head. 'I don't know why this chap should choose to impersonate the Doctor. But I intend to find out.'

'Er – yes, sir. Quite, sir,' said Munro, who was now completely baffled.

The Brigadier turned to the equally puzzled Liz. 'My apologies, Miss Shaw, we seem to have had a wasted journey. Doctor Henderson, is there another way out of this building?'

Henderson looked up from his patient. 'Turn left instead of right and you can get out through the kitchens.'

'Thank you, Doctor Henderson. I'll be in touch. Miss Shaw, Captain Munro.' The Brigadier strode briskly from the room, Liz and Munro following. Liz didn't resent the brusqueness of his tone. She sensed just how disappointed the Brigadier had been by his failure to meet his old friend, the Doctor.

In the entrance hall of the hospital, things were very much calmer. Most of the pressmen had gone, accepting the Brigadier's statement and making the best of it. Mislaid Government space equipment wasn't as good a story as a monster from Mars, but it was better than nothing. Only Wagstaffe was still hanging about and he wasn't quite sure himself why he bothered.

Suddenly he heard the sound of a car. He reached the hospital steps just in time to see the UNIT car drawing away. If the Brigadier's got nothing to hide, why is he sneaking out the back way, thought Wagstaffe irritably. He wandered across to the door to Casualty, where Mullins was still on guard. 'Any chance of a word with Doctor Henderson?'

Mullins shook his head. 'No use asking me. You can wait if you like.'

'Never mind. I'll ring the office and then get back.' He was moving towards the 'phone when Mullins' voice stopped him.

'Somebody's there. Been there ages, he has.'

Wagstaffe looked across to the booth. Beneath the hood he could see the figure of a man standing motionless.

'Know who he is, do you?' asked Mullins. 'Funny bloke. Eyes that go right through you.'

Wagstaffe shook his head. 'Never seen him before. He's not one of the regular boys. You say he's been there quite a while?'

Mullins nodded. 'Ever since that Brigadier came through.'

Wagstaffe moved towards the 'phone booth. 'Better winkle him out, then, hadn't we?'

'Rather you than me,' said Mullins.

Wagstaffe crossed to the booth and tapped his arm.

'Think you could get a move on, old chap?' he said pleasantly. 'You see I've got a rather urgent story to 'phone in and ...'

His voice tailed away as the man in the booth swung round on him. Like Mullins before him, Wagstaffe recoiled from the fierce impact of those glaring eyes. He tried to go on.

'I mean, you have been in there quite a while and ...' The man in the booth brushed past him, walked across the entrance hall and disappeared through the exit doors.

Wagstaffe looked at the telephone. It was still on its rest. He hadn't been using the 'phone at all, he thought. All that time he had just been standing there. Like a waxwork.

'Shoes,' said the Doctor feebly. 'It's most important. Must have my shoes.'

The nurse smiled placidly as she took his pulse.

'I've already told you,' she said, as if to a child, 'you don't need your shoes because you're not going anywhere.'

That's all you know, thought the Doctor to himself. He slumped back on the pillows as Doctor Henderson entered.

'How is he, nurse?'

'He seems well enough, Doctor. But his pulse is pretty peculiar.' She handed Henderson the graph. He studied it gloomily.

'Ten a minute! Still, for all we know that might be normal for him. Heartbeat?'

'Strong and steady, sir. Both of them.'

Henderson sighed and bent over the Doctor. He spoke with professional cheerfulness. 'Hullo, old chap. How are we feeling now?'

'Shoes,' said the Doctor again.

Henderson turned to the nurse. 'Poor chap's mind seems to be wandering.'

'He seems to be worried about his shoes. I think he believes they've been stolen.'

'Well, if he's worried about them, he'd better have 'em. Might as well humour the poor fellow.'

The nurse fished under the bed and produced a rather battered pair of elastic-sided boots. Immediately, the Doctor reached forward, snatched them from her and clasped them protectively to his chest. He sank back on the bed, a blissful smile on his face, and seemed to go to sleep.

Henderson gave him a worried look. 'I wonder if there's any brain damage. I'll run some tests on him as soon as he comes out of it.'

The nurse looked at her peculiar patient. 'He's certainly been acting very erratically.'

Henderson frowned. 'Think I'll test his blood pressure while I'm here. Get the apparatus, will you please, nurse?'

As the nurse left the room Henderson checked the charts on the end of the Doctor's bed, shaking his head in sheer disbelief. How could you treat a patient whose anatomy seemed to contradict all the known laws of medicine? Those incredible X-rays!

On the bed, the Doctor opened his eyes cautiously. Henderson, brooding over the papers, was turned away from him. The Doctor up-ended his shoes, first one, then the other. From the second there dropped a key. With a sigh of relief, the Doctor closed his eyes, the key clasped tightly in his hand.

For a minute or two the little room was silent. The Doctor seemed to doze. Henderson was immersed in the charts. Neither of them seemed to notice when two men, one of them pushing a wheel-chair, slipped silently into the room.

Henderson, vaguely aware that someone was there, glanced up absently, expecting to see his returning nurse. He drew back in horror at the sight of a giant figure looming over him. He opened his mouth to shout, but an enormous hand swatted him to the floor as easily as if he had been a fly. A second before he sank into unconsciousness, Doctor Henderson noticed something peculiarly horrible about that hand. It was completely smooth and white, and *there were no fingernails.*

The two huge figures moved swiftly and efficiently. The Doctor was hoisted effortlessly into the wheel-chair. Surgical tape was slapped as a gag over his mouth. A blanket from the bed was bundled round his night-shirted form and he was wheeled from the room. The entire kidnapping had taken place in a matter of seconds. On the floor, Henderson groaned and stirred, struggling slowly to his feet. Feebly he shouted for help.

The two massive figures pushed the wheel-chair with its silent burden along the corridor. By a side door a man stood waiting. He was immaculately dressed, with handsome regular features. He stood completely still, like a waxwork. The only alive thing about him was his fiercely glowing, burning eyes.

As the two giants with the wheel-chair appeared, he opened a small side door leading to a yard. The two men wheeled the chair through the doorway and the third man hurried after them into the hospital yard.

The little party moved swiftly and silently round the corner. At the top of the steep hospital drive stood a small plain van, the back doors already open. The Doctor in his wheel-chair was pushed rapidly up to the van.

Suddenly the Doctor sprang into life. Gripping the sides of the wheel-chair, he gave a tremendous shove with both feet against the back of the van. The wheel-chair shot rapidly between the two kidnappers and landed backwards in a hedge. Adroitly the Doctor spun it round, and with another tremendous shove launched himself down the steep hospital drive. Gathering speed, he raced down the drive at a tremendous rate.

His kidnappers made as if to follow him, then at a sign from their leader leaped into the van. The leader took the wheel and started turning the van in order to pursue the Doctor.

Doctor Henderson staggered through the hospital foyer, ignoring the astonished receptionist and reeled out onto the steps. He called hoarsely, 'There they are. Stop them! Stop them!'

At this precise moment, Captain Munro drove up in a UNIT jeep. He saw Henderson collapsing on the front steps, the Doctor disappearing through the main gates in a wheel-chair, and two very odd looking men clambering into a van driven by a third. The van went off in pursuit of the Doctor.

Immediately Munro swung the jeep round in a tight circle and set off after the van. Driving one-handed he lugged out his service revolver and tried a few shots at tyres, but with no luck. Tossing the revolver on the seat, he concentrated on his driving.

The Doctor meanwhile was whizzing at tremendous speed down the short, steep hill that led to the hospital. He was very much aware of the pursuing van gaining on him rapidly. It was almost upon him when he spotted a gap in the hedge that bordered the hill. A tiny, narrow track led deep into Oxley Woods. The wheelchair lurched onto its two side wheels and almost overbalanced as the Doctor flung it into a right-angled turn that sent him rocketing down the path.

The kidnappers' van skidded to a halt at the head of the narrow track. The two huge, silent men jumped out, obviously intending to follow the Doctor on foot.

Then behind them they heard the sound of the UNIT jeep coming after them. As if in obedience to some unspoken command, the men jumped in the van, which accelerated off down the road.

Munro skidded his jeep to a halt at the head of the track. Grabbing his revolver, he shot again at the tyres. Again he missed, and the van disappeared out of sight round the corner of the road. For a moment Munro paused, wondering if he should give chase. He glanced down the little track. A few hundred yards down it he could see the wheelchair. It lay on its side, one wheel still spinning. In front of the chair there seemed to be a huddled form. Munro decided that recovering the victim was more important than catching the kidnappers, and set off running down the track.

But when he got to the chair he realised that what he had taken for the Doctor's body was no more than a pile of blankets. Munro paused, listening. Faintly he could hear movement going away from him deeper into the woods.

'Hey, come back,' he called. 'It's all right, you're safe now.'

The Doctor was running at full speed through the tangled woods, ignoring the branches that lashed at his face and body. Totally confused by the sudden flurry of events, there was only one thought in his mind. Like a hunted animal making instinctively for its lair, he wanted desperately to reach the safety of the TARDIS.

In one hand he clutched the reassuring shape of the little key that he'd hidden in his shoe. With the other he scrabbled ineffectively at the plaster over his mouth. He paused for a second to try to get it off. Then behind him he heard shouting and the distant sounds of pursuit. The Doctor decided that running was more important than talking and resumed his flight. He had no way of telling that his pursuer was Munro, who wanted only to help him.

On the other side of the woods, Corporal Forbes and his patrol were running too. Forbes had heard the distant sounds of shooting from the hospital and had instinctively led his men in the direction of the trouble. In different parts of the woods, other patrols were converging on the Doctor.

The young sentry left guarding the TARDIS could hear the noises too. He'd been on duty in this gloomy, sinister forest since early dawn. He was cold, tired, hungry and ready to panic. The crack of the shots from Munro's revolver had already alarmed him. Now from all round seemed to come shouts and the sound of men crashing through the woods. He spun round nervously from side to side, trying to cover every direction at once.

Suddenly he caught a glimpse through the trees of a ghostly white figure bearing down upon him. He brought his rifle to his shoulder.

'Halt,' he called in a cracked voice. 'Halt or Ifire!'

Hemmed in by the sound of the UNIT patrols moving in all round him, the Doctor suddenly caught a glimpse of the square blue shape of the TARDIS through the trees. Summoning up the last of his strength, the Doctor flung himself towards it in a last desperate sprint. As he burst from the bushes surrounding the clearing, he saw to his horror the soldier with his rifle aimed straight at him. The Doctor tried to shout but the tape was still over his mouth. There was the crack of the rifle shot, a searing pain in his head and then blackness. The Doctor spun round and crumpled to the ground.

Seconds later Forbes and his patrol reached the clearing.

'I had to shoot, Corp,' babbled the sentry. 'He attacked me. Came straight at me!' Forbes looked at the still figure of the Doctor.

'Attacked you, did he? An unarmed man, in a hospital nightshirt?'

'I challenged him, Corporal, honestly. He didn't answer.'

Forbes knelt and examined the Doctor, turning him gently over onto his back. 'He couldn't answer. Somebody's taped his mouth up.' He looked at the Doctor's white face. A smear of blood was startlingly red on the forehead. Forbes felt for a pulse in the neck. He could feel nothing.

Munro ran up to the clearing, saw the group of soldiers gathered round the motionless Doctor.

'What's happened, Corporal? Is the man all right?'

Forbes looked up. 'No sir. I think he's dead.'

THE HUNTING AUTON

Captain Munro paced nervously up and down in the hospital entrance hall, rehearsing what he would say in his coming interview with the Brigadier. He sighed. However you put it, it sounded just as bad. He heard the sound of a car drawing up outside and went out onto the hospital steps.

The Brigadier got out of his staff car, cold anger in every line of his stiff figure. Munro threw up a brisk salute. The Brigadier touched his cap brim with his swagger stick in a brief acknowledgement and said, 'Well?'

Munro sighed. It was going to be even worse than he had feared. 'There was some kind of a raid, sir. They knocked out Doctor Henderson and our sentry, and tried to get the patient away.'

'Who did?'

'We're not sure, sir,' said Munro.

'Tried and succeeded, it seems,' said the Brigadier sourly.

'Well, not entirely, sir. I turned up just as they were getting him out of the building. The patient got away in the confusion, they chased him, and I chased them.'

'And lost them.'

'Well – yes sir. You see, the man ran into the woods. He seemed to be making for the police box where we found him. I thought it was more important to get him back.'

'Instead of which the poor chap was shot down by one of our sentries?'

'It was a very confused situation, sir,' said Munro defensively.

'It was a complete and utter botch-up!' snapped the Brigadier. 'How's the poor chap now?'

'Well, that's just it, sir. No one seems to know.'

The Brigadier said, 'I'd better see him.'

'There is one piece of good news, sir,' said Munro hopefully, as they walked along the corridor. 'Our chaps have turned up one of these meteorite things. Or, rather, the bits of one. It's on its way here now.'

'I'm delighted to hear that the Army managed to achieve something, besides the shooting of a harmless civilian,' said the Brigadier as they entered the hospital room.

Doctor Henderson, still a little shaky himself, was leaning over his patient, once more stretched out on the hospital bed. The Doctor lay completely motionless. Henderson and the nurse were applying some instrument to his head.

Henderson looked up and nodded as the Brigadier entered, and said: 'Extraordinary. Quite extraordinary. Look at these readings.'

The Brigadier looked and was none the wiser. He said: 'How is he?'

'This registers the activity of the brain,' explained Henderson. 'Normally this line fluctuates considerably even when a person is unconscious.'

The Brigadier looked at the chart. 'Not a lot going on, eh?' he said, feeling that some comment was expected.

Henderson was impatient. 'There's nothing whatever going on, as you put it.'

'But he isn't dead?'

'No. But you might say he was just barely ticking over.'

'Something to do with that bullet wound,' suggested Munro.

Henderson shook his head. 'That only left a slight graze across the scalp. Couldn't account for this condition.'

The Brigadier was becoming impatient with all this medical mumbo-jumbo. 'Then what does?' he asked.

Henderson rubbed his chin thoughtfully. 'It's only a guess, but I reckon this coma is self-induced.'

'You mean the chap's put himself out?' asked the Brigadier. 'Why would he do that?'

'Again, I'm only guessing,' said Henderson. 'But it could be part of some kind of healing process. A chance for his body to recover from all the stresses it's been suffering.'

The Brigadier moved closer to the bed and studied the sleeping form. Everything about him sounds like the Doctor, he thought. The police box, the strange physical make-up. And he knew me. He really did know me. He knew about the Cyberman and the Yeti. But there's no resemblance. No resemblance at all. The face, the height, the build, the colour of the hair – all utterly and completely different. And yet ... The Brigadier could remember so many incredible things about the man he had known as the Doctor. Was a change of appearance any more unbelievable than all the rest?

He turned away from his bed. 'You'll keep me informed of his condition. I'd like to know as soon as he can talk.'

'Yes, of course,' said Henderson. 'Oh, by the way, we found this clutched in his hand.'

Henderson handed the Brigadier a little key. 'We had to prise his fingers open. He was really hanging on to it.'

'Yes,' said the Brigadier thoughtfully, 'he would do. Thank you, Doctor Henderson.' Followed by Munro, he turned and left the room.

Outside the hospital, a couple of soldiers were standing guard beside a wooden ammunition box.

'That'll be the meteorite fragments, sir,' said Munro. The Brigadier peered inside the box, as a soldier held open the lid. The box was about half-full of chunks of some dull green substance, rather like heat-fused glass.

'All we could find, sir,' said Munro. 'It must have broken up when it hit the ground.'

The Brigadier sniffed. 'Doesn't seem much result for all this effort. Keep searching. See if you can find me a whole one. Oh, and put the box in the boot of my car. Miss Shaw can take a look at it.'

The soldier took the box away and the Brigadier turned back to Munro. 'The police box is already on its way to H.Q. I want a guard on the hospital at all times.'

'Yes, sir,' said Munro. 'We won't lose him again, I promise you.'

The Brigadier looked back at the hospital. 'What puzzles me is, why did those people want to kidnap him?'

'Maybe he was one of them,' suggested Munro. 'They could have been trying to rescue him.'

'Anyone get a good look at them?'

'Better than that, sir,' said Munro proudly. 'We've got a picture of their leader.' He produced a glossy photograph and handed it to the Brigadier.

The Brigadier studied the picture, obviously one of those taken on his first visit to the hospital. The photograph showed the Brigadier talking to the crowd of journalists.

'That's him, there, sir,' said Munro. Over the Brigadier's shoulder in the picture there could be seen a man standing, watching. A well-dressed man with handsome, regular features and staring eyes.

'Several people recognised him, sir,' said Munro. 'He was here posing as a pressman.'

'What about the other two?'

'Couldn't really get much of a description,' admitted Munro, 'only that they were very big. And there was something strange, blank-looking about their faces. Probably wearing stocking masks.'

The Brigadier opened the door of his car. 'Three things, Munro. Keep searching for the meteorites; guard that man in the hospital; and keep investigating the kidnap attempt. Call me at H.Q., the minute there's news.' The Brigadier closed the car door and the driver accelerated away. Munro gazed after the departing car. Is that all, Brigadier, he thought to himself. And what do I do in my spare time?

As Harry Ransome drove down the familiar road towards the plastics factory, his mind was in a turmoil. His thoughts kept circling round the letter, the incredible, unbelievable letter that had been waiting for him on his return from his business trip to America.

I'm not just going to accept it, he thought. They owe me an explanation, and I'm going to get it. He drove through the gates and parked in his usual slot in the company car-park. Picking up the bulging brief-case from the seat beside him, he got out of the car and stood still for a moment, bracing himself. A smartly-dressed, dapper little man in his early thirties, he usually radiated the warmth and charm of the top-class salesman. But Ransome's face was grim and determined as he strode into the factory.

The girl behind the reception desk was new to him.

She had a strange, expressionless, doll-like prettiness. She looked up incuriously as he entered.

'My name's Ransome. We haven't met, but I expect you've heard of me. I work here – or I used to. Head of Sales and Design. Been with the firm for years.'

Still she didn't speak. Ransome took a deep breath. 'Just popping in to see Mr Hibbert. Don't worry, he won't mind. We're old friends. It's all right, I know the way.'

Ransome strode determinedly past her and through the door to the factory floor. Then he stopped in amazement. Everything was different. The jolly white-coated girls who worked on the production lines, the old-fashioned machinery turning out dolls' heads and limbs and bodies – it was all gone. The place was completely deserted. Ultra-modern equipment had been moved in, equipment that hummed and whined, carrying out its tasks alone and unaided.

Automation, thought Ransome. Everything's been automated. He walked between the new machines and crossed to a doorway. The door was locked. A notice read 'Restricted Zone – Strictly Private'. Ransome was indignant. They can't do that, he thought. That's my workshop. Used to be my workshop. He glanced round, suddenly overcome by a strange feeling of unease. Then he crossed the factory floor and climbed the flight of steps that led to Hibbert's office.

The moment he was out of sight, the door he had been trying opened. A man stood there, looking towards the flight of stairs. An immaculately-dressed man with handsome, regular features and eyes that seemed to glow.

Ransome gave a perfunctory tap on Hibbert's office door and threw it open. He stood for a moment, looking at the man behind the desk. Good old George Hibbert, he thought ironically. Hasn't changed a bit – on the outside.

Hibbert rose slowly. 'Harry,' he said, in a flat level voice. 'I wasn't expecting you.'

'Weren't you? Then you should have been.' Ransome snatched an envelope from his breast pocket and threw it on Hibbert's desk. 'What's all this about, George?'

Still in the same expressionless voice, Hibbert said, 'The letter explains everything.'

'It explains nothing.' Ransome opened his brief-case, fished out a large doll and dumped it on the desk. Hibbert looked at it incuriously. It was an elaborately-dressed girl doll, with golden curls and a simpering smile. Ransome fished a remote-control unit from the case and pressed a button. Immediately, the doll struggled to its feet and began to walk slowly across the big leather-topped desk, scattering Hibbert's papers. Ransome pressed a second control and the doll began to talk in a high sweet voice. It said, 'Momma, momma, take me for a walk. Momma, momma, buy me some sweeties. Momma, momma...'

Ransome flung the control onto the desk and the doll became silent. Slowly it toppled onto its face. Ransome drew a deep breath. 'Our famous A.1 Walkie Talkie doll,' he said. 'You do recognise it?' Hibbert said nothing.

Ransome went on: 'When I invented this doll, you promised me full backing. You sent me to the States to try and interest the Americans in joint production. You said if it all worked out, we'd turn the whole factory over to making Walkie Talkies. You were going to make me a partner.'

He paused for breath. Still Hibbert sat motionless and silent. Ransome took wads of papers from the brief-case and slapped them on the desk. 'Well, it's all here. Agreements ready to sign. Advance orders, the lot. And when I get back home, what do I find? A letter cancelling the whole deal and giving me the push!'

Ransome looked appealingly at Hibbert. But still the older man made no response.

Ransome's tone altered. 'George, we worked on this project together. I thought we were friends. You helped me with the plans, you encouraged me. Now you just put the chop on it. Don't you think you owe me some kind of an explanation?'

At last Hibbert looked up. 'There was a cheque enclosed with the letter. The financial compensation was adequate.'

Ransome was ironic. 'Oh yes. All very generous. Only that doesn't happen to be the point. I want to know *why*.'

'There were reasons for the decision,' said Hibbert tonelessly. 'Excellent reasons. I cannot explain further.'

'Why not? Why can't you explain?'

'It's the new policy. We've got a new policy. We are no longer manufacturing dolls. We have turned over to other work.'

'This doll's the best thing we ever came up with,' Ransome insisted. 'You said yourself there was a fortune in it.'

Hibbert repeated, 'We've got a new policy.'

'What about my workshop?' Ransome insisted. 'Why can't I get in there?'

For the first time Hibbert's face showed some animation. In an alarmed voice he said, 'Stay away from there, Harry. You mustn't go in there. It isn't safe.'

'What about my tools, my equipment?'

'We'll send them to you. You must promise not to go near there. You shouldn't have come back here, Harry. It isn't safe.'

Ransome looked curiously at his old colleague. Hibbert's manner had changed completely. The inhuman coldness had gone. Now there were traces of Hibbert's old self. But he seemed frightened, confused.

'Listen, George,' said Ransome gently. 'I'm sorry I blew up at you. Is anything wrong? Are you in some kind of trouble?'

Hibbert shook his head as if to clear it. He said wildly, 'Harry ... Harry, you've got to get away ... they'll kill—'

Hibbert stopped talking as the office door was flung open. A man stood in the doorway. An immaculately-dressed man with handsome, regular features and glaring eyes.

Ransome said: 'Who the blazes are you?'

The man said nothing but it was Hibbert who answered in the same cold flat voice in which he had first spoken.

'This is Mr Channing, my new partner. There's no point in going on with this conversation. The letter explained everything. Good day to you.'

Ransome opened his mouth as if to argue but something about the burning glare in Channing's eyes seemed to destroy his will. He packed the doll and the papers back into the brief-case and almost ran from the office, edging past the motionless figure of Channing in the doorway. He could feel those burning eyes following all the way across the factory floor. Not until he was back in his car, driving fast away from the factory, did he begin to feel safe.

As the sound of his car died away, Channing turned coldly to Hibbert. 'You did not handle the situation well.'

Hibbert said: 'It wasn't easy. He'd worked here for many years. We were – friends.' His voice tailed off. Somehow he knew that friendship was not a word that would have any meaning for Channing.

Channing's cold voice held a hint of puzzlement. 'The letter was clear. The money offered was sufficient. Why did he not accept the situation?'

Hibbert tried again. 'He liked working for me, you see. He was interested in the project, not just the money.'

'The correct letter would have fashioned his response.'

Hibbert rubbed his forehead. He sounded almost angry. 'It isn't as easy as you make it sound. You don't understand people. They're not always so predictable.'

Channing swung round on him. Hibbert backed away in terror as those staring eyes seemed to burn into his brain. But Channing spoke quietly, almost kindly.

'The visit of the man Ransome has disturbed you. But he is gone now. He will not return. All you need do is continue to run the factory as though nothing had changed. That is your sole concern, Hibbert. Do you understand?'

As always when Channing spoke to him in that tone, Hibbert felt calmed and reassured. A sense of clear-headedness and well-being came over him. It was all so simple. All he had to do was follow Channing's orders and everything would be all right. He had to do what Channing told him because ... because ... Hibbert found that he couldn't remember the reason. But he was quite sure that Channing must be obeyed, that there would be the most terrible consequences if Channing became angry with him. Hibbert's face twitched at the memory of some horror buried deep in his mind. Then he became relaxed again, as he heard Channing's soothing voice.

'Do you understand, Hibbert? Do you understand?'

Hibbert said calmly: 'Yes, I understand.'

Channing turned away and stared broodingly out of the office window at the line of trees which marked the beginning of Oxley Woods.

'Two of the energy units are still missing. The Autons have not succeeded in finding them.'

Hibbert said worriedly: 'Perhaps they broke up on landing.'

'Perhaps. Or they may have buried themselves too deep in the soil of your planet.'

'Do you think that man in the hospital found one? Will you try to capture him again?'

'No. It is too dangerous.'

'If the energy units are buried, how will you find them?'

'They will increase the strength of their pulsation signals. The Auton is searching now. It will find them.'

Hibbert looked at him curiously. 'You talk of these energy units as if they were alive.'

Channing turned and looked at this pitifully inadequate human creature. How limited was its intelligence. How easily its mind could be controlled. Soon these ridiculous little animals would be swept away, replaced as masters of this rich planet by the all-conquering mind of the Nestenes. Still, for the moment it was useful. It must be reassured, humoured.

Channing said gently: 'Energy is a form of life, Hibbert.'

Hibbert's worries persisted. 'What about UNIT? Do you think they suspect the truth?'

Channing smiled coldly. 'Even if they do, their minds will be too limited to accept it – until it is too late. I do not think we have anything to fear from UNIT.'

Sam Seeley came out of the back door of his cottage. With a hasty look to make sure his wife wasn't watching, he scuttled down to his shed, a tumbledown building at the end of the long, overgrown cottage garden. He slipped inside and closed the door behind him. Then, furtively he dragged an old tin trunk from under his workbench and opened the lid. Like a child with a new toy, Sam just couldn't resist taking another look at his treasure. The wonderful find that was going to bring him fame and fortune – once those idiots of soldiers realised that it took a man like Sam Seeley to find things in the woods.

Seeley unwrapped the green globe with trembling fingers, till it lay exposed on the crumpled sheet of tin foil. He stroked it gently.

'Worth a pound or two, you are, me beauty. I'll just hang on to you till they all get a bit keener.'

Sam let his imagination wander, dreaming of a huge cash reward from a grateful government. He'd have his picture in the local paper. Maybe they'd even want him to go on telly. Sam was so wrapped up in his dream of wealth and glory that he scarcely noticed when the globe began to pulse with a greenish glow, gently at first, then with increasing strength.

Not far away in the woods the Auton had been standing motionless under a tree. It was shaped like a man but it was not human. It wore dark, serviceable overalls. Its face was a rough copy of a human face, but blank, unfinished, the features horribly lumpy and crude. It stood, silent, motionless, waiting.

At precisely the moment that the globe in Seeley's trunk began to pulse, the Auton came to life. Its whole body swung round like a radar antenna, first one way and then the other. It swung back towards a particular point and then froze. Then, after a moment it began to move forward in a clumsy, shambling run. It ran in a perfectly straight line, snapping off the branches and bushes that were in its path. Only for big obstacles, like trees, would it turn aside. But it always returned unerringly to its course, pounding towards the signal that was summoning it.

Sam Seeley was wakened from his dreams of glory by a familiar voice. 'Sam, Sam Seeley! What you up to down there?' He peered through the shed window and saw his wife, Meg, hurrying down the path. Instantly Sam tried to put the globe back in the trunk but it slipped from his fingers and rolled under the workbench, still pulsing. Sam threw some old sacking over it.

In the woods the approaching Auton quickened its pace as if the signal were stronger.

Sam looked up innocently as the shed door flew open. His wife, Meg, a thin, depressed looking woman in an old flowered apron, stood looking suspiciously at him.

'What you up to in there, Sam Seeley?'

Sam's face was a picture of virtuous indignation. 'Up to? Nothing. Just a bit of sorting out.'

Meg looked suspiciously round the cluttered shed, and noticed the old tin trunk. 'What you doing with that old box?'

'Nothing.'

Meg had been married to Sam for over twenty years, and by now she disbelieved everything he told her on principle.

'You haven't been thieving again, have you? 'Cause if you have …'

'Oh, that's nice, isn't it?' said Sam. 'Accusing your own husband.'

Meg opened the lid of the trunk and peered inside. It was empty.

'Satisfied?' asked Sam. 'Then how about getting me some grub? I'm hungry.'

'Just you watch your tongue,' said Meg indignantly. 'And don't you go bringing any of your old rubbish in my house.' Slamming the shed door behind her, she disappeared up the garden path and went inside the cottage kitchen.

Sam chuckled to himself. He fished out the glowing globe from beneath the pile of sacking, re-wrapped it in the kitchen foil, put it back into the trunk, then closed the lid. He slid the trunk back under the workbench, then left the shed.

In the woods the Auton stopped its remorseless progress. It swung its huge body in an arc, first one way and then the other, searching for the lost signal. Finding nothing, it simply stood there, waiting for the summons to come again. It could feel no impatience, no tiredness, no hunger. These were human qualities, and the Auton wasn't human. It would wait there for ever if need be, until its orders were changed, or the summoning signal came again.

The Doctor lay stiff and straight, eyes closed, in the hospital bed. He looked rather like the model of a crusader on an old tombstone.

Henderson looked down on him. 'Well, he's out of that deep coma. Seems to be sleeping normally now.'

The nurse said: 'Do you think he's well enough to be handed over to the UNIT people yet?' She spoke a little regretfully, as if she'd grown rather attached to this unusual patient.

'Oh, I think so,' said Doctor Henderson. 'But Mr Beavis is coming down specially to examine him. Saw my report and insisted on having a look.'

The nurse gave him a sympathetic smile. Mr Beavis was the hospital's senior Surgical Consultant. He appeared only rarely, spending most of his time in his Harley Street consulting rooms. His eccentric appearance and high-handed, lordly manner never failed to strike terror into the junior staff.

'But Mr Beavis is a surgeon,' said the nurse, puzzled. 'I don't see—'

'Exactly,' said Henderson cheerfully. 'I gather he thinks this chap is some kind of interesting freak. Probably plans to open him up and sort out his innards for him.'

The nurse shuddered, and Henderson grinned at her. 'Come on, let's leave the poor chap to rest while he can.'

Henderson and the nurse both left the room. As soon as the door closed behind them, the Doctor's eyes opened and he sat bolt upright.

'Interesting freak,' he muttered indignantly. 'Well, nobody's going to sort out *my* innards.' He swung his feet out of the bed, stood up and stretched.

'Now then, I wonder where they put my clothes.' The Doctor looked round the room. His clothes were nowhere to be seen. Cautiously he opened the door a crack, peered out, and then slipped out into the deserted hospital corridor. First he'd find himself some clothes. Then he'd go and find the TARDIS.

6

THE DOCTOR
DISAPPEARS

At that very moment two sweating soldiers were wrestling the TARDIS into a corner of the UNIT laboratory, while Liz and the Brigadier looked on.

'Right, that'll do,' said the Brigadier, and the soldiers thankfully stopped shoving and left the room.

'All you need now is a key,' said Liz. 'Maybe the police will lend you one.'

'As a matter of fact, Miss Shaw, I already have the key.' The Brigadier produced the little key that Henderson had taken from the Doctor's hand.

The wall 'phone-buzzer sounded and the Brigadier picked up the receiver. He listened for a moment, said: 'Yes, yes, very well,' and put the 'phone down, frowning. He turned to Liz.

'General Scobie is on his way up.'

Liz raised her eyebrows inquiringly.

'He's our Liaison Officer with the Regular Army,' explained the Brigadier. 'Technically, he's my immediate superior. Very important to keep on good terms with *him*. His men are carrying out the search.'

Liz returned to her workbench. 'As long as you don't expect me to salute him.'

The Brigadier heaved an exasperated sigh. 'Really, Miss Shaw, if you could try to be a little less difficult.'

Liz was still in a bad mood because her experiments were going badly. 'I didn't ask to come here, remember?' she said.

The Brigadier's equally acid reply was cut off by the entrance of General Scobie. Scobie was in his middle fifties, with a grizzled grey moustache. He was a rather shy man who took refuge behind a rough military manner, snapping out orders and questions in a gruff voice. But his bark was very much worse than his bite. He and the Brigadier got on extremely well.

Scobie looked round the laboratory, and at the busily-working Liz.

'Sorry to interrupt, Brigadier,' he barked. 'Just thought I'd look in, you know.'

'Always a pleasure to see you, sir,' said the Brigadier smoothly. 'Miss Shaw, may I present General Scobie? Miss Shaw is our new Scientific Adviser.'

Scobie said gruffly: 'You're a lucky feller, Lethbridge-Stewart – having a pretty girl around the place.'

Liz, who was in no mood for frivolity, gave him a quelling look and went on with her work.

The Brigadier hastened to smooth over the moment's awkwardness. 'Miss Shaw is working on the meteorite operation for us,' he said.

Scobie seized the topic thankfully. 'Ah yes, yes. Anything new on that? Papers seem to be going wild. Martians … space-ships … silly season, y'know.' Suddenly Scobie caught sight of the battered old blue police box standing in the corner. His eyes widened. 'What the devil are you doing with a police box?'

Liz looked up. 'As a matter of fact, General Scobie, it isn't a police box at all. It's a camouflaged space-ship.'

Scobie stared at her, then started to laugh. 'Camouflaged space-ship, hey?' he said. 'I like that. Very good, young lady, very good.' He turned to the Brigadier. 'Like to see a sense of humour among the troops. Good for morale, you know, good for morale.'

With some difficulty the Brigadier managed a tight smile.

'Quite sir. Well, I think we should let Miss Shaw get on with her work. Perhaps a drink in my office, sir?' The Brigadier quickly ushered General Scobie out of the laboratory, shooting an exasperated look at Liz over the General's shoulder. Liz chuckled, and went back to her work, feeling rather cheered up by the encounter.

*

The Doctor strolled along the hospital corridor in his dressing-gown, occasionally exchanging a cheerful nod with a nurse or a fellow patient. Sooner or later, he realised, someone was going to ask him what he was up to. That is if he didn't run slap into Henderson, or his own particular nurse. Suddenly, he heard the familiar sound of Henderson's voice. 'Hope you had a good journey, sir?'

The voice was just round the next corner. Immediately, the Doctor opened the nearest door, looking for a hiding-place. He found himself in a small room, one side of which was lined with lockers. Another door, at the far end, led into a washroom. Footsteps stopped outside in the corridor. Henderson's voice said: 'How were the roads, sir?' Another voice, high-pitched and querulous, answered: 'Shockingly overcrowded, as usual. No room for a decent car these days.' The door to the corridor started to open.

The Doctor dashed through into the washroom. He looked round wildly at the row of washbasins. Then he spotted the shower-stall in the corner ... Hastily he began pulling off his dressing-gown.

In the locker-room, Henderson was helping Mr Beavis off with his driving clothes. One of the old boy's many eccentricities was to drive a vintage Edwardian Rolls. He dressed accordingly.

Henderson slipped the long driving cape from Beavis's shoulders and hung it up. Beavis pulled off his Sherlock Holmes deerstalker. The two men walked into the washroom. Beavis took his jacket off and began to wash his hands.

'What are all those toy soldiers doing round the place?'

Henderson had to raise his voice to answer. Loud splashing and tuneless singing was coming from the shower-stall.

'Searching for lost Government equipment. That's how they found the patient, you know, sir.'

Beavis cackled: 'And then they shot him, eh?'

'It was all a bit unfortunate,' agreed Henderson.

A new thought struck Beavis. 'Listen, I've left me car outside. They won't go muckin' about with it, will they?'

Henderson passed the old man a towel and stood by to help him on with his jacket. 'I'm sure it'll be quite safe, sir. As a matter of fact, I've asked them to look after it for you.'

'I thought perhaps a cup of tea in my office, sir?' said Henderson. 'You could take a look at my notes and records. Then we could go and see the patient.'

Beavis settled his jacket onto his shoulders and turned to go. A note of enthusiasm came into his voice. 'What I thought we could do, d'you see ... just a brief exploratory operation. Open him up, take a poke around, see what's what.'

The old man's voice faded as Henderson ushered him through to the locker-room and out into the corridor. The door closed behind them. The Doctor's indignant face popped out between the shower curtains. 'Poke around!' he said. 'Poke around! Oh no you don't!'

Wrapped in a towel, the Doctor stepped out of the shower and went through into the locker-room. The lockers contained all kinds of different garments, stored for the hospital's in-patients. The Doctor rooted around and found the locker with his own clothes. He fished them out, and looked at them sadly. The coat was wrinkled, the trousers were baggy, and both were far too small. He shook his head. 'You'd think if they changed the body, they'd remember to change the clothes to fit.' Well, he wouldn't get far looking like a scarecrow. He needed a disguise. Ruthlessly the Doctor began to rummage through all the other lockers, hauling garments out and tossing them on the floor with wild abandon.

Ten minutes later he stood looking at himself in a mirror. The dark trousers were quite a decent fit, and so was the velvet jacket. The frilly white shirt, once the property of an aspiring pop star, added a touch of gaiety. So did the floppy bow tie. The Doctor gave his new appearance an approving nod. In his old body, he'd never bothered about clothes, but in his new appearance they seemed rather important to him.

The Doctor spotted Beavis's cape and deerstalker hanging up. Just what he needed. 'Serve the old butcher right,' he said cheerfully to himself. 'And didn't he say something about a Rolls?' He slipped the cloak round his shoulders and pulled the deerstalker over his eyes. Finally he went through the pockets of his old clothes. 'Sonic screwdriver, TARDIS detector ... Yes, it all seems to be there.' Quickly the Doctor transferred his possessions into his new pockets. Then he slipped Beavis's cape round his shoulders, pulled the deerstalker down over his forehead and cautiously opened the door into the corridor.

Hastily he pulled it shut again as once more he heard familiar voices.

'Dammit, Henderson, if those notes are accurate, the feller *must* be a freak,' Beavis was saying.

'They're accurate, I promise you, sir,' Henderson replied. 'But if he is a freak, he seems to be a very healthy one. I don't see that an operation ...'

'Where's your sense of adventure?' asked Beavis. 'Haven't had a really interesting operation for years. It'd be a *challenge*.'

The Doctor shuddered to himself as the voices moved away. Then he opened the door again, stepped out into the corridor, and made off hastily in the opposite direction.

As the Doctor strode across the foyer, with a brief nod to the receptionist, a passing medical student said to his friend, 'Old blood-and-bones isn't honouring us for long. He's only just arrived.'

'Good job too,' said the other. 'He's probably finished off poor old Henderson's patient for him already.'

The Doctor emerged onto the steps. A soldier was standing guard on a very handsome vintage Rolls-Royce.

The sentry looked up in alarm as he saw the tall, imposing figure bearing down upon him. They'd impressed it upon him that the old boy was some kind of VIP.

'All present and correct, sir,' said the soldier as the Doctor climbed on board. 'Very handsome vehicle, sir.'

'Harrumph,' replied the Doctor, thanking his lucky stars that the key was still in the dashboard. The old engine turned over sluggishly, and the Doctor revved it up again.

In the room that had been the Doctor's, Beavis and Henderson were staring, perplexed, at a very empty bed.

'Some kind of prank, is it?' said Beavis querulously.

'He was here just a moment ago,' said Henderson.

A coughing roar was heard from outside. 'My car!' the old man yelped angrily. 'Someone's muckin' about with my car!' He rushed from the room.

With Henderson panting behind, Beavis rushed out onto the main steps, just as the Doctor got the old Rolls engine turning over to his satisfaction.

'Stop, stop,' yelled Beavis. 'Get out of that car at once!' The Doctor raised his hand in a lordly wave, put his foot down hard. He accelerated down the drive, through the main gates, and out of sight.

As the Doctor sped along the road that led through Oxley Woods he caught sight of the Army patrols, still searching. But it didn't arouse much interest in him. As yet, the Doctor had no idea of the significance of the meteorite shower that had accompanied his arrival on the planet Earth. He had only one idea in his mind – to find the TARDIS, and its key, and resume his travels through Time and Space. He glanced down at the device on the seat beside him. In appearance it was like an old-fashioned pocket-watch. But instead of hands, the dial bore a single needle. That needle always pointed unerringly towards the TARDIS. It was quivering now. With a smile of satisfaction the Doctor sped on his way.

Deep in the woods Corporal Forbes and his patrol were bending excitedly over their detection device. They were on the borders of a small stream which ran through a clearing.

'It's a reading, Corp,' said one of the soldiers excitedly. 'I'm sure it's a reading. Can't seem to see anything, though.'

Forbes squatted on his boot-heels. The reading was strongest at the very edge of the stream. Carefully Forbes began to smooth away the muddy soil, digging gently with his strong fingers. Soon his fingers touched a round smooth shape.

'Shovel,' snapped Forbes, and one of the others hastily passed him a short-handled trench shovel from his pack.

As Forbes dug cautiously, the spherical shape of a meteorite was gradually revealed.

'Must have buried itself in the wet mud, see,' said the Corporal. 'Then the water smoothed over the mud, covered the traces, like. Get Captain Munro on the RT, lad. Tell him the good news.'

As the soldier turned to his field radio, the sphere was already beginning to pulse with a green, unearthly light.

Not far away, an Auton came to life. It spun round in an arc, spun back again, getting a fix on the signals from the sphere. Lurching forward the Auton began its march towards the unsuspecting soldiers.

When Munro arrived in the clearing the sphere, now pulsing strongly and regularly, had been completely dug up. It was resting on sacking in the bottom of an ammunition-box.

Munro looked at the sphere with curiosity. 'Well done, Corporal Forbes, jolly well done. Carry it up to the jeep, will you?'

The two soldiers picked up the ammunition-box by its rope handles. With Munro and Forbes in the lead, the little group headed for the road.

'The Brigadier will want this in the lab at H.Q., right away,' said Munro.

'Going to drive it up yourself, sir?' asked Forbes. Munro considered; the idea was tempting. But other patrols were still searching. He was needed on the spot to co-ordinate their efforts. Anyway, thought Munro, fair's fair. Forbes had done well to find the meteorite. He deserved to be the one to hand it over.

'I think that honour should be yours, Corporal,' said Munro as they reached the jeep. 'I'll let the Brigadier know you're on your way.'

Two soldiers lowered the ammunition-box carefully into the back of the jeep. They lashed the box into place to make it secure. Forbes got into the driving seat.

'Quick as you can, Corporal,' said Munro. 'But no accidents!'

Forbes grinned. He was a very experienced driver. He'd never had an accident in his life. At a nod from Munro, he started the jeep rolling and disappeared down the country lane, with a roar of exhaust.

'Lucky blighter,' said one of the soldiers enviously. 'He'll be down the pub tonight, while we're camping out in the wild, wet woods.'

Briskly, Munro turned to them. 'Let's not rest on our laurels, eh? Quite a number of those things came down. So far we've turned up one broken one and one whole one. Got to do better than that, haven't we?'

With an inward sigh, the soldiers shouldered their detection gear and returned to the search.

Once the sphere was in the jeep, the Auton realised that pursuit was hopeless. The energy unit was moving away too fast. The Auton stopped, apparently baffled. But the tiny fragment of intelligence that animated the Auton was also a part of the supreme brain of the Nestenes. Part of it, and in constant communication with it. That particular Auton became motionless. The problem no longer concerned it. Fresh orders had been transmitted to one of its fellows, better placed for immediate action.

Corporal Forbes was whistling cheerfully as he drove through the woods. Decent of young Munro to let him deliver the meteorite to H.Q. Some officers would have hogged that job themselves. Taken all the credit, too. Might be a spot of leave in this, with any luck. Maybe even another stripe.

These happy thoughts were suddenly interrupted. A figure stepped from the woods ahead of his jeep. Big chap, wearing overalls. He just stood there in the middle of the road, waiting. Hitch-hiker probably, thought Forbes. Some hopes, this trip.

He made a negative wave of his hand and moved the wheel to drive round the obstruction. But the figure dodged suddenly in front of the jeep, and Forbes had to jam on the brakes to avoid hitting it. The jeep skidded to a halt, its nose in the roadside ditch. Forbes jumped out, shaken and furious.

'You stupid great oaf,' he yelled. 'Might have got killed. Why don't you ...'

His voice tailed away as, for the first time, he got a clear look at the giant figure bearing remorselessly down on him. The bloke was enormous, he thought. A giant. And the face! Blank and lumpy and shapeless, like a waxwork left in the sun.

Forbes became aware that the giant was ignoring him and making straight for the ammunition-box lashed to the back of the wrecked jeep. From the corner of his eye, he saw that the lid of the box had flown open. The sphere was flashing rapidly with a kind of furious brightness. Forbes ran to the back of the jeep and grabbed his rifle. Training it on the advancing figure, he stood guard over the box.

'Now listen, mate,' said Forbes, his voice showing none of the panic he was beginning to feel. 'This is government business, see, so just you clear off! I don't want to open fire, but just you believe me, if I've got to, I will.'

His words had absolutely no effect on the advancing figure, now coming very close. Forbes, realising that his enemy wasn't even human, opened fire without the slightest hesitation. He emptied a full clip of bullets into the massive chest. The giant was by now so close that Forbes plainly saw the line of holes appear across the breast of the dark coveralls. But there was no blood, thought Forbes frantically.

No blood, and the thing just kept on coming.

Swinging his empty rifle as a club, Forbes landed a tremendous blow on the huge, smooth head. The giant staggered, then smashed the rifle from his grasp, casually, as if swatting a fly. The last thing Forbes saw, as another blow struck him to the ground, was that blank, expressionless face looming over him.

The Auton lifted the body of Corporal Forbes in one hand and tossed it into the ditch. Then moving to the back of the jeep, it took hold of the ammunition-box. The tough manilla ropes snapped like cotton. The Auton lifted the box clear of the jeep, and carrying its flashing, pulsating burden almost reverently, disappeared amongst the trees.

In the restricted zone of the plastics factory, strange alien machinery whirred and hummed and glowed. There came a soft glugging sound as the plastic mix flowed through the pipes. In the centre of the area stood a vast opaque container, shaped very like a coffin. Thick pipes coiled around it, feeding in nutrients. Channing stood watching with quiet satisfaction as deep inside the container something moved and stirred, and grew. Along the walls stood a motionless line of Autons. They seemed to be watching the thing in the tank, waiting eagerly for something to happen.

A buzzer sounded from the doorway. Channing did not move. 'Yes?'

A nervous voice said, 'It's me. Hibbert.'

Channing touched a control button and the door slid open. Hibbert entered cautiously. He hated coming to this place. 'General Scobie has arrived.'

Channing nodded. 'I have almost finished.' He turned his burning eyes on Hibbert. 'I shall need more carbon disulphide tomorrow.' The creature in the tank needed constant nourishment if it was to grow and live. Hibbert glanced curiously at the coffin-shaped tank. He hadn't been told what was in there. He didn't like to think about it.

Channing watched him. 'It would be better if you did not come to this section again. We are approaching a critical point. It could be dangerous for you.'

Hibbert looked at the motionless Autons lining the wall.

'I thought you had control over them. You said they were just walking weapons.'

Channing said softly: 'I have *some* control over them. But they also have a life of their own. Their over-riding function is to kill. You will appear to them as just another target.'

Hibbert shuddered, and thankfully followed Channing from the room. The thing in the tank continued to move and grow. The line of Autons watched and waited. At the feet of one of them was an ammunition-box. But now it was empty.

THE HORROR IN THE FACTORY

Angrily the Brigadier snapped into the 'phone: 'For heaven's sake, man, what happened?'

Munro's voice was apologetic. 'We just don't know, sir. The jeep was in the ditch. So was Corporal Forbes, with his neck broken. No sign of the ammo-box or the meteorite.'

'Could it have been an accident?'

Munro sounded dubious. 'It could, sir. But Forbes was an expert driver. He *could* have driven into a ditch and broken his neck in the fall. The box with the meteorite *could* have broken loose in the crash. But in that case where is it? We've searched the entire area.'

'Well, keep searching! I'll try to send you down some more men. Let me know as soon as there's news.'

The Brigadier went to see Liz Shaw and told her the bad news. 'It seems as if somebody, or something, doesn't want us to get hold of one of those meteorites,' he concluded gloomily. The internal 'phone on the wall buzzed and he sighed in exasperation as he grabbed the receiver.

'Yes, now what?'

'Main gate security here, sir. Someone insists on seeing you.'

'Didn't you give him the usual cover-story?'

'Yessir. Told him this building was a branch of the Pensions Department, and we'd never heard of you. He said nonsense, it was UNIT H.Q., and he insisted on seeing Brigadier Lethbridge-Stewart. Er, he said you'd pinched some of his property, sir,' finished the voice apologetically.

'What does he look like?'

'Tall thin bloke, sir, old-fashioned clothes. Driving an old-fashioned car, come to that.'

The Brigadier was jubilant. 'Whatever you do, don't let him get away.'

'He doesn't *want* to get away, sir,' said the voice. 'He wants to come in and see you. Most insistent he is.'

'Then don't stand there dithering, man,' said the Brigadier rather unfairly. 'Send him in at once.'

He turned to Liz, almost spluttering with excitement. 'It's him. That chap. He's actually had the cheek to turn up here. How the blazes did he find this place?'

'Wait and ask him,' suggested Liz practically. A few minutes later the Doctor was shown into the room.

He strode across to the astonished Brigadier and shook him warmly by the hand. 'Lethbridge-Stewart, my dear fellow!' He looked at the TARDIS and patted it affectionately. 'And here she is, all safe and sound. How kind of you to look after her!'

From behind her laboratory bench, Liz watched the Doctor with interest. This was a very different figure from the deathly-still form she'd seen stretched out on the hospital bed. It was obvious that the Doctor, if that was who he was, was now fully recovered. He was tall and elegant in the old-fashioned clothes that seemed to suit him so well. And he positively crackled with life and energy, completely overwhelming the somewhat stunned Brigadier.

'Now then, old chap,' the Doctor went on briskly, 'there's just the little matter of the key. Don't happen to have it, do you?'

'As a matter of fact I do,' said the Brigadier. 'But it doesn't seem to work.'

'Ah, but it will for me,' said the Doctor, with a charming smile. 'It's personally coded, you see, keyed to my molecular structure.' And he held out his hand.

But the Brigadier didn't respond. 'Not so fast. I've got one or two questions to ask you.'

'Questions? My dear chap, it's not a bit of use asking me questions. I've lost my memory, you see.'

The Brigadier was sceptical. 'Have you now? That's very convenient.'

'Not so much lost it exactly,' explained the Doctor, 'as had it taken away. Not all of it, of course. I mean I remember you quite clearly. But quite a lot of other things are a bit cloudy. Things will probably come back to me in time.' He smiled, as if everything had been made perfectly clear.

'I see. So you claim to be suffering from some kind of partial amnesia?'

The Doctor looked distressed. 'You do like to spell things out, don't you?'

'And you also claim to be the man I once knew as "the Doctor"?'

'That's it, old chap, you're getting there,' said the Doctor encouragingly. Liz suppressed a smile.

'And yet,' said the Brigadier triumphantly, 'your whole appearance is totally different. How do I know you're not an impostor?'

The Doctor seemed delighted. 'Ah, but you don't, old chap, you don't! Only I know that.' He noticed a mirror and immediately began pulling faces into it. 'How do you like my new face, by the way? I wasn't too sure about it myself at first, but it's beginning to grow on me. And it's flexible, you know, very flexible.' To prove his point, the Doctor began to pull a variety of extraordinary faces.

The Brigadier took a deep breath and sank rather groggily onto a laboratory stool. 'All right, Doctor, all right! Say I accept this rigmarole, there are still quite a few things to be explained.'

Liz, deciding she'd been ignored long enough, cleared her throat meaningfully. The Brigadier waved a distracted hand towards her. 'This is Miss Shaw, our new Scientific Adviser.' The Doctor was waggling his eyebrows into the mirror.

'Did you know that on the planet Delphon they communicate only with their eyebrows?' He waggled his eyebrows ferociously at Liz. 'That's Delphon for how do you do.' He grinned infectiously and Liz couldn't help smiling back. There was something very engaging about this colourful madman. 'How do you do,' she said. 'What are you a Doctor of, by the way?'

He waved his hand airily. 'Practically everything, my dear, practically everything.'

The Brigadier harrumphed. 'You arrived last night slap in the middle of a shower of very unusual meteorites.'

The Doctor said: 'Did I really now? How fascinating.'

Briefly the Brigadier summarised recent events. The meteorite shower, the finding of the Doctor, the attempted kidnapping and the disappearance of the one whole meteorite that had been found. The Doctor listened with an air of deep interest.

'So you see,' said the Brigadier, 'I can't possibly let you leave until I'm sure there's no connection—'

The Doctor interrupted: 'That's most unfair. I've no recollection of last night. Even that kidnapping business seems just a sort of nightmare ...' Suddenly his attention was attracted by the fragments on the lab bench. 'What are these?'

Liz said: 'Those are fragments of something the Brigadier thought was a meteorite.'

The Doctor looked at her. 'And you don't?' He began to finger the fragments, turning them over and over. 'Plastic!' he said in a surprised tone. 'Surely this is some form of plastic?'

Liz nodded. 'Apparently. But it's not thermo-plastic, and neither is it thermo-setting. And there are no polymer chains.'

The Doctor's manner was now completely serious. Liz watched in fascination as his long fingers turned the fragments over and over on their tray. He weighed some pieces in his hand. 'Most interesting. I wonder what was inside.'

'Inside?'

'Well, it's obvious, isn't it, this was some kind of hollow sphere?' Deftly his fingers assembled the pieces into a curved shape.

'I'd say the space in the middle was about three thousand cubic centimetres, wouldn't you agree?'

Liz looked at him with new respect. The calculation, if it was accurate, had been done with astonishing speed.

The Brigadier had been watching the two of them with interest. It looked as if they would make a good team. He stood up. 'Do I gather you're going to help us – Doctor?'

'If I do, will you give me back the key to the TARDIS?'

The Brigadier nodded. 'Certainly – once this matter has been satisfactorily cleared up.'

The Doctor looked keenly at him. There was a hint of resentment in his eyes. Then he smiled, seeming to accept the situation. 'In that case,

Brigadier, I suggest you allow Miss Shaw and myself to get on with our work.' The Doctor turned back to Liz. 'Do I have to call you Miss Shaw? Should be Doctor Shaw, I suppose, really. Or even Professor Shaw?'

'Just Liz will do fine.'

'Splendid!'

The Brigadier said, 'Right then, I'll leave you to it.'

'Just a moment, old chap,' said the Doctor. 'How many of these meteorite things came down?'

'About fifty, near as the radar people could estimate.'

The Doctor frowned. 'And all you've found is this?' He indicated the tray of fragments.

'That, and the whole one, which disappeared on the way here.'

The Doctor slipped out of his cape and threw it across a stool. 'Well, it's obvious what's been happening, isn't it? Before your search could get really under way, most of these things were collected.' The Doctor looked from Liz to the Brigadier. 'Collected and taken somewhere. Question is – where?'

Harry Ransome steered his car carefully down the bumpy forest track. One half of his mind knew that what he was planning was completely daft. But he was determined to go on with it.

After his extraordinary interview with George Hibbert, he'd driven very fast to the local market town and treated himself to several drinks. He went over the interview in his mind time and time again … the strange remote manner of old George, almost as though he'd been hypnotised … the way he'd suddenly seemed more like himself as he'd warned of danger … the arrival of Channing with his burning eyes … the way George had suddenly become a zombie again.

The more he thought about it, the more convinced Ransome had become that there was something very wrong indeed at the factory. Perhaps George was being threatened, or blackmailed. Maybe they had him under some kind of drug. After his fourth drink, Ransome was certain that for George's sake, as well as his own, he had to investigate further. He'd thought of telling the police. But what was there to tell them? The grumbles of a discontented ex-employee? No, first he had to find evidence. In this mood, Ransome had left the pub and gone to look for a hardware shop.

The track became too narrow to drive any further. He stopped the car and got out. From the boot he produced a pair of heavy-duty wire-cutters. He moved through the trees to the wire fence that marked the boundary between the factory and the woods.

Inside the factory, General Scobie's tour had come to an end. He'd expressed polite interest in all the impressive new automated machinery. Now the real purpose – the very flattering purpose – of his visit had been reached.

Scobie was a genuinely shy and modest man. It had never occurred to him that anyone would ever consider him as any kind of celebrity. He had been astonished when Hibbert had contacted him, and had needed quite a bit of persuasion before agreeing. 'Just a simple soldier, you know. Doing my duty.' 'Exactly, General,' Hibbert had said, 'that's just the sort of people we want. Not the showy celebrities, always getting in the papers and on television, but the ones who really keep the country going.' Eventually Scobie had agreed to come to the factory.

Now, in the factory's Replica Room, he was feeling a little hurt. The blank-faced dummy he was looking at bore only a very rough resemblance to him. Channing hastened to explain: 'You see, General, this is just the first draft, so to speak. Prepared from measurements and drawings. For the final process we need your actual presence. If you wouldn't mind standing over there?'

Channing indicated a sort of upright coffin, surrounded with complex instruments. Gingerly, Scobie stepped inside. Immediately, the instruments surrounding him sprang to life. They hummed and whirred and clicked and buzzed excitedly.

'Every detail of your appearance is being recorded, General,' explained Channing. 'The measurements of the facial planes are accurate to millionths of a centimetre.'

Scobie grinned uneasily. 'Jolly impressive,' he said as the instruments fell silent, and Channing helped him to step out. 'I hope it all turns out all right.'

'It will, General,' said Channing solemnly. 'I can promise you that.'

Ransome meanwhile was dodging from machine to machine across the factory floor. Not that there was anyone about to see him. The whole place was deserted. He reached the door to the Restricted Area, and set to work, using his wire-cutters and an improvised crowbar. Savagely he wrenched at the lock, and in a few minutes he had it open. He slipped inside.

Once through the door, he looked round him in astonishment. The machinery here was far more advanced in design, more alien in purpose, than anything out on the factory floor. Fascinated, he moved towards the huge coffin-shaped tank that dominated the centre of the area. Lights flashed and machinery hummed, as if in warning as he moved closer, trying to get a clear look at the huge thing that writhed sluggishly inside the tank.

Ransome had failed to notice the line of silent Autons as they stood motionless against the wall behind him. Absorbed in what he was looking at, he didn't see at first when one of them, the nearest, turned its head to look at him, and then suddenly came to life, taking a step forwards. On its second step, some instinct warned Ransome and he looked behind him. He leaped back as the giant figure came towards him.

The thing held out its hand in a curious pointing gesture. Then, to Ransome's unbelieving horror, the giant hand dropped away from the wrist on some kind of hinged joint. The hand dangled limply to reveal a tube, projecting from the wrist. It was like the muzzle of a gun.

For a moment Ransome stood terrified, then he instinctively hurled himself to one side. A sizzling bolt of energy whizzed past his head, drilling a plate-sized hole in the steel wall. Ransome look at it incredulously, and the Auton raised its hand to fire again.

By pure chance, Ransome made the one move that could save his life. He ducked round the side of the plastic coffin, sheltering behind it. The Auton paused. An over-riding point in its programming was that the tank and its contents must not be harmed.

Lowering its wrist-gun, the Auton began to stalk Ransome round the tank, waiting for the chance of a clear shot at him. By keeping the tank between them Ransome was able to edge near the door. He made a sudden dash through it, leaving the shelter of the tank. The Auton fired another energy-bolt, missing Ransome's head by inches, and blasting another hole in the wall. Then it pursued Ransome out onto the factory floor.

Another energy-bolt whizzed past Ransome's head as he dodged between the machinery. There followed a terrifying game of hide-and-seek. Ransome ducked and dodged around the machinery, desperately avoiding the hunting Auton. He realised that the creature must have some kind of intelligence. It consistently managed to block his way to the exit. All the time it was edging closer and closer, confining him to one corner of the factory. With a feeling of terror Ransome realised that he was running out of hiding-places. He could see the Auton coming closer, wrist-gun raised.

Suddenly he heard footsteps and voices. He peered cautiously from behind a machine casing. Coming towards him across the factory area was Hibbert, talking to a man in army officer's uniform. Ransome was about to call for help, when he saw Channing following along behind. Ransome kept silent. Something told him that he would get no help from Channing. As he watched, Channing suddenly stopped walking. Those strange, burning eyes swept round the factory floor. Ransome shuddered and ducked out of sight.

As soon as he made contact with the consciousness of the Auton, Channing knew everything that had happened. He knew of Ransome's breaking in, the hunt across the factory, the fierce desire of the Auton to destroy the intruder. Swiftly Channing weighed up the factors. It was too soon to risk Scobie seeing anything that would disturb him. Channing flashed a mental command and the Auton stepped back in a shadowed corner and became motionless.

Instantly, Ransome seized his chance, weaving between the machinery and dashing out through the doorway by which he had entered.

Channing walked up to Scobie and Hibbert, who had been waiting for him in some puzzlement.

'Everything all right?' asked Hibbert.

'Forgive me, gentlemen,' said Channing, 'just a sudden problem, something I must attend to later.'

'Jolly quiet round here,' said Scobie. 'Doesn't seem to be anyone in the place.'

Hibbert said: 'We're turning over to full automation, General. The factory virtually runs itself.'

Scobie chuckled. 'Splendid. Don't get any of this strike nonsense, eh? Didn't I see a big chap in overalls just now, though?'

Channing said: 'We still have one or two men about the place, for the heavy work. Your car's through this way, General Scobie.'

They walked to where the General's limousine stood waiting. Scobie held out his hand. 'Well, goodbye, gentlemen. Been a most interesting afternoon.' Channing hesitated, hands still clasped behind him. It was Hibbert who stepped forward and shook Scobie's hand.

'Goodbye, sir, and thank you once again for coming down here. We know how busy you must be.'

'You'll let me see the model of me when it's really finished?'

'You will certainly see it, General,' said Channing, '... when the time comes.'

Scobie got into his car, and was driven away. Channing and Hibbert looked after him a moment, and then walked back into the factory.

Ransome meanwhile was struggling through the hole he had cut in the wire. He ran for his car, jumped in, and reversed as fast as he could up the forest track. Not until he was back on the road and driving very fast towards London did he even begin to feel safe. Suddenly, he saw a small group of soldiers emerge from the forest. He jammed on his brakes and wound down the car window.

'Hey ... hey you!'

The NCO in charge of the patrol came up to the car.

'Anything wrong, sir?'

'There's something terribly wrong. They just tried to murder me!'

The Corporal looked at Ransome's wild-eyed face with some caution.

'Better tell the police then, sir. There's a police station down in the village.'

'It's not a matter for the police. Look, let me talk to somebody senior. One of your officers.'

The Corporal considered for a moment, then decided to play it safe. Probably the man was just a nut, but you never knew.

'Captain Munro's in the Command Tent. At the end of that lane, just down there. You could have a word with him.'

Ransome's car was already speeding down the road. The Corporal shook his head, and he and his men resumed their patrol.

In the factory's security area, Channing and Hibbert stood looking at a small screen. Hibbert said: 'You're sure it was Ransome? You didn't actually see him.'

Channing indicated the Auton, now once more standing in line with its fellows. 'The Auton saw him. It comes to the same thing.' Channing looked at Hibbert almost with pity. These humans with their limited, separate minds. How could they understand the essential unity of the Nestene consciousness? He touched a control and a bright cobwebby pattern appeared on the screen. 'The detection scanner has registered his brain-print.'

Hibbert looked frightened. 'What will you do?'

'Send the Autons to destroy him.'

'No, Channing, no! You can't just kill him! He was my friend.'

Channing came close, his burning eyes boring into Hibbert's very brain. He spoke soothingly: 'It is necessary, Hibbert. He saw all this. He saw the Autons. No one can see those things and live. No one except you, Hibbert. Think, and you will see that it is necessary.'

Hibbert's mind became calm. Of course Ransome had to die. It was unfortunate, but logical. 'How will the Autons find him?'

Channing said: 'They are programmed now to detect his brain-print and destroy him on sight.' He looked at the pattern on the screen. 'He is still in the area. Soon they will find him.' As if at a silent command, the line of Autons jerked into life, and marched silently from the room.

Hibbert said: 'You are sending all of them to hunt for Ransome?'

'If they find Ransome they will kill him. But that is not their primary purpose. All of the energy units have been recovered or accounted for. All except one. But that one is the most important of all.' Channing swung round on Hibbert, his eyes burning with a fierce unearthly light. 'Before the invasion can begin, we must find the swarm leader!'

Sam Seeley took a noisy swig from his mug of tea, and looked up defiantly at his wife. 'How do you know it weren't an accident, then, eh? How do you know?'

Meg's voice was hushed with drama. 'The soldiers found one of them things that came down in the woods. Poor lad was driving it back to London, on one of those little jeeps.'

'So he had a crash,' said Sam. 'Nothing in that. Road accidents happening all the time.'

Meg leaned forward. 'His neck were broken, clean through. And his rifle were beside him, the barrel all twisted. They say there was a look of terrible fear on his face.'

Sam shivered. 'Lots of gossip,' he said uneasily. 'Old wives' tales.'

Meg took another sip of tea. 'Maybe so. But I'm glad I never found one of those things.'

'Lucky for anyone who did,' said Sam defiantly. 'You see, they'll be offering a reward soon.'

'Maybe,' said Meg. 'And maybe you wouldn't live long enough to enjoy it.'

She finished her tea and stood up. 'Well, I'm off down the shop.' She gave Sam a peck on the cheek, and put on her coat. Sam was staring into his tea mug, obviously a very worried man. As she came out of the front door, Meg smiled to herself. She knew well enough that her Sam was up to something. He'd been acting funny and mysterious ever since that night in the woods. Well, maybe she'd managed to scare some sense into him. Barney, Sam's old lurcher dog, was dozing in the front garden. He wagged his tail, but couldn't be bothered to get up.

Back in the cottage Sam stood up, undecided. Course, it was just a lot of silly gossip. Still, he couldn't keep that thing in the shed forever. Maybe it was time for a little chat with those soldier boys. Couldn't do any harm to sound them out. He might even drop one or two hints.

In the UNIT Command Tent, Captain Munro looked with concern at the terrified figure on the other side of the trestle table. Ransome's hands were shaking so much that he had to clasp the mug of strong army tea with both hands. His teeth chattered against the rim of the mug as he drank.

Munro said gently: 'I'm sorry, sir, but the story isn't all that clear. You broke into the factory, and someone tried to kill you?'

Ransome made a mighty effort. 'Not *someone*. *Something*. A creature. There were lots of them. They must be making them in the factory. No proper eyes ... no hair ... a lumpy face ... it came after me.' Ransome began to shiver uncontrollably.

'It's all right, you're safe now,' said Munro soothingly. 'Now then, you say it had a gun?'

Ransome spluttered with the effort to explain the horror he had seen. 'Not *had* a gun ... the gun was part of it ... its hand just fell away, hung there ...' He looked at Munro wildly, as if begging him to understand and believe him.

Munro came to a decision. 'Look, sir, all this is a bit above my head. I'd like you to tell this story to my Brigadier. He'll know how to handle things.'

Munro raised his voice. 'Sergeant! I want this man taken to UNIT H.Q., right away.'

Liz Shaw and the Doctor were bent over the tray of meteorite fragments. The Doctor moved the scanning equipment gently across the surface. Liz said, 'Are you getting a reading?'

The Doctor shook his head. 'Nothing.'

'Right, that's it, then,' said Liz in some disgust. 'We've tried every test and, except that we *think* it's some kind of totally unknown plastic, we've got nowhere.'

The Doctor shrugged. 'Well, we did our best. After all, with this primitive equipment they've given us ...'

Liz gestured round the laboratory. 'Primitive? Come on now, Doctor, that's not really fair. We've got lasers, spectographs, micron probes.'

The Doctor sniffed disparagingly. 'What we really need is a lateral molecular rectifier. That'd give us the answer in no time.'

'And what on earth is a lateral molecular thingummy?'

'Nothing on Earth, unfortunately. But I've got one in the TARDIS.'

'You really do keep your scientific equipment in that old police box?'

The Doctor looked at her solemnly. 'My dear young lady, you simply wouldn't believe what I keep in there.'

'All right, then,' said Liz, 'get the thing out. We've tried everything else.'

The Doctor looked crestfallen. 'The trouble is the – er, box is still locked. And the Brigadier refuses to part with the key.' He looked at Liz hopefully. 'You might be able to persuade him.'

In his office, the Brigadier was listening with mounting incredulity to Harry Ransome's story. Ransome was calmer now, more coherent. He went over the whole story from his first visit to America, to his final escape from the Auton. When he was finished Ransome sat back and took a deep breath. He looked at the Brigadier ruefully. 'Don't believe a word of it, do you? Can't say Iblame you.'

Embarrassed, the Brigadier fiddled with a little key on his desk blotter.

'Now, I didn't say that, Mr Ransome. As a matter of fact we, at UNIT, are particularly interested in that part of the world.'

There was a tap on the door and the Brigadier looked up as Liz Shaw entered. 'Excuse me,' she said with a glance at the visitor.

The Brigadier was irritated at the interruption. Time the girl learned some discipline. She was in UNIT now.

'Not now, Miss Shaw.'

'This is rather urgent. You see, the Doctor thinks—'

The Brigadier was outraged. 'Miss Shaw, your work in the laboratory is only a small part of a very complex operation. Mr Ransome has come to me with a very interesting story, and I want to hear it without interruptions.'

Ignoring Liz, the Brigadier rose and pointed to a wall-map. 'Now exactly where is this plastics factory of yours?'

Ransome peered at the map, and then said: 'Just there.'

The Brigadier nodded. 'Exactly. Close to the borders of Oxley Woods. Some very funny things have been happening there.'

The two men had turned their backs on Liz to study the map. She was left standing in the doorway, furious at her abrupt dismissal. Suddenly she saw the little key on the desk. Without a word, she snatched it up and swept from the room, slamming the door behind her with a crash that shook the room.

The Brigadier winced, then resumed his place behind the desk.

'Now then, Mr Ransome, let's just run through the main points of this story of yours again.'

Liz stormed into the laboratory, and thrust the little key into the Doctor's hand. 'Of all the pompous, overbearing idiots,' she said furiously, 'that Brigadier takes the biscuit!'

The Doctor looked at the key in amazement. 'He gave it to you – just like that?'

'Not exactly. I took it.'

'Oh dear,' said the Doctor. 'I'm afraid he's going to be very cross with you.'

Taking the key from her hand, he looked at her with a worried frown. He glanced from the tray of meteorite fragments to the TARDIS and then back at Liz. He seemed torn by indecision.

'Hadn't you better get on with it?' said Liz.

The Doctor sighed. 'Yes, I'm afraid I had. Thank you, my dear. Goodbye.'

The Doctor crossed to the TARDIS and slipped the key in the lock. The door opened and the Doctor stepped inside, closing the door behind him.

Liz looked at the closed door in amazement, waiting for the Doctor to emerge. Why had he said goodbye like that? Suddenly she heard a strange groaning and wheezing coming from the TARDIS. It was like the sound of some powerful but rather ancient engine creaking into life.

That sound reached the Brigadier in his office. He looked down at his desk, registered the absence of the key. To Ransome's astonishment he gave a bellow of rage and ran from the room.

The groaning and roaring was still going on as the Brigadier dashed into the laboratory. The TARDIS was shuddering and vibrating now. Liz had backed away from it and was watching in astonishment.

'The key,' spluttered the Brigadier, raising his voice above the din. 'You gave it to the Doctor?'

Liz nodded. 'He said he kept some vital equipment in there.'

'Equipment?' roared the Brigadier. 'You little idiot! He's escaped! We shan't see him again.'

The roar of the TARDIS rose to a shattering crescendo. 'There you are,' shouted the Brigadier. 'He's going!'

Suddenly there was a loud bang from inside the TARDIS. The groaning noise subsided, the TARDIS door flew open, and a cloud of smoke billowed out. In the middle of the smoke appeared the Doctor, coughing and choking. He waved his handkerchief to clear the smoke and then spotted the Brigadier and Liz. He gave them a rather sheepish smile, and closed the TARDIS door.

'I was just testing, you know. Just testing.'

'Doctor, you tricked me,' said Liz accusingly.

The Doctor sighed. 'I'm afraid I did, my dear. Please forgive me. The temptation was very strong. You see, I suddenly couldn't bear the thought of being tied to one time-zone and one planet.' He turned to the Brigadier. 'Sorry, old chap. I won't do it again.'

'You certainly won't,' said the Brigadier grimly. 'Give me that key, Doctor.'

'Must I?' said the Doctor plaintively. 'As you saw, the TARDIS isn't working any more.'

He looked so unhappy that the Brigadier couldn't help feeling sorry for him. He cleared his throat and said gruffly: 'Well – if you give me your word not to try and escape again.'

The Doctor sank despondently onto a stool. 'I couldn't escape now if I wanted to – not in the TARDIS. They've changed my dematerialisation code.'

'Who's changed what?'

'The Time Lords. Oh, the despicable, underhanded lot!' said the Doctor indignantly.

'You can talk,' said Liz. She hadn't entirely forgiven the Doctor his trickery.

Hastily, the Doctor turned to the Brigadier. 'Well now, about this little problem of yours. Miss Shaw and I have come to a dead end, I'm afraid.'

'It's because we haven't got a lateral molecular rectifier, you see,' said Liz, with a look at the Doctor.

'A what?' said the Brigadier. 'I told you I can get you any equipment you need.'

'Just a little joke,' said the Doctor hastily. 'The thing is, we need something more to work on.'

'I think I may be able to provide it for you,' said the Brigadier. 'Will you both come to my office, please? There's someone I'd like you to talk to. We're all going to take a little trip down to Essex, to visit a plastics factory.'

8

THE AUTON ATTACKS

Sam Seeley shuffled his feet uneasily, twisting his old cloth cap between his fingers. His gaze wandered all round the tent, trying to avoid the sceptical eyes of the young officer behind the table.

Munro said sharply: 'Come on now, Mr Seeley, you're wasting my time. Have you got something to tell me, or haven't you?'

'I'm only trying to help, like,' said Sam vaguely. 'You see, I knows these woods, like, knows every rabbit-hole.'

'Poacher, are you?'

'Let's just say I'm self-employed.'

'I'm still trying to work out why you came to see me.'

Sam groaned inwardly. This conversation wasn't going at all the way he'd imagined it. No one seemed at all interested in his subtle hints. All he was getting was a lot of uncomfortably direct questions.

He tried again. 'See, if I knew a bit about what you was looking for …' Munro's voice was stern. 'I'm afraid I can't tell you that, Mr Seeley. But I can tell you this. The objects we're searching for are extremely dangerous. One man has been killed already.'

Sam made a final try. 'I reckon it'd be worth a fair bit of money – if anyone did happen to know where he could put his hand on one?'

Munro leaned forward. 'It'd be worth quite a long spell in prison for someone withholding information, if someone did know where to find one, and didn't inform us. Of course, if that someone came forward like a public-spirited citizen – well, there might possibly be some question of a small reward. Some kind of finder's fee.'

Sam brightened immediately. Even a small reward was better than nothing. He pulled up one of the wooden chairs and sat down, leaning forward confidentially. 'Well, it were like this, you see … I were checking me traps last night in Oxley Woods when all of a sudden …'

When Sam's wife returned from her shopping the little cottage was silent and empty. She wasn't particularly surprised. Her Sam was in the habit of appearing and disappearing as the fancy took him. She went out of the back door and called: 'Sam, Sam, you out there!' There was no answer. On impulse she went down the garden and opened the shed door. No Sam. She was about to shut the door and go back to the house, when she saw the tin trunk under Sam's workbench. She remembered how oddly Sam had behaved before. On a sudden impulse, she pulled the trunk from beneath the bench and opened it.

This time it wasn't empty. Something round was in the bottom, wrapped in a sheet of her kitchen foil. She smiled in satisfaction and set about unwrapping it. With the kitchen foil removed, she saw a dull green globe, made of something heavy and smooth. It was about the size of a football. She popped it back inside and began to drag the trunk back to the house. Once she had the trunk in the cottage's tiny sitting-room, she opened it again. The globe began to glow softly. Then it started to pulse with light. The pulsing increased in brightness and intensity until the globe was flashing rhythmically. Meg leaned forward, staring at it as if hypnotised.

In the woods a waiting Auton came to life. It swung its body from side to side, searching for the direction of the signal. Then it began to move forward, heading straight for the cottage.

In the security area of the plastics factory a light flashed on a monitor panel. The light flashed in exactly the same pulsing rhythm as the globe. Channing and Hibbert stood watching.

'Less than two miles away,' said Channing with satisfaction. 'We have found the swarm leader at last.'

'Aren't you going to collect it?' asked Hibbert.

'That is already being done.' Channing's eyes narrowed. His consciousness was linked to that of the Auton. He could see what it saw, hear what it heard. 'There – that little building. That is where the swarm leader is being held!' Channing's voice was exultant. He stood rigid and motionless, as if in a trance. Hibbert looked at him in horrified fascination. Channing said softly: 'We are nearly there.' His eyes stared blankly into the distance.

The Auton continued its relentless progress. In the distance it saw the cottage appear through the trees.

Meg suddenly shook her head, as if freeing herself from the hypnotic influence of the glowing sphere. Suddenly she slammed shut the lid, cutting off the flashing light. Then she began to drag the trunk out of the sitting-room. Let Sam keep the nasty thing in the shed if he wanted to, decided Meg. She wasn't going to have it in *her* house.

As the speeding UNIT car reached the edge of the woods, the Brigadier told the driver: 'Take us to the Command Post first. I'll let Captain Munro know we're here; see if there's any news.'

In the back seat of the car sat Liz, the Doctor and Ransome. Ransome had become increasingly silent as they came nearer to the scene of his terrifying experience.

Liz gave him an encouraging pat on the arm. 'No need to worry, this time, Mr Ransome,' she said. 'You won't be going back alone. The Brigadier can pick up some troops to go with us.'

Ransome looked ashamed. 'I'm beginning to think I can't face going back at all,' he confessed. 'I thought I was going to be all right, now, but it all seems to be coming back to me. It's as if they were still watching me.' There was the sound of panic in his voice.

The car was jolting down the forest track now, and they saw the tent with the UNIT sentry outside. The car came to a halt, the sentry saluted and Munro emerged from the tent.

Before the Brigadier could say anything, Munro spoke excitedly. 'This is marvellous, sir, you've turned up just in time. I've got a chap in here who actually found one of the meteorites. A whole one. He's been keeping it in a trunk in his shed!'

Sam Seeley was somewhat taken aback when a whole group of people poured into the tent. His eyes widened when he saw the Doctor. But Sam made no mention of having seen the arrival of the TARDIS. He reckoned he was in enough trouble. Anyway, who'd believe him? This tall chap was one of the nobs. When Sam, rather shamefaced, had told his story again, the Brigadier snapped: 'Captain Munro, do you know where this man's cottage is?'

Munro turned to an Ordnance Survey map spread out on the table. 'It's here, sir. Just a few minutes away.'

'Right, you'd better come with us.'

Liz noticed Ransome. He'd followed them from the car, and was hanging about on the edge of the group, looking completely confused. 'Perhaps I could wait here,' he said.

Munro noticed Ransome for the first time. 'Yes of course. My chaps will look after you. Sergeant, get Mr Ransome some tea.'

Munro grabbed Sam by the arm. 'Come along, man. We need you to show us where the thing is.'

Munro and the Brigadier crammed into the front seat of the car, next to the driver, while Liz, the Doctor and Sam Seeley sat in the back. The car jolted off down the track, heading for the road.

Sam looked round approvingly at the padded comfort of the Brigadier's staff car. 'Very kind of you gentlemen to give me a lift home,' he said amiably. 'Beats riding my old bike.' Nobody answered, and Sam fell silent.

The cottage that they were making for stood still and silent. An Auton stepped from the forest and walked towards the cottage gate. Barney was still stretched out in the little front garden. He raised his head and growled at the approaching figure.

In the shed at the end of the garden Meg gave the trunk a final shove back under the workbench and stood up, dusting her hands. She stopped a moment, listening. How silent everything had become. Even the birds seemed to have stopped singing. From the house came the long drawn out howl of a dog.

Meg yelled: 'Barney, just you stop that racket.'

The dog howled again, on a rising note of terror. Uneasy, Meg moved towards the house. 'Just you shut up that racket now, Barney.'

There was yet another howl, cut short by a sudden yelp. Then silence. Meg stood listening for what seemed ages. Suddenly she heard the sound of smashing glass and splintering wood. Meg ran towards the house. She came into the little parlour and stopped in amazement.

The little room was a complete wreck. Chairs and table were broken, a dresser smashed open. A giant figure, its back turned, was rooting through the contents of a corner cupboard, searching with a sort of savage ferocity.

Meg was too indignant at the total wreck of her home to feel frightened. 'Hey, you!' she yelled. 'What you think you're at, then? Just you get out of here!'

The figure swung round and looked at her, and Meg gave a gasp of terror. The face was blank and smooth, the features crude and lumpy.

Meg whispered hoarsely: 'Now just you get out. My husband's about, you know.' But she knew as she spoke that the creature couldn't hear or understand her. Slowly she backed away. Then turning she ran through the little passage and out of the back door. Snatching the key from the lock, she closed the door and locked it from the outside. Then she ran down the garden path to Sam's shed.

Sam's old shotgun was in its usual place, hanging above the shed door. She grabbed it and broke it open.

There was a shattering crash from the house. Meg looked up. The back door had been burst completely from its hinges. Framed in the doorway, stood the Auton. For a moment it just stood there, watching her. Then it started to walk down the garden path. Meg raised the gun and pulled the trigger. There was a dry click. Of course. Sam never left the gun loaded. Meg searched frantically on the shelf by the shed door and found an open box of cartridges. With trembling hands, she broke open the gun and loaded it. Snapping the gun shut, she looked up. The Auton was almost upon her.

She levelled the gun. 'Now, you saw me load it,' she said shakily. 'You get away from here or I'll blow a hole in you.' The Auton continued to advance.

'I mean it! I'm not fooling, you know.' The Auton was almost within arm's length now. Meg raised the shotgun and fired, first one barrel and then the other. The Auton was rocked backwards by the blast. It recoiled a few paces, and Meg could see the smoking holes in the breast of its rough overalls. Then it began to walk forward again. There was no change in the expression of the blank face. Meg screamed once more. Then she fainted. The Auton stepped over her and went into the shed.

*

395

Channing's face was a mask of fierce concentration. He hissed: 'The signal is muffled but it is near now. It is very near. We must find it. We must find it.'

Everything was quiet as the Brigadier's staff car drew up outside the little cottage. Everyone climbed out of the car and Sam led the way inside.

'Meg!' he called. 'Meg, we got company.' He stopped appalled as he saw the wreckage all round him.

'I think we may be too late,' said the Doctor. Suddenly they heard a bumping noise from the garden. The Brigadier and Munro drew their revolvers. Followed by the others, they ran through the wrecked cottage and out of the shattered back door.

Meg's body lay crumpled at the side of the shed. The Auton was carrying the tin trunk up the path. Before anyone could stop him, Sam Seeley pushed his way to Meg's side. Ignoring the Auton, he picked up his wife and began carrying her out of danger. The Auton looked up, seeming to sense that it was watched. It dropped the trunk and raised an arm, pointing at the Brigadier. The hand dropped on its hinge. A nozzle appeared, projecting from the wrist.

'Down!' yelled the Doctor. 'Everybody down!' He gave the Brigadier and Munro a shove, grabbed Liz and hurled her back inside the building.

An energy-bolt sizzled over the Brigadier's head, blasting a hole in the brick wall of the cottage. The Brigadier and Munro took cover, Munro behind a coal bunker, the Brigadier round the angle of the wall. Both opened fire at once with their heavy service revolvers. The Auton reeled and staggered under the impact of the bullets, but it continued to return the fire, sending bolt after bolt of energy from its wrist-gun.

From his position in the doorway, the Doctor yelled: 'Brigadier, Captain Munro! Hold your fire!' The guns became silent. The Auton too stopped firing, moving its gun slowly from side to side. Speaking clearly and distinctly the Doctor called: 'The platoon must be nearly here. We'll capture it when they arrive.'

In the plastics factory Channing's face twisted with anger.

'Recall,' he hissed. 'Recall, recall!'

At his elbow Hibbert said nervously, 'What's happening?'

Channing said: 'UNIT. Too many of them. It is too soon for a pitched battle.'

At the cottage the little group watched in amazement as the Auton wheeled suddenly and made off through the woods. The Brigadier moved as if to pursue, but the Doctor stopped him. 'Let it go, Brigadier. If you caught it, you couldn't harm it. And it would certainly kill you.'

'What's all this about a relief platoon, Doctor? I didn't order any troops to follow us.'

The Doctor smiled. 'You and I know that. But it didn't.' He gestured in the direction of the Auton's retreat.

'You think that thing actually understood you?'

'Maybe not the thing itself. I think it was just a sort of walking weapon. But whoever is controlling it understood me.'

Forestalling any more questions, the Doctor said: 'Now let's take a look at what it came for.'

The Brigadier looked at Liz, who was helping Sam to revive Mrs Seeley. 'How is she?'

'Just shock, I think. We ought to get her to hospital.'

The Brigadier said: 'Munro, call an ambulance!'

As Mrs Seeley was helped inside the cottage, Sam said: 'I'll want compensation! Look at all this damage! And what about my reward?'

Exasperated, the Brigadier turned on him. 'By making off with that meteorite, Mr Seeley, you brought all of this upon yourself, and gravely hampered my investigations. As for a reward – you and your wife are both still alive and relatively unharmed. Isn't that reward enough?'

Chastened, Sam followed the Brigadier into the cottage. After all, he thought hopefully, there was always the newspapers. A story like his ought to be worth a bob or two. Sam could already see the headlines – 'MY STRUGGLE WITH THE MONSTER'. Still scheming hopefully, he followed the Brigadier into the cottage.

Liz joined the Doctor who was peering into the trunk. 'Fascinating!' he said. 'Quite fascinating. I was right about the size and shape, you see.'

Liz looked at the sphere. It was still pulsing, though now in a more subdued rhythm. The Doctor indicated the silver foil at the bottom of the trunk. 'He'd got it wrapped in this, you see. Aluminium foil. That, and the metal of the trunk, must have muffled the signals.'

'And when that poor woman took it out, it started calling for help! Hadn't you better wrap it up again?'

Deftly, the Doctor began to wrap the sphere in the kitchen foil. 'I think perhaps you're right.'

'Suppose the thing explodes, like the other one?'

The Doctor closed the lid of the trunk. 'There's no reason why it should, if we treat it gently. That is, unless it's got a built-in self-destruct impulse. Still, we'll just have to risk that.' And he beamed cheerfully at Liz.

'Doctor,' said Liz, 'you'll have to unwrap that thing and take it out of the trunk if we're going to work on it in the laboratory.'

'Yes, of course we will.' The Doctor swung the trunk onto his shoulder and started to carry it towards the car.

'Well,' said Liz, 'what do we do if that thing decides to come back and get it?'

The Doctor chuckled. 'That, my dear, is a very good question.'

Munro came out of the cottage. 'The ambulance is here, sir. Seeley's going with his wife to the hospital.'

The Brigadier nodded, and turned to the Doctor. 'Well, Doctor? What do we do now?'

It was curious, thought Liz, how the Doctor seemed to have assumed command. Or maybe it wasn't strange, she thought. There was something very reassuring about the Doctor.

He rubbed his chin thoughtfully. 'Well, it's pretty obvious where that creature came from. Obviously something very similar attacked Ransome at the plastics factory.'

'Right,' said the Brigadier crisply. 'I'll move in at once.'

The Doctor shook his head. 'And maybe face an army of those creatures? Until we know a little more about what's going on, we'd better move cautiously.'

'Then what do we do?'

The Doctor said: 'First we send this trunk back to UNIT H.Q., under armed guard.'

Munro stepped forward. 'I'll see to it right away, Doctor.'

'Mind,' said the Doctor warningly, 'no one's to open that trunk until I arrive.'

'I doubt if anyone will want to!' said Munro.

The Doctor turned to the Brigadier. 'Now I think we should collect Mr Ransome from your Command Post, and pay a nice friendly visit to that plastics factory.'

Channing paced up and down in silent fury. 'We must recover the swarm leader,' he said angrily.

'But if UNIT has taken it – and you don't want a pitched battle yet – how can we?' said Hibbert.

Channing said: 'There are other methods.' Suddenly he noticed the monitor screen. Ransome's brain-print pattern had reappeared and was pulsing brightly. Channing said with savage satisfaction: 'Your friend Ransome has been unwise enough to return to the area. Him at least we can deal with now!'

Alone in the UNIT Command Tent, Ransome swigged the last of his mug of now-cold tea. He was feeling tired and depressed. The idea of re-visiting the plastics factory terrified him, even with the prospect of the Brigadier's protection. And now he'd just been dumped here and left while they all rushed off somewhere hunting meteorites. Still at least he was safe for the moment. Ransome could hear the soldiers moving about in the clearing outside, and the bark of the Sergeant's voice as he supervised the unloading of stores from an army truck. Ransome was bored. He wished that the Sergeant would come back, so he'd have someone to talk to.

Something bumped against the canvas at the back of the tent. Ransome looked up idly, assuming that one of the soldiers had brushed against it. Then to his amazement a long rip appeared in the canvas wall. A figure stepped through it. Ransome leaped to his feet in utter terror. Facing him was an Auton.

Before Ransome could even scream, the hand dropped back on its hinge and a searing bolt of energy smashed him to the ground. The Auton trained its gun on the body and a beam of bright light shot from the wrist-gun. Ransome's body glowed red then white, and then simply vanished. The Auton stepped through the rip in the canvas as silently as it had come.

Minutes later the Brigadier's car drew up at the Command Post. Munro gave orders for sending the trunk to UNIT H.Q. The Doctor, Liz Shaw and the Brigadier entered the tent. They looked round in puzzlement.

The Brigadier yelled: 'Sergeant! Where's Mr Ransome gone to?' The Sergeant appeared in the tent doorway.

'Nowhere, sir, not as far as I know. I left him in here drinking tea. I had to go out and get the supply truck unloaded.'

The Doctor was looking swiftly round the tent. Almost at once he spotted the slash in the tent wall.

'We can only presume he got out this way.'

'But why?' asked the Brigadier aggrievedly. 'Why should the chap just slope off like that?'

'He was pretty scared about the idea of going back to that factory,' Liz said thoughtfully. 'Maybe he decided he just couldn't face it.'

The Doctor moved away from the tent wall. 'We're all assuming he got out. Maybe something else got in.'

'Somebody kidnapped him – from my Command Post?' The Brigadier was appalled at the very thought.

The Doctor shrugged. 'After all, Ransome's story was our only link with the factory. If Mr Ransome's anywhere, that's where he'll be.'

As the car sped towards the factory, the Doctor sat chin in his hands, brooding. Liz sensed that his mind was turning over all that had happened, trying to find a pattern, a reason. He was still silent as they drove through the open gates, with the sign 'Auto Plastics' on them.

'They don't seem to object to visitors,' said Liz as they got out of the car.

'No, they wouldn't,' said the Doctor absently. 'They'd want to keep everything looking fairly normal. Right up till the last moment, that is.'

Liz looked at him curiously, but by now they were in the luxuriously furnished reception. The Brigadier explained his business to the pretty, rather doll-like girl receptionist. He was obviously prepared to over-ride all opposition. But there wasn't any.

'Mr Hibbert will see you now,' said the receptionist in her clear emotionless voice. 'Will you come this way please?' It was almost as if they'd had an appointment, thought Liz. As if they'd been expected.

She looked round curiously as they crossed the deserted factory floor. This was very advanced machinery, fully automated.

The Brigadier stopped for a moment, looking over his shoulder. Liz followed his gaze, and thought she saw someone moving behind one of the machines. Then the Brigadier murmured an apology, and they moved on. The girl took them up to the staircase that led to Hibbert's office, showed them inside, and silently withdrew.

Liz looked curiously at George Hibbert as he rose from behind his desk. He looked very like the average business executive anywhere. Dark striped suit, horn-rimmed glasses, greying hair. There were lines of strain and worry on the face, but no more than on the faces of many other businessmen.

Hibbert settled them all in chairs and then sat down behind his desk. He listened politely as the Brigadier introduced Liz and the Doctor, and explained the reason for their visit. The Brigadier gave a brief summary of the story Ransome had told them. His voice tailed away rather as he came to the end of it.

'And – er – well, there you are. You will appreciate that extraordinary as the story is, we have to check on it.'

Hibbert looked politely puzzled. 'Well, if you say so, Brigadier. Though I would have thought that it was more a matter for a psychiatrist than a security man.'

'You mean that Ransome was unbalanced?'

'That, or simply malicious.'

Liz said: 'So there was no truth in this story at all?'

'Well, there was some. It's true that he used to work for me. It's also true that he designed a new type of electronic doll. It was a brilliant invention but far too complex and expensive for the mass-market. When I refused to produce it here, he went off to America in a huff to try and find backing.'

'And succeeded apparently,' cut in the Brigadier.

'So he told me. But the fact that others were prepared to risk their money didn't mean that I was prepared to risk mine. My attitude

401

hadn't changed and I told him so. He seemed to feel I'd let him down. He became violently abusive and I had to ask him to leave.'

'So you think he made up this whole story just to cause you trouble?'

'I'm afraid so, Brigadier.'

'But why should he tell such a fantastic story?'

Hibbert shrugged. 'Why don't you ask him? I'd very much like to ask him that myself.'

'We were going to bring him with us,' said Liz. 'Unfortunately he disappeared before we set off.'

'I'm not surprised! Didn't dare to repeat all this nonsense to my face.'

The Doctor spoke for the first time. 'What exactly do you make in this factory, Mr Hibbert?'

'I'd be delighted to show you. Perhaps you'd care to have a look at our store-rooms?'

The first room Hibbert took them to was lined with shelf after shelf of plastic dolls. Dolls with hair of every colour, dolls of every shape and size. Row upon row of china-blue eyes gazed at them unwinkingly from shiny pink plastic faces. Liz shivered. Somehow there was something rather sinister about so many of the little creatures in one place.

Hibbert waved his arm in a sweeping gesture. 'This was our original line, of course. However, since then we've broken into new territory. If you'd come through here.'

He took them into another, larger store-room. It seemed to be full of a huge crowd of silent figures, standing and waiting. Hibbert switched on a light.

'This is our big success at the moment. Display mannequins for department stores and shop windows.'

Liz looked round. Row after row of impossibly handsome men and beautiful women. If possible, they were even more sinister than the dolls.

The Doctor said: 'And do these, er … mannequins move?' Hibbert smiled. 'Of course they do.' He went up to the nearest mannequin and shifted its position. Arms and legs and body moved easily, and stayed as they were put.

'It's fortunate you came today. These will all be gone by tomorrow.' Hibbert put the mannequin back in its place. 'As you can see,' he said proudly, 'they're extremely supple and flexible. But I can assure you they don't move by themselves. We call them Autons, after the name of the factory – "Auto Plastics".'

The Brigadier coughed. 'Most impressive. Well, we mustn't take up any more of your time, Mr Hibbert.'

As Hibbert led them back across the factory floor towards the reception area, the Doctor asked: 'These Autons of yours – they're selling well?'

Hibbert nodded proudly. 'You'll find our Autons in every big department store in every city in England.'

Suddenly the Doctor stopped. He pointed across the factory floor to the area marked 'Restricted Zone'. 'I don't believe you've shown us what goes on in there, Mr Hibbert?'

'And I'm afraid I can't.' Hibbert turned to the Brigadier. 'Confidentially, Brigadier, we do a certain amount of work for the Ministry of Technology. Research into heat-resistant plastic for the space programme. Unless you and your party have special Ministry passes ...' Hibbert shrugged apologetically. 'Well, I'm sure you, more than most people, will appreciate the necessity for good security.'

'And if I should get hold of a Ministry pass and come back here?'

'Then I'd be more than happy to show you the Research Laboratory. Though, mind you, I don't understand half of what's in there myself. My partner, Mr Channing, handles that side of our work.'

The Brigadier said: 'It's a pity we didn't get a chance to meet him.'

'Yes, indeed,' agreed Hibbert. 'Unfortunately he's away on a buying trip at the moment.' By now they were back in the reception area. Hibbert said: 'Well, if there's nothing more, gentlemen?'

The Brigadier glanced at the Doctor, who gave an almost imperceptible shake of his head.

'No, I don't think so,' said the Brigadier. 'Thank you for all your help. I hope we won't have to trouble you again.'

Hibbert said: 'Goodbye, Brigadier, Miss Shaw, Doctor. Let me know if I can be of any further assistance.' He watched as the three visitors got into the car and were driven away.

Hibbert turned and walked back into the factory area. Suddenly he seemed to sag, as if exhausted after some mighty effort. Channing appeared from behind the machinery and stood beside him.

'One of the visitors puzzled me. His brain was more powerful than most humans.'

Hibbert said: 'You mean the Scientific Adviser? Probably an exceptionally intelligent chap.'

'You did well, Hibbert. You did very well.'

'Do you think they were satisfied?'

'They are still suspicious. But they have no proof. It will take them time to move against us.'

'If they're not satisfied, they'll come back with more soldiers. They'll search in there.' Hibbert glanced towards the restricted zone.

'We have a way to stop them,' Channing reminded him. 'All we need is a short delay. When the time comes, no amount of soldiers will help them.'

The two of them began to walk towards the Replica Room.

As the staff car sped back towards London the Brigadier was saying: 'Well, that's the place all right. I caught a glimpse of someone skulking about on the factory floor. It was the chap who tried to kidnap you, Doctor.'

The Doctor nodded. 'Caught a glimpse of him myself. The elusive Mr Channing, no doubt. Yes, I think that creature at the cottage was one of their Autons.'

Liz asked: 'What are you going to do now?'

The Brigadier was decisive. 'Move in in force. Put a cordon of troops round the factory, then search the place from top to bottom.'

'Suppose it's full of Autons – like the one that attacked us at the cottage?'

The Brigadier snorted. 'Well, revolver bullets didn't bother that thing much. But we'll see if they can laugh off bazookas or light artillery. Dammit, I'll bomb the place if I have to!'

The Brigadier's moustache positively bristled with military fervour. 'Old Scobie promised me full co-operation,' he went on, 'and I'm going to take him up on it.'

'Why do you have to go to him?' asked Liz.

'UNIT itself only maintains a small token force,' the Brigadier explained. 'For any really big operation we have to ask the Regulars for help.'

Liz turned to the Doctor who was slumped deep in his corner, chin in hands. 'You're very quiet, Doctor. Do you think the Brigadier should invade in force?'

The Doctor looked up. 'Wheel in your big guns by all means, Brigadier. We must close that factory just as soon as we can.'

'Then what are you looking so worried about?' asked Liz.

The Doctor sighed. 'I think we may be underestimating our enemy,' he said. 'Something tells me it isn't going to be so simple.' And he relapsed into silence.

As soon as they were back at UNIT H.Q., the Doctor seemed to revive. The tin trunk was waiting for them at the laboratory, and the Doctor immediately set about rigging up a complicated set of aerials and dials around it.

'To jam its signals,' he explained. Then he carefully took the globe and unwrapped it, fixing it on a specially rigged-up stand. At once the globe began to pulse angrily.

'No good having a tantrum, old chap,' the Doctor told it reprovingly. 'You'll just have to talk to *us*.'

'What do we do with it now?' asked Liz. 'Sit and admire it?'

'Didn't you hear what I said?' asked the Doctor. 'We're going to try and communicate with it. And test its strength.'

The Brigadier meanwhile was talking to General Scobie on the telephone. He told him all that had happened: the attack at the cottage, Ransome's disappearance, the visit to the plastics factory. Scobie was baffled, but co-operative.

'Auto Plastics,' he said incredulously. 'I was down there myself earlier today,' and rather diffidently he explained about the replica of him that was being made. 'Still,' he went on, 'that's neither here nor there. You can bank on me for all the co-operation you need.' The General glanced at his watch. 'It'll take a bit of time to set up, though. Tell you what, Lethbridge-Stewart, I'll get cracking right away. I can set up the mobilisation overnight, and we'll move in first thing tomorrow.'

'Couldn't be better, sir. Thank you again,' said the Brigadier.

'Right,' said Scobie, 'I'll be in touch with you about liaison. Good night, Brigadier.'

Scobie put down the 'phone and sighed. Extraordinary business. Still that's what the Brigadier and his chaps were for, to deal with things like this. Scobie had a flash of regret for the days when soldiering was simpler. A nice straightforward cavalry charge, now! Nothing to beat it. He was just about to pick up the 'phone and call his H.Q., when the doorbell rang.

General Scobie heaved an exasperated sigh. He'd been looking forward to a quiet evening with his collection of regimental memoirs. Who the devil could this be?

Scobie went to the door of the little mews flat and opened it. At the sight of the figure facing him, he fell back in horrified disbelief. Another General Scobie stood there looking at him impassively. As his other self bore down on him, he took a faltering step backward. The other General Scobie stepped after him. Channing appeared behind the second Scobie. 'Good evening, General,' he said. 'As I promised, I have brought your replica to see you.'

Channing and the second Scobie stepped into the flat, pushing the General before them. The door closed. There was a muffled, gurgling scream, and then silence.

9

THE CREATURES IN THE WAXWORKS

Full of his plans for the coming attack, the Brigadier burst into the laboratory.

'Well, I've fixed it all up,' he began cheerfully. 'We're moving in—'

'Ssh!' said Liz, waving him into silence.

Rather hurt, the Brigadier subsided. He stood watching as Liz and the Doctor surrounded the meteorite, or whatever the thing was, with a variety of complicated looking apparatus.

'All right, my dear, is the oscillator connected?' said the Doctor.

Liz was fitting two complex pieces of circuitry together.

'Hang on … yes, okay now.'

'Right. Switch on. I'll watch the graph.'

Liz flicked a switch and then turned a control knob. The apparatus began to give out a low hum.

The Brigadier looked at Liz and the Doctor as they bent over their instruments. He sighed, recognising that he hadn't a hope of understanding what they were up to. No doubt they'd tell him when it suited them. And *he* was supposed to be the one in command! Not for the first time the Brigadier considered applying for a transfer back to normal regimental duties. Life had been so simple then. Parades, inspections, manoeuvres, more parades … He'd been offered the UNIT job not long after that Yeti business in the Underground. Presumably because he was the only senior British officer with experience in dealing with alien life forms. At the time it had seemed like a rather cushy number, carrying as it did the welcome promotion from Colonel to Brigadier. If only he'd known! First that nasty affair with the Cybermen, and now this. The trouble with the scientific approach, thought the Brigadier, was that it left you at the mercy of your scientists.

Then he brightened. For all their scientific mumbo-jumbo it was direct military action that was going to solve the problem. The Brigadier's eyes sparkled with anticipation at the thought of tomorrow's attack on the plastics factory.

Encouraged by this thought, he cleared his throat loudly and said: 'Perhaps you wouldn't mind telling me what you're actually trying to do, Doctor?'

The Doctor looked up. He gestured towards the green globe on its stand. The thing was now beginning to pulse angrily. 'Well, it appears that in there we have what one might loosely call a brain ...' The Doctor took a quick look at the quivering needle that was drawing spidery lines on a recording graph. Fifty megacycles.'

Liz repeated: 'Fifty megacycles.' She turned the control knob a little further. 'Anything?' she asked.

The Doctor shook his head. 'No. Up another fifty, Liz.' As Liz adjusted her controls again, the Doctor resumed his explanation.

'You see, Brigadier, we know it's emitting a signal of some kind. So if we can establish the frequency on which it operates we may be able to counteract its – oh dear!'

While the Doctor had been speaking, the hum of the apparatus had been rising steadily higher. There was a puff of smoke, and a shower of sparks shot from the apparatus. Hurriedly Liz switched off and stood back.

'I rather think we overloaded the circuit,' she said ruefully. She began to inspect the apparatus. 'Yes, look! The thermionic valve's blown.' Liz began to disconnect part of the apparatus.

'Now that really *is* interesting,' said the Doctor in a rather pleased tone. 'It means that there must be an extremely high resistance on the ...'

The Brigadier interrupted hastily: 'Doctor, you say that thing is some kind of a brain?'

'Well, part of a brain. Or call it an intelligent entity. That's probably nearer the mark.'

'And it's signalling somewhere? Where to?'

The Doctor gave him that patient look again. 'To the rest of itself. Surely that's obvious?'

Liz looked up from her work on the apparatus. 'So the other globes that came down – they're all part of one entity? Some kind of collective intelligence?'

The Doctor nodded. The Brigadier peered at the globe with a kind of revulsion. He couldn't help feeling that it was peering back at him. 'Can it see us, or hear us?' he asked, instinctively dropping his voice to a whisper.

The Doctor chuckled. 'My dear chap, it isn't sentient.'

'Our measurements show that there's no physical substance inside it,' said Liz.

'Probably gaseous ions held in a hetero-polar bond. Or something like that,' said the Doctor, as if that made everything perfectly clear.

The Brigadier persisted. 'But it is alien – and dangerous?'

The Doctor looked at the globe thoughtfully. 'Well, it's an intelligent life form, and it isn't here by accident. I'm afraid we must assume that its intentions are hostile.'

'But if it has no physical form, how can it harm us?'

The Doctor said impatiently: 'Once here, it can presumably create for itself a physical form, or even a number of them. Otherwise there would have been no point in its coming.'

Liz said: 'A form like the thing at the cottage?'

'That's right. There may be other forms of it, too. Creatures we haven't even seen yet.'

Liz shuddered. 'I'm not sure that I want to.'

The wall 'phone buzzed and the Brigadier picked it up. He said: 'Yes? Ah, General Scobie … good, put him on.' He listened for a moment and then the familiar voice of Scobie came on the line.

'Lethbridge-Stewart? About this raid on the plastics factory. Not on, I'm afraid. They're doing important Government work, and they mustn't be interfered with.'

The Brigadier could hardly believe his ears. 'But, sir, our investigations all point to the fact that this factory is the centre …'

Scobie's voice cut in coldly: 'I'm sorry, Brigadier, but this is a direct order. Keep away from that factory, or you'll find yourself in very serious trouble. By the way, I'm recalling my men. They're urgently needed elsewhere.' There was a click and the 'phone went dead.

The Brigadier turned to the others, his face grim. 'That was General Scobie. He's cancelled the raid on the factory.' The Doctor and Liz were busily re-assembling their apparatus. The Doctor looked up.

'Well, you'll just have to go ahead without him, won't you?'

'Go ahead? How can I, without any troops?'

'What about all those men you had searching the woods,' asked Liz.

'They were regular army chaps. On loan from General Scobie. Now he's withdrawn them all.'

The Brigadier began to pace the laboratory. 'Well, I'll just have to go over his head. Get on to the Home Secretary. Make him revoke the order. If that doesn't work, I can get on to UNIT H.Q., in Geneva, and ask them to put pressure on the Government.'

The Doctor's face was grave. 'All that's going to take time – and I've suddenly got a nasty feeling that time's running out on us.'

'How do you think the plastics factory people managed to get Scobie to change his mind?' asked Liz. 'Have they got influence in high places?'

'No idea,' said the Brigadier disgustedly. 'Unless they managed to appeal to his vanity with that replica business.'

The Doctor looked up keenly. 'Replica? What replica? Why didn't you tell me?'

'Didn't give me much chance, did you?' said the Brigadier aggrievedly. 'Only just heard about it myself.'

He told them about Scobie's earlier visit to the factory. About the special exhibition of VIPs that was being held at a famous London waxworks.

The Doctor's face lit up. 'A waxworks. My goodness, a waxworks. Yes, of course!' He glanced at the clock. 'Come on, Liz, we might just get there before they close.' Almost dragging Liz after him, the Doctor rushed from the laboratory.

'Hey, wait! Just a moment,' the Brigadier called after them. Then he shrugged his shoulders. Let them go to the waxworks. Let them go to the Tower of London, Buckingham Palace and the London Zoo while they were at it! And much good might it do them. As usual all the real work was left to him. Like children, these scientists!

The Brigadier gave the glowing green sphere a final disgusted glare. Malignantly, it flashed back at him. Then he left the laboratory and went down the corridor to his office. Throwing himself into his chair, he snatched up the 'phone.

'Operator, this is Brigadier Lethbridge-Stewart. Get me the Home Secretary on the security line. I want to fix up an immediate appointment.'

Liz Shaw hung on to her seat as the Doctor raced the UNIT jeep through the London traffic. He'd only been dissuaded from taking Mr Beavis's Rolls by her reminder that it was probably on the stolen cars list. But he was getting quite a turn of speed out of the jeep.

'Nippy little things, these,' yelled the Doctor happily, as they took a corner on two wheels, outraging a passing traffic-warden.

'Doctor, please,' yelled Liz. 'What's the rush? And did you ever pass a driving-test?'

The Doctor was indignant. 'Of course I did! I'm a qualified rocket pilot on the Mars to Venus route. And as for the rush – if we can get to the waxworks before closing time, it'll save us the bother of breaking in!'

The Doctor whizzed the jeep through a narrowing gap between two heavy lorries. Liz shuddered and decided not to distract him with any more questions.

In a few minutes they arrived outside the waxworks.

With a fine disregard for regulations the Doctor parked the jeep on a double yellow line, and hared up the steps, Liz following behind. There was still ten minutes to go till closing time. Liz went to the ticket-box.

'Hardly worth going in now, is it?' said the old attendant at the main entrance, as Liz showed him the tickets.

The Doctor beamed at him. 'Well, as a matter of fact, old chap, we just wanted a very quick look at one particular exhibit – the special VIP room.'

The attendant seemed surprised. 'Don't get many asking for that, sir,' he said. 'Here, you come with me, I'll show you where it is.' Liz and the Doctor followed him along the corridors. Most of the visitors were going the other way, making for the exits. The old man took them to a small room, set apart from the main displays. There was the usual raised platform with a silk rope railing it off. On the platform stood a number of still figures. Most were of ordinary looking men and women in business clothes, though one or two were in uniform. Liz looked at the Doctor in puzzlement. Was this all they had come to see? But the Doctor was looking round with keen interest. Apart from themselves the room was completely empty.

'They don't seem very popular, do they?' he said cheerfully, turning to the old attendant.

'Well, between you and me sir, this lot aren't,' said the old man. 'It's choice of subject if you ask me. I mean, look at 'em.' He waved round the room. 'Top Civil Servants, one or two MPs, high-ranking blokes in the Army, Navy and Air Force, even the Police. All very important ladies and gentlemen, I'm sure. But – well, not a lot of glamour about them, you see. And the public must have glamour.' The little old man nodded his bald head emphatically.

'They do seem rather a dull lot,' agreed Liz.

'Mind you,' said the attendant loyally, 'this new modelling process is marvellous, no doubt about it. I mean, see for yourself. Looks real, even feels real. Every detail perfect. Now if only they'd done a few pop stars, or a decent murderer or two.'

'That wouldn't have been nearly so much use to them,' said the Doctor, almost to himself. Ignoring the attendant's startled look, he said: 'I gather these waxworks aren't made here – in fact, they're not really waxworks at all.'

'That's right, sir. Some factory down in the country do them. Completely new process. Some new kind of plastic.'

'How do they come to be on display here?' asked Liz.

The old man's voice became confidential. 'Well, you see, miss, these people are trying to break into the waxworks line. So they got on to us and offered to provide a whole display completely free, just to see how the things went with the public. This little room was empty, so we agreed. Between you and me, it hasn't been much of a success.'

412

'On the contrary,' said the Doctor, 'I think it's been a great success.' He gave the puzzled old man a charming smile. 'Is the display complete now?'

'Well, we thought it was. One more turned up today, though. That's him over there.'

He pointed to a stiff uniformed figure at the end of the room. Liz and the Doctor walked up to it.

'It's General Scobie!' said Liz.

'Just as I thought,' said the Doctor. He turned to the attendant. 'Thank you so much for being so helpful. We mustn't keep you any more. I know there's only a few more minutes, and you'll be busy closing up. We'll find our own way out.'

'Right you are, sir,' said the attendant. 'You'll find an exit just over there.' And he shuffled out of the room.

Liz turned back to the Doctor. 'What's so surprising about a replica of Scobie? We knew they'd done one.'

But the Doctor wasn't listening. To Liz's astonishment, he swung his long legs over the silk rope and climbed up on the platform. He began examining the model of General Scobie. He tweaked its ear, looked into its eyes, and finally first peered at, then listened to, the watch on the model's right wrist. Then he climbed back over the rope.

'Liz, if you were making a model of someone, would you put a wristwatch on it?'

'I might – if it had to look completely authentic.'

'All right. Would you also go to the trouble of winding the watch up and setting it to show the correct time and date?'

Liz looked at the model of Scobie, then back at the Doctor. 'I don't know,' she said uneasily. 'What are you getting at?'

The Doctor indicated the rows of silent figures. 'All these models must be taken into custody immediately. I'll want to examine them in the laboratory.'

'You can't arrest an entire waxworks display.'

'*I* can't, but the Brigadier can! Change for the telephone, please, Liz.' Urgently the Doctor held out his hand.

Liz fished out some change and gave it to him. With a muttered 'Back in a minute,' the Doctor rushed off.

413

Left alone with the silent models, Liz looked around her. She examined the replica of General Scobie. It did look uncannily lifelike. But surely the Doctor couldn't mean … ? And what about all the others?

She looked up in relief as the Doctor came hurrying back. 'Nobody there,' he said bitterly. 'The Brigadier's gone round to see the Home Secretary and young Munro's on his way back from Essex. Just some idiot soldier who'd never heard of me and didn't understand what I was talking about.'

'I'm not sure that I do,' said Liz. 'What do we do now?'

'If the Brigadier can't help us, we shall have to help ourselves.'

Liz looked at him with horror. 'You're not suggesting we just steal these things?'

'Well, not all of them,' said the Doctor reasonably. 'But we should be able to manage one or two little ones, surely?'

'And what will the staff say when we start walking off with the exhibits?'

The Doctor gave her a pitying look. 'We don't do it right now, Liz. We'll wait till the place is closed and empty.'

Liz drew a deep breath. 'Doctor, if you imagine for one moment …'

From outside in a corridor they heard an attendant's voice. 'Come along now please, ladies and gentlemen. The waxworks is now closed.'

The Doctor grabbed Liz by the hand. 'Come on, Liz. Hide!'

The old attendant came into the room and peered round shortsightedly. The place was empty. He wondered briefly about the strange couple who had been so interested in this display. Must have gone out by another exit, he thought. He turned out the lights and went back into the main corridor.

After a moment, two of the models in the rear rank moved and stirred. Cautiously Liz and the Doctor came out of their stiff poses and climbed off the platform.

'Splendid,' said the Doctor. 'Now all we have to do is wait until things quieten down a bit.'

Liz sat down on the edge of the platform. 'Doctor, when you were talking about the watch – did you mean that's the *real* General Scobie?'

'Oh yes, I think so. Under some form of deep hypnosis, poor chap.'

'Can't you bring him out of it?'

The Doctor looked dubious. 'Too dangerous. I don't know the exact techniques they used, you see. It could do him permanent damage, even kill him, if things went wrong.' The rows of silent figures were now shadowed in the semi-darkness. 'What about this lot? Are they real people too?' said Liz nervously.

'Oh, I doubt it. You see, these replicas haven't been activated yet. They had to use their Scobie replica early.'

'So as to stop the Brigadier from attacking the factory?'

'Exactly.'

'And these others?'

'They'll be activated too. When the time comes. That's why I need to get some of them back to the lab. I've got the apparatus we fixed up for a weapon to use against them, you see. But I'll need to run proper tests.'

'How much longer have we got to wait here then? I keep getting the feeling those things are watching me.'

The Doctor gave her an encouraging pat on the back. 'Cheer up, it won't be for much longer. And it could be much worse, you know.'

'It could?'

The Doctor smiled. 'Just think – we might be in the Chamber of Horrors.'

Channing and Hibbert stood silently, almost reverently, beside the huge tank. The creature inside was much bigger now. It could be seen moving and struggling with restless life, as if ready to break out.

Channing adjusted more controls to speed up the flow of nutrient. Hibbert asked in a kind of fascinated horror: 'What will it look like when it is ready?'

Channing straightened up from the controls and looked at him impassively. 'I cannot tell you that.'

'But you must know,' protested Hibbert. 'You made it.'

'I made nothing. I merely created an environment which enabled the energy units to create the perfect life form.'

Hibbert rubbed his forehead. 'Perfect for what?'

'For the conquest of this planet,' said Channing coldly.

Hibbert's face twisted with effort. 'I don't under—'

Channing looked at him with sudden contempt. 'Of course you don't understand. How could you?'

Hibbert backed away in terror. Channing forced himself to remember that he would need this weak human tool for just a little longer.

'Don't struggle against me, Hibbert,' he said soothingly. 'Trust me. Obey me. We must work together.'

Hibbert relaxed. 'Yes, of course. It's all so clear when I'm with you. It's just that sometimes ...' Hibbert shook his head as if to clear it. When he spoke again his voice was bright and cheerful. He might have been any business executive discussing a routine problem with a colleague.

'What about the swarm leader? It still has to be recovered from UNIT.'

Channing's tone was equally matter of fact. 'That is being attended to now. By *our* General Scobie.'

'But he's only a copy. If he's detected now ...'

Confidently Channing said: 'Until now, Hibbert, you have seen only the basic Autons in action. Crude weapons with a single purpose – to kill. The facsimiles are perfect reproductions, even down to brain cells and memory traces.'

'There is still a difference. They're not human beings.'

'The only difference is the absence of emotion. And emotion is inefficient, Hibbert. That is why the Nestenes are your superiors.' Channing turned to go. 'I am going to activate the facsimiles. You will see then how effective they are.'

Captain Munro paced about indecisively. He was wishing he knew what the blazes was going on. First the Essex operation had been cancelled. All the army men on loan to UNIT had been suddenly recalled. The Major in charge of the withdrawal had been as puzzled as Munro himself. 'Sorry, old chap, direct orders from General Scobie himself. All these chaps are going on special training manoeuvres in Scotland.' Now, back at UNIT H.Q., Munro had learned from the duty corporal that a raid on the plastics factory had been suddenly mounted and as suddenly cancelled. The Brigadier was off trying to secure an interview with the Home Secretary, and the Doctor and Miss Shaw had vanished on some wild goose chase. Apparently the Doctor had 'phoned in some time ago with a wild demand that they should attack a waxworks. Then he'd run off in a huff without saying where he was speaking from. There didn't seem much that Munro could usefully do about anything.

Feeling baffled, lost and generally deserted, Munro decided that he might as well go home. After a night and a day combing those wretched woodlands he could do with a night in a proper bed. Yawning, Munro was just about to go and tell the duty corporal of his intention when he heard voices in the main area. To his astonishment he recognised the familiar tones of General Scobie. Hastily grabbing his cap, Munro dashed from his office. In the reception area he found General Scobie accompanied by two tough-looking armed military policemen. The thoroughly terrified duty corporal seemed to be protesting feebly about something.

Saluting, Munro said: 'Can I help you, sir?' As Scobie turned round Munro noticed that the old boy had none of his usual cheerfulness about him.

Scobie's voice was cold and formal. 'Ah, Munro. This fool here seems incapable of obeying a simple order.'

'I'm sorry to hear that, sir. What's the problem?'

'No problem. I'm taking the meteorite off UNIT's hands.'

'But surely, sir …' Munro protested.

'Where is it?' barked Scobie.

'In the laboratory, sir. But with respect …'

Scobie wasn't listening. Followed by the two military policemen, he marched down the corridor and into the lab. Munro had no choice but to follow.

In the laboratory the meteorite was still standing on its special stand. As Scobie entered the green globe began once more to pulse with light. Scobie looked at it with satisfaction and reached out to take it. Hurriedly Munro said: 'May I ask what you intend to do with it, sir?'

'The Government are sending it to the National Geophysical Laboratory.'

'The Doctor and Miss Shaw had already begun to run a series of tests—'

'And where's this precious Doctor now, eh?'

'I'm not quite sure, sir,' Munro admitted. 'But I'm sure he'll be back soon and so will the Brigadier. If the matter could wait till then ...'

Scobie was insistent. 'Certainly not. This thing's too important to be left to some nameless eccentric.'

Again he reached for the meteorite but Munro managed to edge between Scobie and the stand.

'I'm sorry, sir, but I think the Brigadier ought to be informed. I've no authority to part with the meteorite.'

Suddenly Scobie's eyes seemed to blaze with anger. 'Are you refusing to obey an order, Captain Munro?' There was a cold ferocity in Scobie's voice as he went on: 'I am forced to remind you that, although you are attached to UNIT, you are still a serving officer in the British Army. Will you hand over that meteorite? Or must I take it – and have you placed under arrest on a charge of mutiny?'

Munro was silent for a moment. His every instinct told him that something was badly wrong. For one moment he considered resistance but the effect of years of military training was too strong. He said stiffly: 'You leave me no alternative, sir. But under protest.' He stepped back from the stand.

Carefully, almost reverently, Scobie lifted the pulsing globe from its stand. Followed by the two silent military policemen, he turned and strode from the laboratory.

The Doctor and Liz sat waiting in the semi-darkness. Liz's head nodded forward, and she realised that, in spite of her strange surroundings, she was almost asleep.

The Doctor rose to his feet, yawned and stretched. 'Come on, Liz. I think we've waited long enough. The place should be empty now.'

The silence was shattered by the banging open of a door in the distance. The sound of marching footsteps echoed along the empty corridors, coming towards their room.

'Oh yes?' whispered Liz. 'What's all that then?'

The footsteps were now almost at the door. Hurriedly the Doctor grabbed Liz's hand and dragged her to the back of the room, where a long velvet curtain covered a recessed window. They both slipped behind the curtain.

Light spilled into the room from the corridor, as the door was thrown open. Liz peered out through a tiny gap. Channing stood framed in the doorway. Beside him was Hibbert. And behind them stood two more dim figures. Liz saw that their features were crude and lumpy and the eyes blank. They were Autons, like the thing that had attacked them at the cottage. She could feel the Doctor's hand gripping her arm fiercely, warning her to keep absolutely still and silent.

Channing looked keenly round the room. It seemed as if his eyes could burn through the curtain to reveal their hiding-place.

Channing said suddenly: 'I sense the presence of human life forms in this room.'

Liz edged away from the curtain. She could feel the Doctor tense beside her. She heard Hibbert reply: 'There's only us here, and the facsimiles. And Scobie.'

Channing said: 'Yes, of course. Scobie.'

Then Hibbert's voice again: 'What must you do to activate them?'

'Do? Nothing. They know that it is time.'

Liz couldn't resist looking again through the tiny gap. The silent figures on the platform began to stir. Heads turned, hands and feet moved. Jerkily, hesitantly at first, the figures took a few stumbling paces. Then, seeming to gather confidence, they began to step down from the low platform. In the same eerie silence they marched one by one from the room. Soon only one figure was left. That of Scobie. The real Scobie, Liz reminded herself. Left all alone while his inhuman companions walked away.

'Where will they go?' she heard Hibbert ask.

There was an icy triumph in Channing's reply. 'To take their places. It is time for them to begin their work.'

Channing turned and followed the Replicas. Hibbert stood gazing for a moment into the empty room. Suddenly Liz realised with horror that his eyes were fixed on hers. Liz wondered if he had seen her through the gap in the curtains. Hibbert hesitated for a moment, then followed Channing from the room. The two faceless creatures followed behind him. The door closed.

Liz and the Doctor stepped out into the room. The Doctor said softly: 'We must warn the Brigadier at once! Their plans must be far more advanced than I'd realised.' Suddenly the door opened. They whirled round to face it. Hibbert was standing there. He was alone.

Slowly, hesitantly, he came towards them. He said in a thick, slurred voice: 'What are you doing here? You shouldn't be here. Channing ... Channing will ...'

The Doctor moved forward and spoke in a low urgent voice: 'Channing will kill us if you let him know we're here. He killed your friend Ransome.'

Hibbert's voice was confused. 'Ransome? I had to dismiss him. He had to be dismissed because ... Channing said ...'

The Doctor said in an urgent whisper: 'Channing is controlling your mind. You must resist him. Channing is your enemy. He's the enemy of the whole human race.'

Hibbert looked at him, in distress. 'Channing is my partner. There's a new policy, you see. It's because of the new policy.'

'Now listen to me, Hibbert,' said the Doctor firmly. 'You must get away from Channing. Get away from him and *think*. Come to UNIT. I can help you.'

Hibbert stared at him in anguish. He rubbed his hand over his eyes, shook his head as if trying to clear it. Suddenly there came the sound of echoing footsteps in the empty corridor. 'Remember,' hissed the Doctor, 'they'll kill us.'

Channing's voice called: 'Hibbert! Where are you, Hibbert?' Liz and the Doctor had just time to duck behind their curtain before Channing appeared in the doorway, an Auton behind him.

From the gap in the curtain Liz saw him look round the room. 'What are you doing, Hibbert? Is anything the matter?'

Liz held her breath as Hibbert stared back at Channing. She could almost see the struggle in his mind between the effect of the Doctor's appeal and Hibbert's fear of Channing.

Hibbert said: 'No, nothing's wrong. I was just checking.'

'There is nothing to check. We are finished here. Come.' Channing turned and left the room. Hibbert gave a last glance at the velvet curtain, and obediently followed him. For a moment the Auton stood poised in the doorway as if surveying the room. Then it, too, turned and left.

Liz heard the sound of their retreating footsteps. There was a sudden crash as a door somewhere was slammed. Liz and the Doctor emerged cautiously from behind the curtain.

Liz said: 'Do you think he'll tell Channing we were here?'

The Doctor rubbed his chin. 'I hope not.'

'Why didn't he give us away?'

'Because Hibbert is still a human being,' said the Doctor. 'His mind is being dominated by Channing. But the human mind is a wonderfully resilient thing. It's almost impossible to control it completely for very long.'

Liz nodded in understanding. 'So his real personality keeps trying to break through?'

'That's right. And the control seems to be weakening. It's only completely effective when Channing's actually with him. If he can manage to get away from Channing completely, he may be able to shake off his influence.'

The Doctor listened at the door for a moment. 'They seem to be all gone.'

Thankfully Liz followed him to the door. She couldn't get away from the place soon enough. She stopped in the doorway and looked back. General Scobie stood in solitary state on the now empty platform. 'What about him?'

The Doctor shot Scobie a regretful glance. 'Nothing we can do for him now. The poor old chap is safer where he is. Come on, Liz.'

They made for the nearest exit.

10

THE FINAL BATTLE

As Liz and the Doctor approached the Brigadier's office, they heard his voice raised in outrage and astonishment. 'And you mean to say you simply stood there and let him walk off with it?'

They entered the room to find Munro standing unhappily to attention before the Brigadier's desk.

'There simply wasn't any alternative, sir. He is a General. Besides, he had two armed MPs with him. It was that, or find myself under arrest. And they'd have taken the globe anyway. I tried to contact you as soon as it happened, sir.'

The Brigadier waved Liz and the Doctor to chairs. 'The reason you couldn't contact me, Munro,' he said bitterly, 'was because I have been spending many long hours in the ante-rooms of Whitehall, trying to get in to see a number of important Government officials. With, I might add, a complete and utter lack of success. Either they were tied up in endless conferences, or they'd left early for a long weekend.' He turned to the Doctor and Liz. 'And I now get back here, only to learn that, not content with cancelling the operation, Scobie's turned up behind my back and walked off with the only piece of evidence.'

'Oh that wasn't Scobie, Brigadier,' said Liz. 'Scobie's still at the waxworks. That must have been his replica.'

'Exactly,' said the Doctor. 'They activated that one first because they needed it to deal with UNIT. Now that the rest of them are on the loose, we're going to have *real* problems.'

The Brigadier gazed at them blankly. 'Others? What others? Will you kindly explain what you're talking about, Doctor?'

Briefly, the Doctor and Liz told of their discoveries at the waxworks. At the end of the story, the Brigadier scarcely looked any the wiser.

'Are you trying to tell me that some blessed waxwork walked in here and commandeered that globe?'

Munro said: 'His manner *was* very strange, sir. Sort of cold and inhuman. Not really like himself at all. But I'd never have thought ...'

'Don't you see?' said the Doctor, 'that's the cunning of it. The Replicas aren't *exactly* the same as human beings. Nothing is. A wife, or a child, or a close friend could detect them in a moment. But we're not talking about personal relationships. We're talking about people in authority. Seniors giving orders to juniors.'

Liz joined in. 'After all, Brigadier, if *you* came in here all fierce and unfriendly, and started barking orders at everybody, I don't suppose anybody would notice the slightest ...' Her voice tailed away as she realised what she was saying. Munro concealed a grin behind a sudden attack of coughing.

'All the same, she's quite right,' said the Doctor. 'A lot of the Replicas will probably cause some suspicion. But they'll all be able to achieve a great deal of damage before they're detected.'

'What harm?' said the Brigadier. 'What are these things *for*?'

Patiently the Doctor explained. 'Very soon they'll have taken over all the important positions in the country.'

'What about the originals, the real people?' asked the Brigadier.

'Some of them will have been got out of the way – like poor Scobie. The others, well ...' The Doctor shrugged.

'A number of very important people will start appearing in two places at once, giving contradictory orders. It'll all add to the confusion when the invasion starts.'

'Invasion!'

'Don't tell me you hadn't realised, Brigadier. Everything that's happened so far has been just a preliminary. Before long the full-scale attack will begin.'

'What are we going to do about it?' said the Brigadier. 'I've tried to alert the Government, but no one will listen.'

The Doctor stood up. 'Two things, Brigadier,' he said decisively. 'First Miss Shaw and I must devise a weapon to use against the Autons. Once that is done, *you* must attack the plastics factory.'

'How can I? I keep telling you, Scobie's withdrawn all his men.'

The Doctor frowned. 'You must have *some* men available?'

'Myself, Munro, one or two headquarters staff...'

'Don't forget, there's Miss Shaw – and me!' The Doctor smiled encouragingly. 'Not much of an army, is it, Brigadier? But it'll have to do.'

The thing in the huge plastic coffin was almost complete now. It surged and pulsed, making the whole room vibrate. Channing stood watching it, with an air of quiet satisfaction. After a moment the door to the security area opened and Scobie, or rather Scobie's Replica, joined him. In its hands the Replica carried the pulsing green globe. Channing turned. 'They suspected nothing?'

The Replica answered in the same flat emotionless voice. 'Nothing. The human soldiers accept my orders without question.'

'And what of UNIT?'

'UNIT is being watched. If they move against us, we shall know. And without their soldiers they are powerless. They will not dare to attack.'

'Humans are not totally predictable,' said Channing. 'It is growing harder to maintain my control over the man Hibbert. Now he has disappeared.'

'Hibbert is no longer necessary.'

'No.' There was satisfaction in Channing's voice. 'We need no one now.'

He took the energy unit from the hands of Scobie's Replica, and placed it carefully in a kind of incubator next to the great plastic coffin. The pulsing of the glowing green globe rose to a peak, as Channing pulled a series of controls. Then with a final flash of light the energy unit became inert. The fragment of the Nestene consciousness which it carried had been absorbed. The final element had been added. The Nestene Mind, that vast cosmic will and intelligence that linked Channing, the Replicas, the killer Autons and the handsome display mannequins in windows all over the country, was now complete.

Channing turned to the Replica, his eyes blazing with exultation.

'Tomorrow we will activate the Autons. This planet will soon be ours!'

*

A vast tangle of electronic equipment lay on the laboratory bench. Liz Shaw was helping the Doctor to connect and cross-connect a maze of circuitry.

'Let me see,' muttered the Doctor, grappling with a confusion of multi-coloured leads. 'A red and a yellow makes ...'

'Green?' suggested Liz hopefully. 'Honestly, Doctor, I'd be a lot more help if I knew what this contraption of yours was supposed to do.'

The Doctor looked up. 'Oh, didn't I explain that? Well, you remember the device we were testing the green globe with – when we still had a globe to test?'

Liz nodded.

'Well, this is exactly the same sort of thing. With one or two refinements.'

'As I remember, Doctor,' said Liz, 'that thing fused.'

'Indeed it did,' admitted the Doctor. 'But this one is a good deal more powerful. This time I'm hoping that exactly the reverse will happen. The Auton will fuse!'

Liz watched him as he went on working tirelessly. The long nimble fingers deftly sorted out wires and the cross-connections, working quickly and surely.

Liz yawned. 'Couldn't we take a break, Doctor? I can hardly keep my eyes open.'

The Doctor shook his head. 'Must get finished, my dear.' He looked up at Liz and she saw the lines of tension in his face, the controlled worry in his eyes. 'I don't think there's very much more time, you see,' he said gently. 'We may need this device very soon.' The Doctor went on working and Liz yawned again. She looked out of the lab window. There were a few pale streaks of light in the sky. She looked at her watch. It would soon be morning.

'Just think,' she said, 'most of the rest of London is just starting the day!'

The city was coming to life. Office cleaners were leaving the towering blocks in chattering bands. Commissionaires and porters were reporting for duty. Shop managers and staff were letting themselves into their shops, getting ready to open the doors and face the public.

The earliest of the office workers, and the keenest shoppers, were getting off their buses and emerging from Underground stations. Soon a normal, bustling London day would be in full swing. But this day, in London, and in cities all over the country, was to be like no other. This was the morning of the Auton invasion.

In the shop windows and in the department stores the mannequins stood waiting. A policeman patrolling along Oxford Street cast a casual eye at the window display in one of the big stores. A group of window dummies, dressed in bright, casual sports clothes, sat under a beach umbrella in a cheerful seaside setting. The policeman thought longingly of his own holidays. Only another two weeks ... As he passed on his way the mannequins posing round the table stirred and came to life. Jerkily at first, they rose from their beach chairs and rugs. The tallest raised its hand in a pointing gesture. The hand dropped away on its hinge to reveal a gun nozzle. The rest of the dummies in the group followed suit. For all their handsome faces and bright holiday clothes, these, too, were killer Autons. Swiftly, unhesitatingly, their leader stepped straight through the store window and out onto the pavement.

The astonished policeman heard the crash of glass and spun round. His first thought was that there must have been some sort of accident. He stopped in utter amazement at the sight of the tall figure of the Auton stalking towards him along the pavement. Other figures followed the first Auton through the gap, stepping onto the pavement. From up and down the street came the crash of glass as other Autons came to life. The policeman's next thought was of some kind of enormous hoax. Students, he thought vaguely. They'd gone too far this time. That thought was also his last. As he ran towards the group of Autons, their leader raised its wrist-gun and blasted him to the ground.

By now other groups of Autons were appearing on the pavement. Ruthlessly they blasted down everyone they met. People ran screaming, trying to escape. In streets nearby, in streets all over London, and in the streets of every major city in Britain, it was the same story. People screamed and panicked and ran, and the Autons blasted them down.

The police received thousands upon thousands of calls. But there was little they could do. Arms were issued, but the few rifles and revolvers available were powerless against the Autons. BBC and ITV issued urgent warnings. 'Don't go to work. Don't go out shopping. Stay indoors and barricade yourselves in your homes. Admit no one you do not know.'

Many people were saved by warnings like these, but many others, already out on the streets, were unable to escape. The Autons seemed to be everywhere.

The Government declared martial law and called out the Army. But most of the available troops were mysteriously absent on manoeuvres far away from the big towns. They were recalled at once, but things seemed to go wrong continually. Orders failed to arrive, or were misinterpreted. Troops were told to stay put, or sent to the wrong place. In the other services the story was the same. The Navy and the Air Force armed what men they could, but the men never seemed to get clear orders, or to arrive where they were wanted. It was as though in every position of authority traitors were working against the Government, deliberately confusing the situation.

In an office in Whitehall a young civil servant listened appalled as he heard his Minister on the telephone, deliberately giving orders that would worsen the situation. He rushed into the office to demand an explanation. The Minister stretched out his hand in a curious pointing gesture – and the hand dropped away to reveal a gun.

There were many other similar scenes. Many more of the Replicas were detected, but not before they had done enormous damage, spreading chaos and confusion everywhere.

Commando squads of killer Autons in their dark overalls began to attack communications centres. Telephone exchanges, radio and TV transmitters, underground power cables, all exploded in flames under repeated blasts from the Auton weapons. Radios, TV screens and telephones went silent.

Completely cut off from each other, little groups of soldiers, policemen, Government officials, desperately tried to make sense of the situation, tried to find some way of combating the enemy. And all the while they eyed one another uneasily. No one knew when a familiar hand would drop away to reveal the wrist-gun of an Auton.

There were, of course, one or two successes. A group of quarrymen broke open their explosives hut and blew several Autons to pieces with blasting charges. Here and there tanks prowled the streets, shooting down or crushing the Autons in their path. Little groups of soldiers became tired of waiting for orders and for reinforcements that never came. Acting on their own initiative they raided their own armouries for what weapons they could find and fought desperate little street battles, turning bazookas, trench-mortars and anti-tank guns against the enemy.

UNIT H.Q. was under siege. The sleepy duty soldier who had opened the main doors that morning had been greeted by an energy-blast from a waiting Auton that missed him by inches. He had promptly slammed the doors shut again, and pressed the button that activated a second pair of reinforcing doors in heavy armour-plate. All over UNIT H.Q., emergency doors and shutters slammed down.

In his office the Brigadier had sent out desperate calls for help. Everywhere it was the same story. Chaos ... panic ... confusion ... Then, one by one, the outside 'phones went dead.

The Brigadier had told the Doctor of the situation as far as he knew it. The Doctor nodded gravely. 'Much as I feared,' he said. 'I'd hoped for a little more time ...' And even as he listened, he had gone on working on the complicated electronic device. Now, waiting in his office, the Brigadier wondered if the thing would ever be ready. Not that it mattered, he thought gloomily. There was little they could do now. Maybe take a few of the enemy with them before the inevitable end. The internal 'phone, still powered by the emergency generator, suddenly buzzed. The Brigadier snatched it up. 'We're ready now,' said the Doctor's voice. The Brigadier slammed down the 'phone and ran to the laboratory.

He found Liz and the Doctor contemplating the completed device. Two army knapsacks rested on the bench. The first contained a jumble of electronic equipment, the second a portable power-pack. A long flex connected the first knapsack to the second. The Doctor was busily plugging what looked like a microphone, also on a long flex, into the pack containing the equipment.

The Brigadier looked at the contraption dubiously. 'Is that *it*?'

'Of course that's *it*,' said the Doctor. 'This first knapsack carries the device itself. The second, which will be carried by Miss Shaw, holds the power source.' He beamed proudly at his brain-child.

'And what's this?' said the Brigadier, indicating the microphone-like object. 'I thought we wanted to destroy them, not interview them.'

'This,' said the Doctor, 'is the ... er, business end. A UHF transmitter. The device is effective only at very short range, I'm afraid.'

'He means you practically have to shove it down their throats,' explained Liz.

The Brigadier looked unimpressed. 'Will it work?'

'We shan't know that till we try. Are you ready for the attack?'

'As ready as we'll ever be. I never thought I'd lead a force consisting of headquarters clerical staff, a female scientist and ...' At a loss for words he waved his hand towards the Doctor.

'Cheer up, Brigadier,' said the Doctor. 'It's quality that counts, you know, not quantity. Shall we go?' He passed Liz the power-pack and shouldered the other himself.

A few moments later the Brigadier and his little force, loaded into two jeeps, were waiting in the UNIT garage. The Doctor was at the wheel of one jeep, accompanied by Liz and two soldiers. The Brigadier and the remaining soldiers were crammed into the other. The soldiers were heavily armed with a variety of curious weapons. The engines were already revving up. The Brigadier gave a signal and a soldier pressed the button to open the steel garage doors, and jumped in the back of the jeep. As soon as the doors began to open the Doctor gunned his jeep into a racing start and shot up the ramp. The Brigadier's jeep followed close behind. Energy bolts from waiting Autons whizzed round their heads, but the little jeeps weaved in and out of the attackers and disappeared out of sight.

Afterwards Liz could only remember that journey out of London as a kind of nightmare. By now the streets were empty, so there was no traffic to delay them. There was wreckage and devastation all around. Many buildings were now ablaze but there was no sound of fire engines speeding to the rescue. Fire stations had been one of the Autons' first targets, and by now most fire engines were destroyed.

They passed little groups of fleeing, terrified people. One or two of them shouted out warnings. The route they took went through side streets and back alleys, away from the shopping centres, away from the Autons. Occasionally Autons did appear and fired after them, often missing by inches. Once an Auton stepped directly in front of their jeep, wrist-gun raised. The Doctor put his foot down and smashed straight into it, sending it flying against the side of a building. Liz looked over her shoulder and saw to her horror that the Auton had lurched to its feet and was firing after them.

Soon, to her heartfelt relief, they were leaving the suburbs behind them, speeding down country lanes to the plastics factory where everything had begun, and where everything must be ended if there was to be any hope for mankind.

In the woods just outside the factory a solitary figure had been curled hidden in a ditch for hours. Unaware of all that had been happening in the cities, George Hibbert had been taking the advice given by the Doctor in the waxworks – to get away from Channing so that he could think. Gradually, in the peace and quiet of the forest, Hibbert's brain had cleared at last. The full horror of what he had become flooded over him. But at last he was himself again. At last he could think his own thoughts. And he knew what he must do. Stiffly he rose to his feet and began to walk back towards the factory.

Inside the factory itself Channing stood in silent communion with the creature in the tank. Through the shared Nestene mind he was aware of all the destruction he had caused. Channing was pleased. Everything was going as it should. He was aware, too, that the Doctor and the Brigadier with their tiny force were on the way to attack him. He wondered idly what made these humans struggle so desperately to the last.

The factory was now almost empty of the killer Autons. They had been sent to do their deadly work around the country. Only a small group remained, to guard the creature in the tank. The creature that would soon emerge and take its rightful place as ruler. But Channing was not disturbed by the fact that there were so few Autons. He had made his arrangements. The factory was still well guarded.

A voice behind him said: 'Channing.' He turned. Hibbert was walking towards him, an iron crowbar in his hand. He said: 'Hibbert. There you are. I have been worried about you.'

A wave of hatred flooded over Hibbert at the sound of that familiar voice. He heard Channing say: 'You should not have gone away, Hibbert. It is safer for you to stay with me.'

Hibbert's voice was harsh. 'So that you can go on controlling my mind. Oh no, Channing. The Doctor was right. I can think, away from you.'

'You have spoken again to the Doctor?'

'He was at the waxworks. He knows what you're up to. He'll stop you.'

Channing was amused. 'He may know, Hibbert. But there is nothing he can do. Our invasion of your planet has already begun.'

Hibbert looked at him in loathing. 'Who are you? What are you?'

Channing said: 'We are the Nestenes. We have been colonising other planets for a thousand million years. Now we have come to take Earth.'

'But what's going to happen to us – to *Man*?' The full horror of it suddenly came over Hibbert. 'You'll destroy us.'

Channing's voice was soothing. 'Not you, Hibbert. You are our ally. You have helped us.'

Hibbert said dully: 'And you ... you're not human.'

'I am part of the whole, Hibbert. Nestenes have no individual existence. This body is merely a container, Hibbert. You should know that. You made me.'

And Channing smiled a terrible smile.

All the things which had been blocked from Hibbert's mind now came back to him. He remembered finding the green pulsating globe in the woods, the night of the first meteor shower. He remembered taking the globe back to the factory. He remembered staring as if hypnotised into its flashing green depths.

It had seemed as if the globe was talking, deep within his mind. It had told him of the other globes, and where to find them. It had told him how to design the new machinery, to order the parts, to assemble them himself. It had told him of the special plastics mix that had to be fed into the tanks, and how to attach the electrodes to the globe to transfer its energy.

Night after night Hibbert had worked, secretly in the deserted factory. Luckily, Ransome was on that trip to America. Then finally Hibbert had stood beside a bubbling tank of plastics mix, and connected the electrodes and thrown the switch. The globes had flashed and then died.

The tank of bubbling plastic seethed with life. A shape within it began to solidify, and dripping from its depths rose something in the shape of a man. The something that was now called Channing.

After that things became hazy in Hibbert's mind. He and Channing had made the Autons, and the Autons had made other Autons. All the time Channing's grip on his mind had grown stronger and stronger. Finally, he had had no thoughts of his own at all. He had become merely an extension of Channing's will. But all that was over now. He had broken free.

Suddenly Hibbert gestured to the giant plastic coffin with his crowbar. 'And that thing in there?'

'That is our real form, Hibbert. The form we once had on our own planet, before we shook off the body and became pure mind. We created human forms for ourselves to help begin our invasion. But once the planet is ours, we shall re-create the form that was once our own.' Channing laughed, looking proudly at the tank. 'In there is the repository of all the Nestene consciousness. Would you like to see it, Hibbert?' Again Channing laughed, and the thing within the plastic tank bubbled and seethed as though sharing in his mirth.

Hibbert snatched at one central thought. 'Then if you exist as one, you can die as one!'

He leaped towards the tank, crowbar raised. But before he could reach it an Auton stepped from the shadows and blasted him from existence. At a sign from Channing the Auton blasted at Hibbert's body with its energy-gun until, like Ransome before him, he had totally disappeared.

Channing suddenly stiffened. Through the eyes of an Auton posted in the woods near the factory, he saw the UNIT jeeps flashing by. Channing wondered again at this stupid insistence of the humans on fighting to the very last minute. He left the Restricted Area to prepare to meet them.

*

Jolting across the woodlands between the trees, the Brigadier's little force had driven the jeeps to the very edge of the wire fence surrounding the factory. Swiftly and efficiently two soldiers cut a gap in the fencing. The Brigadier went through first, followed by the Doctor and Liz, carrying the two linked packs. The handful of soldiers followed after them. They moved swiftly and silently to the factory buildings, and up to a small back door. It was locked. At a nod from the Brigadier one of his men blew it open. The little group moved through the shattered door and into the factory itself.

They looked round in amazement. The place was totally deserted now, and the strange alien machines were silent, their work for the moment over.

'Where's everybody gone?' said Liz uneasily.

'They're here – somewhere,' said the Doctor. 'That's the place we want.' He pointed towards the Restricted Area. But before they could take another step, armed men appeared from hiding and sprang up all round them. Liz was delighted to see they wore the uniform of the Regular Army.

'You've got some reinforcements after all, Brigadier,' she said.

The Doctor glanced around. 'I don't think so, Liz,' he said gently. 'Those guns are pointed at us.'

To her utter amazement Liz saw that he was right. The young Captain in charge of the soldiers had drawn his revolver and was covering the Brigadier.

'Brigadier, you and your men are under arrest. Please lay down your arms immediately.'

From the door of the Restricted Area, Channing watched. It had amused him to have his factory guarded with human soldiers.

The Brigadier could scarcely believe his ears. 'What the blazes do you think you're up to, man?' he snapped. 'Don't you realise that we're being invaded, and this place is the centre of it all? Put down that gun and give me some help.'

Confidently the Brigadier strode towards the young officer. The Captain raised his revolver. 'I'm sorry, sir, but I have my orders. I'll shoot if you force me to. Now order your men to lay down their arms, or my men will fire.'

'Then they'll have to shoot, Captain.' The Brigadier's voice was calm. 'We came here to do a job and we're going to do it. Now are you really going to open fire on a fellow officer? Or are you going to be sensible and place yourself under my command?'

Liz glanced at the Doctor. She nodded towards the weapon they carried, but the Doctor shook his head. It might or might not work against the Autons, but against human soldiers it was useless.

Liz looked at the young Captain, wondering what he would do. It was obvious that he had not expected things to go this far.

The Brigadier said: 'Well? Make your mind up. Because I assure you I'm going in there.' He nodded towards the Restricted Area. Concealed behind the doorway, Channing watched impatiently. By now the Brigadier should have surrendered, since he was so hopelessly outnumbered. Again this tiresome human insistence on continued resistance. Were they too stupid to give up? Channing wondered.

There was an edge of panic in the Captain's voice. He stubbornly repeated: 'I have my orders.' The Brigadier took another step forward.

Suddenly the Doctor's voice broke the tense silence. 'I'm no expert in military matters, but surely the Brigadier outranks you. Shouldn't you obey his orders now?' For a moment it looked as if the Captain would give way. He lowered his revolver. Then someone stepped from the shadows. It was, or rather it seemed to be, General Scobie. Liz felt the Doctor tense with excitement beside her. He gave her a warning tap on the elbow and began to edge towards the General. Liz followed with the power-pack.

The Captain turned thankfully to the figure of General Scobie, relieved to be free of his terrible responsibility.

'For the last time, Brigadier, will you surrender, or shall I order my men to shoot you down?' The General's voice was harsh and threatening. Not a bit like the real Scobie, thought Liz. But real enough to convince those soldiers.

By now Liz and the Doctor had edged their way round the group and were standing close to Scobie.

The Brigadier said: 'Now, listen to me, Captain, this is not the real General Scobie.'

'I'm sorry, sir, but it certainly is,' said the Captain. 'I've served on the General's staff. I know him well.'

'Perhaps I can settle the argument,' said the Doctor. 'Would you care to say a few words into this?' He held the microphone-like object close to Scobie's face and snapped: 'Switch on, Liz!'

Liz reached inside the power-pack and turned on the controls.

Scobie said: 'What is this nonsense ... ?' He clasped his hands to his face and fell writhing to the ground. His body became still.

The Captain turned on the Doctor. 'You've killed him!'

'Oh, I don't think so,' said the Doctor. 'You see, he was never really alive.' He knelt by Scobie's body and turned it over. The face had become blank, lumpy, featureless. Like that of an Auton.

(Far away in London the real General Scobie suddenly awoke, and was astonished to find himself alone in the Replica Room of the waxworks.)

The Captain gazed at Scobie's face in horrified unbelief.

'Well,' snapped the Brigadier, '*now* will you place your men under my orders?'

The last vestige of doubt disappeared from the Captain's mind. 'Yes, sir,' he said.

Then from inside the Restricted Area marched a line of Autons.

'Take cover!' yelled the Brigadier. UNIT men and Regulars found what cover they could behind the factory machinery. The Auton hands dropped down on their hinges, and energy-bolts blazed from their guns. The Brigadier and his soldiers did their best to hold the advancing Autons. The bullets from the Regulars' rifles had little or no effect. But the Brigadier had equipped his men with sub-machine-guns and grenades, and the UNIT armoury had even managed to produce one anti-tank rifle. The heavier weapons did have some effect. As the soldiers returned the Autons' fire, the din in the little factory was deafening. Liz watched horrified as several soldiers, struck by sizzling energy-bolts, were hurled clear across the room to collapse like empty sacks against the walls. From the corner where she and the Doctor were hiding, she saw Autons cut to pieces by machine-gun bullets, and blown to pieces by grenades. An Auton arm blown clear from the body continued to lash wildly round the room, spitting energy-bolts like a demented snake.

Liz became aware that the Autons were gaining. Their line was moving ever closer to the spot where she and the Doctor were hiding. She tugged at the Doctor's sleeve. Surely they ought to fall back too? The Doctor shook his head. He gestured to Liz to be ready with the power-pack. Then, quite deliberately, the Doctor rose to his feet. He stepped full in the path of an advancing Auton and thrust the transmitter near its face. Without waiting to be told, Liz switched on the power-pack. The Auton suddenly slumped, collapsing almost on top of them.

Huddled behind the shelter of the Auton's body, Liz and the Doctor waited, as the line of other Autons swept over and past them. Liz's nose was no more than an inch from the Auton's outstretched arm. She looked at the big hand – it was the left one, the one without the gun – and shuddered at the blunt fingers with no fingernails. Then the Doctor tugged her to her feet.

'We've done it, Liz,' he whispered exultantly, 'we're behind the enemy lines.' With the battle raging behind them, Liz and the Doctor ran for the now unguarded door to the Restricted Area.

Once they were inside, both stopped in amazement. The room seemed to be empty. It was dominated by the vast coffin-shaped tank. Inside the tank something enormous heaved, and seethed and bubbled.

Liz looked up at the Doctor. 'There's something alive in there,' she said. 'Oh yes,' said the Doctor mildly. 'I rather thought there would be, you know. It was the logical next step. You remember, poor Ransome told us about it.' The Doctor sounded pleased to have his theories confirmed. To her amazement Liz saw that his face showed not fear, but a sort of detached scientific curiosity.

'Now, I wonder …' said the Doctor, and he walked round the tank as if contemplating a swim in it.

'Doctor, you're not going in there,' said Liz, as the Doctor dragged over a crate to stand on.

'Someone's got to, you know. Our friend in there is the key to everything.'

'Quite right, Doctor. But your discovery has come too late.' Channing stepped from behind the tank, and stood facing them.

'Oh, I don't know,' said the Doctor. 'There's a saying on this planet that it's never too late.'

Channing looked at the Doctor. 'You speak as if you are not one of the humans.'

'As a matter of fact, I'm not.'

'I thought as much when you first came here. Your mind has a different feel to these humans. There are depths in it I cannot reach.'

The Doctor said: 'Like you, I am not of this planet. But I didn't come here of my own choice. Why did you come?'

'We are Nestenes. Our purpose is conquest – always. We must spread the Nestene mind, the Nestene consciousness throughout all the galaxies.'

'We?' asked the Doctor keenly. 'You speak for all your people?'

'I am all my people,' said Channing simply. 'We are the Nestenes. We are all one.'

'A collective brain, a collective nervous system, is that it? And as far as Earth is concerned, all housed in that life form in the tank?'

'Exactly so!' said Channing. His voice rose to an exultant shout. 'Would you like to look upon the true form of the Nestenes, Doctor – before you die?'

The fluid in the tank heaved and bubbled in a final convulsion. The whole side of the tank shattered open, as the Doctor and Liz leaped back.

Standing towering over them was the most nightmarish creature Liz had ever seen. A huge, many-tentacled monster something between spider, crab and octopus. The nutrient fluids from the tank were still streaming down its sides. At the front of its glistening body a single huge eye glared at them, blazing with alien intelligence and hatred.

The Doctor stood peering up at it with an expression of fascinated interest. 'Remarkable,' he said. 'Quite remarkable.' Then he shouted: 'Now, Liz!'

But just as he spoke the Nestene monster lashed out with one of its many tentacles and began to drag the Doctor towards it. Liz switched on the power-pack. Nothing happened.

'Now, Liz! Now!' the Doctor shouted urgently. Again Liz flicked the controls, and again there was no result. Liz realised that when the monster grabbed the Doctor, the lead connecting the Doctor's machine to her pack had been pulled out.

The monster was dragging the Doctor closer and closer. He struggled frantically as a second slimy tentacle wrapped itself round his throat, beginning to throttle him. Liz ducked under the creature, scrabbling for the other end of the lead. She grabbed it and began to plug it in. Angrily, yet another tentacle wrapped round *her*, but with a final desperate effort Liz managed to jam the lead into its socket.

Immediately, there was a hum of power from the Doctor's machine. As Liz turned the power up to its highest notch the Doctor shoved the microphone-shaped transmitter up to the single blazing eye. Immediately, the monster gave a single agonised howl that seemed to shatter Liz's eardrums. The tentacles holding Liz and the Doctor lost their power and they fell to the ground.

Then, as they watched, the hideous creation that had housed the Nestene mind began to blur and dissolve. It seemed to melt away before them like a wax model in a blast of fierce heat.

Finally there was nothing left but a sort of vast spreading puddle of thick, slimy liquid. For a moment that single eye remained floating in the puddle, glaring its hatred at them to the last. Then it, too, dissolved. The Nestene was dead.

Liz and the Doctor picked themselves up. The Doctor saw Channing, face downwards where he had fallen. He turned the body over. Like Scobie's Replica before him, Channing now had the crude blank features of an Auton. The Doctor looked up. 'Nothing to be frightened of, my dear,' he said gently. 'It's only a waxwork.'

A minute or two before, as Liz was struggling to reconnect the Doctor's machine to the power-pack, Brigadier Alastair Lethbridge-Stewart had resigned himself to the end of a not-inglorious military career. He and his men had fought a gallant rearguard action across the factory, many being blasted to extinction by Nestene energy-bolts in the process. The few left alive were now trapped in an angle of the factory wall, under a deadly crossfire from two groups of advancing Autons. The Brigadier cut an advancing Auton in two with a savage burst from his sub-machine-gun. The gun emptied itself, and the Brigadier automatically reached for another magazine from his belt. But the belt was empty. Another Auton appeared in front of the Brigadier, its wrist-gun aimed at point-blank range. The Brigadier gazed into the nozzle of the gun, waiting for the final blast. Then, to his amazement, the outstretched arm seemed to wilt before his eyes. It drooped, and the Auton crashed to the floor. All around, the other Autons were collapsing too.

Suddenly there was silence. Powder smoke drifted in low clouds through the still air of the factory. The Brigadier and his few remaining men looked at each other in astonishment, scarcely able to believe that they were still alive. A voice cut through the silence. 'Brigadier! Where are you, Brigadier!' came the Doctor's voice impatiently. 'Are you all right?' The Brigadier ran for the Restricted Area.

Liz and the Doctor waited in the doorway. Behind them the Brigadier could see some kind of nasty oozy mess spreading over the floor. Tired but happy, the Doctor surveyed the scene. Behind him was the shattered tank, the dissolved monster and the remains of Channing.

In front of him the bullet-shattered factory, the collapsed Autons, and the soldiers who had died holding them back.

'Glad to see you're all right, Doctor, Miss Shaw,' said the Brigadier.

'I'm not sure if I am yet,' said Liz shakily.

The Doctor put a comforting arm round her shoulders. 'I think we've won, Liz,' he said gently. 'But the price has been very high.'

It wasn't until they were safely back at UNIT H.Q. that they realised it was really all over. When the Nestene monster had died at the plastics factory, Autons all over the country had become instantly lifeless, as harmless as the waxworks they resembled. Much damage had been done, and many lives lost. But gradually the country was pulling itself together again, and soon a return to normal life would begin.

In the UNIT laboratory the returned warriors were celebrating in mugs of strong, sweet army tea. Proudly the Doctor was explaining the workings of his machine.

'Basically, it's a sort of ECT machine – electro-convulsive therapy. Only much more powerful. You see, the Nestenes were held together and animated by that one central brain. In a sense they were all literally part of one vast creature. A creature that could split itself up, put fractions of its consciousness into different forms. It put just a tiny bit of itself into the Autons. Just enough so that they could move and think, in the simplest possible way. They weren't really alive at all.'

Liz shivered. 'They were alive enough for me!'

The Doctor took a swig of his tea and went on. 'It put a bit more of itself into the Replicas. They could pick up and reproduce the pattern of a human brain, and give quite a good imitation of a human being.'

'What about this fellow Channing?' asked the Brigadier.

The Doctor rubbed his chin. 'I think it put a tremendous amount of itself into Channing. He was the advance guard. He could think, and plan. I think he could even feel, in a way, though his emotions weren't really like ours.'

'And that creature in the factory?' Liz asked.

'Well, since the Nestenes are really just one creature,' the Doctor explained, 'I suppose it was more comfortable for them to have the part of them that was here all in one body. When Channing really got organised at the factory he set about creating a suitable receptacle. And as soon as it was ready they transferred all of themselves, or rather all of itself, all its vital energy, from the meteorite state into that one collective brain.'

'Putting all their eggs into one basket?' said the Brigadier.

'Just so,' said the Doctor. 'And by giving the creature a kind of brain-storm, you might say I kicked over the basket.'

'You said "the part of them that was here", Doctor,' said Liz. 'You mean there's more of it?'

'Oh, I should think so,' said the Doctor cheerfully. 'I don't suppose the Nestene brain risked all of itself on this planet.'

The Brigadier said: 'Then they might try again?'

The Doctor looked thoughtful. 'It's possible. But they've had a pretty severe setback. And since they seem to communicate by telepathy the rest of the Nestene brain will know how badly they were defeated here.'

Liz said practically: 'Do they know how limited the range of UHF waves are? You practically have to stand on their toes for that thing to work.'

The Doctor nodded. 'That is something I hope they haven't learned.'

The Brigadier said: 'Doctor, if the Nestenes do decide to launch a second attack, can we rely on your help again?'

The Doctor gave him a quizzical look. 'Do I take it that you're satisfied that I'm not an impostor?'

'Oh, I think so,' said the Brigadier. 'Two things combined to convince me, actually.'

'Oh, yes?' said the Doctor curiously.

'The brilliance of your scientific results was one,' said the Brigadier.

'And the other?' said the Doctor, with a modest smile.

'Your uniquely, aggravating temperament,' the Brigadier said crisply. 'There couldn't be two like you anywhere, Doctor. Your face may have changed, but not your character!'

For a moment the Doctor looked offended, then he caught Liz's eye and grinned.

The Brigadier went on: 'I am prepared to offer you the post of UNIT's Scientific Adviser – since Miss Shaw here doesn't seem to want it. What do you say?'

The Doctor looked thoughtful. 'I really think we ought to discuss terms first, old chap.'

'Terms?' said the Brigadier. Liz could tell from his voice that he thought the honour of working for UNIT should be reward enough.

'Terms?' the Brigadier said again. 'Well, I think you'll find the salary adequate.'

'My dear chap, I don't want money,' said the Doctor indignantly. 'Got no use for the stuff.'

The Brigadier looked puzzled. 'Then what do you want?'

'Facilities to repair the TARDIS! Equipment, a laboratory, somewhere to sleep. Oh, and I insist that Miss Shaw stays on here to help me.'

He looked appealingly at Liz. So did the Brigadier.

'Well, Miss Shaw?' he said.

Liz took a deep breath and then nodded. 'I must be raving mad,' she said. 'But all right. If you really want me to.'

The Brigadier said: 'There you are, then, Doctor. Anything else?'

'Good heavens, yes! Do you realise I'm stranded here with nothing more than I stand up in?' The Doctor looked guilty. 'Come to think of it, most of that isn't really mine. Oh dear, and there's that car, too.' He

441

looked appealingly at the Brigadier. 'You know, I really took to that car. It's got character.'

'No, Doctor,' said the Brigadier firmly. 'The car must go back to its owner.'

The Doctor sighed. 'Yes, yes, I suppose it must. But there's no reason why you shouldn't find me another one like it, is there?'

The Brigadier looked as if he was about to explode when the Doctor said gently: 'It would help to persuade me to stay, you know.'

'Oh, very well,' growled the Brigadier.

Liz couldn't help smiling at the Doctor's air of childlike pleasure.

'Oh good,' he said happily. 'When can I go out and choose it?'

'Not just yet,' said the Brigadier patiently. 'At the moment you have no official existence, Doctor. I must fix you up with a full set of papers first.' He turned to go, and then stopped. 'By the way, Doctor, I've just realised. I don't even know your name.'

The Doctor looked from the Brigadier to Liz Shaw. All in all he was quite looking forward to his stay on Earth. Naturally, he wouldn't be there for long. In spite of the Time Lords he'd soon manage to get the TARDIS working and be off on his travels. For instance, he could try reversing the polarity of the neutron flow in the dematerialisation circuit …

He was brought out of his daydream by the Brigadier's voice. 'Well, Doctor?'

Ah yes, a name … he thought. Just for the time he was here. No question of telling them his real name, of course. Time Lord names have an almost mystic importance, and are usually kept closely-guarded secrets. Anyway, they'd never be able to pronounce it. A name … thought the Doctor. Something simple, dignified and modest. He didn't want to draw attention to himself. The Doctor's eyes brightened. He'd got it – the very thing! He turned to the waiting Brigadier.

'Smith,' said the Doctor decisively. 'Doctor John Smith!'

DOCTOR WHO AND THE DAY OF THE DALEKS

1

TERROR IN THE TWENTY-SECOND CENTURY

Moni sat up and looked around cautiously. The enormous dormitory was packed with sleeping forms, dragged into total exhaustion by hours of brutal physical toil. One or two murmured and twisted and cursed in their sleep. A man screamed, 'No, no, please don't ...' and then his voice tailed off into the mutterings of a nightmare. Moni saw that it was Soran. He had been beaten by the guards that morning for failing to meet his work-norm. Soran was weakening daily. He wouldn't last much longer.

Somehow the incident seemed to give Moni courage. It was for Soran that he was fighting. Soran and thousands like him who would die in the work camps from brutal beatings, or worn out after years of grinding labour, unless ... unless ... Moni threw back the coarse blankets and swung his feet to the floor. There was nothing unusual in his being fully dressed. The dormitories weren't heated and most of his fellows slept fully clothed against the night cold. Vaguely Moni remembered having heard of a time when men had special clothes to sleep in – called py-something or other. His mind could scarcely imagine such luxury.

Moni fished his boots from beneath his pillow. He'd put them there automatically the night before. The boots were made of new strong plastic, and in the work camps nothing valuable was safe unless it was within touching distance. Tucking the boots under his arm Moni moved silently across the room towards the door. His bare feet made no sound on the rough concrete floor.

Once in the compound, he paused in a patch of shadow to pull on the boots then crept silently along the edge of the outer wall. Taking off his tunic Moni uncoiled a thin plastic rope from round his waist. He took the crude grappling hook from his pocket, tied it to the rope and swung the grappling hook at the row of spikes on top of the wall. It fell short and landed back at Moni's feet with a metallic scrape. Moni froze in terror. He glanced towards the doorway of the guard's quarters. Surely they must have heard. But there came only the rumble of guttural inhuman speech. The compound was supposed to be patrolled at all times, but the guards were careless and idle. On cold nights like this they kept to their quarters, huddling round the roaring fires in the iron braziers, stuffing down slabs of coarse grey food that their masters provided.

Moni hurled the grapple again, and this time his luck was in. It caught firmly on the spikes and, after testing it with a tug, Moni climbed quickly up the rope, his tunic between his teeth. Once on top of the wall it would make a rough pad to protect him from the spikes. Awkwardly he bestrode the wall, pulling the rope up beside him, and freeing the grappling hook. He lowered the rope to the other side of the wall, dropped his tunic after it, and then jumped down, landing with a thud that jolted the breath out of him. Quickly he put on his tunic, and hid rope and grappling iron beneath it. He set off swiftly down the endless concrete road through the rubble.

Moni had covered several miles before his luck ran out. He was just turning the corner of one of the many ruined buildings when an enormous hairy hand reached out from the darkness and plucked him off his feet. The hand slammed him against the remains of a brick wall, making him gasp out loud. Moni flinched, as a burning brand was thrust uncomfortably close to his face, and as his eyes became accustomed to the light he could just begin to pick out the hulking shape of the creature that had captured him. Nearby was a small campfire with other giant forms huddled round it. Moni cursed his luck. He had run into one of the roving patrols, camping out in the ruins. From the campfire, a guttural voice said, 'Bring!' Moni's captor shambled back towards the fire, dragging Moni after him like a rag doll. Moni let himself hang limp, making no attempt to resist. He had no wish to be torn to pieces. Against human beings he might have stood a chance, but these guards were not human: these were Ogrons.

Thrown sprawling at the feet of the patrol, Moni looked up at the hulking shapes looming over him in the firelight. Often as he had seen them before, the Ogrons never failed to terrify him. Creatures somewhere between gorilla and man, they stood almost seven feet in height with bowed legs, massive chests and long powerful arms that hung almost to the ground. Their faces were perhaps the most awful thing about them: a distorted version of the human face, with flat ape-like nose, small eyes glinting with cruelty, and a massive jaw with long yellow teeth. But the Ogrons had one quality which gave Moni a glimmer of hope, even now: for all their savage ferocity and primitive strength, they were very, very stupid.

Moni scrambled to his feet. Forcing himself to speak slowly and calmly he said, 'I am a section leader of Work Camp Three. I am needed to replace a section leader of Work Camp Four, who has been taken ill.' He looked round the circle of Ogrons to see if his story was being believed. The Ogrons looked back at him impassively. Did they believe him? Had they even understood what he was saying? In the same calm, flat voice Moni said, 'The order for my transfer came direct from your masters. If I am delayed they will be very angry. They will be angry with *you*.'

This time his words had some effect. It was almost comic to see the looks of alarm on the brutal Ogron faces. The one thing which could strike fear to the hearts of these terrifying creatures was the mention of the even more fearsome beings who were their masters.

The leading Ogron gestured into the darkness with a massive hairy paw. 'You go. Go quickly.' Moni turned and ran into the darkness.

It took him another hour of hard, dangerous travel before he reached his destination. He crossed a patch of waste ground. The moonlight showed weeds flourishing over the shattered foundations of a house. Shifting the concealing rubble, Moni found and then lifted a hidden trap-door and dropped down into the darkness. He landed at the head of a still intact flight of steps. Cautiously he moved down them until his eyes picked out a little patch of light at the bottom. It was shining beneath the edge of a closed door. Moni moved quietly to the door and rapped out a complicated series of knocks. After a moment the door creaked open. Boaz stood facing him, blaster in hand. 'All right Boaz, it's me,' said Moni.

Boaz's voice showed the strain he was feeling. 'You're late ... we didn't know—'

Moni interrupted him. 'Ran straight into an Ogron patrol. Managed to talk my way out of it. The others here?' Boaz nodded, and Moni followed him into the cellar.

Anat and Shura were huddled round the charcoal fire that blazed in a makeshift brazier. Moni glanced quickly round the room. It was his first visit to the H.Q. of this particular cell, but they were all much the same. In every city there were hidden rooms like this. Places to store arms and food. Places to meet and talk and plan. Places where men and women met with one burning desire in common – to take back their planet from the alien beings who had stolen it.

Patrolling Ogrons carried out an unending search for these hideouts. Sometimes they found one: Ogron boots kicked in the door and the little group of plotters inside were ruthlessly destroyed. But for every cell that was wiped out, another and still another sprang up to replace it.

Moni looked round at the three eager faces. Boaz, dark, scowling and intense; fiercely brave, but too highly strung, too ready to act without thinking. Shura, the youngest, full of a fiery idealism. Finally, he looked at the girl, Anat. Slim, dark and wiry with close-cropped hair. Anat was still beautiful, in spite of the rough work clothes she was wearing. Here was the real leader, Moni thought. Fierce courage, a passionate hatred of the enemy, and the cunning and caution that made her wait until the best moment to strike.

Anat spoke first. 'Something's happening, Moni. What is it? You wouldn't have called this meeting without good reason. We don't often have the honour of meeting one of the Central Committee!'

Brisk and to the point as always, thought Moni approvingly. He said, 'You're right, of course, Anat. Something *has* happened. Something big, and it involves you all.' He paused for a moment, collecting his thoughts. 'You know the kind of thing we've been doing up till now

– isolated bits of sabotage, sometimes big, sometimes small. But pinpricks, no more than that.'

Boaz burst out: 'Pinpricks? Is that what we've been fighting and dying for? As long as we go on hitting them, at least they know they haven't beaten us.'

Anat put a restraining hand on his arm. 'Let him talk, Boaz. He knows the value of our work.'

'You're right, of course,' said Moni quickly, 'any act of resistance is valuable in itself, but we can't go on for ever like this. They can't stop *us*, but we can't really hurt *them*. We're all losing sight of the big objective because we're too concerned with the day-to-day struggle!'

Anat said, 'Is there an alternative?'

Moni nodded. 'There may be – now. The scientists and historians of the Central Committee have come up with a plan. It's dangerous, maybe suicidal, but it offers a chance to free the entire planet. It calls for a special mission, carried out by just a handful of us. I have recommended you three for the final assault team, that is, assuming you all three volunteer.'

Anat leaned forward urgently, the glow from the fire illuminating her thin face. 'We volunteer. All of us. You know that without asking. Now, tell us the plan.'

Moni paused for a moment looking round at their eager faces. He might well be about to send them all to their deaths. He said, 'I can only give you a brief outline now. Like the rest of you, I have to be back in camp before morning. But I can tell you this much: we want to attempt to send you back through time ...'

The Controller of Earth Sector One pushed aside the remains of an excellent meal. Appreciatively he drained the last of his drink – real wine in a real china cup! Few men on Earth enjoyed such luxury in *these* times. He repressed a twinge of unease at the thought of those of his fellow humans who were less fortunate, those in the work camps. They would be draining their bowls of gruel about now, desperately licking the bowls clean to see that not a scrap of food was wasted ... Before leaving the room the Controller paused before a mirror, smoothing back his thinning hair and adjusting the tunic on his shoulders. More luxury, he thought. The same basic tunic as the others of course, but cloth! Real cloth, none of your plastic! He picked up the sheaf of reports he had been working on through dinner and sighed. He knew how much he was envied and hated. People didn't realise that his rank had its duties too. The constant unremitting work. And now he had to make his report to Them. Something They wouldn't care to hear, what's more.

Bracing himself, the Controller left his private dining-room and strode along the endless corridors of Central Control. Scurrying human slave workers made way for him deferentially. But it was a different story when he reached the doorway leading to the innermost H.Q. The door was flanked by Ogron guards, and as he tried to enter, one of them shoved him away with a hairy paw. The Controller strove to retain his dignity.

'You know who I am. Chief Controller of this entire sector. You will show me the respect I am entitled to.' The Ogron looked at him impassively, and the Controller's shoulders drooped in defeat. He knew that the Ogron saw him as just another human. A slave, like all humans. He said dully, 'You don't understand. I must make a most important report – to your masters.' Unconsciously copying the tactics of Moni the night before, the Controller added, 'They will be angry if you do not let me enter.'

The Ogron grunted, 'You – wait!' Leaving its fellow to guard the Controller it went inside. After a moment it returned and said, 'Come now.'

The Controller went through into the antechamber and then waited. Silently a panel slid open in front of him and he entered the inner chamber.

It was a small, completely bare room with a raised ramp at one end. After a moment another wall-panel slid open and a gleaming metallic creature glided through. Its eye-stalk swung round to look at the Controller, who bowed respectfully. This, after all, was the Black Dalek, one of the supreme rulers of the planet Earth in the twenty-second century.

In its grating metallic voice the Black Dalek said, 'Report!'

The Controller tried to restrain the quaver of terror in his voice. 'I have been studying the recent reports of resistance activity. It has reached a peak in recent weeks. I think they are planning some major operation against you.'

The Black Dalek said, 'The humans you refer to as the resistance are criminals. They are enemies of the Daleks. You will find and destroy them.'

The Controller sighed. It was always the same: the flat, toneless command to do the impossible. The Daleks seemed to have no conception of the courage and cunning of the resistance, nor for that matter of the lumbering stupidity of the Ogrons they expected to catch them. He struggled on. 'There has been one particular feature of the recent wave of activity. Several recent thefts have involved papers or equipment dealing with your research into time travel.'

For a moment the Black Dalek did not reply. When it spoke its grating voice seemed to be pitched a few degrees higher. The Controller shuddered. This, he knew, was a sign of anger. The Dalek said, 'We shall maintain a continuous scan upon the Time Vortex. If the humans attempt to travel in time we shall track them down and destroy them.' The Black Dalek's voice rose higher still as it chanted the threat of destruction that was the Daleks only creed: 'They are enemies of the Daleks. All enemies of the Daleks must be destroyed. Exterminate them! EXTERMINATE THEM! EXTERMINATE THEM!'

2

THE MAN WHO SAW
A GHOST

Suddenly in the clump of trees that huddled close to the side of Austerly House an owl hooted. The UNIT sentry swung round, his Sterling sub-machine gun at the ready. Then he went on with his lonely patrol, grinning at his own nervousness. Mind you, he thought, a night like this was enough to make anyone jumpy: the wind howled eerily in the trees, black clouds streaked past the full moon, so that pitch darkness alternated with bright moonlight. And all the time he heard the mysterious night noises of the countryside. The sentry was a Londoner. He would have been far happier guarding somewhere where there was a bit of life – pavements and street lights and people passing by.

He marched along the gravel path that bordered the house. He glanced up at the rows of windows. All dark – except for one, where light showed through a gap in the curtains of the ground-floor study. Nobody could say the old boy wasn't a worker, thought the sentry. Past midnight and still at it. The sentry remembered what the Brigadier had said at the briefing meeting.

'The international situation has taken an ugly turn. There is a very real possibility that the events in the Near East will escalate into a full-scale conflict. We may well be on the verge of World War Three. The peace of the world depends on the success of the coming Conference. And the success of that Conference depends on one man – Sir Reginald Styles. His safety is in your hands.'

The peace of the world ... thought the sentry. It was a big responsibility for one tall, grey-haired old man. No wonder the old boy was a bit tetchy. Still, Sir Reginald would be safe enough with sentries all round the house, more at the main gate, and patrols in the grounds. With a final glance at the study window, the sentry turned and began to retrace his steps. As he disappeared from view round the corner of the building, there was a curious shimmering in the air. Suddenly a man appeared. One moment he wasn't there, the next he was. He wore dark combat clothing – tunic, trousers, and boots. A massive hand-gun was holstered at his side. He had no badges or military insignia, but looked like a soldier ... perhaps some kind of irregular, a commando or a guerilla.

The man flattened himself against the side of the building. Then he began to edge cautiously towards the lighted French windows of the study.

Inside the study all was silent except for the ticking of the clock and the scratching of Sir Reginald's pen. He was preparing the notes for his speech at the coming Conference. 'It is therefore vital,' he wrote, 'that the Chinese Government accepts the assurances ...'

Sir Reginald stopped writing and looked up. Had there been something at the window? A tapping, a scratching as if the latch was being slid back? No, there was nothing. It was all this security nonsense making him jumpy. How could he work with soldiers clumping round the house. He began writing again. '... accepts the assurances of good faith ...'

The sound came again. Sir Reginald stood up ... maybe one of the sentries was trying the window. Sir Reginald called, 'Who is it? Who's there?' No answer. He strode to the French windows and threw them open.

Facing him was a youngish man in some kind of guerilla uniform. The man was holding an enormous pistol, trained straight at Sir Reginald's head. It was many years since Sir Reginald had been a soldier but the old reflexes still worked. He flung himself upon the man, dragging down the gun arm. He hung on desperately as the guerilla thrust him back into the room. The two men reeled about, sending the lamp crashing from the desk. They tripped and fell over a chair, smashing it beneath them. Sir Reginald hung on to his attacker's gun arm with both hands, desperately trying to get control of the weapon. There could be only one end to the unequal struggle: Sir Reginald was well into his sixties, the guerilla young and strong. Pinning the old man beneath him he slowly brought his gun round to aim at his victim's head. Despite all his efforts, Sir Reginald saw the muzzle of the gun pointing straight at him ... he could see and feel everything with a strange clarity, as if it were happening in slow motion ... the circle of the gun barrel looked enormous ... above it he could see the guerilla's face twisted with savage hatred. He could even see the man's knuckles begin to whiten as his finger tightened on the trigger. He wrenched at the guerilla's sinewy wrist with both hands, but it was as firm as a rock. His hands were slipping. Then, incredibly, they were empty. The guerilla's wrist seemed to melt away. The whole figure of his opponent shimmered, then vanished. As the study door was flung open Sir Reginald found himself flat on his back wrestling with thin air. A UNIT corporal helped Sir Reginald to his feet; he was trembling with reaction and shock. Miss Paget, his secretary, went to him.

She said, 'Sir Reginald, what happened? Are you all right?'

Sir Reginald looked at her wildly. 'Attacked me ... he attacked me. Tried to kill me!'

One of the patrolling sentries stood outside the French windows. The corporal rapped. 'See anyone?'

The sentry shook his head. 'Came running when I heard the noise, Corp. No one came through there.'

The corporal turned back to Sir Reginald. 'Who attacked you, sir? Who did you see?'

Sir Reginald said slowly: 'He vanished ... disappeared into thin air ... like a ghost ...'

Brigadier Alastair Lethbridge-Stewart swung his highly-polished boots onto the top of his desk, tucked the telephone receiver under his chin and waited for the Minister to stop yammering in his ear.

The Brigadier glanced at the headlines on the front page of *The Times* – 'NEAR EAST CRISIS– WAR LOOMS'. If it happened he'd apply to be posted back to his Regiment. It would be nice to wear the kilt again. The Brigadier realised that the voice in his ear had stopped. He said, 'Er, quite, sir. Quite.' The yammering started up again. The Brigadier sighed, interrupting politely, but firmly.

'I have the reports in front of me now, sir. The sentry *outside* the house heard the sounds of struggle, and ran towards the French windows. The sentry *inside* the house also heard the noise and ran through the study door. Except for Sir Reginald himself, the study was empty.' There was a further outburst on the other end of the 'phone. The Brigadier replied, 'No, sir, I was not proposing to ignore the matter!' Since he had in fact been proposing to do exactly that, he had to pause and rack his brains for a moment before going on. Then inspiration came.

'As a matter of fact, sir,' said the Brigadier, lying magnificently, 'I was about to pass the matter over to one of my top men.' The Brigadier allowed a hint of reproach to creep into his voice – 'I was just on my way to brief him when you called ...'

Inside the laboratory of the Scientific Adviser to UNIT everything was still. Mysterious tangles of elaborate equipment straggled over the benches. The solid blue shape of an old police box stood incongruously in one corner. Suddenly the police box began to give out the most agonising groaning sound. It vibrated, shaking the whole laboratory and rattling the retorts and test tubes. The groaning reached a peak, there was a loud bang, the door of the police box burst open, and a tall, lean man shot out of the police box in a cloud of smoke. He slammed the door behind him, cursing fluently in an obscure Martian dialect.

The laboratory door opened. A very small, very pretty girl came in. Quite unsurprised she slapped the coughing Doctor on the back, gave him a glass of water and opened the laboratory window to let out the smoke.

'Foiled again, Doctor?' asked Jo Grant sympathetically.

The Doctor nodded, sipping his water gloomily. 'It's maddening. I'm so nearly there. If I could only cut out their primary override on the dematerialisation circuit.' He picked up a sheaf of notes and studied them gloomily.

Jo looked at him affectionately. Sometimes the Doctor seemed to think she understood the most difficult scientific theories as easily as he did himself. At other times he had an infuriating habit of carefully explaining that two and two made four.

When she had first joined UNIT, Jo Grant had assumed that the Doctor's story of travelling in Time and Space in a police box called the TARDIS (the initials stood for 'Time and Relative Dimensions in Space') was some kind of joke. Recent experiences had changed all that. The TARDIS, temporarily 'grounded' by decree of the Doctor's mysterious superiors, the Time Lords, had suddenly started working again and Jo had found herself caught up in an adventure on another planet in the distant future.* With this in mind she said:

'I thought the TARDIS was working again!'

'My dear Jo, the TARDIS was being operated under remote-control by the Time Lords ... just because they wanted me to do their dirty work for them!'

'But if it works for *them*—' Jo persisted.

'I don't want it to work for *them*,' said the Doctor irritably, 'I want it to work for *me*. No one's going to use me as an interplanetary puppet.'

Suddenly, an inspiration seemed to strike him. 'Of course. Now why didn't I think of that earlier.'

Leaping up, the Doctor dashed back inside the TARDIS. Through its open doors Jo could see that he was bent over the central control column, making careful adjustments to the instruments. As he did so the laboratory door opened. Jo looked up and to her utter astonishment saw the Doctor standing in the doorway.

Amazed, she looked back inside the TARDIS. There was the Doctor still bending over the console. She looked back at the door. There was the Doctor standing looking at her. But there was an even bigger shock to come. Another figure appeared from behind the Doctor. She was looking at herself.

The two Jo Grants looked at each other in mutual astonishment. Then the Doctor, the one in the doorway, spoke.

'Good grief! Oh yes ... yes, of course. I remember now.'

He gave Jo his familiar charming smile. But she could only gaze back at him thunderstruck, as he said reassuringly, 'Now don't worry, my dear. I know you're alarmed, but ...'

He was interrupted by the appearance of the Doctor from inside the TARDIS. But this Doctor shared none of Jo's astonishment. He

---

Doctor Who and the Doomsday Weapon

looked at his other self with a sort of mild curiosity ... 'Oh no! What are *you* doing here?'

The new arrival rubbed his chin and said apologetically, 'Don't worry, I'm not here ... that is ... well in a sense I am here, but you're not there. It's all a bit complicated to explain ...'

The Doctor cut his other self short. 'Well this won't do at all, will it? Can't have two of us running about.'

'Don't worry, old chap,' said the second Doctor cheerily. 'It'll all be—'

And then he vanished in mid-sentence, the second Jo Grant with him. The remaining Doctor gave a satisfied nod, and headed back inside the TARDIS.

'Now just a minute, Doctor,' Jo protested. 'What was all *that* about?'

'I'm afraid I must have overloaded the temporal circuitry, Jo. Must have produced a localised distortion.'

Jo looked at him, still baffled. The Doctor chuckled. 'Very funny thing, Time. Once you start tampering with it, the oddest things happen.'

Jo said: 'But there was another me – and another you. Where did they go?'

'Back into their own time stream of course. Or do I mean forward?'

Jo made a final protest. 'But Doctor ...'

The Doctor waved her aside reassuringly. 'Don't worry, my dear. Just a freak effect. Now I really must get on.'

He was just about to re-enter the TARDIS when the door opened once more. Jo looked up in alarm, but this time it was only the Brigadier. 'So there you are, Doctor. I need your help.' Jo could see that the Doctor was not very pleased by this new interruption. She braced herself for the inevitable clash.

'I'm sorry, Brigadier,' said the Doctor curtly. 'I happen to be extremely busy.'

'So am I, Doctor. Now then, you've heard of Sir Reginald Styles?'

'No,' said the Doctor flatly. He picked up his notes and began to study them.

Jo said helpfully, 'Isn't he the chief British representative at the United Nations?'

'That's right, Miss Grant. And he's the key man in the latest summit conference.'

The Doctor looked up. 'My dear Brigadier, I'm a scientist, not a politician.'

With an exasperated sigh the Brigadier retorted, 'If you weren't always tinkering with that wretched contraption of yours, perhaps you'd realise just how bad the international situation has become.'

'You humans are always squabbling over something,' remarked the Doctor pointedly.

'This particular squabble looks very like ending up in a third world war.'

There was real anxiety in the Brigadier's voice. The Doctor's attitude changed at once. 'As bad as that, old chap?'

The Brigadier sank down onto a laboratory stool. 'The whole thing flared up in the Near East. But really it's a sort of three-cornered quarrel between Russia, America, and China. Sphere of influence, that sort of thing.'

'And Britain arranged for this summit conference,' said Jo, 'so that the three big powers could meet and sort it all out.'

'Exactly, Miss Grant. But at the last moment the Chinese refused to attend. Without them the conference can't even start. Sir Reginald Styles is due to fly to Peking in a few hours' time. The Chinese trust him. There's just a chance he may be able to persuade them to change their minds.'

Tossing aside his sheaf of notes the Doctor said, 'All right, Brigadier. You've convinced me the situation's serious. Where do I come in?'

'Styles has suddenly started acting oddly. Last night he claimed someone tried to kill him at his home. This morning he denies the whole thing. You see the problem, Doctor. If Styles doesn't fly to Peking, the conference may fail. But how can we let him go if he's cracking up?'

'Suppose he isn't cracking up?' said Jo. 'Suppose his story's true?'

'That's just it. According to my men, no one was there. No one could have been there.'

Briefly, the Brigadier recounted the events of the previous night.

The Doctor looked thoughtful. 'From what you say of Styles, he's not the type to invent or imagine things. So obviously *something* happened. The question is what? Did Styles say anything more – last night, I mean?'

The Brigadier shrugged. 'Apparently he just babbled something about a ghost.'

In a clearing in the woods near Austerly House there was a sudden shimmering and distortion in the air. Then a man appeared! One moment he wasn't there, the next he was. He wore the tough, serviceable clothes of a guerilla, and there was a massive hand-gun holstered at his side.

The man looked swiftly around him. He heard movement nearby, and with a swift, practised movement flung himself to the ground, rolling into the cover of a patch of bracken. Seconds later the boots of a UNIT patrol passed within inches of his head. When the patrol had gone on its way, the man got to his feet. He began to move cautiously through the trees towards the house. Then, directly ahead of him, came another shimmering in the air. Three huge forms materialised, blocking his path. The guerilla's mind was filled with panic. Ogrons! They had pursued him from his own time.

Abandoning any attempt at silence, the guerilla turned and ran away from the direction of the house. He heard the sound of the pursuing Ogrons as they crashed through the woods behind him. He knew he could outrun them, at least for a while. Their huge bulk made them slow and clumsy. But he knew, too, that the Ogrons' endurance was almost limitless. When he was utterly worn out and breathless they would still be lumbering after him. And if they caught him … instant death – if he was lucky; otherwise capture, and a return to his own time zone for interrogation by the Daleks. His only chance was to lose the Ogrons in a sudden burst of speed.

The guerilla burst from the edge of the woods into open park land. The going was easier here. Easier too, for his pursuers. They were still behind him. Just ahead a high wall marked the edge of the grounds. With a desperate spurt of speed he ran towards it. The three Ogrons appeared behind him in close pursuit.

Meanwhile a third group had joined the chase. Sergeant Benton of UNIT had been outraged to have the peace of a routine patrol disturbed by what sounded like a herd of elephants crashing through the woods. He led his patrol at a fast trot towards the sound. As they ran they unslung their Sterling sub-machine guns.

The fleeing guerilla reached the wall and hurled himself at the top in a desperate, scrabbling leap. For a moment he hung by his hands from the top of the wall, then, slowly and painfully, managed to heave himself over.

Benton and his patrol emerged from the woods just in time to see the guerilla drop down out of sight. They watched in amazement as the pursuing Ogrons swarmed over the wall with ape-like ease and also disappeared from view. Benton yelled: 'After them!' adding to himself, 'Whatever they are.' The UNIT patrol sprinted for the wall and began to scale it.

The guerilla was panting and gasping now, beginning to slow down. Getting over the wall had cost him time, and the Ogrons were very close. Across the field in front of him he could see a fenced-off strip of land running parallel to the road. Two steel rails ran along the centre of it. Of course – a railway! Some primitive twentieth century transport system. Not far away the rails disappeared into a dark archway. A tunnel. He could hide in its darkness, use the time transmitter and get back to his own time ... He was almost within reach of the tunnel mouth when his foot twisted on a stone. He crashed to the ground, half-stunned.

With a savage roar of triumph, the pursuing Ogrons were upon him. He struggled to rise but his leg gave way beneath him. The huge hairy hands of the Ogrons reached out for him, and a massive blow smashed him to the ground.

Benton and his patrol came running up. 'Give 'em a warning shot!' snapped Benton. A burst of machine-gun fire rattled over the Ogrons' heads. One of the Ogrons drew the strange, massive pistol from the holster at its side and fired back. There was a sharp electronic buzz, and the man next to Sergeant Benton simply disintegrated. He vanished, as though his whole being had exploded into fragments.

'Take cover!' yelled Benton, and the UNIT soldiers hurled themselves to the ground, rolling into whatever shelter they could find. A burst of fire hammered into the Ogrons. The creatures staggered under the impact of the bullets, but did not fall. At a sign from their leader they fled into the darkness of the tunnel mouth, leaving the crumpled form of their prisoner behind them.

The UNIT patrol dashed up to the tunnel. 'One of you look after him,' ordered Benton, indicating the unconscious guerilla. 'You two, cover the other end of that tunnel. Whatever those things are, we've got them bottled up.' Cautiously, with guns at the ready, Benton and his men advanced into the blackness of the tunnel.

3

THE VANISHING
GUERILLA

In Sir Reginald's study at Austerly House, the Doctor, the Brigadier, and Jo Grant were hearing an account of the events of the previous night. Miss Paget, Sir Reginald's secretary, was a thin, sharp-featured woman in her fifties, the perfect picture of the top-ranking senior secretary. It was obvious that she was devoted to Sir Reginald, and had been very shaken by his strange behaviour.

'Please go on, Miss Paget,' said the Doctor in his most reassuring voice.

'I think that's everything really. Sir Reginald *said* someone attacked him. But there just wasn't anyone there.'

'And he definitely used the word "ghost"?'

'Oh yes. I was quite struck by it. You see, he's always been very scornful of—'

Miss Paget stopped talking as though she'd been switched off. Sir Reginald stalked into the room. He looked round angrily.

'What's going on here?'

'These gentlemen are from UNIT,' said Miss Paget.

'And who asked them to come here? We've got enough soldiers cluttering up the place as it is.'

Miss Paget's voice was shaky but determined. 'I asked them, Sir Reginald. Because of what happened last night.'

'Nothing happened last night,' said Styles icily.

Crushed, Miss Paget was silent.

The Brigadier said firmly: 'There does appear to have been *some* sort of incident, Sir Reginald.'

Sir Reginald was obviously not used to being contradicted. He looked as if he might explode at any moment.

Tactfully, Jo Grant said, 'Perhaps if *you* could tell us what really happened, Sir Reginald?' She gave him her most charming smile.

Sir Reginald was too well-mannered to storm at what appeared to be a mere child. Wearily he said, 'I was working late – must have nodded off at my desk. I knocked over the lamp, scattered all my papers. I woke up a little confused. I was picking up my papers when Miss Paget and the sentry came in. All a lot of fuss about nothing.'

Sir Reginald wasn't used to lying, and he did it very badly. Jo couldn't help feeling sorry for him as he gazed fiercely round, trying to hang on to his dignity.

The Doctor meanwhile had wandered over to the French windows, and seemed to be studying the pattern of the carpet. The Brigadier persisted, 'But you did mention ghosts, Sir Reginald.'

'Did I? Must have been having a bit of a nightmare.'

The Doctor said gently, 'What about these marks here?' He pointed downward. 'Muddy feet, Sir Reginald. Someone *was* here.'

'Must have been the sentry.'

The Doctor shook his head. 'According to Miss Paget the outside sentry didn't come into the room.'

Sir Reginald blustered, 'Are you accusing me of lying, sir?'

Hastily the Brigadier cut in, 'You've obviously been under a good deal of strain, sir. Were you feeling at all unwell last night?'

Sir Reginald snapped: 'Felt, and feel, perfectly well. Now, if you'll excuse me, Brigadier, I really can't afford to waste any more time.' He turned to Miss Paget. 'Where's that car? I'm due at the airport in twenty minutes.'

Miss Paget said, 'It's waiting for you now, sir.'

Jo saw the Brigadier look quickly at the Doctor. She sensed the unspoken question. The Doctor said, 'Then we mustn't detain you further, Sir Reginald. Allow me to wish you every success in your mission.'

For a moment Sir Reginald seemed taken aback. Then, with a brief nod of farewell he turned and left the room, Miss Paget scuttling behind him. Captain Yates, the Brigadier's number two, appeared in the doorway. 'Call for you on the RT, sir. Sergeant Benton.'

As the Brigadier went out into the hall, Jo turned to the Doctor. 'What was all that about? Something did happen last night, didn't it?'

The Doctor nodded.

'Then why did Sir Reginald say that it didn't?'

'My dear Jo,' said the Doctor gently, 'whatever happened was so extraordinary that Sir Reginald can't believe it. He thinks he's been having hallucinations.'

'So why doesn't he admit it?'

The Doctor sighed. 'If you were about to begin an important mission would you want to admit you'd been seeing things?'

'I see,' said Jo brightly. 'So that's why you pretended to believe him.'

'Nothing else to be done. He's been shaken up, but he's still perfectly capable. And at the moment this little planet of yours needs his talents very badly.'

The Brigadier appeared in the doorway. 'Doctor, Miss Grant, will you come with me, please? There's been some kind of shooting incident just outside the grounds.'

As Jo, the Doctor and the Brigadier came down the steps at the front of Austerly House they saw Sir Reginald's limousine drawing away. The Brigadier looked after the car for a moment, strain and anxiety plain on his face. Then he bustled Jo and the Doctor into the waiting jeep. Captain Yates started the engine and they shot off, gravel spurting from beneath their wheels.

Five minutes' fast driving brought them to the road near the railway tunnel.

An anxious-looking Sergeant Benton was waiting for them.

'Morning, Sergeant Benton,' said Jo cheerily. But Benton was too worried to give her more than a quick nod.

'This way, sir,' he said, and led them across the fields to the tunnel.

On the way he told his story to the extremely sceptical Brigadier. Jo couldn't help feeling sorry for him as he struggled on. The Brigadier interrupted, 'Let me see if I've got it straight, Benton. This chap appeared from nowhere, and these other – creatures were chasing him?'

Benton said, 'That's right, sir. Sort of ape-like they were. Like stone-age men, or gorillas.'

'I see. Gorillas wearing clothes and carrying guns?' drawled the Brigadier.

Benton nodded dumbly.

'Then where the blazes are they, Sergeant Benton? You said you had them trapped in the tunnel. Presumably you captured or killed them all?'

Benton swallowed hard. 'Well no, sir. We had men going in from both ends. The two patrols bumped into each other. The tunnel was empty.'

'You saw them go in, you sealed off both ends, and the tunnel was empty?' said the Brigadier incredulously.

Again Benton nodded. 'Some kind of trap-door,' said the Brigadier hopefully. 'Maybe a secret passage?'

Benton shook his head. 'We checked, sir. Every inch. It's just a plain, ordinary railway tunnel. Not even used any more. This line was shut down years ago.'

The Doctor was bending over the unconscious man in guerilla's clothes. 'This chap's in a pretty bad way. Concussion, I think. He should be in hospital.'

'Ambulance is already on its way, Doctor,' said Benton. 'We'll get him to the UNIT sick-bay.'

The Brigadier picked up the strange-looking gun lying by the guerilla's side. 'What do you make of this, Doctor?'

The Doctor examined it curiously. 'It's a new one on me, Brigadier. But at the moment I'm rather more interested in this. It was hidden inside his tunic.'

The Doctor held out a small black box with control knobs set into the top. Jo thought it looked like a rather superior transistor radio.

'Some kind of signalling device?' suggested the Brigadier.

The Doctor shook his head. 'As a matter of fact, Brigadier, I think it's a rather primitive form of time machine.'

There was the rhythmic blare of a siren, and they saw a UNIT ambulance driving along the road. It stopped. Two men jumped out carrying a stretcher. The Brigadier turned to Sergeant Benton. 'See him into the ambulance, Sergeant. You'd better travel with him. Take a couple of men with you. I want him kept under constant guard.'

Benton saluted, waved over the ambulance men, then started to transfer the wounded guerilla to the vehicle. The man was muttering and groaning as they lifted him onto the stretcher.

'Do you think he'll be all right, Doctor?' asked Jo.

The Doctor was still absorbed in the strange black box. 'Oh I think so, Jo.'

'As soon as he recovers consciousness,' said the Brigadier grimly, 'he'll have quite a few explanations to make.'

The Doctor looked up. 'No doubt. Meanwhile, we've found two very interesting clues. That gun of his, and this machine. Let's get back to the laboratory, Jo. I think I'd like to run one or two tests...'

The office of the Controller of Earth Sector One was not a pleasant or comfortable place, just bare gleaming metal walls and floor, and a plain functional desk. But to the Controller himself it was evidence of his power and rank. Few humans enjoyed such space and luxury. But after all, he reminded himself, he was the supreme authority in that part of Earth once known as England. Supreme after the Daleks, of course...

Coldly, the Controller studied the Ogron guard. There was a cutting edge in his voice when he spoke. 'You have failed in your mission.'

The Ogron shook its head vigorously. There was almost a tremor in the thick guttural voice as it replied. Ogrons could master human speech only with difficulty, and their vocabularies were very small.

The Ogron growled, 'No, Controller, we did not fail. We found the enemy and destroyed him.'

'You were told to capture him alive. He was needed for interrogation.'

'Human soldiers came. We had to return to this time zone.'

Wearily, the Controller wondered if the Ogron was telling the truth. The creatures were so savage that it was difficult to persuade them to take prisoners. Their instinct was to kill anyone they got their hands on.

'Then you are sure the rebel was dead? If the twentieth century humans captured him alive, he could tell them much.'

There was a flicker of fear in the Ogron's tiny red eyes. It grunted, 'The enemy is dead. We killed him.'

466

The Controller rose from behind his desk. 'I want an intensified effort by all your patrols. These rebellious criminals must be found and destroyed! If not – the Daleks will be displeased. They will punish you. Now go!'

The Ogron lumbered from the room. The Controller sighed. For years now the criminal rebels – guerillas they called themselves – had been resisting the rule of the Daleks. Never more than a pitiful handful of them. Yet in a way, that handful seemed immortal. As soon as one group of resistance fighters was tracked down another sprang up. With their pitifully tiny resources, their cellar hideouts and their home-made weapons they took on all the might of the Dalek technology. Naturally, the rebels could never win. Yet in a way it seemed they could never lose. The Controller was forced almost to admire his fellow humans. They were wrong, of course. Hopelessly misguided. But such courage! Such persistence and cunning in the face of impossible odds. With qualities like these it was easy to see why the race of Man had once been a great one. The Controller sighed again. But it was ultimately all for nothing. Eventually the rebels would lose the unequal fight. They would suffer the fate of everyone who opposed the Daleks. They would be exterminated.

With a deliberate effort the Controller turned his attention back to his duties. The production figures for Work Camp Three were below the norm. If they did not improve the Daleks would be angry. The Controller began to study the sheaf of production reports on his desk.

As the Brigadier strode into the UNIT laboratory he was astonished to see Jo Grant hauling a large stuffed dummy across the laboratory. She propped it up in a chair at the far end of the room, and stood back, looking at her work in satisfaction.

'Bit early for Guy Fawkes' Night, Miss Grant,' said the Brigadier.

Jo turned at the sound of his voice. 'The Doctor wanted it. Don't ask me why. How's that poor man you found?'

The Brigadier shrugged. 'Benton's with him in sick-bay now. Chap's still out cold, apparently. Will be for some time.'

The Doctor emerged from the TARDIS, the guerilla's gun in one hand, the black box in the other. 'Then we'll just have to wait till he wakes up, won't we?' His tone was brisk and cheerful ... Jo saw that he was thoroughly enjoying the task of grappling with this new problem. She couldn't help feeling glad that he'd found something to take his mind from the endless and seemingly hopeless struggle to get the TARDIS working again. The Doctor looked at Jo's dummy slumped grotesquely on its chair at the far end of the laboratory.

'Splendid, Jo. Just what I wanted. Most lifelike, isn't it, Brigadier?'

The Brigadier studied the drooping dummy without enthusiasm. 'Yes, very nice. May I ask what it's in aid of?'

'I thought you might like a little practical demonstration. Now then, if you'll all step this way.'

The Doctor led them to a position by the door. At the opposite end of the laboratory, the dummy slumped grotesquely in its chair. The body was made from an old pair of army denims stuffed with newspapers. It had a paper-stuffed pillowslip for a head. Jo had drawn a crude grinning face on the pillowslip with lipstick.

'Now, Jo, Brigadier,' said the Doctor, 'I think you'd better stand behind me – just in case.' He raised the guerilla's gun, and aimed it at the dummy.

'Steady on, Doctor,' said the Brigadier hurriedly. 'Just in case of *what*, exactly?'

The Doctor looked over his shoulder. 'In case I've mistimed the setting, of course. In which case, we might lose most of the wall.'

The Brigadier was outraged. 'Now just a moment! This building happens to be Government prop—'

But he was already too late. The Doctor had resumed his aim, and activated some kind of trigger. There was a high-pitched electronic buzz. Chair and dummy simply vanished! The Doctor gave a satisfied nod.

The Brigadier walked slowly to the other end of the laboratory. There was absolutely no sign of either chair or dummy. He looked at the gun in the Doctor's hand. 'What the blazes is that thing, Doctor?'

The Doctor put the gun down on a laboratory bench. 'Quite an effective little weapon, isn't it?'

The Brigadier looked grim. 'According to Benton those ape creatures were carrying exactly the same kind of weapon. He lost one of his men. No trace of the body afterwards.'

The Brigadier's voice was angry. Jo knew how much he worried about the safety of the men under his command. To lose even one soldier was a considerable blow.

Gingerly, Jo picked up the alien weapon. It looked something like a cross between a revolver and a blunderbuss. It was heavy, and she needed two hands to hold it.

'What is it exactly, Doctor?' she asked. 'I mean, how does it work?'

'Basically, it's a form of ultrasonic disintegrator.'

Jo tried to translate the Doctor's reply into something she could understand. 'You mean it's some kind of ray-gun?'

The Doctor took a deep breath. 'Er, well, yes, Jo. Sort of ... The point is, it's an extremely sophisticated weapon. Far more advanced than anything yet developed on Earth. Er – I don't think you'd better point it like that.'

Jo realised that she was aiming the gun straight at the Brigadier. Hastily she put it back on the bench.

The Brigadier said, 'You say it wasn't made on Earth? You mean it comes from another planet?'

The Doctor shook his head. 'I've just done a metallurgical analysis: it proved conclusively that the metal from which this gun was made was mined here on Earth.'

Jo was puzzled. 'But you said it couldn't have been made on Earth.'

'Not at the present time, Jo.'

'Kindly stop talking in riddles, Doctor,' said the Brigadier irritably.

The Doctor walked to the other end of the bench and picked up the black box. 'Do you believe in ghosts, Brigadier?'

'Do let's be serious.'

'I am serious, I assure you. Perhaps I used the wrong word: not so much ghosts as apparitions – creatures that can appear and disappear.' He studied the box, turning it round in his hands. 'You see we usually think of ghosts as coming from the past. But what about ghosts from the future?'

He looked from Jo to the Brigadier, smiling gently at the sight of their baffled faces.

Jo said slowly, 'You said that thing was some kind of time machine ...'

The Doctor picked up the little machine and began fiddling with the controls. 'That's right. But I think it must have been damaged when the man fell. I can't seem to get it to ...'

But even as the Doctor spoke the machine seemed to come to life. It gave a sort of low hum. A curious shimmering effect filled the air around it.

The Doctor shouted, 'Good grief, it's working! Stand back both of you!' Frantically he jabbed at the control knobs.

In the UNIT sick-bay, not far away, Sergeant Benton sat beside the unconscious guerilla's bed. The guerilla, now wearing a pair of hospital pyjamas, was twisting and muttering, drifting in and out of a kind of coma. Not long ago he had suddenly shouted in fear, then slumped back into unconsciousness. For the moment he was relatively quiet. Benton's head began to nod, as he was lulled by the peace of the little room. Suddenly Benton jerked awake. A strange shimmering seemed to fill the air. Benton looked on in utter amazement as the guerilla simply faded away. The shimmering stopped and the bed was empty. Benton found himself pulling back the sheets and peering under the pillow, as if he expected to find the man hiding. Then he pulled himself together. The bloke was gone, and that was that. Benton sighed. Guess who'd have to try and explain *that* to the Brigadier ...

The Controller of Earth Sector One stood in the Temporal Scanning Room. All around him was the strange and mysterious machinery of the Daleks keeping continuous watch on the Time Vortex, that mysterious void where Time and Space are one. Girl technicians moved silently about the room. The Controller thought to himself that there was something strange and inhuman about them. They seemed completely emotionless, dedicated to the machines they served. He turned to the girl beside him and said, 'Why did you send for me?'

The girl indicated a faint flickering pulse on one of the screens in front of them. 'A time transmitter is in operation in the twentieth century time zone.'

The Controller felt a sudden excitement. This could only mean more resistance activity. This time, perhaps, he could trap them. He said, 'Can you fix the Space Time co-ordinates?'

Coldly the girl said, 'I will try. The trace is very faint.'

Her hands flickered quickly over the controls on the console in front of her. Slowly the pulse on the screen flickered and died.

The girl said, 'It's no use, Controller. Transmission has stopped. I think a transference has taken place, but it is not possible to be specific.' Her voice was flat and unemotional. She was simply reporting a fact.

The girl's indifference only increased the Controller's feeling of anger and disappointment. Sharply he said, 'Continue scanning. Next time I advise you to be more efficient, or it will be the worse for you.'

The girl was completely unimpressed. In the same emotionless voice she said, 'Everything possible was done. We shall continue scanning. If further transmissions take place you will be informed.' She turned away and returned to her duties.

The Controller looked after her furiously. Then he sighed, accepting defeat, and left the scanning room.

In the UNIT laboratory the Doctor put the machine down with a sigh of relief. 'It's all right. The thing's gone completely dead again.'

'But it *was* working,' said Jo anxiously.

The Doctor sighed. 'Oh yes. Unfortunately it was accidental. I still don't know how or why.'

The telephone rang and the Brigadier snatched it up. 'Yes? All right, Benton, what is it?' The Brigadier's voice rose to a sort of strangled yelp. 'What! He did *what*, Benton?'

The Brigadier listened a moment longer and said, 'All right, Sergeant, I believe you. Yes, I'll tell him.' With a mighty effort he put the 'phone down, slowly and gently. 'That was Benton from the sick-bay. You may be interested to know, Doctor, that at exactly the moment you started tinkering with that wretched machine, our guerilla friend shimmered, and vanished – just faded away out of his hospital bed.'

'Now that *is* interesting,' said the Doctor. 'What's more it proves I was right. The thing's definitely a time transmitter. Somehow I managed to shoot the poor chap back to where he came from.'

The Brigadier gave him an exasperated look. 'I'm glad you find it interesting, Doctor – but it's not particularly helpful is it? When that man vanished, our chance of finding out what's going on vanished with him.'

'Don't be so pessimistic, old chap. This business isn't over yet, you know.'

'It isn't?' said the Brigadier gloomily.

'I very much doubt it. You see, I don't think those behind it have achieved their objectives yet. So they're bound to try again.'

'Try *what* again?'

'I'm not sure about the *what*, Brigadier, but I think I know the *where!*'

The Brigadier said, 'Well, I suppose that's something.'

'Everything that's happened,' the Doctor went on, 'seems to centre round Austerly House. And who ever tried to harm Styles is certain to try again.'

'But he isn't even there! He's in Peking by now.'

'That's right. So the place will be empty.' The Doctor turned to Jo who had been looking on in puzzlement. 'Well, Jo, how about it?'

'How about what?'

The Doctor smiled. 'How do you fancy spending a night in a haunted house?'

4

THE GHOST HUNTERS

Once again the wind whistled eerily in the trees round Austerly House. Once again a nervous sentry jumped at the sudden hoot of an owl. And, once again, one solitary window was illuminated, that of Sir Reginald Styles' ground-floor study.

Inside the study, however, things were very different. Instead of Sir Reginald toiling over his papers, the elegant figure of the Doctor lay sprawled at his ease in an armchair by the blazing log fire. On a little table beside him stood a heavy silver tray. It held knives, plates, glasses, a little basket of biscuits, a bottle of wine and a very large Stilton cheese. The little black box, the time machine, stood on the table next to the tray.

Jo Grant stood beside the Doctor's chair. The Doctor looked up at her.

'You know, Jo,' he said thoughtfully, helping himself to a large slice of cheese, 'you can always be sure of one thing with politicians whatever their political ideas: they always keep a well-stocked larder.'

Jo looked at the loaded tray with an air of some disapproval. 'I'm not sure that you really ought to help yourself like that,' she said dubiously.

'Nonsense, Jo. You heard what Miss Paget said. We're to consider the place our own.' The Doctor took another bite of cheese by way of underlining the point.

Jo looked around uneasily. In spite of the warmth and comfort of the firelit study she was very much aware that the rest of the big, old house was dark and empty. And outside the house itself was the black night, with strange noises coming from the gloomy woods. Of course, Captain Yates, Sergeant Benton and armed UNIT patrols were guarding the house. But that hadn't helped Styles. He'd still been attacked.

Jo shivered. 'I wish you hadn't sent all the servants away.'

The Doctor poured himself a glass of Burgundy. He held up the glass to admire the rich red colour of the wine. 'Had to be done, Jo. How can you expect ghosts to walk in a house full of people?'

Jo shivered again and the Doctor stopped his teasing. 'Look, there's really nothing to worry about. Have a piece of this delicious cheese.'

'No thanks, Doctor. I don't seem to be hungry right now.' Jo came and perched herself on the arm of his chair.

Munching away at his cheese the Doctor said indistinctly, 'Really ought to eat something, it's liable to be a long night.'

Jo said, 'I know. That's what I'm worrying about.'

Outside the house the wind howled and it was starting to rain. Captain Yates stood in the shelter of the main doorway and watched the wind thrashing about in the tree tops. Sergeant Benton hurried around the corner of the building and joined him. Benton's army waterproof was spotted with big drops of rain.

'Everything quiet, Benton?'

'Yes, sir, quiet as the grave.' Benton shuddered, wishing he'd found a more cheerful expression.

'Right, carry on.'

Benton saluted and plunged back into the darkness.

Throughout the grounds little patrols of armed men moved quietly through the pitch-black night, exchanging pre-arranged signals and passwords.

There were no sentries around the abandoned railway tunnel. It was some way from the house, and it hadn't struck the Brigadier that there was any point in guarding it.

Inside the darkness of the tunnel there came a faint shimmering and glowing. Three figures materialised one by one. First the girl, Anat, leader of the resistance cell that Moni had visited at such peril. Next Boaz, scowling with grim determination. Finally Shura, young and eager, trembling with nervous excitement. All three were loaded down with equipment.

Once all three were materialised, Anat produced a tiny light-cell. Dimly it illuminated the rough brickwork of the tunnel. Boaz said exultantly, 'We made it, Anat. We made it!'

Swiftly they began to unload the heavier equipment. Shura found a hiding place for it, a crevice in the wall of the tunnel. He covered the equipment with loose rubble, and looked up excitedly. 'Well, this is it!'

Anat was more cautious. 'The place *looks* right. But the tiniest error in the temporal co-ordinates and we may be too soon. Or too late.'

Shura said, 'There's no chance of that. We'll succeed this time.'

'We've got to,' said Anat grimly. 'Now listen to me, all of you. You heard what Moni said before we left. We're the last chance. Two others have tried before us and failed. The Daleks are getting closer all the time, and they can track our equipment. If we fail, we'll be lucky to get back to our own time zone alive. And we'll have lost the chance of defeating the Daleks.'

Boaz said, 'We won't fail, Anat.'

'We mustn't,' Shura added eagerly.

Anat said, 'We'll make our way to the house. You've all memorised the old historical maps?' The others nodded. She went on, 'Remember it'll be very different outside the tunnel. You'll see fields, roads, houses with people in them. The kind of world we should have had. The kind of world we can still have if we succeed. Are you both ready?'

Again the two men nodded. 'Then we'll make our way to the house. There'll be army patrols, but we'll avoid them.'

Boaz said fiercely, 'If they try to stop us ...' He patted the holstered gun at his side.

Anat cut in, 'Remember, they are not our enemies. We have only one enemy. The man we have come to kill.'

Swiftly and silently the three guerillas slipped out of the tunnel and began moving across the fields to Austerly House.

The Doctor took another appreciative sip of his Burgundy. 'Ah, yes. Amost good-humoured wine, this. A touch of the sardonic perhaps, but not cynical. A truly civilised little wine, one after my own heart.'

Jo looked at him impatiently. 'Do stop chuntering on, Doctor.' She got out of her chair and moved to the door. 'I'm going to the kitchen to make myself a cup of tea.'

The hallway was empty and dark. There were suits of armour by the staircase and a stuffed stag's head stared glassily at her from the wall. Everything looked strange and sinister in the gloom.

Jo was making for the kitchen when suddenly the massive front door began to creak. She tried to call to the Doctor, but her voice seemed to have gone. Terrified she crouched against the wall as the door swung open. A huge figure loomed in the doorway. With a sigh of relief Jo realised it was Sergeant Benton.

In the darkness outside, the three guerillas had come to the high wall surrounding Austerly House. Working with trained efficiency they climbed it and dropped to the other side. All three froze into cover, face downward. Their dark combat clothes blended perfectly into the woodland floor. The boots of a UNIT patrol passed by within inches of them. Once it had moved away they got up. Slowly, they began to work their way towards the house. They moved in utter silence – just like ghosts.

Jo said indignantly, 'Sergeant Benton! You took years off my life, creeping about like that.'

'Didn't want to disturb the Doctor. What's he up to anyway?'

'Nothing very much. He's either tinkering with that black box you found, or carrying on like a one man Wine and Cheese society!'

At the mention of food and drink Benton cheered up. He was a big chap, and he needed a lot of fuel to keep him going. He leaned forward confidentially. 'Couldn't spare me a bite, could you, Miss Grant? I'm famished.' He did his best to look undernourished.

Jo said, 'You wait here.' She marched back into the study.

The Doctor had cut himself another piece of Stilton and poured out another glass of wine. He was contemplating them with anticipation when Jo entered and took both plate and glass from his hand.

'Jo!' he said protestingly.

'All in a good cause, Doctor.'

The Doctor watched her disappear through the door. He sighed, and reached for the cheese knife.

Benton beamed as Jo put the plate and glass on a hall table beside him. 'You've saved my life, Miss.'

He was just reaching out when a familiar voice said, 'And what do you think you're doing, Sergeant Benton?' Captain Yates stood in the main doorway.

Benton straightened up to attention and saluted. 'Just checking up, sir.'

'I see, Sergeant. Then perhaps you'd like to check up on number two patrol?'

Benton said, 'Yessir.' With an anguished glance at the little table, he disappeared into the darkness.

Mike Yates seemed to notice the plate and glass for the first time. 'Why, Jo, how very kind of you!' He swigged down the wine and popped a piece of cheese into his mouth.

Jo looked at him severely. 'Mike Yates, that was mean.'

'R.H.I.P.,' said Mike indistinctly, his mouth full of cheese.

Jo looked at him blankly. 'Come again?'

'R.H.I.P.,' he repeated. 'Rank Has Its Privileges.' He gave her a smile, and followed Benton out into the night. Jo went back to the study.

The Doctor looked up. 'So what was all *that* about?'

'Oh nothing. Just feeding the troops.'

The Doctor nodded approvingly. 'Quite right. I remember saying to old Napoleon, you know, Boney, I said, always remember this ... an army marches on its stomach.'

Jo sniffed. 'Well Mike Yates certainly does.' A gust of wind rattled the window panes and she looked up nervously. 'Doctor, did you mean what you said to the Brigadier about ghosts?'

The Doctor smiled. 'I also said there were different kinds of ghosts.'

'I know, ghosts from the past, and ghosts from the future. Which kind did you have in mind?'

The Doctor looked at her seriously. 'Isn't it far more a question of whether they have us in mind?'

By now the guerillas were very close to the house. They had concealed themselves in a clump of bushes close to the study window. Boaz said, 'In there. He must be in there. Come on.' He was about to move forward, when a UNIT patrol crunched along the gravel path. Boaz pulled himself down into cover again.

Another gust of wind rattled the study windows, and rain lashed against the panes. The Doctor crossed to the French windows and pulled back the heavy curtains. 'It's certainly a wild night, Jo. I don't envy those poor chaps on patrol.' He stood for a moment looking out into the blackness.

In the clump of bushes Boaz raised his gun and took aim. The tall figure in the window made a perfect target.

Suddenly his arm was pushed aside. He looked angrily at Anat.

'For heaven's sake, Anat,' he hissed, 'it's him, the man we came to kill! One shot and it's all over.'

'No,' Anat said fiercely. 'We must be sure. We'll go inside the house.'

'Too late now, anyway,' said Boaz sourly. The figure had left the window.

Anat said, 'We'll wait a moment longer. Then we go in.'

Inside the study Jo said, 'I never got that cup of tea!' Once more she set off for the kitchen.

The Doctor picked up the black box, and began to examine it for the hundredth time. Restlessly he turned it over and over in his long fingers.

He slipped off the back and began to peer at the maze of alien circuitry inside.

'Thing's a complete botch-up,' he grumbled to himself. 'Shouldn't work at all, but it does. Or did. Must be a booster somewhere or you wouldn't get the power.' Muttering to himself he bent absorbedly over the little box.

At a signal from Anat the three guerillas burst from the bushes. They knew that their moment of greatest danger would come in crossing the little patch of open ground between the bushes and the house itself. Just as they were completely in the open a two-man UNIT patrol rounded the corner of the house.

For a split second the soldiers peered at the dim figures before them. One of the soldiers snapped, 'Who goes there? Give the password.'

When there was no answer the UNIT men raised their guns. But Boaz and Shura were already shooting. There was a high-pitched electronic buzz, and the UNIT patrol vanished, totally disintegrated.

Anat gave an anguished look at her two fellow guerillas. But she knew there had been nothing else for them to do. This mission had to succeed, even at the cost of innocent lives. She gave Shura a quick signal. He moved to the French windows. Anat and Boaz slipped through the front door of the house.

In the study, the Doctor gave up the time machine in disgust. Nothing he could do seemed to make it come to life again. He slammed it down on the table. Immediately, it began to give out a low hum, and the swirling shimmering effect appeared very faintly around it.

The Doctor looked at the device in amazement. 'Hey, Jo,' he called. 'I've got it working again. Come and see. Jo, where are you?'

Jo heard the Doctor calling her from the kitchen, though she couldn't hear what he was saying. Still, it might be urgent. She abandoned her tea-making and headed back to the study.

Shura peered through the gap in the curtains. To his utter amazement he saw a time machine standing on the table. And it was operational! The one thing that was certain to bring the Daleks and their Ogron killers down upon them.

Shura crashed his booted foot against the lock of the French windows. They flew open, and he shot into the room amid a shower of glass.

The tall man had been standing in the doorway, but he whirled round with amazing speed at Shura's entrance.

Shura had temporarily forgotten that he had come to kill this man. He only wanted him to turn off the time transmitter before the Daleks picked up the signal. But before he could even speak an amazingly long leg shot out and kicked the gun from his hand. Shura dived desperately for the time machine. But the tall man obviously mistook this for an attack.

He dodged, reached out, and Shura found himself gripped by long steely fingers. Somehow he was spun, twisted and sent crashing into the wall. He slid to the floor half dazed. The one thought in his mind was that the man must, *must* be made to turn off the time transmitter, which still pulsed away.

In the Temporal Scanning Room the Controller of Earth Sector One peered eagerly at the screen. The tiny pulse was very faint. He turned to the girl technician beside him. 'This time, you *must* fix the co-ordinates.'

'We are attempting to do so now, Controller!' A panel in the far wall slid open. A squat, black metallic figure glided towards them. Its eye-stalk swung round onto the Controller, and the harsh, metallic voice grated, 'What is happening? Report.'

The Controller said, 'We have located a time transmitter operating in the twentieth century zone. We're fixing the co-ordinates now.' He shot a quick look at the impassive girl technician beside him and hoped desperately that his words were true. Hastily he went on, 'Security patrol are standing by.'

The Black Dalek swivelled round, turning its eye-stalk towards the faint pulse on the screen. The Dalek voice rasped: 'Whoever is operating the time transmitter is an enemy of the Daleks. They are to be exterminated.' Once again the voice rose almost to a shriek. 'Exterminate them! EXTERMINATE THEM! EXTERMINATE THEM!'

In Sir Reginald Styles' study, Shura struggled desperately to his feet. He pointed to the pulsating time transmitter and croaked, 'Please turn it off. You must turn it off or they'll kill us all!'

The tall man hauled Shura to his feet and dumped him down in an armchair. 'To be quite honest I don't think I *can* turn it off. I'm not even very sure how I turned it on. Now then, my friend, I want to ask you one or two questions.'

From the doorway a girl's voice said: 'Get away from him.'

The Doctor turned from his captive. He saw a thin, dark girl in guerilla costume. Next to her another guerilla, a man. He had Jo Grant held firmly in front of him, a gun at her head.

Obediently the Doctor moved away. The girl went straight to the time machine, and with a few complex manipulations of the controls managed to turn it off.

In the Temporal Scanning Room, the Controller's heart sank as he looked at the blank screen. He turned to the girl technician, hoping against hope … Perhaps there had still been time to trace the transmission.

The usually impassive technician's voice held a tremor of fear as she said, 'I'm sorry. We've lost the trace.'

The Black Dalek swung round on her angrily. Then it swung back to the Controller. The Dalek gun was pointing straight at him. The Controller knew that he might well be blasted into extinction then and there. The Daleks had no mercy on those who failed them. He stood perfectly still, not daring to breathe, trying not to even think. There was a long and terrible silence. Then the Black Dalek turned and glided out of sight.

5

CONDEMNED TO DEATH!

With an air of grim satisfaction the guerillas surveyed their prisoners.

Jo stood motionless, still held by Boaz, who had grabbed her in the hall. The Doctor leaned his shoulders against the mantelpiece and looked round the room. He appeared utterly calm and relaxed, yet Jo could see that his eyes were bright and alert, his long thin body poised for instant action.

The Doctor nodded towards Boaz and said mildly, 'I think you might let the young lady go. She's scarcely likely to harm you.'

Boaz suddenly felt rather foolish holding his gun to the head of such a very small girl. He let her go. She gave him an indignant glare and walked across to the Doctor.

Ignoring Jo completely, Anat walked towards the Doctor, gun in hand. She looked up into his face. 'So you're the man. Outwardly so innocent looking, yet capable of such terrible crimes. Who would ever know?'

The Doctor gave her a puzzled look. 'I'm sorry, young lady, but I haven't the faintest idea what you're talking about.'

Anat snapped: 'Silence! You have done enough talking. It is time for your execution.'

Jo looked at the girl appalled. Why would anyone want to execute the Doctor? She felt the girl was working herself up into a kind of frenzy – as though she couldn't quite face the idea of killing in cold blood.

The same thought had occurred to the Doctor. The girl wasn't a natural killer, but she had it within her to shoot him down in certain circumstances. In a deliberate attempt to lower the emotional temperature he said, 'Execution? Don't I even get a trial?'

Anat said, 'We have our orders.'

'No doubt. But whose orders?'

'That does not concern you.' Anat stepped back. 'Boaz, Shura!'

All three guerillas trained their guns on the Doctor. Desperately, Jo threw herself in front of him. 'Please, leave him alone. He's never done anyone any harm.'

Gently, the Doctor took Jo by the shoulders and moved her out of danger. Then quite undisturbed by the three gun muzzles pointed at him he said, 'Young lady, may I say one thing?'

'A last-minute speech of repentance?' said Anat contemptuously.

'Not exactly. You see, I rather think you're making one terrible mistake.'

'And that is?'

'A simple question of identity. You think I'm Sir Reginald Styles, I imagine?'

'Of course you're Styles.'

'Ah, but that's the mistake you see. I'm not Styles at all.'

Anat looked at him scornfully. 'Very feeble, Sir Reginald. Is that the best you can do? You answer Styles' description. You're in his house.' She indicated the tray. 'You drink his wine and eat his food. But you're not Styles.'

Once again the three guerillas raised their guns. Jo was frozen with horror. She remembered the dummy she had made, the way it had shimmered and vanished. She tried to rush forward again, but Boaz caught her and threw her into an armchair, holding her down with his free hand.

'I admit that it does all sound a little implausible,' said the Doctor calmly, 'but perhaps you'd care to look at the newspaper on that table.'

Anat moved to the table and picked up the newspaper. It was last night's evening paper. The headline read 'STYLES FLIES TO PEKING IN TALKS CRISIS'. 'There's even a picture of him,' said the Doctor cheerfully. 'As you can see we're not really very alike.'

Worried, Anat looked at the headline, the picture of Styles and then back at the Doctor. 'If you're not Styles – why are you here?'

'Believe it or not I was waiting for you.'

Boaz, who had been listening with increasing impatience, raised his gun. 'We're wasting time, Anat. Here, I'll do it.'

Anat knocked the gun aside with surprising force. 'I command this mission. We are soldiers, not murderers. Now get outside, I want you to keep guard.'

For a moment Boaz didn't move. Then he nodded and moved to the door.

Anat turned back to the Doctor. 'Now then, suppose you answer my question sensibly. How could you be waiting for me? You couldn't have known we were coming.'

'Oh but I did. You tried to kill Styles once. It was logical to assume you'd try again.'

'And you deliberately took his place? Why?'

'Because I wanted to talk to you. To discover *why* you want to kill Styles. To find out where you came from, and equally important – when.'

Anat looked up sharply. That last remark showed familiarity with the idea of time travel. Suddenly Boaz burst into the room. 'Soldiers! Coming up the path.'

Anat said, 'We must hide. Bring them!' and she pointed to the Doctor and Jo.

Quickly the guerillas hustled their captives out into the hall. The crunch of army boots could be heard coming up the path. Anat looked round. There was a big, wooden door beneath the staircase and a flight of steps leading downwards. 'Down there,' she ordered.

Pushed by the three guerillas, Jo and the Doctor stumbled downwards into the darkness. They heard Anat hiss, 'You are both covered by our guns. One sound and you will be dead.' The little group huddled silently in the darkness.

Sergeant Benton and his patrol looked round the empty hallway. He called, 'Doctor! Jo! Where are you?' There was no reply.

Benton said to the soldiers: 'Take a look in the other rooms.' The soldiers clattered off, scattering through the house.

Benton spotted the door under the stairs and pushed it open. He found a light switch and pressed it. A single grimy bulb illuminated a flight of wooden steps leading down to a whitewashed cellar. Row upon row of wine racks stretched away into the darkness. Benton yelled: 'Anyone down there?' There was no answer.

Only a matter of inches away from him a silent group crouched behind the massive cellar door. Jo and the Doctor could feel the cold metal of guns pressing against their foreheads. Benton paused uneasily ... something didn't feel right ... Then he heard Captain Yates calling him. He turned out the light and closed the cellar door.

Yates was standing in the hallway, his face grave. 'Number two patrol failed to report in, Sergeant Benton. They seem to have vanished.'

Benton said, 'So has the Doctor, sir. And Miss Grant. Study window's smashed open, and there seems to have been a struggle. You reckon they've been kidnapped?'

The soldiers came back into the hall. One of them said, 'We've checked every room, Sarge. Whole place is empty.'

Yates looked at his watch. 'It'll be light before long. We'll make a full-scale search of the ground and check with all the other patrols. Someone must have seen something.' He turned and led the way out of the house.

When the noise of the soldiers' departure had faded away, Anat pressed the light switch again. She looked down the steps into the cellar and said, 'This will do for the moment. Tie them up and gag them!'

Boaz and Shura shoved the Doctor and Jo down the steps. Anat went out into the hall, back into the study and peered cautiously out of the window. Dawn was very near now. There were already pale streaks of light in the east. Dimly, Anat could see the woods and lawns of Austerly Park. She gazed at the peaceful landscape with a kind of wonder. Then she looked around the study; for the first time she realised that she had actually journeyed into the past. The comfort and luxury of old houses, well-furnished rooms such as this, had long been things of the past when Anat was born. She reached out and touched the softness of the velvet curtains.

The entrance of Boaz and Shura recalled her to the realities of her mission. They were not here to enjoy Earth's past, but to change its future.

Boaz said, 'They'll be no trouble for a while.' He turned to Anat with a hint of challenge in his voice. 'Well, what happens now?'

'I'm going to ask for fresh orders. The whole situation has changed.' She produced the little sub-temporal voice transmitter from her tunic and spoke into it. '*Mission intercept to base ... mission intercept to base ...*' There came only a crackling. Anat shook her head, 'It's no good. There's some kind of disturbance in the Time Vortex.'

Shura said, 'Why don't I go back to the tunnel, Anat? The big booster transmitter's there. That'll get through.'

Anat thought for a moment. 'All right. Tell them what's happened. Ask them for a prediction on Styles. They may be able to look up the date of his return here. Now hurry, it'll be light soon.'

Shura slipped out of the French windows and faded away into the darkness.

Anat sank into a chair, realising for the first time how tired she was. Boaz looked down at her and said, 'Surely it's obvious what we should do?'

'Is it?'

'We're *here* now. Actually in Styles' house. We wait till he returns and then kill him.'

Anat looked at him wearily. 'And suppose Styles *doesn't* return? How long do you think we can stay here undetected? What about those two down in the cellar?'

'They might come in useful as hostages.'

'And if they don't? If they become a danger to us?'

Boaz shrugged. 'Then we kill them.'

Down in the cellar the Doctor was wiggling his neck and chin in the most amazing manner. With a last desperate twist, he managed to free the gag from his mouth and chin. 'Ah, that's better,' he exclaimed with a sigh of relief.

'Mmmmm,' said Jo indignantly. 'Mmm mmmm mmmmm mm?'

The Doctor regarded her thoughtfully. 'I'm not at all sure I shouldn't leave you like that. It's very peaceful.'

There came a fresh outburst of indignant 'mmm's from Jo, and the Doctor rolled over to her. After a bit more effort he managed to pull her gag away with his teeth.

Immediately Jo burst out, 'Doctor! Who are these people? Why do they want to kill Styles? Where do they come from?'

The Doctor said, 'One thing at a time, Jo. And it's not where, but *when*. In terms of technological progress, I'd say they're about two hundred years ahead of your time.'

'The twenty-second century?' said Jo.

'Visiting the twentieth,' said the Doctor thoughtfully, 'on a special mission through time to find a certain politician and kill him. But why?'

'You're the one with the answers, Doctor.'

'Well, for a start, they're not criminals.'

'Oh aren't they?' said Jo indignantly. 'They were going to murder you, remember.'

'The word they used was "execute". They're political fanatics. I think they've come here to try and change history. And that's a very fanatical idea.'

The Doctor was quiet for a moment, then he said, 'Let me have a go at getting your ropes off, Jo. At least it'll help to pass the time.'

The Controller stood watching as Dalek scientists supervised the installation of a massive and complex piece of equipment in the Temporal Scanning Room. He turned and spoke to the Black Dalek at his side. 'We are maintaining a constant watch upon the Time Vortex. If we detect a transmission that continues long enough and strong enough, we shall certainly be able to trace it to its source.'

The Black Dalek intoned, 'All enemies of the Daleks must be tracked down and destroyed.'

The Controller said, 'This new equipment ... I am not quite clear as to its purpose.'

'Since you are unable to capture the criminals unaided, the science of the Daleks will help you. This is the Magnetron. If the time transmitter that was traced is used again, anyone so doing will be diverted in the Space Time Vortex and materialise here.'

'But only if that particular machine is used?'

'It is necessary to set the Magnetron to the frequency of a particular transmitter.' The Black Dalek's answer sounded almost sulky.

The Controller wasn't very impressed. If one particular time machine was used they *might* be able to capture the person using it. Since the resistance fighters knew that all transmissions risked being traced, it was highly unlikely that the machine would be used again. But the Controller knew better than to express his doubts. Humbly he bowed his head.

The Black Dalek said, 'It is likely that the criminals will have returned to the spatial co-ordinates where the first criminal was located. You will despatch another security patrol to that place and time zone.'

The Controller looked up sharply.

'With respect, is that wise?' he asked. 'If they are seen ...'

The Dalek rounded on him fiercely, its voice rising to a pitch almost of hysteria: 'Do not dispute with the Daleks! The function of the human is to obey!'

Again the Controller bowed his head, and followed the Black Dalek from the room. The Daleks were becoming frightened, he thought. Fear could have only one result – to make them even more ruthless than before. And that meant harshness and oppression for Earth. As he followed the Black Dalek along the endless corridors of Central Control his mind was busy.

What were the resistance guerillas up to in the twentieth century time zone? What did they hope to achieve that the Daleks were so desperate to prevent? The Controller entered his office and gave the orders that would despatch a patrol of Ogrons back to the railway tunnel where the first guerilla had been found.

It took Shura a long time to reach the tunnel. He was helped by the fact that he was alone instead of one of a group of three. But it was beginning to get light now, and the grounds were alive with searching UNIT troops.

For a long time Shura hid in a tree near the outer wall. When at last the patrols had finished searching that particular area he dropped down from his tree and began to scale the wall. At the last moment he was spotted. He heard a shout of alarm as he dropped down on the other side of the wall and sprinted for the tunnel. He guessed the soldiers would follow him.

Once inside he paused to get used to the darkness. He fumbled his way along to the hidden cavity where he had stowed their equipment. Moving aside the two heavy Dalekenium bombs, he fished out the big transmitter, and started to use it. 'Mission intercept to base ... mission intercept to base ...'

But even the powerful main transmitter picked up only crackling and static. There was obviously some kind of massive disturbance in the Space Time Vortex, thought Shura. Maybe some new invention of the Daleks. Their time travel technology was constantly improving.

He was about to try again when a massive booted foot stamped down on the transmitter, smashing it beyond repair. Shura looked up to see an Ogron grinning savagely down at him. The Ogron hauled him to his feet, and smashed him against the tunnel wall. His gun was ripped from his holster, before he could use it.

Shura was young and strong, and he fought desperately. But like any human being he was helpless against an Ogron's strength. The Ogron gripped him in a savage bear hug, then hurled him to the ground. As he tried to rise a booted foot smashed him savagely in the ribs. He rolled away desperately as the Ogron kicked again.

Shura had one advantage in the unequal struggle. He guessed that the Ogron didn't want to kill him. Or rather it wanted to, but had been ordered instead to take him alive. The beating-up was merely a way of relieving its frustrations at being deprived of the pleasure of destroying him. Shura rolled towards the cavity and groped inside. Next to the bombs was a spare disintegrator pistol. As the Ogron reached for him again Shura rolled and came up with the gun in his hands. He fired, and the Ogron was blasted into nothingness.

Shura sank down against the side of the tunnel wall, gasping for breath. He took stock of his injuries: several ribs were broken for sure, and one arm. There must be other Ogrons about, he thought muzzily. He wouldn't survive long if they found him. There was only one possible hiding-place.

Scrabbling aside the rubble with his good hand, Shura enlarged the cavity they had used as a cache. He dug out a space big enough to lie in, pulled the ruined transmitter and the gun in after him, and then covered the supplies and himself with rubble.

Minutes later other Ogrons came lumbering along the tunnel. Shura heard shouts, and then shots. He heard the Ogrons muttering briefly in low guttural voices. Then there was the familiar hum of a time transmitter; Shura guessed that the Ogrons had been spotted by the UNIT troops, and were returning to their own time zone. Soon he heard more human shouts, and the sound of army boots.

Shura should have been found by the army patrol. But the UNIT troops had already had one experience of chasing Ogrons into the tunnel and finding it empty. Perhaps, too, they weren't too keen to linger long in the tunnel, just in case those gorilla things *hadn't* all gone. In any case, the soldiers rushed in quickly one end and out the other.

Shura heard one of them call: 'No good, Corp, they've faded away again.' That shout was the last thing Shura heard for quite a while.

Battered and exhausted, suffering not only from his wounds but from the strain of the last few hours, he felt himself drift into a state of unconsciousness. Soon, curled up in his nest of rubble, bombs and pistol clasped to his chest, Shura was fast asleep.

Anat and Boaz waited for Shura's return with increasing unease. Both jumped when the telephone began to ring. Although neither had seen or used a telephone before, they knew well enough what it was.

They stared at it helplessly, wishing it would stop. But the ringing went on and on. Anat reached a hand out towards the 'phone. Boaz snapped: 'Leave it!'

'They'll be suspicious if no one answers,' said Anat desperately. She came to a decision. 'Those people in the cellar. Bring them up.'

Boaz dashed from the room, and Anat waited for what seemed an agonisingly long time. Still the telephone kept up its unending ringing and ringing.

Boaz came back into the room, herding Jo and the Doctor before him with his pistol. Anat said, 'Untie him.' Boaz cut the ropes from the Doctor's wrists and pushed him towards the 'phone. 'Answer it,' said Anat. 'Tell them everything's all right.' Boaz held the gun to the Doctor's head.

Slowly, the Doctor picked up the receiver and said 'Hello?'

'Sorry to bother you so early,' said the Brigadier. 'Been up all night with this conference crisis.'

'That's all right, Brigadier. As a matter of fact, I've been up all night myself.'

'Ghost-hunting, eh?' The Brigadier chuckled. 'Anything happen?'

Anat moved her head close to the Doctor's, so that she too could hear what the Brigadier was saying.

'Nothing happening,' responded the Doctor calmly. 'Everything's very quiet here.'

'Jolly good. Thing is I had some kind of garbled report from Yates and Benton that you'd vanished. They looked in the house and couldn't find you. Said the place was deserted.'

The Doctor said, 'Did they? Oh yes, must have been when we were down in the cellar. Did I tell you old Styles has a fascinating collection of wines?'

'Now listen, Doctor, you're absolutely sure everything's all right at that house? Because Styles is coming back there tomorrow night. He is taking the main delegates to his house for an informal preliminary conference.'

Boaz and Anat exchanged exultant glances. Before anyone could stop him the Doctor said, 'I'm not sure that's wise, Brigadier.'

Boaz, thrust the gun closer to the Doctor's head. Anat gave him a look of warning.

'Oh really? Why not?'

The Doctor didn't reply.

After a moment the Brigadier said, 'You're sure everything *is* all right, Doctor?'

Speaking clearly and distinctly the Doctor said, 'I assure you, Brigadier, there's nothing to worry about. Tell Styles that. Tell the Prime Minister. And, Brigadier, be particularly sure to tell it to the Marines.' Hoping that his knowledge of twentieth century slang was accurate, the Doctor put down the 'phone.

At UNIT H.Q., the Brigadier turned to Yates and Benton. 'You were right. The Doctor's in trouble. I think he's been made prisoner. We're going back to Austerly House right away.' He paused at the door. 'Oh, and send a message to the patrols. They're to keep the house surrounded, but they're not to go inside.'

Anat and Boaz were jubilant. 'He's coming here!' exclaimed Anat. 'Sir Reginald Styles is coming here! We can carry out our mission.'

'Of course,' said Boaz, 'the conference is here tomorrow night. Our dates were right after all.'

'You certainly showed a remarkable ability to predict the future,' agreed the Doctor, 'though I suppose it's not so remarkable really, since our future is your past.' Boaz and Anat were scarcely listening to him.

Nor was Jo. Before the guerillas had brought them up from the cellar, she and the Doctor had practically succeeded in getting the ropes off her wrists. Although the Doctor's wrists had been tied he had still been able to use his fingers, and by standing back to back he had been able to untie most of the knot. Now Jo was finishing the job herself. Suddenly, she was free. And no one seemed to be worrying about her.

The Doctor made a second attempt to talk to Anat. 'Isn't it about time you told me what you think you're up to? Why do you imagine that killing Styles will make any difference to the future you come from?'

Anat said, 'It will make every difference.'

'Styles isn't a bad man ... At the moment he's doing all he can to stop a world war ...'

'You believe that?' said Anat. 'You really believe that?'

'Most certainly.'

'Then I've got some rather startling news for you. Your friend Styles isn't trying to stop a war – he's going to start one ... unless we can stop him.'

Jo dashed across the room and picked up the time machine. She raised it threateningly above her head.

'Right,' she snapped, 'you can both drop your guns.'

Anat and Boaz made no move to obey her.

'If you don't do as I say,' said Jo determinedly, 'I'm going to smash this machine to bits. You'll be stranded here for ever. You'll never get back to your own time.'

The Doctor said, 'Jo, you've got it all wrong ... Put that machine down before it starts working again.'

Jo ignored him. Looking at Boaz and Anat she said, 'I warn you, I mean it.'

Anat sounded almost sorry for her. 'My dear child, we don't need that machine. We have others of our own.'

Jo looked at her uncertainly. 'You're just bluffing.'

'I assure you I'm not,' said Anat. 'Now put that machine down and stop being silly.'

To Jo's amazement the Doctor said, 'Jo, do as she says.'

Confused, Jo gripped the machine tighter. Unconsciously her fingers tightened over the control knobs. Suddenly the machine hummed into life. A shimmering effect filled the air around Jo's body. She felt herself in the grip of some terrible force, drawing her away … and before the Doctor's horrified gaze, Jo, still clutching the time machine, just faded and vanished away …

6

PRISONER OF THE DALEKS

Jo Grant was twisting and turning in a sort of strange misty nothingness. Soon she lost all sense of up or down. Over and over, round and round she went. All the time she could feel the tug of powerful forces that seemed to be pulling her apart. She felt sick and dizzy and terrified. Just when she could bear it no longer all the different pulls seemed to combine. She felt herself being drawn steadily in one particular direction.

Gradually it seemed that she was becoming more solid, more real ... the misty nothingness was fading away ... she was in a real place again ... she could feel a solid floor beneath her. It was cold and metallic.

Cautiously, Jo opened her eyes and looked around her. She was in some kind of control room, surrounded with gleaming alien machinery. Towering above her was a group of huge, ape-like creatures with savage cruel faces. They carried guns, big pistols like those used by the guerillas. The guns were all pointing straight at her.

The Doctor called: 'Jo! Jo!' but it was too late. She had completely vanished. He turned to Anat. 'What's happened to her?'

Anat's look was almost sympathetic. 'The machine was faulty. She's probably been disintegrated, dispersed for ever into the Time Vortex.'

Boaz said, 'That's if she was lucky.'

'And if she wasn't?' said the Doctor grimly.

Again the look of sympathy from Anat. 'If the machine was still working, it's possible that she'll be re-embodied in our time.'

'Believe me,' Boaz added ominously, 'she'd be better off dead.' He indicated the Doctor with his pistol. 'What do we do with him?'

'Put him back in the cellar. Tie him up again.'

While Anat covered him with her gun, Boaz put the ropes back on the Doctor's wrists. The knots were cruelly tight. No chance of undoing them again, thought the Doctor.

When the binding was finished Boaz stepped back. 'All right, get moving.' The Doctor ignored him, and looked at Anat. 'There's nothing you can do to save my friend? Nothing at all?'

Anat shook her head. 'Believe me, I'm sorry. But she brought it on herself. We didn't want to harm anyone unnecessarily.'

Boaz came up to the Doctor and jabbed the gun in his ribs. 'Now listen, you! Anat may be soft-hearted but I'm not. As far as I'm concerned you're just a nuisance, and I'd as soon kill you. Now get back to that cellar.'

It was obvious that Boaz meant what he said. The Doctor went out of the study and into the hall. Boaz opened the cellar door, and shoved him down the steps.

The Doctor lay in darkness on the cold stone floor. For a moment a wave of despair washed over him. At the moment it seemed that the guerillas might well succeed in their plan to kill Styles and start another war, though why should they want to do that? The Doctor sighed. And now Jo was gone, perhaps dead, perhaps stranded in some alien and terrifying future.

It wasn't in the Doctor's nature to give up for very long. Surely the Brigadier had understood his message? Anyway, the one thing you could always do was try. Patiently the Doctor began to work on the ropes that bound his wrists.

Guarded by two of the ape-like monsters, Jo Grant was being marched along a series of endless, gleaming metal corridors. From time to time they passed shabbily dressed men and women bustling about on mysterious tasks. The place was like an anthill, thought Jo. Everyone seemed cowed and terrified, standing aside rapidly, and showing no curiosity at the sight of Jo.

They reached a sort of office, and Jo was thrust into a chair. Behind a desk sat a thin, dark man with a haggard, haunted face.

The two monsters took up a position behind Jo's chair. The man waved them away. 'You can go now.' For a moment they didn't move. The man said again, 'Go!' They turned and lumbered from the room.

The man smiled at Jo. 'They're only servants, you see. And so stupid! Nothing to be frightened of really.'

Jo said, 'What are they?'

'A kind of higher anthropoid. They used to live in scattered communities on one of the outer planets. They make useful servants.'

For a moment Jo had a ridiculous picture of one of the hulking gorilla-things coming in with a tea-tray. She giggled. 'Servants? What do they do?' she asked.

'We use them as a kind of policeman, or rather to help the police.'

'I see,' said Jo brightly. 'You mean they're sort of police dogs?'

'Exactly. They are very faithful, very loyal.'

Jo was beginning to feel less frightened. The explanation did make the creatures less terrifying. After all people had used guard dogs for ages, and it was the same thing really. And the man seemed to be friendly enough.

'Look, I know it sounds silly, but could you please tell me where I am?' she said.

'You're at Central Control in Sector One. In fact, I'm the Controller of the Region.' There was pride in the man's voice. His rank was obviously important to him.

'Yes, but where? What planet?'

The man seemed puzzled. 'Why, Earth of course. Where else?'

'But it's all so different,' said Jo helplessly.

'That's because you've travelled in time. You see, this is the twenty-second century.'

For a moment Jo's head reeled. The Controller said reassuringly, 'Don't worry. We can get you back to your own time. Is that what you want?'

Jo nodded eagerly. 'Yes, of course.'

The Controller sat back in his chair, 'First I'd like you to tell me everything that happened to you before you found yourself here.'

The Controller sat back and listened as the girl told her story. He congratulated himself on his handling of the situation. It had been obvious from the start that the girl was no guerilla. But her possession of the time machine meant she must have been in contact with them, probably quite innocently. And her story was bearing out his theory.

When Jo had finished, the Controller sat back for a moment, trying to digest the flood of new information. He wished his knowledge of twentieth century history were better. What was so important about this man Styles?

Jo said, 'The really worrying thing is, the Doctor is still their prisoner.'

Her heart sank as the Controller said solemnly, 'I'm afraid your friend is in very great danger.'

'But why? They know now he's the wrong man.'

The Controller's face was grave. 'You don't know these people as I do, Miss Grant. I've spent years trying to track them down. They've been responsible for the most terrible crimes. And if anyone gets in their way, they're totally without mercy.'

Jo remembered the burning fanatical eyes of the three guerillas. She shuddered. 'I can well believe it,' she said.

The Controller leaned forward across his desk. 'Now, we may be able to mount a rescue operation to save this friend of yours. But we'll need your help.'

'Yes, of course. Anything at all.'

'We know where these criminals are holding your friend. We have maps that show where Austerly House once stood. But equally important is the "when". Can you remember exactly what time they arrived?'

Jo nodded. 'Just after midnight.'

'Yes, but the date, the month, the year?'

Puzzled, Jo told him. The Controller gave a sigh of relief. 'Excellent. I'm sure we'll be able to help your friend. Now I must ask you to excuse me. I must start arranging the rescue expedition at once.'

'And you'll take me with you, get me back to my own time?'

The Controller came from behind his desk and took Jo's arm.

'Naturally, naturally. Now I'm sure you're tired, hungry and thirsty. We have special refreshment suites for honoured guests. Let me take you to one ...'

He paused at the door. 'When the criminals transferred to your time, did they arrive near the house itself?'

'I doubt it,' said Jo. 'The UNIT guards would have seen them.'

'Have you any idea where they did arrive? Some kind of hideout in your time, perhaps?'

Jo frowned. 'There's an old railway tunnel near the house. That's where we found the wounded man, and the time machine. They could have hidden in there. It's a very long tunnel, and completely abandoned.'

'A tunnel?' said the Controller. 'Excellent. Now come with me. I'll let you know as soon as there's any news.'

A few minutes later, the Controller stood once more before the Black Dalek.

'I have won her trust completely. Thanks to me we now have the information we need.'

The Controller knew that there would be no word of praise for his success. Daleks spoke only to condemn failure. Their servants were expected to succeed, or pay the penalty.

The Black Dalek said, 'The criminals are using the tunnel as a transfer point. We will prepare an ambush in the twentieth century time zone.'

'Security forces are standing by,' the Controller said quickly. 'If you wish I will take charge of things myself.'

The Black Dalek swivelled its eye-stalk towards him. With a tinge of contempt in the guttural voice it said, 'This expedition is too important to be entrusted to a human. Some of us will accompany you. *The expedition will be led by the Daleks!'*

7

ATTACK OF THE OGRONS

Boaz looked out cautiously from behind the curtains. 'There are patrols all round the house, but they don't seem to be coming near it.'

Anat said, 'Well, why should they? They think the place is empty, apart from the Doctor and that poor girl.'

Boaz turned away from the window. 'They're bound to send people here before Styles comes back. I know from the history books – such a man will have many servants.'

Anat shrugged. 'It's a big house. We'll find somewhere to hide. In the attics perhaps, or down in the cellar with our prisoner.'

'Yes, of course,' said Boaz. 'Or we could take the servants hostage. We only need to survive until Styles arrives. Once we kill him, we either escape or die. Doesn't really matter which, does it?'

Anat looked at him with concern. She wondered how much longer Boaz would be able to stand the waiting. He could only bear it by screwing himself up to a pitch of fanatic dedication. Her own nature was calmer, more determined. She bitterly regretted the deaths they had caused – the girl, the UNIT patrol ... But she accepted them as a necessary part of the price that must be paid if they were to succeed. In the same way she accepted that her own death might well be a part of that price.

Suddenly there came a familiar sound. They rushed to the window.

Ogrons were materialising outside the house. Boaz raised his gun and blasted the first one before it had time to get its bearings. Anat joined him at the window.

For a while it was a kind of grim target practice. An Ogron would materialise, look round, and be instantly shot down, vanishing as fast as it had arrived. But they couldn't get rid of them all. Others were materialising out of their line of fire and coming to join the attack.

The air was full of the savage buzzing of the disintegrator guns. Soon the rattle of machine-gun fire was added to the din.

Boaz said exultantly to Anat, 'It's the soldiers!'

UNIT patrols began to arrive, opening fire on the Ogrons. The soldiers tried to form a protective line in front of the house.

The UNIT soldiers fought at some disadvantage. The weapons of the Ogrons were far more effective. It took a full clip of machine-gun bullets to kill an Ogron. Anything less and the monsters just went on fighting, roaring with rage and pain, but hardly even slowed down. But one direct hit from an Ogron pistol could blast a UNIT soldier into extinction.

Boaz and Anat, shooting from the now shattered French windows, had disintegrator guns of their own, and the atomic power packs built into the handles were practically everlasting. But they were only two, and the Ogrons outnumbered them badly.

In the cellar the Doctor heard the sound of battle, and speeded up his attempt to escape. By flailing his legs about he had managed to upset a whole rack of wine bottles. They had fallen to the floor in a crash of broken glass. Now the Doctor was rubbing his bonds against the jagged end of a broken bottle.

A UNIT soldier blazed away at the nearest Ogron. Roaring, the creature sank slowly to the ground. The soldier reached for a new clip of bullets, but before he could fit it, another Ogron blasted him into oblivion at close range. The Ogron swung its gun onto another soldier, but Anat disintegrated it with a shot from the window.

Boaz yelled: 'The soldiers can't hold them!'

Anat saw that it was true. The UNIT forces had lost too many men. Before long the Ogrons would break through the protective cordon and get into the house. Anat saw that defeat was just a matter of time. 'We'll have to get back to the tunnel,' she shouted. She took a final shot at an Ogron and ran from the room.

Boaz waited a moment longer, firing from the window to cover her retreat. Then he too turned to go, only to find himself facing a very angry Doctor, covered with dust and cobwebs and bleeding from several cuts on the wrists.

Before Boaz could even speak the Doctor was upon him. A long arm reached out, and Boaz went hurtling across the room, his gun skidding across the floor before he had a chance to use it.

As the Doctor moved to pick up the gun a voice said: 'Keep still.' He felt the cold metal of a gun barrel on his neck. Anat was in the doorway. She said to Boaz, 'Out – get to the tunnel!' and he rushed from the room. Anat gave the Doctor a sudden shove, and turned to run after Boaz. As she did so there was a shattering crash and an Ogron burst through the French windows, smashing the few remaining panes of glass in the process.

At once the Doctor grappled with the Ogron, trying to get hold of its gun. The creature's strength was enormous, and the Doctor strove in vain to wrench the gun from the hairy paw; at the same time he fought to restrain the creature's other hand from grasping his throat. The Doctor knew he could never match the immense strength of his opponent. Instead he applied the judo principle of turning an enemy's strength against him. Giving way before the Ogron's rush, the Doctor rolled onto his back, shoved his feet into the Ogron's stomach and sent it flying. The top of the Ogron's head thudded into the wall. Plaster dropped from around holes in its surface, and the creature slid to the ground, stunned. The Doctor tried again to get its gun, but the weapon was still tightly gripped in the hairy paw. He remembered Boaz's dropped gun, scooped it up, and ran after the two guerillas.

The Doctor ran along the passages of the old house, through the kitchens and into a paved courtyard. He ran through a back gate and found himself on the gravel path at the rear of the house.

Quickly working out his bearings he decided to make for the tunnel. Something told him that his only hope of rescuing Jo was to stay with the guerillas. Two Ogrons ran round the corner of the house, cutting off his retreat. The Doctor raised Boaz's gun and fired. There was a buzz, and the Ogron exploded into nothingness. He turned the gun on the second Ogron, and fired again, but nothing happened. The thing was jammed, or empty. The Doctor hurled the gun at the monster's head, but missed. The Ogron grinned savagely, showing its yellow fangs. Slowly it raised its gun, enjoying the moment ...

The Doctor braced himself, wondering what it would feel like to be disintegrated. There was the noise of an engine, and the Ogron turned to face a new enemy.

The Brigadier came roaring round the corner in a jeep. Before the Ogron could fire, the Brigadier drove straight into it, sending it flying through the air, then he slammed on the brakes.

As soon as the Ogron hit the ground it was up again, charging the jeep. Coolly, the Brigadier snatched up his Sterling from the seat beside him and emptied the full clip of bullets into the Ogron. Rocked back on its heels by the impact, the Ogron staggered, then slumped to the ground.

The Brigadier jumped down from the jeep, stepped over the Ogron's body, and walked up to the Doctor's grimy and bleeding figure.

'Are you all right, Doctor? What the blazes have you been up to?'

The Doctor gave him a weary grin. 'I'm fine – thanks to your most timely intervention.'

'Then perhaps you'll explain what's going on,' said the Brigadier sternly. 'What are these creatures?'

'I'll try to explain later,' said the Doctor. 'At the moment I'm in a bit of a hurry.' To the Brigadier's indignation, the Doctor jumped into the jeep and shot off.

'Come back, Doctor! Come back at once!' the Brigadier yelled. But the only response was a cheery wave as the jeep disappeared out of sight.

The Doctor sped through the grounds of Austerly House, and along the road that led to the tunnel. As he came in sight of it he saw Anat and Boaz running across the fields towards the tunnel mouth.

The Doctor took the jeep as close to the tunnel as he could. Then, abandoning it, he ran across the fields after the two guerillas.

Once inside the tunnel, he was in almost total darkness. He groped his way forward, cautiously. Ahead he could hear echoing footsteps. The footsteps stopped. A tiny point of light glowed in the distance. The Doctor made his way towards it.

A strange humming noise came from behind him and he turned round. In the darkness a kind of glowing circle had appeared from which was emitted an eerie light. Within the circle a shape began to form. It was a shape the Doctor knew only too well, that of his oldest and bitterest enemy. A Dalek was materialising in the tunnel!

In a moment the process was completed. Still glowing with the same sinister light the Dalek swivelled round its eye-stalk as if getting its bearings. The Doctor froze, flattening himself against the tunnel wall. Behind the Dalek, Ogrons were beginning to materialise.

As if it sensed the Doctor's presence the Dalek spoke. The familiar grating, metallic voice said, 'Stop! You are all enemies of the Daleks. Surrender, or you will be exterminated!' The Dalek began to trundle down the tunnel towards him.

8

A FUGITIVE IN THE FUTURE

Again the Dalek voice echoed through the darkness of the tunnel, 'You are all enemies of the Daleks. Surrender at once or you will be exterminated!'

The Doctor realised the Dalek hadn't seen him at all. It was addressing the guerillas. Somehow it must know they were in the tunnel. He turned and ran on at full pelt through the darkness, towards the tiny glowing point of light.

As he got nearer he saw that the light came from a little torch-like device, held by Anat. She and Boaz stood side-by-side, hands joined. Each held a pulsating black box in the other hand. The two time-machines were pulsating rhythmically and already, the shimmering effect was beginning to build up.

As the Doctor ran up to them Anat screamed, 'Get back!'

Almost out of breath, the Doctor gasped, 'There's a Dalek ... more Ogrons ... in the tunnel behind me!'

The two guerillas turned. They saw the Dalek and the Ogrons bearing down on them. The Doctor pointed the other way. From that direction another Dalek, with Ogrons in support, was approaching. 'You're trapped,' said the Doctor.

The shimmering effect of the time field grew even stronger. Anat yelled, 'Get back! If you're caught up in the time field you'll be taken with us!'

The Doctor had no intention of being left behind ... not with Daleks and Ogrons arriving from both sides. Instead of arguing, he wrapped his arms around Boaz in a determined bear-hug. The guerilla tried to break free, but the Doctor couldn't be budged. It became clear that wherever Boaz was going, the Doctor was going with him.

As their pursuers converged upon them, the little group shimmered and faded from sight. Like Jo Grant before him, the Doctor found himself twisting and twirling in the Time Vortex. Since he was used to time travel, he was much less frightened than Jo had been. He couldn't help thinking that time travel by this method was very different from time travel in the TARDIS. It was like comparing a trip in a luxury liner with going over Niagara Falls in a barrel.

Still holding grimly on to Boaz, the Doctor became aware that the Vortex was fading away. They were back in the real world. With a sudden jolt the Doctor found himself on firm ground. Letting go of Boaz, he looked round. They were still in a tunnel, but a very different one, more modern in design.

The two guerillas were checking equipment, and stowing away their time machines. Anat said, 'We warned you.'

The Doctor was looking around with interest. Only a single rail ran along this tunnel. They were in part of a monorail system. Probably built some time in the twenty-first century, and by now abandoned. Anat followed his glance. 'This may come as a shock to you,' she said gently, 'but you've travelled in time.'

The Doctor gave her a quizzical look. 'My dear young lady, I'm probably rather more familiar with time travel than you are.'

The guerillas started to move away. The Doctor said, 'Wait. Those Daleks we saw – where did they come from?'

Anat looked at him curiously. 'You know of the Daleks?'

'Indeed I do. You might say we're very old enemies. What are they doing on Earth in this time zone?'

Anat said flatly, 'They've ruled the Earth for almost two hundred years.'

'And if you knew about the Daleks you're a fool to have come here,' said Boaz.

'I came to find Jo Grant. As long as there's a chance that she's alive ...'

Boaz said, 'Come, Anat, it's dangerous to stay here.'

'Please,' said the Doctor, 'how do I set about finding her?'

Boaz said, 'That's *your* problem!' He made another attempt to pull Anat away.

She hesitated. 'We can't just leave him to fend for himself.'

'I can,' said Boaz. 'Now, are you coming or not?'

Hurriedly Anat whispered to the Doctor, 'If the Daleks have got her she'll be at Central Control. But don't try to rescue her, it'd be suicide.'

Suddenly Boaz yelled, 'Run, Anat!' More Ogrons and Daleks were rushing at them out of the darkness.

The guerillas turned and ran. The Doctor ran too. This new set of tunnels was a complete maze, with openings in every direction. Here and there the tunnel roof was broken away so that patches of daylight lit up the gloom. The Doctor took a wrong turn and ran almost straight into an Ogron patrol! He turned and ran back with Ogrons pounding close behind him. As he turned into the opening of yet another tunnel, he saw a patch of light gleaming above him. In the half-light he looked around and saw some kind of hand-rail. The Doctor leaped for it and found himself hanging on to a maintenance ladder bolted to the wall. He clung there while the Ogrons ran past below him. Then, deciding that up was as good a direction as any, he started climbing the ladder.

It led up to a rusty trap-door. The Doctor managed to get his shoulder under it, and shoved hard. Reluctantly, the trap-door creaked open. Cautiously, the Doctor poked his head out, and wriggled through the trap-door into daylight.

All around him was a scene of complete and utter desolation. Every inch of the countryside, as far as he could see, seemed to have been built up till not an inch was left, then methodically hammered down. A sea of rubble stretched before him. Here and there a wall or two was still standing.

The Doctor fished a tiny instrument from his pocket. It was a sort of miniaturised Geiger counter. He tested the rubble around him. The little instrument began a subdued clicking.

The instrument was registering minute traces of radioactivity. Atomic war had brought about this ruination. The radiation had faded as time went by.

The Doctor climbed a little hill of rubble and looked around him. In the distance a group of buildings stood out from the desolation. They were stark and ugly, made of rough concrete. They looked bleak, and functional, with nothing attractive or welcoming about them.

They looked – there was only one word for it – 'Daleky'. The Doctor sighed. Unattractive as the buildings were, they made a point to aim for. There must still be people left on Earth. Perhaps someone would help him. He began to pick his way through the rubble.

The Controller of Earth Sector One was talking for his very life. After the latest failure to capture the guerillas, he had been summoned to appear before the High Council of the Daleks, the supreme ruling body of the planet Earth.

He stood, isolated in a pool of light, in a long, bare metallic room. It was completely featureless except for the raised area at the end. Here the dreaded Black Dalek and its superior, the even more powerful Golden Dalek, stood, with other Daleks grouped around them.

Briefly, the Controller ended his report. 'Security guards combed the tunnels, both here and in the twentieth century time zone. Nothing and no one was found. Our forces had to leave the twentieth century zone because of increased opposition from the human soldiers.'

For a moment there was silence. Then the Golden Dalek said, 'You have failed the Daleks. You will be punished.'

The Controller knew that appeals for mercy would be useless. He decided to speak his mind. At least he could die with dignity. 'Am I responsible for this failure? Ogron security guards carried out the mission. And was it not led by the Daleks themselves?' There was a stunned silence. Not for more than a hundred years had any human dared question the authority of the Daleks. The Controller went on, 'The Ogrons are stupid and clumsy! They are useless for operations of this kind. As guards in the work camps, perhaps ... but definitely not for anything that calls for intelligence or initiative!'

There was a note of uncertainty in the voice of the Black Dalek. 'The Ogrons are loyal servants of the Daleks.'

'No doubt. But it takes humans to deal with humans. Now, if you would allow me to recruit *human* security guards ...' (The Daleks used humans mostly for manual labour and simple administration.)

The Black Dalek said, 'Humans are treacherous and unreliable.'

'Not all humans,' replied the Controller, a little amazed at his own daring. 'I have served you loyally all my life.'

The Golden Dalek spoke again, 'Do not dispute with the Daleks. Obey without question. The hunt for the enemies of the Daleks must be carried on unceasingly. All enemies of the Daleks will be exterminated.'

The Controller sighed. He hadn't really expected any concessions. He was being turned away with the usual propaganda. At least he was still alive.

The Black Dalek said, 'Is your report concluded?'

'Except for one thing. It seems likely that a human returned from the twentieth century time zone with the guerillas. According to the patrols it must be the man the girl spoke about. She called him "the Doctor".'

He turned to leave. The Black Dalek's voice rose almost to a shriek –

'Stop! Doc-tor? Did you say, Doc-tor?'

The Controller was astonished at the strength of the reaction. The word 'Doctor' was pronounced jarringly in two syllables, and he could almost feel the hate in the Dalek's voice.

Now the Golden Dalek joined in, pronouncing the Doctor's name with the same venomous intensity. 'The one known as the Doc-tor is not human. He is the supreme enemy of the Daleks. He must be found and exterminated.'

Now the other Daleks took up the chorus. As the Controller left, their voices rang in his ears. 'Exterminate him! EXTERMINATE HIM! EXTERMINATE HIM!' But there was something different about those voices. They held some quality the Controller had never heard before, and as he walked from the council hall he recognised it. The quality was *fear*. For the first time in the Controller's experience of them the Daleks were actually afraid.

The Doctor had been travelling for many hours across the ruined landscape. Progress was slow. There were no roads to speak of, and the Doctor avoided those he saw. He had to be constantly alert for Ogron patrols, and always be ready to shelter in a ruin or a ditch. Once he had lain for what seemed ages in the cellar of a wrecked house while a resting Ogron patrol sat almost on top of him, chomping food from their pouches and talking in low guttural voices. At last they had moved on and he had been able to go on his way.

Now he had reached the edge of the enormous building which he had seen shortly after emerging from the trap-door. A high stone wall ran round it, with savage spikes at the top. Although the Doctor didn't know it a resistance leader called Moni had climbed that wall a few nights before. Looking for an easier way in, the Doctor moved along the wall cautiously. He passed what looked like a kind of lamp-post. But on top of it was not a lamp, but a monitor-lens. The Doctor unwittingly activated it when he passed through its field of vision. It swung round to follow him as he moved by.

On a screen somewhere inside the building a little spot of light began to move, recording the Doctor's progress. A girl technician leaned forward and spoke into a microphone. '*Alert, alert, intruder detected by outer wall. Description corresponds to that of wanted man known as "the Doctor".*'

'Allow him to enter the area, and then surround him. He must be captured alive.'

The Controller himself gave that final order. He knew the Daleks would probably prefer the Doctor to be killed on sight. But he was anxious to meet the man who could actually produce fear in the Daleks. He wasn't sure exactly why he felt like this. He only knew that he had to meet and talk to the Doctor before he let the Daleks dispose of him.

The Doctor meanwhile had found a small door in the wall. He was busy picking the simple electronic lock with the aid of his sonic screwdriver. Soon he had it open, and had slipped inside. He found himself inside a bare concrete yard which gave onto a number of barn-like buildings. Automated trucks on rails rumbled into them. The trucks were filled with crushed rock, obviously some kind of mineral ore.

He slipped across the courtyard and peered inside one of the long, low buildings. An endless conveyor belt ran right across it. Ragged, thin workers were standing beside the belt, sorting through the mineral ore with their bare hands. Others were staggering from the trucks to the belt with rock-filled baskets, keeping the conveyor supplied. The sorted-out ore moved off in another set of trucks, the rejected rocks were carried away and dumped onto another belt which took them out of sight. Ogron guards with whips stood by the workers. There was also a human guard who seemed to be in overall charge.

The Doctor watched the whole process with horror and indignation. The minerals arrived, were sorted, and were carried away. The whole process went on endlessly, and could obviously have been carried out entirely by machines. Probably the Daleks found it simpler and cheaper to wear out human beings instead, the Doctor thought angrily.

A thin old man stumbled and dropped his basket. Instantly, the human guard's whip cracked across his shoulders. The Doctor was quite unable to stop himself. He leaped from his cover, and next second the guard found himself flying through the air. He landed with a thump inside one of the trucks. The workers at the conveyer belt stopped working in astonishment. The Ogrons drew their guns.

Then a voice called, 'No!' It was the human chief guard climbing shakily out of the truck. 'The orders were to take him alive. And you needn't be gentle about it!'

Two Ogrons closed in on the Doctor. He ducked under the grip of one, and sent it spinning into its fellow. Both Ogrons fell. The Doctor sprinted for the door. Beside it stood two more Ogrons. They fell on him savagely, and within minutes the Doctor was beaten into unconsciousness. The Ogrons dragged him away. The human chief guard turned to the workers. 'Get on with your work – unless you want some of the same.' Hastily, they went back to their tasks, the Ogrons standing over them with their whips at the ready.

Moni slipped across the rubble and down the flight of stairs. It was dangerous to risk a daylight meeting, but the situation was urgent. As far as he knew this hideout was still secure. If Anat and the others had escaped ...

He rapped out a complicated series of knocks on the door and to his relief the door was opened. Boaz was there, pale and weary. Beside him was Anat. Moni glanced round the cellar. 'Where's Shura?'

Anat said, 'We lost him. He went to contact H.Q., and never returned. They must have got him.'

Boaz said angrily, 'We were nearly caught getting back here ourselves.'

Moni listened silently while they told the story of the failure of their mission. He said, 'There's a girl being held prisoner at Central Control – she must be the one you're talking about. Can she tell them anything?'

Anat said, 'She knows we want to kill Styles. She can tell them that.'

Moni sighed wearily. Everything seemed to be going wrong. The mission had been a shambles from the start.

Anat asked, 'What about the man – the one who came back with us? Have they caught him yet?'

Moni shook his head. 'Not yet. But it's just a matter of time ...'

511

9

ESCAPE FROM THE OGRONS

Jo Grant pushed her plate away with a sigh of pleasure. 'No more please. I couldn't eat another thing.'

The Controller leaned forward with a wine bottle. 'A little more wine?'

'No, honestly, nothing. It was a terrific meal.'

Actually, thought Jo, it hadn't been all that hot … coarse bread, tough meat and a mish-mash of strange vegetables. And she didn't think the Doctor would have thought much of the wine.

'I'm glad you enjoyed it,' he said. 'Few people eat so luxuriously these days.'

Jo thought he had a strange idea of luxury. She smiled, and said nothing. 'Nowadays,' the Controller went on, 'we have to get most of our main food elements from pills and tablets.'

The Controller sat back and smiled at her. 'Do go on telling me about your friend, the Doctor.'

'I don't think I can tell you anything more,' said Jo frankly. 'We've covered just about everything.' And indeed they had. The Controller seemed fascinated by the Doctor, and had asked question after question about him.

'You really don't know what he was doing *before* he joined this UNIT organisation?' asked the Controller.

'No idea,' said Jo firmly. 'No one knows very much about the Doctor, he's a very mysterious character. Look,' she went on hurriedly, 'please don't think I'm ungrateful, but you did say something about rescuing the Doctor, and getting me back to my own time.'

The Controller said, 'It isn't easy, you know. Our scientists are working on the problem.' He paused. 'As for your friend the Doctor, well, there's something I haven't told you. There's reason to believe that he followed you to this time zone.'

Jo was overjoyed. 'That's marvellous! Do you know where he is?'

'I'm afraid not. He was travelling with the criminals. No doubt they kidnapped him. We're carrying out a search for him at this very moment.'

A girl entered the room, bowed to the Controller and handed him a note. He waved in dismissal and she scuttled away. He opened the note, looked up at Jo and smiled. 'Good news, Miss Grant. Your friend the Doctor has been found. I'm going to fetch him now.'

Jo jumped up. 'Can I come with you?'

He shook his head. 'That isn't advisable. But don't worry, I assure you he's safe and well.'

At that particular moment the Doctor was in a bare metal cell, feeling on the very contrary both unsafe and unwell. He was at the end of a long and gruelling interrogation. The purpose seemed to be to get him to admit that he was in some kind of resistance movement. The guard hoped to impress his masters by producing a confession by the time they arrived. But despite some brutal handling the Doctor wasn't co-operating.

Again the guard yelled, 'Tell us who you are!'

'You'd never believe me,' said the Doctor wearily.

'Name your contacts in the criminal resistance movement.'

'Haven't got any.'

'What are you doing here?'

'Looking for a girl called Jo Grant. How many more times?'

'As many as it takes to get the truth out of you. Shall I hand you over to our friends here? They don't get much fun.' The guard indicated the two Ogrons holding the Doctor down in his chair.

The hairy paws were gripping his shoulders with brutal force.

'Poor fellows … that's too bad, but I'm not in the mood for games.'

The cell door opened and a small plumpish man entered. He wore plain dark clothing, with a civilian, rather than military look.

'Any progress?' he enquired.

The guard said, 'He's not being very co-operative.'

'How unwise of him. Perhaps I can persuade him. The rest of you wait outside.'

The guard looked rebellious for a moment. 'I said outside!' the newcomer repeated with an edge to his voice. At a nod from the guard the Ogrons released the Doctor and trooped out of the cell. The Doctor wriggled his aching shoulders. What next, he wondered.

The plump little man started to say, 'I am the manager of this work camp, and I advise you …' But as soon as the cell door closed behind the Ogrons, he changed his tone. He leaned close to the Doctor and hissed, 'Which group are you with?'

The Doctor sighed … 'Don't you start. I've just been telling your hairy friends … I'm not with any group.'

The manager's voice was frantic, 'You don't understand. I'm in the resistance myself. I want to help you. Now, who sent you here? What were you supposed to do?'

Angrily the Doctor said, 'Nobody sent me! I am *not* a spy *or* a guerilla. I'm simply trying to find …'

But the little man wasn't listening. As the cell door started to open he grabbed the astonished Doctor by the collar and did his best to shake him.

'You're a spy! Admit it, you're a spy!'

The new arrival entered the cell and said severely, 'Stop this at once! Why is this man being treated like this?' He turned to the Doctor and said, 'My dear Doctor, please permit me to apologise. I'm the Controller of this Sector. You're an elusive fellow, you know, I've had quite a job tracking you down.'

Gingerly, the Doctor rose to his feet. 'I'm glad you finally succeeded!'

By now he was beginning to feel that he must have broken into a madhouse.

'I've been looking forward to meeting you for some time. Miss Grant has told me so much about you.'

'Jo Grant?' said the Doctor eagerly. 'She's safe?'

'Safe and well and longing to see you again.' The Controller turned to the guard. 'See that the Doctor is taken at once to the guest suite at Central Control. I'll join you there later, Doctor.'

Deciding to make the most of his new status as an honoured guest the Doctor said simply, 'Thank you,' and allowed himself to be ushered from the cell.

Once the Doctor had gone the Controller said, 'Perhaps we might go to your office, manager?'

The manager was deferential. 'Of course, Controller. This way.'

As they walked along the manager said, 'Excuse my asking, Controller, but who was that man? Why is he so important?' They reached the manager's office and went inside.

'That's no concern of yours,' said the Controller. 'What does concern you is the recent drop in production figures for this work camp. You are becoming too soft. As from next month your work targets will increase by ten per cent.'

'It's impossible, Controller. I can't do it!'

'Shall I replace you with someone who can?' asked the Controller coldly.

'I'm sorry. I'll do the best I can.'

'That's better. We'll consider this a friendly warning, shall we?'

'You're very kind, Controller.'

With a farewell nod, the Controller left the room. The manager waited for a while, looking out across the work compound. Then he closed the door, unlocked a drawer in his desk and produced a tiny communicating device. He spoke into it softly, '*ZV ten to Eagle, do you connect?*'

The crackling voice came back at once: '*This is Eagle, ZV ten. We connect. What is your message?*' (Eagle was the emergency channel of the resistance, manned twenty-four hours a day.)

The manager said, '*Time is short. I think they suspect me. Today a man was captured in the grounds. The Controller himself came to fetch him. I don't know who he is but he's important.*'

'*Do you know why he's important?*'

'*Negative. Check with your source at Central Control. Ask them why—*'

The manager broke off short as his office door was smashed open. An Ogron stood in the doorway, the human security guard behind him. There was no time to conceal the communicator. Its tinny voice said, '*ZV ten, this is Eagle. Do you connect?*'

Deliberately, the manager smashed the communicator to the ground. He waited hopelessly as the hands of the Ogron reached out for him ...

In the guest suite at Central Control the first rapturous greetings were over. The Doctor was listening to Jo's account of life in the twenty-second century with more than a little suspicion.

'Honestly, Doctor, it's not so bad. I quite like it here. Everyone's been very kind ... not like those nasty guerillas ...'

The Doctor rubbed his chin. 'I'm glad you're being treated so well, Jo. I met some people earlier today who were anything but kind I can assure you.'

The Controller entered in time to hear this remark. 'Now be fair, Doctor. That was a regrettable error, which I put right as soon as I could. You mustn't jump to conclusions.'

The Doctor's manner was distinctly cool. 'Better than jumping to the crack of a whip from some security guard. Tell me, do you run all your factories like that?'

The Controller smiled. 'That isn't just a factory, Doctor. It is a rehabilitation centre for hardened and violent criminals.'

The Doctor was unimpressed. 'Including a large proportion of old men and women?'

'I can assure you,' said the Controller, 'life on this planet has never been more efficiently or more economically organised. People have never been happier or more prosperous.'

The Doctor snapped: 'Then why do you need so many guards around? Don't the people like being so happy and prosperous?'

Jo Grant had been listening to this conversation with increasing dismay. Reproachfully she said, 'You're being a bit unreasonable, Doctor. The Controller only wants to help us.'

'Does he now?' said the Doctor. 'I wonder why?' Turning back to the Controller he said, 'I find it rather surprising that, with a few rather remarkable exceptions, the human population of this planet seems to lead a life below the level of a dog. It makes me wonder who really rules this Utopia of yours.'

Jo had never seen the Doctor so angry before. The Controller seemed to wither at the sound of the cutting voice. He said haltingly,

'I'm afraid I must leave you. I have work to do. If you'll excuse me, Miss Grant.'

The Controller turned and almost stumbled from the room.

Jo looked after him, worried. 'You shouldn't have spoken to him like that, Doctor. You don't know the whole picture.'

'Neither do you, Jo. Don't you see, Earth has become a slave planet. That man's no more than a sort of superior slave himself. Humans don't rule their own world any longer.'

Jo felt completely baffled. 'Then who does?' she asked.

'The most evil, ruthless life form in the cosmos – the Daleks!' said the Doctor. 'Now just you listen to me.'

He told Jo all he had learned of the true state of affairs in the twenty-second century. Jo was horrified. 'Then why is he being so nice to us?'

'They want to get information. It's an old technique. They've tried the hard treatment. This is the soft. I don't think I want to wait till the hard comes round again.'

Jo shivered. 'Nor do I.'

The Doctor said, 'I got myself captured deliberately. I thought they'd put us together. But now I've found you we need to get away from here!'

Jo lowered her voice. 'There's a guard in the corridor outside.'

The Doctor said softly, 'Don't worry, Jo. I can deal with him.'

The Controller strode down the metal corridors towards the innermost Dalek H.Q. He could still hear the sound of the Doctor's scornful voice. Well, he'd tried to help the man ... tried to treat him decently. Now the Daleks could take over. They'd been right all along ... it was a waste of time being considerate to such criminals. With thoughts like these the Controller tried to drown the memory of the Doctor's accusing voice. But it was no good. In his heart he knew that everything the Doctor had said was true.

Jo Grant stood in the middle of the guest suite and screamed just as loud as she could: 'Help! Help! Please help me!'

The Ogron guard lumbered through the door and stood looking at her suspiciously. All it could see was the small human girl jumping

517

up and down and screaming. No danger there. It made no attempt to draw its pistol. It stood staring at Jo in amazement as she shrieked, 'Help! Help!'

The Doctor stepped from behind the door and delivered one of his celebrated Venusian karate chops. In theory the Ogron should then have slid quietly to the ground. Unfortunately, it did no such thing. The nervous system of the Ogron race is very resistant to shock, and is also protected by layers of incredibly tough muscle. As a result, the Ogron turned round slowly, and snarled at the Doctor, rather as though he'd stepped on its toe.

Somewhat taken aback the Doctor yelled 'Hai! Hai!' and delivered three more devastating blows – left hand, right hand, left foot – guaranteed to pulverise any life form in the universe. The only result was that it irritated the Ogron even further. It advanced on the Doctor roaring with rage, and the great hairy paws reached out and grabbed him. Before the Doctor could dodge, the Ogron's hands were locked round his throat. The pressure of the mighty arms sent him slowly to his knees. As consciousness started to slip away the Doctor thought that this was a useful lesson: never underestimate an opponent. Unfortunately, it looked like being the last lesson he would ever learn.

At this point Jo Grant took a hand in things. She jumped on the table, snatched up a full wine bottle and smashed it down as hard as she could on the top of the Ogron's head.

The result was instant and dramatic: the bottle shattered and the Ogron collapsed on top of the Doctor, out cold, wine trickling down its face.

The Doctor wriggled from underneath it, rubbing his throat. 'Thank you, Jo,' he said a little hoarsely.

He remembered the Ogron he had sent crashing into a wall, back in Austerly House. 'Top of the head seems to be their only weak point.' He grinned at Jo. 'Seems a terrible waste of wine, though. Come on, we'd better get moving.'

They moved out into the metal corridor, not running, but walking briskly as though they had a perfect right to go wherever they were going. The people they passed ignored them. In this world of the future, it was safer to mind your own business.

A buzzer sounded, and Jo looked up at the Doctor in alarm. He shook his head, telling her not to worry. Suddenly, the corridor seemed to fill with people all hurrying in one direction. Jo and the Doctor let themselves be carried along with the tide.

Lost in the bustling crowd, they were swept into a big lift which then went down and down for a long time, then out they emerged into a sort of wide entrance hall. Through the big main doors they could see daylight.

The hall was very congested. They followed the crowd out through the doors. A second crowd was trying to get in. 'Shift-changing time,' whispered the Doctor in explanation.

There were Ogron guards at the door, but their only interest seemed to be in keeping the crowd moving with guttural yells, and occasional blows from their whips. They obviously didn't see the crowd as individuals at all, and the different clothes and appearance of the two fugitives seemed to pass unnoticed.

In the Inner H.Q., the Controller was reporting the Doctor's capture to the Black Dalek. He finished his story and waited. Surely this would bring at least a word of praise.

For a moment the Dalek was silent. Then it grated, 'Your description of the Doc-tor does not tally with our files. Repeat.'

Puzzled, the Controller described the tall lean man with the shock of white hair. 'Do you mean this isn't the man?' he asked.

The Dalek said, 'Evidence indicates that the Doc-tor has changed his appearance.' It turned to a Dalek at a control console and said, 'Immediate visual display of suspect!'

The Dalek at the console said, 'I obey.'

It touched a control knob and a screen lit up showing the guest room suite. It was empty except for the Ogron now struggling slowly to its knees ...

For a moment the Dalek seemed stunned. Then the Black Dalek screeched: 'Emergency, Emergency ... The Doc-tor has escaped! Sound the alarm!'

The Dalek at the console touched another control and a strident alarm began to blare out. The Dalek said, *The Doc-tor has escaped. Alert all security units. He must be found and exterminated.*

The Black Dalek intervened. 'No! We must capture him alive. We will use the Mind Analysis Machine to discover if this *is* the Doc-tor.'

The Controller shuddered. He had seen captured guerillas after they had been under the Daleks' Mind Analysis apparatus – shambling idiots, with all their intelligence drained from them. Death would be better than that.

The Dalek at the control console spoke into its microphone. '*Cancel previous instructions. The Doc-tor and the girl prisoner are to be captured alive and taken to Mind Analysis area.*'

Jo and the Doctor were crossing a wide, busy compound. Doorways on the far side led to long halls where crowds of people were standing in line to get bowls of grey, unappetising stew. At the end of the compound was a huge, main gate. Through its bars they saw the familiar vista of endless rubble.

The gates were standing slightly open, but there were more Ogron guards on duty there. Unlike those at the doors of the building they were scrutinising keenly all those who went in and out, checking passes and permits. Jo realised that getting out of the building was one thing; getting out of the entire compound was going to be much harder. Which way should they go? They would never get through that main gate. There seemed no point in going back into the main block either. Sooner or later someone would notice them and ask questions.

The Doctor said, 'Look, Jo,' and drew her attention to the main gate. An extraordinary vehicle was jolting across the rubble. It looked like a sort of giant tricycle. It had enormous balloon tyres, and their purpose was obvious: the odd-looking vehicle sped over the rubble as easily as if it were on a paved highway.

The tricycle shot through the gates and into the compound. The Ogron security guard riding it parked it near the gates, jumped off, and clattered up some stairs, carrying some kind of despatch box.

The Doctor looked at the tricycle with interest. 'Useful little vehicle, that,' he murmured. 'Specially developed for crossing all that rubble.'

Jo looked up at him, alarmed by the gleam in his eyes. 'Now, Doctor …' she said, warningly.

A strident alarm began to blare out through the compound. The Doctor yelled, 'Come on, Jo, I think that's for us.' Dragging Jo behind him he ran across the compound to the parked tricycle. He jumped into the driver's seat, and Jo perched up behind him. It took the Doctor only a moment to work out how to use the simple controls. With a roar of power the machine shot through the main gates past the astonished guards, and out across the sea of rubble.

Jo hung tightly to the Doctor as the tricycle sped across the ruined landscape. The little vehicle seemed to be able to cross virtually anything, and they flashed over ruined buildings, occasional bits of road and once even the scrubby and patched remains of a field.

All around was nothing but destruction and desolation, with here and there the jutting towers of the Dalek compounds breaking the horizon. The Doctor pulled up at the top of a little hill, and looked round. Three or four more giant tricycles ridden by Ogrons, were coming from the compound they had just left.

'Can't we outrun them?' asked Jo. 'We've got a good start.'

'We might,' said the Doctor. 'But what about those – and those?' He indicated the other compounds in front of them. From each one was speeding a group of more tricycles.

'We're surrounded!' said Jo anxiously. 'What are we going to do, Doctor?'

'Only one thing we can do,' said the Doctor cheerfully, 'give them a run for their money. Ever wondered how the fox feels, Jo? Hold tight!'

Jo closed her eyes and hung on to the Doctor as hard as she could. The rest of the journey was a nightmare. She saw it only in glimpses as she opened her eyes from time to time, only to close them again hurriedly. The Doctor did incredible things with the giant trike, weaving it in and out of the rubble and the ruins. Jo could have sworn that once they drove up the side of a house and dropped down the other. They zoomed along the tops of walls, leaped over gaps in the ruins, and ploughed through weed-choked ditches. But every time Jo opened her eyes, the circle of their pursuers was drawing in closer.

In a final desperate effort to break through the cordon, the Doctor drove straight off the edge of a small cliff of rubble. The trike shot through the air, and Jo screamed as they landed, bounced, and then crashed into a tangle of broken timbers. There was a jarring impact, and then silence.

The Doctor said gently, 'Open your eyes, Jo. It's all over.'

Jo looked around. Their trike, its handlebars buckled, was jammed in a pile of timbers, wedged far too tightly to move. Around them was a circle of grim-faced Ogrons, guns in hand. The Doctor sighed, 'Well, it was fun while it lasted.'

10

INTERROGATION BY THE DALEKS

'Rescue him? Why should we risk our lives to rescue the Doctor?' In the guerilla's underground cell, Boaz stared at Moni in disbelief.

Moni's voice was low and urgent. 'I tell you we *must*.'

Anat said, 'Why?'

'When the work camp manager reported the Doctor's capture, he said he was important to the Daleks in some way.' Moni paused. 'He couldn't tell us any more. They must have got him just afterwards. He was executed this morning.'

Anat sighed. The plump, frightened little man had been an old friend of hers. Thanks to his position he had been one of their best agents. But she was used to such losses. They all were. She said, 'Go on.'

'I checked with our contact at Central Control,' Moni continued. 'She's a clerk on the Controller's personal staff.'

'And what did she tell you?' asked Boaz. 'What's so important about one man?'

'It seems the Doctor is a sworn enemy of the Daleks. He's fought and defeated them in the past.'

Anat murmured, 'He did say he'd encountered them before.'

'According to our contact, the Doctor is the one man the Daleks actually fear. Don't you see how important that makes him – to us? He must know a tremendous amount about them. If anyone can help us, he can.'

'Why should he?' asked Anat. 'He's no reason to be grateful to us. We threatened to kill him.'

Moni said, 'That was all a misunderstanding. If we rescue him he'll owe us something. And if he hates the Daleks as much as we do, he's bound to be on our side when we explain.'

Boaz looked dubious. 'An attack on Central Control. It's suicide. A lot of us will be killed even if we succeed.'

'But it will be worth it,' said Moni urgently. 'Look, I need you two because you know the Doctor by sight. Well, what do you say?'

Deep inside the Central H.Q. of the Daleks the Controller looked on impassively as the Doctor was strapped to a long, low table by Ogron guards.

The walls of the little room were lined with strange alien equipment. Dalek scientists monitored control panels. A giant screen filled the whole of the fourth wall.

Once the Doctor was totally immobilised, the Ogrons strapped a silvery helmet over his head. Leads from the helmet ran to the equipment nearest the screen. When all was ready, the Ogrons stepped back. At a nod from the Black Dalek, a Dalek scientist operated some controls. The screen lit up, but only a fuzzy swirling nothingness could be seen.

The Dalek scientist said, 'He is deliberately suppressing his thoughts.'

'More power,' ordered the Black Dalek. The hum of power rose higher and higher. Still the swirling clouds on the screen did not change.

The Black Dalek said, 'You will admit your identity. Who are you?'

As the power rose yet higher a face began to appear on the screen. An old man with a sharp querulous face.

There was a note of triumph in the Black Dalek's voice. 'It is the face of the Doc-tor as we knew him on Skaro. Confess! Confess!'

The Controller saw the Doctor's face distort with the effort of his mental resistance. But it was in vain. Slowly the first face disappeared and a second one took its place. This showed a younger, dark-haired man with a humorous, rather comic face. 'That is also the Doc-tor.' The voice of the Black Dalek rose to a shriek of triumph. 'You *are* the Doc-tor. You are an enemy of the Daleks! Now you are in our power! You will be exterminated! YOU WILL BE EXTERMINATED! YOU WILL BE EXTERMINATED!'

Every Dalek in the room aimed its gun-stick at the Doctor's helpless form.

11

THE RAID ON DALEK HEADQUARTERS

The Black Dalek and his aides gathered round the table to which the Doctor was tied. Their guns were swivelled round to aim at the Doctor. It was obvious that he was to be executed on the spot.

The Controller stepped forward and shouted, 'Stop!' The Daleks swivelled round to face him.

The Black Dalek said, 'Be silent.'

'To kill him now would be a mistake,' said the Controller firmly. 'Don't you see? He can give you valuable help.'

'The Doc-tor is an enemy of the Daleks. How can he help us?'

'He's been in contact with the resistance groups. We know that. Don't you see? He may well be the brain behind them.'

The Black Dalek seemed to consider for a moment. 'You have proof of this?'

'We know that he's been working with them,' said the Controller urgently. 'Why else did he break into the work camp? It must have been to make contact with the manager – a leader of the resistance who has just been executed. Why did he take that risk? Perhaps there is some new plan to attack you.'

The Black Dalek turned back to the Dalek scientist. 'Continue to operate the Mind Analysis Machine. We shall force the truth from his mind.'

The Controller pointed to the Doctor. He was limp and unconscious, his head lolling back against the restraining straps. 'Look at him. You've practically had to kill him just to establish his identity. He'll die before he tells you anything more.'

Again the Black Dalek considered. 'What is your plan?'

'Let *me* interrogate him.'

'Why should you be more successful than the Daleks?'

'I understand how his mind works. I can gain his confidence. Bring pressure on him through the girl.'

There was a moment's silence. Pressing home his advantage the Controller said, 'When I've finished with him we'll have enough information to smash the whole resistance network.'

The Black Dalek swung round to the Ogrons and indicated the Doctor. 'Release him.'

The Ogrons unstrapped the Doctor from the table and dragged him to his feet. The movement seemed to revive the Doctor. Slowly his eyes opened. He looked at the Daleks all round him.

When he spoke his voice was low and determined. 'I've defeated you before. I defeated you on Skaro. I defeated you here on Earth, too.'

The Black Dalek's voice was triumphant. 'The Daleks have discovered the secret of time travel. We invaded again. We have changed the pattern of Earth's history.'

Defiantly, the Doctor said, 'You won't succeed, you know. In the end you will always be defeated.'

'*You* have been defeated, Doc-tor! The Daleks' empire will spread through all planets and all times. No one can withstand the power of the Daleks.'

With the triumphant sound of the Dalek voice ringing in his ears, the Doctor was dragged from the room.

In the guerillas' underground hideout there was a scene of quiet activity. Guns were being cleaned and assembled. Little packs of plastic explosives were being made up. They were getting ready to raid Dalek Headquarters.

Boaz looked round the cellar. It was strange to see new faces in the place that he had shared with Shura and Anat all this while. Another three-man cell had been called in to make up the assault party.

The leader was Mark, a short, stocky man, with hands scarred from years of work in the Dalek mines. It was said that he'd escaped by strangling an Ogron guard. Looking at those broad tough hands, as they assembled a disintegrator gun, Boaz could easily believe it.

Then there was Zando, a round-faced, red-headed lad, with an expression of mild innocence. He looked too young and timid to be a guerilla – a fact which had often saved his life.

Finally, Joab, a shy and timid man who was expert with all forms of explosives. Boaz watched as he rolled a batch of plastic Dalekenium compound into balls the size of a man's fist.

'Steady on,' he protested, as Joab slapped the plastic around like baker's dough. 'Isn't that stuff pretty unstable?'

Joab gave a shy grin. 'Only when it hits a Dalek.' In this form, Dalekenium exploded on impact with a Dalek outer casing.

Boaz crossed to where Moni and Anat were studying a map. Moni was joining their group to replace the missing Shura. He would lead the expedition.

Moni and Anat seemed cheerful and confident as they planned possible routes. Boaz looked at the others in the little cellar. 'You'd think they were planning a day's outing,' he thought bitterly. 'In a few hours' time, some, perhaps all of us, will be dead. And why are we risking our lives? To rescue some mysterious character who'd probably refuse to help us anyway.'

'And to think we had him as our prisoner,' thought Boaz with continuing bitterness. 'If we'd known he was so important, we could have brought him here in the first place.'

Moni folded up the map. 'Well, that's it then. Everybody ready?' There was a murmur of assent. 'We'd better get moving. Time is short.'

Boaz packed up his equipment and followed them from the cellar. Well, Doctor, he thought, you'd better be worth it.

Back in the guest suite the Controller was watching in astonishment as the Doctor made a rapid recovery. When he had been carried from the Mind Analysis Machine the Doctor had seemed broken and exhausted. Now with a little food and wine, and a chance to rest, he was almost his old self again. So much so that he was paying very little attention to the Controller's efforts to convince him that he should co-operate with the Daleks.

'My dear chap,' the Doctor was saying a little impatiently, 'how can I possibly tell you what I don't know myself?'

'But you were in contact with the guerillas,' the Controller persisted.

'Not from choice,' Jo chimed in indignantly. 'They were going to kill him.'

The Controller turned his attack to Jo. 'Can't you see, I'm trying to help him? I've already saved his life.'

'True enough, old chap, and I'm grateful,' said the Doctor, 'but wasn't that just so that you could impress your Dalek masters by getting information out of me?'

The Controller was silent. To be truthful he wasn't sure of his own motives. Certainly that had been part of the reason. But he had also felt a strange reluctance to see the Doctor killed. He tried again.

'Unless you give me information about the resistance – the names of their leaders, the location of their hideouts, their future plans – the Daleks will destroy you.'

The Doctor took another swig of wine and said coolly, 'I don't doubt it.'

The Controller looked curiously at him. 'You value your life so little?'

'On the contrary, I value it enormously. But the Daleks will try to kill me whatever I tell you. They've had it in mind for years.'

'But if you co-operate with them—'

'As *you* co-operate with them?' The Doctor looked at the Controller with a kind of pity. 'You really think it possible to *co-operate* with the Daleks?'

'They can be reasonable,' said the Controller defensively. 'They value my services.'

'They tolerate you,' said the Doctor. 'They allow you to live, as long as you're useful.'

The Controller said angrily, 'I am a senior government official!'

'You're a slave,' said the Doctor simply. 'A slave who has a few privileges in return for helping to oppress his fellow-slaves.'

Suddenly the Controller yelled: 'Be silent!' and Jo saw that he was literally shaking with emotion.

There was a moment's quiet. Then the Controller spoke in a low, hoarse voice.

'You don't understand,' he said. 'No one can understand who doesn't know about those terrible years. Towards the end of the twentieth century a series of devastating wars broke out. There were long periods of nothing but destruction and killing. Nearly seven-eighths of the world's population were wiped out. The rest lived for a long time in holes in the ground, starving, reduced to the level of animals. The entire planet was in ruins.'

Jo and the Doctor were silent, overcome by the horror of the picture he had drawn. Then Jo said softly, 'And that's when the Daleks took over?'

The Controller replied, 'There was no power on Earth to resist them.'

'So Earth became a giant factory,' said the Doctor. 'All the wealth, all the minerals, carried away to Skaro.'

'But why do they need to do all this?' asked Jo.

The Doctor looked grim. 'Because the Dalek empire is continually expanding. They need a constant flow of raw materials for their war machine. And the planet Earth is particularly rich in minerals.'

The Controller nodded. 'Everyone who is strong enough works in the mines. The rest work in factories, sorting and grading the ore, helping to build weapons for the Daleks. As you say, we're all slaves.' The Controller rubbed his hand over his eyes. It was years since he had allowed himself to think the truth, let alone speak it out aloud.

Jo said, 'How did you come to work for them?'

'Everyone has to work for the Daleks,' said the Controller simply. 'This is better than the mines or the factories.'

'Is it?' said the Doctor. 'Is it really?'

The Controller tried to defend himself. 'I've used my position to help others. I've gained concessions, even saved a few lives.'

'Wouldn't you have helped more by using your skills to lead the fight against the Daleks?' said the Doctor.

The Controller sighed. 'It's hopeless ... no one can fight the Daleks.'

'That's not what the guerillas think.'

'A handful of fanatics ... most of them killed off already. Believe me ... there's nothing they can do to change things.'

In a small courtyard at the back of Dalek Headquarters, an iron hatch began to slide open. Moni, Anat, Boaz and the other three guerillas emerged. They looked around them. The courtyard was narrow, dark and windowless. On one side, an archway gave onto a bigger courtyard. On the other, a low ramp ran up to a metal door set into the side of the main building.

The group clustered round Moni, who indicated the metal door. 'This exit is hardly ever used. It's reserved for the Daleks. The door will be locked.'

'We'll open it,' said Joab, fishing out a pack of plastic explosive.

'Up the stairs, along the corridor and we're there,' said Moni. 'It's the nearest exit to the guest suite. Boaz and Anat come with me … the rest of you hold this courtyard, we have to go back the same—' He broke off as an Ogron came into the yard. It reached for its pistol, but immediately Zando tripped it and Mark smashed it over the head with his gun. The Ogron fell without a sound. Moni said, 'Well done.'

Zando grinned. 'We've had a lot of practice.' Anat and Moni moved towards the ramp.

Seconds later it seemed that the little expedition was doomed before it began. Two Ogrons, guns in hand, rushed through the archway from the next courtyard. At the same moment the metal door opened. A Dalek came through it and glided down the ramp, heading straight for Anat. Its gun swung round to cover her.

Zando and Mark and Joab all fired through the little archway at once, blasting the Ogrons out of existence.

At the same moment Boaz grabbed the ball of plastic explosive dropped by Joab. He ran straight at the Dalek menacing Anat and slapped the explosive onto its outer casing. There was a tremendous explosion and Boaz and the Dalek disappeared in a cloud of smoke.

Anat turned blindly to Moni. 'That stuff's *designed* to explode on contact. He must have known.'

'He knew,' said Moni, 'but it doesn't always go off when you throw it. He wasn't taking any chances.' He shook her roughly. 'Now come on! Do you want him to have died for nothing?'

Moni and Anat rushed through the open door and up the stairs. The second group stayed behind as arranged. Zando and Mark kept up a steady fire through the archway, while Joab lobbed balls of plastic explosive.

They were in a good position, but hopelessly outnumbered. They couldn't hope to hold out for very long.

*

In the guest suite the Controller continued his vain attempt to convince the Doctor that he should furnish information about the guerillas. 'Think what you like of me,' he said wearily, 'but I did save your life. I won't be able to keep you alive unless you give me something to tell the Daleks.'

'I simply don't have any information,' said the Doctor, 'and quite frankly, I wouldn't give it to you if I had.'

Suddenly there came the thump of plastic explosive, and the high-pitched buzz of disintegrator guns.

The Controller leaped up in alarm. He looked round wildly as the sound of firing came nearer. 'Guards!' he shouted 'Guards!' A figure dashed through the doorway, gun in hand. But it wasn't an Ogron guard. It was Anat.

With her was a man they didn't know. He looked at the Controller. 'No use calling for your guards, my friend. They're all dead.'

Anat said, 'Doctor, Jo, are you all right?' Before they could answer, she went on, 'You've no reason to trust me, but please come with us. We need you to help us fight the Daleks. This is Moni, one of our leaders.'

The Doctor said, 'Come on, Jo.' They made towards the door.

Suddenly the Doctor stopped. The other guerilla, Moni, was aiming his gun to shoot down the Controller. 'And as for you ...' he was saying.

The Controller stood motionless, waiting. The Doctor said, 'No!'

Moni looked at him in astonishment.

'Killing him won't do any good,' said the Doctor, 'he's not the real enemy.'

Moni said, 'But he's helped them. If you knew of the blood on his hands ...'

The Doctor replied, 'They'd always have found someone. Leave him.'

Anat called, 'Moni – let's go.' Reluctantly Moni lowered his gun. Jo, the Doctor and the two guerillas sprinted down the corridor. The Controller stood perfectly still where they had left him. He was stunned, unable to grasp what had happened. He could scarcely believe that he was still alive.

531

12

RETURN TO DANGER

Wrapped in an old blanket Jo Grant huddled close to the wood fire in the brazier. She sipped gratefully at a tin mug full of steaming herbal tea. She looked round the cellar curiously. It was a grim enough place, yet the firelight gave it a homely look. She preferred it to the shining metallic luxury of the Dalek quarters.

The Doctor sat next to her. He too was sipping tea. There was a constant buzz of conversation between the Doctor, Moni and Anat who were all gathered round the fire. Jo knew that three more guerillas had been lost in the rescue. One had been killed fighting a Dalek. Two others had sacrificed themselves to cover their retreat.

Jo's mind drifted back to their escape...everything had happened so quickly. She and the Doctor had followed the guerillas down corridor after corridor and then down a flight of endless steps. Eventually they had emerged into a courtyard. There had been shooting and the thud of explosives, yells and roars and clouds of smoke.

Then they'd all crawled through a little hatchway and along narrow tunnels. Finally they'd crossed what seemed like miles of rubble, stopping to hide from Ogron patrols.

At last they'd ended up here.

Jo tried to concentrate on the conversation going on around her but she kept nodding off. Dimly she was aware that they were talking about Sir Reginald Styles,

The Doctor was saying, 'But how do you know all this? How do you know Styles was responsible?'

'There were still history books,' said Moni impatiently, 'even after the catastrophe. We know.'

Anat took up the story. 'You see Styles only pretended to be working for world peace. Really, he wanted power for himself.'

The Doctor took another swig of his tea. 'So you're saying that this conference he called was a trick?'

'Exactly that,' affirmed Moni. 'He managed to lure all the leading delegates to his house.'

The Doctor said, 'I was told that he was planning a sort of preliminary conference, just before I, er ... left Austerly House.'

'Once they were at the house,' said Moni, 'there was a tremendous explosion. The house was completely destroyed. Styles was killed with the others.'

'That wasn't very clever of him,' commented the Doctor.

Moni said, 'Obviously he must have set a bomb. Perhaps he mistimed the fuse.'

'There were charges and counter-charges,' said Anat, 'and of course the conference was finished. Soon after that war broke out. First with conventional weapons, then with atomic. Thereafter a succession of wars led us to this –' She waved her hand round the cellar.

Moni nodded in agreement. 'And after that the Daleks came and took over what was left.'

The Doctor stared thoughtfully into the fire. 'So you decided to go back in time and intervene in your own history ... to kill Styles before he managed to carry out his plan?'

'That's right,' said Moni.

'We stole the plans of time machines from the Daleks. We stole parts and equipment, and managed to build machines of our own.'

Anat joined in. 'At first things didn't go too well. The transference was unstable. People appeared for a while in your time, and then just faded away.'

'That explains the ghost that Styles saw,' said Jo. 'And the man who vanished from the UNIT sick-bay.'

The Doctor nodded. 'Then you three turned up – which is more or less where I came in. By the way, what happened to the other one? That young chap ...'

Anat frowned. 'Shura? He simply vanished. We think an Ogron patrol must have got him.'

Moni said, 'Somehow the Daleks learned what we were trying to do. They sent Ogron security guards back into your time to stop us. Shura probably ran into one of them.'

The Doctor looked round the circle of intent faces. 'There's one thing you still haven't told us. Why did you go to so much trouble to rescue us?' He looked quizzically at Anat. 'After all, our first meeting wasn't very friendly.'

Anat said, 'I'm sorry about all that, Doctor. At first we thought you were Styles. When we found out that you weren't, you were just a nuisance. Our mission had to succeed at all costs.'

The Doctor looked across at Moni. 'You still haven't answered my question. Why *did* you rescue us?'

Moni leaned forward. 'We learned later that you were an old enemy of the Daleks, that you'd fought and defeated them before. Surely you'd help us to beat them here?'

The Doctor said, 'If I can – certainly. What do you want me to do?'

Moni said urgently, '*You* can succeed where we failed Doctor. We want you to go back to your own time and kill Styles!'

There was a good deal of bustle and activity around the tunnel near Austerly House. The area was floodlit by spotlights, and by the headlights of army jeeps.

Captain Yates stood before the Brigadier's jeep, with some odds and ends of guerilla equipment. There was food, the shattered booster transmitter, and a stubby looking cylinder with controls set into it.

'We found this stuff in a sort of hiding place, hollowed out beneath some rubble, sir.'

The Brigadier looked at the odds and ends and grunted. 'This all?'

'Yes, sir. No sign of anyone or anything else.'

The Brigadier sighed. He had spent a very long day clearing up after the battle at Austerly House, and carrying out a search of the area. Now he had extended the range of his search as far as the tunnel. Except for this bundle of odds and ends, there had been absolutely no results.

Equally useless had been the Brigadier's efforts to convince the powers-that-be to abandon the idea of a conference at Austerly

House. As was often the case in UNIT operations, the Brigadier's reasons were too fantastic to be believed. In addition there was an embarrassing shortage of evidence. The disintegrator guns used by both Ogrons and guerillas destroyed all trace of their victims. Even the bodies of Ogrons killed by bullets had mysteriously faded away. All the Brigadier could produce to support his story were the signs of battle in Styles' study, and the fact that numbers of his own men had vanished.

A sceptical official from the Ministry had looked at Styles' wrecked study and muttered disapprovingly about 'vandalism'. Squads of painters and decorators had worked hard all day to repair the damage, and now even *that* evidence was gone.

The main obstacle though was Styles himself. At present he was in London greeting the other delegates as they arrived. And he was firmly opposed to any change of plan. Arranging the Conference, he said, had been a delicate, almost impossible business. The slightest change in plan might arouse suspicion in the delegates, and send them rushing home again.

The Brigadier could see the old boy's point. And the prize of world peace no doubt justified the risks. But it still left the Brigadier with the problem of trying to protect the Conference.

There was the roar of a motor-bike and a despatch rider halted by the jeep. The Brigadier took the offered message and tore it open.

'Well, that's it, Mike. No change in plans will be considered. Styles and the other world leaders will arrive first thing tomorrow.' He crumpled up the signal in disgust.

'All we can do is keep searching, Mike. Constant patrols at all times. We'll extend the radius of the search. I want a completely safe area all round the house and grounds. Oh, and keep a heavy guard on this tunnel; it seems to be the centre of things.'

'What about this lot, sir?' asked Captain Yates, indicating his finds from the tunnel. The Brigadier poked the collection with his cane – 'Be careful, sir!' said Yates in alarm. 'The cylinder looks very much like a bomb.'

'Oh, send it all back to UNIT H.Q. The Doctor might like to look at it – *if* we ever see him again.' The Brigadier started his jeep and drove back towards the house. Yates dumped his finds in the back of a UNIT truck. He wondered if the Doctor would ever turn up to examine them. Jo Grant, too, come to that. Mike shook his head wearily and went back to organising the search.

The Brigadier and Captain Yates didn't know it, but two important items were missing from their find in the tunnel. The most important was Shura himself. Then there were the things he was carrying, stuffed into a bulky parcel inside his tunic: a disintegrator pistol. And a Dalekenium bomb.

After the noise and shooting of the Daleks' failed ambush at the tunnel, Shura had drifted off into more uneasy sleep.

When he awoke, his condition was worse rather than better. His exhaustion, his wounds, the long spell in the cold damp tunnel had sent him into a high fever. When he awoke he was almost delirious. Only one thought filled his mind: the others had gone, abandoned him! But he himself must complete the mission. He must get back to Austerly House and kill Styles.

Just as darkness began to fall he had emerged from his hiding place, limping along slowly, like a wounded animal. He came out of the tunnel into the cool night air, and stood gasping for a moment. Then he lurched across the fields towards the house. Just as he reached the edge of the field he heard the noise of soldiers coming towards him. He stumbled into a ditch and lay still, covering himself with leaves and bracken. He heard the sound of army vehicles as they parked on the road. Men jumped out, there was a clatter of booted feet, shouted orders. Footsteps thudded by him, within inches of his head.

When it was quiet Shura got to his feet and staggered on leaving the little cluster of vehicles behind him.

Although he didn't realise it, this was Shura's greatest stroke of luck. As the Brigadier's men were spreading outwards from the house, he was moving towards it. Once he'd passed through the line, he and the searchers were moving in opposite directions.

It took him a long time to get into the grounds. He was too weak to climb the wall, so he went round to the main gate and waited. The gate was guarded. Shura waited patiently under cover until a UNIT lorry drove up. While the sentry was checking the driver's pass, Shura somehow scrambled over the tailboard and inside the lorry. It was full of food and drink, cases and cases of it. Sir Reginald and his guests had to be well fed. Shura hastily added a loaf of bread and a bottle to the bundle inside his tunic.

The lorry soon jolted to a halt at the back of the house, and Shura jumped out, slipping into the shadows as the driver came round to unload. The kitchen door stood open, but there were lights on, and he could hear the sound of voices.

Shura moved along the side of the house, looking for a way in. His boots clanged on metal and he looked down. At his feet was a round manhole cover. Shura fished a knife from his pocket and managed to prise it up. Unhesitatingly, he took off his tunic, made a bundle of all his possessions and lowered them through. Then he swung his legs into the dark circle and slid down. He found a foot-hold on something lumpy and shifting. Reaching up again through the hole he dragged the cover back into place. Minutes later a UNIT sentry came round the corner. His boots clanged on the manhole cover just as Shura had it back in place.

Shura fished a light-cell from his pocket and looked around him. He was in a tiny cellar filled with lumpy black stone. He remembered his history. Of course ... coal! They used to burn it for fuel ...

Shura's incredible luck had served him well again. It was almost as though he was meant to succeed ... as though fate was co-operating with him. Austerly House had long ago been converted to oil-fired central heating. But the old coal cellar, and the remnants of the coal, were still there. Nobody ever came to the cellar now.

Shura hollowed out a nest for himself in the coal and settled back. He knocked the top off the wine bottle and took a swig, then stuffed handfuls of bread into his mouth.

Under the influence of the wine and the fever that possessed him he was floating aloof and carefree above the world. Everything was going well. When Styles arrived he would kill him. The mission would be completed. In the pitch blackness of the coal cellar, gun and bomb clutched to his chest, Shura felt calm and happy. All he had to do now was wait.

*

Jo woke up with a start from her doze by the guerillas' fire. Something was happening in the cellar. Voices were raised in excitement. The Doctor was on his feet, pacing about the room.

'Don't you see, man,' he said, 'you're asking me to commit murder! How can I agree to do what you want?'

Anat said, 'We're asking you to kill one man – and to save many more lives.'

'It's still murder,' said the Doctor stubbornly.

'Isn't it justified,' insisted Moni, 'if it would save the human race from the Daleks?'

'Ah, but would it?' said the Doctor, resuming his pacing about. 'Would it?'

Anat looked at him in puzzlement. 'We've told you how it all happened.'

'And suppose your history books got it wrong? Oh, not the basic facts, but their interpretation of them?' He turned to Moni. 'Won't you return us to our own time? Now we know the facts there may be other things we can do to help you.'

'Doctor, please,' said Moni. 'The relationship between our time zone and yours is fixed. A day has gone by here, a day has gone by in your time. Soon it may be too late. Won't you promise to help us? We'll send you back if you'll give us your word to kill Styles.'

'My dear chap,' said the Doctor, 'I'm completely with you as to the ends, but I can't accept your choice of means ... and more than that ... something feels wrong about the whole idea ...'

Jo yawned and stretched. Everyone looked round when she spoke up. 'Thing that puzzles me is, I just can't believe in Styles as a ruthless mass murderer. I mean he got a bit stroppy, but basically I thought he was quite a nice old boy.' She yawned again.

The Doctor swung round on her enthusiastically. 'That's it, Jo. That's it! Just what was worrying me ... that's what I feel, too!' He turned to the guerillas. 'Styles is a *good* man; vain, arrogant, pompous if you like, but underneath it all, good. He really does want world peace, I'll swear it. He couldn't have caused that explosion.'

Anat said, 'Then who did?'

'Let me see that book of yours again,' said the Doctor. Anat passed him the tattered book. Worn almost to pieces by constant handling it was obviously one of the guerillas' greatest treasures. He peered at the

538

faded print and began to read aloud. *'The explosion in the cellar was of such shattering force that it was suspected that a small atomic bomb had been used. But later tests showed no trace of radioactivity. It was charged that the Government had developed some new and deadly "clean" form of atom bomb. This was strongly denied, and no such bomb was ever used in the wars that followed.'*

The Doctor closed the book. An incredible idea was beginning to form in his mind. 'An explosive unknown *at that time*,' he said softly. He looked at Anat. 'And one of you didn't get back from your mission!'

'That's right – Shura. He went to try and contact base. We never saw him again.'

The Doctor said thoughtfully, 'What sort of equipment did you take to the twentieth century?'

Anat said, 'Usual battle gear: disintegrator guns, booster for the sub-temporal radio, food supplies, explosives ...'

The Doctor stopped her. 'Explosives?'

'We took two Dalekenium bombs. Just in case ...'

'What did they look like?'

'Stubby black cylinders, about so big.' She gestured with her hands. 'Small, but tremendously powerful. We stole them from the Daleks!'

'I don't remember ever seeing you with these bombs,' said the Doctor. 'When you were at the house did you have them with you?'

'Shura hid them for us in the tunnel when we arrived. We didn't have time to pick them up on our way back.'

'Exactly,' said the Doctor. 'Shura hid them in the tunnel where he went to make his attempt to call base. And Dalekenium is a clean explosive. All the power of the atom, but no fall out!'

'Well yes, but ...' Anat stared at him in horror. 'No Doctor. It's impossible.'

The Doctor said remorselessly: 'It all fits. An explosive unknown on Earth at the time ... Shura, abandoned, wounded perhaps, but determined to carry out his mission ... and Styles returning to the house with the other delegates.'

The Doctor looked round the circle of horror-struck faces. 'Don't you see? You want to change history. But you can't. You're part of it, trapped in a temporal paradox. Styles didn't kill all those world leaders. He didn't start the wars that led to the Dalek conquest. *You* did. You did it all yourselves!'

13

THE DAY OF THE DALEKS

Once again the Controller stood before the High Council of the Daleks.

The Black Dalek, the Golden Dalek and their aides surrounded him, menacing and threatening ...

Dully, he listened to the accusing voice of the Golden Dalek. 'You have failed the Daleks. The Doc-tor has escaped.'

'He will be recaptured,' said the Controller. 'I swear it.'

'He must be found and destroyed.'

Wearily the Controller said, 'I am sure he will attempt to return to his own time zone. When he does, and if the guerillas are helping him, they will use the old monorail tunnels. It gives them a fixed reference point near Austerly House in the twentieth century. I can set another ambush – fill the tunnels with guards.'

The Black Dalek said, 'If you fail us you will pay with your life. This is your final chance.'

The Controller turned and walked from the room.

He returned to his office and summoned Zeno, his senior assistant, a sharp-featured, ambitious young man. Briefly, the Controller gave instructions for the ambush. 'I leave the whole thing to you. Don't trouble me with details.'

Puzzled, but happy at a chance to distinguish himself, Zeno returned to his own office. A few moments later his good mood was shattered when he received a summons to appear before the Black Dalek. Hurriedly, he made his way to the inner H.Q., where he waited trembling until the Black Dalek appeared.

Zeno looked at the Dalek in awe and horror. Though he had worked for the Daleks all his life, it was very seldom that he actually saw one.

Particularly one of this exalted rank. The Daleks ruled by proxy, and were seldom seen.

The Dalek said, 'We are not satisfied with the loyalty and efficiency of the Controller. It may be necessary for you to replace him!'

Zeno bowed, 'I'm sure that you know best,' he said.

'You will observe him closely during the coming operation. Then you will bring us your report.'

It was still dark when Jo, the Doctor, and the two guerillas made their way across the rubble. Jo was very tired now. She stumbled several times, and the Doctor steadied her with a hand on her arm.

She could remember the hours of argument that followed as the Doctor tried to get the guerillas to accept his theory ... their final, reluctant acceptance. Jo hadn't followed all the ins and outs of the argument; all she knew was that at last they were going home, away from this horrible world of Daleks and Ogrons, back to their own time.

Moni halted at the tunnel entrance. 'This is it, Doctor. Anat will take you to a point that is equivalent to the railway tunnel in your own time. Then you'll be transferred. Goodbye and good luck.'

Moni shook hands briefly and turned back. The rest of them plunged on into the darkness. Anat led the way, flashing a little light-cell occasionally to give them their bearings. They plodded on for what seemed an endless time, through the tunnels. At last Anat said, 'We're here!' She shone round her light, and the Doctor recognised the point of his first arrival. Anat produced a time machine. 'It's already set. All you need do is press the operating button.' She, too, shook hands. 'Goodbye, Doctor. I hope you're right about it all. Do what you can for us, won't you?'

She was about to hand over the machine when they were all caught in the beam of a fierce spotlight. A voice said, 'Stay where you are, all of you!'

Ogron guards appeared all round them.

The Controller walked forwards. 'It has ended as I said it would, Doctor. No one can defeat the Daleks. It is madness to oppose them.'

The Doctor walked up to the Controller. He spoke in a low urgent voice.

'I can free this whole world from their rule. I know what happened, how they were able to conquer this planet. I can set Earth's history back onto its proper path. Are you going to stop me?'

In an agonised voice the Controller said, 'If only I could be sure ...'

The Doctor said, 'You spoke of the war, the suffering, the starvation ... I can stop that from ever happening. We can stop it! Will you help me?'

'You saved my life,' said the Controller slowly. 'You could have let them kill me. And now you offer freedom.' He turned to the surrounding Ogrons and said, 'Go! I will deal with these criminals alone! Go I tell you!' Confused, the Ogrons shambled back into the darkness.

The Controller turned back to the Doctor. 'You go, too. Go quickly!'

The Doctor beckoned to Jo. She ran to join him. He looked at Anat. She shook her head. 'I'll stay in my own time, Doctor. Besides, the machine will only transport two.'

Swiftly, the Doctor activated the machine. The glow of the time field surrounded the two figures. Slowly Jo and the Doctor began to fade away.

Zeno came running down the tunnels, armed Ogrons at his heels. He bellowed, 'Stop! Stop them!' But it was already too late – Jo and the Doctor had vanished.

Zeno looked at the Controller. 'You have let them escape. You will pay the penalty for this, Controller.' He turned to Anat, 'And so will you.'

But Anat's gun was already in her hand. She shot out the spotlight and disappeared into the darkness. Zeno made a determined grab for the Controller. To his surprise the Controller was standing quite still: he made no attempt to escape.

Anat ran swiftly through the dark tunnel. She slipped easily through the milling crowds of Ogron guards, shooting out any spotlight that appeared. The Ogrons panicked and fired wildly, killing each other in the process.

Anat came to the point where the Doctor had left the tunnels. The maintenance ladders were an old and familiar escape route. She climbed nimbly upwards and emerged into the fresh air.

She stood for a moment looking over the sea of rubble, the only world she had ever known. There were streaks of light in the east. Dawn was breaking. If the Doctor succeeded it might be a new dawn for all of them. If not, she could always go on fighting. She began to clamber across the rubble, towards the hideout.

After the same mind-twisting voyage through the Time Vortex, Jo and the Doctor found themselves back in the railway tunnel of their twentieth century. 'All right, Jo?' queried the Doctor. She nodded. 'Come on then. There's very little time.'

They ran out of the darkness of the tunnel and cannoned straight into Sergeant Benton who was in charge of the tunnel guard. 'Jo, Doctor!' he yelled. 'Where have you two been?'

'No time for explanations!' snapped the Doctor. 'What's happening at the house?'

Benton looked at his watch. 'Delegates will be arriving for the Conference at any moment. Styles is there already. Wants to make an early start.'

'We may still be in time then,' said the Doctor. 'Lend me a jeep, Sergeant, I've got to get over there right away.'

Benton shrugged. 'I've got to stay here. The Brigadier wants this tunnel guarded. Help yourself, Doc!' He indicated a jeep parked on the road nearby. The Doctor made for it at a run.

Jo said helplessly, 'Hello, and goodbye, Sergeant.' She set off after the Doctor.

For the last time, the Controller of Earth Sector One stood before the Dalek High Council. Somehow he seemed a different man. His shoulders had lost the cowed slump of slavery, and he was free at last from fear, since he had nothing now to lose. He listened quietly while an eager Zeno made his report.

The Black Dalek swung round on the Controller accusingly. 'You will be exterminated! You are a traitor to the Daleks.'

Its gun-stick swung round to cover him. So, too, did the guns of the other Daleks.

The Controller's voice was calm as he said, 'Oh no. I have been a traitor to humanity all my life. But not any more.'

The Black Dalek shrieked with rage, 'You will be exterminated!'

The Controller smiled. 'Who knows? I may even have helped to exterminate *you*.'

The smile was still on his face when the blast from all the Dalek guns caught him. His body twisted for a moment in an intensity of white light, and then slumped to the ground.

The Black Dalek turned to Zeno as Ogron guards dragged the body of the Controller from the room. 'You have proved yourself worthy to be the new Controller. But be warned … the Daleks expect total loyalty from those who serve them!' Zeno bowed and walked from the room.

The Daleks began to talk amongst themselves in grating metallic voices. It was not so much a conference: since all Daleks think alike it was more a chorus of agreement. The Golden Dalek, the senior, spoke first.

'The Doc-tor is a Time Lord. His intervention may be able to return the course of history to its original path.'

Then the Black Dalek: 'We must follow him to the twentieth century time zone and destroy him.'

'The war amongst the humans must break out,' pronounced the Golden Dalek.

'The Dalek conquest of the planet Earth must not be reversed,' agreed the Black Dalek.

The Daleks left the room to prepare for their expedition. This time they would invade the twentieth century in force.

In spite of the early hour, there was a little crowd of spectators around the gates of Austerly House. They watched with interest as one by one the diplomats arrived in their long, black limousines. There was even a television news team. The commentator was working very hard to make a series of pictures of middle-aged men getting out of cars sound exciting.

'And it is no exaggeration to say that the peace of the world may well depend on what happens here today. On the steps you can see Sir Reginald Styles greeting the Chinese delegate as he steps from his car. The last-minute agreement of the Chinese to attend has given this Conference its greatest chance of success. That agreement is due almost entirely to the efforts of Sir Reginald himself. Beside Sir Reginald, on the steps, is Brigadier Alastair Lethbridge-Stewart. The Brigadier is, of course, head of the British section of UNIT, the United Nations Intelligence Taskforce, and he is in charge of security at the Conference.'

The commentator paused, racking his brains for something else to say. He was wishing that something, anything, would happen when his wish was suddenly granted. A jeep, driven *very* fast, suddenly shot up the drive and came to a screeching halt at the front steps. A very tall man in rather tattered clothes leaped out, followed by a very small young lady. The tall man rushed up to Styles and the Brigadier, and hustled them inside the building.

The commentator caught a protesting cry of 'Doctor – what do you think you're ...' and then the trio disappeared inside the hall.

Inside the Doctor was saying, 'Never mind where I've been. You must evacuate this house at once!'

Styles said furiously, 'Is this man mad?'

'Please, do as he says,' said Jo. 'If you don't, you'll all be blown up!'

'That's right, Brigadier,' said the Doctor. 'Somewhere in this house there's a bomb.'

'Impossible,' the Brigadier said flatly. 'Whole place has been searched.'

'Then search again,' replied the Doctor, 'but clear this building first!'

Styles said, 'I flatly refuse to leave, Brigadier. And I insist this man be removed.'

In the cellar beneath the house, Shura was priming his Dalekenium bomb. By lifting the lid of his manhole a little earlier he'd been able to hear the noise and bustle of the arrivals. He'd even heard a passing sentry calling, 'Smarten up, there. Old Styles is just arriving.' For Shura that was evidence enough. He'd waited a little longer, finished the last of the bread and wine, and now the bomb was primed. Little figures began to click over on the dial of the bomb. Then they stopped. Shura peered at them muzzily with his light-cell, but they seemed blurred. The timing mechanism had jammed. But it didn't matter. He could easily do without it!

On the road near the tunnel Sergeant Benton leaned against a wall and stretched. He wondered how much longer he'd have to go on guarding this rotten tunnel. Nothing had happened there for ages. He peered into the darkness of the tunnel mouth. Something seemed to be moving.

In the hall of Austerly House time was ticking away and the argument still raged. Styles was adamant, and finally the Doctor gave up. 'Brigadier, get Styles and the rest of them out of this house at once; use force if you have to!'

The Doctor dashed to the wine-cellar door and opened it. He switched on the light. The cellar was empty.

'Cellar, the book said a cellar,' he muttered to himself. Rejoining the group in the hall he said abruptly, 'Sir Reginald ... is the wine-cellar the only cellar in the house?'

Sir Reginald looked at him in amazement, convinced by now that the Doctor was quite mad. 'Yes, of course!' he snapped.

The Doctor shook him by the shoulder. 'Think, man, think ... there must be another!'

'There's a little coal-cellar by the back kitchen,' said Styles after a moment. 'Never used now, of course.'

As the Doctor was about to rush away the Brigadier's walkie-talkie crackled into life. The Brigadier listened to the agitated voice and said, '*Do your best to hold them, Benton. If you can't, fall back slowly. I'll reinforce you as soon as I can.*'

He turned to the Doctor and said, 'Some kind of attacking force is coming out of the tunnel. Those ape things and something else. Some kind of robots ...'

'Daleks,' whispered Jo. 'Daleks and Ogrons!'

The Doctor nodded. 'They're coming to blow up the house and kill Styles – make sure that history goes their way.'

The Brigadier understood none of this, but he was at his best in a military situation. The attack from the tunnel gave him the excuse he needed. He turned to Styles and said crisply, 'You, Sir Reginald, the diplomats and all their staff will evacuate this house at once! Don't argue, man, you can make your protest later. Captain Yates, get them moving!'

Seconds later the television commentator saw the extraordinary sight of a number of very distinguished foreign diplomats being practically thrown into their cars by UNIT troops and driven away at speed. He had no chance to describe this for the viewers however, for minutes later he and his team were being bustled into a jeep and driven away likewise.

In the now rapidly-emptying house the Doctor ran to the little coal-cellar. He burst open the door and saw Shura, lying on the coal, covering him with a pistol. On the coal beside Shura was the stubby little bomb. The Doctor drew a deep breath. 'Shura,' he said quietly. 'You've got to listen to me.'

The invaders from the tunnel advanced remorselessly upon the house. The UNIT troops fought bravely, but could not hold them back. The Ogrons could be killed, though with difficulty. But the Daleks – they seemed invincible. Nothing stopped them as, flanked by their Ogron guards, they glided effortlessly forward. They swept up the drive and were now very close to the house. The Brigadier blazed away from the front steps. Men were being shot down all round him, and he knew that it was only a matter of time ...

Jo Grant looked from a window with horror at the advancing Dalek army. Instinctively, she ran to warn the Doctor.

In the coal-cellar doorway, the Doctor, still covered by Shura's gun, was saying persuasively, 'Shura, if you set off that bomb, you'll be sacrificing yourself for nothing. Styles has gone now – he isn't in the house I tell you.'

Shura's hand was resting on the little black plunger. He said dreamily, 'Must kill Styles, must stop the war ...'

The Doctor looked at him sadly. Shura's face was gleaming with sweat, his eyes unnaturally bright. The Doctor recognised the signs of high fever. There was little chance of getting through to Shura now.

Jo Grant ran and joined him in the doorway. 'Doctor, come away! The Daleks are attacking from the tunnel! They're almost in the house ...'

She stopped talking as she saw the grim figure of Shura, crouched on the coal, the bomb beside him.

Shura reacted to Jo's voice. 'Daleks? Daleks ... here?'

'That's right,' said the Doctor. 'They've come to make sure their version of history isn't changed. Shura, *please*, won't you come with us? We can save you.'

Shura seemed to become suddenly rational. An attacking force of Daleks was something his fevered mind could grasp. 'You two get out of here. Leave them to me. Just let them get into the house ...'

Jo said, 'Shura, no! Make him come with us, Doctor.'

'This is Dalekenium,' said Shura. 'The only stuff that will deal with the Daleks – their own bomb!'

'We could rig up a time fuse,' said the Doctor desperately. 'Shura, there must be some other way ...'

'The time mechanism is broken,' said Shura. 'Anyway this stuff's too unstable. I'll use the contact plunger. Only way to be sure.' His hand hovered over a black plunger in the side of the bomb. 'Now are you getting out, Doctor? Or do you both want to be here when I press this?'

The Doctor gave him a last look, then said, 'All right, Shura. Come on, Jo!'

The two ran through the empty house to the front steps where the Brigadier, and what was left of his men, were fighting a last desperate rearguard action. Some of the Ogrons had fallen, but most of them were still advancing, the apparently invincible Daleks at their head.

The Doctor ran up to the Brigadier and yelled, 'Fall back! Everyone fall back! Let them into the house. It's the only way.'

The Brigadier shouted, 'You heard the Doctor! Everybody pull back! Re-group on the hill behind the house.'

Led by Jo and the Doctor, the Brigadier and his few remaining troops turned and ran. Triumphantly, the Daleks and their Ogron army came on.

From the little hillside behind the house the Doctor and the others watched as a triumphant flood of Ogrons, led by the Black Dalek and the Golden Dalek swept up the drive and swirled into the house. Softly the Doctor muttered, 'Now, Shura, *now!*'

Inside the house the Daleks and their Ogron guards milled about the empty rooms. From his hiding place in the cellar, Shura could hear the angry Dalek voices. 'Where are the delegates?'

'Where is the man, Styles?'

'They must be found and exterminated.'

'The Dalek conquest of the planet Earth must not be reversed.'

'The Daleks will be victorious!'

Shura said softly to himself, 'Oh no, not this time. This time it's going to be different.' With that he pressed the black plunger on the bomb.

From the hillside the Doctor and his group saw the tremendous eruption. It destroyed the house in a single, savage blast. The noise was shattering. As the black smoke drifted away they saw that the house had completely vanished. No ruins, no debris, just a gaping black hole in the ground …

The Doctor turned to Styles, who was standing nearby. 'Your conference has been saved, Sir Reginald. I hope you make sure it's a success. You still have a choice of futures.'

Styles looked at him wonderingly. 'Don't worry. We all know what will happen if we fail.'

'So do we,' said the Doctor. 'We've seen it, haven't we, Jo?'

Ignoring the puzzled looks from Sir Reginald and the Brigadier, Jo and the Doctor walked down the hill.

14

ALL KINDS OF FUTURES

'I'm sorry, Doctor,' said Jo obstinately, 'I still don't understand.'

They were walking along the corridor towards the laboratory.

'It's quite simple, Jo. Somehow the Daleks managed to pervert the course of history so they could conquer the Earth. The guerillas tried to change things back, but because they were a part of history, their intervention just repeated the pattern. I was able to intervene and put history back on its proper tracks.'

'I know,' said Jo impatiently, 'because you're a Time Lord. But that still doesn't explain how' – she stopped in amazement as the Doctor flung open the laboratory door. Another Jo Grant was there, looking at her with equal astonishment.

The Doctor said, 'Good grief, yes, of course, I remember now.' He looked at the second Jo Grant. 'Now don't you worry, my dear. I know you're alarmed but—'

To Jo's astonishment a second Doctor came out of the TARDIS. He frowned at them. 'Oh no, what are you doing here?'

Jo heard the Doctor reply. 'Don't worry, I'm not here, that is ... well, in a sense I am here but you're not there ... It's a bit complicated to explain.'

'Well, this won't do at all, will it?' said the second Doctor severely. 'Can't have two of us running about.'

'Don't worry, old chap,' said the Doctor. 'It'll all be ...'

Suddenly the second Doctor and the second Jo disappeared. Calmly the Doctor walked into the lab and took off his cloak.

'Wait a minute,' said Jo, 'that all happened before. Only they were us and we were them.'

The Doctor smiled. 'Don't worry about it, Jo. I told you time was a very complicated thing.'

The Brigadier entered looking a little shaken. 'I think I've been having hallucinations. For one ghastly moment I thought I saw two of you.'

'Nothing for you to worry about, old chap,' said the Doctor soothingly.

'Ah well,' said the Brigadier. 'Now then, what did I come in for? Oh yes, good news from the Conference. Seeing that explosion seems to have done 'em all good. According to old Styles they're all co-operating beautifully.'

'I'm glad to hear it,' said the Doctor. 'Now if you'll excuse me, I've got work to do.' He opened the door of the TARDIS.

Jo saw that he was about to plunge back into wrestling with the problem of the grounded TARDIS. Before he could disappear she said, 'Doctor!'

The Doctor paused. 'Yes, Jo,' he said patiently.

'That future we saw – with the Daleks ruling the Earth … is it going to happen, or isn't it?'

'It is, and it isn't,' said the Doctor not very helpfully.

'Oh come on, Doctor,' said the Brigadier, coming to Jo's support. 'What sort of answer is that?'

'I meant exactly what I said,' protested the Doctor. 'First it is – and then it isn't. There are all kinds of futures you know.'

'Futures with Daleks in them?' asked Jo.

The Doctor said, 'It's possible, Jo.'

'But surely those Dalek things were all destroyed?' said the Brigadier.

The Doctor said, 'That was a mere handful … the Daleks exist in many places, and many times. I thought I'd destroyed them once before, but I was wrong.'

The Doctor stood for a moment, gazing into the distance … as if he were looking through time itself, thought Jo, wondering when and where his old enemies would attack again.

The Doctor came out of his daydream and gave her a smile. 'I've just *got* to get the TARDIS working again, Jo,' he said. 'I've got a feeling I'm going to need it.'

With that he disappeared inside the TARDIS and closed the door.

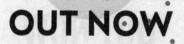